W. J. Burley lived near New̲ ̲ ̲ ̲ ̲ ̲ ̲ ̲ ̲ ̲ ̲ ̲ ̲ and was a school-
master until he retired to concentrate on his writing. His many
Wycliffe books include, most recently, *Wycliffe and the Guild of
Nine*. He died in 2002.

The Wycliffe Novels

W.J.BURLEY

This omnibus edition first published in Great Britain in 2011
by Orion Books, an imprint of
The Orion Publishing Group Ltd
Orion House, 5 Upper Saint Martin's Lane
London WC2H 9EA

An Hachette UK Company

1 3 5 7 9 10 8 6 4 2

Wycliffe and the Three-Toed Pussy Copyright © W. J. Burley 1968
Wycliffe and How to Kill a Cat Copyright © W. J. Burley 1970
Wycliffe and the Guilt Edged Alibi Copyright © W. J. Burley 1971
Wycliffe and Death in a Salubrious Place Copyright © W. J. Burley 1973
Wycliffe and Death in Stanley Street Copyright © W. J. Burley 1974

A CIP catalogue record for this book
is available from the British Library.

ISBN 978 1 4091 3276 9

Typeset at The Spartan Press Ltd,
Lymington, Hants

Printed in Great Britain by Clays Ltd,
St Ives plc

The Orion Publishing Group's policy is to use papers
that are natural, renewable and recyclable products and
made from wood grown in sustainable forests. The logging
and manufacturing processes are expected to conform to
the environmental regulations of the country of origin.

www.orionbooks.co.uk

Contents

Wycliffe and the Three-Toed Pussy 1

Wycliffe and How to Kill a Cat 165

Wycliffe and the Guilt Edged Alibi 339

Wycliffe and Death in a Salubrious Place 505

Wycliffe and Death in Stanley Street 659

Wycliffe and the Three-Toed Pussy

I apologize to the local council and to the planning authority for planting a village of two hundred and fifty people on the coast between St Ives and Zennor without the necessary permits.

I apologize also to the few residents on those beautiful cliffs for saddling them with such obnoxious neighbours.

Of course Kergwyns has no existence outside the pages of this book and neither have the people who live in it.

W.J.B.

1

Pussy Welles.

Slumped on her plain oatmeal carpet in ultimate relaxation, in the abandoned posture of a child asleep; one arm beneath her body, the other flung out, fingers flexed but not clenched. Her auburn hair shone lustrous in the sunlight, splayed on the pile. Her simple cornflower-blue frock made a splash of colour on the neutral ground. One leg – the right – drawn up under her, only visible below the knee; seamless nylon and a neat, though by no means elegant, flat heeled suede shoe. Her left leg straight and bare, no stocking, no shoe.

The foot was deformed.

Two toes missing, the first and second; obviously a congenital malformation, not a consequence of accident or surgery. All these things ought to have seemed trivial in contrast with the jagged hole between her breasts and the dark red viscous mass clogging the fabric of her dress and the pile of the carpet. But it was not so for the two men who stood over her.

The sergeant was deeply moved by the sight of her deformed foot, a gross flaw where he had supposed only perfection. For the super-intendent, it had always been the fact of death and not the means that shocked him; the dissolution of a personality. But they both bent over her in professional scrutiny.

They could not see the wound of exit – if there was one, it must have been hidden by a fold in the material of her dress; but the entry was horrifyingly apparent. They did not touch her; she would have to be photographed, examined and inspected by a gaggle of experts before she was moved. The superintendent looked round the room; all the furniture stood on legs, easy to clean underneath, no draper-ies, nowhere to lose anything, just an expanse of carpet from wall to wall. The cartridge case lay plain to see against the white skirting board, under a china cupboard.

'An automatic,' the sergeant said, ensuring his credit. 'It looks like a .32.'

'We shall know soon enough.'

Wycliffe wanted to stop the sergeant talking. Soon there would be more than enough talk, an avalanche of facts, fictions, surmises and explanations; for the moment, he wanted to form impressions of his own. He knew the girl's name – at least, he knew what they called her – Pussy Welles. And Pussy Welles was dead, apparently shot through the heart. He could start from there.

As far as he could tell, she must have been about twenty-five or six. He thought her beautiful, and, in death, she had a look of innocence. Deceptive? Why should he think so? Perhaps because a girl is unlikely to be called *Pussy* for her innocence. Feline – but of what kind? I love little pussy, her coat is so warm – that sort? Or green eyed, sleek and stealthy? He could find out by asking the sergeant who was bursting to tell all he knew of the girl, but the superintendent preferred to wait. In any case, he thought he knew already the kind of cat she must have been.

She had money, or at least, she spent it. It was only a cottage, one of those four-square little granite blockhouses with slate roofs that form the nucleus of every Cornish village, but like many of them nowadays, it had been elegantly modernized, gutted and reconstructed from within. This one room ran the length of the cottage and it had two bow windows. The furniture was good quality reproduction stuff – or was it genuine?

Superintendent Wycliffe stood at one of the windows looking out. The little front garden was paved with granite sets and succulents grew in the cracks, sedums and houseleeks. The wooden palings were painted pale blue, a colour which seems to be the badge of those cottages which have undergone their metamorphosis. Beyond, a narrow lane, a stone wall, and the lichen covered roofs of more cottages, grey-green and orange, then the grey square tower of the church rising out of a clump of sycamores just coming into leaf.

A strange spot for the kind of girl she seemed to be. It occurred to him that she was not freckled as most auburn haired people are; her skin was clear, rather pale, translucent. He could swear that she was a natural blonde but what could it matter if she dyed her hair? Most girls do. In any case it would all be in the report.

Deceased met her death as a result of a gunshot wound. The bullet was

6

*fired from a Webley .32 automatic pistol and entered the body between
the sixth and seventh ribs slightly to the left of the sternum. The wound of
entry indicates that the shot was fired at close range, the weapon being
held at less than fifteen inches and more than nine inches from the surface
of the body . . .*

It would all be there, in a wealth of boring detail, essential for the
court, if it ever came to court, but very little help in detection.
Crimes like this, nine times out of ten, are an explosive result of
a build up of tension in human relationships. When those relationships are known, the criminal is known though the technical
data may be needed to convict him.

Two men were walking down the lane, dawdling, obviously trying
to see as much as possible during their brief passage, unwilling to
stop and stare openly. One was heavily built, florid, fortyish; he wore
a black polo-necked jersey. The other was younger, slim, small; only
head and shoulders visible above the palings, but it was enough;
green corduroy jacket, orange cravat; thin, pale, sensitive features,
black hair scrupulously parted. He caught sight of the superintendent
and looked away at once. As they disappeared down the lane he was
gesturing vigorously in conversation with his companion.

Wycliffe smiled. Unlikely that these boys would tangle with a
woman!

Her deformed foot was beginning to trouble him, not for the
reason it worried the sergeant. The superintendent knew that total
perfection is so rare that when it seems to be, one looks the more
diligently for flaws. His was a more practical point. Why only one
stocking and shoe? Even if she had started to undress in her sitting-
room, the other stocking and shoe should be there, and they were
not.

He nodded unconsciously in confirmation of a conclusion,
having convinced himself that this was a deliberate advertisement of
deformity.

A police car came to a halt in the lane, blocking it completely and
a second pulled up, hard on its heels.

'They've come. I'm off!'

The sergeant's surprise and obvious disapproval annoyed him, so
that his manner became peremptory. 'Ask the inspector to see that
everything is put back exactly as they find it and nothing to be taken
away without my permission.'

'Where will you be, sir? – in case the inspector wants you?'

'At the pub – there is one, I suppose?'

Although he was successful, having what is called a distinguished record, he always lost confidence in himself at the beginning of a case; he would avoid his subordinates for fear of sensing their mute criticism, and, forced into their company, he became aggressively dictatorial. Those who knew him shrugged. He'll be all right when he's run in.

Now he escaped through the backway, through a little modern kitchen with a dining alcove, into the garden. It should have been a potato and cabbage patch, hard won from the thin, black stony soil of the moor, but somebody had transformed it into a delightful walled garden with rhododendrons, azaleas, camellias and laurels. Obviously not the dead girl; the garden was made before she was born. A door in the high wall brought him out on to the moor for the house was on the very outskirts of the village. Gorse, heather and brambles grew almost to the door but there was a path of sorts and he reached the lane and made off down it like a guilty schoolboy, away from the police cars. A hundred yards and the lane turned sharp right and on the corner, facing back up the lane, a substantial farm house meticulously cared for; a white gate with a varnished plaque:

CLEMENS AND REED. ANTIQUE DEALERS.
INSPECTION INVITED.

Anybody in that house sufficiently interested would know a good deal of what went on in the dead girl's cottage.

The turn in the lane brought him to the square; the church opposite, the pub on his left and a score or so of cottages completing the square. A war memorial in the middle. A pleasant little place, sleepy at this time of year but, no doubt, busy enough in the season.

It was deserted now at any rate but there were plenty of discreetly curtained windows and those who watched, saw him pause, resting on his stick, taking things in. Unless they knew, they would hardly suspect that he was a policeman; he prided himself on that. Barely the regulation height, slender in build, it was difficult to believe that he had ever walked a beat, but he had – twenty years ago. He looked comfortable in his tweeds, not a bit like a bobby off duty. With binoculars slung over his shoulder, he might have been one of the

8

bird watchers who frequented the neighbouring cliffs and coves. But he had no binoculars, just his stick.

Wycliffe never felt like a policeman. Often during his twenty-odd years of service he wondered why he joined. He hated discipline, hated regimentation and sometimes he hated order; but he hated violence more. Perhaps that was why he stayed, but he had joined for no better reason than to get out of the family business. The Wycliffes were large scale market gardeners in Hereford.

Pussy Welles had been murdered; there could be no doubt of that. Perhaps she was not much loss, but violence must never be tolerated. That was his creed. By the same token he was, unlike most of his colleagues, opposed to capital punishment. No compromise! Otherwise you are on the road to Belsen and Hiroshima. For whatever reason he had become a policeman, that was why he remained one.

'Good morning, superintendent, what will you have?'

A modest fame which should have flattered but merely irritated. His answer was surly but the man behind the bar was not easily put off.

Mike Young, licensee, in striped shirt and fancy waistcoat. A heavily built man, running to fat, a high colour and blond, thinning hair. But it was his face which captured reluctant attention. One side of it was a caricature, a series of livid scars from well above the normal hair line down to his jaw bone; the ear pinna was missing altogether and his neck was deeply furrowed by the scars of complex lacerations.

Wycliffe sipped his whisky. There were only two other customers, the two men he had seen passing the cottage. They sat close in the window seat, silent. The older one had a tankard of beer, the other, some short drink, probably gin. Wycliffe had his back to them but he knew they were watching him with interest and apprehension.

'A nasty business, superintendent! Who would want to kill a girl like Pussy Welles?'

'You knew her?' A fatuous question in a village of two hundred people but Young seemed anxious to answer.

'Everybody knew her – and liked her – she brought a bit of life into the place. I'd like to get my hands on the bastard that killed her!' His great thick fingered hands closed convulsively; a man of violence. He picked up his cigarette that smouldered in an ashtray, drew on it deeply and exhaled the grey smoke through pouting lips. Then he leaned forward and lowered his voice confidentially.

'I might as well tell you that the cottage is mine.'

'You mean that she rented it from you?'

The landlord nodded and Wycliffe sensed an embarrassment though he could not divine its cause.

'She took it four or five years back when my mother and father died.'

'Did she have relatives here?'

'Not that I know of.'

Wycliffe filled and lit his pipe, watching the landlord over the undulant flame of the match. 'An odd place for a young woman to settle, a village like this, don't you think?'

Young raised his massive shoulders expressing unwillingness to comment.

'Was the cottage furnished?'

'No, she brought her own.'

'Did you get your rent?'

Hostility and suspicion flared in his eyes. 'I don't know what you mean!'

'I mean did she pay her rent?' The menace in his voice was the more effective in that it was unconscious. He disliked the landlord.

Young reached below the bar for a cloth and began to wipe the polished surface in a reflex action. 'She always paid,' he said sullenly.

A complication here, and Wycliffe thought he could guess what it was. After a prolonged silence, Young looked at him sheepishly. 'I suppose you'll be staying to lunch, superintendent?'

'And I'd like a room for two or three days.'

'I'll go and fix it now.' He was anxious to be gone. Wycliffe detained him.

'As you rented her the cottage, you must know something about her – references – that sort of thing.'

'No, I knew nothing about her, superintendent. She paid me a substantial deposit when she took over and that was good enough for me.' He edged away, like a guilty schoolboy, itching to go before he commits some indiscretion.

'One more thing,' Wycliffe said, 'the antique dealers, what sort of people are they?'

10

No mistaking relief in Young's distorted grin. He nodded towards the pair in the window. 'You're in luck, superintendent, meet Mr Clemens and Mr Reed.'

Wycliffe took his second whisky to the window and drew up a chair. It was pathetic; they waited for him to speak in frozen attitudes so that he felt like a predator. He introduced himself – superfluous – but it enabled him to be friendly and they responded, tentatively. Harvey Clemens and Aubrey Reed. (Why, for God's sake? – do they change their names when they feel the call, like film stars?). Aubrey was the younger; Nature had played a shabby trick, endowing him with the essential attribute of masculinity when, in all else, he was a woman.

'We know why you are here,' Harvey said.

Wycliffe smiled. 'I suppose the whole village knows by now. Mrs Vines, the lady who found her, will have spread it round a bit.'

Aubrey made an angry gesture. 'She's an old witch! We used to have her to do our cleaning – didn't we, Harvey? – but we had to get rid of her. You don't want to take notice of anything she tells you!'

'I'll bear that in mind,' the superintendent said.

'What do you want from us?' Aubrey was petulant, suspicious.

'Just that your cottage overlooks the dead woman's and you may know who visits her – her friends, if you like.'

'Men,' Harvey said.

Aubrey looked nervously at the bar but the landlord had gone. 'We don't spy on our neighbours, superintendent.'

Wycliffe let his cold eyes rest on Reed for some time before he spoke. 'Perhaps we should continue this conversation at the police station in a more formal atmosphere.'

Aubrey made a little grimace of shocked distaste. 'We don't want to go to the police station, do we, Harvey?' He put his hands meticulously together and locked them between his knees. 'She had a lot of men friends.'

'Disgusting!' Harvey said.

'Who, for example?'

Aubrey nodded towards the bar. 'He used to be one.' It was obvious that he hated the landlord; equally obvious that he was afraid of him.

Wycliffe refilled his pipe and carefully pressed down the tobacco with a fitting on his penknife. 'Used to be?'

11

'Until he had that accident. Now, I suppose even she . . .'

'It must have been some accident! – what happened?'

Harvey cut in. 'He was thrown through the windscreen of his car! Right through the glass! They couldn't see him for blood when they found him.'

Aubrey shuddered. 'Harvey! He was driving home from St Ives late at night, and his car skidded on a patch of oil.'

'Oil?'

'Yes. A five gallon drum of oil all over the road. They think it must have fallen off the back of a lorry or something.'

'He was drunk,' Harvey said.

'Anybody else?'

Aubrey kept his hands tightly locked and swayed gently from side to side.

'There's Dr Barnes,' Harvey said. 'He's a lecturer in archaeology at the University. They've got the cottage going down at Kitt's Cove.'

'They?'

'He and his wife; they spend their vacations down here.'

'Are they down, now?'

'He is,' Aubrey said, 'I saw him yesterday.'

The superintendent lit his pipe and puffed until it was drawing to his satisfaction. 'Did you happen to notice anyone going to the cottage yesterday?'

Aubrey considered. 'Yesterday we worked all day . . .'

'Worked?'

Mild contempt. 'In our showroom. We are dealers in antique furniture and *objets d'art*.'

'And your showroom?'

'Is round the back of the house, a converted barn, so we couldn't be expected to see what went on.'

'But you didn't stay there the whole day, surely?'

'Until the light went.'

'And then?'

'Well, we couldn't see anyone then, could we?' Harvey giggled. He had the same infuriating pertness as Alice's March Hare.

'As a matter of fact it was dark when I saw Barnes,' Aubrey volunteered. 'I was out with Abélard.'

'Abélard?'

'Our pussy. We had him neutered, you see,' – from Harvey.

12

'One of us takes him out for a few minutes each night before going to bed.'

'And you saw Barnes – where?'

'At the cottage. That's what you wanted to know about, wasn't it?'

'Going in or coming out?'

'I don't know; he was standing on the step.'

'At what time was this?'

Aubrey considered. 'A little after ten. I remember the church clock striking just before I let Abélard out. By the way, what happened to her cat? Is somebody looking after it?'

'You mean that Miss Welles had a cat?'

'A silver point, like Abélard; a magnificent animal.'

Wycliffe suddenly wearied of the precious pair; they were even less prepossessing in their new found confidence than when they were scared. Did they think they were hiding the obvious? Or that he cared?

It was quiet, peaceful. The sun shining through the fake bottle glass windows made intricate green patterns on the marble table tops and on the floor. Now and then he could hear the *ping* of the shop doorbell from right across the square. Half past twelve. A turn round the square before lunch.

He walked in the sunshine. Gulls soared overhead in the faded blue sky and he could smell the sea. A lane ran down beside the inn, the entrance marked by a finger post:

FOOTPATH TO CLIFFS.
RESIDENTS' CARS AND CALLERS ONLY.

Select. He would have liked to walk within sight of the sea but it would probably take too long. The six months since his appointment to the regional squad, after twenty years in the Midlands, had not accustomed him to having the sea always round the corner. Instead, he walked by the churchyard. He looked idly at the headstones, slabs of slate, deeply incised with the vital history of the parish and crusted with mosses and lichens. Even the preposterous later crosses and curbs were achieving a decent obscurity. He wondered whether the mortal remains of Pussy Welles would find their way to this consoling place, there to decay in peace. A Mini car shattered the silence, coming into the square; it made its way down on the opposite side of the central green and pulled up outside the inn. He stopped to watch; a young man and a young woman got out, slammed the doors and went through the bar entrance.

He wondered about the village children. Where were they? There seemed to be none; evidently a tidy and well ordered little village. On the surface. He reached the shop and went in to buy tobacco, aware that he was interrupting a discussion. Three women with shopping bags watched him being served and he was certain that the little hole of silence he had made would soon be healed.

A hell of a way to conduct an inquiry, strolling around like a tourist! But he completed the circuit of the square and arrived back at the inn. The bar was empty so he found his way to the dining-room. Three of the tables were laid and the couple from the Mini sat at one. Again he knew that he was interrupting something – a quarrel this time. On closer inspection, they were not so young; little short of thirty, either of them. She was fair, petite, determined; he, mousy, a little blundering and anxious. They avoided each other's eyes, and his.

He sat at a table laid for one.

The waitress, a sluttish young girl in a black dress too tight for her, went to the couple's table. 'Soup for you, Dr Barnes?'

Dr Barnes.

Wycliffe went back to the cottage in a mood of acute depression, with no relish for the tasks ahead. A young constable standing disconsolate outside the door saluted.

'Inspector Darley is inside, sir.'

'Alone?'

'Yes, sir.'

Wycliffe nodded. 'You can get back to your duties. No need to hang about here.' He hated the least semblance of military routine.

Since his appointment he had come to terms with Inspector Darley. The two men had complementary qualities. Wycliffe was imaginative, impatient of routine, inclined to be lazy. Darley follow-ed the book, believed that every one of the twenty-four hours was made for work when there was work to be done, and was never bored. Even physically they were extremes, Wycliffe was slight, almost frail; Darley a giant, bulging in his clothes. All of which scarcely added up to any liking between them.

They talked in her sitting-room but she was gone. The place

where she had been was marked with a black outline of her recumbent form and by the rust brown stain on the carpet.

'Anything to tell me?'

Darley spoke with ponderous slowness, his words, like his movements suggested a film run at reduced speed. 'Dr Slade thinks that she died between half past nine and eleven – off the record, of course.'

'No sign of a gun?'

'No. It was a .32 automatic but you probably know that already. There are eight licensed weapons of that description in the division and they are being checked but nobody in Kergwyns has a licence for a .32.'

Wycliffe filled his pipe and passed the pouch to Darley. 'Any indication as to why she should settle in a place like this?'

Darley paused in the act of thumbing down the tobacco in his pipe and stared at the bowl. 'In a way. The local sergeant knows the story. Apparently she arrived in St Ives about five years ago with her husband . . .'

'Husband? – Never mind, I just hadn't thought of her with a husband.'

Darley ignored the interruption. '. . . a man called Horner, Arthur Horner. He leased a shop with a flat over and they set up in business – fancy goods, postcards, paperbacks, that sort of thing.'

'What happened?'

'Happened?'

Wycliffe snapped. 'Well, she's not there with him now, is she?'

'He died six months after they took the shop.'

'Oh? What did he die of?'

A hint of a smile. 'Falling over a cliff.' Darley had the satisfaction of seeing that he had made his point.

Wycliffe thawed. He sat himself in one of the fragile armchairs. Darley remained standing, discomfort and efficiency went hand in hand in his opinion.

'Accident?'

'So it seems.' Darley re-lit his pipe. 'She had nothing obvious to gain by his death and she wasn't there to push him anyway. All they had was the stock and furniture and that was sold to pay the rent.

'After the husband died, she came here and started to use the name of Welles. I gather there was a convenient arrangement with the landlord of the inn who owns this cottage. Since then there have been other men – according to the gossips.'

Wycliffe sighed.

Darley frowned. 'What a way to live! An attractive young woman, still in the twenties.'

But Wycliffe thought – What a way to die! An instant of violence cutting off a life. Like dropping the curtain at the beginning of the second act. How he hated violence! But Pussy Welles was dead and nothing would bring her back. How many in the village took satisfaction in that fact? For how many of them was her death a reassurance? For which of them was it a desperate necessity? His job to find out.

'What about relatives?'

Darley frowned. 'A girl of her age must have close relatives but there's nothing to show that she was in touch with them. Of course, I've arranged to follow up what leads we've got.'

'Letters, papers, bills . . . ?'

The inspector jerked the stem of his pipe upwards. 'There's a sort of study or office next to her bedroom but somebody got there before us – the killer, I suppose. All her stuff has been tumbled out from the desk. There's no way of knowing what's missing but it's unlikely to be anything of intrinsic value; she had a few bits of jewellery and there was thirty pounds in cash in the desk.'

'It's pretty obvious she lived by her wits and it's possible she was going in for a spot of blackmail.'

Wycliffe drummed his fingers on the arm of his chair. He looked at the chalk outline and saw vividly, for a moment, a mind image of the girl lying there; her slim bare leg outstretched, her deformed foot. 'Did you find her other shoe and stocking?'

Darley shook his head. 'Certainly not the shoe. I don't know about the stocking, there's a drawer full of them up there and they all look the same to me.' He smoothed a massive hand over the broad shining band of baldness that parted the greying vestiges of his hair. 'There were scratches on her thigh, high up where the suspenders fasten to the stocking top, as though somebody had ripped the stocking off with considerable violence.'

'Before or after death?'

'After, Slade thinks.'

Wycliffe was accustomed to Darley's habit of telling the story in

16

his own way. He was perfectly capable of discussing a case for ten minutes before producing a crucial piece of evidence linked to some private theory.

Wycliffe nibbled. 'What are you suggesting?'

'I wondered if this could be a sex crime.'

'Sex murder by bullet?'

The inspector shrugged. 'No, I agree, it doesn't make sense.'

'All the same, those scratches are very odd, coupled with the missing shoe and stocking. As soon as you get Slade's report let me know.'

While he sat, discussing her murder as though it was an academic exercise, Pussy Welles' body would be lying on a slab in the pathologist's laboratory, subject to every conceivable indignity, just to provide the report he mentioned so casually. He stood up, walked to the window, and stood with his back to the room. The sky had clouded, smoky clouds from the south-west billowing overhead drizzled rain. Every last trace of colour drained from the landscape, nothing left but shades of grey. He pushed open the window and let in the moist air that carried with it the tang of the sea.

'Well! Let's take a look up there.'

On the narrow stairs Darley had to turn sideways at the bend and the treads protested. There were two rooms, a bedroom with a window facing the village and a study with its window overlooking the moor. The bedroom was simple, cheerful, and in good taste. A double divan bed neatly made up, a candy-striped bedspread, white walls with prints and a whole wall of floor-to-ceiling cupboards with white sliding doors. A chair, and a minute dressing table with an oval mirror fastened to the wall. A room, chaste in its functional simplicity.

The study was smaller, hardly room to move about. A desk, a chair, shelves crammed with books and a record player with a stack of records. The superintendent glanced over the shelves, modern novels, poetry, books of reference and the records were highbrow too.

'She must have been intelligent and educated,' Wycliffe said. 'You don't associate this sort of thing with a woman who lives as she seems to have done.'

Darley grunted. 'I don't know why not! It isn't a question of education but of morals.' He was a lay preacher when he could spare

17

the time. He pointed to the record player. 'When our chaps went over the place the little red light was still on. It looks as though she might have been playing it when her visitor arrived.'

'The bed was undisturbed?'

'Made up as you saw it.'

Wycliffe lifted the lid of the record player. The top record of a stack was an LP of Verdi's *Nabucco*. It was possible that she died while her cottage was filled with the ineffable sadness of the slaves' lament.

On the writing desk there were two neat piles of papers and the empty drawers were stacked on the floor. Wycliffe shuffled among the papers and was surprised by what he found – a small pile of crossword blanks with handwritten clues. He saw that they were difficult – the academic kind that appear in the more expensive Sunday papers and literary magazines. The other, a pile of quarto sheets closely written in her neat script.

'She's writing a novel!'

'Apparently.' Darley was unimpressed. 'This was all; it was scattered about. I had it collected together and sorted but nothing has been taken away. There doesn't seem to be much that's useful; no engagement book, no addresses or telephone numbers, no letters, no bills even.'

Wycliffe picked up the pile of manuscript, fascinated by the new twist it gave to his ideas on Pussy Welles. By the end of each murder case he was impressed and a little repelled by the extent of his knowledge of the victim, for he seemed to know more of the dead than of the living. And it was beginning here. The personality of Pussy Welles was growing and taking shape in his mind. Five hours ago he had never heard of her; then she was the victim of a shooting, just another victim – no more than an outline, like the outline of her body on the carpet. Seeing her had filled in some of the detail; she was young, good-looking – beautiful, he thought – and she had a deformed foot. She lived in a well appointed little cottage which she had furnished in good taste. Then people began to talk to him about her, telling him that she was a widow, hinting that she lived by her wits, that she was a woman belonging to men. The kind to get herself murdered? Now he had more facts which hardly seemed to fit; she had been well educated, sufficiently so to contrive sophisticated crossword puzzles and to write a novel.

18

'I'll take this with me.'

Darley raised his eyebrows. 'Here's her birth certificate – Anna Patricia Holst. Her father was of Austrian birth, naturalized British, a musician. She was born in Colchester.'

'If she married a chap called Horner, where does the name of Welles come in?'

Darley shrugged.

'No marriage lines?'

'No. From what I hear she was a bad lot.'

Darley believed that immorality was a disease of the pubic region and Wycliffe was irritated. He found the girl's room deeply moving, an horizon in her life which she could not have known to be her last.

'An inclination to ring the changes in bed doesn't render a girl eligible for murder!'

'I'm aware of that, sir!'

'I suppose you've laid on a house to house?'

'Thomas, Evans and May have been at it since before noon. They're taking their time about it!'

'What sort of brief did you give them?'

Darley raised his massive shoulders. 'The usual. Anybody seen in the vicinity of the cottage last night; anybody who heard a shot; and – more discreetly – who were her regulars?'

'A blank cheque for gossip,' Wycliffe grunted. 'You'll be lucky if they finish tonight!'

Darley was nettled. 'It has to be done, sir!'

The doorbell startled them.

'That'll be them now. I'll go down.'

Wycliffe went to the window. He could not see anyone at the door because of the porch but he stared gloomily across the cottage roofs to the church tower. The drizzle had turned to rain and the wind was freshening; the grey granite, crumbling under encrusting lichens, seemed to soak up water like a sponge. He heard voices downstairs but not those of the detectives; then Darley's heavy tread on the stairs.

'It's a Mr Lomax; he thinks he's got something to tell us.'

Probably some village crank anxious for notoriety but in a murder case everybody has to be heard. He went down to find the man perched on the edge of a chair, his mackintosh dripping on to the carpet. In the forties, lean to the point of emaciation, studious

19

looking – an impression helped by the thick lenses of his spectacles. He looked about him nervously with quick, bird like glances. Every now and then his eyes rested on the tell-tale chalk marks, but only for an instant.

'Your men came to see me but I thought it would be better if I talked to whoever is in charge . . .' He peered from the inspector to the superintendent.

'Superintendent Wycliffe,' Darley introduced.

'Thank you. It seems dreadful to come here – almost ghoulish, but there is no police station in Kergwyns and I did not know how else . . .'

'You were perfectly right to come here if you have something to tell me.'

Lomax could not settle his gaze, nor apparently, compose his thoughts.

'Perhaps you should begin by telling us who you are,' Darley suggested.

'Who I am? Yes, of course. My name is Edgar Lomax and I am a naturalist, a student of animal behaviour. At one time I was a lecturer in the subject in the University of London.' He spoke with a certain pride. 'Then I came into a little money and resigned my university appointment to pursue my own work with greater freedom – that was when I came to Kergwyns.'

'So that now you are independent, and very nice too!' Wycliffe wondered when he would get to the point.

Lomax nodded. 'In a manner of speaking, yes. With the income from my books I manage very well. Natural history is big business these days and there seems to be an insatiable demand for articles and books at the popular level. It pays for my more serious work and I am able to live very comfortably.' He produced a large white handkerchief and mopped his forehead free of the little droplets of water that drained from his saturated hair.

He looked like a starved, nervous and very wet rabbit.

'You were acquainted with Miss Welles?'

'Yes, indeed. Certainly we were acquainted.' He seemed distressed but marshalled his courage to come to the point. 'This is a small village, superintendent, and we live, so to speak, in each other's pockets. No secret is a secret for long. You will probably know already that Anna – Miss Welles – had a certain reputation where

20

men were concerned.' He paused, as though waiting for confirmation but Wycliffe was silent and he continued, picking his words with care. 'She had a very rich and many sided personality and you will find that she had many friends . . .' He hesitated, then added, 'most of them, it is true, were men, but not all of them were on the same . . . ah . . . footing. I was a very close friend . . .'

He was obviously trying to say that he didn't sleep with her.

'I was, to a certain extent, in her confidence, and I have been aware for a week or more that she has been worried. She admitted as much, and although she did not tell me the cause of her trouble, I gathered that she needed to raise a sum of money.' He coughed uneasily. 'I told her, of course, that she could count on me but she wouldn't hear of it. "No Edgar," she said, "you owe me nothing, but there are those who do." '

He stopped speaking with obvious relief and sat, staring at the toes of his heavy shoes, caked with mud.

Wycliffe thought he understood the man; nervous, sensitive, inhibited, he would revel in the friendship of an intelligent woman with a reputation for reckless living. Playing with fire without much risk of getting burnt.

'You don't know precisely, Mr Lomax, what it was that was troubling Miss Welles?'

He looked up, startled. 'No! Indeed I do not – I wish I did!'

'And you have no idea what she meant when she said that there were others who owed her something?'

Lomax locked his fingers together and regarded them intently. 'I suppose that she meant there were people who owed her money, but I have no idea who they were.'

'When did you last see her?'

His answer came promptly. 'The night before last.'

'The night before she was killed?'

He nodded. 'That was when she admitted to me that she was worried and I offered to help . . .'

'You visited her here?'

'Oh, no! We met at the Dampiers' – I walked home with her and it was then that she told me.'

'These Dampiers were friends of hers?'

'Yes. John and Erica, brother and sister, they have a house beyond the inn.'

'Tell me about them.'

Lomax looked puzzled. 'About the Dampiers?'

'If you will, Mr Lomax. We have to get to know as much as we can about this young woman and we can do that best through her friends.'

Lomax accepted this rather specious explanation. 'Dampier writes children's books and his sister illustrates them. They are an accomplished pair, but he is a cripple, poor fellow – a hunchback. He goes out very seldom and he is dependent for his social life on a few friends who visit him for a game of Mah-Jongg and a chat.'

Mah-Jongg! It sounded pleasantly nineteen-twentyish – ragtime, ear-phones and all that.

Wycliffe started to fill his pipe, after offering his pouch to Lomax who said that he did not smoke.

'This little village seems to have more than its share of talent. The Dampiers, yourself – author and naturalist . . .' He puffed strongly, persuading his pipe to draw. 'Then, I gather, Miss Welles made up crossword puzzles for publication.'

Lomax smiled. He was more relaxed. 'She did indeed, and very good ones. The Dampiers put her on to it, they seem to have a great many contacts in the newspaper and publishing world. As to the rest, I suppose that Kergwyns is typical of many villages in this county, a refuge for intelligent cowards.' He laughed. 'A place where it is possible to hide from the harsher realities of life in the second half of our century; to pretend that they do not exist, or to write about them with an Olympian detachment.'

'Was Dr Barnes one of your Mah-Jongg party?'

Lomax looked surprised. 'Dr Barnes? No, he was not. It is true that he and his wife sometimes come along when they are down but they are not regulars and I doubt . . .' He broke off. 'What made you ask?'

'Who else was at the Dampiers' that evening?'

Lomax was nettled by the new brusque note of interrogation and his manner became constrained. 'Our usual party; in addition to the Dampiers, Anna and myself, there were Harvey Clemens and Aubrey Reed, the antique dealers, and the Mitfords.'

It was not necessary for Wycliffe to speak, only to raise his eyebrows and Lomax went on: 'A couple who live in the village; he is a teacher at a school in Penzance. A keen sportsman, he used to be an amateur rally driver.'

'You are being extremely helpful, Mr Lomax,' Wycliffe said. 'It is essential for us – strangers – to be able to fill in the background and you are greatly simplifying our task.'

Silence while the two policemen smoked and Lomax looked round, a little reassured.

'You said just now that Miss Welles had friends – what about enemies?'

Lomax drew in his thin lips. 'Enemies! – that is being a little dramatic, surely? Most people don't have enemies and I don't suppose she had . . .'

'She was murdered, wasn't she?' Darley snapped and put Lomax off his stroke; his eyes went furtively to the chalk marks once more.

'Yes, of course, it's difficult to grasp. Obviously she had an enemy but it's almost impossible to believe that someone would do such an awful thing. There were some who disliked her but . . .'

'Who, for example?'

Lomax smiled faintly. 'Women in general, I suppose.'

'Men?'

Lomax shifted uncomfortably in his chair. 'I think there was some trouble between her and Aubrey Reed . . .'

'The antique dealer?'

'Yes, they certainly quarrelled.'

'But she still played Mah-Jongg with him at the Dampiers' on the night she was killed?'

'Oh, yes, nobody would do anything to upset that, it was an institution.'

'Have you any idea what they quarrelled about or when?'

Lomax sighed. 'It was quite recent – within the last two or three months at any rate, and I think it was about their cats.'

'Cats?' Darley was incredulous.

Lomax seemed to apologize for human follies. 'You know how these things are. They both have male Siamese but Reed's is neutered while hers is not – she says that she wants it to enjoy the simple pleasures of life. Anyway like many Siamese males it is aggressive and there were fights in which Reed's cat got the worst of it.'

'Hardly motive for murder!' Darley remarked scathingly.

'You evidently don't know many cat owners,' Wycliffe muttered.

Lomax looked round vaguely. 'That was one of the reasons I came over – somebody will have to feed and look after him . . .'

'I have't seen a cat about the place, have you, Darley?'

'No!' With emphasis.

'Odd, but cats are strange creatures, I expect he'll turn up. If so, perhaps you'll . . .'

'Yes, of course, we'll let you know.'

They all seem more concerned about the cat than the girl.

Lomax still had something he wanted to say but found difficulty in saying it; finally, it came: 'You don't think she might have committed suicide?'

'Do you?'

He was taken aback. 'It seems so much more likely than murder.'

'What about the gun?'

'Somebody could have taken it.'

'Who and why?'

A trace of irritation. 'How should I know? But it could have been somebody's gun, somebody who came in and found her and didn't want to be involved.'

Wycliffe nodded. 'An interesting suggestion.'

Another silence.

'Is that where . . . ?'

'Yes, that's where we found her, one leg doubled up under her, the other outstretched.'

'You know when she was killed?'

'Somewhere between nine and midnight.'

Lomax stared at the black outline, openly now. He shuddered. 'Horrible!'

'She was shot at close range from the front, the bullet passed right through her body, penetrating the heart and damaging one of the great vessels. That accounts for the effluxion of blood. You can see it on the carpet.'

Darley looked at his chief in astonishment and Lomax was pale but Wycliffe seemed not to notice. 'After shooting her, the murderer started to undress her.'

'Undress her?' His voice was little more than a whisper.

'Yes, he tore off the shoe and stocking from her left leg with considerable violence, lacerating and bruising her thighs.'

'Horrible!'

'Yes, murder at close quarters is rarely the cosy business we read about in detective stories. Incidentally, her left shoe and stocking have not been found . . .' He stopped, as though struck by a new idea. 'By the way, Mr Lomax, can you account for your movements last night?'

Lomax winced. 'I was at home all the evening.'

'Alone?'

The wretched man nodded, then he brightened. 'At a little before ten, I rang Dampier.'

'Did you speak to him?'

'I spoke to his sister, she said he was out.'

They were interrupted by the telephone. Darley went to the porch to answer it and they could hear his side of the conversation. 'Yes, he's here, I'll ask him to come to the telephone.' His great moon-face peered round the door. 'It's for you from Dr Slade.'

'I must go,' Lomax announced. He seemed to welcome the chance and pushed past the superintendent on his way to the telephone. 'If I can be of any further help . . .'

Wycliffe watched him go out into the rain, then picked up the receiver. 'Wycliffe here.'

'This is Slade. That girl was pregnant.' The pathologist never wasted words.

'How long?'

'Eight or nine weeks.'

'So that she would have known?'

'What do you think?'

'Anything else?'

'Nothing you don't already know.'

'Right, thanks for ringing; the information may be useful.'

'We do our best,' Slade said and rang off.

Darley was gloomily complacent. 'These girls really ask for it!' He was more concerned to discover why Wycliffe had been so brutal with Lomax but the superintendent was enigmatic.

'It was just an experiment and he'll get over it.'

25

2

Wycliffe could not sleep and by seven o'clock he was standing in the doorway of the inn smoking his first pipe of the day. Sylvie, the girl who had served his meals the day before, was already at work, cleaning up the bar, slow moving, her eyes still clogged with sleep. She had taken pity on him and made some coffee.

'Do you know who did it?'

'No. Do you?'

She rested her plump bare arms on the bar counter and wrinkled her brow. 'I'll tell you one thing, it was a woman.'

The superintendent sipped his coffee and said nothing.

'They had it in for her and no wonder!' She ran her fingers through a tangled mop of brown hair, sweeping it back from her eyes. She looked like a child newly awakened. Later in the day when she had done herself up she would look coarse, vulgar. 'No man was safe from her.'

'Good coffee!' He emptied his cup and she refilled it. 'You didn't like her?'

Screwed up features. 'I didn't have anything against her; it takes all sorts, I suppose.' She paused. 'But she wasn't a snob which is more than you can say for some of 'em round here.'

Wycliffe disliked leading the girl on, imposing on her youth, but a policeman has to get his gossip from somewhere. Oddly, in his old city division, he had questioned scores of girls younger than Sylvie, expecting them to be wise in the ways of vice, surprised to discover occasional innocence. Here in the country it was different, Sylvie reminded him of girls in the village where he had grown up. 'Was your boss one of . . . ?'

Sylvie nodded. 'Before my time – years ago. Not since his accident.'

'So she drew the line at that.'

She laughed. 'You don't know much about women, do you? It wasn't her who laid off, it was him. I know that for a fact. In any case, what are a few scars compared with a humped back?'

'A humped back?'

'Dampier, or haven't you got to him yet?' A malicious grin. 'His sister, Erica, doesn't like it one little bit!' she added in a travesty of refinement. 'That sort make me sick!'

How old was this girl? Eighteen? Nineteen? Certainly no more, yet she treated him like a schoolboy.

'Sylvie!' The landlord stood at the entrance to the bar. He wore his pjyama tunic tucked into the top of a pair of greasy flannels; he was unshaven, unwashed, bleary eyed.

'Good morning, superintendent.' His acknowledgement of Wycliffe was perfunctory. 'Sylvie, it's time you started on the breakfasts.' He evidently disapproved of their tête à tête.

'OK. I'm coming!' She winked at Wycliffe and waltzed off after her employer.

So Wycliffe stood on the steps of the inn alone, smoking his pipe, waiting for the village to come to life. A better day; the rain had gone with the night and the sun was up, behind the church; the sky was powder blue. Too good to last. He heard a milk lorry rattle along the road a quarter of a mile away and he persuaded himself that he could hear the sea. With more than an hour before breakfast, he decided to go and take a look.

Down the lane beside the inn there were a few more cottages then four or five large bungalows, nineteen-thirty vintage, their gardens choked with *Senecio* and *Olearia*. Each gate displayed a little card with the name of the occupier. There was one for *Mr and Mrs A. Mitford* and the last one read, *John and Erica Dampier*. He could see nothing of their bungalow except the roof from the lane but on the sea side, a huge dormer window topped the grey-green jungle of their wind-break. The ground shelved a couple of hundred yards to the cliff edge so the window commanded a panoramic view of the coastline, all the way from Godrevy to Pendeen. It was too perfect to be real, the sun glittering on the water, the white lace of foam at the foot of the cliffs, the golden gorse scenting the air. He stood on the cliff edge and looked down at the inshore water, a little sinister under the precipice of rock. As he watched a seal bobbed up, then another and another, he had never seen seals before except in zoos. He was

27

so absorbed in watching them that at first he failed to notice a more singular phenomenon closer at hand. A little to his left, a precipitous path led down to a tiny cove, a broken, crumbling, and in the superintendent's opinion, totally impracticable path, but a man was scrambling up, a contorted figure, moving with furious energy, using his hands and arms almost as much as his legs and feet. Every now and then he would look up, presumably to gauge his progress and Wycliffe glimpsed a black bearded face, striking even at that distance, by reason of the high domed forehead.

So Dampier took his exercise in the early morning, presumably to avoid an audience. Poor devil! And what exercise!

Wycliffe would have walked away to avoid thrusting himself on the man in these circumstances but glancing back to the bungalow he could see the form of a woman at the upstair window, watching, and for some reason he felt that it would be cowardly to retreat. In a surprisingly short time Dampier reached the top and stood for a moment, panting and mopping his forehead with his sleeve. His deformity was extreme, affecting his legs as well as his spine but his head was magnificent, a young Socrates. Wycliffe was reminded of those seaside photographs where the victim is persuaded to push his head through a hole thereby lending a face to a grotesque figure. But it's not funny when nature herself plays the joke.

'Good morning.'

Dampier answered with a quick smile.

'My goodness, that was a stiff climb!' Wycliffe said.

'It's quite easy when you do it often and it's good exercise.'

He had a pleasant cultured voice, assured despite a certain shyness of manner. 'Are you a visitor?'

Wycliffe introduced himself and Dampier smiled.

'No need then, for me to tell you who I am.'

'I intended to come and see you, but not at seven-thirty in the morning. I'm out for a pre-breakfast stroll but I'll trouble you a little later in the day if I may.'

He saw Dampier's involuntary glance back at the bungalow.

'No time like the present.'

'Good! You knew Miss Welles, of course?'

'Very well.'

'How long?'

Dampier considered. 'I met her first about seven years ago when she was down on holiday but I have known her well only since she came to Kergwyns to live – about five years, I suppose it must be.'

'When did you last see her?'

'She was at my house on Wednesday evening along with other friends.'

'Mr Lomax?'

Dampier's eyes narrowed. 'Among others, yes.'

'Did she seem to be her usual self?'

'Her usual self,' Dampier repeated the words as though they presented a problem. 'It's difficult to say, she seemed depressed but that was not unusual.'

'Do you know any special reason why she might have been depressed on that occasion?'

A slight shrug of irritation. 'She wasn't by nature a sanguine person.'

'You don't know, for example, that she was pregnant?'

No sign of surprise. Dampier had himself well in hand; a formidable man. 'I didn't know that she was pregnant,' he answered, without expression.

'Does it surprise you?'

He hesitated. 'Yes, I think it does.'

'Can you make any suggestion as to the father of the child?'

'No.'

'Could it possibly have been you?'

Dampier returned the superintendent's stare, unflinching. 'It's possible but extremely unlikely.'

Wycliffe relaxed. 'Thank you, that was very frank.'

It was natural for them to walk back together through the gorse, both of them uneasily conscious of being watched from the window.

'I live in the first bungalow.'

They stopped at the gate. 'You realize that we may have further questions for you or your sister, Mr Dampier, but that is all for the moment.'

Dampier nodded. 'I quite understand.' As he opened the gate a huge tabby cat padded towards him and rubbed round his legs. 'That reminds me, what happened to her cat?'

The superintendent was curt. 'I've no idea.'

He was getting the feel of the place, getting to know the people who knew Pussy Welles and that was something. It might not be the

29

best way to conduct an inquiry but for him it was the only way. He had to think himself, almost live himself, into the world which had been the victim's. Darley would look after the routine with superb efficiency and feel with some justification that he was carrying the brunt of the case, but Darley was made for martyrdom and enjoyed it.

He went into breakfast and was given VIP treatment by Sylvie who seemed to have taken him under her wing.

After breakfast Darley telephoned.

'She was definitely married to that fellow Horner. The marriage took place in a Willesden Register Office only a month before they settled in St Ives. She was married in the name of Welles because her parents both died when she was very young and a couple of that name adopted her. They had a bookshop in Richmond but they're retired now and nobody seems to know where they've gone. The girl worked as a secretary but again, nobody can remember where.'

'You've dropped a word to the press – asked for their co-operation et cetera?'

'Of course!'

Of course! He had only said it because Darley expected him to say something. 'I'm surprised that the press haven't turned up here yet.'

'They will.'

An awkward silence.

'Have you any special instructions, sir?'

'What? No, I don't think so. I expect you'll keep busy.'

'I've got the inquest at eleven.'

'Yes, and, incidentally, let me know the arrangements for the funeral. If a relative doesn't turn up . . .'

He dropped the receiver feeling that he had gone down one step further in Darley's estimation. Then he went out into the square, as peaceful as ever; a postman delivering letters, a white dog sunning himself in the middle of the road and a little boy sitting on the steps of the war memorial reading a comic. An old yellow bus rattled in and pulled up by the church. The driver shut off the engine, got out and lit a cigarette, leaning against the wall of the churchyard. Soon people began to arrive in ones and twos, mostly women with shopping bags but sometimes a couple, the men in dark suits which only saw the light once or twice in a week.

30

'Where are they going?' Wycliffe strolled over and stood by the little boy.

'Penzance. It's Saturday.' He didn't look up from reading his comic.

Wycliffe thought it would be a good time to call on the Barneses. He continued across the square and followed a winding lane between granite hedges, out on to the road. As he stood at the junction, the yellow bus passed him and chugged off in the direction of Penzance. He watched it snake round the bends until it was out of sight then took the opposite direction. He found the path to the cove, walked past the farm, past the Barnes' car parked in a clearing and on to the cottage. The door was open but there was nobody about so he knocked. A young woman in a quilted dressing gown came down the passage and he recognized her as the girl from the Mini. It was obvious that she recognized him but they were formal.

'Mrs Barnes? – Superintendent Wycliffe. I would like a word with your husband.'

'I'm afraid my husband isn't up yet; perhaps you will call back later.' Firm, distant.

'It's important and I'd rather wait.'

Then a man's voice from upstairs. 'For God's sake let him in, Ursie, and tell him I'll be down in a minute.'

She shrugged. 'In there.'

A little sitting-room, low ceilinged and dimly lit, the window almost blocked by ivy.

'I'm sorry to come at an inconvenient time.'

No answer. When he was seated in an armchair with broken springs, she said, 'My husband will be down shortly,' then she went out, closing the door behind her.

He could imagine the crisis between them, the armed truce that now prevailed. Barnes had probably counted on an impulsive emotional confession demanding quick and loving absolution; penitence in a warm embrace.

'I can't think what came over me! To treat you the way I did . . . I must have been mad!'

And she was supposed to say: 'Don't think of it, darling – you know it doesn't matter between us – not really . . .'

But it had mattered to Ursula. She was profoundly shocked and

31

she didn't want to talk about it or anything else. All she said was: 'You must give me time to think. I must get used to the idea.'

Now, twenty-four hours had passed and she was still tight lipped and silent. Well, she probably had more shocks coming to her, poor girl.

Wycliffe wished that he had waited outside where he could have smoked his pipe. He felt imprisoned in the dim little room, silent except for the noise of the stream by the gate. They must have taken over the furniture with the cottage; a chiffonier, and Edwardian version of *His* and *Her* chairs, a grotesquely ugly overmantel. Either they had an academic detachment which allowed them to live with it or they were the trend setters in a cult of Edwardiana. He was plucking up courage to go out into the garden when he heard footsteps on the stairs and a moment later Barnes came in, sullenly apologetic. He looked haggard and he was unshaven and unwashed. Wycliffe noticed the weakness of his mouth and chin; a man who might kill from fear but not for jealousy or revenge. He slumped into a chair by the window.

'This is a terrible business.'

'I want to ask you about your association with Miss Welles.'

He nodded. No attempt at evasion.

'When did you last see her?'

The question seemed unexpected and he shifted uneasily in his chair. 'On Wednesday afternoon, the day before she died. I called at the cottage after lunch.'

'You didn't see her again on the Thursday?'

'No.'

Wycliffe sat forward in his chair, causing it to creak alarmingly. He spoke quietly. 'It is fair to tell you, Dr Barnes, that you were seen in the neighbourhood of the cottage after ten o'clock on Thursday night. According to the pathologist the shooting occurred somewhere between nine-thirty and midnight.'

Barnes said nothing.

'You see that your position is serious unless you offer some explanation.'

'I did go to the cottage on Thursday evening but I did not see her.'

'Why not?'

'For the simple reason that she didn't answer the door. I rang but there was no answer.'

'So what did you do?'

'I came away.'

'Were there any lights on in the cottage?'

'Yes, upstairs and down.'

'And yet you came away?'

Barnes seemed embarrassed. 'Yes.'

'Did you hear any music coming from the cottage?'

'Music?'

'The record player.'

'No.'

'Did Miss Welles often fail to answer the door to you?'

'It happened. It meant that it was not a suitable time to call.'

'Perhaps you had a special ring?'

He nodded. 'Yes.'

Wycliffe got up and stood with his back to the fireplace looking down on the seated Barnes. He felt restless, cramped, unable to concentrate in this dark poky little room. 'When you saw her on Wednesday or at any earlier time, did you form the impression that she might be in serious trouble?'

'No.'

'Or danger?'

'Certainly not!'

'Did she ever attempt to blackmail you?'

'How could she?'

'By threatening to tell your wife.'

'No. In any case, she wasn't that sort of girl. She was highly intelligent and sensitive. I can't imagine her trying to blackmail anybody.'

'Did you pay her?'

Barnes made an angry gesture. 'She wasn't a common prostitute!'

Wycliffe frowned. 'I'm not mincing words, Dr Barnes; this is a murder case and you would do well to remember it. This girl was, to say the least, unconventional in her relationships with men and I am asking whether you paid her for her favours to you?'

'It wasn't like that.'

'Then what was it like?'

'From time to time there were small loans.'

'Loans not intended to be repaid, is that it?'

He nodded.

'And what did these loans amount to?'

'A few pounds at a time, not a great deal.'

'Enough to be financially embarrassing?'

A momentary hesitation. 'No.'

Wycliffe's manner became conversational again. 'Were you in love with her?'

'No.'

'Then why did you become involved?'

Barnes looked at him as though the question was an absurdity. 'Surely you understand that some men feel that they are missing something in marriage?'

'And look elsewhere for it?'

'I wasn't actually looking.'

'You mean that it was offered?'

'I suppose you could say that.'

'Are you in love with your wife?'

'Yes!'

As though upon her cue, Ursula Barnes came in; she had changed into a well washed linen dress, pale green and rather too long to be fashionable. She sat down on an upright chair without looking at her husband. 'You don't mind, superintendent?'

'It's up to your husband, Mrs Barnes.'

Barnes shrugged, probably implying that what he thought wouldn't make any difference. Wycliffe continued.

'Did you know that Miss Welles was pregnant?'

'Pregnant?' His surprise seemed genuine. 'I don't believe it!'

'A pathologist doesn't make that kind of mistake, Dr Barnes.'

'Did she know?' He looked nervously at his wife but she seemed indifferent. 'I mean . . .'

'It was eight or nine weeks so she must have had a pretty good idea.' Wycliffe cursed himself for allowing Barnes to sit between him and the light. 'Is it possible that you were the father?'

'No, it is quite impossible.'

'How can you be sure?' The question came not from the super-intendent but from his wife. 'After all, Richard, you were involved with her in a way that has been known to have that result.'

Wycliffe was revising his ideas of Ursula. She had not come in to protect her husband but to derive a malevolent satisfaction from his humiliation. Barnes looked at her with a pained expression before replying.

'If you must know, she was fanatically careful.'

It was Wycliffe who wanted to change the subject. 'Where did you first meet her?'

'We met her at a party, about a year ago.'

'At the Dampiers'?'

'Yes.'

Wycliffe reseated himself in the chair with broken springs. 'What were your impressions of the dead girl, Mrs Barnes?'

She swept the hair from her brow with a quick movement. 'I distrusted her from the start; she was the sort of woman who preys upon men.'

'I am being indiscreet, but my questions are necessary. When did you begin to suspect that your husband was having an affair with her?'

The answer was immediate. 'I didn't suspect; I thought he had more . . .' She stopped herself; perhaps she was going to say more sense or more integrity, but whatever it was, she changed her mind. 'I neither knew nor suspected anything until Richard told me about it after she was dead.'

'Why did you tell your wife at all?' Wycliffe turned to Barnes.

'Why? I should have thought that was obvious.'

'Because he thought I would be sure to find out.' Ursula spoke with a sneer. Reconciliation was still a long way off.

The superintendent changed his ground once more. 'Did she ever speak of her past life – of her life before she came to Kergwyns?'

'Never.'

'But you knew that you were not the only man in her life?'

'I knew that there had been others.'

'Had been?'

'All right, still were.'

'Dampier for one?'

'Yes, Dampier.'

'That was understandable,' Ursula put in quickly. 'If you have seen John, you must realize that he couldn't . . . that it would have been difficult for him to lead a normal life – to marry and have children. The way he sees it, it would be impossible. Even if he

35

found a woman willing to have him, he couldn't allow himself to impose his misfortune on her, to let her carry his burden . . .'

'But surely, his sister is doing precisely that, and Pussy Welles . . .'

'That is quite different!' Ursula interrupted. 'Erica is devoted to him and as for that girl . . .'

Obviously she was less than a woman; a mere safety valve for the noble repressions of the hunchback. Wycliffe had had enough. He stood up. 'Thank you for your help; I shall probably have to come again but meantime, I will send someone along to take your statement, Dr Barnes.'

'My statement?' Barnes looked surprised.

'Of course, about your visit on Wednesday afternoon and your second visit on Thursday evening.'

Barnes walked with him to the gate. The sky had clouded over and heavy drops of rain threatened a downpour but Wycliffe lingered. Now he was in the open he felt in no hurry. 'Can you suggest anyone who might have feared or hated her enough to kill her?'

'No, I can't. The very idea seems absurd.'

'And yet she is dead.'

Wycliffe knew too well that in a case of murder it is a mistake to search for a dramatic or even an *adequate* motive; most killings are done for reasons that seem trivial to all but the killer and so the victim's death appears mysterious and unaccountable. Barnes shivered; perhaps because he was coatless and the cold raindrops made large damp patches on the material of his shirt, perhaps because his thoughts were harrowing.

'I can't imagine who would want to kill her.'

Wycliffe looked at him thoughtfully and murmured half to himself, 'She was killed by a jealous lover, a jealous wife or a very frightened man.' He turned up the collar of his raincoat and hurried off up the path, leaving Barnes looking after him, worried, puzzled, apprehensive.

By the time he reached the road it was raining in earnest. He could have stayed out the shower at the cottage but he liked to withdraw at what he considered to be the right psychological moment. He had no faith in sustained interrogation, little and often was his recipe. Just keep coming back.

The fact that she was pregnant probably explained why she had been worried, why, according to Lomax, she needed money. It fitted with her 'you owe me nothing but there are those who do'. Presumably Barnes was one. He suspected that Barnes had parted with more money than he would admit. If she had pressed him hard, might he have killed her? A weak character driven to desperation. Then there was Dampier – no weakness there, but deformity. Is it possible for a *normal* mind to cohabit with such gross deformity of body? He had seen Dampier on the cliffs exhausting himself in frenzied purposeless endeavour like Quasimodo on the bells. For the first time it occurred to him to associate the tortured malformation of Dampier's body with the secret blemish on the murdered girl. Had she been so morbidly conscious of her own aberration that she could identify herself with his monstrosity? Was the removal of her shoe and stocking after death to be seen as a declaration? Then there were the women to be remembered – Ursula Barnes, Erica Dampier and how many others?

He had been walking almost oblivious of the rain until he realized that he was wet across the shoulders, that water was dripping down his neck from his sodden cap. The whole moorland seemed like a green-brown sponge oozing rivulets of brown water over the tarmac. At one point where a farm entrance bridged the ditch, a blockage sent a river of fluid mud across the road so that he was forced to wade almost ankle deep. He reached the inn at last and went to his room to change without seeing anyone. A warm appetizing smell spiced with garlic came up from the kitchen which seemed to be beneath his room. He could hear the rattle of pans and crocks and a girl's voice singing. He wondered if Sylvie did the cooking as well as everything else.

When he was standing in his shirt, there was a tap at the door and he put on his dressing gown. It was Sylvie, holding an envelope by one corner.

'What is it?'

'It's for you, it came just after you went out, dropped into the letter box with the rest of the post. I haven't shown it to him.' She was conspiratorial.

A cheap envelope addressed in pencilled capitals. He was familiar enough with these.

'Didn't you ought to test it for fingerprints?'

37

The message, also in pencilled letters was brief:

BARNES HAS OR HAD AN AUTOMATIC PISTOL

Nothing remarkable under the circumstances about an anonymous letter. Every murder case brought a crop of them, some malicious, most of them crazy, the odd one now and then, informative. But they all had to be investigated. He had to admit that few were as explicit as this one and if Barnes did possess an automatic and if it turned out to have been recently fired and if . . . Well, put all the ifs together and there might be the beginnings of a case.

3

At the start of his affair with Pussy Welles, Richard Barnes could look back upon four blameless years of marriage to Ursula. On the whole, they had been four good years, they got on well together. Ursula liked to manage people and Richard had no objection to being managed, they were both involved in interesting academic work and neither of them wanted children. It seemed a pretty good recipe for marriage and it worked. But as time went on Richard began to be troubled by vague dissatisfactions, he felt that in the even tenor of their ways, in their tacit acceptance of each other, in the very stability of their relationship, they were missing something. At least, he was. And he was not long in reaching a conclusion about the source of his discontent. There was no adventure and little romance left in their marriage. He blamed Ursula for this; she had domesticated sex. Before their marriage, she had been very thoroughly into the subject of marital love through the media of both literature and expert consultation and even after they were married she continued to study their relationship as though it was a subject for a projected thesis. In short, and in Richard's opinion, she had acquired an objective and clinical approach which came near to sterilizing their embraces. He could still derive the keenest anticipatory pleasure from her petite blonde body but in its climax, their lovemaking seemed to be at the level of hygienic eroticism.

It is probable that like thousands of other couples they would have gone on making the best of this rather poor bargain if Ursula had not come into money. From the modest competence of their combined university salaries they entered upon relative affluence. And the first thing they did was to buy a cottage in a charming valley near the village of Kergwyns on the north Cornish coast. It was during their first vacation in the cottage that they met Pussy Welles and it was during that same vacation that Richard made her his mistress. At least that was how he saw it.

Richard, like most men, thought of himself as having a way with women, though he would have had difficulty in finding justification for thinking anything of the kind. But it was confidence born of this unwarranted assumption which encouraged him to enter so light-heartedly into his relationship with Pussy Welles. It was all so delightfully simple and it solved his problem. True, there had to be a little deception, but as life with Ursula seemed to benefit rather than otherwise, he was not troubled in his conscience for long. By the end of the Easter vacation he felt that he had discovered the secret of the good life. There was nothing sordid about it, their assignations were occasions for gaiety and mirth and they achieved undreamed of satisfaction in each other's arms. From time to time, quite suddenly and inconsequentially, Pussy would say, 'Oh, Richard! – lend me a few quid, I have to pay the milk bill.' So that he was never in a position of having to actually pay her; she was far too civilized and sophisticated for that.

During the following summer and Christmas vacations their liaison continued and flourished. The sums which Pussy 'borrowed' increased, causing Richard some misgivings. 'I wonder if you could manage a fiver to tide me over until Saturday, Ricky, darling . . .' Luckily, and surprisingly, Ursula had become quite casual about money so that a few pounds here or there hardly seemed to matter. And it was well worth it. He was a new man; his work prospered, his outlook grew more mature, more tolerant, and he felt affectionately protective towards Ursula. Such benefits accrue when the sacred and the profane are kept decently apart.

His main difficulty had been to explain his absences to Ursula but he soon acquired an astonishing facility at contriving situations in which it seemed natural for them to be apart so that he was able to achieve three and sometimes four meetings a week while they were at the cottage.

The crisis came during their second Easter at Kergwyns. Ursula was a moderator for some intermediate examinations and she had to remain up during the first week of the vacation. The opportunity was heaven sent, but he must be discreet.

'I don't want to go down without you, darling.'

'Don't be silly, Richard. You'll have a week of peace and quiet to spend on your book.'

'Well, there is that . . . if you don't mind . . .'

'Silly boy!'

He wrote to Pussy Welles at once telling her the good news.

And so, early on a fine Monday morning, he stacked the car with clean linen and provisions and set out. By midday he was approaching St Ives with the great panoramic sweep of the bay on his right; the blue-green sea shattering the sunlight into a million dazzling fragments; the lighthouse on its little island, whiter than white. Too good to be true – a story book picture – *First Day of the Holiday.* Five minutes edging through the narrow streets of the town, a long climb, and he was out on the moor in sight of the sea again. The gorse was more golden than he had ever known, the dead stalks of last year's bracken made great splashes of rusty red, and the grey-green lichens softened the giant granite outcrops so that they looked tamed, amenable.

A mile along the road, within sight of the square squat tower of Kergwyns church, he turned off down a rutted track in the direction of the sea. Past the entrance to a farm the track petered out in a clearing almost enclosed by blackthorn and goat willow. He left the car there and followed a footpath for fifty yards, over the dark waters of a little stream to a second clearing where the cottage was, hemmed in on three sides by a coppice of sycamores. The stream and the footpath continued together past the gate of the cottage towards the cove, half a mile down the valley. Apart from the noise of the stream it was a silent place, still; even in the sunshine the light was mellow. To some it might seem sinister but Richard loved it; he looked forward especially to these first moments of arrival and savoured them as a connoisseur of sensual pleasure. The little garden was choked with ferns and the cobbled path carpeted in moss; the air was moist and laden with the blended indefinable scents of thrusting growth and equally vigorous decay.

He removed the white card from the front door: *Ursula and Richard Barnes. Redirected mail to . . .* and their address. They never locked the door, which was foolish, but it was another way of emphasizing that this was their special place, that it was different. First he would light the fire to air the place, then he would unpack the car . . . His eyes rested on the telephone – their only amenity –

Ursula called it. Should he ring now? Or save it until he had done the chores? He was like an adolescent, unsure of the reception he would get from his first love, eager to put it to the test. He picked up the receiver and dialled her number. The tantalizing wait, punctuated by those absurd noises that mock at our most profound emotions. He willed her to be there and to answer. She was in the kitchen preparing her midday meal; the muffled ringing came through from the little hall at the front of the house. She was wearing her blue flowered housecoat, her auburn hair caught with a slide at the back, like a little girl's. She never hurried. He imagined her drying her hands, walking calmly, gracefully, through the sitting-room, opening the little white door with the glass panels, reaching for the receiver . . . he waited for the click . . . but it never came. He waited through an interminable number of rings before deciding that she was out. He was just replacing the receiver when he heard her voice, musical, controlled, 'Kergwyns 42'.

'It's me – Ricky.'

'Oh, so you're down already.'

'I told you in my letter. Ursula has to stay up for another week, so I'm alone . . . Can I see you?'

'When?'

'Tonight at the cottage?'

'Why at the cottage?'

'I told you I'm alone, and you remember the last time?' He tried to breathe warmth and tenderness into the telephone.

'All right, then.'

'What time?'

Hesitation. 'I'll come when I can.' She dropped the telephone.

Her coldness rebuffed him, but it would be different when she came. He set about his tasks, trying to shake off a lingering sense of anti-climax. After lunch out of tins he walked down to the cove killing time. Early in their acquaintanceship, Pussy had warned him in her bantering way.

'All you want from me is the one thing your wife doesn't give you; ours is a convenient arrangement, an accommodation. It's not romance.'

She was right, of course. He tried to reconcile himself to the knowledge that she had other men. Why should it matter? But it did.

From six o'clock, he was on tenterhooks. Would she come for a meal? Once, when Ursula had gone away overnight she came to the cottage and they cooked omelettes on the bottle gas cooker and ate them in front of the fire, drinking a whole bottle of wine between them. She had stayed the night, the only time in his life when he had actually slept with another woman. Well, he had plenty of eggs and cheese and tomatoes and wine, and he had aired the bed. He sat in the living-room with the wireless playing softly, watching the window, watching the light turn yellow, then fade almost to darkness before she came.

'I couldn't come before.'

He took her coat and she stood in the firelight. She looked chaste in her white blouse and black skirt, just standing there, but when she walked, the sway of her hips and the way she held herself so that her breasts protruded . . . He took her in his arms but she disengaged herself.

'Later, Ricky!' She chided him like a fond mother, her voice reproving, but full of promise. She kissed his cheek. The old magic.

'Will you have something to eat?'

'No thanks, I've had a meal.'

'Drink?'

'All right, make it a gin if you've got some.'

He handed her the drink and sat opposite her, feasting his eyes. It seemed incredible that directly she would allow him to possess her. She was the kind of girl that every man would stop to look at as she passed down the street; the very antithesis of Ursula. Not but what Ursula had a lovely body, but clothed in her habitual woolly jumper and tweed skirt, she looked dumpy, homely. Pussy's skirt clung to her – like fur.

The little bedroom was warmed by the flue from the fire below. The double bed and a dressing-table filled almost all the space and the soft light from an oil lamp, suspended, glowed on the motley colours of Ursula's patchwork quilt.

He watched her undress, slowly, deliberately, gracefully. It occurred to him that she was a professional doing her job in a thoroughly professional way, studying the needs of a client and meeting them. He banished the thought as unworthy. He preferred to believe that she enjoyed making love; certainly if she had been entirely mercenary, she could have done a great deal better for herself. He could never make up his mind about Pussy.

Making love with her was like playing an intricate game which you know you are going to win in the end. She had the art of turning each encounter into an opportunity for fresh conquest, seeming to resist each phase in the progress of love until overcome by blandishment; defeated by the consummate skill of her lover, she could resist no longer. In another age and another place, she might have been one of the great courtesans.

She stayed the night. When Richard woke in the morning he was momentarily shocked by the auburn head on his wife's pillow, then he remembered and reached out a hand to stroke her body. She turned over on to her back, wide awake at once, like someone who sleeps on guard. She sat up, pushing her hair back with a sweeping movement of both hands. Outside everything was grey and raindrops chased each other down the little window panes.

'Damn! It's raining.'

'It doesn't matter, I'll run you back in the car.'

'You can drop me at the corner, I don't want to give them more to gossip about than they've got already.'

She lit a cigarette; he fondled her bare breast without achieving the slightest response.

'Ricky . . .'

He raised himself on his elbow. 'What is it?'

She studied the glowing end of her cigarette. 'I need some money.'

'Well?'

'A lot of money.'

'How much?'

She exhaled the blue smoke slowly, watching it rise in a thin spiral column to the ceiling. 'A hundred and fifty pounds, and I need it quickly – before the week is out.'

'But . . .' He was scared, but before he could say more she stopped him.

'Before you start to argue, Ricky, listen!' Her voice was hard, her features cast in a mould that he scarcely recognized. 'You've had what you wanted from me at less than the price of a street girl. What I'm asking for is just something off the arrears; something on account.'

She got out of bed and began to collect her clothes. With complete irrelevance he realized for the first time that she dyed her hair. She was fair – like Ursula! Why hadn't he seen that before? Certainly not for the want of opportunity. She was a cheat! Absurdly, irrationally, this distressed him as much as her demand for money.

'But I don't think I can get hold of a hundred and fifty pounds without Ursula knowing . . .'

'That's your problem!' She sat on the foot of the bed, brushing her hair.

He was silent, calculating. He might just manage it.

'Well?'

'I'll see what I can do.'

'Good! You mustn't run up debts you can't pay.'

With that, she reverted to normal. They had breakfast together, she chatted away, giving him the latest news, and when he dropped her at the corner where the road to the village left the main road, she said:

'Shall I see you tonight?'

He stopped himself from saying 'Yes', just in time. 'No, not tonight, I must get in some work on my book.'

He turned the car and drove back over the shining wet road muttering to himself in time with the sweep of the screen wipers. 'Bloody fool! Bloody fool! Bloody, bloody, bloody, fool.' He parked the car in the clearing and returned to the cottage. He would have liked to tell Ursula the whole story, to throw himself on her mercy, but he dared not.

'It isn't that I'm narrow minded. Rationally, I know that a man sleeping with another woman may mean almost nothing, but in practice, I don't know . . . If you ever did it, Richard, I think I should feel that I had failed you – let you down. I should lose confidence in myself – I don't think I could carry on. I really don't.' That had been Ursula's reaction to the misconduct of one of Richard's colleagues.

'I mean, a successful marriage is so much a matter of mutual trust . . . No, I just couldn't face it.'

They ran a joint bank account but since his association with Pussy Welles, he had opened a secret account, paying in small sums whenever he could to provide for his vacation expenses. He thought that there was something over a hundred pounds in his account and he could draw that out with, perhaps, twenty from their joint account; that would be as much as he dared and it would have to

45

do. He went back to the car and drove to St Ives, to the bank, coming away with a hundred and thirty-six pounds in notes – the price of folly. Suddenly the whole affair had become squalid, it had turned sour on him. Why? Was it because he was being asked to pay the market price for what he wanted instead of getting it on the cheap? However he thought of it he could find no shred of comfort, no salve for his injured pride. My God! – but he would know better in the future! And then he thought of Ursula with shame and humility and warm affection – he would make it up to her.

Next morning – Wednesday – he had heard nothing further from Pussy Welles and they had made no arrangement for him to hand over the money. He wanted to be clear of it, to close the episode; and Ursula would be arriving on Friday. He decided to lunch at the inn, to fortify himself with a few drinks and to go along to Pussy's house afterwards. He walked to Kergwyns in the watery April sunshine. The square was empty and silent, the grey granite and the grey-blue slate made it seem grim, almost sinister. The churchyard boasted a little coppice of wind stunted sycamores, now in pale green leaf, otherwise only the lichens provided any splash of colour.

The bar was empty except for the landlord, reading his newspaper spread on the counter.

'Morning, Dr Barnes. I heard you were with us again.'

'Morning, Mike.'

'The usual?'

Richard's usual was a light ale. He would have liked a short drink but he was flattered at having his taste remembered.

'Have one with me, Mike.'

He was of a timid disposition and he felt gratified to be on easy terms with a great brute of a man like the landlord.

'Mrs Barnes not with you?'

He entered into a more detailed explanation than was necessary and stopped himself too late when he saw Young looking at him, an amused, slightly contemptuous smile on the expressive half of his face. He changed the subject hastily. 'I suppose you can fix me up with lunch, Mike?'

Young turned over the page of his newspaper. 'I suppose I shall have to, Dr Barnes, it wouldn't do if we bachelors didn't stick together, would it?'

★

After lunch he went along to the cottage resolved to be distant, matter-of-fact and to make an unequivocal break, but his antagonism had evaporated. He was prepared to admit that he owed her more than an occasional pound or two changing hands under the euphemism of a loan. When she answered the door she looked preoccupied and tired but she seemed pleased to see him. She had been working in the sitting-room and there were reference books scattered on the floor and a clip-board of crossword blanks on the arm of her chair.

'I'm trying to make my deadline.'

He said that he didn't want to interrupt but she brushed this aside.

'I'm glad of the excuse.'

Richard was an earnest young man, not to say a little dull, and making up crosswords was an employment unworthy of academic talent. 'I can't understand why you don't do something really creative. Pussy. With your brains and imagination you could *write*.'

She laughed. 'I like doing it and they pay me.'

'But it's only a sort of game.'

'Of course, but what's wrong with that?'

'You could do something *worthwhile!*'

She was teasing him as she often did. 'It depends on what you believe to be worthwhile.'

He stopped to think, trying to say something challenging. 'If you had Aladdin's lamp, what would you do?'

She frowned and pursed her lips. 'I think I'd put myself at the head of a great financial empire – the tycoon of all tycoons.'

'For the money?'

She shook her head. 'No, I don't think the money would interest me. I should do it for the satisfaction in making decisions and watching their repercussions. I should plan and predict then sit back and watch.'

'But you'd have to have some purpose in mind – an aim.'

She looked at him suddenly serious. 'Why? You throw a stone into a pond just because you want to watch the ripples. That's reason enough.'

'But if it's power you want, why not be a general or a field marshal?'

'All right! I'll settle for a field marshal's baton – but only in

47

wartime; peacetime soldiers are pathetic; children playing with rather stupid toys.'

He was uncomfortable, unable to gauge her mood. 'I hope you'll stick to crosswords.'

'Why?'

'Because people who want power for its own sake are dangerous.'

She was lying back in her chair, relaxed – *available*. He knew that with very little persuasion he could take her upstairs and resume where they had left off. He was tempted but he recalled his panic over the money. It couldn't happen again without Ursula knowing. Suddenly he realized that she was laughing at him.

'You are a timid soul, Richard! Don't you ever feel that you want to live dangerously?'

He was angry. 'No, I don't!'

She looked at him, thoughtful and detached. 'But it isn't your choice is it? Decision is the privilege of the strong.'

He took the envelope containing the money from his pocket and dropped it on the table. 'There's a hundred and thirty-six pounds there. It was all I could manage.'

She glanced at the envelope but said nothing.

'Will it be enough?'

'For what?'

He gestured angrily. 'I think I had better go.'

She did nothing to stop him but she followed him to the door and stood on the step while he covered the little distance to the gate. 'Goodbye, Richard.'

He did not answer. In the lane he met Lomax who looked at him queerly. He had rarely been so angry, never so humiliated.

Ursula was arriving on Friday morning – less than forty-eight hours to go. In that time he must try to close a chapter in his life, banish this girl from his mind, forget the humiliation he had suffered. He was accomplished in the art of forgetting but it took time, and he was anxious that Ursula, quick to sense any sudden change in him, should not probe with solicitous questions. The recipe was exercise and hard work and he followed it conscientiously. His book, a psychological novel, long projected, painfully begun and intermittently pursued, had never received such concentrated attention, and on the Thursday afternoon he walked by the cliff path to St Ives, returning on foot by the road. He was tired but relaxed. He had certainly not forgotten but his recollection was already blurred at the edges, he was in the mood to write it off to experience. Soon his memory would be so hazy that it would be easy to accept a more flattering view of the facts.

He felt hungry and took trouble over preparing his meal, he opened a bottle of wine, found a detective novel which he hadn't read, and settled down to eat. Afterwards he cleared away and washed up ready for Ursula's arrival in the morning. He looked forward to it with warm and tender anticipation. Good old Ursie! Read until bedtime.

4

Wycliffe sat back in his chair and placed the palms of his hands together as though in prayer. 'That clears up the details of your visit to the cottage on Wednesday afternoon, Dr Barnes. Now we come to Thursday evening. In your original statement you said that you were not admitted, that you rang the bell and although the house was lit up, no-one answered your ring. This was not unprecedented so after a little wait you returned home. That is what you said – is it in fact what happened? Or do you wish to revise this part of your statement also?'

'No! I mean that it is not exactly what happened and I do want to revise it.'

He looked exhausted and ill, the colour drained from his cheeks, his whole body sagging in the chair. He was demoralized – not because he had been harshly treated – Wycliffe seemed to go out of his way to be courteous, almost respectful in the manner of his questions but he could not disguise their implication. For the first time in his life he had been caught out in a pattern of clumsy lies. Never since he was a schoolboy facing his headmaster had he been so called to account. 'But that was not what you said, Dr Barnes . . .' It was devastating: a demeaning experience.

How long had he been there? He had no idea. It seemed that he had spent a significant part of his life slumped in that chair, staring at the window behind the superintendent. The glass had been obscured with white paint which had flaked off, giving a mosaic view of a red brick wall. The light was yellowing so it must be evening. They had given him some tea but he had lunched at home with Ursula. Incredible!

A man has been at St Ives Police Station since two o'clock this afternoon, helping the police with their inquiries . . .

That is what they would be saying on the *News* and in the evening papers. People round their television sets and in pubs would feel just a little more cosy and secure. 'So they got him!'

It had started with the pistol.

After the superintendent's visit and after his statement had been taken, it seemed that with luck the worst might be over. He set about reassuring Ursula, winning her back, and he seemed to be making progress. Oddly, it was by telling her in detail of his affair with Pussy that he began to gain her sympathy and even her understanding. 'You poor simpleton, Richard! Really, you need someone to look after you! But the police can't seriously suspect you of having killed her, can they?'

'Of course not!'

But he didn't tell her of the hundred and thirty-six pounds he had paid to Pussy, nor did he mention the gun. That was left to Super-intendent Wycliffe.

It was the Sunday following the murder; they had just finished lunch and Ursula was making coffee while Richard sat at the table, reading. Ursula answered the superintendent's knock.

'I hope I'm not spoiling your lunch, Mrs Barnes. I'll try not to be too long.' He did not wait to be invited but followed her into the living-room. 'Ah, Dr Barnes – just one or two more questions.'

Richard sat immobile, waiting.

'I understand that you were once a member of an archaeological expedition to the Middle East?'

'Yes, about five or six years ago.'

'You were issued with a .32 automatic pistol?'

'Yes.'

'You did not hand it in at the end of the expedition?'

'No, it was an oversight. Nobody asked for it and I forgot about it until months later.'

'Where is it now?'

'Until recently it was where it has always been with my field gear in a box upstairs.'

'And now?'

He passed a hand over his brow, a hackneyed gesture of despair. 'I don't know; it's gone.'

'Richard!'

'It's true. After I knew that Pussy Welles had been shot, I thought of the gun and I went to look for it – you know how it is – just in case . . .' He seemed to be appealing to the superintendent for understanding but Wycliffe was inscrutable.

'After keeping the gun illegally for a number of years you didn't report its loss?'

'No, I was scared.'

'Is this your gun?' Wycliffe produced a pistol from his pocket. 'We can check, of course, but it will take time.'

Richard took the gun and examined it. 'Yes, I think it's mine – in fact, I'm sure.'

Wycliffe nodded. 'It is also, according to the experts, the gun that killed Miss Welles.'

'But that doesn't mean . . .' Ursula began, then stopped.

'It means that she was shot with a gun for which your husband was responsible. I think you should make a further statement, Dr Barnes – at the station.'

'All right, I will drive over this afternoon.'

'I have a car and driver waiting on the road, Dr Barnes. I think we should get it over.'

But it wasn't over yet; only beginning. They were just getting to the most difficult part.

'After leaving Miss Welles on bad terms on Wednesday afternoon, why did you go to see her again on Thursday evening?'

'She telephoned me at about a quarter to ten saying that she must see me. If I didn't come, I should regret it.'

'She threatened you?'

'I suppose that's what it amounted to but at the time it seemed that she was more distressed than threatening. I didn't want to become involved again but I felt that I must find out what was happening. Pussy wasn't the sort to flap but when I tried to question her on the telephone, she just rang off.'

'So you took your car and drove to Kergwyns. What happened?'

Barnes made a little gesture of revulsion and when he spoke his voice was barely audible so that Wycliffe had to lean forward to catch his words. 'When I arrived, the cottage was lit up as I said and there was no answer to my ring. In the ordinary way, I would have gone back home but in view of her telephone call I had to see her. I banged on the door and it pushed open – it was unfastened – so I went in.' He stopped as though the scene presented itself afresh to his eyes. 'She was lying on the floor – dead.'

Wycliffe waited for him to continue, thinking it best that he should tell his own story, but the silence lengthened and at last, he prompted, 'What did you do?'

'Do? I just stood and looked at her; I was too shocked to do anything.' He spoke like a man drugged, every sentence seemed to cost him a disproportionate effort of thought and enunciation.

'Did you notice anything odd about her?'

'Odd? Yes, she had on only one shoe and stocking and her bare foot was deformed. That somehow made it worse.' A glimmer of animation brought life to his eyes. 'I know it sounds ridiculous but it shocked me almost as much as seeing her dead.'

Wycliffe frowned. 'But you must have known that she had a deformed foot.'

'You would think so, but I didn't. She always wore ankle socks, even when . . . even when she was going to bed. I had never seen her feet uncovered, she used to say that she suffered from bad circulation.' He seemed to dwell on these thoughts and Wycliffe was about to bring him back with a question when he carried on of his own accord. 'I was going to telephone the police – I even went to the porch where the telephone is, then it struck me that Pussy's death would bring everything out into the open. I wanted to avoid that if I could; it would do her no good and it might finish me with my wife . . .'

'What about the gun?'

For the most part Barnes had avoided the superintendent's eyes, now he looked straight at him. 'I don't know what you mean.'

Wycliffe betrayed the first sign of impatience. 'Dr Barnes, it must be clear to you that if someone stole your gun for the killing, he would have no reason to remove it from the scene of the crime. If he did, it would be a dangerous embarrassment.' He paused to allow his reasoning to sink in. 'But if you recognized the gun, lying beside the body, it would be quite natural, though unwise, for you to take it and hide it.'

Barnes would have interrupted but Wycliffe wouldn't let him.

'Let me finish! Your gun was found, quite by chance. A culvert beneath a farm entrance between your cottage and the village was blocked so that the drainage water flooded the road. In clearing the culvert, your gun was found, otherwise it might have stayed there for years.' Wycliffe leaned forward and spoke with great earnestness.

'Now, Dr Barnes, let me advise you to be absolutely frank, did you remove that gun and hide it?'

'No, I saw no gun.'

Wycliffe nodded but it was impossible to judge whether he accepted the denial as truth. 'Very well then, what *did* you do?'

It seemed to take a little while for Barnes to reorientate his thoughts. 'I went upstairs to the bureau to see if she had kept any of my letters or anything else that might involve me, but somebody had got there first; there were no letters or anything of that sort and I found nothing.'

'Nothing, Dr Barnes?' The superintendent waited, then added, 'Remember you are making a fresh statement.'

He seemed to debate within himself and Wycliffe made no attempt to hurry him. At last, he had reached a decision. 'All right! I found the hundred pounds in ten pound notes – still in the paper band as I had it from the bank.'

'And you took it?'

He nodded. 'Not that I wanted the money back but I thought that the bank were bound to have the numbers and that the police would try to trace the money.'

'You still have those notes?'

'No.' He looked sheepish. 'I stopped the car on my way back and stuffed them down a hole in the hedge.'

'A hole in the hedge.' The superintendent's voice was expressionless. 'You could find the place again?'

'I think so.'

'So that having looked for anything that might involve you and having taken the money, you walked out.'

'Yes. I must admit that I was scared.'

There could be no doubt that he had been scared or that he still was. Could his foolish, incriminating behaviour be attributed wholly to that? Or had he been so frightened that as weak men sometimes will he had resorted to a desperate remedy?

Wycliffe asked many more questions. Who visited the cottage regularly? Who else might have known about the gun? Had he ever seen any evidence of intruders? But nothing fresh emerged. The light in the dingy little room faded and the lamp was switched on. Barnes made a new formal statement and signed it. Gradually it was being borne in upon him that he really was under suspicion of murder. Perhaps the superintendent was convinced of his guilt and believed that it was only a matter of time before he admitted it.

'What time is it?'

'Nine o'clock.'

In connection with the Cornish murder a man has been at the St Ives Police Station for seven hours, assisting the police with their inquiries . . . That was what they would be saying on the *News*. And the gossips would say: 'They must be sure of their ground to keep him there like that.'

For long periods of time they seemed to ignore him. People came and went as though he was just part of the furniture but they never left him alone, there was always somebody in the room. If they were going to detain him all night, would they have to charge him? He wouldn't ask questions of that sort – not let them see that he had even considered the possibility. What would happen if he said, 'I am going home. If you want me again, you know where to find me!'? He was deliberating whether to try it when the superintendent came back again after a lengthy absence.

'Well, Dr Barnes, that is all for the moment. Your wife is outside with your car, waiting to take you home.'

For an instant he felt like an animal whose cage is suddenly thrown open, incredulous, suspicious. 'I can go?'

Wycliffe looked at him gravely. 'I have insufficient evidence to detain you, Dr Barnes.'

The man who has been at St Ives Police Station for over eight hours, assisting the police with their inquiries into the Cornish murder, left at a little after ten o'clock this evening. In a brief statement to the press, Superintendent Charles Wycliffe said that he did not envisage an early arrest.

A set-back for the listeners and watchers.

But the evidence that was to turn the scale came next day, the day of the funeral.

All Darley's efforts had failed to produce a relative. Her mother, by adoption, was dead and her father in a home for the confused elderly. To Wycliffe's surprise, it was Lomax who sought and obtained the coroner's authority to make arrangements for the funeral. And so she was buried in the little churchyard among the slate headstones, an interloper in a company of Nances, Pascoes, Kessells and Trewins.

In a thin grey drizzle a little group of men in raincoats stood round the grave while the vicar read the shortened service. Wycliffe was there, intrigued by his fellow mourners. No women. He was surprised to see Barnes; perhaps his wife thought it impolitic for him to stay away. The innkeeper was there, lugubrious and solemn; Harvey Clemens and Aubrey Reed shared an enormous umbrella and Dampier braved the public gaze for once. Lomax was chief mourner and he was accompanied by a tall, fleshy young man whom Wycliffe identified afterwards as the school teacher, Mitford.

The strangest group of mourners in the superintendent's wide experience. Despite the rain a little knot of villagers waited by the churchyard gate. He could imagine their gossip and scolded himself for seeing a certain humour in the situation.

Mainly because he did not want to walk back with the others, he lingered by the graveside while they trooped to the gate under an archway of dripping sycamores. Then he saw a woman in a plum coloured raincoat, with an umbrella to match, picking her way among the graves towards him, her absurd little high heels clutching at the spongy ground with every step.

'Superintendent Wycliffe? Elsa Cooper.'

She was younger than he had supposed, now that he could see her face, not much over thirty, a plump, self contained woman, her features a little coarse and hard. She obviously managed something, a small hotel, a hairdresser's, a dress shop – perhaps a café. She had that indefinable air of experience which Wycliffe had known so well among a certain class of women in the city. Not easily frightened. 'I wanted to speak to you. I was a friend of Pussy Welles.'

A woman friend!

Wycliffe was wet already and getting wetter. The woman's umbrella was merely an irritation, a threat at the level of his eyes. 'Let's find somewhere dry.' And they moved into the shelter of the church porch and sat side by side on the wormeaten bench like lovers escaping from the rain.

It turned out that she owned a boarding house in St Ives.

'I got to know Pussy when she came to St Ives on holiday; she stayed at my place there years running, though it wasn't mine then, mother was still alive.'

'Did she come alone or with her family?'

'Oh, she was alone. She was a typist or secretary or something in London and she wasn't short of money.'

'She would have been about nineteen or twenty, I suppose, when you first knew her?'

'About that. She was four years younger than me. Anyway, when she got married and they came to St Ives to live, we stayed friendly – not what you might call close, but she would occasionally drop in of a morning for coffee and we would have a shopping spree now and then in Penzance. After Arthur, that was her husband, was killed, we kept in touch; she moved out here and whenever I felt like a gossip I would ring her up and she would do the same. That's what happened on Thursday evening.'

'Thursday evening?'

'The night she was killed.'

'You rang her up?'

'No, she rang me.' She stood up, divesting herself of her raincoat, and began to shake it vigorously. 'This damned rain! There's no end to it! She wanted my advice.'

She seemed to expect the superintendent to ask the obvious question but as he remained silent she went on: 'Pussy was pregnant and she wanted to know if I would help her.'

'In what way?'

She gave him a look of contempt. 'What sort of help does an unmarried girl need when she's pregnant? Do I have to spell it out?'

Wycliffe was unperturbed. 'Are you an abortionist, then?'

'No, I'm not! And if that's all the thanks I get for coming to you, I can go again.' The superintendent said nothing but she made no attempt to go. 'I am not an abortionist but neither am I wet behind the ears. I've been around and I might have helped Pussy if this hadn't happened. You see, I'm being frank.'

'The world is hard on us women and we've got to stick together,' Wycliffe said tonelessly.

Her anger flared in a look. 'You know all the answers, don't you?'

'I've heard them so many times before. Never mind, what happened on the telephone?'

She shrugged. 'If it wasn't for the thought of him getting away with it, I wouldn't bother, I'm damned if I would!'

'Who, getting away with it?'

'Dr bloody Barnes. He was with her when she phoned me.'

'How do you know?'

'She told me. I asked her if she knew who the father was and she said that she did. Ricky Barnes. Then she said, "He's here now, I'm trying to work out the details with him." I said I hoped the details included some cash and she laughed and said that I needn't worry.'

'What time was this?'

'About a quarter to ten. I was watching a programme on the telly which finished at a quarter to ten and when I came back from talking to her it was over.'

'You are prepared to make a statement?'

'I shouldn't have come if I wasn't.' She fiddled with the clasp of her handbag and seemed ill at ease. 'There's something else.'

'Something else?'

'Pussy was laughing as I told you, then she suddenly got serious. She spoke almost in a whisper so that I could hardly hear her. "If anything happens to me, Elsa," she said, "remember I told you." I asked her what she meant but she wouldn't say any more. When I pressed her she said to forget it, that she was only joking. You could never tell with Pussy.'

'Did you take her seriously?'

'Not at the time – not really.'

'But you do now?'

'What do you think?'

Wycliffe regarded her gravely. 'This happened last Thursday evening and you must have heard on Friday that she was dead, now it's Monday. You haven't hurried yourself.'

She stood up and began to put on her raincoat. 'I've had dealings with the police before and the local bunch don't have a very high opinion of me. I might easily have got short changed. Then I thought of coming to see you. Anyway, you can make what you like of it, I've got to get back.'

'Wait! You knew Pussy Welles three years before she came to live here, did she know anyone else in the district at that time?'

She gave him a knowing look. 'You mean any of the Kergwyns lot? She got herself mixed up with Mike Young, he was quite the lad about town in those days, believe it or not. She used to go out to Kergwyns so I suppose she must have come across the others but she never mentioned them to me that I can remember.'

'Did she ever speak to you of her home or her people?'

'I don't think so; not much anyway. I remember her father kept a shop of some sort in Richmond and she worked in the City I think, but that's about all.'

'No talk of boy friends?'

'Not really. I remember her telling me once that there was a man who had taken a fancy to her, giving her expensive presents, that sort of thing. I had the impression he was her boss but I may be wrong. Anyway he must have been a lot older than her for she spoke of him as "my old man".'

'It couldn't have been Arthur Horner?'

She shook her head decisively. 'No. That was a whirlwind court-ship and marriage; in any case he was very little older than her.'

'One more question: you say you were her friend, what did you think of her?'

She seemed surprised by the question and looked at him doubt-fully before answering. 'Think of her? – I suppose I thought she was a queer sort of girl. Not my sort really; for one thing she was well educated and I think she came from a good home, but she had to have men.' She paused, screwed up her snub little nose. 'I've never understood her. She didn't do it for the money, that's certain; she could have made a living easily enough without that. And yet she hated the men she went with.'

'Hated them?'

'That's what I said. At least, she despised them. Not at first, of course, when they were new, but it wasn't long before she would change. The funny thing was, she was reluctant to give them up . . . as I said I never understood her. There was something strange about her attitude to men – something a bit frightening.'

'Frightening?' Wycliffe tried to get her to enlarge on the word but she couldn't or wouldn't. He watched her tapping her way down the path to the gate and sat for some time before getting up to follow.

Well, he had more than enough evidence for an arrest. Not from the best sources but it was enough to force his hand. He walked slowly back through the rain to the inn where Inspector Darley was waiting for him. He took no satisfaction in the prospect of this arrest. It was not the logical outcome of a process of patient investigation and study, of fact and reason; it was a course forced upon him by an accumulation of damning evidence which he had not even sought. He did not necessarily believe that Barnes was innocent, equally, he was unconvinced of his guilt, but there is a point beyond which a police officer must act on the evidence whatever he thinks of it. Darley could not understand him.

'The court will decide whether he's guilty; it's not our problem.'

This trite statement of the obvious did nothing to improve the superintendent's temper.

They were sitting in a little private room at the inn which the landlord had offered for their use. There were wicker chairs and small circular tables with beer mats and little else.

'All right, let's hear the case as we shall put it to the DPP.'

Darley rubbed his chin and prepared to expound. 'In the first place, Barnes was having an affair with the deceased. On his own admission, she had been making increasing demands for money and the day before her death, he claims to have paid her more than a hundred and thirty pounds – the sort of sum he couldn't raise twice without his wife's knowledge.' Darley had produced his notebook and was leafing through the pages, his great index finger followed the lines of a paragraph here and there.

'We know that the girl was pregnant and, according to this Cooper woman, she believed that Barnes was the child's father. Cooper also says that she was trying to secure an abortion and, presumably, it was for that she needed the money.'

'But he had already paid her the money,' Wycliffe intervened. 'There is nothing to suggest that she was asking for more.'

Darley smiled. 'I've thought of that. Barnes certainly drew a hundred and thirty-six pounds from the bank but we only have his word for it that he paid it over. All we found of the money was thirty odd pounds. I know he claims to have taken back the tenners and hidden them to protect himself but that money hasn't been found and he seems unable to help.'

Wycliffe sighed. 'I don't know where that gets us, but go on, anyway.'

Darley heaved his great bulk forward in his chair to get a better light on his notebook. 'Then, of course, there's the pistol. He used a weapon which he had had by him for years and which no-one was supposed to know about; afterwards, he hid it. Should we have found out about the pistol if somebody hadn't written an anonymous note? Finally he is seen on the doorstep of the girl's cottage at ten o'clock. He says that he had just arrived but, according to Elsa Cooper, he was at the cottage when Pussy Welles rang her at a little before quarter to ten.'

Wycliffe stood up and walked to the window. It looked out on a yard stacked with barrels, blocking the light; a high wall shut off the yard from what must be the open land to the cliffs. 'Barnes insists that he wasn't there, that he had only just arrived when Reed saw him.'

'Well, he would, wouldn't he?'

Wycliffe was irritated by the inspector's complacency but he had no answer for it. 'If anybody comes forward to say they saw Barnes on the road between nine forty-five and ten, the whole case will blow up in our faces.'

'Nobody will!' Darley was aggressively final.

'I hope you're right.' Wycliffe let his pipe go out but continued to suck it moodily. The silence lengthened and Darley was getting uncomfortable.

'You think he's innocent?'

'It's possible though it's equally possible that we've got the right answer for the wrong reasons. The whole thing came too pat for my liking.'

'There are no holes in it that I can see.' Darley was patient.

'Who wrote the note about his gun?'

The inspector was ponderously reasonable. 'Somebody with no good blood for Barnes, obviously, but it was probably a lucky guess. Somebody who knew Barnes had a gun and wanted to make sure we knew too. These villages are hotbeds of gossip and backbiting.'

But Wycliffe was deeply troubled in his conscience. He was going to arrest a man of whose guilt he remained unconvinced. An introvert, he had been able to survive twenty years of dissecting his own actions and questioning his motivation, he had been able to succeed as a policeman, only because he believed that he was doing an essential job with integrity. Like every other policeman he had brought charges which failed to stick but never, either before or after a hearing, had he felt any doubt about the guilt of the accused. Now he had doubts, serious doubts, and in a case of murder. Looking at the evidence, he could find little justification for his misgivings, but it only irritated him to have Darley point this out. 'I have to *believe* in my cases,' he muttered to himself, 'and this Barnes doesn't *smell* like a murderer.' That was the rub. Wycliffe did not believe that given the circumstances all men are potential murderers. The very idea was repugnant to him. 'Killers are born,' he was fond of saying. 'Not all of them end up by killing but given the circumstances, *they will kill*; for the rest, murder is inconceivable.'

He thought enviously of the colleagues with whom he had worked during twenty years; estimable men, yet he found it difficult to believe that they had ever been troubled by ethical niceties. 'You charge a man and you do your damndest to make it stick!'

5

At St Ives police station yesterday evening a man was charged with the murder of twenty-seven year old Anna Welles, found dead on Friday morning at her cottage in the little village of Kergwyns on the north Cornish coast . . .

'So they did get him!' Everybody pleased and just a little relieved that the law wins sometimes. Everybody except the man himself, and his wife, and Superintendent Wycliffe. But you can't please everybody.

'This case isn't over yet, don't make any mistake about that!'

Inspector Darley shrugged massive shoulders and wisely said nothing.

'The inquiry goes on; you understand?'

'As you say, sir.'

They sat opposite each other in a dingy little office at the back of the station. A dusty sunbeam from a window high up crept along the opposite wall. The superintendent's thoughts led him in a circle. A vague figure stood, just a couple of feet from Pussy Welles, facing her, holding a gun, and shot her dead. He tried to impose on that figure the form and features of Richard Barnes but he failed. The girl fell and her killer stood over her. Did he hesitate? Did he gloat? In any event, he stooped, wrenched off her shoe, reached up under her corn-flower blue dress and ripped off one stocking, lacerating her thigh. At that moment he must have looked on her with hatred, hatred so intense that the action was in the nature of an orgasmic release. Could anything stir the wretched Barnes to such a distorted emotional climax? Weak, rather ineffectual, essentially amiable – that was how he saw the man he had charged with murder.

He lit his pipe and studied his colleague over the leaping flame of the match. He had to carry Darley with him, no point in creating antagonism. 'Just to humour me, John' (the Christian name always helped), 'let's suppose for a moment that Barnes didn't do it and see where that gets us . . .'

'In Queer Street, I should think, seeing we've just locked him up!' Darley, ponderously jovial.

'It seems to me that this crime must have been the work of someone to whom violence came easily, almost naturally.'

'Why?'

Wycliffe was engagingly tentative. 'I'm not sure. I'm certainly impressed by the way in which he *exhibited* her deformity. That strikes me as the action of a man given to violence.'

'Or a timid man obsessed by fear and the hatred born of fear. The timid ones are the worst when the crunch comes.'

'You may be right, but . . .'

'Or I could imagine a jealous woman doing something of the sort.' Darley was warming, thawing out.

Wycliffe nodded. 'An interesting idea; I hadn't thought of that.' He smoked placidly as though turning the notion over in his mind. 'But it bothers me that she was shot at close range from the front with no sign of a struggle.'

'You can't defend yourself against somebody with a gun, not unless you have one too.'

'But you can try. It wouldn't be in keeping with what we know about the girl to suppose that she was petrified with fright. If some-body threatened you with a gun held only a few inches from your chest, what would you do?'

'Try to knock it up and grab it.'

'Exactly! And that's what I would expect from this full-blooded emancipated young woman. If she tried, she probably wouldn't have succeeded but she would have deflected the shot, yet the bullet entered her body horizontally, no sign of deflection.'

'He might have produced the gun and caught her unawares.'

'It's possible but unlikely; very few people are capable of shooting without hesitation – fortunately. Even with the firmest intention to kill there must be an instant when the killer screws himself up to the crucial act of pulling the trigger.'

'So?' The sunbeam in its migration now shone on Darley's bald head and he had to shield his eyes with his hand, squinting at the superintendent.

'Why don't you move?'

'What?' It would never occur to Darley to avoid discomfort but he shifted himself now, irritated by the interruption. 'How do you explain the absence of any deflection?'

Wycliffe studied the stem of his pipe as though it provided enlightenment. 'Three possibilities: she thought her assailant was playing the fool; she thought he hadn't the guts to fire; or, *she wanted to die.*'

Darley laughed. 'There's only one of those for my money. People don't play with guns in my experience and if she wanted to die it's unlikely that she would sit tight until somebody happened to come along with homicidal intentions.' He was pleased with his neat summing up. 'Which brings us back to Barnes, she wouldn't think he had the guts to fire but she was wrong.'

They sat in silence, Darley beating a little tattoo on the arm of his chair. No point in talking. Wycliffe had never found any real help in talking over a case with colleagues; he did it because it was expected. Even a painfully reasoned analysis of the facts, made in the privacy of his office, seemed to cloud rather than help his judgement. He had to let facts and ideas jostle one another in the back of his mind, on the fringe of his consciousness. He had to live in the case, soaking up the atmosphere of the place and people, then, if he was lucky, some promising notion might crystallize out. But already there had been pointed enquiries from Regional HQ. When did he expect to return?

To sit at a desk and fill out bloody forms.

Darley was growing impatient of wasted time; he picked up a copy of the case file and opened it, spreading the pages with his huge spatulate fingers. 'All right, sir! If we have to look elsewhere, what about Young, the innkeeper? If ever I saw a violent man, Young is one.'

'He hasn't got a record.'

'By the skin of his teeth! A few years back he was up on a GBH charge but the defence pleaded provocation and he got away with it. Before that he had two narrow squeaks, one for assault and the other for an offence against an under age girl. The local super doesn't like him having that licence but without an actual conviction there isn't much he can do about it.'

Darley paused, waiting for a comment but Wycliffe merely gazed at him with expressionless eyes. Darley was not put off. 'By all accounts Young was intimate with the dead girl before his accident

65

and there's talk that he still goes there – to do the garden!' He made this seemingly innocent employment sound like a monstrous depravity. 'Then there's Dampier . . .'

'Yes, Dampier.' Wycliffe had thought a lot about him. But he had to stop Darley pricing the field. He stood up. 'I want to know more about this girl's past – about all their pasts. They're none of them locals. What brought them here? Was there any connection between any of them before they came? Start digging – there's a good fellow!' He walked to the door, picking up his stick from the corner. 'I'm going back to the village to do a bit of snooping on my own account.'

'You'll need a car.'

'Why?'

'You came in on the bus, didn't you?'

'I shall walk.'

'Walk! It'll take you the best part of an hour!'

'So what? I'm in no hurry.'

Darley shook his head slowly from side to side and watched him go.

He climbed the hill out of the town, past the new houses, past the pottery and came at last out on to the moor. A sunny April morning, warm; a moistness in the air that seemed to fix the scents of the moor, of gorse and the faintly acrid smell of decay from patches of bog. He stepped out briskly, beginning to enjoy himself. It was silent as the grave, easy to believe that there was no other living soul in the landscape.

The night before he had read Pussy Welles' novel, what there was of it, in bed. *God and Maggie Jones.* A strange uncanny story. If she had finished it there could be little doubt that she would have found a publisher. Maggie Jones, like Joan of Arc, heard voices and believed them to be of God. She was convinced that she was a divine instrument but, far from being overawed, she regarded the relationship as a business one. 'I need Him and He needs me!' The instructions or requests which Maggie received from her exalted patron were even more partisan and parochial than St Joan's, being concerned with the welfare or downfall of individuals rather than armies or nations. And she had no hesitation in using her privileged position to secure the advancement of her friends and the con-founding of her enemies. What redeemed the book from absurdity was its impudent irreverence, the piquancy of the dialogue between

Him and Maggie and the Machiavellian schemes they exulted in contriving to achieve His will and purpose.

He was impressed by the book but it made him uncomfortable. If Pussy Welles got her kicks from manipulating people more or less in her power, the field must be wide. Pushed far enough even the veriest mouse may turn and fight back. Cat and Mouse! How feline can you get?

A butcher's van passed him, driven slowly, and he was aware of the scrutiny of the man at the wheel. He must be getting known in the neighbourhood or perhaps it was the oddity of seeing an obvious visitor strolling along carrying a brief-case. Scarcely realizing that he had covered the distance he found himself in the square; the sombre grey granite looked almost mellow in the sunshine. A car, its roof-rack stacked with baggage stood outside the inn, vanguard of the army that summer would bring. Apart from the car, only two old men sunning themselves, contemplating the churchyard. He was warm and thirsty but he walked past the inn and entered the lane which led to the cliffs; he was calling on the Dampiers.

Erica took him upstairs to a room which occupied the whole of the roof-space of their bungalow. It had a magnificent dormer window overlooking the sea and it was a room after his own heart, stacked with books, littered with the impedimenta of both their trades, yet comfortable. Originals of Erica's book illustrations were propped against the walls or tacked to the slope of the ceiling. A paint stained easel, a free standing drawing board, two desks, a studio couch, chairs, bookshelves, piles of manuscript, books and always more books. A pot-bellied iron stove vented into an island chimney and the floor was covered with sisal matting and strewn with rugs.

Then there were cats. He counted six but couldn't be sure that he hadn't counted one twice or missed a couple. There was nothing patrician about these cats, they were shameless hybrid moggies but they possessed the house and carried more than their share of feline dignity because of it.

Dampier sat near the window in a rocking chair specially made for him, a cat on his knees. Seated there he looked almost normal and it was easy to forget his deformity. Wycliffe sat on the couch and Erica had a straight backed padded chair opposite her brother. She hardly took her eyes off him. She was good looking but a sharpness of feature, an air of suspicion and a scarcely veiled threat of antagonism, robbed her of beauty.

Wycliffe seemed relaxed; one of the cats jumped on to his lap and he stroked it gravely until it settled. The Dampiers waited for interrogation but instead he began to talk about children's books.

'My two were brought up on your stories,' he confided. 'They had only one fault, we couldn't get enough to satisfy the demand.'

Erica purred and Dampier was suitably confused. Dampier lit one of his cheroots and encouraged the superintendent to bring out his pipe. The thaw set in.

'So you have children, superintendent?'

'Twins, a boy and a girl, but they've gone beyond fairy stories now, I'm afraid.' Then he took a breath and plunged. He remarked on the preoccupation of children's stories with monsters, with human deformity and with beast-men. For a moment the conversation seemed to totter, then, for no obvious reason, it recovered and Dampier's self-consciousness and restraint diminished. His interest kindled. He developed a theory that childhood fascination with monstrosity is a racial memory of the palaeolithic childhood of the race, monsters envisaged in the eerie fire-lit entrances of the great limestone caves.

'Monsters and mystery are the seeds of religion and religion is the adult fairy tale,' Dampier announced. 'It emerges in each new individual as it evolved in the history of our kind.'

Wycliffe smoked placidly, apparently content to gossip. 'Yes, I suppose riddles and puzzles are as much an ingredient of children's literature as monsters. I gather that some of the less comprehensible nursery rhymes are to be interpreted as riddles and certainly a great many fairy stories centre upon the solution of a puzzle or the answer to a riddle.'

Dampier nodded. 'So, of course, do the great stories of classical mythology and this supports my recapitulation idea . . .'

'And you may add almost the whole of modern crime fiction, I suppose,' Wycliffe remarked with a grin. 'Am I right in thinking that the best writers for children have what I call a *chess* mentality, or is this a myth founded on Lewis Carroll?'

Erica had listened in silence, nodding approval from time to time, now she intervened decisively: 'Oh, it's no myth! I've always said that John has a great deal in common with Lewis Carroll. They have the same mastery of nonsensical but seemingly irrefutable logic and the same *glee* in contriving puzzles. John is an expert bridge player which is closely similar to chess in its intellectual demands and his mathematics master at school . . .'

'For God's sake, Erica!' A strangled cry of protest and pain, but with magnificent recovery of self control, Dampier went on in an almost normal voice, 'Really! To listen to Erica you might think I was a genius instead of a children's hack!'

Erica flushed and there was a moment of painful silence before she too recovered. Evidently such crises were not new to them. She turned to Wycliffe. 'Well, if you don't mind, superintendent, I'll see about the lunch.'

When she was gone Dampier apologized but Wycliffe seemed not to notice.

'Speaking of puzzles, wasn't it you who suggested that Pussy Welles might get her living from crossword puzzles?'

'Yes, it was – why?'

'She published a fair number?'

'Hundreds, I should think.'

'Wouldn't she have kept copies?'

'Of course; in fact I know that she did – several box files of them.'

'They're not there now. All we found was a few blanks.'

'How extraordinary!' Dampier was either genuinely surprised or a good actor. 'Why on earth would anybody want copies of published crosswords?'

'I've no idea.'

Dampier rocked in his chair for a moment or two, gazing out over the sea; then he swivelled round to face the superintendent. 'Look here, I know you've come to ask questions. Your little prologue has done the trick, I'm softened up so let's get on with it.'

'All right! Where were you on the night she was killed?'

Dampier smiled in spite of himself. 'So you don't really believe that Barnes did it?'

'It's my job to find the truth.'

'Then you'd better let poor old Barnes go. He's a weak mortal but he wouldn't kill a fly.' Dampier rocked to and fro. 'As to my whereabouts, there's no mystery about that, I was walking on the cliffs as I do most nights. I go out in the early morning and late at night for the obvious reason that I don't care to parade myself in daylight. It was Erica who told you chaps that I was in all the evening but I don't think they believed her.' He stopped speaking and smoked in silence for a while before asking, 'Is that all you wanted?'

'You know damn well it isn't.'

Dampier nodded. 'You want me to tell you about her.'

'And about yourself, your sister and the people who made up her circle of friends and acquaintances.'

Dampier tapped the accumulated ash from his cheroot, a long grey cylinder that dissolved into dust. 'Erica has made a life for the two of us here, a life so skilfully tailored to my deformity that sometimes I am deluded into feeling normal. Erica is one of those women with the instincts of a mother but not of a wife. If Mother Church recognized artificial insemination for spinsters Erica would be fulfilled, but instead, she mothers me. If she didn't have me it would be some other chronic invalid or hypochondriac or dogs. You understand?' He turned his blue eyes, almost childlike in their gaze on Wycliffe, tentative, afraid of being misjudged. 'I know it sounds ungrateful and ungracious but the fact that I see things pretty clearly doesn't mean that I don't appreciate what she does. The trouble is that I have the instincts of a man though I look like a caricature. I am a Toulouse Lautrec without the consolation of talent or the amenity of the brothel; not a tragedy but a bad joke.'

Wycliffe said nothing and he continued.

'I was not in love with Pussy Welles but she was necessary to me.'

'Was she in love with you?'

'You're joking!' He looked out of the window again where the scene was beginning to lose its picture postcard quality, there was a blurring of the horizon presaging rain. 'But I think she needed me too. Men don't have a monopoly of sexual aberration, super-intendent.'

'So I'm told.'

Dampier laughed without humour. 'Pussy preferred cripples, which was lucky for me.' He crushed out the remains of his cheroot in the ash-tray. 'I've been frank with you because I don't want you wasting your time thinking I did it. I lose more than anyone by her death.' His face twisted in an involuntary spasm. 'I wish to God whoever shot her, shot me at the same time.' After a moment he smiled. 'That's how I feel at the moment, but I shall probably get over it.'

'Did you ever see her feet?'

'Her feet? What the hell are you at now?' He stopped. 'She certainly had a thing about her feet, she used to say she suffered from bad circulation and would never take off her ankle socks, even in bed.'

'She was deformed.'

'Rubbish!'

'She thought herself to be. She had only three toes on her left foot.'

'Well I'm damned! I never knew that.'

'The murderer did.'

Dampier was watching the sea once more. He must have known its every mood. Grey smoky clouds were climbing up the sky reaching out for the sun. 'It's difficult for me to be objective about her, she was a strange girl. She had a thirst for power which I imagine is uncommon among women. She exploited the power of her sex and I think she got a kick out of her crosswords mainly because she was determining how several thousand people would spend two or three hours of their leisure. I know it sounds fantastic but that was how she thought. I remember her saying to me once: "I wish I had pots of money, John." I asked her what she would do with it and she smiled. "I haven't thought but I'd get a hell of a kick making my will!" Another time, apropos of nothing, she said, "It is simple to gain control over another human being; all you have to do is to discover his weakness. Everybody has one, a tender spot, a heel of Achilles; find it and you are in the saddle." I asked her if she had such a weakness and she laughed. "Of course! But I take damn good care not to let anybody know about it!"'

'Was she happy?'

Dampier looked at him in surprise. 'Does it sound as though she was? For that matter, who is? Certainly not the ones who are cursed with an insatiable desire for new experiences and sensations. In my opinion she never knew a moment of contentment let alone of happiness. The best she knew was a pleasurable excitement which quickly yielded to disappointment. She could *not* be satisfied, it was not in her nature, so that her only pleasure came in anticipation.'

'Did you ever hear her speak of death – her own death?'

Dampier hesitated. 'I think you mean, did she contemplate suicide? Of course, I don't know, but she said a strange thing to me

71

once. The circumstances you can imagine; she said, "I wonder what it will be like to strip away this eighth veil of our flesh? Will it mean death or release?" '

'What did your sister think of her?'

'What would you expect? She hated her. But I think she looked upon her as a sort of prophylactic medicine for me. She was made welcome here and everything was friendly on the surface.'

Wycliffe rested his hands on his knees and seemed to study his fingers. He spoke without looking at Dampier. 'When her body was found it was fully clothed except for her left shoe and stocking which were missing. Her deformed foot was exposed and there were scratches suggesting that the stocking had been removed with considerable violence after death.'

'And you think little Barnes did that?'

'What do you think?'

'That it must have been a woman.'

Wycliffe said nothing, allowing the full implication to sink in. Two or three times Dampier started to speak then changed his mind. The seconds ticked by.

'What about the others?' Wycliffe asked.

It seemed to be a relief for Dampier to talk about the Barneses, the Mitfords, Lomax, the innkeeper and the queers but he had little of interest to say. It was evident that he liked the Barneses but he had a strong antipathy to the Mitfords.

'School teachers! Janice is all Cheltenham Ladies' and Young Conservative while Alfred is convinced that he was singled out by providence to mould the minds and bodies of the young. Poor devil! I think she'd given up hope when she hooked him.'

'They don't sound like congenial company for Pussy Welles.'

Dampier agreed. 'But I think Alfred's unassailable pomposity was a challenge to her.'

'Do you think he resisted successfully?'

Dampier grinned. 'If Janice got to know that he didn't your murder would be solved.'

Wycliffe left Dampier standing at the gate, a cat perched on his crooked shoulder, another nuzzling at his legs. What to make of him? Deeply conscious of his deformity, he had the strength to come to terms with it, to smother his bitterness and to live a life as normal as intelligence and an iron will could make it. He was armoured

72

against the world, but if someone – a woman – pierced that armour, kindling emotions it was designed to shield . . . If Pussy Welles got her kicks from manipulating people, Dampier was terrifyingly vulnerable and highly dangerous. A man with nothing to lose.

6

The church clock chimed the quarter; a quarter past twelve. Time
for a drink before lunch. The bar was empty except for the landlord
reading his paper, spread on the counter. He seemed to be a fixture
at this time of day. Wycliffe asked for a light ale and took it to a table
by the window, anxious to avoid conversation, but the landlord
didn't want to talk either. Wycliffe was still thinking of the Dampiers. People who earned their living by any sort of freelance creative
work intrigued him, perhaps he had romantic notions about them.
At any event, he envied them their freedom, even their fundamental
insecurity. He had always had a literary bent; if things had been
otherwise when he left schoool . . . if he had taken his chance of
university. But the twins had made it. Which reminded him that he
had promised to ring his wife. He was on his way to the telephone in
the lobby when he met Darley coming in, Darley looking glum.

'The money's been found.'

'What money?'

'The hundred quid in tenners which Barnes hid in the hedge.'

'So he did hide it?'

Darley nodded. They moved back to the superintendent's table.

'Drink?'

'I'll have a tonic water, thanks.' He removed his trilby and placed
it carefully on the bench beside him. 'Last night, one of the car
patrols up near the border picked up an old tramp – Jimmy Ellis –
drunk and disorderly and they found forty quid in tenners on him.
This morning, when he's sobered up, he admitted having another
fifty stashed away.'

'Did he say where he got it?'

'From a hole in the hedge on the coast road near Kergwyns.'
Darley spoke with disgust. 'There's an old tumbled down shack by
the roadside and Jimmy was preparing to doss down for the night

74

when he saw a car stop, a man got out and hid something in the hedge. Of course, when the car drove off, Jimmy took a look and he found the notes. Surprisingly enough he's pretty definite about time. He knows it was Thursday and he says the church clock had struck ten three or four minutes before. Having got this windfall, Jimmy was too scared to spend it but when he got away up the other end of the county he began to feel safer and temptation was too strong for him.'

'He didn't by any chance see the fellow hide a gun in the culvert?'

'No such luck! The culvert is only fifty yards down the road so he would have been sure to see if there was anything to be seen. Actually he says that he waited for the lights of the car to disappear before he started to investigate.'

Wycliffe shrugged. 'Well! That doesn't help the case against Barnes.' He stopped abruptly and looked at Darley. 'Have you got something else up your sleeve?'

Darley was sheepish. 'I'm afraid so. Ellis says the same car – a red Mini – passed him on the road a quarter of an hour earlier, going in the opposite direction – that is, towards Kergwyns.'

The superintendent sighed. 'So that's that!'

'I've no doubt he could be shaken. I mean, red Minis . . .'

'Rubbish! This lets Barnes out and you know it!'

The bar was filling, several locals and a few obvious visitors. Wycliffe said, 'Let's get out of here!'

They strolled along the path towards the cliffs. 'We've been taken for a ride! I was afraid of it. Barnes was framed. That girl deliberately involved him in a murder charge.'

Darley was satirical. 'Her own! She frames Barnes for her own murder – it's ingenious and I doubt if it's been done before.'

But Wycliffe was in no mood for banter. 'Look at the facts, man! At a quarter to ten, just a few minutes before she died, Pussy Welles telephoned her friend, Elsa Cooper, to tell her that she was pregnant, that Barnes was the father of her child and that he was with her discussing what they should do. It's an unlikely story at best. Why did she ring the Cooper woman?'

Darley was nettled. 'She rang, because she wanted to protect herself from Barnes by telling someone else the facts *in his presence.*'

'But he wasn't there!'

'We've only the word of a drink sodden old tramp for that.'

'And Barnes' own word – don't forget that. It's corroboration we've got now, and disinterested corroboration. If Barnes arrived at the cottage when he says he did, then he didn't kill her. But that telephone call to Elsa Cooper and the one to Barnes himself, fixed him with both motive and opportunity; the means was his anyway. Admittedly, he made things blacker for himself by going off with the money and hiding it, but remember, there is no evidence that he hid the gun.'

'I can't believe that the girl rigged her own murder.' Darley was doggedly obstinate.

'I could believe almost anything of that girl but that doesn't alter the situation as far as Barnes is concerned. We've no case.'

Darley looked at the superintendent curiously. 'You sound pleased.'

Wycliffe nodded. 'I am; though God knows why.'

They had reached the end of the lane and stood among the bracken facing out over a sparkling sea, but neither of them saw it.

'They'll be serving lunch; come back and have some with me.'

But Darley was not to be wooed. 'No thanks. If what you say is true, we're back to square one and I've got work to do – sir.'

'Suit yourself.'

They walked back in silence for a while then Wycliffe said, 'Pussy Welles' husband fell over a cliff, one of her lovers met with a curious road accident that was almost fatal, now Pussy herself has been murdered and another of her lovers framed for the crime. All this in a little over five years – it's too much!'

'I don't see what you're getting at.'

'Neither do I but I don't like it.'

Outside the inn, Wycliffe said, 'I shall be at the cottage this afternoon if you want me.'

'Doing what?'

'I've no idea. Snooping, brooding.'

'We've been over that place . . .'

'. . . with a fine tooth comb – I know. Anyway, don't let me keep you.'

He enjoyed his lunch; lentil soup, chicken with half a bottle of white wine, apple tart and cream. Good plain food, well cooked, that was what he liked. The dining-room was more than half full and Sylvie had her work cut out but she made sure he wasn't kept waiting. 'When are you going to let that poor man go?' she whispered as she changed the plates. He gave her a black look but she only winked.

Afterwards, feeling a little drowsy, he walked out into the watery sunshine, along the unsurfaced lane to the cottage, without seeing a soul. He unlocked the glass panelled door and entered the little white porch with its telephone. The tulips were still on the telephone table, dropping now, their petals all over the floor. He still hadn't spoken to his wife; he dialled.

'Is that you, dear?'

Who else?

'You sound dreadfully tired; don't overdo it.' His wife was convinced that he overworked. What would Darley have said?

'The twins? They've gone to Sidmouth this afternoon. They both hope your case will be over soon so that you can spend a bit of time with them before they go back . . .'

Using Pussy Welles' phone, he couldn't help trying to make comparisons between her and Helen; they were both women but there the resemblance seemed to end.

' 'Bye, love, see you soon.'

He went into the sitting-room. The charcoal outline and the stains were still there. Already the cottage smelt of mustiness and disuse and it was chilly. He looked round at the unconcealing furniture on stilt legs, at the spread of carpet and at the formal prints on the walls, and shook his head. He passed into the kitchen; stainless steel and laminated plastic; a dining alcove with seats for four, a radio on a ledge and over it a framed abstract glowing in reds and orange.

About as personal as an operating theatre.

But he explored the drawers and cupboards of the kitchen fittings, finding only expected things; though there was a red covered account book; a detailed record of her housekeeping expenses; separate sections for milk and bread, paid for by the week; and for goods from the village store, paid for by the month. Difficult to reconcile this careful housekeeper with the improvident wanton, living on her wits. But perhaps even whores keep accounts.

He dropped the book back into a drawer and started to poke about in the coke boiler. A heavy tarry deposit round the flue suggested that someone had burned a great deal of paper. 'And cleaned the thing out afterwards,' Wycliffe muttered. It must have been recent, a good coke fire would have shifted it. For some reason, most of the records of her work were missing, her letters and the host of personal papers that one accumulates. Had they been burned here? It seemed likely. By the murderer? Hardly. It would have been too big a risk and taken too long. In any case, why should he burn her business papers? And if so much had to go, why leave the few crossword blanks? Why leave the manuscript of her novel? Wycliffe was convinced that there had been deliberate selection; equally convinced that it had been made by Pussy Welles, herself. What was left was intended to speak for her, or at least *of* her in a particular way. Did this mean that she expected to be murdered? Incredibly, it seemed so and this tied in with her attempt to implicate Barnes.

Wycliffe had the tantalizing feeling that he was skirmishing on the fringe of the truth. An image had formed in his mind but it was blurred and indistinct, it would not focus. He knew from experience that it was no good trying too hard. He climbed the twisted little stair, only glanced into the bedroom, and entered her study. Here, if anywhere, she belonged; despite her reputation he believed that her broadest contact with life was on the plane of the intellect. Perhaps he was unduly influenced by her novel.

Afternoon sunshine flooded the little room and it needed no great effort of the imagination to see her seated at the desk, the sun glinting on her auburn hair, turning up references, filling in clues, her forehead puckered in a frown of concentration. Was it more or less difficult to imagine her on the other side of the partition, wrestling with her hunchback on the bed or cynically tempting another of her lovers to the limit of erotic abandonment? He believed that the disparate elements of her personality came nearest to reconciliation when she was sitting at this desk, recording the outrageous activities of Maggie Jones. Did she chuckle at her own audacity? Wycliffe thought not. Pussy rarely chuckled or laughed; an occasional smile, a Mona Lisa smile.

He perched himself on the edge of the desk and surveyed the room. Books. They were a literary lot in this case. And she had catholic interests, everything from archaeology to literary criticism, from modern poetry to the theory of games. He snooped, picking out a book here and there, and so he came upon a little nest of erotic works; nothing special about them except that they were all inscribed on the flyleaf, some with amatory message, others without, but all.

From A. Alfred Mitford? Perhaps. The dates spread over two years and the last was three years old. Each of the books he examined, he held by the covers and shook the pages, gathering only a bus ticket, two anonymous scraps of paper and a receipted bill. He sat down in the armchair by the desk and started again, just gazing blankly at the books, the walls, the floor, the records . . .

The only pictures were a few framed photographs; they might be interpreted as trophies, but there was no knowing how Pussy regarded them. A profile of Dampier which looked as though it had been enlarged from a snapshot; probably he would never agree to a photograph. A portrait of Lomax, seated at his desk, pen in hand, Rembrandt lighting. Very distinguished. A photograph of Mike Young, barely recognizable; a slimmer, younger, undamaged version; undoubtedly he had what used to be called sex appeal. And a picture of Mitford; Mitford standing in front of a rakish looking sports car, holding a cup. The picture must have been taken several years ago; at least there was no sign of his present, well matured pot belly. Wycliffe took the pictures down and laid them on the desk. In doing so, he noticed that the one of Mitford was bulkier than the others, there was something between the picture and the backing and the sealing tape was new. He ripped it off, lifted out the millboard backing and uncovered a little pad of folded newspaper cuttings which he spread on the desk.

FATAL FALL AT CLEGAR
DEATH OF ST IVES BUSINESS MAN

A verdict of accidental death was recorded by the Coroner, Dr J. L. Goody, on Mr Samuel Arthur Horner of 26 Rush Street, St Ives, at an inquest on Friday. Mr Horner fell 200 feet to his death from the notorious Clegar Cliff while bird watching on the evening of the 6th September.

In evidence it was stated that Mr Horner had formed the habit of strolling along the cliffs on fine evenings with his binoculars, watching the seabirds coming in to roost on the ledges. One witness said that he had frequently observed Mr Horner to stand dangerously near the edge in his efforts to obtain a better view. Mr Horner's body was not recovered until the following day.

79

Newcomers to St Ives

Mr Horner, who was 32, was a comparative newcomer to St Ives having started the business in Rush Street only six months ago, after moving from London with his wife. Mrs Horner said that she had often been concerned at her husband's apparent indifference to danger when he was absorbed in his hobby. The coroner expressed deep sympathy with the widow and hoped that the tragedy might serve to remind other coastal bird watchers of the risks attendant on over enthusiastic pursuit of their hobby.

The other two cuttings were more recent and dealt with Young's car smash:

LICENSEE IN CAR SMASH
SERIOUS ACCIDENT ON COAST ROAD

On Friday night at a little before eleven, Mr Michael Young, licensee of The Inn at Kergwyns was driving homewards from St Ives when his car skidded at Kitt's Corner. Mr Young was thrown through the windscreen and received multiple injuries. He is now undergoing treatment at the Royal County Hospital where his condition is reported to be 'serious'.

Mr Young might have lain unconscious at the scene of the accident for several hours but for an anonymous telephone call to the police.

Mystery of Anonymous Call

The police are unable to offer any explanation of the anonymous call but inquiries are proceeding. There are no houses in the immediate vicinity of the crash and during the winter months hardly any traffic on the road after nightfall. The nearest public telephone is situated in the square at Kergwyns, one and a half miles away but the police are convinced that the call was made within minutes of the crash. It is understood that the voice of the caller was distorted as though by an attempt at disguise.

Oil on the Road

The accident appears to have been caused by the presence of a large quantity of motor oil on the road. A five gallon drum, almost empty, was found at some distance from the smash and appears to have been struck by the car. The police are investigating the possibility that the drum fell from a passing lorry but so far their inquiries have been unrewarding.

Mr Young has been licensee of the Kergwyns Inn for five years and is well known to all football enthusiasts as the energetic chairman of the Penwith Club.

The final cutting was a paragraph only:

KERGWYNS ACCIDENT

The motor accident to Mr Michael Young, licensee of the Kergwyns Inn, reported in our last week's issue, remains something of a mystery. The police have been unable to trace the anonymous caller who notified them of the accident or to discover the source of the oil on the road which caused the accident. Chief Inspector Judd of the County CID stated that there was no suspicion of foul play.

Mr Young is reported to be making slow progress towards recovery.

Wycliffe read the accounts slowly, carefully. There could be no doubt that the cuttings had been deliberately hidden in the picture; but why? Anybody could go to the newspaper office and look them up. To make sure, he removed the other photographs from their frames but found nothing. He piled them together on the desk, except Mitford's which he slipped into his case, and got up to leave. It was then that he noticed someone in the little walled garden below. At first he thought it was someone hiding, for the figure which he had only glimpsed had disappeared behind a laurel bush but he was soon disillusioned, the innkeeper emerged into sight, calmly hoeing round the shrubs. There was no reason why he shouldn't; the place belonged to him and although the police held the keys of the cottage they had placed no ban on the garden. Still, it seemed a trifle provocative. He would go down and see what Young had to say for himself. But on his way downstairs, the telephone rang. It was Darley.

'A bit more information from the Yard. On Lomax. He was Pussy Welles' sugar daddy when she worked in London, the chap who, according to Elsa Cooper, used to give her expensive presents.'

'Lomax!'

'Exactly. You never can tell. He was a lecturer, as he said, and she worked in the Registry. To cut a long story short he seems to have lost his head completely and when she let him down with a bump, he took to drink and finally had to resign. That's when he came down here. According to the Yard, he's a bit of a joke in zoological circles with his research on lemmings . . .'

'On what?'

'Lemmings. Apparently his life's work is concerned with social behaviour in lemmings but it never comes to anything. Meanwhile he makes a pretty good living writing popular natural history. I gather it's all a bit pathetic . . .'

'I don't know about pathetic but he was very foolish not to come clean. I think I'd better have a chat with Mr Lomax.'

'I somehow thought you might. Shall I have him brought in?'

'Wycliffe hesitated. 'No, we'll keep it on a friendly basis for the moment.'

He forgot Young in the garden and had locked the front door when he remembered. He was tempted to leave it but bitter experience had taught him not to ignore anything in the slightest degree unusual so he went back through the house.

Young was unperturbed. 'I've always kept an eye on the place; gardening wasn't much in her line and she was glad for me to come along and keep it tidy.' He held his head so that the good side of his face was towards the superintendent, giving the disturbing impression that he was speaking to someone else.

'It's my cottage, as I told you, my father and mother lived here after they retired until they died and I suppose I shall move in when I've finished over yonder.' He nodded in the direction of the inn. He rested one enormous hand on the hoe and though he spoke amiably enough, his hand seemed to twitch as though impatient for some violent activity.

'I was surprised to see you here,' Wycliffe said, shortly. 'There's no reason why you shouldn't continue to look after the garden but you mustn't attempt to get into the house until we hand over the keys. You understand?'

'You can rely on me, I've no call to want to go in there.' His manner became insinuating. 'How's the case going, superintendent? Dr Barnes is a nice enough young fellow and I can't really believe he did it. Do you think he did, sir?'

'He's been charged,' Wycliffe snapped. Then he changed the subject abruptly. 'About your accident.'

'My accident?' Young was not only surprised but uneasy.

'Are you satisfied that it was an accident?'

'Of course it was! I don't understand what you're getting at, superintendent.' No mistaking his alarm now.

'You didn't receive a warning?'

'A warning?'

'A warning that you might have such an accident.'

He was breathing hard and his hands were restless. He said nothing for some time then he made a sudden movement. 'You mean a premonition.' He laughed. 'I don't believe in that sort of thing.'

'Neither do I!' Wycliffe snapped. 'I'm talking about a warning, a threat if you like.'

The innkeeper looked straight at him now and his expression was ludicrous. 'I don't know what you're talking about!' He tried to sound truculent but he wasn't in full control of his voice.

Wycliffe spoke lightly. 'I think you understand me perfectly. Just think it over. It may not be healthy to keep secrets for too long.'

'That sounds like a threat to me.'

Wycliffe's temper flared. 'Don't be a bigger fool than God made you! If you didn't get a warning the first time, I'm giving you one now.'

Young made no response; he continued to rest on the hoe, staring away from the superintendent.

'You mentioned your parents just now, I understood that you were adopted.'

Young faced round and regarded Wycliffe with his good eye. 'That's right.'

'How old were you when you were adopted?'

'Eight.'

'What happened to your real father and mother?'

'I can't remember, perhaps I never knew.'

'Did your foster parents have this pub when they adopted you?'

He seemed more nervous than ever but his answers were straightforward. 'No, they had an off-licence in Ealing; they bought this place and came down here to live when I was twelve. They wanted to live in the country.'

'What was your name before you were adopted, Mr Young?'

He raised his shoulders irritably. 'I can't remember. If you had the sort of childhood I had you would try to forget it.'

Wycliffe moved off towards the cottage but the innkeeper called him back. His manner had become conspiratorial. 'I'll show you something, here against the wall.' At the foot of the wall, lying beside a mound of rotting leaves was the body of a cat, a Siamese; fur was missing in patches and the body was beginning to show signs of decay. 'It was her cat, I came across it by accident, buried under that pile of leaves.'

'This afternoon?'

'Yes. Whatever you might think, superintendent, I haven't been near this garden until this afternoon since she died.'

'All right, no need to get excited. Have you got a bag we can put it in?'

Young seemed disposed to continue his protestations but changed his mind. 'There may be something in here.'

Wycliffe followed him into a small lean-to built against the garden wall. It was dark, damp and earthy; when his eyes got used to the light he could see a bag of fertilizer propped up on a couple of blocks, shelves with flower pots and a jumble of tins and bottles. 'Was she troubled by rats?'

'I shouldn't think so – why?'

Wycliffe held up a rusted tin of rat poison, a branded product.

'I shouldn't think there were any rats about now but there might have been a year or two back when they had horses next door. There used to be a stables the other side of this wall but it's all derelict now.' He held out a large plastic bag that had once contained fertilizer, 'Will this do?'

They put the cat in the bag and Wycliffe went off with his trophy. But it was not the dead cat that occupied his mind. Four names chased each other round and round: Horner, Young, Pussy Welles and Barnes. Two were dead, one was grossly disfigured and one was in gaol on a murder charge. Isolated misfortunes? Or a closely knit pattern? And something even vaguer troubled him – a resemblance which he had noticed yet now eluded recollection.

Back in the square, two small boys and a girl played with a ball and Wycliffe watched them with satisfaction. The almost total lack

84

of overt activity in the little village was beginning to get him down. It was like a film set between takes.

Lomax lived in a house immediately behind the church, reached by a track which left the road from the village just beyond the square. Wycliffe loped along between high hedges without even a glimpse of the church tower to remind him of the proximity of the village. It was so quiet, he could hear cows ripping off grass in a hidden field and a bumble bee, busy with the primroses, sounded like an aeroplane. After a little while a farm gate, painted white, straddled the path and admitted him to the cobbled courtyard of the house. It had once been a farmyard but now sedums and sea-pinks grew between the cobbles and a Cornish Cross had been erected on a granite plinth in the middle. A black and white cat, sitting in the sunshine, stopped licking its paws to watch. He rang the bell on the house door. No answer. He tried again. Silence. He crossed the yard to a large outbuilding, pushed open the wicket and entered a semi-darkness alive with muted rustlings, squeaks and twitterings. The lemmings. As the superintendent's eyes accommodated to the dimness he could see a great battery of wire cages each about eighteen inches cube and housing one or a pair of lemmings. He watched them aimlessly for a while and they took notice of him, some of them posturing aggressively, rising on their hind legs, grunting and squeaking. The cages took up only a fraction of the shed space which was otherwise empty except for a wheelbarrow, gardening tools and bins for the lemmings' food. An area of oil stained floor indicated where Lomax kept his car.

A nervous, querulous voice demanded, 'Who's there?' So he went out, apologizing.

'What were you doing in there?' Lomax seemed really agitated, but Wycliffe soothed him.

'I've had such a lot of trouble with my animals recently.'

'Trouble?'

'Deaths unrelated to age.' Lomax nodded jerkily; all his movements were jerky, bird-like. 'I can't account for it. In all the years I've reared these creatures, I've never encountered anything like it and I keep the fullest demographic records . . .'

'I'm here to talk about Pussy Welles, Mr Lomax.'

He looked hurt, a little shocked at the interruption but he nodded. 'Yes, of course, you must come inside.'

The inside of the house surprised Wycliffe, it had turned into a modern villa with all the trimmings and Lomax displayed it with pleasure and pride. 'I live alone of course, and I do most things for myself, just a woman from the village three half days a week . . .'

One room occupied the whole of the front of the house downstairs and looked out on a lawn bordered with shrubs and surrounded by a high wall. The garden adjoined the churchyard but only the tower and the wind blasted sycamores appeared above the wall. The room had been equipped and arranged to present its owner as a scholar, a *savant*. Glass fronted shelves of gleaming mahogany held volumes of *Proceedings* and *Transactions* of a dozen learned societies; box files in neat rows were labelled with subject cards, a recessed bench held an impressive microscope and lighting devices and a polished table near the window was clear except for writing materials and a pile of galley proofs. All that was needed was that he should sit in the padded leather chair, take up his pen and be ready for the photograph that would appear first in *Nature* and later, perhaps, in his biography. *Dr Edgar Lomax at work in his study.* What strange carrots lure us donkeys on!

'This is where I work.'

But when they were seated he reverted to Pussy Welles of his own accord. 'I miss her, superintendent. She was a remarkable girl. You would be surprised at the subjects we discussed – everything . . . And she could listen . . .' His vagueness measured his difficulty in defining let alone filling the gap in his life.

Had Pussy Welles submitted to boredom by this man? Or did she get some sort of kick out of the unlikely association? At every turn it was the enigma of her character which clouded the emerging outlines of his ideas and reduced them once more to flux. It was easy to feel sorry for Lomax but there was more to it than that.

'Why didn't you tell me that you knew her in London?'

'So you found out.' He nodded in acceptance of the inevitable. 'I had to resign. I behaved very badly, but she was cruel. It is strange that running through her kindness, her patience and her generosity, there was this vein of cruelty – of sadism.'

'But you followed her down here?'

A wry smile. 'I had to.'

Wycliffe said nothing and after a moment Lomax felt driven to fill the silence. 'I never deceived myself that she loved me but she was the nearest I ever came to . . . to . . .' He searched for a word and failed to find one. 'I was never a good mixer. Even at school I was the boy who lurked in the corner of the playground half hoping for friendly notice, half afraid of being laughed at or bullied.' He smiled selfconsciously. 'You can imagine that I never made a hit with girls. Until I met her I had never known what it was to possess a woman. That amused and attracted her.' He took out a handkerchief and patted his forehead and lips which glistened with sweat. 'You will understand that I was in no position to lay down conditions, I could not afford the luxury of jealousy.'

Wycliffe was touched and shamed at the spectacle of such humility. There is something profoundly wrong with a society which fails to educate its youth in the things that really matter. But he was a suspect.

'Who killed her?'

Lomax was not taken by surprise. 'I told you before that in my view, suicide is the most likely explanation of her death. She was deeply unhappy.' He was dissatisfied with this statement and search-ed for words to express himself more precisely. 'Unhappy is not the word, she was plagued by a gnawing discontent . . . I can't explain it but anyone who knew her was aware of it.'

Dampier had said, 'In my opinion she never knew a moment of contentment . . .'

'You knew her husband?'

'Only vaguely; he was a member of the local natural history society. An amiable, quiet man, he seemed to be. As a matter of fact, I used to wonder why she married him.'

'You thought you would have made a better match?' Cruelty to dumb animals.

'No, I did not think that. I wondered if she had married him for the same reason as she . . . associated with me.'

'And what was that?' Crucify him! It's all in the sacred name of justice.

'I hinted at it just now. I think that she took pleasure in broadening one's experience of the – ah – erotic aspects of love. If it didn't sound absurd coming from a middle-aged man, I would almost say that she took pleasure in the corruption of innocence.' He was obviously distressed but, apparently determined to tell the truth as he saw it. 'I

87

know this sounds ungrateful but she was, as I have said, a complex personality.'

Wycliffe had left his chair and walked over to one of the bookcases. He had his back to Lomax, scanning the titles. Give him back a grain of self respect. 'Your relationship with her must also have been more complex than you suggest.'

'In what way?'

'Well, you shared certain intellectual interests.'

'Yes. That is true; that is very true.'

'I see you have a copy of *Cook's Psychology of Deformity*.'

Lomax answered with apparent casualness. 'Yes, the subject interests me, why?'

'I happened to notice a copy of the same book on Dampier's shelves.'

'Which shouldn't surprise you, surely!' Lomax said.

7

The curtains were drawn over the great window of the Dampiers' upstair room and some of the stuff that usually cluttered the floor had been cleared. Three card tables with chairs round them were set for Mah-Jongg, the walls of tiles already built and the counters apportioned. The old iron stove in the centre of the room cast its orange glow and roared in competition with the gale outside. Spring had slipped back into winter in a single day as it is apt to do, and the wind came from the north, a bitterly cold breath from the Arctic sea. John Dampier sat in the firelight waiting for his guests while Erica busied herself downstairs. His massive ungainly body fitted the rocking chair so that it seemed part of him and he rocked to and fro, smoking one of his cheroots and stroking the sleeping cat on his lap. He was experiencing a rare contentment. For the most part, his waking hours seemed to be a struggle against boredom, against frustration and against the crushing burden of his deformity, but now and then, for no reason that he could tell, he would find himself unexpectedly at peace, not only resigned but content. It was like coming in from a storm and shutting the door. He wished that he was spending the evening alone but his serenity was too deep to be unduly disturbed. He wondered vaguely what Wycliffe was playing at.

On his second visit, the superintendent had been decidedly less amiable, at least to begin with, but when he was leaving he said, 'You haven't thought of having another of your Mah-Jongg evenings?'

'No. In any case, it's too soon; noboody would come.'

'They would if they knew I was interested.'

'You want me to lay on something?'

'It might help.'

'A bit unorthodox, surely?'

'So is murder.'

'At least it means that he doesn't suspect you,' Erica said when he told her.

'Of course, it means nothing of the sort!' It had been his own first thought but it irritated him to have her put it into words.

'In any case, you've nothing to fear,' she said in self reassurance.

Nothing to fear. It was true that he was not afraid but that was because he had so little to lose – less now. It was one of his few compensations that he could view the worst with equanimity. For a man without belief there is only death to fear and he was certainly unafraid of death; sometimes it seemed to beckon him kindly, as a friend, a promise, not a threat. He would look down from a cliff edge at the dim mysterious water and wonder why he bothered to cling to life. He knew why – because it was interesting, though less so now that Pussy was gone. She had been an unfailing source of surprise, even on that last day – her last.

It was that day the superintendent wanted to know about.

'It was a Thursday – *your* day, wasn't it, Mr Dampier?'

Nasty! But true. All the village knew that. Bit by bit, without much need for persuasion, Wycliffe got the story – most of it.

He had walked along the cliff then struck inland arriving, as usual at the back door of the cottage. Not that he cared about people knowing but he hated to be stared at. It was four o'clock and they chatted, then had tea. And after tea, bed. It was their routine. When it was over and they were lying side by side, recapturing the perspectives of normality, she said, 'I'm pregnant, John, and it's yours.'

He was surprised but not unduly concerned. Her particular brand of sensuality demanded risk and he had considered the possibility.

'I'll make arrangements for you to go into a clinic in town.'

'No. I want you to marry me.' Just like that. He was astounded.

'Erica will have to go, of course,' she added, an apparent after-thought.

Then he understood – or thought he did. 'There's no question of Erica being forced out of her own home.'

'Don't fret yourself; she'll go of her own accord.'

'I wouldn't count on that.'

She got out of bed and stood, naked, stroking her belly and smiling. 'When she realizes that the alternative is an abortion which will destroy your child, she'll go fast enough. Erica couldn't live with that thought to plague her. Your child, even by me, will be sacro-sanct.' Anger or hatred suddenly flared. 'My God! If it wasn't for her conventional little mind she would be in bed with you herself!'

And that was as far as Wycliffe could persuade him to go.

'You believed that she really intended to marry you?'

'At the time.'

'And since?'

'I've had doubts.'

'What happened after that?'

'I've said all I intend to say.'

'I can't accept reservations in a murder case, Mr Dampier.'

'You can go to hell!'

It wasn't obstinacy or even self preservation, he could not bring himself to admit that for once his armour had been pierced and emotions roused which he had long believed dead. He would not order his thoughts to reconstruct those moments of anger and humiliation.

Wycliffe had stared in silence for some time, then: 'Very well! But if the charge against Barnes is withdrawn you may be forced to answer my questions.'

Then he made his proposition – a Mah-Jongg party – it sounded bizarre, put like that.

The door bell.

Ten minutes past seven. Curiosity (or apprehension?) had so far overcome good manners as to bring somebody twenty minutes early. Erica would be annoyed, she was still preparing refreshments. He wondered if Ursula Barnes would come; he had seen her only once since her husband's arrest and she had been tight, resentful, antagonistic, just as Erica would have been. Everybody to blame. Women are irrational animals. But it looked as though she wouldn't have to suffer much longer.

The early arrival was Janice Mitford; he might have known. He could hear her high pitched chatter, always on the fringe of hysteria, and Erica's cool replies. Where was Alfred? Of course, he might be there without having spoken yet.

But Alfred wasn't there, she came up the stairs alone.

'Hullo, John, I came early because I wanted the chance of a word before the others come.'

She had cultivated what was supposed to be an easy

91

companionable manner with men which raised his hackles. Bloody bitch! What he had against her was nebulous; she led Alfred a dance but he despised Alfred. The real trouble was that she didn't know how to behave like a woman and she groped desperately, disastrously, to find out. One ought to be sorry for her but instead she had the impact of an ill-timed joke.

'Do you mind if I switch on the lights? I can't stand the semi-darkness.'

She sat in the chair opposite him, shooing off one of the cats. The Mah-Jongg evenings had never been occasions for dressing up but her jumper and slacks were something new. The V-neck and the clinging thin wool advertised what was underneath.

'I'm worried, John, desperately worried!' She lowered her voice. 'In fact, I'm frightened and I've nobody to turn to but you.' She blinked rapidly, touching her eyes with a rolled up handkerchief. 'It's Alfred, he's in some sort of trouble over Pussy Welles.'

Dampier shifted impatiently in his chair so that the cat on his lap stretched and clawed the air once or twice before settling down again. Perhaps she was frightened but he was damned if he was going to be comforting.

She drew a packet of cigarettes from her handbag, tapped one nervously on the packet and forced Dampier to disturb the cat once more in order to light it. 'I'm a bundle of nerves, John; sometimes I hardly know what I'm doing!' She smoked with frequent short inhalations until the cigarette had a quarter gone, then she crushed it out in the ash-tray. It seemed that she had screwed herself up to the pitch of courage.

'It started with her coming to the house on the afternoon of the day she was killed. I was out in the back garden and when I came in he was talking to her in the porch. Of course, she soon went but it was obvious that what she said to him was upsetting. The next day when we heard she had been shot, he just went to pieces. He wouldn't eat and he couldn't sleep and he wouldn't tell me what was wrong. The last couple of days he seemed to be getting over it but this morning, Inspector Darley came and he's as bad as ever again. Really, John, I don't know what to do. Thank God it isn't term time.'

Dampier regarded her without compassion. 'You think Alfred might have killed her – is that what's worrying you?'

The fright in her eyes was unmistakably genuine. 'Good God, no!' She put a hand to her mouth. 'I never said that. I just want to know what hold she had over him that even now she's dead puts him in such a panic.'

'Somebody killed her,' Dampier said, 'and even the police are beginning to realize it wasn't Barnes, but it must have been one of our little set.'

She looked at him wide eyed, on the brink of hysteria but she controlled herself. 'This is awful! I don't know what to do!' She had her knuckles in her mouth like a child trying to hold back tears.

'Is Alfred coming?'

She looked at him vaguely and he had to repeat the question.

'Of course he's coming. I came early because I wanted to talk to you, now I wish I hadn't.'

The door bell again. Janice got out her make-up and set about repairing the ravages. 'Heavens! I look a sight.'

This time it was Mike Young. His low pitched guttural speech was unmistakable. He came upstairs heavily like a desperately tired man, and when he spoke he seemed to have trouble finding the words and enunciating them. Dampier wondered if he had had a mild stroke until he realized that he was merely drunk.

'Glad you were able to come, Mike.'

Young nodded. 'It seemed like a bloody command performance so I thought I couldn't afford to miss it.' He slumped heavily into a chair. Hitherto he had maintained a vulgar smartness in his dress – fancy waistcoats and check suits, now he looked seedy, his clothes creased and soiled. He took a packet of cigarettes from his pocket and lit one with the precision of a drunken man, then he seemed to notice Janice for the first time.

'Hullo! Where's Alfred? Isn't he coming?'

She looked at him with annoyance and distaste; his use of their Christian names had been a sore point for a long time and she had blamed it on Alfred. ('You never know how to keep your distance with people!') But she answered Young civilly, 'He's coming later – why?'

Young shrugged. 'I feel sorry for him, that's all.'

'Why should you feel sorry for my husband?'

He shook his head and laughed as though at a very good joke.

Janice stared at him and her mouth slackened, she might have

93

screamed if Dampier hadn't cut in, not angry, but authoritative, 'You're drunk, Mike! Either you behave or you get out!'

The tension evaporated. Young mumbled an apology, Janice controlled herself and Dampier felt justified in his expectation of an eventful evening.

Lomax, Harvey Clemens and Aubrey Reed arrived together and Ursula Barnes a few minutes later. She was pale and she had dark rings under her eyes to tell of sleepless nights. The black wool frock she wore accentuated her pallor but gave her an air of distinction that was not lost on Dampier. There was really no obvious reason why Richard should shop elsewhere. She spoke to Dampier briefly, acknowledged the others then sat a little apart, making it clear that for her this was no social occasion. Janice moved to sit beside her but got a cold reception. Alfred came at last and Erica brought him upstairs. He had evidently walked in the rain a good deal further than the distance between the two houses. His eyes sought his wife's anxiously. Dampier missed nothing.

He saw his sister standing at the top of the stairs surveying her guests and watched her with the eyes of a stranger. She had the bleached dignity and charm of faded chintz but her face, even her eyes were empty of vitality. He was to blame for that; he was a parasite, draining away her life and she encouraged him. Why? Did she have any regrets? He had no idea. She spoke, raising her voice to gather their attention: 'There's no reason why we shouldn't start playing if that's what everybody wants.'

'Yes, let's start. The suspense of waiting for that terrible man is killing me!' Aubrey Reed, heavily facetious.

Erica smiled, then her gaze fell on Young, lying back in his chair, sleeping it off, and her smile faded. She turned to Lomax. 'All right! Edgar and Janice, I know you both like to go for limit hands so will you make one pair? John and Ursula make another, then I think the rest of us prefer to play as a foursome – Alfred, Harvey, Aubrey and me – is that all right?'

Nobody answered but they moved to their tables, leaving Young asleep by the stove, his heavy breathing blending with its roar and with the noise of the muted wind. Erica put a shovelful of coke on the fire then joined the others.

Mah-Jongg is not a game for conversation. The rattle of the tiles, an occasional cry in the mysterious language of the initiate, these are the only sounds until a player shouts, 'Mah-Jongg!' Then his tiles are checked, scoring begins and chips pass from hand to hand in settlement of debts. Afterwards the tiles are reshuffled and the walls rebuilt for the next game. It is during this last operation that recriminations may break out but these are rare for Mah-Jongg is not a game for partners, every man is for himself alone.

Dampier found it an odd experience to be playing the game again. In the past he had always been paired with Pussy Welles and between them they had acquired a reputation for phenomenal limit hands and for playing without a word spoken. Even the declaration of Mah-Jongg was made in silence, the player would merely brush his hand over the tiles so that they fell face upwards on the table. Pussy was always absorbed in the play – out to win, which she usually did; she had a card-index memory and a sixth sense for his intentions. He could recall the faint smile on her lips as she made a deft exchange of tiles and placed the new one in its appropriate place. He was finding it disturbingly easy to recall her at any time; unsought and uninvited her image would steal into and take possession of his mind. Sometimes, as now, he saw her in some remembered context of pleasure or relaxation but mostly she appeared as she had been on that last afternoon of her life and he would strive vainly to close his mind to the recollection.

'Mah-Jongg.' Ursula said without the smallest grain of interest. She laid her tiles on the table, the poorest of hands yielding only a meagre score.

He smiled at her, touched by a sudden sympathy. Why should she have to submit to playing this nonsensical game when all her thoughts were concentrated on her husband awaiting trial for murder?

'You're bored and no wonder! You don't have to play.'

She looked at her watch. 'The superintendent hasn't come yet. Do you think they will release Ricky?'

'I'm sure they will.'

At Erica's table, Aubrey Reed was being temperamental, it was obvious that he and Harvey had quarrelled, she knew the signs. Aubrey drummed on the table top with the tips of his manicured nails while Harvey hunched over the tiles, studying them as though he was deciphering an obstinate code. Most of the time she could put up with them for John's sake. He liked to have them round, they amused him, but tonight her nerves were on edge, she sensed trouble and the two of them were an added irritant.

Aubrey tapped viciously on the table with a tile. 'For God's sake, Harvey, hurry up! It's like watching a bad film in slow motion.'

Harvey said nothing but continued to deliberate over his discard, arranging and re-arranging the tiles in his hand. Aubrey turned to Erica conversationally:

'When I was in Singapore the Chinese used to say, "The sound of tiles falling should be as the patter of raindrops in a summer shower." Speed is the essence of the game, don't you agree?'

She would have liked to smack his sallow effeminate face or, at least to say something that would bite into his smug self esteem but she contented herself with silence.

'He read that in the book of instructions,' Harvey said.

'What did you say?' Aubrey demanded, his voice rising.

Harvey raised his eyes and surveyed his adversary mildly. 'I said that you read that bit about the patter of raindrops in the instruction book. You were only forty-eight hours in Singapore, in a transit camp, and I doubt if you saw a Chinaman.'

Aubrey went white. 'What do you know about where I've been and what I've done?' His calm was ominous.

But Harvey was single-minded and determined to elaborate his theme. 'In any case I don't think they have summer showers, more like tropical downpours . . .'

'Will you shut up and play the game?' Aubrey was leaning forward over the table, glaring up into Harvey's bland and rather stupid face.

'It's like a lot of these so called Chinese sayings – made up to sound clever. I've heard that most Chinese play the game with cards and they wouldn't make a noise anyway . . .'

'You bloody fool!' Aubrey hissed. 'My God, why do I put up with him? He nauseates me!'

She should have intervened – poured oil, but she had no intention of doing so. Let the little rats fight if they wanted to. But Mitford was acutely embarrassed, his fair complexion flushed.

'Really!' He shifted uncomfortably in his chair.

Aubrey turned his aggression on him. 'You were going to say?'

'Just that we should get on with the game,' Alfred said. He might be a lion on the rugby field but he was a coward off it.

She could not help comparing the men she met with her brother and none of them came well out of the comparison. Despite his deformity he was the only real man amongst them; she was proud of him, but her pride blended with a profound pity and recently, with fear.

She was sitting where she could see the whole room. Lomax and Janice Mitford seemed to be absorbed in their game but John and the Barnes girl had given up all pretence of playing, they were deep in conversation. At least, he was talking and she was listening, hanging upon his every word. She found that she resented Ursula Barnes but she could not say why. Perhaps in some self protective illogical fashion she was blaming the girl because they looked like releasing her husband. It had been such a satisfactory solution but now, who knew what might come? John was missing the Welles girl; there could be no doubt about that, and he would continue to miss her until someone else came along. Well, that could be arranged, plenty of girls would be flattered by his attention once they got to know him. Now that she understood that it was essential to him there would be no problem; she had not understood at first. But no more of the intellectual type! She tried to bring her attention back to the game which she had been playing automatically while her thoughts ranged wide. It was useless to think of and plan for the future until she was sure that there would be one. Everything depended on what this policeman found out; what there was for him to find out.

The door bell.

Erica went downstairs to receive him.

Wycliffe came upstairs, blinking in the light and looking less like a policeman than ever. He was smiling, a little nervous, diffident. He might have been a benevolent don looking in on an undergraduate party. A mouse where they looked for a lion.

He said polite things and Erica led him to a seat on the couch. She offered him a glass of white wine. 'We always do cheese and wine, it's become a tradition. I hope it suits you. You can have red if you prefer it.' The superintendent smiled and nodded, trying not to miss anything. He turned to Ursula Barnes, 'I have some good news for you, Mrs Barnes, I'm sure you won't mind the others hearing it, your husband is likely to be released on Monday; the charge will be withdrawn.'

An involuntary exclamation from Ursula, incredulity and relief.

Then a little silence followed by them all congratulating her. Alfred Mitford's pleasure in the news seemed to subside first, he tried to make his remark sound casual, man to man, 'I suppose this means that you start all over again.'

Wycliffe shrugged. 'Not altogether, Mr Mitford, we have quite a lot to go on.'

Dampier tried next. 'Is Barnes being released because of fresh evidence?'

The superintendent seemed to consider the question. 'There has been a certain amount of fresh evidence but it is mainly a matter of our making a new approach. At first this crime was considered in isolation, now we believe that it is linked with others.'

'Others?'

'Another murder and an attempted murder.'

Dampier looked unbelieving. 'And where are these crimes supposed to have happened?'

Wycliffe was casual. 'Oh, in this neighbourhood.'

Reed's irritating high pitched laugh. 'But even in this village murder is unlikely to pass unnoticed.'

'You think so, Mr Reed?' Wycliffe sipped his wine. 'I can assure you that murder is all too likely to pass unnoticed when it is skilfully undertaken.'

Lomax had spoken little, now he intervened as though to make an academic point. 'But surely, superintendent, we are told that the murderer who displays ingenuity is more likely to be caught.'

Wycliffe nodded. 'That is probably true but I think you are confusing ingenuity with skill. One of our victims was pushed over a cliff – that was a very skilful murder but it could hardly be called ingenious. In the absence of an eye-witness there can be no proof against the murderer.'

'Horner!'

'Yes, Mr Dampier, Pussy Welles' husband. I have little doubt that he was murdered.'

'And the attempted murder?'

The superintendent looked at the sleeping Young. 'He was lucky to escape with his life, don't you think? There was no intention that he should. That was an attempt at murder which was ingenious but not skilful. A full investigation at the time would almost certainly have brought the criminal to book.'

98

'But who . . . ?'

The landlord stirred in his sleep and opened his eyes. He looked round, vaguely at first, then when he realized that he was the centre of attention he became mildly truculent. 'What's all this, then?'

'We were talking about Arthur Horner,' Wycliffe said quickly.

'Pussy's husband.' He blinked sleepily.

'Yes.'

'He fell over the cliff at Clegar – killed himself.' He turned the uninjured aspect of his face to Wycliffe, sufficiently awake now to be self-conscious.

'That's what they said in the papers but do you think he *fell*?'

'He might have jumped for all I know.'

'Or have been pushed?'

The landlord was silent, evidently deciding how to react. He took out a cigarette and lit it, ostentatiously deliberate. 'I suppose you know what you're talking about, superintendent.'

'You should know better – you were there.'

Young faced him and it was strange to see the colour drain from the living side of his face so that it rivalled the other in its pallor. 'What the hell *are* you talking about?' The words were aggressive but their manner was not. He looked round nervously, furtively.

'At the time Horner died the police had no reason to suppose that it was anything but an accident and so their inquiry was superficial. Recently my men have been delving a little deeper and although five years have passed they found a witness ready to swear that you were on the cliff at Clegar that evening at about the time Horner was supposed to have fallen.'

Young puffed at his cigarette, thoughtful, cautious. 'I'm not denying that I was on the cliff that evening.'

'But you didn't volunteer the information at the time.'

The landlord was aggrieved. 'Why should I? There was no call.'

'Not if you had a conversation with Horner shortly before his death?'

'But I didn't! Whoever says that is a liar! Look here! I don't know what you're trying to pin on me but I never spoke to Horner that night nor laid a finger on him!'

Wycliffe spoke in a low voice that hardly carried across the room. 'You may be speaking the truth but in that case you saw someone else talking to him and for some reason you chose to keep quiet about it. You continued to keep quiet when two years later you were almost killed in a car smash that was deliberately contrived. Why?'

Young was a pitiful sight but he spoke firmly. 'You're mad! You make it up as you go along.'

Wycliffe shrugged and returned to his seat. Young sat staring at the stove, the ash on his cigarette lengthened. Dampier lit one of his cheroots; Reed, still sitting at the Mah-Jongg table, tapped irritatingly with his nails on the wood. Erica stood up. 'I'll get some coffee.'

Janice Mitford watched her go and sighed, a sigh that was almost a sob.

'What's the matter?' Ursula, in her relief, felt magnanimous.

'It's all right for you, but I'm scared; scared almost out of my wits.'

Harvey Clemens walked over to the window and parted the curtains. 'The rain has stopped; it's moonlight – lovely!'

Aubrey Reed stopped his niggling. 'Superintendent, is the criminal here tonight?' His manner was childish, bantering.

Wycliffe seemed to take the question seriously. 'I suppose it depends on your point of view.'

'That's a damned queer answer.'

'The fault was in the question.'

Mitford still sat by his table but he had swivelled round to face the others. He looked flushed but he was one of those fair complexioned people who have a perennially high colour and the heat of the room was troubling him. His jumbo ears were bright red and little beads of sweat trickled down his lips. He stared at the fire with unblinking eyes, then he seemed to brace himself to speak. 'What possible motive could anybody have for committing these crimes? If what you say is true, somebody murdered Horner, tried to kill Mike Young and succeeded in killing Pussy. It doesn't make sense, does it?'

'Don't forget that the same person framed Barnes, for framed he certainly was,' Wycliffe said.

Dampier fingered the ends of his beard and looked at Mitford, smiling. 'You might say that we've been lucky – so far.'

'Lucky?'

'Nobody's tried to kill us yet.'

Mitford understood; he eyed his wife nervously but Janice was

100

paying no attention, she was following her own thoughts and she wanted to talk.

'She was a *wicked* woman. I know it sounds absurd but I am still more afraid of her dead, than I am of whoever killed her. She had a way of looking at you . . . as though you were a *thing*.' She shook herself, perhaps to dispel a memory. 'I know the exact moment when she decided to take Alfred away from me. I can't explain it but she had been talking to me – just gossiping, she could make herself very agreeable, then, suddenly, she glanced across at Alfred and back at me – no more than that, but I knew and I remembered.'

Ursula was getting bored, she wanted time to relish her own good news but Janice was gathering momentum.

'Of course, men are fools. She had only to lift her finger to have any one of them come running – *you* know that.'

Ursula felt compelled to say something. 'By all accounts Mike Young managed to resist her – after his accident.'

Janice nodded. 'That always puzzled me. I think he was afraid of her.'

'Perhaps he is sensitive about his disfigurement.'

Janice laughed unpleasantly. 'Are you joking? He manages well enough with that little slut at the inn. In any case, he and Pussy Welles were two of a kind – vicious!' She took a packet of cigarettes from her handbag and offered one to Ursula who refused. 'I've only taken this up since I found out about them – Alfred and her. You have to do something.'

A silence which Ursula refused to bridge.

Soon Janice began again. 'How that woman . . . !' She lowered her voice. 'When I had proof, I made Alfred tell me everything – every detail. You wouldn't credit what she did!' She eyed Ursula appraisingly. 'Of course you're married and you know what men are like. I mean they're all dirty minded and more than dirty minded if you give them a chance, but a woman . . .' She edged closer so that Ursula was enveloped in the smoke from her cigarette. 'She used to make Alfred strip her, then beat her across the buttocks with a cane! Can you believe it? Isn't it disgusting?'

Ursula had had enough. 'I don't know, it might be rather fun. I must see what Ricky thinks . . .'

Fortunately Erica returned with the coffee and there was a general commotion. Young seemed to rouse himself from a deep reverie, looked at his pocket watch and stood up. 'It's time I was going. I must be back in time to cash up.'

Perfunctory farewells, then Erica went downstairs with him. They heard the front door bang and she came back up, looking relieved. She sat by Ursula. 'A strange man, I feel sorry for him. You'd never think that before his accident he was the most eligible bachelor in the district. What a tragedy! Of course it's not only his disfigurement, it's the drink.'

'He frightens me,' Janice said. 'A violent man.'

'Oh, no!' Erica was just a little too quick, too emphatic. 'Before all this he was the kindest of men, a rough diamond perhaps, but kind and gentle.' She was blushing. 'It was all her fault, none of this would have happened if it hadn't been for her. I'm glad she's gone but it's too late now, somebody should have killed her before she had the chance to sow the seeds of so much wickedness.'

Wycliffe was looking at her with interest. 'That is what she did, Miss Dampier. She sowed the seeds of wickedness.'

Dampier saw the animation in his sister's face and wondered; it was a rare phenomenon. He wished they would all go home, he wanted to think. Wycliffe would get somewhere, that much was obvious but would he recognize the truth when he saw it? Pussy had delighted in weaving complex patterns, she contrived, collected and relished the memory of situations, gloated over them as a connoisseur and achieved what pleasure she knew in planning others. To discover any truth about her it was necessary to break clean through the web of her contrivance. He had reason to be grateful to her for five bearable years but she was a dangerous woman and if ever he had doubts of that, their last afternoon together would have dispelled them.

They were going, thank God! The Mitfords first. Janice, her voice harsh and brittle, tight-lipped. 'Goodbye, John. Thanks for putting up with me.' Alfred's soft clammy hand. 'Thanks for a pleasant evening, John.'

A pleasant evening!

Lomax hovered uncertainly, then in a moment of decision said, 'I must go,' and went. Reed and Clemens, Ursula Barnes: 'Don't worry about me now, John.' She smiled; suddenly she seemed beautiful.

Wycliffe was cryptic. 'Stir the mixture and allow to stand over night.'

Dampier heard Erica seeing them off. The liturgy of farewell. Then the front door slammed, she shot the bolt and after a moment, came back upstairs. She stood by his side, ruffled his hair. 'You're tired, boy. Time for bed.'

Silver moonlight and a bitter wind off the sea; more like Christmas than Easter. Wycliffe hurried up the lane from the Dampiers', the church clock struck twelve, some of the strokes loud and clear, the sound of others snatched by the wind and scattered over the moor. The square etched in the cold light, deserted, no lights in the houses, none in the windows of the inn. He let himself in very quietly and tip-toed across the lobby to the telephone. Afterwards he went out again and walked up and down the square, smoking his pipe, until he was joined by a young constable. It was nearly one when he finally went indoors leaving the constable to watch until morning.

'What do I do if he comes out, sir?'

'Follow him but let him see you're doing it, then he won't go far.'

'I'm bound to be seen when it gets light.'

'Doesn't matter. Keep an eye on the back and the front doors. When people start moving about you can go home; put in your report at the station.'

He remembered similar nights when the whim of a superior had kept him from a warm bed. 'Are you married?'

'No, sir.'

'That's something then, isn't it?'

8

Wycliffe couldn't sleep; his mind was over active and his stomach was soured by the red wine he drank with his dinner. Easy to get into bad habits away from home. He tumbled and tossed for an hour then switched on the light, got up and turned out the contents of his briefcase, looked for something to focus his attention. Pussy Welles' crosswords, they should be better than counting sheep. He found a ball-point and got back into bed. He picked one at random and it was easier than he had expected; he was not an addict but he could manage this.

Beheld both monarch and mouse, two words, five and three.

'*A cat may look at a king provided she doesn't take him for a mouse?*' The solution was obviously, *Pussy cat*, but he had the quotation wrong.

Pussy cat, pussy cat, where have you been?
'I've been to London to see the Great Queen.'
Pussy cat, pussy cat, what saw you there?
'I saw a little mouse under her chair.'

That was it. Too many damned cats in this case. Try this: *Ruler of all the dim rich city*, six letters. Ah! It was Tennyson who first kindled his love of words. *For all the sacred mount of Camelot and all the dim rich city, roof by roof* . . . Even at two in the morning he could thrill to their music. He wrote in *Arthur*. Getting on nicely. Three or four more and his eyes began to feel heavy; the medicine worked, he switched off the light and fell asleep. He had a muddled dream and at the climax he was in a car being driven furiously by Mike Young along a cliff road when suddenly the road wasn't there, they were falling . . . falling . . . falling . . . He woke, clutching at the bed-clothes, certain that he had called out and feeling foolish. It was broad daylight. The pages of Pussy's crosswords were scattered over the floor.

He met Sylvie on the stairs. 'No time for coffee this morning and you'll have to wait for breakfast. He's in bed.'

'What's the matter with him, is he ill?'

She grinned. 'You could say that.'

'Hangover?'

She nodded. 'He must have been at it for a good part of the night.'

'Is he often like that?'

She looked at him, seemed about to say something but changed her mind. 'I must be off else you won't get your breakfast.'

Darley turned up before Wycliffe had finished. 'Coffee?'

'No thanks, I had mine two hours ago.' He had obviously taken umbrage. Soon it came out. 'You had the inn watched last night; I saw the constable's report at the nick.'

'Did he see anything?'

'Not of Young. He kept back and side door under observation all night but according to his report, he saw nobody but Mitford.'

'What was Mitford doing?'

'Standing by his garden gate smoking, for over an hour, between two and three.'

'Turned out by his wife I shouldn't wonder. Did Mitford see our man?'

'Apparently not. Our chap kept in the shadow; he wasn't sure of his brief and he thought he'd better play safe. But he could see Mitford all right, in the moonlight.'

'Did he have him under observation the whole time?'

'Not quite. He didn't actually see him go indoors – one minute he was there and the next he was gone. You know what it is, keeping observation on a man a hundred and fifty yards off in the moonlight. The eyes play tricks. Why? What's it all about, sir?'

'Just a hunch that didn't come off,' Wycliffe said. 'I'm glad I'm not married to that woman.'

'I'm glad I'm not married to any woman,' Darley growled.

'Then you'd better come with me, I'm going to talk to Aubrey Reed and his friend.'

Inspector Darley was not amused and the superintendent went alone.

Even years of police work and a tolerant disposition had never

105

reconciled him to queers and this worried him for he half believed that what we hate most in others is what we fear in ourselves. He consoled himself with the thought that never since puberty had he turned his eyes from a pretty girl.

Reed answered the door, wearing jeans and a polo necked jersey. He seemed a little resentful, rather more, apprehensive. Wycliffe was taken into the sitting-room, a large room with nineteen-twentyish furniture; two overblown settees upholstered in brocade and armchairs to match; a china cabinet with some nice pieces, a screen with tapestry panels, two or three poufs and a couple of standard lamps. The only pictures were four Beardsley drawings and Burne Jones which could have been a reproduction, over the mantelpiece. Heavy curtains, partly drawn across the windows shut out the sunlight and although there was a fire in the grate, the room had an unused feel, it was like the period rooms one sees in museums, selfconscious and depressing. Wycliffe had to sit in an armchair which was like being trapped in the embrace of a feather bed, but Reed sat himself on one of the little stools by the fire and jabbed at the coals with a brass poker. His figure was boyish but his face had long since lost all trace of the mobility of youth, the lines were set and deepening. Thirty-two or three.

Wycliffe took his time. Reed lit a cigarette and ignored him. If it was a game to see who would speak first, it was never played out for Harvey Clemens opened the door and stood, looking surprised and uncertain on the threshold. He wore a blue and white apron and clutched a tea-towel. He muttered something and would have gone but Wycliffe stopped him. Reed snapped:

'If you're coming in, for God's sake take off that ridiculous apron; you look like a butcher boy!'

Whatever had inspired and sustained his rebellious mood of the night before, Harvey was submissive now; he took off his apron and rolled it up with the tea-towel. 'I was washing up, I didn't know there was anybody here.' He perched on the edge of a chair and looked round, apprehensive but determined to be affable. He had left the door ajar and a Siamese walked in, inspected the other occupants of the room and jumped on to Harvey's lap, flexing its claws through the jeans so that he winced. Reed eyed him with disdain.

'I told you yesterday evening that Dr Barnes is to be released tomorrow.'

'Does that mean that you are back where you started or do you have someone else in mind?' Reed was jaunty, ironic.

'It means that despite Dr Barnes' foolish behaviour, we are satisfied that he did not kill Miss Welles. We still have to find out who did.'

'She deserved it anyway, didn't she, Abel?' Clemens spoke to the cat.

'It must have been one of her men friends.' Half a statement, half a question from Reed.

'Did you count yourself as one of those, Mr Reed?'

Aubrey made a sinuous movement of the shoulders, wholly feminine. 'Of course not!'

'What about you, Mr Clemens?'

'I hated her, she was a bitch!' He fondled the cat on his lap. 'Among other things, she tried to poison Abélard, didn't she, old boy?'

'Don't be a bigger fool than God made you,' Reed snapped. 'She didn't poison the cat!'

Clemens looked injured. 'The vet said he'd been poisoned and you said . . .'

'Never mind what I said, it was intended as a joke. In any case, the superintendent doesn't want to listen to gossip.'

Wycliffe toook a sheaf of typewritten papers from his briefcase and turned the pages. 'We have to consider every possibility,' he said, without obvious relevance. 'How long have you lived in Kergwyns, Mr Reed?'

Reed looked surprised. 'Oh, eight or nine years.' He considered. 'Yes, we came here, bought this place and set up in business nine years ago.'

Wycliffe stroked the side of his face with his fingertips and mused over his papers. 'I know very little about the antique trade but surely this was a very odd place to choose?'

'You think so? You can set up an antique business anywhere, once you have a connection.'

It was Clemens who answered the unspoken question. 'We had a good start. My father had a business in Bristol on quite a big scale. When he died, we sold up and came down here.'

'We?'

'Aubrey and me. Aubrey worked for my father as a buyer going round to sales, that sort of thing.'

Wycliffe nodded. So that was it! 'And you, what did you do in your father's business, Mr Clemens?'

Clemens wriggled like a guilty schoolboy. 'I didn't have much to do with the business.'

'So it was your capital and Mr Reed's experience?'

'I can't see what all this has to do with you, superintendent!' Reed was petulant.

'Background, Mr Reed, just background. In any case, there's nothing dishonourable in a partnership between capital and experience, is there?'

However they interpreted the rhetorical question, both Reed and his partner seemed to find it disquieting. Wycliffe turned over the pages of his document.

'In your statement to Inspector Darley, you said that you had known Miss Welles only since she came to Kergwyns to live.'

'Well?'

'I want to know if that is strictly true. It appears that she was in the habit of spending her holidays in St Ives before she came down here to live and that she used to visit Kergwyns in company with Mr Young at the inn. This is a small village and you may have heard or seen something of her.' Wycliffe left the invitation vague, unspecific. 'We want to know everything there is to know about her life both before and after she settled here.' He saw them exchange looks but seemed not to notice.

'We knew her by sight, of course,' Reed admitted.

'And by reputation,' Harvey added.

'A bit wild,' Wycliffe suggested.

'Mike Young was the centre of a lively set in those days, most of them a good deal younger than he was. She was with them.' It was obvious that Reed wanted to appear cooperative without giving anything away.

'Nude bathing parties at night – that sort of thing,' Harvey said and earned a black look.

'A few youngsters out for mischief,' Reed was tolerantly contemptuous.

'Anyone who lives in the village now? – apart from yourselves that is.'

Harvey was dying to tell the story, he was a born scandal-monger. 'Alfie Mitford was one of them but they were mostly strangers – visitors.'

'But there was more to these parties than just bathing without costumes,' the superintendent prompted.

Reed shrugged. 'There was a certain amount of pairing off, you don't want us to draw a diagram, do you?'

'And fights,' Clemens put in. He was excited, like a child with a story to tell.

'Fights?'

'She used to take flashlight photographs.'

'Who did?'

'Why, Pussy Welles. She used to organize everything.'

'Look here, superintendent, there's no point in raking all this up. It was years ago and we were all a lot younger and a lot sillier. It's best forgotten.' Reed's squeaky voice was almost pleading.

Wycliffe eyed him with distaste. 'I shall be glad to forget it, Mr Reed, once I am satisfied that it has nothing to do with my case. Until then, I expect you to answer my questions. About these fights . . .'

'It was really all-in wrestling,' Clemens said, 'like you see on the television. I fought Mike Young three times and beat him every time. You wouldn't think so would you? I'm a lot stronger than I look, aren't I, Aubrey?'

'And while you were wrestling, Pussy Welles took photographs?'

'Oh, yes, she used to photograph everything.' He needed no more encouragement and Reed was powerless to stop him. With the enthusiasm of a boy recounting his favourite story he told his tale of vicious sensualism incited and directed – stage managed – by the dead girl.

She couldn't have been more than nineteen!

'She was certainly an unusual young woman. Did she try to use any of these photographs?'

Clemens was suddenly canny, he looked slyly at Reed. Aubrey was scornful. 'There's no point in holding back now, you fool! Of course she used them – after she came to live at Kergwyns. Where do you think her furniture came from? Every piece in that cottage is rightfully mine. She used to give me instructions like a wealthy client – money no object. But she wasn't satisfied with that. When she had all the furniture she wanted, she started trying to get cash.' He stood up and took a cigarette from a box on the mantelshelf, lit it and leaned nonchalantly with his elbow on the shelf. 'I drew the line at that.'

Wycliffe heaved himself out of the armchair and walked to the window, perhaps to remind himself that the sun was shining outside. 'How?'

'I told her she could do what she liked with the photographs.' He warmed to his role now that there was no purpose in concealment.

'And how do you explain this sudden access of courage?' Wycliffe threw the question over his shoulder without bothering to turn round.

'I had the sense to stop and think. Until then I did what she wanted without stopping to make a rational appraisal of her hold over me – a mistake made by many victims of blackmail, I imagine.' (He was right there!) 'What could she do? She could send copies of the photographs to a few of my friends, shock one or two of my customers. She might even try to involve me with your people but the photographs were five years old and I was prepared to take a chance.' He preened himself.

'What happened when you refused to pay?' Wycliffe still had his back to the room.

'Once she understood that I meant it, she took it very well. She laughed. "Photographs? There aren't any, I destroyed them years ago." So you see, superintendent, I – we, had no reason to harm her.'

The smirk on his lips as he sat down left no doubt that he believed himself well out of a tricky situation.

'But she might have blackmailed others – not so strong-minded.' The superintendent was scathing.

'Alfie Mitford, for instance,' Clemens said.

'Shut up, you fool!' Reed's voice was almost a shriek.

'Why shouldn't I tell him? She came here the day she was murdered . . .'

Reed sprang at him like a cat, clawing at his face. 'I'll kill you! I'll kill you!' But Clemens stood up, lifting Reed with him like a baby, and catching his arms he pinioned them and Reed yelped.

Clemens released him. 'I didn't mean to hurt you.' Reed collapsed on to the settee, shaking with temper and sobbing. Clemens stood

110

over him, his great moon-face creased with concern. 'He's easily upset, you can never tell . . .'

'I'll leave you to console him,' Wycliffe said.

'But don't you want to know what she said?'

'Well?'

'She didn't usually come here but she came Thursday morning and after talking for a bit she asked if we'd heard any rumours. She said it was going around that Mike Young's accident wasn't an accident at all but that somebody tried to kill him. Aubrey wouldn't say anything, he's good at playing it cool, he just said why did people want to bring that up after all this time? She said it didn't matter but perhaps somebody ought to ask Alfie Mitford where the oil came from.'

'Where the oil came from?'

'Yes; ask Alfie Mitford that.'

'Is that all?'

Clemens was crestfallen. Wycliffe let himself out, slamming the front door so that it rattled. 'Bloody little rats!'

He had forgotten that it was Sunday – Easter Sunday – but the square reminded him, it was more lively than he had yet seen it, people coming out of church and gossiping in the sunshine. Women in new hats, several of the men in sober suits and well brushed bowlers. Erica Dampier looking more bleached than ever in a beige two-piece, talked earnestly to the vicar. Janice Mitford, alone, looking haggard, she seemed on the point of coming over to him but changed her mind. Even the dogs were having a day out, sniffing at this and that and at each other.

A film set, Wycliffe thought, would be more convincing.

The bar was crowded, Sylvie and a little rat faced man with a dangling cigarette, coped as best they could but Sylvie caught the superintendent's eye and with a gesture as plain as words told him, 'He's still in bed.'

Lunch was late and served by a harassed elderly woman who mixed up the orders. Evidently there was disorganization behind the scenes and the food was cold. Not that Wycliffe was critical, he ate mechanically and brooded.

Barnes had been fixed by the dead girl; now he was inclined to wonder whether she had not played the game another move ahead. Had she foreseen that the case against Barnes would come unstuck and provided another candidate in Alfie Mitford? Bloody ridiculous! And yet he was being led by the nose to interest himself in Mitford; first the photograph with the newspaper cuttings concealed in the frame, then this devious procedure to set Clemens gossiping. What other motive could she have had? 'Somebody should ask Alfie Mitford where the oil came from.' Presumably the oil that caused Young's smash. Mitford had been an amateur racing enthusiast and the picture showed him with his car. Was the whole thing too silly or was it what he might expect from the twisted mind of the author of *God and Maggie Jones?* He groaned and a visitor at the next table looked across sympathetically. 'Not very good is it? The meat's like leather.'

Why couldn't it have been a nice straightforward case with a jealous lover waiting to say 'Yes, I did it and I'd do it again'? If he was right and he was still dancing to Pussy's tune, then she had wanted him to take Mike Young's smash into account. He had to bear in mind the possibility that Mitford really was the culprit. He toyed absently with a couple of tinned peaches swimming in a milky gravy.

9

For Ursula Barnes Sunday morning was an anti-climax. After the strain she seemed to have entered a limbo of the emotions which denied her even a sense of relief. Instead of the excitement of anticipation, instead of pleasure or even satisfaction she experienced only a numbing emptiness, an intolerable detachment. Most of the time her throat felt constricted and she was on the brink of tears. She had the sense to know that it would come right when Ricky was back but she had to get through this endless day. She forced herself to do the cottage chores, trying to believe that she was getting it ready for him but it was unreal. What if something went wrong and they didn't let him go? She cooked a meal which she hardly touched. She told herself that within twenty-four hours he would be sitting opposite her again and tried, desperately, to see him in the eye of her mind but all she achieved was an anonymous blur. It was the last straw and the intolerable tension dissolved into a paroxysm of weeping.

Then she felt better. She washed her face in cold water and decided to go for a walk. She followed the path by the stream towards the cove but when it reached the rocky defile above the beach she chose instead the cliff path and climbed to a grassy promontory and sat there. A quiet spring afternoon, the sea shining like silver in the sun, the air sweet and balmy, the gorse full blown in flower and bumble bees stocking up for their broods. The old recipe trotted out every year but always a best buy.

She began to relax; she had a lichen covered boulder at her back and the turf was springy. She watched midget waves breaking in a lace of foam, a dog pursuing an uncertain scent along the crumbling bank of the stream, gulls swooping and quarrelling over something on the flat rocks at the other side of the cove. She felt drowsy and perhaps she dozed for she was startled by heavy foot-falls that seemed close, a man hurrying along the cliff path towards her. He was tall, heavily built and he wore a navy track suit.

'Alfred!'

'Ursula!'

He was out of breath and seemed embarrassed. She hoped that after saying polite things he would go away but he didn't, he loomed over her and fumbled for words. 'Getting some exercise; since I've given up actually playing games I find it difficult to keep my weight down. I do a lot of reffing of course but it's not the same.' This came in disjointed phrases with long pauses in between.

'No, I suppose not,' Ursula said when it seemed certain that no more would come.

'Do you mind if I sit down? Just for a moment?' He sat beside her, his arms round his knees and stared out to sea. 'Janice and I were delighted to hear about Ricky. You must be relieved.' He didn't sound delighted.

'Yes.'

'It's really odd why that superintendent hasn't been to see me, I thought he was interviewing everybody . . . everybody in any way connected with Pussy Welles.' He spoke her name as though it was an indelicacy which had to be got over. 'The inspector took a statement from me in the beginning but that was all. I suppose I ought to be glad – I mean glad that they are not interested in me but now I'm a bit worried if they are going to start all over again.'

Ursula had little sympathy or patience with men who, like infants, want to be kissed and made better, and she resented the implication that everything was all right as long as Ricky was the scapegoat. So she gave him no encouragement but he blundered on.

'A school teacher is especially vulnerable to ill-natured gossip and Janice is very . . . To be quite frank, I only told the inspector part of the truth . . .'

'You can soon put that right.'

But he was not to be snubbed. 'You see, I knew Pussy before she came to Kergwyns to live. She used to come here for her holidays.'

Bit by bit the story came out punctuated by excuses, apologies, explanations. She heard about the nude bathing, about the fights on the beach, about the photographs and most of all about his infatuation for Pussy Welles which he seemed to regard as a disease for which he deserved pity rather than blame. 'I was very young and irresponsible.' (He must have been in his early or middle twenties.) 'I had a difficult childhood; my parents were over protective.' (All parents are either over protective or indifferent.) 'The gradual initiation into sex which most youngsters manage in their teens was telescoped for me into a few weeks, years late.' Once he had stopped and looked at her with concern, 'I hope I'm not shocking you.'

'No, you're not shocking me,' Ursula said. But he was though not in the way that he feared.

'I was a young teacher at the same school as now and terrified that all this might get out – it would have finished me.' He picked at the loose threads of his trousers and collected his thoughts to begin again.

Ursula watched the sky and sea, sometimes she would follow the flight of a bird or shift her position to sit more comfortably. He was puzzled by her detachment; how could she be so indifferent to his confidences?

'Then I met Janice at a conference and after a short engagement we were married. The next I heard of Pussy Welles, she was married too and although she had come to live at St Ives, I thought that she would be as anxious to forget the past as I was. For a time it seemed that I was right, then her husband was killed and she took that cottage of Mike Young's. I mean, why did she have to come to live in the village?'

With a naive egoism he told how Pussy Welles established herself in the village. He tried to keep out of her way at first but Janice involved him in the social life of the place so that they were bound to meet and in the end he was paying her clandestine visits. 'It wouldn't be true to say I didn't want to.' He was blushing like a schoolboy. 'I mean Pussy Welles was a very attractive girl – not only physic-ally . . . and she couldn't be shocked. You never felt *dirty*.' He said the word then winced as though he had been hurt. 'But she was hard! There was no sentiment, no affection, no love. I think she was incapable of love.'

Ursula was learning a lot about men which might be good for Richard.

'Of course, I knew that I was doing wrong – deceiving my wife and so on. I also knew that I was bound to be found out eventually, so I decided to explain to Pussy and to stop seeing her. But when I told her, she looked strange and said, "I was going through a box of

115

junk the other day – you know the sort of thing – stuff I hadn't looked at for years, and I came across some old photographs. You remember the nights we used to go bathing?" I knew what she meant, she didn't need to threaten.'

When he arrived he had been hot from exertion, beads of sweat on his brow and running down his cheeks, great damp patches under the arms of his track suit; now he shivered. 'It was horrible after that – I mean being *made* to do the most intimate things . . . She used to put me through what she called *love tests* – I got to hate her! Then Janice found out and I had to stop going there. In a way I was relieved but it didn't really solve anything because she still had the photographs and she could still ruin my career any time she felt so inclined.'

'But she didn't.'

Mitford shook his head. 'She really didn't have much chance, it wasn't long after Janice found out that she was killed.'

Ursula was mystified. Why should he be so anxious to establish that he had a motive for the crime? Was this a preamble to confession? For a moment she felt uneasy. Was it so unlikely that a murderer should confess his crime, explain it, justify it, then kill his confidante? She shivered. To be washed up on the shore one fine morning.

'You're cold! How utterly thoughtless of me to keep you here like this!'

Then she felt a fool. 'No, I'm not cold, not a bit.' To punish herself she added: 'I suppose you realize that what you've told me is an admission that you had a strong motive for killing her?'

He sat, shoulders drooping, scuffling the ground with his feet. 'I know.'

'Then why tell me?'

'Because I've got to talk to somebody and I can't talk to Janice.' He was silent for a long time, then he burst out, 'And you haven't heard everything yet, there was the business with the oil . . .'

'The *oil*?'

'Pussy came to my house on the afternoon of the day she died; she hadn't been there for months. Luckily, Janice was in the back garden. She talked for a few minutes then she said, "If anything happens, Alfie, I should tell them about the oil. If you don't they'll get to know just the same, then it would look bad for you."' He shuddered. 'She was a devil! – I asked her what was likely to happen and she just laughed, then Janice came in and she went.'

'But what's all this about oil?' Ursula was losing patience.

He spoke so quietly that it was difficult to hear. 'The oil that made Mike Young skid came from my garage, a five gallon drum I used for waste from the sump. It was in the days when I used to do rally driving.'

'Did you put the oil on the road?'

'Oh, God, no!'

'But the drum of oil came from your garage. Stolen?'

He nodded.

'Which gives a strong presumption that Young's crash was no accident but an attempt to kill him – just as the superintendent said last night.'

Mitford writhed. 'He knows. I'm sure he knows, just like she said he would. And it makes me an accessory.'

'Why didn't you report the loss of the oil at the time?'

'Pussy advised me not to get involved.'

'You told her?'

He nodded. 'What shall I do?'

Ursula was angry but she realized that it was useless to tell him what she thought. 'I don't know what you should do but I'll tell you this much, if Ricky had told the police the truth he wouldn't be in prison now.'

Mitford waited but when he saw that there was no more to come, he got up. 'I'll think it over. It was good of you to listen . . . You won't say anything?'

'I won't say anything.'

'Thanks. You're a good sport.'

Christ, I hope not! Ursula was learning fast. She watched him loping away down the path to the valley then she got up herself and set off in the opposite direction.

She had walked some distance along the cliff path before she thought of where she was going. She couldn't face a return to her solitary vigil at the cottage so she decided to continue along the cliffs to the village and to call on the Dampiers or to have tea at the pub. For once she needed to be among people. She reached the ruins of a mine engine house with a truncated stack perched on the cliff edge and from the ruin a grassy track ran in the direction of Kergwyns church tower. It occurred to her that this might be a short cut to the village and she decided to follow it. As she moved away from the sea the sense of desolation increased and soon the broad track petered out into a maze of rutted paths among the heather but she could see the tower straight ahead and there seemed no reason why she should not reach it. Overhead a buzzard lazily quartered the ground but otherwise there was no sign of life.

As she approached the village she had to cross a couple of tiny fields bounded by low walls of huge granite boulders but then she came up against a higher wall of properly mortared stones that she could not possibly climb. It was infuriating, the church tower was less than a hundred yards away, but to her left the wall ended in a marsh with standing water and to her right it seemed to lose itself in a bramble thicket of indeterminate extent and quite impenetrable. She swore with vigour and realized that her behaviour was almost hysterical. 'What the hell is wrong with me? I've just got to go round; it's a nuisance but what of it?'

It was quiet, so quiet that she could hear her heart beating. She set out along the wall and just before the brambles started she came to a little door set in the wall and surmounted by a pointed arch which gave it an ecclesiastical air. If she could open it and if it led into the churchyard, all would be well. It opened easily enough but not into the churchyard. She found herself in the cobbled yard of a farm-house with outbuildings on two sides and the house on a third. A white painted farm gate separated the yard from a gravelled drive that must lead to the village. There was no sign of life in the house, the windows looked blind and she had only to cross the yard. Just then a little animal scuttled across almost at her feet and disappeared behind a pile of logs. A rat? She hadn't seen it clearly. Then she saw another. In the centre of the cobbled yard there was a Cornish Cross and seated on the plinth, a little brown, stubtailed creature nibbled at one paw. A lemming! Then she knew where she was. She walked over to the cross and found two more on the plinth at the other side and yet another crouched between the cobbles a yard away; the place was alive with them. The wicket in the big double doors of the outhouse was open and she watched another put its little snub nose out into the sunlight then beat a hasty retreat. She walked over to the shed. When her eyes had adapted to the light she could see the bank of cages with all their doors open and there were lemmings all over the floor. Some were scurrying about, others were crouched, panting and glassy eyed, more lay on their sides, eyes closed, apparently dead.

She hurried out of the shed, closed the door and crossed to the house. As she pressed the bell the door itself yielded, opening into a square hall with stairs on one side, the open door of the kitchen on the other and a glass door with multi-coloured panes straight ahead. Lying in the rainbow pattern of light from the coloured glass, on the floor of the hall, a black and white cat, stretched out in death. For the first time since she entered the courtyard she felt afraid.

'Mr Lomax!' Her voice sounded absurdly tremulous and faint. She tried again. 'Mr Lomax!' This time it was almost a scream but nobody answered. 'Is there anybody in the house?' She hardly knew what to do. Caution and common sense counselled that she should go for help but she hated to go with half a story. She looked into the kitchen, it was empty, a pile of dirty dishes on the draining board, a stove crepitating gently, a couple of tea towels on the rack. On the floor a congealed mess testified to the illness of the cat. She opened the glass door having to step over the cat's body to do it, and found herself in Lomax's study. Lomax was there too, seated at his table, the sunlight streaming down on his greying head. He seemed to be asleep, his head resting on his left arm, but he was dead, shot through the temple. She stood looking down at him feeling quite calm and no longer afraid. She wondered how long he had been dead. Could the killer still be in the house? She strained her ears; nothing but the majestic ticking of the grandfather clock. Then she noticed the gun, lying on the carpet by the chair, just a few inches from the trailing fingers of his right hand. Suicide! The church clock chimed a quarter past three and startled her by its nearness.

There was nothing she could do. She crept out of the room, stepped over the cat and left the glass door ajar. The flowered porcelain knob must already carry one set of her prints. Not that it mattered, she supposed. She reached the yard and then she ran, sending the lemmings scuttling for cover. The drive brought her into the lane just a few yards from the square. She forced herself to walk and to breathe deeply. The square was deserted except for the old men on their seat and a solitary herring gull perched on top of the war memorial like a weather cock.

Lomax was dead. He had shot himself. Did this mean that he was guilty?

At the inn she was lucky to catch both the superintendent and the inspector. She told her story sounding more composed than she felt.

'You go along. I'll telephone the boys and join you later.'

When Darley had gone Wycliffe said, 'Are you all right? . . . Sure? . . . Good girl! This must be the last straw for you.' He sounded genuinely concerned and she hoped she didn't look like a plucky little woman.

Lomax was dead so Lomax could wait. The superintendent went through to the back premises of the inn and up the private stairs. On the landing he hesitated then turned right and threw open the first door. In the room the curtains were drawn and the air was heavy with the smell of stale spirits. Mike Young lay on the bed fully dressed except for his jacket and shoes, snoring in a drunken sleep. An empty whisky bottle lay on the floor.

Wycliffe swept back the curtains and slammed down the window, letting in the sunlight and a breath of air but the only effect on Young was a brief interruption in the rhythm of his breathing. Wycliffe stood over him. 'Even if I succeed in waking him he'll be too drunk to talk!' He put his head into the passage and bellowed: 'Sylvie!' His voice must have been heard half across the square.

But Sylvie was already coming down the passage, pulling a dressing-gown round her. 'What's going on? I was getting ready to go out. Is he gone round the bend?'

She stood in the doorway of the bedroom watching the super-intendent with more interest than surprise. The main item of furniture in the room was a chest of drawers, the veneer chipping off, its surface greasy with the grime of years. Wycliffe had yanked out one of the small top drawers and was throwing its contents on to the floor. Handkerchiefs, socks, clean and dirty, ties, loose collars and a few paper backed novels.

'When did you see him last?'

She walked into the room, stepping over the debris. Wycliffe was through with one drawer and starting on the next.

'Just before lunch. I came up to ask him if he wanted anything.'

'And did he?'

She grimaced like a little girl. 'He was just like now. Why? What's he done?'

'I'll ask the questions! What time did he get in last night?'

She had to think. 'Just after closing time – half after ten. He cashed up.'

'Then?'

'I went to bed.'

'Where do you sleep?'

'The room at the head of the stairs. If you want to know, I heard him come up about a quarter past eleven.'

'But he could have gone out again at any time during the night without you knowing?' Wycliffe was busy now with one of the long drawers and the pile of clothing on the floor grew.

'He could have but he didn't.'

'How do you know?' The superintendent stopped what he was doing to give her his undivided attention.

She shrugged. 'Do you want me to tell you what happened or don't you? He did go out and I heard him. Just after two. He'd been moving about in here, keeping me awake, then I heard him pass my door and go downstairs. After a minute or two he opened the back door – the bolt makes a noise.'

'Did you hear him come back?'

'No. I never saw or heard any more of him until just after eight this morning. I looked in here and he was just like you see him now.'

'You mean he's been sleeping it off since then?'

She grinned. 'The bottle was only half empty then.'

'Have you ever seen a gun among his belongings?'

'A gun! What's he supposed to have done, then?'

Wycliffe repeated his question. She tossed her head, clearing the straggling brown hair from her eyes. 'I've never seen him with a gun and I'm never allowed in here. He always locks the door when he goes out and I'm not even allowed to clean it – *as* you can see for yourself.'

'But you told me . . .'

'That I sleep with him. I do sometimes but he always comes to me.'

Wycliffe had reached the bottom of the second long drawer and came up with a battered briefcase. It was locked but he opened it with a safety pin. A few papers. He spread them on top of the chest of drawers. Two birth certificates, a will and a photograph. The first certificate recorded the birth of Charles Michael Holst and the other that of Anna Patricia Holst, eight years later.

'They were brother and sister!' Sylvie looked at the man on the bed in astonishment. For once, something had surprised her. She turned to the superintendent, 'You knew?'

'No, I wondered. They were alike.'

'*Alike!*'

Wycliffe picked up the photograph, a snapshot taken on the pavement outside a dreary looking terraced house, a youngish woman with a baby in her arms and a little boy standing at her side. On the back someone had written in a feminine hand, *Michael 8. Anna 3 months.*

'It looks as though papa's music didn't pay very well.'

Wycliffe collected the papers and put them back, relocking the case. Young snorted vigorously in his sleep and turned over on his side. A man's voice downstairs called, 'Anybody about?'

'See who it is.'

Sylvie went out but came back almost at once with a uniformed constable who looked as though he had just come out of training school. He stared at the cluttered floor and at the man on the bed.

'Well?'

'Inspector Darley would be grateful if you would join him at the house, sir.'

Wycliffe nodded. 'You'll be all right?'

Her smile was contemptuous. 'Is it all right to tidy up?'

He was about to say something, changed his mind, shrugged and went out. The constable followed him.

10

The church clock chimed then struck five. In the courtyard of Lomax's house you could hear the mechanical throat clearing that preceded each stroke and the dissonant overtones that followed. Wycliffe sat on the plinth of the Cornish Cross, morose, introspective. The place was alive with policemen, a car and a van were parked in the courtyard and there was another car in the lane. Half the village seemed to have turned out to watch. A constable at the gate stopped them from coming in but they were out in the lane and some had climbed onto the hedges to get a better view. Not that they could see much; only the comings and goings and the superintendent sitting there.

Now and then a lemming flitted across the cobbles to disappear into the shed and the dead ones were still there.

'They're ready to move the body, sir.' Wycliffe merely growled, but after a while he knocked out his pipe, got up and went indoors.

'Something's happening!' The watchers could hardly be expected to know that the principal in their drama felt redundant, that all the real work was being done without his help or intervention.

Darley had established his headquarters in the kitchen.

'Any idea of when it happened yet?'

Darley smoothed his bald head. 'The doctor says he's been dead for at least fourteen and probably sixteen hours or more. Say, between eleven last night and three this morning with a preference for the earlier time. Slade may be able to give us a better idea when he gets hold of the body.' Darley hesitated, looked down at the papers in front of him, then went on, 'Are we to continue to treat this as murder? That's the first question that has to be answered.'

'Or?'

Darley frowned. 'Suicide, of course.'

'And what do you think?'

'There's no doubt in my mind that he killed himself.'

'Why?

Darley resented being forced to spell it out. 'It seems to me that there's only one explanation of his suicide – guilt.'

'So it's all tied up and we're wasting our time – is that what you're saying? You may be right, but let's get this straight! It's almost certain that already in this case, murder and attempted murder have been passed over as accident. Certainly an innocent man has been arrested. I don't intend to repeat those mistakes. We'll treat this as suicide only when there is no possibility that it could have been murder.'

Darley reddened but said nothing.

'Now, is there anything, so far, in the slightest degree inconsistent with it being suicide?'

Darley nodded towards the stove. 'There's that. It's still alight, which means that it must have been refuelled say, after eleven last night. I understand that they are designed to go for twenty to twenty-four hours once they're fully banked up, and there's still several hours burning left in the fuel bed. I know it seems unlikely that a chap would bank up his fire before shooting himself but you and I know they do some queer things.'

'Any heating in the room where he was?'

'A night storage heater and a coal fire which had gone out.'

'What about the animals? – the cat and the lemmings.'

'You mean the fact that they were poisoned?'

Wycliffe nodded.

'I don't see that kind of behaviour as inconsistent with suicide. Quite the reverse. If the animals were important to him he might well feel that he must take them with him, so to speak.'

'By poison?'

'That might seem the only way open to a man of a sensitive nature.'

'A very good point,' Wycliffe admitted.

In the big front room Lomax had been photographed from every possible angle, seated in his chair, his papers on the desk in front of him but these photographs would never appear in *Nature* nor was it likely that anyone would write his biography. Whatever notoriety he achieved now would spring from his connection with a series of crimes, either as a victim or as their perpetrator.

124

The technical people had taken over and until they were through, Darley and the superintendent were in the way. A detective held the revolver, suspended by its trigger guard and examined it carefully. 'Two chambers fired, sir.'

'*Two?*' Wycliffe was startled.

'No doubt of it, sir.'

'OK to shift him now, sir?'

Other men lifted the body in which *rigor* had so far advanced that they were forced to lay him on his side on the stretcher. Despite the gaping hole in his temple, his features were composed and only a little paler than in life. They covered him with a sheet and whisked him away to the van outside. For once, the watchers had something to watch.

'There he goes, poor chap!' A middle-aged woman with a large bosom and a soft heart.

'You don't want to waste your sympathy on the likes of him. They say he shot himself because he killed the girl.' An old man with a military moustache who had once been an RSM. 'No room for murderers, hang 'em I say.'

'Well, if he did kill her, she had it coming to her,' the woman retorted.

Back in the house they found the second bullet. It had entered the spine of a book at the end of the room, penetrated through the pages and bedded itself in the plaster. Darley held the mutilated book in his hands, *Eysenck's Handbook of Abnormal Psychology*. 'If he committed suicide, this must be the first, not the second bullet.'

'What?' Wycliffe seemed worried and vague. 'Oh yes, of course, but why did he fire it before turning the gun on himself?'

'I've heard that suicides – genuine ones who really mean to go through with it, have a horror that it won't work. Lomax wanted to make sure that the gun was in working order, he probably hadn't fired the thing for years – if ever.'

'But is it his gun?'

'Oh, yes. It's registered in his name all right. You're not suggesting, sir, that he was firing at someone else?'

Wycliffe shrugged. 'No.'

The fingerprint men were busy with drawers and cupboard doors. Wycliffe watched them; his manner was apologetic. 'Once you start a murder routine you have to go through with it.'

As each piece of furniture was fingerprinted two other detectives began a meticulous search. If they came across anything of the slightest interest it was put on the desk to be examined by Darley. Wycliffe took up a position by the desk and watched, idly, as the heterogeneous collection increased.

'I suppose you will get them to do a paraffin test on his hands?'

Darley nodded.

'Both hands?'

'Both? No. The gun was found within reach of his right hand. What would be the point of testing the other?'

'I don't know, but have it done.'

The church bell began tolling for evening service, a monotonous clang on the tenor bell. Evidently somebody had decided that the usual cheerful cascade of sound would be inappropriate. There wouldn't be many in the congregation anyway. Wycliffe looked out of the window; the church tower was silhouetted against a brilliant sky, blue with white wisps of cloud turning gold at the edges.

'I'll take a look upstairs.'

'Help yourself.' Darley was preoccupied and glad to see him go.

Wycliffe went out into the passage and up the stairs; stairs and landing were carpeted from wall to wall in plain blue. There were four doors, three bedrooms and one that had been converted to bathroom and lavatory. One of the bedrooms was a lumber room and of the other two, one was a very comfortable looking guest room. Lomax's bedroom was plain and bare by comparison, white walls with no pictures, the floor varnished boards with only a couple of thin mats. The furniture was massive, a mahogany chest of drawers with a mirror over it, a Victorian wardrobe and an armchair upholstered in black leather. But it was the bed that caught attention, a brass bed, the ancestor of them all, gleaming and splendid, complete with patchwork quilt and valances of white damask with lace insertion. Straight out of grandmother's room, a distaff heirloom in which, no doubt, Lomax's mother had been conceived and born. On the wall by the bed, a hanging bookcase crammed with novels, novels of adventure and romance, Scott, Stevenson, Dumas, Hardy, Buchan . . . all tattered through endless re-reading. So Lomax commuted between two worlds of fantasy, one, the world of the great scientist, the other, that of the great adventurer.

And he had tangled with Pussy Welles in the hope that she would give substance to his dreams. Wycliffe wondered how complete and utter disillusionment might subvert such a man. Would it render him capable of killing his Guinevere and viciously displaying her secret flaw? It was certainly possible; in such straits the flesh and blood romantic may not confine his tilting to the windmills. But while his dream world was still intact, could he then, plot with her to kill? Could Lomax have killed Arthur Horner and contrived the crash which almost killed Young? It seemed less likely though not incredible if the besotted man could persuade himself or be persuaded that he was serving his love. Even *Dickson McCunn* fought a bloody battle in defence of his private ideal of chivalry.

On the chest of drawers there were three photographs in oval silver frames, one of Lomax himself, one of Pussy Welles and the third of an old lady with thin lips and hard eyes. Mistress and mother. He picked up the photograph of Lomax, a younger Lomax, a studio portrait which was vaguely familiar – probably because it was the one which appeared on the dust covers of his popular books on natural history. An intelligent face but the intelligence inhibited by destructive self awareness. Thin lips turned down at the corners; a man unhappy with himself but contemptuous of his fellows. Under great stress he might be capable of anything, and suicide would be his ultimate escape.

Pussy Welles had been dead for ten days. Wycliffe felt unusually depressed, he had been involved from the beginning and there had been another death, but he had to admit that far from being able to offer proof of guilt he was still unsure in his own mind where the guilt lay. He told himself that the difficulty arose from the composite nature of the case as it presented itself; in part, and essentially, it was a series of events deliberately planned by the dead girl to relieve her boredom, to exact retribution or merely to demonstrate her power, but superimposed on this pattern was another, the product of expediency and fear. The difficulty was to separate the two. He was not even sure to which category of events Pussy's own death belonged. It was like a jig-saw puzzle in which a number of 'foreign' pieces had been substituted and you had to begin by weeding them out. There could be no doubt that Pussy Welles was the real criminal but it was equally certain that she had not herself performed all the criminal acts. The law was only interested in identifying her accomplice and demonstrating his guilt. Lomax? Possibly. Young? He was her brother but did this tell in his favour or against him? In any event, he was a victim – how to explain that away? Mitford? Introspective, emotionally immature, under petticoat rule; perhaps nobody had paid enough attention to him. Ursula Barnes had said something about meeting him on the cliffs but it had been lost in the excitement created by her other news. Mitford must be remembered. Dampier? Wycliffe had to admit to a prejudice in his favour; of all the people who figured in the case Dampier was the only one with whom he felt able to achieve a common bond of either understanding or sympathy. But the fact remained that he was mentally able and physically crippled, a man unlikely to be restrained by the same sanctions which are effective with those who are either less intelligent or less frustrated.

Then there were the queers. Wycliffe was unable to take them seriously; for him they were a joke in bad taste. But he had an ingrained revulsion against homosexuality which no amount of objective argument could destroy. Reed was mean and he was prepared to believe that he was also vicious but it seemed extremely unlikely that Pussy Welles had ever made him a partner in anything.

He became aware that the light was fading, that he had been daydreaming. The sky behind the church was flushed with the afterglow of sunset and soon it would be dark. He went downstairs and found Darley alone in the study; he was sitting at the dead man's desk going through those items which his subordinates had thought worth his attention.

'I take your point,' he said, 'Lomax was left handed.'

'What?' Wycliffe found this ability to resume a conversation exactly where it had been left off an hour ago, disconcerting. 'Oh, you mean the business of the paraffin test? I happened to notice that the other evening, he seemed to use his left hand for preference, then this afternoon I saw that the written material on his desk suggested left handedness.'

Darley nodded. 'He might still have used his right hand on the gun; many people who have a left handed tendency are almost ambidextrous.'

'Of course, but it would be interesting to know the extent to which he used his right hand. What about fingerprints on the gun?'

'His own, quite a good set from the right hand, blurred as you would expect in firing two shots.'

Darley switched on the desk lamp and the twilight outside suddenly gave way to darkness. They could hear singing from the church, an Easter hymn:

> Jesus lives! thy terrors now
> Can, O Death, no more appal us;

'I would like your opinion on these.' He picked up a slim wad of papers, letters, written on sheets of different sizes and colours, all in the same neat, small hand. 'They're from Pussy Welles to Lomax and they go back six or seven years – to the time when he was still at the university and she worked there as a secretary.' He pointed to a length of blue ribbon on the desk. 'They were tied up with that – imagine it, in a man of his age! But they seem to settle our case.'

Wycliffe brought another chair into the circle of light and settled down to read. There were about two dozen letters spread unevenly over the period, presumably she wrote only when they were separated for more than a day or two and this was confirmed by phrases from the letters:

'*since you've been away . . .*' '*I've missed you, especially at the weekend . . .*' and '*I shall be home all Thursday evening so if absence has made you fonder . . .*'

The earlier letters were full of affectionate regard, the young girl impressed and flattered by the attention of a distinguished older man.

> You shouldn't apologize for writing often, surely you realize that I'm flattered by your interest . . .

Later, written while she was on holiday in Cornwall:

> If you must justify our relationship by precedents, remember that Beatrice was only fourteen when Dante found her. I am twenty-one!
> No! You never bore me with details of your work, I revel in being associated, even distantly, with anything creative . . .

'He must have lapped it up, poor devil!' Wycliffe said.

Darley was going through Lomax's other papers – drafts of

articles, business letters, bank statements. He looked up with a tired grin. 'No fool like an old fool!'

Then the tone of the letters changed:

Really, Edgar, you can't expect to monopolize me. I know you would be the last to want me to feel that I had been bought by your presents, much as I appreciate and value them.

A little later:

No, I do not mean that things are finished between us but I have never led you to believe that our relationship was or could be an exclusive one. You are very foolish to try to get consolation from drink, that will solve nothing and may cost you your job. Try to realize that you have not 'discovered a guilty secret of mine'. I have never tried to make a secret of my life and certainly do not feel any guilt. You must understand that in my own way, I too am rather a 'special person' and I have no intention of belonging to anybody.

Then there was a gap in the letters. When they resumed, Lomax had settled in Kergwyns and Pussy had married and was living with her husband in St Ives.

A woman pays for her mistakes, but in all honesty I must admit that I have nobody to blame but myself. When I think, dear friend, of what you offered me compared with what I now have! But there is no going back . . .

You can't imagine how I look forward to our little meetings but they make me sad for I cannot help but be reminded of how things might have been . . .

And then, on the day of the inquest on her husband:

I have never been so happy, it is like being reprieved from a life sentence! Thank you, thank you, thank you! I will make sure that you never have any regrets. But we must be circumspect, my dearest, that is what I find most difficult! When the coroner (pompous old fool!) expressed sympathy with the widow, I nearly laughed in his face! But we must be careful for the time being, there must be no hint of suspicion. What would I do if . . . ? There, I can't bring myself even to write of the possibility.

Another long gap, almost three years, then:

. . . you are welcome at the cottage now as always, it is childish of you to write. It is not I who have changed . . . You have become morbidly introspective and a source of concern to your friends . . . Sometimes I fear that you are developing a persecution complex. Perhaps you should get advice, I am sure that John will know a good alienist . . .

The last letter was dated two days before Pussy Welles died:

My Dear Edgar,
    You are becoming extremely tiresome in your persistence. I have always despised jealousy as the most futile of emotions. Either you have the courage to do something about it or you haven't. I have told you more than once that you have no special claim on me and your threats are merely ludicrous. By all means come to the cottage if you wish – Thursday evening will suit me – though I can't promise that you will be reassured.
    Pussy.

Wycliffe put down the little pile and sat back in his chair. Darley sat back too. 'Well? What do you think of them?'

Wycliffe seemed reluctant to talk, the letters had affected him strangely, his features registered only blankness and he regarded the inspector dully. 'I don't know what to think. That is the most incredible collection of documents I have ever come across.'

Darley was surprised. 'Incredible? I wouldn't say that; surely you've been telling me all the way through, what an extraordinary girl she was – these only prove you right. Utterly amoral, she got her kicks by manipulating people as though they were puppets which is more or less what you said about her.'

Wycliffe said nothing and Darley went on, 'In the end, one of her performers proves to be flesh and blood after all, and gets his own back. I can't say I blame him, although he's a murderer twice over.

131

'Isn't that how you see it?' he demanded when Wycliffe remained silent and inscrutably blank.

'I don't know.'

'But surely you agree that Lomax shot himself?'

'It certainly looks like it.' Wycliffe raised his hands in a gesture of bewilderment. 'But why?'

'Why? You ask that after reading those letters? The wretched man had lost his job, committed murder and goodness knows what else for this evil little baggage but instead of the reward he hoped for, he got the brush off. So he killed her, and you ask why, after all that, he committed suicide!'

'I suppose you are right.'

The inspector shuffled the papers on the desk impatiently. 'I'm sorry, sir, but I really can't understand your attitude.'

'So it's all over?'

'Yes, bar the shouting, and there won't be much of that. Nobody is very interested in a murderer who commits suicide, the great British public will feel that they've been done.'

'It seems such an unsatisfactory ending.'

Darley looked at him in astonishment. 'Unsatisfactory! But we aren't writing detective stories! This is for real!'

Wycliffe smiled. 'For real! – I shall remember that.'

He got up and moved towards the door. Darley watched him uneasily.

'I'll see you in the morning.'

The superintendent walked slowly back to the inn. The watchers had tired of their vigil for it was dark. There were few lighted windows, even on Sundays the villagers seemed to avoid the front of their houses and, in any case, most of the men were at the inn. As he entered the bar conversation faltered and died. They watched him and made way for him to reach the counter where Sylvie and the little rat-faced man were busy.

'How is he?'

Sylvie tossed her head. 'He's had some black coffee and he's getting dressed. I think he'll live.' She drew a pint of bitter, pushed it across to a customer, picked up the wet money and gave change. 'I've tidied up and I doubt if he'll notice if you don't tell him.'

'I won't,' Wycliffe promised. 'In fact, I'd say nothing to anybody of what happened last night or this afternoon.'

132

She grimaced. 'I know how to hold my tongue; I've had enough practice.'

'Good!'

After dinner he walked on the cliffs and watched the rain clouds creep in over the sea, shutting out the stars. Once more that night he found sleep through the devious pattern of one of Pussy's puzzles.

Rodent Operator and Musician, four and five. *Pied Piper!* Wycliffe was pleased with himself. That gave a *P* to start one across. *Small dog in leading strings?* That checked him for a while. Six letters. He thought of pup and he thought of pet but it was some time before he put them together: *Puppet . . .*

He heard the church clock begin to chime midnight but he was asleep before the twelve strokes had doled themselves out. Two or three times in the night he woke and found himself thinking about the case. His thoughts seemed unusually lucid which probably meant that his critical faculty was still asleep, but he felt peaceful and contemplative so that when he finally woke he wasn't surprised to find that he was on the brink of decision.

Half past six; rain with a wind behind it, driving water down the window panes. Since coming west he was getting to like rain. He got out of bed and stood looking out of the window. Below him, the backyard of the inn, stacked with barrels, glistening in the rain and surrounded by a high wall; beyond a stretch of gorse and heather to the cliff edge and the sea, but today his vision was bounded by the sheeting rain. Even so, by bringing his face close to the glass he could see the roofs of the bungalows in the lane.

'Bloody fool!' He muttered to himself, then he put on his dressing-gown and slippers and went downstairs.

It gave him a perverse pleasure to hear Darley's sleepy voice at the other end of the wire.

'I hope I haven't got you up.' He waited while Darley made certain unspecified preparations for a more extended conversation. 'About the two bullets fired from Lomax's gun – I want you to ask the ballistics people whether they can offer any evidence at all as to which was fired first, the one that went into the book or the one that killed Lomax . . .'

'So you still think it might be murder?'

'Perhaps, but never mind about that . . .'

'But surely it's impossible for ballistics to tell anything of the sort?'

Wycliffe was impatient. 'Ask anyway. Remember that the gun probably hasn't been fired for a very long time before this – if ever. And get on to them first thing. I don't want this balled up.' It never took long for Darley to ruffle his sunniest mood.

'And the letters – the letters from Pussy to Lomax – get them tested for prints . . .

'Anybody's, yours, mine, the dead man's, Pussy Welles', Uncle Tom Cobleigh's. Then I want them examined by a handwriting expert. Gordon Cleaver who used to work for the Home Office lives somewhere in this area – take them to him . . . Yes, you can take a specimen of her writing along if you like but I'm not questioning that she wrote them. I'm sure she did.

'And Darley . . . come and have lunch with me here.' He was pleased with himself; no doubt about that. Darley was impressed and mystified too. But he would look a damn fool if it all went wrong.

As he left the booth he could hear Sylvie in the kitchen and he went to get some coffee. She was hollow-eyed.

'You look tired; you're overdoing it.'

'You can say that again; he's been with me most of the night – after sympathy and you know what.'

'You don't have to put up with it.'

He watched her pour the coffee from the percolator into the cups.

'He's asked me to marry him.'

'And will you?'

'I could do worse, I suppose; this place could be a gold mine.'

He sensed that she was asking his advice and he thought of Mary, his own daughter, not much younger than Sylvie. He was deeply touched but there was no advice he could give her, the contexts were so different.

'Good morning, superintendent.' It was Young, early abroad, in pyjama tunic and trousers. He looked ill. But he was amiable and a little shamefaced. 'Sylvie told me you wanted to talk to me yesterday about poor Lomax. The fact is, I had the father and mother of a hangover – I expect you guessed. But if there's anything I can do now?'

'Two questions, Mr Young, that's all.'

Young took a crushed cigarette packet from his trousers pocket, picked out one, straightened it and lit up. 'Fire away!'

'The man you saw talking to Horner on the evening of his death was Lomax?'

'What do you think?'

Wycliffe nodded. 'Now, on the night of your car crash, you told the police that Lomax was in St Ives, though Lomax himself said that he was at home.'

Young raised his shoulders and grimaced. 'I know he was there; I saw him and I saw his car in the car park, not far from mine.'

'Ah! And when you went to fetch your car, did you notice whether or not his was still there?'

The innkeeper turned full face as he spoke. 'It was gone, the car park was empty.'

'So you've known all along?'

Young's eyes narrowed. 'Not *known*, superintendent, I had no proof.'

'And you did nothing.'

He stubbed out the butt of his cigarette. 'Once when I showed the slightest sign of stepping out of line, I was nearly killed in that smash. It taught me a lesson. A single unguarded remark about Arthur Horner, here in this bar, led to that in twenty-four hours.'

'So when I pressed you on Saturday night in front of Lomax, you went home and drank yourself into a stupor because you were scared?'

'I'm not denying it.'

'But there's nothing to be scared of now.'

'No.' Young agreed in a curiously level voice. 'As you say, there's nothing to be scared of now.'

'Well, thank you, Mr Young.' Wycliffe moved to the door, then turned back. 'It may interest you to know that there was a constable on duty here all Saturday night, so that the risk was not overlooked.'

Young's face was impassive. 'I've never had much faith in the police, superintendent, but thanks all the same.'

11

Tuesday evening at Lomax's house, and another gathering of those who were known to have the strongest reasons for interest in Pussy Welles, dead or alive. This time there was no subterfuge, no attempt to cloak the purpose of the gathering in a socially acceptable guise; all of them knew why they had been asked to come and any doubts were dispelled by the place of their meeting. You can't make merry in a dead man's study, at least, not before he is decently buried. (Lomax was not buried, his body rested transiently in a refrigerated drawer at the county mortuary.) The same people would be there, except for Lomax himself, and Ricky Barnes would take his place.

A fine evening after two days of almost continuous drizzle, a waning moon and starlight. The Barneses parked their Mini in the square and walked back, arm in arm, very close, revelling in mutual self abasement and the cosy business of making it up. But Barnes was edgy, his wounds still raw. No-one answered the bell but the outside light was on and the door stood ajar.

'They said we should go in.'

There was no-one else about but the lights were on in the study and a wood fire blazed and crackled on the hearth. Somebody had arranged chairs and there was a table with drinks and glasses.

'I don't know why we had to come.'

Ursula was patient, as with a child. 'We didn't *have* to, darling, but it seemed a good idea. We might as well *know* what's happening; we have a right to that at least.'

Richard went to the drinks, poured himself a whisky and splashed soda.

'I don't suppose they'll mind,' Ursula said.

'I don't care a damn if they do!' He sipped his drink and wandered moodily round looking at the bookshelves. 'I've never been in here before – queer bird, Lomax. I wonder why he did it?'

'There was something very odd about him.'

Barnes laughed bitterly. 'I expect they said that about me – "I always thought he was a bit shifty – he didn't quite ring true if you see what I mean," – know-all bastards!' He stopped suddenly and faced his wife, 'You don't think they've got me here on false pretences? I mean there's still plenty they could charge me with . . .' His look was pleading, he seemed to beg for reassurance and she gave it, bolstering up his courage until he became aggressive again.

The bell rang and Ursula went to let in Alfred Mitford and Janice. They seemed surprised and put out and Barnes instantly concluded that it was because of him. Alfred sat on a fireside stool, hands clasped over his knees. Janice poured herself a gin; she was tense, excited, her movements were exaggerated and twice she spilt some of her drink down the front of her dress. 'This all seems very odd to me. I mean why are they throwing us together like this? What do they expect to gain by it?'

'I suppose they think we are entitled to some explanation,' Ursula said.

'Explanation!' Janice was contemptuous. 'This is a police trap, my dear, and don't you make any mistake about it!'

'Trap? What for?' Barnes was anxious and she was flattered by his appeal to her.

'What for? To catch the murderer. They've let us think it was Lomax, that he committed suicide because he was guilty, but I heard on good authority that he was murdered . . . Poor Edgar!' She added as an afterthought, 'He never did anybody any harm.'

'I don't believe it!' In her anxiety to shield her husband, Ursula was too emphatic for good manners and Janice bridled.

'You believe what you like, but we shall see before the night is out. In any case, you've nothing to worry about, Ricky's been acquitted. The accused leaves the court without a stain on his character! Isn't that what they say? And you can't be tried twice for the same crime.'

'Janice!' Even Alfred was constrained to protest at his wife's indiscretion. 'You must be out of your mind.'

Janice laughed hysterically. 'I expect I am, and is it any wonder?' She looked at Ursula. 'You might as well know that I'd give a lot to be in your shoes.'

'In *my* shoes? I don't know what you're talking about, Janice.'

'You know they can't touch your husband, he's safe, but what about mine?'

Alfred groaned. 'For God's sake, Janice!'

Either the Dampiers didn't ring the bell or they weren't heard; they just walked in and their arrival served to distract Janice. Dampier made for one of the armchairs and never spoke until he was settled, it was as though he believed himself invisible until he opened his mouth. Erica seemed aware of the tension, she looked pale and haggard, but she smiled. 'I don't suppose this is going to be a jolly evening.'

'At least they've laid on something to drink,' Dampier said. 'Pour me a whisky, Alfred – No soda, just a dash of water, don't drown it . . . thanks, that's fine.' He tasted his drink and looked round with twinkling eyes; whatever the others might think, he was determined to get what enjoyment he could out of the evening. 'First time I've ever been here. It's not what I expected and yet it's Edgar, Edgar to the "T", sober, pompous and . . . what's the word? . . . fatuous.'

'John!' Erica protested mechanically.

'Well, that's what he was and we all know it, being dead doesn't alter that.'

'I wouldn't have said it was a very apt description of a murderer,' Barnes said, and he spoke with careful articulation like a man who is a little drunk and afraid of showing it. 'There must have been more to him than we thought.'

'Murderer?' Dampier was contemptuous. 'Edgar never murdered anybody, he wouldn't kill a chicken.'

'There! What did I tell you?' Janice seized on an ally.

But Dampier's mood was expansive, he swept on, 'By the way, Richard, I haven't said how glad we are to see you back in circulation. How does it feel?'

Barnes poured himself another whisky. 'I haven't had a chance to find out yet, the repercussions are only beginning.'

'Repercussions?'

'The University have offered me a Sabbatic term, you can guess what that means.'

'It means that they are sympathetic and want to help,' Ursula asserted.

'Nonsense! It's a broad hint and the opportunity to look for another job.'

Dampier fondled his beard; he seemed to take pleasure in its black profusion. 'I'm more concerned about who will take your place.'

'Take my place? Where?' Barnes was sharp, ready to take offence.

'Why, in gaol, of course!' Nervous laughter with Mitford looking disapproving, as though they were being sacriligious.

A minor commotion in the passage and Aubrey Reed came in, followed by Harvey Clemens. Reed stood for a moment, hands thrust deep into the pockets of his suede jacket; his eyes shone, he was excited. It occurred to Dampier for the first time, that he probably doped. 'Well? Where is everybody? Where's the super-intendent?'

'Why don't you get yourself a drink?'

Reed poured gin, Clemens opened a bottle of ale. The church clock chimed and started to strike. Everybody listened and counted as though they didn't know the time already.

'Eight o'clock. Sounds close, doesn't it?' Clemens remarked. He looked round, 'Quite a party, aren't we? Like Christmas.'

'We could play games while we wait,' Reed said. 'So this is where the great man worked. I've never been in here before, have you?' He put the question, pointedly, to Mitford. 'But perhaps I shouldn't ask that, inviting a man to incriminate himself.'

Mitford flushed but said nothing. Janice went white.

A crisis was averted by the arrival of Mike Young; he blinked in the light, muttered a word of greeting then made quickly for a chair close to Dampier. 'What's all this about then?'

Dampier was gruff. 'What makes you think I know?'

Young looked round, saw that the others were drinking and poured himself a stiff whisky. 'Who's paying for the drinks?'

'No idea. I suppose we must be guests of the police.'

'Catch those bastards paying for anything.' He took a good pull at his whisky, then looked approvingly at what remained in his glass. 'A drop of the good stuff, anyway!'

When Wycliffe arrived the moonlight was still bright enough to fill the little courtyard with haunting and deceptive shadows. But no lemmings now. He let himself in, hung his coat in the passage and opened the glass door into Lomax's study. A change to see it full of people, who sat about, drinking, presumably chatting, a bright fire crackling away. A meeting of village notables at the home of one of them to organize a protest about something or other. Spoilation of the countryside, drains or re-rating.

Wycliffe sat with a little table in front of him, completing the illusion he was taking the chair. Only the silence measured tension. Nobody had even greeted him.

Dry, speaking with scarcely any inflexion, he thanked them for coming. Informal get together . . . no compulsion on anyone . . . nevertheless co-operation appreciated . . . Everyone present more or less directly concerned with events to be discussed . . . Inquiries had reached the stage when it seemed best to acquaint them with certain facts. Having heard what it was about, did anyone want to leave?

Almost tangible relief. Nobody for the way out.

'Good!'

Wycliffe looked from one to another of his audience slowly, deliberately, as though he wanted to memorize their faces, then he began to talk, so quietly and with so little emphasis that they had to listen carefully in order to follow him. He might have been a don conducting a seminar, fully in control of his subject, but too detached to employ oratorical tricks or to make any attempt to involve his hearers. He suggested that the personality of Pussy Welles was the key to the case and proceeded to offer them a character sketch.

'I have been told that she wanted power for its own sake, that she wanted it badly enough for it to have become an obsession. In such degree, this is not a common phenomenon even among men and, fortunately, it is very rare among women. But when it occurs, it can be more dangerous, for, in my experience, women have a pragmatic approach to morality and they are capable of showing scant respect for taboos which might restrain a man.

'Pussy Welles attempted to achieve her ends through the weapon of her sex. She needed men, but she also used them, seeking a complex satisfaction which had its physical component but derived mainly from the humiliation and servitude she was able to impose on her conquests and in the fear of exposure which she exploited. Where her sex was of little avail, she was quick to use other means.' His eyes rested momentarily on Aubrey Reed. 'Blackmail of one sort or another was her speciality but not usually for material gain and this was her strength.'

He talked on, dry, precise. What the Sunday newspapers would have done with the same material! But Wycliffe never failed to grip his audience and not only because they were so deeply involved. He had the gift of riveting attention.

'When she was killed – murdered, it seemed – there was no shortage of eligible culprits. The most cursory investigation uncovered credible reasons why any one of you, or Lomax, might have killed her. What material clues there were pointed uncertainly to Barnes. He behaved foolishly and by demonstrably false statements, drew attention to himself, then, two apparently damning pieces of evidence precipitated his arrest. An anonymous letter led to the discovery that his pistol was the murder weapon and he was further implicated by the testimony of a woman whom Pussy Welles telephoned only a short while before she was killed. In that telephone conversation, Pussy Welles said that she was pregnant, that Barnes was the child's father and that he was with her discussing what to do. She also hinted that she felt at some risk and the telephone call was intended to ensure her safety.'

Wycliffe matched his finger tips together and studied them in silence. Richard Barnes sat, hunched in his chair, staring at the carpet, and Ursula reached out to place her hand over his. Dampier was restless. He seemed to be on the point of saying something but couldn't quite make up his mind. Suddenly he burst out.

'But this is incredible!'

Wycliffe stared at him, mild eyed. Dampier looked quickly at his sister and away again. 'You know quite well that on the afternoon of the day she died, Pussy told me that she was pregnant and that I was responsible.'

'Well?'

'She threatened me.' He seemed to challenge the superintendent to press him further.

Young was looking at him but it was impossible to judge his thoughts.

'With what?'

Wycliffe cut in quickly. 'You saw fit to keep this to yourself when it might have affected my attitude to Barnes if I had known of it.'

Dampier said nothing and he continued. 'However, it was of little consequence in the long run for I was far from convinced of his guilt. I felt from the beginning that this case had deeper roots, that the death of this girl was part of a pattern. If Barnes had killed her, then it was an intrusive incident, not part of the design.

'I had a number of reasons for coming to this conclusion and they will emerge as I go on. Even when I was compelled to arrest Barnes I continued the case on the assumption of his innocence. But if he was innocent, he had been "framed" and *Pussy Welles was a party to it.*'

Aubrey Reed had sat through the exposition so far with the air of a bored spectator. He lit one cigarette from another and from time to time, sipped his gin. Now he laughed contemptuously. 'I've nothing against Ricky Barnes, but surely, it would be easier to believe that he did it rather than to accept the fantastic notion that Pussy Welles helped to frame him for her own murder.' He turned to the others for support. 'I mean, it's an ingenious idea for a thriller but hardly credible in real life, is it?'

'Lot of nonsense!' Young muttered. He had already had two stiff whiskies and went for the decanter once more.

'What do you think, Mr Dampier?' Wycliffe enquired.

Dampier fingered his beard. 'I could believe almost anything of that girl, but planning her own murder and contriving a trail pointing to the wrong man – the imagination boggles!'

'What about suicide made to look like murder?'

'Ah! That, as they say, is a horse of a different colour.'

'*Did* she commit suicide?' Erica Dampier, strained and white.

'She would have needed an accomplice.' Alfred Mitford spoke for the first time.

Wycliffe turned his attention to Mitford and he shrank back in his shell, wishing that he had had the sense to keep quiet. 'She *had* an accomplice. There's no doubt about that.'

Mike Young was chuckling. Such an unusual phenomenon that everybody loooked at him.

'Mr Young?'

The innkeeper patted his face with a grubby handkerchief. 'It's only that I'd never thought of it – the possibility that Pussy committed suicide, I mean. It would be just her idea of a joke if she intended to do away with herself, to do it so as to cause a hell of a fuss and, my God, she succeeded!'

'And what about her accomplice?'

Young became suddenly wary. After a moment he said, 'Lomax committed suicide, didn't he?'

Janice Mitford had scarcely spoken, she had followed intently everything that passed, looking from one speaker to another apprehensively as though any one might say the thing she dreaded to hear. But now she seemed to have worked herself up to a pitch of almost uncontrollable indignation. 'You mean she killed herself? That she deliberately caused all this misery and anxiety for nothing?' Her voice rose; as with most hysterical women her excitement was a self propagating chain reaction, but Young cut her short. He was venomous, menacing.

'Shut your mouth, Janice Mitford! Whatever Pussy did or didn't do, she was a real woman which is more than can be said for you!'

She looked as though she had been slapped; then she stood up, gathering the shreds of her dignity. 'I'll not stay here to be insulted! Alfred!' But Alfred caught her by the arm and pulled her back to her seat.

'For God's sake sit down and be quiet!'

Wycliffe went on as if nothing had happened. He reiterated his belief that the deaths of Pussy Welles and Lomax were linked with Arthur Horner's and with Young's accident. 'Grown men don't usually fall over cliffs when they are out for a summer evening stroll; neither is it common for five gallon oil drums to fall off lorries on lonely country roads, late at night. That these things and two other violent deaths should happen within the circle of a dozen acquaintances is improbable to the point of impossibility.' He stopped, his eyes on Young who was after his fourth whisky. 'I shouldn't, Mr Young!' He tidied the papers in front of him as he spoke. 'If you are going to follow my argument you'll need a clear head.'

Young looked aggressive, shrugged and sat down. 'I suppose it's your whisky.'

Wycliffe smiled vaguely. 'To continue: at the time of her death Pussy Welles had almost completed a novel called, *God and Maggie Jones*.'

'A novel!' Exclamation from Richard Barnes who had seemed to take little interest in what was going on.

'A remarkable account of a girl, Maggie Jones, who enters into a sort of working partnership with God and between them they set out to play merry hell with the tight little community to which Maggie belonged.'

'Odd she never mentioned it to me,' Barnes said. He didn't explain that it seemed strange because he had bored her with his novel whenever the opportunity arose. He seemed yet to feel some obscure slight and Ursula looked at him sharply.

Wycliffe hesitated. 'In my opinion, it is an extremely clever novel, sometimes mischievous, penetrating and irreverent, but often cruel, vicious and frightening. There is no justice in it; the punishment never fits the crime but is always wildly excessive. One is reminded of the grotesque spite vented by Elisha on the children of Bethel, or some equally senseless atrocity. Often there is no offence at all, punishments are meted out with a sort of sadistic glee and some-times it seems to be virtue itself which is pilloried. Certainly it is a book from an able though warped mind.'

Dampier adopted a rather patronizing manner, reasonable, judi-cial. 'I think I see your point. You are saying that Pussy Welles tried to give substance to her fantasy and that she put these inverted notions to work.'

Wycliffe said nothing and Dampier went on: 'I knew of her novel though the possibility that it was a sort of blueprint for action never occurred to me, but it would be in character and she was capable of bringing it off. It explains a lot.'

'I would like to manipulate people rather than ideas.' Barnes again, and everybody looked at him in surprise.

'That's what she said to me shortly before . . . before she was killed. She was talking about power and how she yearned for it. I suggested that in another incarnation she might like to be a general, and she said, "A general by all means, but only in wartime, peace-time generals are pathetic figures, children playing with rather stupid toys."'

'So she made her own war,' Dampier said. 'Getting back to the novel, doesn't it strike you as interesting that her partnership was with God rather than the devil? It suggests that she wanted to give her ideas – her actions if you are right – at least the colour of morality.'

Wycliffe shook his head. 'I disagree. I think her choice of God rather than the devil was her ultimate piece of cynicism. But what-ever the intention, her book left me in no doubt that she had planned

144

the sequence of events which led, at last, to her death though whether her death was part of the plan could be argued.'

Erica Dampier actually shivered. 'I've always known she was a *wicked* woman, she brought untold evil into this village.'

Wycliffe nodded. 'But no matter how wicked she was, she wasn't alone, she had an accomplice, someone equally culpable in law and the question for me has been – who? Who was her accomplice?' He let the question hang in the air and a new wave of disquiet seemed to ripple round the room.

Dampier smoked one of his cheroots, eyeing the superintendent through the smoke haze; Young, next to him, presented the good side of his face creating an illusion of disinterest by gazing into a far corner of the room. Ursula Barnes sat, legs together, feet tucked in, skirt pulled down – unassailable, but she stole frequent solicitous glances at her husband. He lay back in his chair, legs thrust out, prickly, aggressive. Gaol might have reversed the roles in that household and in the long run he might come to think it cheap at the price. Erica Dampier sat bolt upright, her hands fiddling with the clasp of her handbag like a rosary. Anxious virgin; if anything happened to her brother, she would turn Catholic and enter a nunnery. Good thing too, better than dogs. Aubrey Reed, cross-legged, nonchalant, watched the smoke spiral from his cigarette; Harvey Clemens seemed to doze, incapable of sustained attention. Janice Mitford, showing leg to her suspenders, rolled the little ball of her handkerchief but never took her eyes off Wycliffe. Alfred looked profoundly gloomy but it was impossible to judge the depth of his emotion. He avoided meeting anyone's eyes.

'Let me say at once,' Wycliffe went on, 'that I had little hope of answering my own question. But for Lomax's death, it may have remained unanswered.'

Was there an audible sigh? Certainly the tension evaporated.

'You mean that you accept his guilt?' – Dampier driven to probe but perhaps as relieved as the rest.

Wycliffe shrugged. 'I'm here to give you the facts, you must choose your own interpretation. Lomax can't be put on trial so there is no question of a conviction.

'From the beginning it seemed to me that each one of you had motive and, with one exception, opportunity to kill Pussy Welles. But I was convinced that her death must be viewed in the light of other, earlier crimes that involved her and an accomplice. This narrowed the field but it did not focus on any single person. As I saw it, the women were out – no woman could have sustained a partnership with Pussy Welles. By the same token, Reed and Clemens were hardly to be taken seriously as suspects and, in any case, it turned out that they had their own reasons for a bitter antipathy that excluded collusion.' Wycliffe looked straight at Reed, but Reed said nothing. Perhaps he thought that he was getting off lightly. 'And Barnes was out. He might have killed the girl but he couldn't have participated in crimes which took place before he came to the village. That left Dampier, Mitford, Young and Lomax. It rested between them. But Young was a victim – very nearly a dead one.'

'So then there were three.' Clemens, with unexpected awareness.

'Three,' Wycliffe agreed. He seemed to be sluggish, heavy. It was as though he wanted to damp down interest, draw off steam and, intentionally or not, he was achieving an almost hypnotic calm. Long gaps with only the sound of crepitating logs and the pulse of the grandfather clock.

The church clock chimed.

'A quarter past nine,' Janice Mitford said.

'There seemed no getting beyond that point. I had suspicions – suspicions strong enough to be called convictions – but no proof and a very poor prospect of getting any.'

'And the only proof you have now is that poor old Lomax conveniently killed himself.' Dampier shifted in his chair, impatiently, powerfully, making the castors screech.

Wycliffe shook his head. 'Not quite. There were pointers even before Lomax died. The police made routine inquiries into the antecedents of everyone connected with the case . . .'

A little flutter of concern which Wycliffe seemed not to notice.

'. . . and established that Lomax was intimately acquainted with Pussy Welles while she was a secretary at the Registry and he had his lectureship. A classic sugar daddy situation you might think, expensive presents and the rest, but he so completely lost his head over her that when she started to play him up he went to pieces and had to resign.'

'Edgar Lomax? – I don't believe it!' Unexpected display of loyalty from Janice Mitford.

146

'No fool like an old fool!' Clemens seemed to have a stock of hackneyed aphorisms that he felt bound to work off.

'And then,' Wycliffe went on, 'there was always the possibility that we might persuade Young to talk.' His eyes rested on the inn-keeper who continued to stare at one corner of the room. 'He tells us now, that he saw Lomax talking to Arthur Horner near where he was killed, shortly before it was supposed to have happened. He also admits now, that Lomax was on the road ahead of him on the night he had his smash. If Lomax had lived, we might still have got this information from him.'

Dampier swung round to face Young. 'If you can say all this now, why couldn't you have said it when he was alive? Are you trying to pretend that you kept quiet to save Lomax's neck? If you are, you'd do well to think of a better one!'

'I kept quiet to save my own neck. I knew, but I couldn't prove a thing.'

'Rubbish! Bloody rubbish!'

Young was controlled but firm. He loooked Dampier straight in the eyes and spoke with a certain dignity. 'You believe what you like, Mr Dampier, but it was because once, when I'd had too much to drink and hinted something in front of Lomax, that I had my smash. That was why I was scared stiff when the super started to press me at your place last Saturday. It's all very fine to talk, but Lomax was a killer and he didn't need more than a suspicion.'

'I don't believe it!'

Wycliffe intervened. He produced an official looking envelope, opened it and took out a little wad of photostats.

'Perhaps these will change your view.' He passed the photostats to Dampier. 'They are letters from Pussy Welles to Lomax and they cover several years.'

Dampier put on a pair of heavy, horn-rimmed spectacles and began to read the letters.

'You will see that the more significant passages have been marked.'

At first, Dampier read casually as one compelled by courtesy to consider evidence for an argument patently absurd. But his manner changed. As he read he allowed ash to grow on his cheroot until it fell in a grey shower onto his jacket, unnoticed. The others watched in silence. Young, in particular, never took his eyes from the letters.

147

Wycliffe drew complex doodles on the empty envelope and waited. Richard Barnes got up to put another log on the fire, raising a great shower of sparks from the embers. At last, Dampier took off his glasses and handed back the photostats. He was subdued, chastened. He made a gesture of acceptance, murmured an apology. 'How little we know each other!'

Wycliffe glanced round at the company. 'These are copies of private letters, but both the parties are dead and if any of you wish to see them, you may. You have seen that their contents caused Mr Dampier to change his view of the case.'

Nobody spoke and he collected the letters and put them back in the envelope.

A moment of silence then conversation broke out. Tongues were freed and wagged on the subject of Lomax's guilt. Janice Mitford and Reed with returning courage asked to see the letters.

'It's difficult to believe that it's all over,' Erica Dampier said to no-one in particular. 'We can go on almost exactly as we did before.'

'I still can't believe that Edgar . . . Of all the terrible things! He seemed such a mild man, wouldn't say "boo" to a goose.'

'A bachelor at a dangerous age,' Ursula Barnes pronounced, now firmly aligned on the side of marriage.

'He was a queer bird,' Clemens summed up. 'A queer bird.'

'His epitaph, poor devil!' Dampier said.

In the general relaxation Young poured himself another drink.

12

'When did you first discover that she was your sister, Mr Young?' Wycliffe asked the question conversationally but it brought a silence as abrupt and complete as a gunshot.

Young's whisky spilt down over his shirt front; Wycliffe stood by his chair, looking down at him. 'Don't waste time making up stories, Mr Young, there's no point now, is there? No reason why people shouldn't know the truth. It's all over – just a few stray ends.'

Young still said nothing, he sipped his whisky and stared at the floor.

'She told you herself didn't she? Probably handed you that copy of her birth certificate, laughing, as though it had all been a good joke. When did it happen? The date on the certificate is a little while after your accident.'

'What about it?'

'That was when she told you – when you were in hospital?'

He nodded. 'I didn't believe it at first . . .'

'But she convinced you. All she had to do was to take off her sock. You knew about her deformed foot, didn't you?'

'Of course I knew about it, I was eight when she was born.'

'You never made any attempt to find her?'

'Not really. I wondered about her sometimes; wondered whether we had ever run into each other without knowing it. And all the time . . .'

'You were separated soon after she was born?'

'A few months. Our parents were both killed and there was nobody to look after us so we went into an orphanage. People want babies so she was adopted but I was there for a goodish while. Then I suppose you might say I struck lucky.'

The superintendent's manner was puzzling. His interest in the conversation seemed to be peripheral but he continued to probe.

What was more surprising he appeared to be unaware of the interest he was creating. The proverbial pin might have escaped notice but not much else.

'I was puzzled why a girl like Pussy Welles should identify herself so completely with Cornwall and with this part of it in particular. From her late teens until she died she seemed to spend all the time she could here. When did you first meet?'

Young was gaining in confidence and he showed no reluctance to talk. 'When she was eighteen, down here on holiday. She came into the bar one lunch-time with a mixed bag of other youngsters.'

'You think she knew you then?'

'Looking back, I'm pretty sure she did. She made a dead set at me.' He put his hand to the injured side of his face. 'I didn't think much about it at the time, I was used to a bit of attention from the girls but this was different, she singled me out . . .'

'And then?'

He lit a cigarette before replying. 'You haven't been snooping round here for the past fortnight without finding that out. Whenever she was down we spent a lot of time together. I fell for her; leave it at that.'

'Until she married.' Wycliffe sipped a gin someone had passed him. 'That must have been a shock.'

'I couldn't believe it. I'd always assumed it would come to that between us. There'd never been anything . . . you understand – so far and no further.' He passed his hand over his forehead. 'Which surprised me a bit, I must admit because I had good reason to think she hadn't been so coy with others. Still, if that was how she wanted it, it was good enough for me.'

He drew deeply on his cigarette and watched the rising smoke from his lips. 'She was a witch! She wasn't long in persuading me that she'd been duped into marrying Arthur Horner and that if ever she got free of him we'd take up where we left off. And all the time she knew . . .'

Another version of Pussy Welles. Wycliffe listened and understood things that had puzzled him. Young spoke so quietly now that his voice hardly reached the others and they hadn't the temerity to come closer.

'Lomax was her cat's paw, her *creature*, besotted with her, ready to do anything – *anything*.' He looked up at Wycliffe, a caricature of a smile on his lips. 'But who am I to talk?'

'What about your car smash?'

'His doing – he was jealous, though God knows why. She came to see me in hospital several times and once, when I was getting better, she brought the certificate – as you said, treating it as a joke. I could have killed her then. "We're two of a kind now, brother," she said, "we're both freaks but I can cover mine up and you can't."' He broke off suddenly. 'Do you believe me?'

'I believe you,' Wycliffe said.

'By Christ! I wouldn't blame you if you didn't. Sometimes when I think of her I can hardly believe she was real.'

'Why did Lomax kill her?'

He shrugged. 'You've seen the letters. She drove the poor sod beyond endurance.'

'Is that all?'

'All?'

'All you've got to tell me.'

Young looked puzzled, a little apprehensive. 'I suppose so. I don't know what you mean.' He hesitated. 'After Pussy was gone, I felt safer from Lomax, she was the brains and the *guts*.' He laughed. 'I even had a notion to get a bit of my own back, I nipped into his shed one night and mixed rat poison with the food he gives his lemmings.'

'When was this?'

'I did it more than once.'

'But you didn't kill him?'

'Kill him? He committed suicide!'

Wycliffe said, 'No, Lomax didn't commit suicide, he was murdered. There's no doubt about that.'

'Murdered!' From Erica Dampier.

'There! What did I tell you?' Almost a scream of triumph from Janice Mitford.

Wycliffe held up his hand. 'Lomax was murdered, Mr Young.'

The innkeeper was looking once more at the far corner of the room. Animation which had brought some life to his features a few minutes before, vanished, leaving him sullen, inscrutable. 'All right, if you want to tell fairy tales, I can't stop you.'

Wycliffe perched himself on the arm of Young's chair. 'Two bullets were fired in Lomax's study that night; one killed him and the other bedded itself in a book across the room. Of course, it was possible that not having used the gun for years, he wanted to make sure that it was in working order. In which case the bullet that killed him would have to be the second one fired. Experts will testify that although they can offer no *proof* they are of the opinion that it was the first bullet which killed Lomax and the second which bedded itself in the book. The gun was substantially corroded when it was fired and the interference with the rifling on the bullet due to rust, is significantly greater on the bullet that killed him. Similar confirmatory evidence is given by the cartridge cases.

Dampier was dissatisfied. 'But why should anybody fire twice if the first shot killed him? Just a greater risk of drawing attention.'

Wycliffe nodded. 'The murderer wanted to make sure that the death would be treated as suicide and he knew enough to realize that the police might apply the paraffin test. After shooting him therefore, he placed the gun in Lomax's hand and fired it a second time ensuring not only prints but powder marks as well. Of course, the police applied the test and found the powder marks on his right hand.'

'On his *right* hand?'

'You are going to say that Lomax was left-handed – he was, as far as writing is concerned but to what extent he was ambidextrous, I don't know.'

'He held cards in his right hand and played with his left,' Dampier said.

Wycliffe continued to stare at Young as though he expected enlightenment through attentive observation. Young was on edge, he darted glances here and there round the room, like a bird seeking a possible way of escape. 'You're talking bloody nonsense in my opinion,' he said at last, 'but if Lomax was murdered it wasn't by me. I left Dampier's place before half past ten, cashed up and went to bed.'

'But you got up again, Sylvie heard you.'

'Did she now? Well, if you must air my affairs in public, you might as well know that I went down to get a bottle of whisky from the cellar to get pissed – which I did.'

'You went out. Sylvie heard you undo the bar of the back door.'

'She was mistaken. What she heard was the bar on the cellar trap.' He seemed to be gaining rather than losing confidence. 'Anyway, how could I get out of the place without being seen by your bloody copper? Tell me that.'

'Over the back wall.' Wycliffe answered so promptly that Young was shaken. 'Then you circled the village over the moor and came into Lomax's by the road. At least, that's what you could have done.'

The innkeeper laughed. 'Could have done, might have done – you're wasting your time. The fact is, I didn't!'

'You were seen,' Wycliffe said.

'What's that?'

'I said that you were seen.'

The crucial moment. Wycliffe was strung up to the highest pitch of tension, his whole being concentrated on saying the right thing with the right inflexion, leading Young to the moment of truth and this was it. He had just gambled although to the others he seemed to speak casually; he seemed relaxed.

'Mitford saw you climbing over the wall, didn't you?' He turned to Mitford.

Mitford studied the tips of his toes. His reply was barely audible but it was, 'Yes'. Then he added in a stronger voice, 'I was standing at my garden gate, in the shadow, smoking a cigarette before going to bed.'

Wycliffe knew a tremendous surging wave of relief but the others seemed not to notice anything. Even Young was buoyant.

'Trust you to be where you're not bloody well wanted. I suppose she turned you out of bed again!' He lit another cigarette. 'Anyway, it doesn't prove anything.'

'It proves that you're a liar and in a murder case a man is a fool to lie unless he has something to cover up.'

'I admitted poisoning the lemmings.'

Wycliffe nodded. 'So you did.'

The superintendent knew that a plainclothes sergeant was just outside the window, that Inspector Darley was standing in the corridor on the other side of the glass door, that six uniformed men were strung out round the house. All this in case Young made a break for it. They had him marked as a violent man. And Wycliffe sat on the arm of his chair, close enough, just in case . . . The church clock chimed, then began to strike. Everybody counted – ten.

Wycliffe took the photostats of the letters from his pocket and weighed them in his hand. 'You didn't ask to see these just now.'

Young looked up momentarily, 'No.'

'You already knew what was in them.'

'How could I know?'

Wycliffe spoke patiently, reasonably, as to a child. 'When I asked you why Lomax killed her, you said, "You've seen the letters. She drove the poor sod beyond endurance."'

'What of it? I've got imagination the same as the next man and I knew her.'

'The originals have been tested for fingerprints.'

'So?'

'None of those letters dated after Lomax's arrival in Kergwyns have his prints on them.'

'He must have handled them with gloves on.' Sneer.

'Why?'

'How the hell should I know?'

'You must admit that it's odd.'

'All right, it's odd.'

'There's something even odder: those letters were examined by a handwriting expert . . .'

'You're going to say she didn't write them?'

Wycliffe shook his head. 'No, she wrote them.' He chose one of the photostats and handed it to Young. 'Read that one.'

Young did as he was told or appeared to do so. 'Well?'

'What do you think of it? She is apparently thanking Lomax for killing her husband.'

The innkeeper shrugged. 'She was a fool to write it and he was a bigger one to keep it.'

'You noticed the date?'

'Between five and six years ago.'

'Yes. But the experts are prepared to swear that the original of this letter and of all those dated subsequently, were written within the past eight or ten weeks. They can tell by the ink.'

'Big deal! But it's nothing to do with me.'

Young had adopted a jaunty air but it was wearing thin. Every now and then he shifted nervously in his chair, barely controlling, it seemed, an impulse to violence. But he did control it.

Wycliffe thrust the photostat under his very nose. 'I think this *is* to do with you. The original of this letter and of two others have your prints on them. You were careful but not careful enough. Your sister

154

set up Lomax's death as she had previously set up her husband's and in both instances you were the executioner. She knew that he had kept a few letters of hers and where he kept them; she knew too that he had a gun. After you killed him with his own gun, you added a few more to the pathetic collection of her letters which now branded him as a murderer and as her accomplice, making his suicide not only credible but almost inevitable.'

Young gesticulated, protested, determined to stem the flood of accusation but Wycliffe rested a hand on his shoulder and spoke quietly but with such unmistakable menace that Young quailed as though before an expected blow. 'You will be quiet until I have finished, then you can talk as much as you like – if you still have anything to say.'

From that moment they all knew that Young would not resort to violence. He was afraid. Wycliffe continued in a voice like silk.

'Your sister did not live to see the outcome of her planning. You had murdered her as she intended that you should. You were her pawn, her *creature* – the word was yours – in that as in all else. She was wicked and intelligent while you are wicked and a fool!'

Wycliffe stood up and turned his back on the wretched man. There was no stirring of sympathy for Young but at that moment the room was almost equally antagonistic to the superintendent. He was like a circus trainer with a miserable animal at the end of a big whip.

But the whip was his personality.

He sat himself once more by the little table. 'It is impossible to see clearly into the mind of the girl you killed. She wanted power, certainly, but more than anything she was possessed by an insatiable desire for sensation, a sensualist, a hedonist, she discovered as others have done that the appetite grows with what it feeds upon. The common experiences of life were miserably inadequate to the titillation of her emotional palate so she decided to create situations, to dramatize reality. Egocentric, narcissistic as she was, other people's feelings, even their lives were expendable in her pursuit of perverse and elusive satisfactions. Indeed, her schemes had to be destructive of the welfare and peace of others for only in this way could she appease her envy and express her contempt. Always thumbs down for the loser! Of course, she failed. There can be no success in the denial of the social nature of man. Dampier said of her: "The best that she knew was a mood of feverish excitement which always and

155

quickly yielded to disappointment. She could not be satisfied, it was not in her nature."

'You may think as I did that this was a possible recipe for suicide.'

He looked slowly round at the half circle of faces. In the silence a wind stirred outside, grew and rattled the windows, then died away. Soon it would rain.

'But it would have been out of character for her to do anything so straightforward. She would be at great pains and contrivance in her final production. She would be murdered and in circumstances that would cast the net of suspicion wide.

'How did she set about it?' He addressed the question to Young who looked up, seemed about to speak then shook his head.

'Never mind! The broad outline is clear. Just now, you called her a witch; you said that you could have killed her when she presented you with her birth certificate, when she taunted you with your disfigurement.'

'So I could! I wish I had!' His voice was scarcely more than a whisper.

'But you didn't. Instead you tried to keep out of her way. The whole village observed the change and put varying interpretations on it. But you were not allowed to escape entirely, she knew more than enough to keep you dangling – and you knew that she was reckless – capable of risking her own security to destroy yours. So you continued to provide her with a house, you did whatever little menial tasks she demanded of you, you came when you were called.

'And you were called on that Thursday night, sometime between nine and half-past. *Dampier saw you when he was leaving.*'

The others were merely spectators now, as little likely to interrupt as the audience at a play. Wycliffe and his victim seemed to be isolated from them, unaware of their existence.

'I don't know what exactly happened in that encounter between brother and sister but I can guess a good deal; certainly you learned for the first time, the truth about your car smash. Until then, you had been foolish enough to believe it an accident. That night you were given a circumstantial account of how she had driven to Kitt's Corner, parked her car beyond it, waited for the headlamps of your car, then released the oil over the road. She stood the drum in your path so that you would be certain to brake and swerve. The oil, she obtained from Mitford's garage.'

156

Young looked at the superintendent as though mesmerized; no attempt now to avert the injured side of his face. 'You knew that?' His voice was distorted with emotion, he seemed to be near to weeping, overcome by self-pity. 'My God! Can you believe it? Her own brother!'

'So you killed her to even the score.'

Young made a gesture, vague, evasive, but said nothing.

'You will be charged with the murder of Lomax, make no mistake about that. If what happened that night with your sister is in any way an extenuation of the crime, you would be a fool not to use it. You went to her cottage that evening, the murderer of Arthur Horner – a crime that could never be proved against you. You came away having killed your sister and with her blueprint for murdering Lomax . . .'

Young began to speak; he was not answering any question, nor was he challenging or denying the accusations against him. In a way he was not responding to any external stimulus, he spoke to relieve an inner tension which had mounted beyond endurance. A violent man, but weak; now that violence had failed, he cracked. At first words came with difficulty, there were gaps when it seemed that the flow might fail altogether but slowly his voice gathered strength and he achieved greater fluency.

'It was about a quarter past nine and the house was all lit up. As I rang the door bell I heard her start the record player upstairs and when she let me in the music was so loud I could hardly hear what she said . . .' He raised a hand to his ear as though the sound still troubled him. 'She gave me an envelope and told me to keep it safe, otherwise it might do me a lot of harm. I couldn't make her out; she was excited, feverish, I'd never seen her like it before. I asked her if she was ill and she laughed. "No, I'm not ill but I'm going to die tonight." Of course I didn't know what she was talking about.'

He stared at the floor. Perhaps he was seeing again the girl in the cornflower blue dress living out the last minutes of her life. As he told his story Wycliffe gathered intense visual impressions, almost as though he watched the actual events from behind an impenetrable screen, cut off, incapable of intervention. The girl, infected with a madness bordering on ecstasy, transported by the illusion of power, setting on foot great events; the man, disfigured, sullen, scared, utterly at a loss, conscious only of standing on the brink of disaster.

157

'She was mad! Insane!'

She goes to a little cabinet. 'Do you want to die, Mickey?'

No answer but she has a gun levelled at him. 'You think I wouldn't do it but I tried once and nearly succeeded. You knew too much about me and you were becoming a bore . . .'

The music was drowning his senses, he couldn't concentrate but she was telling him about the night of his accident. Accident! She told her story as if it was a fairy story told to a child and he accepted it with the same childish blend of incredulity and belief, horror and fascination.

'Miraculously, you survived, then I realized it didn't matter. You were such a mouse, you would always do as you were told.' She came closer. 'And you will do, won't you, brother dear? If not, I'll shoot first you, then myself, which isn't at all as I planned. Answer me!'

'Yes.' A strangled ejaculation.

She laughs. 'I knew you wouldn't disappoint your sister.' She looks at her watch. 'Time for the telephone calls; everything to the minute.'

Two telephone calls which mystify him. All the time he is forced to sit so that she can see him from the little porch where the telephone is; all the time she has her gun at the ready. First she speaks to Elsa Cooper then to Barnes. All the time the music fills the little cottage and he is hard put to follow what she is saying but one fact is driven home.

'Is it true that you are pregnant?'

She smiles, the same smile that once captivated him. 'Oh yes, that's true enough.'

'And is Barnes the father?'

She laughs. 'They'll never know and neither will you.' Serious again, business-like. 'Time is short! Barnes will be here in a quarter of an hour and he mustn't find you.'

Now the real nightmare. She gives him his instructions, clear, concise; she produces a second gun – an automatic – and gives it to him. 'Remember! The automatic belongs to Ricky, the pistol to Edgar. Don't get it wrong.' Calm now, cautionary, a mother sending a dull child on an errand. Mickey, Ricky, Edgar – they might all be children playing games.

158

'Now!' She is six feet away, facing him, her pistol still on him. 'Now!'

Still like a child he wails, 'I can't.'

Upstairs the tempo of the music changes. He has no ear for music, no knowledge, but the chorus of voices is a lament of infinite sadness.

'Now!' She takes a step closer. 'I shall count down from five, and I shall fire if you have not . . . Five . . . four . . . three . . .'

She slips to the floor as though in a faint. He has not heard the sound of the shot, is unconscious of having pulled the trigger but she is dead, crumpled on the floor at his feet and he is standing over her with the gun in his hand. The music has stopped. Utter silence.

His first emotion is neither panic nor remorse but anger; anger that he has been tricked. He longs to injure her and there she is, at his mercy. He stoops, rips off her shoe, pulls up her dress, fumbles with her suspenders, tears off her stocking. There! My God! that will humiliate her! Let them find her like that! Then fear and prudence take over and he follows instructions. Just in time. Christ! The door bell! He is through the kitchen, through the little garden and out on to the moor. Barnes, the fool! He has her shoe and stocking stuffed in his pocket.

'So you see, I was driven to it. It was her or both of us.' (I couldn't help it, sir.) Immaturity without innocence.

They seemed to be awaking from sleep and a disturbing, haunting dream. Outside the rain had arrived, driven in from the sea by a violent squall, it beat against the window panes.

Wycliffe stirred himself, emerging slowly from the final pathetic drama conceived in the mind of the dead girl and recreated in the halting phrases of her killer.

'And Lomax?'

He put the question with infinite reluctance. Enough is enough.

Young shivered as though from a sudden chill. When he spoke, he was peevish, petulant, hard-done-by. 'She promised me that I would be safe, that they couldn't possibly suspect me, but she lied and she knew she was lying . . .' He sighed. 'The envelope she gave me – in it there was a letter to me. "You are safe now," she said, "as I promised – *except for Lomax* . . ."' He passed a hand wearily over his brow. 'All the plan was there, the letters, and I had the gun. I decided not to do anything, to take the risk; then they weren't satisfied with

Barnes. You didn't believe he did it and you seemed suspicious of me. That night at the Dampiers' I knew you were after me and Lomax was there. If she was telling the truth, all he had to do was speak . . . I couldn't take the risk after all. *She knew what would happen!*' The words came in a hiss of venomous hatred.

'Are you willing to make a statement?'

Young nodded. 'Anything . . . get it over.'

13

Another Thursday evening and Wycliffe was back with his wife in their Exeter flat. Although it was dark they hadn't bothered to draw the curtains so the city lay mapped in lights, stretching to the horizon. He thought it beautiful but knew that he would change it if he had the chance for one of those bungalows in the lane that led to the sea at Kergwyns. The cathedral clock chimed distantly and struck ten. Three weeks ago at this time Ricky Barnes was ringing the doorbell at the cottage and getting no answer while Mike Young was stealing out the back way on to the moor. Puppets still though their puppeteer was dead. She lay, shot through the heart, a red stain seeping through the material of her cornflower blue dress. Now Young was dead; he had contrived to hang himself in his cell the day after his arrest, so there would be no trial. The case had left a deeper impression on the superintendent than any in his experience for he too had danced to the dead girl's tune, another puppet on a string. And because of it Lomax had died, poor deluded Lomax who wouldn't hurt a fly.

The Deputy had shrugged his immaculately tailored shoulders. 'But my dear fellow! It's an occupational hazard . . .'

One bright spot: a letter from Sylvie, written in erratic spelling with a temperamental ball-point pen: *In his will he left me every-thing . . . He must have meant it about marrying me . . . He was weak but he wasn't all bad . . . They say I shall have to put in a manager. If you and Mrs Wycliffe want a holiday down here . . . it will be on the house . . .*

Helen, his wife, knew all about the case but they hadn't spoken of it for a long time. Now she took the risk. 'Charles, who killed her cat?' No need for explanations, she didn't have to introduce the topic, it was still so much in their minds.

'Young, it was one of the little jobs she gave him to do.'

161

'When she was planning her own death.'

'I suppose so.'

Silence for a while then Helen started again. 'Charles, about the crosswords . . .'

'What about them?'

'I finished them yesterday.'

'Good for you.'

She hesitated, then took the plunge, 'It's all there, Charles, her confession, if you like to call it that, though it's more like an advertisement.'

'What are you talking about?'

'There are fifteen crosswords and if you arrange them in the right order there is a simple code.'

'A code?'

'Yes. The solutions to the first clue across in each case and to the third one down, taken together give thirty words and those words are a message. It's telegraphic but it's intelligible; I've written it out.'

'Switch on the light.'

Intelligible all right, telegraphic, certainly, but the truth about four violent deaths, four purposeless deaths.

His wife tried to fill the silence. 'Certain words and names struck me – they seemed too much of a coincidence – Pussy – Arthur – Young – lemmings . . . I mean, taken together . . .'

Taken together, the final cynicism, the ultimate cocking of the snook.

REAL HUMAN PUPPET THEATRE INVOLUNTARY ACTORS STARRING KILLER YOUNG BREATHLESS EXPLOITS INCLUDE DEATH DIVING ARTHUR SISTER MURDER FAKED SUICIDE SUPPORTING LEMMINGS SPECTACULAR AUTOMOBILE SMASH THRILLS MOTIVATION ANIMATION PRODUCTION BY PUSSY.

Punctuation was scarcely needed but Helen had written out a punctuated version: *Real human puppet theatre. Involuntary actors. Starring Killer Young. Exploits include death diving Arthur, sister murder, faked suicide. Supporting lemmings. Spectacular automobile smash. Thrills! Motivation, animation, production by Pussy.*

Wycliffe walked to the window. 'I might have known she would leave nothing to chance. Nobody must miss the point, but I did.'

'She must have been mad!'

'Her brother called her a witch and she was certainly the wicked witch in this fairy tale.'

Wycliffe and How to Kill a Cat

To Muriel —
collaborator, critic and wife

1

Detective Chief Superintendent Wycliffe, Area CID, in a fawn linen jacket, checked shirt and grey slacks, looked even less like a policeman than usual. He had the right, he was on holiday though paying a courtesy call at the local police station.

'Don't be all day, Charles!' Instructions from Helen, his wife.

'Back to lunch, dear. Promise!'

'Is Inspector Warren in?'

'No, sir, afraid not. Can I help?'

Wycliffe introduced himself. 'A friendly call, sergeant. The inspector and I used to be in the same squad and I thought I would look him up. I'm in the town on holiday.'

Ferocious grin, the best the station sergeant could manage in the way of charm. 'Inspector Warren has been ill with stomach ulcers for more than a month, sir.'

'I'm sorry to hear that.' Conversation languished.

'As you're from Headquarters, sir, you might like a word with . . .'

'No, this is unofficial, sergeant, I expect you've got enough to do at this time of year.'

'Run off our feet, sir.'

And that might have been that, had not a constable appeared from one of the offices, handed the sergeant a slip of paper and murmured something in his ear.

'Right! Get hold of the police surgeon and send him there. Tell Wilkins to stay with it and I'll contact Division.'

'Trouble, sergeant?' Wycliffe, on the point of leaving, lingered.

'Woman found dead in a hotel bedroom, sir. They called in one of our chaps from a patrol car and he's just radioed in.'

'Is that all?'

'Our man thinks there's a good reason to suspect foul play.'

169

'You mean that the woman has probably been murdered?'

'Yes, sir.'

'Then why not say so?'

The sergeant said nothing.

Wycliffe hesitated, then plunged. 'I'll take a look, where is it?'

'Marina Hotel, Dock Crescent, sir. It's a bit of a dump, they cater for merchant seamen mainly. We had trouble there once before.'

'What sort of trouble?'

'Seaman stabbed a tart, sir. A year or two back that was. I believe the place has changed hands since then.'

'Right! You get on to Division, tell them I'm on the spot and ask them not to roll out the waggon until they hear from me.'

'You'll want a car, sir.'

'I've got one.'

Outside the sun was shining. They were queueing for the beach buses, mothers with bulging picnic bags, kids trailing plastic spades, girls in brief summer dresses and some playsuits conscientiously displaying their navels. The superintendent in holiday attire was not out of place, but he attracted curious glances as he crossed the square to the car park. Perhaps it was because he looked pleased with life. Few people do, or are. In fact he was humming a little tune; he caught himself doing it and wondered. The reason for his complacency would scarcely bear examination. True, it was warm and sunny; true, he was on holiday, but it was not these things, it was the prospect of a case which made him sing. He felt in his bones that he was at the beginning of a case which he would remember, one which would go into the books. To be brutally frank then, he was happy because a woman lay dead in a sleazy hotel bedroom. Did he delight in crime? Surely a vicarious pleasure in vice must be at least as reprehensible as indulgence?

He got into his nice new shining black Zodiac and eased his way into the line of traffic. He was secretly proud of his car though Helen said that it was a trifle vulgar. He liked to cruise slowly, almost silently, aware of the power he had boxed up, waiting only for the gentle pressure of his foot. In fact, he had the Rolls mentality without the Rolls pay packet.

Now he had to crawl through the impossibly narrow main street where a carelessly parked wheelbarrow can snarl everything up. Then the shops thinned and he was running along by the harbour with a row of large, terraced Victorian houses on his right. Just before he came to the docks some of the houses were calling themselves hotels and one of these was the Marina. A couple of tired looking Dracaenas in a weedy patch of gravel and a rusted slatted iron seat. The stucco was peeling off the pillars of the porch and a snake of Elastoplast sealed over a crack in the plate-glass of the swing doors. Constable Wilkins was waiting for him in the vestibule.

'The sergeant telephoned to expect you, sir.'

'Doctor arrived yet?'

'Not yet, sir.'

'Where is she?'

'Second floor, sir, a little passage off the landing leads to the extension. It's the door on your left at the end of the passage.'

Wycliffe grunted. 'Wait there, send the doctor up when he comes. What about the inmates?'

'I've told them to stay in their rooms, sir. Most of them are out anyway.'

The staircase had some elegance of design but the carpet was so threadbare that pattern and texture had long since disappeared. Paper peeled off the walls and a faint sickly odour suggested dry rot. But the place seemed reasonably clean. He braced himself for what he might find. After twenty years in the force he was still not shockproof. He could have asked the constable but that was not his way, he liked to form his own impressions from the very start.

As he turned on the first landing to tackle the next flight, he made up his mind that the woman would be fortyish, fleshy, blonde and strangled. She would be lying in a tangle of bedding staring up at the ceiling, fish eyed, her face and neck heavily cyanosed. He had seen it all before. This place was a likely hunting ground for whores and if one of the sisterhood got herself murdered it was ten to one on strangulation, frenzied and brutal.

But he was wrong in most of his surmises.

The figure on the double bed was that of a girl, twenty-one or two at most. Slim, petite, she lay on her back, sprawled across the bed. She was naked but, though her posture was suggestive enough, there was something innocent and virginal about her. Her auburn hair was splayed on the pillow, golden in the sunshine, and it was easier to believe her asleep than dead – until he saw her face. Her face, turned towards the wall and hidden by her hair, had been battered. Without disturbing the body it was difficult to determine the extent and nature of her injuries but Wycliffe noticed at once that the amount of swelling and bruising was disproportionately small for the bone damage which had been done. The upper lip and an area round the left eye were encrusted with dried blood but there was no sign of a free flow. Wycliffe was no doctor but he had seen enough of violent death to know the probable answer to that one. The odds were that the facial injuries had been inflicted after death. In which case, how had she died? Perhaps the initial blow had killed her but it seemed unlikely. Would she have lain there waiting to be clubbed? Not unless she was asleep. But she was lying naked on top of the bed clothes . . .

Wycliffe bent closer to examine the neck and found what he half expected, a tale-telling bluish tinge below the surface of the skin and a faint bruising on either side of the trachea above the larynx. She had been strangled, but by someone who had restrained the impulse to unnecessary violence – or never known it. And that was odd in view of what must have followed. What sort of nut would strangle a girl with such finesse, then smash her face in?

But he was running ahead of himself, time enough to speculate when he had the views of the experts.

He looked round the room – a back room. The window, which had its top sash wedged open an inch or two, looked on to a small yard and a railway cutting beyond with the back gardens of a row of houses on the other side. An iron fire escape crossed diagonally just below the window. There were net blinds but the Regency striped curtains would not draw. The carpet was worn through in places and of no discernible pattern. A built-in clothes cupboard with a full length mirror in the door, a dressing table, an upholstered chair with loose stuffing – these, with the bed, made up the furniture. The girl's underclothes were strewn over the chair and a sleeveless frock in gay op-art material hung from a hanger hooked over the picture rail. A nightdress and a quilted dressing-gown lay in a heap on the floor by the bed. A white pig-skin travelling case, elegant and incongruous, stood by the dressing table which was littered with expensive looking cosmetics. Among the bottles and jars he noticed a few items of jewelry, a pair of earrings, a garnet bracelet and a silver clip with another red stone inset. He looked at everything but touched nothing.

He went out on to the landing when he heard footsteps on the stairs. The police surgeon, tall, slim, immaculate in pepper and salt suiting, iron-grey hair faultlessly parted, and bifocals. A questioning glance at Wycliffe's informal dress.

'Chief Superintendent Wycliffe? Dr Rashleigh. Where is she?'

'As little disturbance as possible if you please, doctor.'

A faint lift of the eyebrows. 'We must assume that we know our respective jobs, superintendent.'

'Perhaps. But don't move her!' Wycliffe snapped. Pompous ass! He went downstairs; doctors always put him in a bad temper. 'Constable!'

'Sir?'

'Radio information room for the murder squad, pathologist, forensic – the lot. Then find the proprietor.'

While he waited, Wycliffe opened a door labelled *Lounge*. A large front room with a bay window which could have been pleasant. Several upholstered armchairs in varying styles and stages of decay, an octagonal table in veneered wood of revolting aspect, a nickel-plated flower stand and plastic flowers. A black iron grate stuffed with crinkly red paper and an overmantle with fairground ornaments. The room reeked of stale tobacco. They would need somewhere to interview witnesses and this would have to be it. He decided to ask for some kitchen chairs to spite possible fleas.

The proprietor was a little man, bald on top with a fringe of grey hair. He was thin except for his paunch, which he carried low. He was smoking a home-made cigarette and his lips were stained yellow. A near down-and-out like his premises, but he had lively brown eyes which missed nothing.

'What's your name?'

'Ernest Piper.'

Wycliffe lowered himself on to the arm of one of the chairs. 'Who is she, Mr Piper?'

The little man raised a hand to his ear and stroked the lobe. 'According to the register she's Mrs Slatterly. Address given, W1.'

'When did she arrive?'

'Sunday evening, she's been here three nights.'

'Alone?'

He nodded. 'She said she was waiting for her husband to join her.'

'And did he?'

'Not to my knowledge, he didn't.'

173

'Had she booked in advance?'

'Telephone call the day before to reserve a double for three or four nights.'

'Not a common experience for you.'

Piper put in some more time fiddling with his ear. 'I don't know what you mean.'

The superintendent took out his pipe and began to fill it. He was entering into the spirit of the thing, beginning to get its flavour. 'I mean that you don't get many bookings, certainly not from husbands and their wives.'

A slow grin revealing blackened teeth. 'I don't have to draw pictures for you, do I?'

'What was your impression of her when she arrived?'

'Classy. Pretty too, a real eye catcher. Pity she got spoilt like that. To be frank, I couldn't make out what she was doing in a place like this . . .' He hesitated then added in a burst of confidence, 'Look, superintendent, I got nothing to hide in this business and I hope you'll bear in mind that I'm being frank.'

Wycliffe struck a match and lit his pipe, puffing great clouds of smoke towards the ceiling. 'We'll see. Did she have any visitors?'

'Not to my knowledge.'

'Which doesn't take us very far.'

Piper shrugged. 'Well, you know how it is.'

'Did she go out much?'

'I passed her in the hall a few times. In any case she had to go out for food, we don't do meals other than breakfast.'

'Any mail?'

'One letter waiting for her when she arrived.'

'Postmark?'

'I didn't notice.'

'Who found her this morning?'

'Kathy, the girl who does the rooms.'

'When?'

Piper looked at his watch, a silver turnip which he took from a pocket in his unbuttoned waistcoat. 'About an hour ago. Say half nine. Kathy came to me in the kitchen and said, "I think something's happened to the girl in fifteen. I think she's dead."'

'Just like that.'

Piper nodded. 'Just like that, Kathy don't scare all that easy.'

'Then?'

'I went up to take a look.' He relit his cigarette which had gone out.

'Touch anything?'

He shook his head. 'Only her – just to see if she had really croaked. I didn't see her face at first. Of course she'd been dead several hours, I should think.'

'You know about such things?'

'I seen a bit.'

'How long since you were last inside?'

A moment of reflection. 'Must be all of ten years.'

'Immoral earnings?'

He nodded. 'No violence though. I never been done for violence.'

Wycliffe noted and approved the precision of statement. The two men smoked placidly in complete accord.

'She was no trollop, super.'

Wycliffe sighed. 'They all have to start.'

The doctor interrupted them, shirt-sleeved and peevish, 'I suppose there is somewhere I can wash in this place?'

'Down the passage on the right, doctor, I'll show you.' Courtesy and service à la Marina! Wycliffe chuckled. He felt better and better. It wasn't crime which gave him pleasure, it was people. He made himself comfortable in the armchair. To hell with fleas!

Dr Rashleigh came back alone. 'I suppose you have notified the pathologist?'

'Of course! Perhaps you will be good enough to look in again when he is here?'

'Very well!' Rashleigh was still stuffy. 'But you may wish to hear my preliminary conclusions?'

Pretentious bastard! 'Certainly, doctor.'

Rashleigh smoothed his tie (Greyhounds 1934). 'I don't want to be too specific, but I think I may say that death was probably due to strangulation. The indications of asphyxia are slight and though there are marks on the neck they are faint.' He squinted up at the ceiling through his bifocals as though reading his lines there and mumbled something about 'vagal inhibition'. Then he went on, 'The facial injuries were almost certainly inflicted after death. As to time of death, I would say that she has been dead from eight to twelve hours.'

'Between ten and two, then?'

'That would certainly agree with my preliminary findings, super-intendent. If I were pressed I should incline towards the earlier time.'

'Very helpful, doctor. Anything else?'

Rashleigh hesitated. 'The girl was not a virgin, superintendent.'

Big deal! Surely he must know if anybody did that virginity beyond the age of twenty is a wasting asset?

'In fact, certain signs lead me to suppose that sexual intercourse probably took place shortly before death.'

'Not after?'

Rashleigh looked flustered. 'I'm not in a position to answer that question on the evidence I have seen.'

Surely the old goat must realize that it mattered! Never mind, the pathologist would see to all that.

When the divisional inspector arrived with his squad he found Wycliffe alone. He was standing beside the window, staring out at the docks. Born and reared and having lived most of his life in the Midlands, the sea and all that pertained to it fascinated him. Those tankers with their ugly grey hulls had probably rounded the Cape not so long ago on their way from some sun-scorched oil port in the Gulf . . .

Inspector Fehling coughed. He had not previously met the chief superintendent, who was a comparative newcomer to the area. His first impression was unfavourable and the inspector set great store by his first impressions. Wycliffe did not even look like a policeman, it was difficult to believe that he was tall enough and he seemed almost frail. A teacher, some kind of academic, perhaps a parson, but never a policeman.

'Inspector Fehling, sir.'

'How do you spell it?'

'F – E – H . . .'

'Ah, the solution, not a lack of success.'

'Sir?'

'Fehling's solution – Prussian blue stuff they used to use to test urine. Never mind, an unusual name, Inspector.'

'So they tell me. Now, do I have your permission to go ahead, sir?'

Wycliffe smiled as though at a secret joke. 'By all means. The pathologist should be here at any minute and the forensic people will be on their way. Let me know if you find anything – I shall be here.'

When Fehling reached the door he called him back. 'Mr Fehling, I object to working in the middle of a circus – no cars outside this building. They must park on the car park down the street; and no uniformed men in evidence . . .'

Fehling was shocked. 'But there are several of our vehicles out there now . . .'

'Then please get them moved – damn quick!'

When Fehling was gone Wycliffe returned to the window. Delegation is a magic word. When you have the rank you can get out of almost any job you don't like doing. Not that chief superintendents are expected to search rooms, look for prints or photograph corpses. He had done his share in the past but never with much enthusiasm or faith. You may need such evidence to convict a man but crimes are about people and relationships. Wycliffe was of a contemplative disposition and he liked, on occasion, to talk. He was remarkable in that he had contrived to turn these dubious attributes into professional assets.

'He said you might like a cup of coffee.' A sleek, black-haired little West Indian girl carrying a tray with a cup of coffee on it, milk and sugar. She looked no more than sixteen but was probably twenty.

'Thanks, I would. Who are you?'

'I'm Kathy – Kathy Johnson – I work here.'

'It was you who found the dead girl?'

She nodded. Another surprise, he had expected some superannuated old pro with swollen legs and carpet slippers. 'I found her.'

'You sleep on the premises?'

'In one of the attics, yes.' She spoke with the attractive staccato precision of her people and she had a gravity of expression and demeanour which gave special weight to all she said.

'What do you know of the dead girl?'

'Not much. She was very pretty. I see her on the stairs once or twice and wish her good morning or good afternoon but that is all except one time . . .'

'What happened?'

She put her hand to her forehead in a quick gesture of recollection. 'I think it was on the first evening she is here, a man come and ask for her. No! it was the next evening – Monday.'

'Did this man ask for her by name?'

'Pardon?'

177

'Did this man say, "I want to speak to Mrs Slatterly" – that is the name she gave in the register isn't it?'

'Mrs Slatterly, that is right. No, I find him in the hall looking at the register and when I ask him what it is that he wants, at first he is unwilling to say then he say, "This Mrs Slatterly, is she young with auburn hair?" and I say, "Yes, but she is out".'

'What then?'

'He thinks for some time then he ask if there is a telephone in her room.' Kathy laughed at the very idea. 'When I say that there is not, he go off without another word.'

'Have you seen him since?'

'No, I do not see him again.'

'When you told Mrs Slatterly of his visit, did she seem worried?'

The little brown nose wrinkled. 'No, not worried.'

'Why don't you sit down?'

'Thank you.' She perched herself on the edge of one of the chairs, her tray in her lap. 'I do not think her name was Mrs Slatterly.'

'Why not?'

'When I have to tell her about the man who come to see her she is half way up the stairs, you understand?'

Wycliffe nodded.

'I say, "Mrs Slatterly!" and although she is sure to hear me she does not turn round. Twice I say it, then I have to go up after her.'

'You are a clever girl.'

'Thank you.'

'About this man, what was he like?'

'Not very tall, a bit fat, and he wore a dark suit with little stripes. It fitted very good, very smart and expensive looking. His hair is sandy coloured.'

'Oldish?'

'Pardon?'

'How old do you think he was?'

'Forty, maybe a little more. He is red in the face a little, perhaps he has had too much to drink, you understand?'

'Perfectly; anything else?'

She frowned. 'There was something about his face, something a little strange, like it was fixed.'

'You mean that his face lacked expression?'

She hesitated then gave up. 'I cannot say what it is that I mean, I am sorry.'

'But you would know him again if you saw him?'

'Of course!'

'Thank you, you are an excellent witness but you may have to say all this again so that it can be written down.'

'That is all right.' She got up, picked up his cup and was at the door when he said, 'You never saw her talking to anyone, I suppose?'

She turned, frowning. 'I almost forget. Yesterday morning when I am making the bed in one of the front rooms I happen to look out of the window. Mrs Slatterly was standing on the pavement by the gate talking to a man.'

'The same one?'

'No, I told you I do not see him again. This is a very tall thin man and, I think, younger, but I could not see him well. I know that he had on a cap and a mackintosh, but I cannot tell you any more.'

'Did they stay talking for long?'

She shook her head. 'I cannot say, I did not stop to watch.'

Progress, or so it seemed. It might not be too difficult to run down the chap in the natty pinstripe – if he was a local. Perhaps Fehling would find firm evidence of the girl's identity by the time he was through upstairs. It was more than likely. But if not . . . Wycliffe sighed and returned to the window, refilled his pipe and lit it. Never go to meet trouble. Two of the dockside cranes were performing complex evolutions, moving along their tracks and swinging their jibs in perfect harmony. Why did they do it? They never seemed to lift anything. Choreography by the shop steward.

Back to the sandy-haired chap in the pinstripes. If he had intended to kill the girl he wouldn't have made himself so conspicuous unless he was a kink. If he killed her it was probably unpremeditated, a sudden flare of anger or lust. Most murders by strangulation were like that but, a big but, the murderer invariably uses force far in excess of what is needed to kill. In this case there was remarkable restraint and restraint implies forethought. But what about the maniacal attack on the girl's face after death? It didn't add up. Wycliffe remembered a young thug in his old manor who made a study of the technique of strangulation, treating it as an art form. Four girls died before he was caught red-handed with the fifth, and none of them had showed any outward sign of the cause of death.

Broadmoor. Detained at Her Majesty's Pleasure. He remembered the case with acute loathing, he had hated that youth and he hoped that Her Majesty would get a hell of a lot of pleasure. Violence of any sort appalled him and senseless self-indulgent violence left him biting his nails.

The pathologist and the forensic people arrived. Wycliffe had met the same team before and they exchanged amiable greetings, then the newcomers went about their business with that air of bored indifference which is their professional equivalent to the bedside manner. The little room was overcrowded and stuffy, but each man knew his job and scarcely a word was spoken. Wycliffe waited on the landing with the police photographers who had already taken pictures of the undisturbed room and were waiting to take more when the pathologist gave the word for the removal of the body.

It took them less than an hour. Dr Franks, the pathologist, a chubby little man, always in a hurry, bustled out. 'Ready now, superintendent. Perhaps you will get one of your chaps to bring up the shell.'

The girl's body would be put into a plastic shell, a temporary coffin, to be carted off to the mortuary.

Franks went into the bathroom and began to run lots of water. Wycliffe could hear him whistling to himself as he washed. It was all in the day's work for him too. 'Bit of a bug-house this, isn't it? What's a kid like that doing in this sort of dump? – Don't tell me, I'd rather keep my illusions. Where the hell is the soap? She was strangled all right. Bit of a fancy job or else a lucky hold by a tyro. Perhaps it was unlucky. Pressure on the jugulars. Even that mightn't have killed her by itself. I'll tell you more this afternoon, but not much. This bloody towel . . . For Christ's sake send somebody for a clean towel . . . Intercourse, as they say, had taken place – *was* taking place for all I know. Not the usual thing though, is it? Then he bashes her face in afterwards. Dear me! A nasty fellow he must be!'

A constable arrived with a fresh towel.

'Ah, that's better! I suppose Rashleigh told you how long she's been dead?'

'Between ten last night and two this morning.'

Franks nodded. 'I'd say after midnight.' He ran a pocket comb through his thinning hair. 'Are you going to join us this afternoon?'

'I shall be looking in.'

Wycliffe went downstairs to the lounge so as not to be in the way. A few minutes later he heard the men carrying her body down. The siren at the docks wailed. Half past twelve; lunchtime. A minute later a flood of bicycles burst through the gates and jammed the road outside. Fortunately they seemed too anxious to get home to bother about what was going on in the Marina.

Fehling came in looking important, a large briefcase under his arm. He whisked the flower stand with its plastic flowers on to the floor, removed the table runner and dusted the table top with a yellow duster from his briefcase. Then he displayed his finds. A photograph in a transparent polythene envelope with blue circles to indicate fingerprints, ten bundles of used pound notes, and a handbag.

'I'm not quite through yet, sir, but I doubt if there's much more of importance. Forensic have been over this lot.'

Inspector Fehling was a very large policeman, but he prided himself on the precision and economy of his movements. A gorilla, but a very refined gorilla. His simplest action was an exhibition – a performance, and one had the uncomfortable feeling that applause was expected. He reminded Wycliffe of those extraordinary athletes who contort themselves improbably while balanced on a narrow beam. He emptied the contents of the girl's handbag on to the table. Compact, lipstick, comb, unmarked handkerchief, five pound notes and some loose change, a tube of aspirin, and a little pocket knife with a mother-of-pearl handle. 'There was a cigarette case and lighter in the pocket of her outside coat.'

Wycliffe pointed to the bundles of notes. 'How much?'

'A thousand pounds, sir. It was in a drawer of the chest under some of her clothing.'

'Anything else?'

Fehling considered. 'Her clothes, of course, they seem to be of pretty good quality, a few pieces of jewelry and a sachet of oral contraceptives. She wore a ring but there is only a superficial mark on her finger so she probably put it on for the occasion.' He produced the ring in a plastic envelope; a gold wedding ring in an antique style, engraved inside with a monogram: W & J, entwined. A moment of hesitation, then, 'That room had been searched before we got there, sir, I'd take my oath on it.'

'They couldn't have been looking for money.'

Fehling was ponderously judicial. 'That's what puzzles me. You wouldn't think they would pass up a thousand quid in singles.'

'Is it possible that they wanted to remove anything that might identify her?'

'Could be! Could be, indeed, sir.' Fehling nodded his great head in approval. 'The West Indian girl says there was a framed photograph of the dead woman on the dressing table, but it's not there now.'

Wycliffe picked up the photograph in the plastic envelope. A half-length portrait of a young man with an electric guitar slung over his shoulder. A thin-faced youth with vacant eyes and the gloomy constipated look common to his kind. No signature, nothing written on the back. It was a studio portrait or the work of a good amateur but too glossy, like the publicity handouts from the big stars.

'Are you an authority on the Charts, Mr Fehling?'

'The charts, sir?'

'The Top Twenty.'

Fehling was disdainful. 'I'm afraid I'm too busy to bother with that nonsense.'

Wycliffe pushed the photograph towards him. 'Then you'd better consult an expert. If he's one of the idols he probably has nothing to do with our case, but if he's the boyfriend then we badly need his help.'

'What sort of expert would you suggest, sir?'

Wycliffe counted ten to himself then answered mildly, 'Try Kathy Johnson.'

'Kathy?'

'Kathy Johnson, the girl who seems to do all the work round here.'

'Oh, the West Indian girl!'

Wycliffe sighed. 'One more thing, the proprietor has got form but I don't want it rammed down his neck. Keep him sweet, he could be very useful.' Wycliffe began to fill his pipe. 'What do you make of it so far?'

The inspector picked up a bundle of notes and flicked them through as though he was about to perform a conjuring trick. 'This money suggests only one thing to me, sir – dope.'

'You think she was here to buy?'

Fehling hunched his immense shoulders. 'Stands to reason! I mean, this is a seaport, she's staying in a sleazy boarding house run

182

for merchant seamen and she's got a thousand in used notes. She wouldn't be selling, would she? Not in this neck of the woods. I reckon we're on to something, sir.'

'In that case, the deal didn't go through – she was still in possession of the money. So she wasn't killed for it. So what was she killed for?'

This extraordinary verbal gymnastic did not baffle the inspector. 'Her boy friend probably knows something about that!'

'This laddie in the picture?' He shook his head. 'In that case we are dealing with two separate crimes both centred on the girl. It's not impossible but William wouldn't like it – neither do I.'

'William, sir?'

'Of Occam, a thirteenth-century gent who enunciated the axiom that in logic, entities must not be multiplied.'

'Ah!'

'Useful to remind oneself that the simplest possible explanation is probably the right one.'

'Quite so, sir.' (Christ! Where do they dig 'em up?) 'Well, sir, what next?'

Wycliffe opened the door and called, 'Kathy!' When she came he showed her the photograph of the boy with the guitar. 'Know him, Kathy?'

'I do not know that boy, superintendent.'

'Would you if he was famous?'

She grinned. 'Oh, yes! I have all their photographs in my room.' Wycliffe thanked her. 'And Kathy! I want you to write out a description of the man you found going through the register. Take your time over it and make it as complete as you can, then give it to Mr Fehling.'

Kathy went and he turned to Fehling. 'Have you found the blunt instrument?'

'Sir?'

'Whatever was used to hit her.'

'Ah. No, sir, we haven't found it, but there's a door stop missing. The door doesn't fasten properly from the inside and Piper put a seven pound brass weight there to keep it shut. Apparently it's one of those with a ring in the top to hold it by.'

'So, whoever it was didn't come prepared.'

Fehling chuckled. 'And it's not every bedroom in which you can count on finding a brass weight handy . . .'

Wycliffe looked at him blankly. 'You'd better set about finding that weight, hadn't you, Mr Fehling? And Mr Fehling, pass the word round, I don't want it known that the girl was disfigured. We'll keep that to ourselves for the moment.' He got up, searching in his pockets for sixpences for the telephone. Fehling stopped him at the door. 'There's one more thing, I forgot it – this, I found it under her bed.'

'What is it?'

He held out a shining ball the size of a marble. 'It's a steel ball-bearing, probably nothing to do with the girl. I expect it fell out of the pocket of the chap who had the room before her.'

Wycliffe took the little ball and slipped it into his pocket. 'I expect you're right.'

2

Wycliffe's hotel also overlooked the harbour, but higher up the estuary, away from the docks, next to the yacht club. The dining room was built out over the water and the racing dinghies often sailed brazenly close to the windows before going about. Wycliffe poured himself another glass of Chablis. 'Very pleasant wine, this, in fact they do us very well here altogether, very well.'

Helen laughed. 'Too well for your waist line, I think.'

He was feeling mellow after a good lunch. The water was like a mirror and if you looked with half closed eyes the whole scene dissolved into a living mosaic of colour, blue, yellow, red and white hulls with the green hillside beyond. It would be pleasant to hire a boat and potter about the harbour for the afternoon. There was a little village of grey stone houses across the water and it would be fun to tie up at the jetty and stroll round the village, perhaps to have tea there. But he had a photograph in his pocket, a photograph of a young man who might, just possibly, be a murderer. He had put off telling Helen, not that she would fuss, she had been too long a policeman's wife, but it might have taken the edge off the enjoyment of their lunch.

'Something cropped up this morning.'

'I thought as much.'

'How could you?'

'You had that half smug, half guilty look I know so well, and you were late for lunch. Is it serious?'

'Murder. I should have been sent for anyway.'

Helen sighed. 'Oh, well, perhaps they will let you charge your hotel bill.'

Comforting woman.

As a concession to convention he changed his linen jacket and slacks for a lightweight suit of worsted and at two o'clock he was walking along the narrow twisting main street, smoking his pipe, one of the crowd returning to work. He would have liked to have been really a part of it, to have exchanged familiar greetings with the people he passed, to have known why the shutters were up at number forty-four, why the tobacconist at thirty-six was wearing a black arm band and the real story behind the newspaper placard which read: COUNCILLOR HILL WITHDRAWS.

This was a credible size for a community, you could identify yourself with it, live its life.

In the newspaper office a mini-skirted girl took time off to be polite. 'This is only a branch office but if you'd like to wait you could see Mr Brown, the local reporter. He's out to his lunch.'

In course of time Mr Brown arrived smelling of his liquid lunch, a red-headed young man, breezily efficient. 'Always ready to help the police, superintendent, what can we do for you?'

In a little office which had a desk, a chair, a typewriter, a telephone and nothing else, Wycliffe produced his photograph.

Brown studied it critically. 'Nasty business at the Marina, super-intendent.'

'Very.'

'Is this the bloke?'

'Not as far as I know. Have you seen him before?'

As Brown spoke a cigarette danced up and down between his lips. 'They're all alike, aren't they? All the same I should probably know him if he was a local lad. Can we print this? Say it was found on the scene of the crime?'

Wycliffe retrieved the photograph. 'We shall put it on the regional telly tonight. If that doesn't work I shall probably circulate it, you can print it then.'

'Who was she, super?'

Wycliffe shrugged. 'I wish I knew. Perhaps you could help, keep your eyes and ears open.'

Brown nodded. 'On a quid pro quo basis. I got precious little out of your chap at the Marina.'

'I'll see to it personally.'

'Thanks.'

'Any time!' The superintendent strolled out into the sunshine and this time he made for the car park.

He drove in a leisurely fashion the ten miles to the county town, infuriating other drivers who could only pass at those rare spots where the road had been straightened and widened. It took him twenty-three minutes. The white Jag chuntering behind would probably have done it in thirteen. Ten minutes lost! Save fivepence on the large packet! The kind of economics Wycliffe would never understand.

The afternoon sun beat down on the hospital campus so that the asphalt was soft underfoot and he was grateful for the cool tiled corridors of the pathology building. He made for the mortuary. It was overrun with people, some of whom had been at the Marina earlier. The police photographers were there with the tools of their trade, the people from forensic and a covey of policemen in and out of uniform. Wycliffe had arranged to meet some of his own Area squad there and he saw Chief Inspector James Gill pushing his way through the crowd towards him.

'Long time no see, sir! Must be all of a week!' Gill was young for his rank, craggy, tough and cynical enough to make Wycliffe feel, by contrast, comfortably warm-hearted. He liked working with Gill and had sent for him on this occasion.

'Who's with you?'

'Hartley, Wills and Manders, all we could spare. What's the Divisional set-up?'

Wycliffe shrugged. 'You'll meet Inspector Fehling directly. Impressive – that's the word, Jimmy, impressive.'

They were making their way through gossiping groups to the far end of the room where Franks and two of his assistants were working on the body of the dead girl. The acrid fishy smell of formalin was strong.

'Anything for me?'

Franks looked up. 'As far as the girl is concerned, nothing you'll want to hear. She was healthy, well nourished, between twenty and twenty-two, she had never given birth. No scars, no nice identifiable old fractures. She has a large mole on her left breast, her teeth have been well cared for, no extractions and only two fillings . . .'

Dr Bell of forensic joined them by the table. 'And there's no joy from the clothing either – there isn't much of it anyway.' He was bald headed, a little wisp of a man, with an oversized pipe which he sucked whether it was lit or not – 'Nipple fixation', he called it. 'Our job would be a pushover if women still wore calico drawers and shifts.'

'I can tell you one thing,' Franks said. He always saved the best till last. 'The man who made love to her is AB.' He looked absurdly pleased with himself, like a little boy who has just said his party piece. 'I ran the usual grouping tests on the seminal fluid and for once we hit the jack-pot.'

Wycliffe was unimpressed, or pretended to be. 'Big deal! If I remember rightly, about three per cent of the population are in the AB group, so, leaving women and children aside, that gives us a round half million suspects in the UK to choose from.'

Franks's baby face wrinkled into a grin. 'You chaps want your job done for you! As it is we do most of it.'

Wycliffe looked down at the figure on the dissecting table. He was hardened by long usage, but it was in any case difficult to connect this gruesome cadaver with the eye-catching girl who had booked in at the Marina on Sunday night. It was that girl he wanted to know about, her living and her loving and the web of circumstance which had finally put an end to them both. He had to put the clock back to Sunday night at least, probably much further, and try to live with her that borrowed time.

He sent Chief Inspector Gill in search of the police photographer. 'I want you to work on your shots of the face and with Dr Franks's help, bring her alive. Let's have a photograph we can publish, one that her friends will recognize.'

Both men were doubtful but they agreed to try; and Kathy, Wycliffe said, would check the result.

Chief Inspector Gill rode back with Wycliffe in his nice new Zodiac to be put in the picture. Gill watched the countryside gliding sedately by and listened. It was one of Wycliffe's consolations that he didn't have to spell everything out for Gill; they had evolved a kind of conversational shorthand which, despite differences of temperament, they could use because their logical processes were similar.

'Three sets of prints on the photograph of the guitarist, one set belonging to the girl. Copies have gone to Area and to CRO.'

'So if he's got form, there's a chance, otherwise . . .'

'It's possible that none of the dabs are the killer's anyway.'

Gill let another mile or so slide by – they were trailing a green double-decker bus at twenty with a queue of traffic behind waiting in vain for Wycliffe to make a move.

'Been this way before, Jim?'

'No sir, first visit. Seems pleasant enough, trees and all that.'

'You should bring your wife and kids down for a holiday.'

'Holiday? What's that? I thought it was something they gave to school kids. Going back to the case, this grouping test of Franks's, is it the same as a blood test?'

'Same thing.'

'Then it could help?'

Wycliffe drew to a halt behind the bus which had stopped to set down passengers. 'If we had a line-up of suspects it might, but we don't even know who the girl is. That's our first job and our best bet there is . . .'

'The laddie with the guitar.'

'Exactly. With any luck the photograph should be in all the papers tomorrow and it might be on television tonight.'

The cars behind had taken advantage of the bus stop and were streaming past. Finally the bus got going again and Wycliffe fell in behind.

'I suppose you couldn't pass that thing, sir? The diesel fumes . . .'

Wycliffe seemed surprised. 'Do they bother you? Anyway it's hardly worth it now, we're just coming into the town.'

They were cruising along a suburban road lined with Dracaenas and villas in a bewildering variety of architectural styles, each with its Bed and Breakfast sign. A canvas banner between two lamp-posts advertised a summer show at the Council's theatre.

Inspector Fehling had been busy establishing a murder hunt HQ at the station. The recreation room had been cleared and equipped with tables and chairs, an epidiascope and a slide projector. A projection screen was fixed to one of the walls flanked by maps of the town and surrounding areas. Telephone engineers were busy installing additional instruments. Fehling looked at his achievement with pride.

'What are the magic lanterns for?' Wycliffe asked.

'A slide projector and epidiascope, sir, for projecting transparencies and prints.'

'Ah!'

'Visual aids, I think they call them, sir,' Gill said. 'All the rage in progressive forces.'

Opening off the main room were two little rooms which Fehling had set aside for the 'brass'. 'You take your choice, sir,' he offered generously, 'but this one is a bit bigger so I've taken the liberty of putting the reports there.' He pointed to a wire tray on the table containing an alarming bundle of typescript.

Wycliffe sat himself in one of the bentwood chairs on the wrong side of the desk and Gill chose the other. Fehling was left standing.

'For God's sake, sit down, Mr Fehling!'

So the inspector had to fit himself into the armchair behind the desk and he bulged over the arms. He started to sort the reports. Obviously he was good at paper work, which is the way to get on. If you make enough copies of bugger-all people think it and you must be important. Wycliffe filled his pipe, refused any papers and said, 'Tell us about it, Mr Fehling.'

Fehling passed a great hand over his brow and back over his thinning curls. 'There is only one new lead so far. You remember the house on the other side of the railway cutting?'

Wycliffe nodded. 'Their backs overlook the back of the hotel.'

'Exactly, they're good class houses, sir – respectable.'

'What's that got to do with it? Are you thinking of buying one?'

'Just that they're the sort of people who make reliable witnesses.'

Wycliffe questioned the assumption but said nothing. In his experience the more respectable people were, the more they had to hide. They didn't want to be mixed up in anything that wasn't quite nice.

'The lady at number twenty-six, a Mrs Foster, says that at a little after midnight she happened to be looking out of her landing window when she saw someone standing on the fire escape of the hotel.'

'Man or woman?'

'She thinks it was a man though she could only see a silhouette against the lighted window.'

'Which window?'

'Top floor of the extension, she says. It must have been the girl's room or the bathroom.'

'What was he doing?'

'Just standing there according to her. She says she watched him for nearly ten minutes.'

'The window of the girl's room won't open.'

'No, sir, it's screwed up.'

'And the curtains won't draw.' Wycliffe lit his pipe and blew clouds of smoke ceilingwards. 'What was she doing looking out of her window at that time of night?'

'I don't know, sir, but she says she's complained on several occasions to the police about goings on in that place.'

'I'll bet!' He caught Gill looking at him quizzically, wondering why he was knocking poor old Fehling who seemed to be doing a pretty good job. He hardly knew himself, not until he stopped to think, then he knew. It was the tacit assumption of Fehling and his like that the world is divided into two camps, the good and the bad, the respectable and the contemptible, the cops and the robbers. Never would Fehling look at one of his victims and say, 'There but for the grace of God . . .'

'Anything else?'

Fehling looked aggrieved, as well he might. 'The other two rooms on that floor of the extension, sir – one was occupied by an elderly tradesman sent down from Newcastle by his firm to do some special job on that cruise liner which is being refitted in the yard.'

'Could he tell you anything?'

'Nothing. He said he'd had a few drinks and slept like a log. The other room – the room next to the girl's – was let to a young man waiting to join his ship when she docks on Sunday. He was the worse for drink too and his recollections are hazy. But he had a girl with him . . .'

'What does she say?'

Fehling stroked his smooth chin which, in a few years, would extend in rolls down his neck. 'We haven't found her yet, sir. He picked her up in one of the pubs and he can't remember much about her except that she cleared off early this morning.'

'What about Piper?'

'Sir?'

'The proprietor of the place – what does he say about the girl?'

'Says he had no idea she was there, if he had he would have thrown her out. Respectable house, all that malarkey.'

'So what are you doing about it?'

'My chaps will be doing the rounds of the pubs tonight.'

'No.'

'Sir?'

'I said no, I expect they've got something better to do than a subsidized pub crawl.'

Fehling raised his eyes to the ceiling and pursed his lips. Chief Inspector Gill was enjoying himself.

'What about the other people staying in the place – anybody suspicious?'

Fehling fished some papers out of the wire tray. 'Here are the reports, sir.'

'Tell me about them, Mr Fehling.'

'Well, sir, there were nine other people staying in the hotel. All were men and all have been questioned by my chaps. They've given credible accounts of themselves, but we're checking, and they've been told not to leave the town without notifying us. Most of them – all but two, in fact – are waiting to join their ships. They've got seamen's books which seem to be in order.'

'What about the other two?'

'Lorry driver and his mate, sir, down here to pick up some turbine rotors which have to go back to the works for balancing.'

Wycliffe stood up. 'Well, I'm off! I'll leave you and Chief Inspector Gill together. No doubt you'll find that you have much in common.'

'Christ! Is he always like that?'

Gill looked at the door which had barely closed behind the Chief Superintendent. 'Mostly, but you'll get used to it.'

'I don't know that I want to,' Fehling grumbled. 'It's like tight boots, there don't seem to be much point in starting.'

Wycliffe left his car on the park and walked in the direction of the main street. It was just on six according to the clock over the post office, and visitors were streaming off the quay, returning from the afternoon boat trips, making for their lodgings and dinner. The children trailed behind and were scolded while the toddlers had to be carried on daddys' shoulders. Wycliffe watched it all with interest and approval. He never tired of watching people, people about their business and their pleasure. Some men watched animals, building little hides to spy on badgers, birds or deer, but Wycliffe could not understand them. From a window on to a street, from a seat in a pub or a park, or strolling round a fairground, it was possible to observe a far more varied species, more complex, more intelligent, more perceptive and vastly richer in the pattern of their emotional response.

The narrow main street was almost deserted, the shops closed, the pubs and fried fish bars just opening their doors but with no customers as yet. Wycliffe ambled along window shopping. The bookshop he had noticed before, an especially good bookshop for a small town. Two large windows, one devoted to new and the other to secondhand books, well displayed and priced. A card invited inspection of *twenty thousand secondhand books inside – many of antiquarian interest and importance.* He promised himself that he would find time to spend an hour there. Good bookshops were getting all too rare. He noticed the name on the signboard:

W.P. COLLINS & SON.
NEW AND SECOND HAND BOOKSELLERS
Estab: 1847

Good for the Collinses!

He made his way through the street on towards the docks and the Marina. Apart from a few people on the pavement gawping, it looked serenely undisturbed. He pushed his way through the swing glass doors and found a constable in the hall. 'Is the room sealed?'

'Yes, sir.'

'Then report back, no need to waste your time here.' The constable went. 'Anybody home?' Silence. An appetizing smell led him by the nose to the kitchen. In better days it had been a conservatory and some of the smaller panes were red or blue or orange glass so that gay splashes of colour cropped up in unexpected places. Piper was seated at a large table covered with oilcloth, reading a racing paper and eating curried stew with a spoon. Opposite him, sitting bolt upright, prim as a maiden aunt at the Vicar's teaparty, Kathy, eating her stew very skilfully, with a fork.

Ernie Piper was too old a hand to be put off his food by a policeman. He looked up and grinned. 'Sit yourself down, superintendent, what can we do for you?'

'You like curry, superintendent? I make it myself and there is plenty.'

Wycliffe realized that he was hungry. 'It smells good!'

'She cooks like an angel,' Piper said. 'That's why I keep you, isn't it, Kathy?'

Kathy smiled but said nothing.

The curry was good – and hot. He had to suck in his breath after the first mouthful. Piper laughed. 'Try some bread, superintendent,' and he passed the board with the best part of a two pound loaf on it. 'She makes her own bread too. It makes going straight worth while.'

For a time they ate in silence. Piper opened a couple of bottles of beer and decanted them into glasses. Wycliffe wondered what Inspector Fehling would make of it if he could see them now.

'Who was the girl in sixteen last night?'

Piper shrugged, 'I told the inspector . . .'

'I know what you told the inspector, I also know your sort, my lad. Is your front door locked at night?'

'Well, no . . .'

'And is there, or is there not, a board in the hall which shows the rooms which are occupied?'

'I told you, I'm going straight, superintendent.' Piper took a great gulp of beer and wiped his lips with the back of his hand.

Wycliffe grinned. 'That's as may be but you're not going soft! Are you trying to tell me that any pick-up can have a free night's lodging and enjoy the other amenities of your establishment if she cares to bring her bloke here?'

Piper looked sheepish. 'Well no, but I can't stop the chaps who lodge here bringing back a bird if they feel that way, can I? I mean this isn't a Sunday school.'

Wycliffe had finished his curry and he was fiddling with the crusty top of the loaf. He broke off a generous chunk and began to nibble. It reminded him of when he used to be sent to buy bread when he was a kid – before they turned it into sponge rubber.

'Have some butter with it?'

'Not likely!' He chewed happily. 'I wouldn't like to be the girl who came back here with one of your boarders if she wasn't on your visiting list or if she didn't leave the proper cut. Where do they put it? Do they drop it in the potted palm as they go out?'

Piper chuckled. 'I'll say one thing for you, you know the score! It was Millie Ford, 46, Castle Hill. She's a good girl so don't you go upsetting her.'

'And don't you push your luck!' Wycliffe growled.

194

It was a mellow evening, a golden light over the harbour, softening the colours, blurring the outlines, the water still and gleaming.

Castle Hill was on his way back to the hotel, a minor hump in the low lying ground which fringes the harbour. You climb steeply from the main street between two rows of small and, for the most part, derelict shops, then the road falls away more slowly to the level of the harbour and the hotel. Millie lived over a shop which displayed a dusty collection of china and glass ornaments calling them, hopefully, antiques. The shop was shut so he knocked at the side door. An immensely fat woman across the street, standing in her doorway, shouted, 'You got to go up, dearie!' Despite all his years in the Force he was embarrassed.

The door opened on to a flight of wooden steps and at the top he was faced by three doors. He knocked on one marked *FORD*, and a voice called, 'Come in!' Of course the room overlooked the ubiquitous harbour, he couldn't escape from it, not that he wanted to. It was a bedsitter, a bit threadbare and over-used, but clean and tidy. 'What do you want, love?' Millie Ford in a housecoat and mules was standing by a tiny electric stove, waiting for a saucepan of milk to heat. 'I'm making some coffee, want some?'

Wycliffe refused. She was thirtyish, plump, a bit overripe, but attractive. 'I'm a police officer.'

She laughed in a bored way. 'I've heard that one before, dear, but I can spot a dick a mile off. Now, what do you want? Are you after something special?'

Wycliffe flapped his warrant card and she looked at it, incredulous. 'On the level? I wouldn't have said you was big enough, they must be making 'em in the handy pocket size. A chief super, too . . . !' She pointed to the only chair in the room. 'You better sit down.' She poured the milk into a half filled cup of coffee. 'Sure you won't? Well, what have I done now?'

Wycliffe looked round the room. He'd seen hundreds like it, most of them a great deal more squalid. She had been ironing a frock and the ironing board was wedged into the little space between the bed and the window. Over the bed there was a piece of poker-work: *Bless this house!* She caught his eye and grinned. 'I expect you know why I'm here,' he began.

She shook her mop of black hair. 'I don't, love, honest.'

He looked at her suspiciously but she seemed to be telling the truth. 'A girl was strangled at the Marina last night.'

She stopped short in the act of sipping her coffee. 'But I was . . .'

'. . . there last night, I know.'

She was shocked and scared. She put her cup down on the stove, sat on the bed and faced him. 'Was it one . . . ?'

He shook his head. 'A stranger, we don't know who she was.'

She was relieved and he didn't blame her. She brought out a packet of cigarettes from the pocket of her housecoat and looked vaguely round for matches. He gave her a box and she lit a cigarette which set her coughing.

'She was in seventeen, next door to you.'

'Ah!'

'Now I want you to tell me all you can remember about last night from the time you picked up your man.'

She blew her nose after the coughing fit and seemed to be collecting her thoughts. 'I usually do The Ship, and I was there last evening. I got into conversation with a chap and we had a few drinks although he was three parts cut before we started. When they shut at half ten he asked me to come back with him, I asked him where and he said the Marina, so that was all right. He was only a youngster and when we got out in the air he made heavy weather of it so that it took me some time to get him there and then he just flaked out on the bed. Not that I was bothered, I got into bed and tried to get some sleep . . .'

'You didn't see anybody?'

'In the Marina? Only Ernie, he was poking about in the little office when we came in and he helped me to get his lordship upstairs.'

'Well?'

She drew on her cigarette thoughtfully. 'I could hear a couple next door and I thought it must be one of ours with a client. I couldn't get off to sleep so I lay there trying to guess who it was . . . you know how you do . . .'

'What could you hear?'

'Just voices, a man and a woman talking but I couldn't hear what they were saying. I only wished they would shut up. Oh yes! – the man coughed a lot – a smoker's cough.'

'Were they quarrelling?'

196

'No, just talking. A lot of men pick up a girl because they want a woman to talk to – funny really.'

Wycliffe sat there staring out of the window watching the purple dusk steal over the harbour like a mist and he was happy. He was feeling the texture of another life with sympathy and understanding – these encounters were the reward, not the penalty of his work. 'Then?'

'Well, it must have been around midnight when I heard somebody come out of the room and pass my door. I thought it must be the girl going home and wished I could go too but my fellow hadn't forked out and I would have to let Ernie have his cut anyway.'

'You're sure that this was around midnight?'

'No, I couldn't be sure of the time – not really.'

'And you heard nothing more all night?'

'Oh yes I did. Probably I dozed for a bit but some time later I heard them talking again and that seemed odd. She must have come back and I couldn't understand it. This time they did seem to be quarrelling but they kept their voices low . . .'

'The same voices?'

She looked puzzled. 'Well, they must have been, mustn't they?' Wycliffe said nothing and she went on, 'Then they stopped talking and started . . .'

'What?'

'To get down to it – I mean, there's no doubt about it with those beds in the Marina.'

'Anything more?'

'No, I didn't hear any more, I must have gone off to sleep properly after that. The next thing I knew it was getting light and my chap woke up. I told him I wanted my money and after a bit he pulled out his wallet and told me to take it. He had the father and mother of a hangover and I don't think he had a clue where he was or who I was . . . Anyway I took four quid and beat it . . . After all it wasn't my fault if. . .'

Wycliffe agreed.

'To think that next door that poor girl . . .' Millie found a handkerchief and dabbed her eyes. The most poignant grief of all when one can say, 'There but for the grace of God . . .'

Wycliffe walked back to the hotel and found Helen in the lounge reading. She looked up with a welcoming smile. 'Have you had a meal?'

'What? Oh, yes thanks.' He was still in a different world from this air-conditioned lounge with its soft lights, thick carpets and silent waiters. This world was less real to him, less comprehensible; it was not that he wanted to . . . He sighed. 'I had curried stew.'

Helen laughed. 'Was it good?'

What would she say if he told her that he had been entertained by a pimp and his Jamaican tart? 'Yes, very good.'

They had a drink together, then Helen said that she felt like bed.

'I'll be with you in ten minutes.'

He lit his pipe and went out on to the terrace. He stood, his arms resting on the balustrade. The waters of the harbour, dark and mysterious, dozens of riding lights sending their quivering ribbons of yellow across its surface. Well away to the right, the docks, a blaze of light, the only sounds a low pitched hum from some machinery and the hiss of escaping steam.

One man was with the dead girl until around midnight. They talked amicably. Had this man left before another appeared on the fire escape? Was the man on the fire escape spying on the couple? It seemed probable that he had come in through the bathroom window, the official way on to the escape in an emergency. In which case the girl had unfastened the window for him. This time the talk was less friendly: 'They seemed to be quarrelling but they kept their voices low'. But this visit had ended in copulation – and in murder.

Two men? It seemed so. So far he had heard of three in the case – four if he counted Ernie Piper. The boy with the guitar, the man in the pinstripes whom Kathy had found going through the register and the chap in cap and mackintosh she had seen talking to the dead girl. Was it one of these who had spent an hour with her? And another of them who had strangled her, then battered her face beyond recognition?

3

A morning conference in the superintendent's little office.

'As I see it, the bloke came the first time to make contact, to find out if she had the money and was able to do a deal. She satisfied him and he went off to get the stuff . . .' Fehling spoke in a ponderously judicial way which was one more source of irritation to Wycliffe.

'You still think that she was buying dope?'

The inspector blew out his cheeks. 'Oh, I don't think there can be any doubt on that score, it's another matter to decide what went wrong.' He studied his finger-tips then added, 'Quite another matter.'

Wycliffe was standing looking out of the window of the office. It was as though he had to keep in touch with the world outside, a room without windows would have been torture to him. The view was uninspiring, an exercise yard and beyond a great expanse of corrugated asbestos, the wall and roof of a garage. 'What do you think, Jim?'

Chief Inspector Gill's ugly expressive features creased in dissatisfaction. 'It sounds likely enough on the face of it but according to what you've just told us they must have spent the best part of an hour together just gossiping. That hardly sounds like a preliminary session to spy out the land – more as if they were old friends. But if they knew each other so well, why didn't he bring the goods with him? In any case, why was she killed?'

Fehling took up the challenge. 'There are at least two possible explanations. When he came back with the dope it's feasible that she wasn't satisfied, or that she tried for a better deal – the girl says she heard them quarrelling.'

'So he makes love to her, strangles her, bashes her face in, then goes off without the money.'

Wycliffe's manner made Fehling flush. 'It sounds a bit thin, but you know as well as I do that you can't predict what a man will or won't do under stress.'

'You said that there were two possibilities – what was the other?'

'That they didn't quarrel about the deal but that her friend decided to round off the evening by giving her a tumble and she put up a fight.'

'So he strangled her?'

'It wouldn't be the first time!' Fehling was on the defensive.

'It couldn't have been much of a fight: Millie Ford heard nothing of it and she was next door.'

'But the girl was strangled and she did have her face battered.'

Wycliffe turned back to the window. 'Yes, and a thousand pounds was left untouched in a drawer. In any case, what about the chap on the fire escape? Where does he come into it?'

Fehling nodded. 'I've thought of that, I believe he was the same man. The front door of the hotel is fitted with a Yale-type lock which is kept clipped back but I found out from Piper that the catch is liable to slip and you find yourself locked out.'

'You think that's what happened to your friend?'

Fehling was pleased with himself. 'I do. Think of it, sir. After his first session with the girl he goes to get the stuff and when he comes back he finds the door locked. Naturally he doesn't want to rouse the house so he nips round and up the fire escape, taps on the girl's window and she lets him in through the bathroom.'

Chief Inspector Gill chuckled. 'That's very ingenious.'

Wycliffe grunted but said nothing. He hadn't a very high opinion of Fehling but he had to admit that there was some sort of case. If the girl wasn't buying dope, why would she hang around with a thousand pounds in used notes in a dockland hotel? Or had she *sold* something? He sighed. Speculation was useless until he knew who she was. 'What are you going to do next?'

Fehling felt that he had scored. 'I thought of looking into the docks angle. What ships are in? Itinerary of last trip? Who was sleeping ashore? – that sort of thing. I also planned to send out circulars – anybody in the vicinity of the Marina between, say, eleven and three.'

Wycliffe nodded. Fehling was right, whatever the reason for the crime it seemed to be linked with the docks or at least with the sea and seamen. 'I think you're on the right lines,' he said in a belated attempt to make amends.

Gill offered round a case containing thin black cheroots which were refused. He had changed to cheroots maintaining that they were less hazardous than cigarettes. He allowed himself only five a day, so that smoking one added something special to any occasion as the advertisement said that it would. Wycliffe lit his pipe in self defence. 'Yesterday evening,' Gill said, 'Inspector Fehling and I made a round of the cafes in the main street and as far as the docks. The Marina doesn't do meals other than breakfast and she must have eaten somewhere. It seems that she used a place almost by the dock gates and not above a hundred yards from the hotel. The chap who runs it had noticed an "auburn-haired dolly" whom he described "as the sort of bird to keep a man awake at night".'

'Poetic, really,' Wycliffe said. 'Was she always alone?'

'Always. The café owner was puzzled by her, she wasn't the sort he expected to get in a place like his.'

'What sort of place is it?'

Gill considered. 'It's really a lorry drivers' caf. Clean enough, friendly, but not much choice beyond the bangers and mash and a cuppa. I imagine it's used mainly by lorry drivers taking stuff in and out of the docks.'

'Not by the locals?'

Gill looked at him sharply. 'No, do you think that's why she went there?'

Wycliffe wished sometimes that Gill did not know him so well. He made an irritable movement to save a reply. He turned to Fehling. 'Why was her face battered in? That's what I want to know.'

'The chap went berserk, scared out of his wits,' Fehling said.

'Is that what you think?' Wycliffe's blank stare was turned on Gill.

The chief inspector shook his head. 'No, either her identification would lead direct to her killer or there are local associations which he doesn't want known.'

'Or both.'

'Could be.'

The telephone rang and Wycliffe answered it. 'Wycliffe.' It was the station sergeant. 'The guitarist, sir, whose photo went out on the telly last night – he's on the telephone, wants to know what it's all about.'

'Is he a local?'

'He's living in the town; he's got a flat in Marine Walk, chap by the name of Graham.'

'Tell him we'll send somebody along to talk to him – say during the next hour, then find out all you can about him from your chaps.'

'We could bring him in, sir.'

'No!' Wycliffe believed that when you brought a man into the police station you saw only half of him. He decided to interview Graham himself.

'He must be a cool one,' Gill said. 'The average man seeing his picture on the telly like that would be on to the nick before the news-reader got to the next item.'

'There aren't any average men left!' Wycliffe growled.

Before he left for Marine Walk he was briefed by the station sergeant. 'Kenneth Graham, sir, he runs a pop group and is known professionally as Kenny the Man. They seem to make a fairly plush living in the season, playing at several resorts up and down the West Country.'

Wycliffe set out.

A chief superintendent's place during a murder inquiry is usually established in the nearest police station but it can be in a village hall or even a caravan. As the officer in charge of the inquiry it is his job to remain at the centre coordinating all aspects of the investigation, receiving reports and deploying men and resources to the best advantage. The most Wycliffe had ever conceded to this official view of his duties was to telephone in at reasonable intervals or to keep in touch through his car radio. He had to get out and about, to get the smell of the chase. He had to meet witnesses in their normal surroundings. 'Field work,' he called it. He could, of course, have had his witnesses brought in. He could have carried out formal interrogations in the stultifying atmosphere of the police station where innocent people soon begin to behave like crooks. But Wycliffe believed that what he called *personal* crimes are more likely to be solved by getting to know the people involved, getting to know them so well that you begin to think as they do.

Two criticisms had been levelled at him at every stage of his career: 'He does not take well to discipline', and 'He often becomes too emotionally involved with his cases'. Damning criticisms of a policeman – Wycliffe never understood why they hadn't blocked his promotion, but he suspected that it was because the solemn Jacks who insisted on reams of paper rarely read what was on it. And he had a good reputation as a villain catcher.

Marine Walk circles the promontory which divides the harbour from the open sea. On the harbour side its low cliffs overhang the docks and on the sea side a fringe of sandy beaches, too small for exploitation, provide refuge for holidaymakers who enjoy peace and quiet. The houses are on the sea side and he drove round catching tantalizing glimpses of the sea through the trees which grow on the gentle slopes almost to the water's edge.

Graham lived in the upper flat of an Edwardian villa which had been modernized and converted into two flats with an outside staircase. The stairs ended on a glass roofed balcony with a magnificent panoramic view of the whole bay.

'Are you a copper?'

Kenny wore tight jeans and a floral shirt but he had changed his hair style since the photograph: instead of allowing it to hang lankly round his hatchet face he was now giving it the wave and set treatment.

'Chief Superintendent Wycliffe.'

'You'd better come in.'

To Wycliffe's surprise, the flat could hardly have been more conventional. Everything shone and though the taste was a bit *Coronation Street*, it had all been carefully chosen and cost money. In the lounge there was everything from a gleaming cocktail cabinet with chrome fittings to the most stupendous fake-log electric fire Wycliffe had ever seen, as well as china ducks clinging to the wall in frozen flight. Wycliffe was fascinated by the seeming incongruity of it all. 'Do you live with your parents?' It seemed the most likely explanation.

But Kenny shook his head. 'You're looking at the gear? No, it's just that I like somewhere nice to come home to and I'm not short of a few bob. As a matter of fact I share with one of my mates.' He sat on the arm of a magenta-coloured cut moquette easy chair. 'Well, what's this all about then? It don't do a chap in my position any good to be put on the telly by the police. People will think I've done something.'

Wycliffe was perched on the edge of a settee trying to stop himself falling back into its monstrous clutches. 'About the photograph, Mr Graham, is it one you use for publicity purposes?'

'No, definitely not. We're a group and we sell as a group – private enterprise is out. That's one other reason why putting me on the telly won't do me any good.'

'The girl who had this photograph was murdered.'

'Yeh?' He sounded impressed and shocked. 'Who was she?'

'That's what we want to find out and it's why we need your help.'

Kenny took a cigarette from a dispenser on one of several little tables scattered about the room. He lit it and gave his attention once more to the superintendent. 'Got a photo?'

'No.'

'Well, I can't help, can I?'

'She was twenty-one or two, auburn haired, good looking, small, and she had a mole under her left breast. People who saw her when she was alive describe her as "eye-catching".'

Kenny had stopped smoking and was looking at the super-intendent with close attention. 'Tell me some more.'

'There's not much else to tell, but these are some of the things she had with her . . .' He took a small parcel from his pocket, un-wrapped it and spread out the few bits of jewelry they had found in her room. 'Recognize any of it?'

Kenny picked up the garnet bracelet. 'I gave her that. She had a thing about rubies but I couldn't run to that so we settled for the next best thing.'

'So you knew her.'

Kenny nodded, his eyes staring distantly, then he sighed, 'She was a doll!'

'What was her name and when did you know her?'

At that moment the door opened and a tousle-headed brunette in a baby-doll nightie came in. She was stretching her arms and yawn-ing. 'What time is it?' She took a cigarette and looked vaguely round the room for a light. Wycliffe might not have been there for all the notice she took. 'God! I feel awful this morning!' She saw the jewelry. 'Are they for me?'

Kenny went over and took her by the shoulders. 'Go back to bed, Chick, or get yourself dressed.' He propelled her out of the room and rounded off his instructions with a resounding slap on her rump which made her squeal. He came back looking sheepish. 'Sorry about that.'

'All part of life's rich pattern,' Wycliffe said. 'Now, you were telling me . . .'

'Dawn Peters she was called, she did a summer season at the Voodoo last year.'

'The Voodoo is a club?'

'Yes, a plush place if you go by the prices. Anyway they hire two bands for the season, one pop and one trad. We was there last year and she was one of two strippers. *The Fabulous Dawn*, they billed her and for once they were right. She used to have the old men sitting on the edges of their seats and begging. Every man in the place was convinced she was doing it for him and that included me – and I'm used to it.'

'You got to know her outside the club?'

He lit another cigarette. 'Yeh.' He was less anxious to talk now.

'Well?'

'Well enough.' He upset ash down the front of his shirt and took time off to brush it on to newspaper. 'I would have married her.'

'Did she live with you here?'

'I didn't have this place then; anyway she shared a flat with the other girl – Sadie. Sadie's still at the Voodoo, but she isn't in the same league.'

'You asked her to marry you?'

'Yeh, and she turned me down. I was lucky.'

'Lucky?'

He crushed out his cigarette in a huge plated ashtray with a press-down middle. 'That's what I said. For one thing she was married already and for another . . .' His voice trailed off. 'She was a case! She had the devil in her. It was any man any time but there was more to it than that.' He paused again, searching for words to describe something which had impressed him. 'She would always go to the limit and a bit further – you know what I mean? That sort of bird's fine to have fun with, but when it comes to the old steak and chips then you want something a bit more steady. Get me?

'It was the same in her act – I mean there are limits even for a stripper in a private club. When she turned it in at the Voodoo they lost a packet but old Quackers, the proprietor, told me himself that he was glad to see her go. With her antics on and off the stage she would have got the place shut down.'

'Where did she go when she left the Voodoo?'

Kenny shrugged. 'Up to the smoke but don't ask me where. She said she had a West End contract and she was probably telling the truth.'

'You said she was married. I take it she wasn't living with her husband?'

'I told you she was sharing with the other girl. I was new to the town then and I never knew the details but I heard gossip. Apparently she was married to some local square who took a pretty dim view of her goings on.' He grinned. 'I can't say as I blame him for that.'

Wycliffe stood up. From the window he could see the whole sweep of the bay from the lighthouse round a ten-mile stretch of coastline to the jagged teeth of the Meudon Rocks. He wondered if Kenny ever looked out of the window, or was it just another status symbol?

'Well, thank you for your help, Mr Graham. You haven't got a photograph of her, I suppose?'

Kenny shook his head. 'I never keep photos of dames, it makes for trouble, but there should be plenty at the club.'

Wycliffe moved towards the door. 'Is your group working at the moment?'

'Oh yeh, we're doing a season at the Scala.'

'Every night?'

'Except Tuesdays and Sundays. They have Bingo on Tuesdays.'

'Where were you on Tuesday night, then?'

Kenny looked shaken. 'Here! Come off it! You coppers are all alike.'

'Routine, Mr Graham, just routine. Where were you?'

He was aggrieved. 'I took the chick to that Indian place in Market Street for a nosh then we came back here early and went to bed.'

'Have you got a car?'

'Yeh. What of it?'

'Nothing. Did you know that Dawn Peters was back in the town?'

Kenny's aggressiveness increased with his nervousness. 'No, I didn't know, and if I had I wouldn't have been interested, copper!'

Wycliffe let himself out into the corridor and turned for a final word: 'Do you think Dawn Peters was her real name?'

'How the hell should I know?' Kenny the Man was disillusioned.

Wycliffe caught himself chuckling as he went down the steps, but if anybody had asked him why, he couldn't have told them. He would probably have grunted or he might have said, 'Just people.'

He drove back slowly to the centre of the town and parked on one of the quays, then he strolled in the main street. It was past one o'clock and the population of the town seemed to have its whole mind on food. It was too late to go back to the hotel for lunch but getting a meal otherwise was a competitive business and he was discouraged by the heat, by the crowded tables, by the queues and by the fact that every available potato seemed to have undergone a metamorphosis into chips. He took refuge in a pub and made a meal off ham sandwiches with mustard and a pint of beer. All round him the talk was of cricket, in which he had no interest. No-one so much as mentioned the murder. He stayed until two and followed his beer with a whisky.

'The Voodoo? They don't open till evening but you may find somebody there . . . Anyway, it's after you pass the church next to the off-licence.' Wycliffe walked once more in the sunshine while others were hurrying back to work. The afternoon heat was oppressive, perspiration made his collar limp and his shirt stuck to his back. The Voodoo had no frontage, only a discreet entrance with a neon sign over the door, unlit. He pushed open the door and found himself at the top of a flight of carpeted stairs which led down below street level. At the bottom he was in a foyer with a cloakroom counter on his right and a couple of padded doors labelled by some retarded character *Adams* and *Eves*, respectively. Red, upholstered banquettes occupied every spare foot of wall space and above them there were framed photographs of show-business personalities, some of them well enough known to be vaguely familiar to the superintendent. Two showed an insipid looking blonde with nothing on but a head-dress and these were autographed *Sadie*. A pair of swing doors with figured glass panels opened into a very large dimly lit room with a curtained stage at one end, a central dance floor and tables and chairs disposed in two ranks on the carpeted fringe. The pervading colour was red, and the walls were hung with huge grinning masks and grotesque totems against a mural background depicting mythical monsters in vaguely erotic involvement. The stage and the bar on the far side were flanked by ten-foot-high figures which looked like refugees from Easter Island but were probably made of polystyrene. A faint smell of stale tobacco and alcohol blended with an indescribable synthetic scent out of an aerosol. But it was cool, like a cellar. There was nobody to be seen. 'Anybody about?'

After a second and a third try, a woman came down the steps from the stage. A bottle blonde, older than she tried to look; inclined to be fleshy, she looked naked rather than provocative in a psychedelic mini-dress which revealed too much white thigh. 'Who are you?'

'I want to see the owner.'

'He's not in.'

'I'm Chief Superintendent Wycliffe, Area CID.'

'What do you want?'

'I'll tell the owner when you've found him.'

She looked him over, then went back the way she had come. Wycliffe sat himself in one of the comfortable armchairs provided for the paying customers and lit his pipe. In about three minutes a man came down from the stage, forty plus, foppishly dressed in cavalry twill slacks, a modish shirt with green stripes and gold links, a green waistcoat with gilt buttons. His face was pink and rather podgy. His blue eyes looked out through rimless glasses and he spoke in an authoritative manner, intended to subdue. He was smooth, too smooth by half. 'Good afternoon, superintendent, nothing wrong, I trust?'

'I hope not, Mr . . .'

'Masson-Smythe – I'm the proprietor.' 'Quackers', Kenny the Man had called him, but not, Wycliffe was prepared to bet, to his face.

Wycliffe remained seated in his chair, smoking his pipe, Masson-Smythe stood over him, rocking on his heels. 'I am making enquiries about a Miss Dawn Peters, do you know her?'

The proprietor straightened the cuffs of his shirt, displaying the gold links. 'We had a cabaret artiste of that name who worked here last season.'

'A stripper?'

Masson-Smythe raised his eyebrows in disapproval. 'She was a speciality dancer and her act possessed great artistic merit.'

'I'm sure it did. She's been murdered.'

The eyes behind the spectacles widened.

'Was Dawn Peters her real name?'

'It was the name she used in her dealings with me.'

Wycliffe's manner hardened. 'But you employed her! What about insurance, income tax, S.E.T.?'

Masson-Smythe was curt. 'All our artistes have contracts, they are self-employed.'

'Was she good at her job?'

'She attracted patrons.'

There was something about Masson-Smythe's face which had been troubling the superintendent, now he realized what it was. Words came from his lips as from a ventriloquist's doll; there was scarcely any change of expression. 'You must have had photographs of her for display purposes?'

'Certainly.'

'I would like to see them.'

For some reason this seemed to touch a tender spot and the man lost something of his aggressive self-assurance. Wycliffe noticed little beads of perspiration on his upper lip. Something to hide. 'I'm sorry, we do not keep photographs of artistes who are no longer under contract with us, the rapid turnover in the entertainment business makes it . . .'

Wycliffe mentioned two or three names off the photographs in the foyer. 'Are these people under contract with you at present?'

'They are in quite a different category, superintendent, they are celebrities and the fact that they have performed here in the past is, itself, an advertisement.'

Wycliffe smoked placidly and Masson-Smythe continued to stand over him. 'I would like to know on what date Dawn Peters started to work here and under what circumstances she was offered a contract.'

For a moment it seemed that the man might refuse but after some hesitation he shrugged and said, 'Then we'd better move to my office.'

His office was on the street level but at the back of the building. It could have been the office of a prosperous accountant, and it occurred to Wycliffe that Masson-Smythe himself looked more like an accountant than a night club owner. He went to a filing cabinet, unlocked it, and drew out a file. He seated himself in an upholstered swivel chair behind his desk and waved Wycliffe to one of the client's chairs. 'Her contract is dated May tenth, and was to run for four months. I have a note here that I interviewed her first on the twenty-second of April.'

'Was she recommended to you?'

Masson-Smythe spread the papers on his desk and pretended to consult them. 'No, she turned up at a rehearsal and asked for a job. At first I didn't take her seriously; too many girls down on their luck think all they have to do is to take off their clothes in public to make their fortunes. It is not as simple as that.'

'Did she appear to be down on her luck?'

He considered. 'No, she was well dressed and well groomed, but she said that she needed money. I asked her if she had had any experience of cabaret work and she said that she had not. I was on the point of sending her away but there was something about her . . . She was an extremely attractive girl but in this business that isn't enough – a girl needs a certain personality and I thought that she might have it.'

'You gave her an audition?' (Do you audition a stripper?)

'There and then.' He took a cigarette from a box on his desk and lit it. 'She was a natural. It is not an easy thing, even for an experienced girl, to give a good performance under rehearsal conditions – no lights, no audience, no glamour, but despite all that she managed to make her performance intimate and provocative.'

'Yet you were not sorry when her contract ended?'

The blue eyes behind the glasses were cold. 'Indeed?'

Wycliffe fixed him with a bland stare. 'I have been told that you were glad to be rid of her, is that true or not?'

'Perfectly true!' It was the woman Wycliffe had seen downstairs. She came in and stood by Masson-Smythe's chair.

'My wife, Thelma, superintendent. I think that you have already met.'

After the civilities, he went on, 'The superintendent is making enquiries about Dawn Peters . . . Apparently she has been murdered.' No news to the little wife who had obviously been listening outside the door.

Wycliffe turned to her. 'You agree that you and your husband were glad to see her go – why?'

'She was a whore and this place is not a brothel. Does that answer your question?'

Masson-Smythe flushed but said nothing. His wife still stood by him, one hand on his chair as though asserting possession. A formidable woman, Wycliffe thought. Seen in a good light, the hard line of her jaw, a mean little mouth and slightly protuberant eyes disposed of what appeal she seemed to have in the dim light downstairs. Wycliffe knew the sort: hard with men, vicious with other women. Some of them had found their true vocations in the Nazi women's gaols.

'She persisted in dating the patrons which, of course, is strictly against the rules.'

And not only the patrons, Wycliffe thought. Hubby had probably taken a turn with the rest.

'When did she leave the Voodoo?'

Masson-Smythe glanced uneasily at his wife then referred to his papers. 'On August twenty-eighth.'

'Before her contract expired?'

'My husband was forced to terminate it.'

'Do you know where she went after she left?'

'I'm afraid her plans had no interest for us.'

Wycliffe took out his notebook and opened it. 'The other girl who worked with you last season is still with you, I should like her name and address.'

'Sadie Field, 4a, Mount Zion, but she can tell you nothing you don't know already.'

Thelma laughed. 'The original dumb blonde – that's Sadie.'

Wycliffe wrote down the address, put away his notebook and stood up. Thelma came out from behind the desk. 'One question, superintendent, was it Dawn Peters who was found strangled in a hotel bedroom?'

'It seems so.'

'I read about it in the papers.'

'Yes.'

Wycliffe had nothing against these people but he wished like hell he had. With most of the people he met, even the bent ones, it was all too easy to discover the common bond of their humanity, but not with this couple. Perhaps they had never been and never would be in trouble with the law but they repelled him. Mean. They lacked charity. St Paul said, 'Though I speak with the tongues of men and of angels and have not charity, I am become as a sounding brass or a tinkling cymbal.' Wycliffe thought so too.

The club owner came with him to the foyer and watched him as he walked up the stairs. As Wycliffe opened the street door he almost collided with a man coming in. A small dark chap with heavily lined features, shabbily dressed. Wycliffe had known plenty like him as bookie's runners before the new laws and he would probably never have given the incident another thought had it not been for the man's obvious nervousness. Before closing the door Wycliffe glanced down the stairs at Masson-Smythe who seemed anything but glad to see his visitor.

Outside the heat reflected from the pavements was like a blast from a baker's oven.

4

Mount Zion, where Sadie lived, was a narrow, steep lane off the main street. It was so steep that there were steps at intervals and a rail running down the middle. Her flat comprised only two rooms and a share in the usual offices of an old tenement building which had been more or less modernized. It was on the second floor and overlooked a concrete yard festooned with washing. The living room, which had a curtained alcove for a kitchen, was furnished with a studio couch, a couple of easy chairs in faded chintz covers, a scratched dining table and two high-backed dining chairs, 1930 vintage. Evidently Sadie was dumb enough to be cheap.

'Miss Sadie Field?' Wycliffe introduced himself.

Sadie looked scared. She had a delicate prettiness, fair hair and freckles, and her figure was of the kind called 'trim', nothing exotic, certainly nothing erotic about her. When the patrons of the Voodoo watched Sadie take off her clothes they must have imagined themselves to be spying on the girl next door. She pulled her housecoat round her and retied the sash. 'Isn't it hot?'

'You were a friend of Dawn Peters?'

Nervous. 'We used to share this flat. Is there something wrong?'

He encouraged her to sit and took a seat beside her on the couch. He had to shift a copy of the *Daily Mirror* and a paperback with a picture on the cover of a Dr Kildare character in gentlemanly embrace with a pretty nurse. A report on the finding of the body had a two-column spread at the foot of the front page of the *Mirror*. He pointed to it. 'Have you read this?'

'Yes.' Wide-eyed. She was gripping her hands together so tightly that the knuckles whitened. 'Was it her?'

'I'm afraid so.'

She looked as though she was going to cry but didn't.

'We know almost nothing about her and we need your help.'

213

She was staring out of the open window at the silhouettes of the buildings across the court. Between them you could glimpse the tops of the masts of craft in the harbour. 'I don't know much about her before she came to live with me and I haven't heard from her since she left . . .'

'When did she come here? Was it when she started to work at the club?'

She shook her head. 'Before. It was nearly two years ago – late August or early September.' She grinned. 'We met in the launderette, we got talking and she asked me if I knew of any cheap lodgings. The girl who shared with me had left so I brought her back. She liked it and stayed.'

'Did you know that she was married?'

'I didn't when she came here first, but people told me soon enough.'

'She didn't tell you herself?'

'Not till she'd been here a good while.'

'I understand that she was married to a local man?'

Sadie nodded. 'A man called Collins, he owns the bookshop. He's a lot older.'

'So that her real name wasn't Peters.'

'No, she wasn't called Dawn, either, her name was Julie.'

Julie Collins.

'I suppose you suggested that she should try for a job at the club?'

She looked surprised. 'No, I had no idea that she was even thinking of it until she turned up one afternoon at a rehearsal and Mr Masson-Smythe gave her an audition. She was like that – kept things to herself.'

'She lived here for eight or nine months before she started work at the club?'

'About that.'

'What did she live on?'

The translucent skin of her forehead wrinkled. 'She had money. It might not have been much but it was enough to live on. And she went with men though I don't know whether they paid her.'

A statement of fact with no overtones of comment but he felt suddenly irritated. Would nobody tell him what he wanted to know about this girl? She must have done most of the same things as other people, and some different, but all he could learn of her was that she went with men. 'Did she go out much?'

'Not much. For days at a time she wouldn't put a foot outside the door.'

'What did she do all day?'

Sadie picked at a loose thread in the chintz cover. 'She used to read a lot.'

'What did she read?' Probably a useless question.

She spread her hands in a little helpless gesture. 'Books from the library and she used to buy books sometimes.'

Wycliffe stood up and started to wander round the room. He was restless. Here he had his first chance to make some real contact with the dead girl. She had lived in these rooms for more than ten months. There must be something! He reached the door of the bedroom and pushed it open, Sadie close on his heels. 'It's not very tidy!' It wasn't, but neither was it dirty or squalid. Two single beds with nondescript coverlets, an old-fashioned dressing table with triple mirrors, a wardrobe with a front mirror and a grotesquely fretted top, a couple of wicker chairs littered with underwear. In an alcove there were shelves and on one of them books. 'Are these hers?' Hopeful.

'What? Oh yes, she left them behind.'

The random fall-out from almost any library: two or three book club selections, Durrell's *Justine*, a couple of Maigrets, a Nicolas Freeling, Dostoevsky's *Possessed* . . . the Collected Poems of Dylan Thomas, *Ulysses* . . . *Ulysses* had an inscription on the fly-leaf:

> 'To my love.
>> 'Can men more injure women than to say
>> They love them for that, by which they are not they?
>> W.'

More ways than one of taking that. In any case it was an odd thing to quote to your girl friend. But literary. The other books were older and had passed through one or more secondhand shops, their decline recorded in pencilled prices on their fly-leaves. Several were books of poetry, Burns, Shelley, Keats . . . the rest were novels, *Wuthering Heights, Tess of the d'Urbervilles, Ann Veronica* . . .

A literary whore? Why not? Wycliffe was broadminded and had

never believed in demarcation. And surely the tapestry of history must be the richer for its cultured courtesans?

He turned away from the books. 'You still share?'

'A staff supervisor from Wandell's.'

'Dawn . . . Julie, didn't tell you much about herself?'

She stood beside him, nervous, anxious to please. 'Not much, she didn't talk much about anything.'

'Have you got a photograph of her?'

'No, but there must be plenty at the club.'

'You got on with her? I mean, was she easy to live with?'

A small frown as she spotted and dived for a pair of tights lying on the floor. She picked them up and stuffed them under a cushion. 'Oh, yes.'

'No quarrels?'

A faint flush. 'Not quarrels . . .'

'Differences then – what about?'

'Several times she brought men home and I didn't like that so in the end I stopped it.'

'Apart from these men, did anybody ever come to see her?'

'Nobody.'

He caught the momentary hesitation in her manner. 'Sure?'

She sat on the edge of her bed and swept back her hair with the unselfconscious grace of a little girl. 'I don't know. One afternoon as I was coming up the stairs I saw a man coming out of our flat. It was just after I'd told her I wouldn't have men . . . Anyway, when I got in I asked her who the man was and she pretended there hadn't been anybody. I called her a liar and after a minute or two she said, "If you must know, that was my husband, he's been trying to persuade me to come back to him".'

'You believed her?'

'I don't know, I think so.'

'When was this?'

'Not long before she finished at the club and went off to London.'

'Surely you must know this man Collins?'

'Not really, I've seen him once or twice but the stairs are very dark – it could have been him.'

'Did she tell you anything about her husband?'

'Not really. I remember I said, "Why did you leave him?" and she said, "He needed a mother not a wife; he didn't know what it was all about".'

'Perhaps he failed to love her for that by which she was not he.'

'What's that?' She looked at him sharply.

'Just thinking aloud.'

He wandered back into the living room and Sadie followed, watching his every move, puzzled by this strange man who was nothing like any policeman she had known. His questions, when they came, seemed almost incidental to some deeper preoccupation. And this was so: his mind was a turmoil of impressions, ideas, recollections, without pattern or purpose. At such times he seemed to lose his judgement, every fact seemed to carry the same weight, every possibility to be equally credible. Once, this state of mind had bothered him, he had supposed that his job demanded crisp, incisive logic; only when he found, to his surprise, that he was looked upon as successful, did he slowly acquire confidence to stifle his misgivings. Now, he rationalized his muddled thinking, saying that ideas crystallized from it.

The curtains of the kitchen alcove were drawn back and he found himself staring out through the little window above the sink. It gave a view of a cluster of mellow slate roofs which had changed little in a century and a half. They climbed steeply to a rising mound until, not far away, they cut the skyline in bold, jagged thrusts.

'Did she smoke?'

'Julie? A little, five or six a day, like me.'

There were so many possibilities. A slut sprawled on the couch all day, not bothering to dress until she put on her war paint to go to the club or to search for a man. Reading Dostoevsky.

'Drink?'

'Not more than you have to in our sort of job. I mean, we have to act as hostesses as well . . .'

Idly he opened the doors of one or two cupboards, a few utensils, a few groceries. A tiny refrigerator under the draining board, he stooped to open it. Half a small chicken, a bottle of milk and three or four bottles of Coca-Cola. He couldn't focus an image.

'The waiters know and whatever they bring is always watered down unless we ask for different.' She didn't seem to mind him poking about but she was puzzled by it.

'Was she sacked?'

'From the club? – No.'

'She left before her contract expired.'

'Because she wanted to.'

'That's not what they told me at the club.'

'You've been talking to Thelma, she hated her.'

'Because Julie went to bed with her husband?'

She frowned. 'That might have been part of it but they were at daggers drawn apart from that. Thelma is inclined to throw her weight about and Julie wasn't the sort to be put on.'

'They told me her contract was terminated because she dated patrons of the club.'

'Oh.'

For the first time she was holding out on him, her face resolutely closed.

Wycfiffe sighed. 'She's been murdered. A man made love to her, then strangled her.'

She turned away quickly, her hand to her throat.

'We've got to find who did it – you agree?'

She still did not face him but she said, 'Yes.'

'All right! She broke one of the terms of her contract, Masson-Smythe says he sacked her for it, you say not . . .'

She faced him now, her face once more composed and frank. 'I think they wanted to get rid of her but they didn't dare.'

'Why not?'

'I think that she knew something about them – something which could have got them into serious trouble.'

'What?'

'I don't know. All I know is what happened one Monday after-noon – we have rehearsals then and this time it was the final one for a completely new show so everybody was on their toes. We had lights, costumes, everything, just like a real show. Dawn – Julie, had a new routine like the rest, this time she came on as a Firebird, dressed in dozens of chiffon scarves, all the colours of flame. She had to do a bit of ballet dancing in flickering red and orange lights as she got rid of the scarves and she did it very well. In the end of course she was naked and when she stood in the spot everybody gave her a hand – everybody except Thelma, that is.'

'She comes to rehearsals?'

'Thelma? She produces. She says she was once a Windmill girl and she seems to think that makes her an authority. Not but what she hasn't got some very good ideas.' Sadie was nothing if not fair. 'Anyway, when Julie finished her act, she said, "Well, dear, you aren't exactly a ballerina but I suppose it will have to do!" Julie didn't say anything, it wasn't easy to make her mad and Thelma went on, "After all, it isn't your dancing they come to see, is it?" Julie still said nothing and it would have passed off but when we were back in our dressing room – we shared – Thelma comes in. I could see she was up to something from the look on her face. She went straight up to Julie and said, "I didn't want to embarrass you in front of the others but I think you should have a bath before you do your act. Your legs, my dear – it shows under the lights".'

Sadie paused and moistened her lips like a little girl telling a story. 'Julie was sitting in front of the mirror brushing her hair and I could see her face in the glass. She went white then she turned round and looking up at Thelma she said, "You're doing your best to provoke me but it would be a big mistake. I know enough to put you and lover-boy out of harm's way for a very long time." You would have thought Julie had hit her. She never said another word, just stood there, then she walked out. But from then on there was never a criticism of anything Julie did, not so much as a sly dig.'

'You didn't discover what it was all about?'

'No. When she went out I asked Julie but she was quite rude. "Whatever it was about, Cheesy," she said, "it's nothing to do with you. It's better you don't know".'

'Cheesy?'

'That's what they call me, it's short for Cheesecake.' She seemed pleased to tell him.

'When did this happen? Was it shortly before she left?'

'Not long after she started to work at the club, perhaps four or five weeks.'

He made a move to go then hesitated. 'Did you like her?'

'Like her?' She echoed the words, stalling for time. 'She was easy to live with – I mean she wasn't catty like a lot of girls . . . in some ways she was quite kind.'

'But?'

Sadie searched painfully for words. 'She frightened me, I didn't understand her – she was *wild*.'

'Wild?'

219

'Reckless – always doing things just for kicks. You never knew what it would be next.'

'What sort of thing?'

She looked at him nervously then away again. 'She's dead now, so it can't hurt her. When she first came here we used to go shopping together and suddenly, in one of the shops, she would say, "We're going to have this on the house, Cheesy!" and she would nick something really valuable – not because she wanted it, either.'

Wycliffe nodded his understanding.

'It used to scare me rigid! But she was never happy unless she was taking risks . . .'

Food for thought, quite a lot of it; more might mean indigestion. 'You've been very helpful, Miss Field, I'm grateful and I may have to come back again.'

She had unwound during the time he had been there, now she was taut and nervous again. 'You won't say anything at the club? I can't afford to lose my job . . .'

'I'll be the soul of discretion.'

Four o'clock and the town shimmering in the heat. Over the sea, a canopy of purplish-black cloud slowly creeping up the sky like a giant shutter excluding the sunlight. He drove back to the station and as he got out of the car he felt a sudden chill with the sky darkening overhead. A moment later, a flicker of lightning and an explosive thunder clap heralding the rain. It came hissing and sweeping across the square like a wall of water as he hurried inside.

Fehling was in the HQ room typing his report, Gill was there too, his chair tilted back, his feet on the table, drinking tea. The lights were on because of the storm.

'The Deputy Chief has been asking for you.'

'Here?'

'On the blower. He wants you to ring him back at his home number.'

'What does he want?'

Gill lowered his feet to the floor. 'That's a moot point at the moment, sir. Something with blood in it, I should think, preferably yours.'

Wycliffe poured himself a cup of cold tea. 'Well, what's new?'

'Not much. Fingerprints have matched one of the sets of dabs on your photograph of the guitar player and we've got the gen from Criminal Records.'

'Well?'

'A small-time crook who stepped out of line and tried for the big league. With four others he was concerned in a wages snatch – thirty thousand quid. They held up a security van in Battersea, the others got away but Allen was coshed by one of the security men and he got nicked.'

'Where is he now?'

Gill smiled. 'That's the point – he skipped while he was waiting to go up the steps – literally. He was below stairs in the Magistrates' Court waiting to be brought up and somehow he managed to get away. Nobody seems to know quite how but I gather there are some red faces.'

'It was all in the Crime Report a fortnight back,' Fehling volunteered.

'Was it.' Not a question, a mild snub. 'What do we know about this Allen?'

Gill picked up a typewritten sheet. 'Frederick Charles Allen, 27, five feet nine, one hundred and ninety pounds . . . blah blah . . . No fixed address . . . Approved School . . . Borstal at eighteen . . . six months housebreaking and assault in '61, two years for robbery in '64 . . . three months and six months for possession and trafficking in '66. There's a photograph.' Gill pushed over the information sheet with an attached photograph – a full-face and a profile. A square-faced young man with puffy unhealthy cheeks, deep-set eyes, a weak mouth and a low forehead, a mop of dark hair.

'He's still on the run?'

'Seems like it. Of course he could have got his mitts on that guitar player's photograph anywhere, there's nothing to say that he's in our manor.'

'There's nothing to say he isn't!' Wycliffe snapped. 'Is there any mention of a girl friend?'

'According to the notes he's a bit of a lad with the birds but no special one.'

They were interrupted by the most brilliant flash of lightning yet and a simultaneous clap of thunder which shook the building. The lights flickered but recovered. Wycliffe pointed to the photograph of Allen. 'Have you shown this to Piper at the Marina?'

'It's only just arrived. The chap I spoke to at the Yard was a bit toffee nosed but from what I could gather they're puzzled about Allen. This snatch was way out of his class.'

Wycliffe grunted. He was impatient, irritable, with the uncomfortable feeling that he was being side-tracked. 'Ask them to let us have all they can get on him.'

Then he told them about his own day. 'The Voodoo is being used as a cover for something and the girl found out about it. Admittedly that was months ago but it may still be the reason she was killed.' He turned to Fehling. 'I want you to put a round-the-clock watch on the club, but discretion above everything. If one of your flatfoots gives himself away . . . !' He made a dramatic gesture. 'And find out what you can about the Masson-Smythes, whether they've got any form, but I don't want the birds frightened off their nest. You'd better tell your fellows also to keep a special eye for Allen, if he puts in an appearance there it would mean something though I'm damned if I know what! The question is, what are they up to? What did the girl find out?'

'Trafficking. It's obvious!' from Fehling. 'Ties up with the money and with this chap Allen, he was done for possession and trafficking.'

Wycliffe took out his pouch and began to fill his pipe. 'I'll say one thing for you, you don't give up, but you may be right. It's possible that the girl bought herself into the racket as the price of her silence.'

'A dangerous thing to do, as we all know,' Gill said. He got out his cheroots and went through the ritual of lighting one. 'There are signs that cannabis is slipping through the south-western ports and that the traffic is getting organized with a distribution set-up in the area. Perhaps we've hit on it.'

Fehling drew the plastic cover over his typewriter and patted it like a pet dog. 'I'm sure of it.'

Wycliffe smoked in silence for a while. 'The resin would probably sell on the market for two-fifty a pound. What would they pay at the port?'

Gill shrugged. 'Say twenty-five to thirty.'

'So a thousand pounds should buy somewhere in the region of thirty-five or forty pounds – a tidy weight for a girl on her own.'

'We don't know that she would have been on her own, she said she was expecting her husband.' – Fehling, anxious to sustain his advantage.

'Why was she killed?'

'Probably because she was a thorn in the flesh of the Voodoo crowd.'

'Why was she battered after death?'

'I think you're making too much of that, sir.' Fehling, getting venturesome.

Wycliffe shook his head. 'If she was working for them would they kill her and leave her in possession of a thousand pounds of their money? In any case, does it *look* like the sort of killing you get when rogues fall out?' He stood up and walked to one of the windows of the long room. He stood there, his hands on the sill, his pipe clenched in his teeth, looking down on the square. The rain had stopped, the clouds were thinning and people were on the move again. He got a kick from the fact that nature could still bring the ant-hill to a stop. 'It's possible that you are right, she may have been mixed up in a small time dope ring but that wasn't why she was killed. She was killed in a moment of passion, incidentally, perhaps almost accidentally . . .'

Sardonic grin from Gill. 'Incidental death by accident – that's a new one for the book.'

Wycliffe turned to face them. 'You're getting cheeky, my lad! Anything else?'

Fehling picked up the sheet he had been typing between finger and enormous spatulate thumb. It was a wonder he didn't hit three keys at once when he typed. 'She arrived in town on Sunday night by Royal Blue coach.'

'From London?'

'She took her ticket and boarded the bus at Victoria Coach Station. The driver remembers her because she was "so small and pretty". She got off the coach in the park here and while he was getting her luggage from the boot she said, "I have to get to the Marina, do you think I'll be able to pick up a taxi?" The driver got her a taxi and saw her into it.'

'There are times when I wish I was small and pretty,' Gill said. He watched a chance smoke ring rise from his cheroot, spread and vanish. 'Do you think we've got enough to start leaning on these Masson-Smythes?'

Wycliffe was definite. 'No! For the present we just watch.'

'What about the husband – the girl's husband – Collins, I think you said?'

'I don't know, I haven't seen him.'

Gill and Fehling looked at him in surprise. Gill said, 'You want one of us . . . ?'

'No.' He glanced at the clock. 'The shop will be shut in a few minutes anyway.'

Fehling was on the point of asking what that had to do with it when a warning glance from Gill stopped him. Wycliffe added, as though in self justification, 'The girl's body was only found yesterday morning, it's not as though she'd been dead a month!'

He would have found it impossible to explain his thinking. He could hardly claim that it was logical. All he knew was that underneath his apparent acceptance of what Fehling and Gill had said, he didn't believe a word of it. He was certain that as yet they did not know what the case was about; they had been sidetracked. He knew of old that lift of the spirit which comes when you have one end of the thread in your hand. Suddenly there is a feeling of certainty. You *know*. He was a long way from that! But until then it was necessary to walk softly, to put out antennae, to get the feel and the smell of things. He would never do that if he gathered facts too quickly, there must be time to digest. He said, as though he still required to excuse himself, 'I'll see Collins in the morning. Meantime, Jim, I want you to do some snooping round the docks.'

'To find what, sir?' Gill thought it was best to get his brief clear.

'How the hell should I know? Just snoop.'

'I've been into that angle pretty thoroughly, sir.' Fehling was piqued.

'There's no reason why the chief inspector shouldn't go there himself, is there?' Fehling sighed, audibly, and Wycliffe went on, 'You know the score, Jim. One of the local lads must have a snout inside.'

'I think I get the message.'

'Good!' He envied Gill this job; loitering round the docks, hobnobbing with the men, snooping round the ships, having the odd drink with a hospitable skipper . . . You make a hell of a sacrifice for promotion. 'Have a chat with one or two of the blokes who tend on the ships; you see them lounging about the quay with their tongues hanging out so it shouldn't be too difficult or too expensive . . . And Jim! see if you come across a little dark chap with heavily lined features . . . fortyish – a little rat of a man. Reminds you of a bookie's runner. May have been a seaman, perhaps he still is.'

Gill's raised eyebrows forced him to go on, 'I saw a chap answering that description going into the Voodoo this afternoon, and I don't think Masson-Smythe was too pleased to see him.'

He was on the point of leaving when he remembered the Deputy Chief. He went into his temporary office, picked up the telephone and asked to be put through.

Deputy Chief Constable Bellings was an administrator, possibly a good one, Wycliffe was no judge, but he knew that Bellings could never have been a real policeman. No doubt he had once hammered a beat, no doubt he had done his share of CID work at the dirty end, house to house, drinking with snouts, hanging round warehouses, sleazy hotels and railway stations, questioning pimps, tarts, tearaways and, later, villains in the big time . . . But for Bellings this had been solely a means to an end, the distasteful and hazardous way to the top. Now he was nearly there, he had reached the stage where you could be objective about the disturbing variety of human weakness and wickedness which we call crime. He could smooth it all into a statistical curve and make it a matter of accounting. No wonder he disliked pegs which refused to stay in their proper holes.

'Mr Bellings? Wycliffe here, sir. I understand that you wish to speak to me.'

'To be accurate, I wished to locate you.'

'This is my HQ for the inquiry, sir.'

'I am delighted to hear it. I hope that it will be possible to contact you there. Good night, Charles!'

'Good night, sir!' And the same to you with embellishments!

He passed through the HQ room on his way out. 'I'm off!'

Fehling looked after him, mystified. 'He's cheered up! I thought he was in for a bollocking.'

'It takes him that way,' Gill said.

5

Wycliffe and his wife stood side by side, arms resting on the balustrade, watching the harbour. The rain had gone leaving a fresh clean smell behind, everything looking sharp and incisive. The sun had set behind them but the sky was still a pale washed-out blue with smoky grey wisps of cloud tinged with gold. Out on the water a radio played a nostalgic waltz tune; further along the terrace a honeymoon couple stood close, arms round each other. Wycliffe rested his hand on his wife's. Twenty-four years ago, almost to the day, he had been a beat copper, standing on the pavement, watching people coming out of a cinema. A pretty fair girl hurried down the steps and dived past him in the direction of the bus stop. She wore an oatmeal summer coat and a saucy brown beret. And that might easily have been that, for the bus swept past and pulled in at the stop. But with only a few yards to go, she tripped and fell, badly ricking her ankle. He had rendered first aid. Helen Wills, typist; Charlie Wycliffe, copper. They had come a long way since then but for a long time the words, 'When I'm a sergeant', had seemed to be the Open Sesame to gracious living. 'We'll be able to afford a little car . . .' Now he was a Detective Chief Superintendent and they stayed at four star hotels as a matter of course – or almost.

'A penny for them?'

'I was thinking what a smug bourgeois couple we've become.'

'Do you mind very much?'

'I don't know. I like to think I do.'

Somewhere a clock began to strike the hour. They counted though they knew the time. 'Nine o'clock.'

'Will Detective Chief Superintendent Wycliffe kindly come to reception?' A pause, then the message repeated by the young lady with a plum in her mouth, over the hotel loudspeaker system. 'Thank you!' Click! The voice had come faintly through the open windows of the lounge. Wycliffe went in obediently, stared at by the guests. Television should have convinced them that detectives don't have handcuffs hanging out of their pockets, or two heads. The girl in reception pointed to one of the telephone booths.

'Gill here, sir. I thought I'd better tell you that Ernie Piper at the Marina recognized Allen's photo. He's been staying there since Sunday in the name of Rawlings. Room twenty-one. He's one of those on Fehling's list supposed to be waiting for a ship and he's got a merchant seaman's book.'

'You've brought him in?'

Perceptible pause. ' 'Fraid not, he's skipped.'

Wycliffe's reply drew the attention of the girl in reception.

'He didn't sleep in his room last night. Piper had spotted him as an ex-con but he says he had no reason to think that he was a wanted man. Reasonable enough if you believe . . .'

Wycliffe did not try too hard to sound reasonable in return. 'If Piper could spot him what's wrong with the wall-eyed cretin who questioned him? What's Fehling playing at?'

'I don't think you can blame Fehling . . .'

'You must be joking! Anyway the thing is, what to do? It's too late to set up road checks, he's had twenty-four hours.' He hesitated. 'You'd better get on to the Met, they'll want to amend their circular – and Jimmy, get on to our own boys and stir them up a bit – make the fur fly.'

He was nothing like as sore as he sounded; he rarely was. Early in his career he had realized that you have to put on a show. A reputation for bloody-mindedness which doesn't go too deep is an asset. Actually he was not displeased with the turn of events; something happening in a case is better than nothing, it gives you the chance to take a fresh hold.

'I have to go out, dear.'

'Will you be late?'

'I don't know but don't wait up for me.'

'The story of my life.'

He was going to take the car but, on an impulse, decided to walk. No point in rushing around. It was getting dark, the street lamps were on but the air was soft and balmy. Girls in their summer dresses without coats, young men in shirt sleeves. They paraded through the town and through the dusk in mixed groups, effervescent, noisy, predatory; looking for trouble. Most of them were restrained from making it by a flimsy barrier of convention. On that barrier, getting thinner every year, order and security depend. The educationalists ride their bandwagons, some of them doing the splits on two at once as an insurance. Some day, somebody will knock their heads together and tell them that education is about living. Meanwhile it's your job to seal the cracks, copper!

Beyond the main street he followed the road round the harbour to the Marina. A light high in one of the attics. Kathy's room? Or was she too parading the streets? He hoped so for her sake, anything is better than loneliness when you are young.

The vestibule of the Marina was dimly lit by a fly-blown bulb over the reception desk. Piper was there in his shirt sleeves, entering figures in a cash book. One of Gill's men was half asleep in a wicker chair by a dusty potted palm. He sprang up and tried to look efficient. 'Mr Gill left word that he will be at the station, sir.'

Wycliffe went straight for Piper. 'Where has he gone?'

Piper pulled the lobe of his ear. 'I haven't a clue, super, straight up I haven't! All I know is the bastard skipped without paying his bill.'

'Did he have any contact with the girl while he was here?'

'Not to my knowledge. I've never seen 'em together but you know how it is.'

'Did he go out much?'

A bit more ear pulling. 'Come to think of it I never saw him go out at all. I only ever saw him at breakfast and he was late for that.'

'What about his other meals?'

Piper shrugged. 'I suppose he must have gone out same as the rest.'

Wycliffe rested his arms on the desk and stared at the potbellied little man, compelling his reluctant gaze. Piper shook his head. 'It's no good leaning on me, Mr Wycliffe, I don't even know what all this is about. What's he done? He never murdered the kid, did he?'

Wycliffe straightened up. 'Where's Kathy?'

Piper brightened perceptibly. 'Probably in her room, I'll get her.'

'Don't bother! I'll find it.' He made for the stairs. What would Piper have thought, or Gill, if they knew that out of simple curiosity he wanted to see Kathy's room?

The attic passage was covered with lino instead of threadbare carpet and seemed cleaner because of it. There was only one room

228

with a light under the door and he could hear the muffled sound of a transistor radio. He knocked. The radio clicked off. 'Who is it?' Kathy opened the door and invited him in.

He was not disappointed. She had impressed herself on the little room. The sloping boarded ceiling was half covered with photographs of pop stars, there was a shelf with a few books, an ancient record player, a table, a chair and a bed with a bright orange coverlet. The sash window was wide open, the radio stood on the sill, and she had obviously been sitting by it sewing, for an embryonic garment lay, a little heap of green silky material, on the chair, needle and cotton stabbed into it. She cleared the chair and made him sit down, perching herself on the bed, knees together, dress pulled down. 'You have come about Mr Rawlings?'

'His real name is Allen and he is wanted by the police.'

'I am sorry, he seemed a harmless man.'

'You liked him?'

'I was sorry for him.'

Sitting by the open window he seemed to be almost on top of the docks; although it was night, clanking and hissing and a massive underlying throbbing filled the room. The superstructure of one ship, a pyramid of lights, seemed only a stone's throw away. 'Doesn't the noise keep you awake?'

'I'm used to it. It did at first.'

'Why were you sorry for him?'

'He was ill, always coughing. Although he was such a big man I do not think he is very strong, he must have something wrong with his lungs.'

'Did he go out much?'

She lowered her eyes. 'He did not go out, he spend most of his time in bed reading.'

'How did he manage for food?'

'He go down for breakfast but I bring him the rest. If not I think he would have gone without.'

'You brought him food; did Ernie know?'

She shrugged. 'Ernie!' Gentle, good-natured contempt.

Wycliffe regarded the solemn face, serene, composed. He wondered from what inner strength she derived her composure. The young need a sense of security! The answer to that seemed to be a raspberry. You were forced to blame it on the generation gap and give up trying to understand. 'Did he make a pass at you?'

'No, it wasn't like that.'

'Did he tell you anything about himself?'

'Only that he was waiting for his ship and he was afraid he would not be well enough to join her. He asked me not to talk about him for if the ship people hear he is ill they will not take him.'

'Did you ever see him with the girl who was killed?'

The question seemed to surprise her. 'But he never left his room except . . .'

'Let's take a look at his room.'

Room 21 was on the same floor as the dead girl's but in the main part of the house facing the front, a narrow room over a passage on the floor below. 'Is this how he left it?'

'Just as he leave it, I only pull back the curtains.'

Which meant that he had probably waited until after dark before leaving. It might help though he hadn't much hope. The room stank of eucalyptus, a smell which always revolted him. He looked round, pulling open the drawers of a rickety chest. Two or three sexy paperbacks, a dirty handkerchief. He turned to the tin which served as a wastepaper-basket. Three empty cigarette packets, dead matches and ash, an evening newspaper and part of a sheet of stiff paper, torn raggedly. On one side, the address of the hotel written in pencil, a feminine hand, on the other, at the torn edge, half – the lower half – of a scrawled signature, and below that, typewritten: *per pro Summit Theatrical Costumiers Ltd.*

A slender link but it might mean something. He fished out a plastic envelope and slipped it in. If Thelma Masson-Smythe had written that address – then . . . Then what? He could have pushed his reasoning powers a bit further but that had never been his way. Let it all mill around. He went to the window and looked out; the same view as from Kathy's room but a floor lower. He noticed a long low building on the other side of the road almost by the dock gates. A blue neon sign read: *SNACKS & CAFÉ.*

'Is that the place where she had her meals?'

'I think so, it is where most of our people go, but of course it is always men.'

'You wouldn't think it worth their while to stay open at this time of night.'

'Ah! In the day they serve men from the docks but at night a lot of young people from the town go there, almost like a club. It is cheap and they have a juke box and if he is in a good mood Joe will let you push the tables back and dance. Sometimes I go there, it is very good.'

A few minutes later Wycliffe was down in the street again. It was properly dark now; if you turned away from the glare of the docks you could see the stars against a velvet sky. He crossed the road to the café, looked up and saw Kathy at her window once more, waved and went inside.

A warm chippy smell. A counter with a coffee machine, a tea urn and a cash register, a few bar stools and behind the counter a fat man with a bald head reading the evening paper. But from the other side of a glass partition, plenty of noise, a juke box in full cry. Behind the counter an open door led into a kitchen.

'Evening.' The fat man stirred himself reluctantly.

Wycliffe produced his warrant card. The fat man, who must be Joe, looked at it indifferently. 'I suppose it's about that business across the way?' He nodded in the direction of the Marina. 'Your chaps have been in here already.'

'I know. You told them the girl came in here for her meals and that she came alone.'

'That's right. She did.' Joe looked at the superintendent through innocent china-blue eyes. 'Since they was here I been thinking and the more I think the more convinced I am – I seen that girl before.'

'Here?'

'Where else? I never go anywhere.'

A waitress came through from the other side of the partition, filled two cups at the coffee machine, rang up one and four and withdrew.

'You have a lot of young people in and out of here in the course of an evening, do you know them all?'

He shook his head. 'No, not all but I don't encourage strangers unless they got somebody I know with 'em. It's easier to keep the peace that way. You know where you stand.' He smoothed a massive hand over his bald head. 'How old would you say she was?'

'Twenty-one, give or take a few months.'

'That means she could have been coming in here anything up to say five or even six years ago.' He shook his head. 'I shall have to think about it.'

The street door opened and a girl put her head round, 'Joyce here tonight, Joe?'

'Ain't seen her.'

The head hesitated then made up its mind. 'OK. Thanks. See you!'

'Are you married?'

The fat man looked surprised. 'Me?' He laughed. 'I'm married all right with three kids and they're married too.' He looked at Wycliffe speculatively. 'Like a coffee?'

Wycliffe nodded and waited while Joe drew two cups. When they were steaming on the counter he produced half a bottle of rum and added a tot to each. 'I've never known a copper yet who didn't prefer it this way.'

Two youths came through from the inner room. 'Night, Joe!'

'You're off early tonight, what's up?'

'We're going fishing with Freddie Bates, there's mackerel out in the bay – millions of 'em.'

Wycliffe and the fat man sipped their coffee. In the mellow mood of the moment he would have given a great deal to go fishing all night in the bay with Freddie Bates, or he would have swopped jobs with the fat man if that had been possible. Of course, what you see of another man's life is just the tip of the iceberg. He brought out his pouch and offered it across the counter but Joe refused. 'Don't smoke.'

'You must know a good many of the docks people?'

'I've been on their doorstep for thirty years.'

Wycliffe put a match to his pipe. 'If somebody wanted to get a man out of the country through this port – no questions asked – could it be done?'

The china-blue eyes studied him with disquieting serenity. 'I suppose it could; there'd be a risk of course.'

'How would you set about it?'

Joe smiled showing two rows of ostentatiously false teeth. 'I wouldn't, I like my peace of mind too much. But I suppose it could be done in one of two ways. A suitable man might get hold of false credentials and sign on as crew . . .'

'A suitable man, you say – that means he'd have to be a seaman?'

'He'd need to know his way round a ship.'

'And if he didn't?'

232

'Then he'd have to stow away and if he was going to do that and get ashore in a foreign port he'd need at least one friend in the crew, preferably somebody with a bit of authority.'

'You think it could be done?'

Joe smoothed his bald head. 'Of course it can be done. It would probably be more difficult with the bigger ships but one of the small-ish foreigners . . . You might not have to search too long before you found even a skipper with a blind eye provided there was a big enough bait.'

'A thousand pounds?'

A shake of the head. 'I'm not up with the prices but in my opinion you'd get all you want for that.'

'Thanks.'

Joe grinned. 'Thinking of emigrating?'

'Something like that.'

Wycliffe moved away from the counter and pushed open the glass panelled door which led to the café. A long room with tables down both sides, green painted walls with advertisements for cigarettes and soft drinks, a couple of bagatelle machines and the juke box. Most of the tables were occupied by long haired youngsters of indeterminate sex. No dancing tonight, presumably because Joe's mood was inauspicious. He walked up the aisle between the tables glanced at indifferently. You would need to be a Siamese dwarf with three legs to really engage their attention. The waitress was at the end tables. Her skirt was so short that every time she bent over a table she showed her behind, but she seemed amiable. 'The girl that was killed? Yes, she used to come here. Are you a reporter?'

'Police.'

'Oh!' Her disappointment was obvious.

'Where did she sit?'

'This one by the window.'

'She arrived in the town on Sunday evening and she died on Tuesday night. How many meals did she have here? Lunch and evening meal on Monday, lunch and evening meal on Tuesday – four meals – is that it?'

'She came here Sunday night.'

'All right – five. Five meals but she sticks in your mind as though she'd been a regular customer for months . . .'

The girl swished crumbs from the plastic top of an empty table and wiped the surface with a damp cloth. 'Well, she would. I mean at lunch time she'd be the only woman in the place except me and Nelly and in the evening, well, she wasn't one of this lot, was she?'

'Too old?'

The little carmine lips screwed up. 'Not so much that but she was different.'

'How?'

'I dunno. The way she was dressed for one thing. She had style, and, for another, there was something about her, she was so small and yet she was . . . well, I know it sounds funny but she was perfect. I mean you could look at her as much as you like and you couldn't find anything wrong with her . . .'

'Did she spend long over her meals?'

'Quite a while. She brought a book and read, and after she had finished eating she would sit there with a cup of coffee, reading. She wasn't in any hurry to go.'

'She had lunch here twice when the place must have been full of men, did any of them get fresh with her?'

She shook her head. 'No, they watched her but they never spoke a word to her, not even a whistle.'

'So that each time she came in she sat at that table alone and spoke to no-one but you – is that right?'

'Well yes, except for one lunch time, it must have been Tuesday, a man came in and sat at her table.'

'A stranger?'

'No, a local, a man called Pellow – Dippy Pellow; he comes in for a meal now and then. He runs one of the launches that tend on the boats.'

'What sort of chap is he to look at?'

She screwed up her face. 'A dark little man, he must be forty-five to fifty. If you ask me a nasty bit of work.'

'In what way?'

She shrugged. 'For one thing he can't keep his hands to himself. I mean, at his age – it's disgusting!'

'Did you get the impression that he came here to meet her or was it by chance?'

She hesitated. 'I never thought, but now you mention it, perhaps he did. Don't you whistle at me, I aren't your dog! Some people!'

The rebuke was for a youth, trying to attract her attention by whistling.

'Did the girl do more than pass the time of day with him?'

'Oh yes, they seemed quite matey. I was surprised.'

'You didn't hear anything of what they said to each other?'

She frowned. 'Believe me, mister, I got something better to do here at lunch time than listen to the customers. Which reminds me,' she added curtly, 'I got work to do now.'

'Wait!' His sudden peremptory manner brought her up short. 'Did she have anything to say to you?'

'Nothing more than just to give her order and say the usual things – nice weather an' all that.'

'You've lived in the town a long time?'

'All my life.'

'You didn't recognize or feel that she was familiar?'

The waitress looked puzzled. 'No, should I have?'

Wycliffe shook his head. 'I've no idea!'

He walked back to his hotel. A moist breeze had sprung up from the west and the air was chilly. Rain tomorrow. He pulled up the collar of his jacket and wished that he had worn his raincoat. The street was almost deserted and he felt depressed. An evening newspaper placard fluttered in the breeze: *Police Baffled by Hotel Murder*. For once they were dead right. Thirty-six hours after the discovery of the girl's body he ought to know a great deal more about her. Was she working for the Masson-Smythes? And if so, doing what? According to them they had kicked her out but according to Sadie she had left of her own free will knowing enough to put them both in gaol. Had she tried her hand at blackmail? That would account for the money and in certain circles blackmail is as good a way to get yourself murdered as any other. But surely not in the way this girl had been killed? Unless Masson-Smythe . . . But would he pay her hush money, make love to her, kill her and go away leaving the money? It didn't make sense. And why at a fifth-rate dump like the Marina? And where did the fugitive Allen come in?

At the back of his mind he had an idea which made sense of a good deal. He had scarcely realized that it was there until he had spoken to the café owner about stowaways. Now, to cheer himself up, he elaborated it in unaccustomed detail.

Assume that the girl had left the Voodoo as she said to go to a job in London. There she takes up with Allen, a smalltime crook with ambitions beyond his class. He is nicked and charged, among other things, with attempted murder but he gets away. What if the Masson-Smythes were Travel Agents? Travel Agents for the underworld? Such organizations exist. From time to time the police uncover one and clean it up but where there is a demand . . . This might not be a bad base, especially with agents in some of the other ports of the south and west. If the girl had ferreted out their secret while she worked at the Voodoo the knowledge would seem heaven sent with her boy friend on the run. Allen is sent to lie low at the Marina until the girl arrives with the money. There she is contacted by Dippy Pellow who runs a launch . . . But why does it fall through? Why is she killed? Above all, why is she disfigured?

Wycliffe sighed audibly and drew curious glances from a couple in a shop doorway. He had to admit that there was only one aspect of the case which interested him – the fact that a girl of twenty-one had been strangled. Crimes of violence appalled him and murder most of all. There can be no restitution. Wycliffe numbered among the people he would call friends thieves, pick-pockets, pimps and forgers, but never once had he felt the least glimmer of sympathy or understanding for the man who used violence as one of the tools of his trade.

It was half past eleven when he reached the hotel and still there were two or three dedicated drinkers on the bar stools, the barman yawning behind his hand. Wycliffe ordered a brandy and drank it off.

'Good night to you.'

'Good night, superintendent.'

Now that they knew who he was there would be no chance of maintaining the illusion of being on holiday.

He went upstairs to bed and at last slipped in beside his wife. She spoke drowsily: 'Anything happened?'

'Enough.' He kissed her good night, turned over and fell asleep at once.

6

Drizzling rain from a slate grey sky. Friday morning. Wycliffe sat at a table in the HQ room looking at a photograph. Gill was having his first smoke of the day, perched on the edge of the same table, like a gargoyle. A detective constable hammered away at his report, his papers among the empty teacups. Wycliffe was absorbed: the photograph showed a girl with shoulder length hair gleaming in the light, fine open features, the forehead broad; thin, gently arched eyebrows, eyes wide, with long curving lashes, delicate nostrils and exquisite lips slightly parted and glistening with moisture as though she had just drawn her tongue across them. Yet this was the picture of a dead girl, the product of the pathologist's knowledge of anatomy and the police photographer's skill. Wycliffe had only to supply colour from memory and imagination, the hair was auburn, the eyes blue – almost violet, the skin . . .

'It's a work of bloody art!' Jim Gill said. 'It could have been on the front page of every newspaper tomorrow morning, now it's wasted.'

Wycliffe put the photograph down. 'She hasn't been officially identified yet so let them go ahead and publish. It will be interesting to see who admits to knowing her – and who doesn't.'

He stood up. 'I'm going to see Collins.'

The rain was hardly enough to keep people indoors but enough to make them wonder why they came out. The clock over the post office showed nine thirty-five and already visitors were trailing through the streets wondering whether to risk a boat trip or, if they didn't, what to do with the day. The narrow street was completely blocked by lorries unloading and several shopkeepers were still washing down their fronts.

At the bookshop a little man with brown eyes like buttons was cleaning the windows and had to move his ladder for Wycliffe to enter. Inside two girls were dusting down the shelves with feather dusters and one of them came over to him.

'I want to see Mr Collins.'

The girl obviously wanted to ask him his business but the blank impassive stare which he had cultivated as part of his stock-in-trade discouraged her and she went off down the shop, wiggling her bottom to show that she was not really impressed. He thought that she had gone to fetch Collins but he was mistaken. After a minute or two she came back with an older woman, a woman in her middle thirties, prickly with efficiency, the sort who has convinced herself that a business career is superior to a man in bed. 'Can I help you?'

'I want to see Mr Collins.'

Pursed lips. 'I'm Miss Rogers, I look after most of the firm's affairs.'

Defeated after all. 'This is personal. I am Detective Chief Superintendent Wycliffe.'

He saw her quick frown and, though her manner remained distant and slightly aggressive, he felt that she had become uneasy.

At the rear of the shop, hidden by bookcases, was a white painted iron spiral staircase, and a sign, pointing up it: *Secondhand Department*. He followed her up the steps and into the distilled mustiness of thousands of old books, a bitter sweet smell even to the booklover. The room was of indeterminate size, crammed with bookcases except for a clearing at the top of the stairs where there were two desks set near a window which overlooked the harbour. At the one nearest him an old lady sat knitting. She had an old fashioned boxtill, an account book and a notice which read: *All purchases to be paid for here*. The other desk was littered with papers but there was no-one sitting at it.

'Where's Mr Willie?'

The old lady stopped knitting and looked at Wycliffe. She had cultivated her age; silver hair meticulously cared for; pouting, rather bad-tempered lips, lightly rouged; soft skinned fleshy cheeks with a dusting of powder to hide an unhealthy flush. 'Who is this?'

'A gentleman to see Mr Willie – where is he? Is he up in the flat?'

A measured silence through which the old lady asserted her refusal to be questioned. 'I'm Mrs Collins, you wish to see my son? What about?' She turned to the younger woman. 'No need for you to wait, Miss Rogers.'

238

It was an absurd situation though the tension was obvious. Miss Rogers stood irresolute for a moment, thought better of making a scene, and clattered off down the iron stairs making them vibrate. The old lady watched her go then turned to Wycliffe. 'You were saying?' But Wycliffe was saved the trouble of having to repeat himself.

'You wish to see me?' Willie Collins himself. Excessively tall, a scholarly stoop, pebble glasses distorting his eyes. He looked forty or more but a second look decided that he might be younger; his close-cropped sandy hair was almost boyish though his clothes drooped from his shoulders as though from the wasted frame of an old man.

'Detective Chief Superintendent Wycliffe, Mr Collins.'

Willie blinked down at him. 'Perhaps we should go somewhere where we can talk.' He darted bird-like glances from his mother to the superintendent and back again, the light glinting on his spectacles.

'Willie . . .'

'Yes, mother?'

The old lady hesitated. 'All right, take the superintendent up to the flat, I'll be there directly.'

'There's no need, mother.'

'Of course I shall come up!'

A small gesture of resignation. 'This way, superintendent.'

Through the bookcase maze to a green baize door and out on to a carpeted landing. Stairs down to a tiny hall and up to the flat.

'We have a side entrance, you see.'

Their sitting room overlooked the narrow chasm of the street and it was not a pleasant room. Wycliffe was vaguely aware of a sense of oppression, not entirely due to the poor light, the massive old-fashioned furniture, the sombre browns and fawns. But more to a feeling that this was a room in which people never lived. He would have sworn that the piano in its walnut case was never played, there was no wireless, no television, no books, newspapers, magazines – no knitting even. Yet within seconds the door opened and a woman bustled in. 'Oh! I didn't know there was anybody here.' Obvious that she was lying.

Willie was put out. 'This gentleman wants to talk to me, Aunt Jane.' But her fixed bland smile forced him to introductions. 'Miss Collins – my father's sister . . .'

She was at least twenty years younger than Willie's mother; leaner, harder, with a hint of fanaticism in her protuberant eyes and thin hard lips. Perhaps she had been born to be a nun and missed a turning somewhere, but she would certainly have looked at home in a convent of one of the stricter orders. She had mannish features accentuated by an Eton-crop hairstyle, a bi-tonal voice like an adolescent boy's and her frame was innocent of curves. 'My dear Willie! What have you been doing to bring a Chief Superintendent visiting us? I'm sure that it must be something quite dreadful!' Her boisterously arch manner irritated. She made no move to go and after an awkward silence she seated herself on a straight-backed chair and waited.

Wycliffe was by the window, peering out between the narrow gap in the curtains; he could look into a room across the street where two girls sat at a table piled high with flowers. They were putting them into bunches. Another world.

'When did you last hear from your wife, Mr Collins?'

Willie was still standing, fiddling with a china ornament on the mantelpiece.

'My nephew's wife left him two years ago and he hasn't heard from her since. It distresses him to speak of her, superintendent.' The melting glance she threw at Willie was not lost on the superintendent.

He produced the reconstructed photograph. 'Is this your wife, Mr Collins?'

Willie took the photograph and stared at it myopically. 'Where did you get this?'

'Is it your wife?'

'Yes.'

'Let me see it, dear.' Aunt Jane took the photograph from him, glanced at it and handed it to Wycliffe. What she had seen seemed to reassure her for she became more relaxed. 'It's her all right.'

'What is it, Willie?' His mother, flushed and out of breath. 'So you're here, Jane!' She looked from her sister-in-law to her son. 'Do you really want your aunt to hear all your business, Willie?'

Willie shrugged.

Wycliffe got down to business in self defence. 'I expect that you have heard of the death of a young woman at the Marina Hotel?'

Willie must have guessed what was coming but he gave no sign.

'I'm sorry to tell you that it was your wife who was killed – murdered.'

'Murdered.' Willie repeated the word in a curiously flat tone which seemed to signify complete acceptance.

'She was strangled.'

An incredibly smug look on the old lady's face. 'Well, it's nothing to do with us, superintendent! That girl walked out of here two years ago.'

Wycliffe said nothing. Willie might not have heard for all the impression the news seemed to have made on him. The old lady went on, her voice complacent like the cooing of a well-fed pigeon. 'Something was bound to happen to a girl like that – she was *wicked*! If she's been punished it's no more than she deserves.'

Aunt Jane remained unmoved but she frowned at her sister-in-law. 'That's foolish talk, Ada, it's natural that the superintendent will want to ask us questions.'

Wycliffe produced the ring which had been taken from the dead girl's finger. 'Was this her wedding ring?'

Willie reached out to take it but his mother forestalled him. She turned to Wycliffe, 'This ring belonged to my mother, she was called Jessica and she married William. You can see the two initials inside. Willie gets his name from both sides of the family . . .' She fingered the ring for a moment and her face softened in recollection, but then the customary pout returned. 'That girl had no business to take it!'

'Don't be silly, Ada! You gave it her, it was her wedding ring!' Aunt Jane snapped. 'In any case you've changed your tune, when she first came here nothing was too good for her. I saw what she was from the start but you'd take no notice of me!'

Wycliffe never ceased to marvel at the scarcity value of human compassion and the meagre currency of charity. 'You are required to identify your wife's body, Mr Collins, and after that you will be asked to make a statement.' These people sickened him.

The old lady bristled. 'I really don't see why my son should be involved in the scandal surrounding this woman. He is respected in the town . . .'

'For God's sake shut up, mother!' Willie bleated and the outburst was so obviously unprecedented that it was followed by stunned silence.

His mother recovered first. 'How dare you speak to your mother like that!'

Wycliffe happened to be looking at Aunt Jane and saw the satisfaction on her face. He was physically as well as mentally ill at ease, the room was close, airless, and he could feel the perspiration round his neck soaking into his collar. Willie looked at him, a pleading look. 'Let's get out of here!' Willie got up and he followed him out of the room and across the passage. 'This is my room, I work and sleep here . . .'

The room looked out on the harbour, it was large, oblong, and more of a study than a bedroom. A narrow bunk tucked against one wall was the only apparent concession to sleeping. Apart from this the two long walls were occupied by benches with drawers below and shelves above. Several of the shelves were crowded with rank upon rank of brightly coloured toy soldiers, drawn up in parade ground order. The walls between the shelves were entirely hidden by coloured prints of eighteenth and nineteenth century uniforms. Under the benches, the smaller drawers were labelled: *Colours; Artillery; Small Arms* . . . the large ones, with the names of battles: *Ramillies; Waterloo; Sedan* . . . The wall by the door was a single nest of bookshelves reaching from floor to ceiling and all the books seemed to be concerned with warfare and the strategy of war, lives of famous generals and technical works on weapons.

Wycliffe looked round with appreciation. This was the sort of room of which he approved – professionally. It told him something of its owner, in this case, probably enough to prise off the lid of Willie's reserve. But he would have to go warily. He picked up a splendid hussar from the array of cavalry and examined it, expressing his admiration. 'I suppose these are accurate?'

'Of course! There would be no point in having them otherwise. I don't play with toy soldiers!' A practised answer to the soft impeachment.

'You are a student of warfare?'

The eyes behind the thick lenses were cautious. 'Of the eighteenth and nineteenth centuries. I know little of earlier times and less of modern war, the very thought of which appals me.'

Wycliffe nodded, replacing the horseman carefully in his rank. Collins pointed to a comfortable looking wing-backed chair. 'Sit down, smoke if you want to.' He spoke in nervous jerks. 'I don't smoke myself.' He seated himself in a swivel chair by his desk and seemed to gain confidence in doing so. 'You wanted to ask me some questions about Julie?'

Wycliffe filled and lit his pipe. Collins seemed to be taking the news of his wife's death remarkably calmly – if it was news. But you could never tell with his sort; often, in self defence, they seemed able to contrive barriers of the mind, compartments in which unpleasant events could be more or less isolated, held for a time in cold storage. 'You don't strike me as a violent man, Mr Collins.'

Collins's quick glance darted round the room. 'Violent?' He made a broad gesture. 'You mean all this? No, I'm not in the least violent, quite the contrary. That's probably why my interest in war is historical. The present and the recent past are too immediate for me, but the battles of Marlborough and Napoleon are sufficiently remote for me to be objective about them. I can look at the strategy of a war or the tactics of a battle in much the same way as I might consider the problems presented by a game of chess.' He was undoubtedly shy, reticent, but he could not resist the chance to explain himself, probably because such opportunities came seldom. He fiddled with his blotter and scribbling pad, placing them geometrically on his desk, then he added, 'I *abhor* violence!'

'You think that it is never justified?'

A period of hesitation. 'I do think that but I also think that it is inevitable, human nature being what it is.'

Wycliffe dimly apprehended that as long as his questions remained general the scholar in Willie would see that he got honest answers. But he was less certain what would happen when the questions became personal. At heart, he believed, Willie was still the gangling gawky youth who had been the butt of his schoolfellows, the one who skulked in a corner of the playground, dreading to be noticed.

But Willie was still worrying away at the problem posed by Wycliffe's last question. 'I think that for any man, however mild, there is a point beyond which he may resort to violence.' He smiled vaguely. 'Call it the threshold of violence. We each have our different thresholds and those for whom it is low soon acquire a reputation for habitual violence while others have to be faced with extreme provocation before . . .' His voice trailed off.

'But even the worm will turn at last – is that what you are saying?'

Collins looked at him, hesitated for a moment, then nodded. 'Yes.'

'How old are you, Mr Collins?'

'I am thirty-eight.'

'And your wife?'

'She is – was, twenty, almost twenty-one.' He crossed his spindly legs and started to beat a tattoo on his knee with his fingers. 'I married Julie two-and-a-half years ago when she was eighteen.' He spoke the name Julie in a special way; it occurred to Wycliffe that it was in a similar manner that priests spoke the name of Christ.

'Her parents?'

'She was an orphan, both her parents were killed in an air crash while she was still a child and she was in the care of the local authority – boarded out, I think that is the expression.'

'She was unhappy?'

'On the contrary, I think that she was quite at home with her foster parents. She had been with them for nine or ten years and they regarded her as their daughter. I think that they would have adopted her but for some legal quibble.'

'They raised no objection to her marrying a man seventeen years older?'

'No. Julie had to apply to the Court but her application was supported by her foster parents and by the local authority.'

'Was she pregnant?'

The restless fingers stopped tapping. 'She was not!'

Wycliffe hardly knew what to ask. He wanted some flesh to clothe the bare bones of this unlikely romance. A young, attractive girl immures herself with two shrewish women in order to marry a shy studious man twice her age. There must have been something.

'How did you first meet her?'

It was obvious that the question revived memories which had become painful. He spoke in a low voice and with long pauses. 'She was at school studying for her "A" levels. She was very serious about her work and her foster parents encouraged her. She read widely and she came to the shop first to buy cheap second-hand books – cheap copies of the poets. Then she found that I was interested in literature and she began to discuss her work with me. She would come in after school or on a Saturday and spend a lot of time in the bookroom. I would join her when I could and we would talk about what she had read, about her lessons, and we would plan her future work.'

'At that time you never met her outside?'

'I told you ... .'

'Always in the bookroom with your mother sitting at the cash desk?'

'Why yes. Mother is always there when the shop is open; she doesn't have to be there but it was her job when father was in the business and it would hurt her if she thought she was no longer needed.'

'Rather onerous conditions for courtship, surely?'

Willie flushed. 'There was no question of courtship!'

'But you married the girl!' He felt that he was moving in a realm outside the usual flesh and blood one that he knew, a world, perhaps, where an apt quotation took the place of hot hands in the back of the stalls. Not one that Julie would be at home in, of that he felt certain. 'Whose idea was it? Yours or hers?'

Willie took off his glasses and began to polish them for they had misted over. 'Actually it was my mother's.'

His mother's! Unexpected but it made sense. 'Your mother had a good opinion of Julie, then?'

'Yes, mother thought her a pleasant, well brought up girl.'

And mother thought too, 'A young girl can be guided – *moulded.*' With Willie well on the wrong side of thirty the alternative might be some mature woman with a mind of her own. Wycliffe thought that he could set the scene and write the script:

'*It's time you thought seriously about getting married, Willie.*'

'*I'm in no hurry. In any case, the chance would be a fine thing!*' Forced joke.

'*Don't be absurd, Willie! Scores of girls would jump at the chance.*'

'*All I can say is, I never come across them.*'

'*One in particular.*'

'*Oh?*'

'*Julie.*'

'*Julie! Don't be absurd, mother! She's only a child.*'

'*She's a woman, Willie. She knows it if you don't!*'

'*In any case it's ridiculous, Julie never thinks of me like that. To her I'm just an old buffer who helps her a bit with her work – just like another teacher.*'

'In Julie's eyes you can do no wrong – I know.'

'Nonsense!'

'Ask her.'

And in the end, of course, he did, as he did most things his mother wished. And because he was already in love with her youth and her mind, because he had a romantic vision of a relationship which was intellectual but deeply affectionate, because her foster parents saw it as a good match and because Julie wanted to get out of her council house home – they married.

That was it, or something like it.

The room was quiet, Wycliffe smoked peacefully, Willie stared at the carpet.

'Can men more injure women than to say

They love them for that, by which they are not they?'

The sentiment might well have appealed to Willie, but not, Wycliffe felt sure, to Julie, not to the girl he had seen lying dead at the Marina.

'What happened?'

Outside the pleasure boats were setting out across the harbour, some bound for the creeks and wooded reaches of the river, others for the more adventurous trip across the bay. A watery gleam of sunshine gave them encouragement. The siren of the ferry boat blasted, sharp, angry, as she changed course to avoid running down a dinghy drifting across her path with sails flapping. Wycliffe could see it all, just sitting there. In such a room he would never do any work.

'What went wrong?'

A stupid question about a situation which had never been right but Collins would not see it like that.

'I don't know. At first everything seemed to go well, then Julie started going out in the evenings, she would stay out late and offer no explanation. In the end she just went off.'

It seemed impossible to make any contact, to find common ground. 'Was she a virgin?'

Willie coloured. 'No.' His eyes darted round the room like an animal trying to escape. 'She told me that she had been . . . that she had been raped by a boy when she was fourteen.'

'Did you believe her?'

It was cruelty. 'I don't know.'

246

'The sexual side of your marriage – was it satisfactory?'

Willie could not have suffered more on the rack. 'I don't know. Why do you ask me these questions?'

'When she left you, where did she go?'

The relief was painful to see. 'She got a job in the town – in cabaret. Mother could never forgive her for that, she thought she did it on purpose to humiliate us.'

'And you – could you forgive her?'

The glasses glinted in the light. 'I had nothing to forgive, it was I who was wrong. I realize now that there was no life in this place for a young girl. I should have known, but if she had told me I would have given her anything . . .' There was pathos in his simplicity.

But it wasn't difficult to imagine the situation. Julie treading on eggshells until she began to feel secure. Timid at first, overawed, watched by the two women. 'We don't do it that way dear! Never mind – you'll learn. We all have to be patient, don't we?' And a husband who believed that love could be equated with romance.

Was that how it had been? Or was there something more sinister behind it all?

'What did you do in the evenings before Julie started to go out?'

He looked surprised by the question. 'In the evenings? Julie used to play three-handed bridge with mother and my aunt.'

'And you?'

'I worked in here.'

'Did you expect her to leave you?'

'No, it came as a great shock.' He matched the tips of his fingers together and studied the result. 'She left a letter for mother which upset her very much.'

'Did you try to get her back?'

He nodded. It seemed for a moment that he could not trust himself to speak. 'Then she went away altogether.'

'And you didn't see her again until . . . until when, Mr Collins?'

'I never saw her again.'

'When she left, did she take any money with her?'

'She may have had a few pounds – not much.'

'She did not steal money from you or from the business?'

'Certainly not!' Collins looked startled. 'Why do you ask?'

Why did he ask? Wycliffe looked at the lean anxious face, at the tense body. Not a modicum of repose. What did he expect the poor devil to say in answer to all his questions? I killed my wife? Was that the object of the exercise? That, or to prove that he had done no such thing. Either way it was preposterous. If this man had murdered his wife it was because at thirty-eight he was still adolescent, because all his self control, all the restraints that were normal to him had been eroded by consuming jealousy; it was because he had a silly, selfish mother; because he had been a fool to marry a precocious child. Because of anything except wanting her dead. Now he had to live with his remorse – if he was guilty. What good would questions do him or Julie or anyone? And if there was no guilt then Wycliffe's very presence in the house was an impertinence.

The mood came and went. Julie was dead by violence and violence must be contained. When he had doubts about his calling, and he had them often, that was his answer.

'Who were her foster parents? I shall have to see them.'

'They are called Little. He is a welder at the docks and they live on the Three Fields Estate – 3, Trevellas Way.'

Wycliffe made a note. There was much more he wanted to know but he believed in short interviews with return visits. He stood up. 'Well, Mr Collins, if you are ready, we will get it over.'

'Now?' A scared look behind the thick lenses.

'These things won't wait.'

'All right. I'd better tell them. How long will it take?'

'You should be back in two hours.'

Wycliffe waited while Willie talked to his mother and aunt. Then they had to walk to the police station where Wycliffe had left his car. As they made their way through the busy streets a surprising number of people greeted Willie in a friendly fashion but he hardly seemed to see them.

'You are very popular in the town.'

'I've lived here all my life.'

They had to drive ten miles to the County Hospital and Willie sat staring at the road ahead. Wycliffe tried to start a conversation several times without result. It was only as they were pulling into the hospital car park that he started a topic of his own.

'Was there anything found in her room?'

'What sort of thing?'

He was quick to disclaim any preconceived idea. 'I don't know – anything.'

'A thousand pounds in used notes.'

Willie said nothing.

Dr Franks was in the pathology building and Wycliffe went to see him first. 'I've brought the husband.'

'Husband?' Franks's brows went up. 'I hadn't thought of her with a husband, is she local?'

'More or less. I wanted to ask you, did she dope?'

'Dope? No. There's no evidence of habitual drug taking – why?'

Wycliffe shrugged. 'Don't bother with it.'

As they went in, Franks whispered, 'You've warned him?'

'No.'

The white light shone down on Julie's shrouded form. 'Just one good look, Mr Collins, and I must warn you that what you will see will distress you.' He nodded to the attendant who lifted the sheet. 'Is that your wife, Mr Collins?'

Willie looked down at the body, he stared as though mesmerized; then he gave a queer pathetic little cry and collapsed on the tiles.

7

'Shall we eat out tonight?'

'If you like. Anywhere in mind?'

'A club, a place called the Voodoo, food, drinks, dancing and a floorshow.'

She looked at him suspiciously. 'It hardly sounds your sort of place.'

'It isn't but I think it might be interesting.'

Since the previous evening the club had been under observation. They had been lucky, an ex-policeman kept a tobacconist's shop across the road from the club and it was a simple matter to put a man in the stockroom over the shop. He had a personal radio and there was a telephone in the next room. His brief was vague, to note all the comings and goings when the club was closed and to try to spot any *known* persons entering or leaving when it was open. The watcher had Allen's photograph and instructions to look out for him in particular.

'He wouldn't be fool enough to try to hide out there,' Gill said but Wycliffe was less certain.

Keeping 'obo' sounds simple enough until you have tried spotting someone from a photograph, simple enough if you have the sort of memory which is an index of faces. Really simple only if you have a sixth sense for the job. Wycliffe had kept obo on countless occasions; having a room for it was luxury. For him, sitting in the soft darkness, looking out on the life of the street would have been a pleasure rather than a chore. A flask of coffee and a packet of sandwiches . . . But it is not a permissible recreation for chief superintendents. All the same he refused to be left out entirely. He decided that he wanted to put Masson-Smythe on edge without making any overt move against him. So he found himself an excuse for dining there.

Membership was by no means exclusive, a pound paid at the desk and a signature in the register, but the food and drink were expensive and there was a minimum charge.

Helen looked round the room with interest. It was dimly but cleverly lit by a red glow from hidden lamps so that the totem figures, the voodoo masks and the murals achieved their maximum effect. When they arrived several couples were dancing but most were at the tables eating. They were shown to a table not far from the stage and presented with monstrous menus which were difficult to read in the dim light.

'Why are these places always so dark?' Helen grumbled.

'I think it's supposed to make you feel naughty.'

'It makes me wonder if the cutlery is clean.'

They ordered roast lamb masquerading as *Filet d'agneau au four* and a bottle of Beaujolais.

During the meal Wycliffe saw Thelma from time to time. She moved among the tables saying the right things to the right people but she did not reach the tables near the stage. Her blue gown, high waisted in the classical style, made the best of her Junoesque figure.

'A striking woman,' Helen said.

'I prefer something more cuddly,' Wycliffe said. 'With her I should always be afraid of being eaten afterwards. Shall we have liqueurs?'

They were about to order when Wycliffe spotted Masson-Smythe himself, immaculate in evening dress, brooding over the floor. He saw them and came over, suave, ingratiating. Wycliffe introduced him to Helen.

'You are having liqueurs? Curaçao? Allow me. I insist!' He instructed the waiter. 'I have a rather special Triple Sec which I keep for my friends . . . May I?' He seated himself at their table.

Wycliffe was astonished at the change in him but felt that this solicitous restaurateur act was a bit overdone.

Helen congratulated him on his club. 'Surprising to find such a place in a small town.'

'It doesn't make a fortune.' Masson-Smythe laughed. 'In fact, during the off-season we do no more than break even but we have to stay open to keep the nucleus of a competent staff.' He looked round with a certain pride at the well filled room. 'As you see at this time of year we do pretty well.'

'Have you always been in this business, Mr Masson-Smythe?'

He beckoned to the cigarette girl and selected two cigars from her tray. 'Mr Wycliffe?'

'That's very civil of you,' Wycliffe said, accepting a cigar.

When they were smoking he turned once more to Helen. 'No, I haven't always been in this business. I was chief steward on one of the Atlantic liners for a number of years. When I got tired of shuttling to and fro and had made enough money, I went to work for a London club to learn the business, then I started here.' Was there a challenge in the look he gave the superintendent? From time to time he dabbed with a white silk handkerchief at the beads of perspiration on his upper lip and once he removed and polished his glasses, squinting painfully while he did so.

Soon Helen was telling him about the twins. 'Have you a family, Mr Smythe?'

'Unfortunately, no. This business and a family don't mix I'm afraid.'

'You don't find it necessary to employ a bouncer?' Wycliffe showing a professional interest.

Masson-Smythe grinned. 'We get very little trouble and if the need arises I can give quite a good account of myself.' His candour was disarming.

They chatted amicably until the cabaret was due to start then he left them.

'What did you make of him?'

Helen was thoughtful. 'Smooth. Did you notice his face? He's had some sort of operation and plastic surgery to disguise the scar.'

Of course! That explained the facial immobility – his lack of expression.

'I also noticed that Thelma hardly took her eyes off us the whole time he was here.'

The bandleader announced the first act of the cabaret in a throaty contralto which made the audience laugh, putting them in the mood. A comedian told a seemingly endless stream of blue jokes and he was followed by a female impersonator whose sex might have been questioned anyway. A pretty girl with a guitar sang folk songs and the audience joined in the choruses. Picked out by a pink spotlight in the darkened room she looked young and appealing in her white mini-dress and everyone felt sentimental. Then it was Sadie's turn. It took her seven minutes of more or less graceful pirouettes and postures before she finally parted with her G-string and made her tour of the tables, her modesty protected by two Japanese fans. What her act lacked in skill was made up by her obvious desire to please and in this, to judge from the applause, she succeeded. When she saw the superintendent, she blushed.

Wycliffe looked at his watch. 'Eleven fifteen.'

'They don't close until three and there's another show with different acts in an hour . . .' Helen was enjoying herself.

Wycliffe stood up. 'I'll be back.' He made his way across the floor now crowded with dancers, out into the foyer. One or two couples were sitting out on the banquettes and a noisy crowd of Midlanders, just arrived, were being persuaded to sign the book. He pushed open the door marked *Adams* into the elegant washroom, all white tiles and gleaming chrome. He presented himself to the wall thinking vaguely about the case but he had had enough to drink to feel gratifyingly detached and benevolent. A cistern flushed in one of the cubicles behind him and he heard the sound of a door catch. A vague reflection of movement in the shining tiles and then a violent blow to the base of his skull drowned his senses in a great wave of pain.

When he recovered consciousness he was still lying on the tiled floor but now two men were bending over him, one was a stranger but the other was Masson-Smythe. His eyes were magnified by his glasses and Wycliffe was fascinated by them.

'What happened, superintendent? This gentleman found you lying here.'

The question irritated him and the base of his skull ached abominably. 'Somebody slugged me, what do you think happened?' He realized that he was very angry.

'There's a doctor in the club, I've sent for him.'

Wycliffe struggled to his feet. 'I don't need a doctor!' He looked at his watch and his eyes took a moment to focus; it was eleven twenty-five, only ten minutes since he had left Helen. 'Have you told my wife?'

'No . . . Shall I send . . . ?'

'No!'

A third man joined them, the doctor, a dapper little man with white hair but a springy step. Wycliffe was taken, protesting, to the staff rest room and made to sit while the doctor examined him.

253

'You've got a slight concussion, strictly speaking you should spend the night in hospital but if you promise . . .'

'I'm going back to my hotel but first I want a telephone . . .' And nothing they could say made any difference. The little doctor took himself off, grumbling, and Masson-Smythe hovered while he shut himself in the plush call-box. He dialled the station.

'Wycliffe here. I strongly suspect that Allen has just left the Voodoo, I want . . .'

'He's been picked up, sir. Wilson, who's on obo opposite the club, saw him come out and radioed in. He was picked up by a Panda . . . Excuse me, sir.' A momentary break. 'They're just bringing him in, sir. Do you want . . . ?'

'I want him locked up!' Wycliffe snapped and slammed down the receiver.

Outside Masson-Smythe had worked himself up into a state of indignation about the outrage committed on his premises but Wycliffe brushed past him growling, 'You need a good bouncer! But if you want to do something you can get me a taxi.'

Back at their table Helen looked at him startled. 'What's wrong?'

'Nothing much. Something's cropped up. Let's go.'

She knew him well enough to keep quiet until they were in the taxi and Masson-Smythe had made his final obsequious apology. 'Now!'

He told her, playing down the incident. 'It's bed for you, my boy!'

His head still ached and he wanted to take a couple of sleeping tablets but Helen was adamant. 'Not on top of all that alcohol!'

Actually he slept soundly until first light. When he woke, his head was still sore, though the pain was more localized. He had a raging thirst which the water from his bedside carafe, flat and warm, did little to cure, and he was tantalized by recollections of the heady chilled beer they serve on the terraces of continental cafés. He tried to occupy his mind with the case. There seemed little doubt that Allen had been hiding out at the Voodoo. If Masson-Smythe was fixing a passage for him it would be the logical place to go when he was forced out of the Marina. It might seem to him to be the last place the police would think of looking for him. Allen could reasonably assume that they would expect him to get as far away from the Marina as possible – not simply to move down the street. But, seeing Wycliffe, his logic deserted him and he panicked.

But what had all this to do with Julie? The only link seemed to be that they were both at the Marina . . . It was no good, he couldn't just lie there with his tongue seeming to swell in his mouth and a taste like sour vinegar. With the greatest care he slid slowly out of bed, but he might have saved himself the trouble.

'What's the matter?'

He mumbled something about the lavatory.

'Are you all right?'

'Fine!'

'You're sure?'

He put on his dressing gown and went out on to the verandah. The harbour lay under a pearly mist which merged into the sky. The land on the other side was a vague insubstantial shape. He could hear the steady chug-chug of a motor launch close by but could not see it, then it emerged abruptly from the mist, glided by and vanished again. An old man wearing a peaked cap and smoking a pipe stood with the tiller caught in his back, immobile as a statue. From somewhere below came the smell of coffee. He stole out of the room and downstairs where his status as a celebrity enabled him to get a cup from the kitchen staff who had just come on duty. He felt better. 'More hangover than concussion,' he told himself and hoped that he was right.

Instead of clearing, by breakfast time the mist had thickened to fog and at intervals they could hear the dismal blare of the fog-signal from the lighthouse in the bay. At nine o'clock, despite protests from Helen, he left for the station on foot. It was not actually raining but water condensed from the supersaturated air as from a steam-bath. He lit his pipe but the tobacco tasted like damp straw.

Saturday morning. The men of the new leisure wondering how to spend the time until *Grandstand*, their women bustling round the house, anxious to get out to do the weekend shopping before the best of everything was sold. Wycliffe felt dull, he had no clear idea what he intended to do. Presumably he would question Allen. The HQ room was empty save for a constable who had been typing and was now collecting his work into neat piles. He was young, probably ambitious.

'What's your name?'

'Rees, sir. Detective Constable.'

'What have you been typing?'

'Sir?'

'I asked you what you've been typing?'

'My report, sir.'

'On what?'

'Enquiries at the railway station, the bus station, taxi ranks and car-hire firms about Allen.'

'Allen is in custody.'

'I know that, sir, but I still have to make my report.'

'Do you think that all this paper work helps you to catch villains?'

The young man was too clever to fall head first into that one. He considered. 'I think that catching villains is a team job, sir, and the team must know what all its members are doing. In the long run full communication saves work.'

'You've been brainwashed.'

'Sir?'

'You don't believe in the lone-wolf approach?'

'I think that it's out of date and dangerous, sir.'

Catch 'em young! He wondered if he was out of date and dangerous. To be more accurate, he knew that he was out of date and merely wondered whether he had reached the stage of being dangerous. He had no doubt that Deputy Chief Constable Bellings would say that he had. He went into his little room and stood by the window watching the condensed moisture run down the panes. His head still ached. Gill came in and found him there. 'How's the patient?' Wycliffe said nothing and he went on, 'We shall have to box a bit clever on this one. After all, he's already been charged with one major crime and the Yard'll want him back, pronto.'

'They can have him when we've finished with him. I want him as a witness in a murder case and for assaulting a police officer.'

Gill was about to say something but changed his mind. 'I'll be off.'

'Where?'

'To the docks, looking for a bent skipper.'

'Where's Fehling?'

'He's there already, waiting for me. I think he's avoiding you.'

'And well he might!'

When Gill had gone he picked up the telephone. 'Send Allen up . . . and send DC Rees with his notebook.' He hadn't prepared for the interrogation, never given it more than a fleeting thought. After all, he believed in playing things by ear. The great exponent of off-the-cuff detection. Old-fashioned! You get a feeling or you stop being a copper – that's what his first DI used to tell him.

His first reaction on seeing Allen at close quarters was one of incredulity. The man was built like a heavyweight wrestler; yet to hear Kathy talk you would have thought that he was a pitiably weak creature. And to imagine him with the fragile delicacy of the dead girl! The imagination boggled.

His eyes were brown, restless, they shifted focus like the eyes of a nervous animal. Probably his violence sprang from fright. Not that that was any excuse.

Wycliffe looked him up and down coolly. 'I've had you brought here to answer questions concerning the murder of Julie Collins at the Marina Hotel last Tuesday night. I am not concerned with the crime you have been charged with in the Metropolitan Police District – is that clear?'

'I don't know anything about any murder.'

'I said, "Is that clear?" '

'Yes.'

'Sit down.' He nodded to the uniformed constable who removed the cuffs.

Allen sat down and Wycliffe signed to the constable to leave. Rees came in and took his seat in a corner of the room.

'How old are you?'

'You've got it on the sheet.'

'How old are you?'

'Twenty-seven.'

Wycliffe relit his pipe, watching the man over the flickering flame of the match. 'Do you smoke?'

'Cigarettes.'

Wycliffe always carried a packet though he never smoked them; he tossed them over. 'Help yourself.'

Allen's fingers were clumsy and he bruised the cigarette as he drew it from the packet. He stood up, bending over the table for Wycliffe to light it, then he puffed greedily. A moment later he was shaken by a violent spasm of coughing.

'What's the matter with you?'

'I've got a weak chest. I was TB as a kid, perhaps I am again.'

A bid for sympathy? From time to time the bright little brown eyes lighted on Wycliffe only to flit away again as soon as they met

257

his, but they kept coming back. 'He's wondering what to make of me.' Which was all to the good.

'You were staying at the Marina when that girl was killed, why were you there?'

A slow shrug of the massive shoulders. 'It's as good a place as the next to keep out of the way.'

'What was your connection with the girl?'

'None.'

'Your prints were found in the girl's room.'

Allen blew smoke through his nostrils. 'You can't con me, copper!'

'On a photograph in her handbag. How did you get to know her?'

An uneasy movement but no reply.

'She was strangled, then disfigured, her face beaten in with a brass weight which had been used as a door stop. You can imagine.'

The man's hands grasping the arms of his chair tightened and relaxed but he gave no other sign.

'Do I bore you?'

A quick frown.

'Where did you meet her?'

Silence.

Wycliffe reached for the telephone. 'You and I are going for a little trip.' He spoke into the mouthpiece. 'Have my car brought round and tell the constable who delivered Allen to come up.' He was play-acting and he hardly knew with what purpose. 'You too, Rees.'

The constable arrived and Allen was escorted down to Wycliffe's car. He was put into the back seat between his gaolers and Wycliffe drove to the county hospital. The fog was beginning to clear inland, the sun was struggling through and vapour rose from the wet roads and fields. He parked the car and led the way to the pathology building. Allen and his guards were left in a waiting room while he went in search of Dr Franks.

After half an hour Allen was escorted to the mortuary. The central lamp shone down on a covered trolley. Wycliffe and Franks stood on one side while Allen was brought to the other. 'Uncover the face.'

Allen's eyes darted round the room but were drawn at last to the mutilated face of the girl on the trolley. He had prepared himself but even so he could not suppress a movement of revulsion. 'This is your girl friend, Allen, somebody did this to her.'

Allen turned his head away. 'Let me get out of here!'

'Stay where you are!' Wycliffe's voice was like a whiplash. 'What's the matter with you? Don't you recognize her?' He drew the covering sheet further back. 'Perhaps you recognize the mole – look!' Brutal! But the only kind of language Allen and his like would understand.

Allen made a violent movement to shake off the two men who held him but failed. Wycliffe replaced the sheet. 'Have you ever had a blood test?'

It was obvious that the man was near the limit of endurance, but impossible to say which way further pressure would affect him. He might go berserk or simply fold up.

'I want you to have a blood test now; Dr Franks will prick the lobe of your ear and take a drop of blood.'

Allen looked at Wycliffe as a tormented dog looks at its tormentor, dumbly, uncomprehending. Franks came round the trolley, an assistant dabbed Allen's right ear lobe with surgical spirit and Franks produced a tiny lancet and phial. Allen winced as Franks squeezed a few drops of blood into the phial; then another dab of surgical spirit and it was done.

'What's it for?'

Wycliffe glanced at him indifferently. 'Just to check.'

'If you would care to wait in my office . . . ?' As they had planned, Franks led Wycliffe down the corridor to his office. Allen and the two policemen followed. Wycliffe seated himself in the swivel chair behind the metal desk and signed to Allen to take the other chair.

'Wait outside,' to the policemen.

It was a repetition of the scene in Wycliffe's office but now Allen was paler, even more nervous and less sure of himself. 'I didn't kill her.'

Wycliffe regarded him with a detached, impersonal stare. 'We shall see.' He looked round the white aseptic room; even the books and files looked as though they had been sterilized, but the window opened on to a little garden with fuchsias in flower and gladioli flaunting themselves. He had to shift his chair to avoid the direct path of the sunlight.

'Are your parents alive?'

'I don't know.'

'Why were you sent to an approved school in the first place?'

'What does it matter?'

'Was it a sex offence?'

'No!' The denial was prompt and vigorous.

'Women like you, I expect. I mean that you can have all the women you want?'

A glimmer of a smile which vanished at once. 'I've never had to twist their arms.'

'But you despise them?'

He raised his hands in a gesture. 'I take them as they come.'

'I gather that this girl who was murdered was pretty keen on it.'

No answer.

'Do you know what they were doing when he killed her? He was having her. Does that surprise you?'

Allen was sitting bolt upright in his chair, tense, scared.

'Have you ever felt like killing a woman at the very instant when . . .'

'I didn't kill her.'

Wycliffe went on as though he had not spoken. 'Of course, there is another possibility, her room is next to the fire escape, you could have been standing out there watching and then . . .'

The brown eyes were focused steadily on Wycliffe's now and Allen half rose from his chair. What would have happened if Dr Franks had not come bustling in is impossible to say. Ostentatiously Franks handed Wycliffe a slip of paper. 'This is what you are waiting for.' As he went out he gave Allen an inquisitive glance. Wycliffe looked at the paper: *Group A. Rh.+ve.* He folded it and put it carefully into his wallet, then he turned again to Allen. 'I think that you were on the point of telling me something.'

Allen hesitated, there was a moment while decision hung in the balance, then he suddenly went limp. 'All right, I'll tell you what I can.'

'You recognized the body in there as that of the girl who stayed at the Marina?'

'Yes.'

'She was your girl friend?'

'You could call her that.'

'What was her name?'

'She called herself Dawn Peters but I think that was for the business . . .'

'You are willing to make a statement?'

'I've said so, haven't I?'

Wycliffe relaxed. From now on it would all be plain sailing as far as Allen was concerned. A born bully, he hadn't the guts even to be a good crook. Wycliffe stood up and went briskly to the door. 'Right! We'll get back to the station.'

The two policemen escorted Allen out and Wycliffe, after a brief word with Franks to satisfy his curiosity, followed them. It was half past twelve when they arrived back and now Wycliffe was looking at Allen with a proprietary air, he was almost jovial. 'Hungry?'

'I haven't had anything since seven this morning.'

'Take him down, see that he gets a good meal, then he can have a sleep.'

Wycliffe had decided to go back to the hotel to lunch with his wife but when he went up to the HQ room he found Gill and Fehling there.

'I think Fehling has hit upon something, sir.'

Fehling, looking sullen, like a schoolboy with a grievance, said, 'I doubt if it's of any importance but this morning, when Mr Gill told me that you suspected the money might have been intended to get Allen out of the country, it set me thinking. My mind had been on drugs but if it's a question of an illicit passage, that narrows the field. There are very few ships where you could get away with that these days.'

'Well?'

'There's a freighter alongside the Eastern breakwater, the *Peruvia*, four thousand tons, Liberian registered. She was towed in several weeks back having had a fire which badly damaged her super-structure and accommodation. She's due to sail on Monday which would have suited Allen. The girl was there with the money . . .'

'I suppose it's a line of enquiry,' Wycliffe said without much enthusiasm, 'but we shall need more than that . . .'

'There is more,' Gill cut in with impatience. 'The skipper is a Spaniard but he speaks English of a sort, and he's been seen several times lately drinking ashore with Dippy Pellow, the chap who runs one of the tender launches. And finally, when she sails on Monday, she's bound for Barranquilla.'

'Never heard of it.'

'It's the Caribbean port of Colombia.'

'And that's supposed to mean something to me?'

'It will if you read this, it's the Yard's reply to your request for further information about Allen.' He handed Wycliffe a typewritten sheet. After details of the offences for which Allen had received his various sentences, the memo went on:

Allen comes from a respectable family. His father was a school-teacher in Surbiton. Both parents are now dead but he has a sister who married an oil engineer and is believed to be residing in Venezuela. He seems to have had no contact with his parents after . . .

Wycliffe handed back the sheet. 'Geography is not my strong point but I assume that Venezuela is next door to Colombia – is that it?'

'That, sir, is it. I suggest we have a go at that skipper and that we pull in Pellow for questioning.'

'Have a go at the skipper by all means but Pellow will keep, he can't run away.'

Wycliffe could hardly admit it but he was bored with this side of the investigation, for he was convinced that it had no direct bearing on the girl's death and that was all that interested him. Why had she been strangled? And above all, why had she been disfigured? He was on the point of telling Gill to carry on when it occurred to him that here was a chance to potter round the docks in the line of duty and there must be some privilege for rank. 'I'll see this Spanish skipper.' He was cowardly enough to add, 'Then if there's any legation trouble it will be my problem.'

Fehling's face betrayed his thoughts. 'In that case, sir, I'll be off to lunch.'

'You're coming with me, Mr Gill can eat for both of us.'

For once Fehling's petulant expression changed to a smile.

They drove through the town to the dock gates. As they passed the Marina Wycliffe wondered what Fehling would say if he suggested dropping in on them for lunch. If he could have been sure of another curry he would have been sorely tempted. On the waste ground beside Joe's café four or five articulated lorries were drawn up. 'Do you fancy something?'

'In there?'

'Why not? He does a good line in coffee with a dash of rum.'

After a moment Fehling decided to treat this as a joke. Wycliffe pulled up at the police barrier which was immediately raised. Evidently they recognized Fehling. Inside the gates he drew into the car park.

'We can drive to the ship, sir.'

'Let's walk.'

Despite the interest of the place Wycliffe almost wished that he had taken the car. Against Fehling's immense bulk he felt insignificant and as Fehling had the length of leg to go with it he found himself hopping over railway tracks, dodging hawsers and almost running to keep up. Finally he had the courage to set his own pace, which forced the inspector into line. He grinned to himself. Easy really!

It was Saturday and the place was almost deserted. They skirted the four main graving docks but Wycliffe made a small diversion to look into the basin of the largest, which housed a monstrous tanker. From the twin propellers his eye swept up over the great bulbous curve of grey steel plates to the rail towering above him. *British Emblem. London.*

'Seventy thousand tons,' Fehling said.

It was high tide and along the wharf the steeply angled gangplanks to the high riding unladen ships worried Wycliffe who had no head for heights. But the *Peruvia*, when they reached her, seemed tiny by comparison. Her renovated superstructure gleamed with fresh white paint but her hull was mottled with great splashes of red oxide where rust had been chipped off. Near the head of the gangway, which Wycliffe climbed easily, a swarthy little man in blue dungarees lent on the rail smoking. He seemed not to see them until Wycliffe addressed him. 'We are police officers and we wish to see the captain.'

The man, without moving from the rail, looked them up and down and without a word returned to his contemplation of the wharf. Fehling's reaction was swift and effective. '*Policia! Captain Hortelano immediatamente!*'

Whether it was the basic Spanish or the drill sergeant's voice and manner, the little man was galvanized into action. 'You have hidden talents, Mr Fehling,' Wycliffe observed.

'His lot have a healthy respect for the police,' Fehling confided.

They were led up a companionway to the bridge and ushered into the presence of the captain with a single word, '*Policia!*'

The captain was small and dark and sallow, a wiry little man in a dusty creased uniform with tarnished buttons and braid. His breath smelt of whisky and his speech had that special precision of enunciation which comes when a hard drinker is at a particular stage of drunkenness. His manner was ingratiating and his English good. 'You will drink with me, gentlemen?'

'No thank you.'

'That is a pity, I look for an excuse as it is not good to drink alone. All the same . . .' He fetched a bottle from a wall cupboard and poured himself a generous double.

They were in his day cabin, which was fresh from the hands of the painters, and Wycliffe had the impression that the captain was not at home in it. Perhaps he was accustomed to a cosy squalor. 'Do you carry passengers on your ship, captain?'

'Passengers? She is not a passenger ship – no. But you understand it is sometimes done that we take one or two. To keep the law they must sign as crew but they do not work and they pay. Last year we have a famous English writer and he stay with us three trips.'

'You are proposing to take a passenger when you sail on Monday?'

The captain drank half his whisky in a single swig. 'No, it was spoken of but the gentleman had not the proper papers.'

Wycliffe was standing at the curtained porthole, staring out over the harbour; the dinghies were racing in the Roads beyond the breakwater. Fehling, monumental and immovable, stood by the door. The skipper's nervous gaze flitted from one to the other.

'The gentleman in question is under arrest.'

'So? It shows, does it not, how careful one must be?'

'You did not know that this man was wanted by the British police for robbery with violence?'

The brown eyes widened. 'But certainly I do not know! Would I ever . . . ?'

'Then why do you suppose he was going to pay a thousand pounds for his passage?'

'*Dios mi!* A thousand pounds? That Pellow – he is . . . he is *sin vergüenza!* He has talk to you, señor, but you are not correctly informed. One hundred pounds is all I was to get for this man's passage to Barranquilla. One hundred English pounds!'

Wycliffe had turned away from the porthole and he was now facing the captain. 'Perhaps you will give me the address of your owners?'

'Owners? What is this? They must not hear of this man, it was not an official arrangement, you understand, and I am in much trouble already because of the fire. If I am in more trouble my career at sea will be finish!'

Wycliffe shrugged. 'If you want to sail on Monday and you don't want your owners to know about this spot of bother, all you have to do is to tell the truth.'

'But I have told you . . .'

Wycliffe took a step towards the door. 'We'll get the address from the docks office.'

'But señor, wait!'

'Well?'

'I was to have five hundred pounds to put this man ashore in Barranquilla.'

'Without passing through immigration?'

He nodded.

'That's better. Now listen to me! If you leave the docks premises or attempt to communicate with this man Pellow or anyone else before you sail on Monday, I'll have you arrested. You understand?'

'I understand, señor. Be assured . . .'

Wycliffe strolled out on to the bridge and stood for a moment by the wheel, looking for'ard over the holds to the bow and beyond. He could see her pitching into a great wall of water, shipping it green, the decks awash, then the shuddering recovery as she began to rear like a porpoise, only to be ready for the next plunge . . .

'Captain Mac Whirr, I presume!'

'Cheeky devil! So you read Conrad?'

'I like yarns about the sea.'

Wycliffe wondered if he might have to revise his opinion of Fehling.

The docks' clock on its steel tripod, rising above the sheds, showed a quarter to two. 'Is there anywhere we can get some lunch?'

'I know a good steakhouse . . .'
'With a glass of beer?'
'At two o'clock? You must be joking!'
'Well let's make for the nearest pub and have one before we eat.'

8

Allen looked more composed when they brought him to Wycliffe's room in the afternoon. He sat in the chair by the desk and waited. Wycliffe stood by the window which looked out on to the blank garage wall. Detective Constable Rees, the young man to whom Wycliffe had talked that morning, installed himself in a corner with his notebook. This day had a special significance for him: he had heard much of Wycliffe's reputation and had followed all his cases; now, in a manner of speaking, they were working together. With ball-point poised he waited for the great man to begin. Wycliffe turned from the window, seemed about to sit down then changed his mind. He felt in his pocket for his pipe, brought it out, lit it, then threw over a packet of cigarettes to Allen. 'You're going to need these.' He smoked for a while then said, 'Well, my friend, I'd better caution you – you are not obliged to say anything unless you wish to . . .'

The little alarm clock on the shelf showed a quarter past three. Allen was smoking and staring at the floor. Wycliffe was moving restlessly round in the tiny space between his desk and the window, like a caged animal.

'When did you first meet her?'

'Six months ago. She was working for a group of three Soho strip clubs. You know the sort of thing – they employ a dozen or so girls who shuttle between the clubs getting in twelve or more acts apiece between two and midnight, six days a week.'

'She must have been making good money.'

Allen lit another cigarette from the stub of the old. 'Seventy-five a week.'

'What were you doing?'

Allen looked blank.

'All right! Save it! You were looking round for a likely bird who would keep you until you did your next job.'

Allen was indignant. 'What if I was? It wasn't immoral earnings!'

Wycliffe chuckled. 'There could be two opinions about that! Anyway you turned on your charm and she fell for it.'

Allen made a gesture of dissent. 'I didn't have to turn on any charm with that one, she was like a bitch in heat and after the first time I couldn't be in a room with her for five minutes before she had her pants off.'

'Where was she living?'

'She shared lodgings with another girl in Bayswater.'

'Address?'

Allen hesitated. 'I can't remember, somewhere behind Paddington Station – Sussex Place, Sussex Gardens, Sussex something . . . I could take you there.'

'You moved in?'

He shook his head. 'It wasn't on, the landlady was an interfering old bag, in any case I didn't want that . . .'

'She came to your place?'

'No, I didn't want that either; if a chap is known by his bird it gives you coppers a bit of a lever.'

'So what did you do?'

'Hotel rooms – some nights and Sundays.'

'What was she like?'

'In bed? She'd been around and she knew all the tricks.'

'And yet you hooked her.' Wycliffe wondered what the young constable was making of all this. Was this the sort of interrogation he had expected?

Allen looked modest. 'She said she never got any satisfaction from other men.'

Wycliffe did not even smile. 'Did she tell you anything about her life before she met you?'

'Not much, she said that she had worked in a club down this way.'

'Nothing else?'

Allen grinned. 'She said she was married.'

'Did she give any details?'

'She said he was an old geezer.'

'Anything else?'

'She said he was creepy.'

268

'What does that mean?'

Allen shrugged. 'He played with toy soldiers like a kid.'

'Why did she marry him?'

'God knows! Why do women do things?' He paused, then added, 'She said she was an orphan and I think she lived in some sort of home. She wanted to get out and this guy had money.'

'And where did this idyll take place?'

'Search me!'

Poor Willie! He had been no more than an episode in her life. Amusing to look back on, to tell her friends about. A creep who played with toy soldiers. Why had she married him? To escape from a childhood hedged in by foster parents, children's officers and the featureless omnipotence of bureaucracy. By marrying Willie she transformed herself into a woman, a woman free to explore wider horizons from a secure base. And the base served its purpose. The truth? Even as the thoughts passed through his mind he knew that they were a ludicrous over-simplification. Julie must have had her fears and her frustrations, her disappointments and her moments of bitter self reproach. Times when she felt sorry for her amiable husband and remorseful for what she was doing to him. But in the story she told, all this would be left out.

What was DC Rees thinking in his corner? Of the silences in particular? No doubt he had been told that when questioning a suspect the pressure must be kept up, never allow time for pre-varication, change ground often . . . But now the suspect's eyes were closed, the room was warm and it was possible that he was dozing. The chief superintendent himself seemed near to it as he sat, elbows on the desk, his chin in his hands, staring into space.

'Was she still in these lodgings when she came down here?'

Allen opened his eyes. 'No, she'd moved to a flat.'

'Address?'

'Queensberry Mansions, Felton Terrace, Hampstead.'

'Up in the world.'

'You can say that again. She packed in with the strip joints about two months ago when she found she had a voice. Some agent took her up and she got a job in cabaret – real West End stuff . . .'

'Did you live in the flat?'

'No, she wanted me to but it suited me to carry on as before. You don't want to get in too deep with a bird.'

Wycliffe nodded as though he were in complete accord with this sentiment. 'And next thing she's staying at a crummy joint here in the far west with you on the same floor, pretending not to know her. And she gets herself murdered.' His manner changed suddenly from a lazy somnolence to vigorous aggression. 'Now, my lad, I want it straight. I know most of the story so don't try any tricks unless you want the murder rap slapped on you.'

Allen was wide enough awake now and resentful. 'I said I would talk and I will, there's no need for threats. You see, I got nicked for this wages job . . .'

'I don't want to hear about that, start from the time when you skipped.'

A moment for reorientation. 'Well, I was lucky and I got away clean. I dodged about for the rest of the day then when it was dark I made for her flat. She always said I could count on her if I was in trouble and now was her chance.'

'She knew you were bent?'

'She knew I'd done a few jobs.'

'She approved?'

He grinned. 'She seemed to get a kick out of it. She couldn't hear enough, wanted every detail. She used to egg me on, "Why don't you try something big? So far you've been taking risks for peanuts!" – that sort of talk.'

'So you went to her flat.'

'Yeh, and to give her her due, she made no bones about taking me in, she was tickled to death at the thought of the cops looking for me. I hadn't been there long when she asked me if I'd like to get out of the country. I said the chance would be a fine thing, then she said, "You told me you had a sister in Venezuela, would she take you if you could get there?" I said she would, partly because I believed it and partly because anything is better than going back inside. It may be some people's idea of a rest cure but not mine. I asked her what it was all about but she wouldn't tell me, she just said I'd be surprised at the contacts she had. Anyway, I didn't really believe her. We went on for a few days then one evening she came home and said it was all cut and dried. She told me to get a passport photo from a place down the road and some new clothes. When I was fitted out she gave me fifty quid and said I was to come down here and book in at the Marina. I was to pretend that I was a seaman waiting for a ship and she would join me later. She told me to keep out of the way and not to let on I knew her when she arrived . . .'

'You didn't know the details of her arrangements?'

'No, she was queer like that, you had to let her make a mystery out of everything.'

'When did you arrive at the Marina?'

'I travelled down Saturday night and got there Sunday morning.'

'When did the girl arrive?'

'Sunday evening but I didn't see her until breakfast-time Monday. She didn't make any move then but she looked in my room afterwards and told me to come to her room that night round eleven. She said, "Later on I shall have company and it wouldn't do for you two to meet." '

'Well?'

Allen shifted his chair to avoid the sun which now streamed into the room from above the roof of the garage. 'Well, I went along at eleven and she told me everything was fixed. She was like a kid with a new toy – excited. She said I was to be put aboard a ship on Sunday night and that I should sail on Monday. Once outside British waters I would be treated like an ordinary passenger and on the other side they would put me ashore in Colombia with no questions asked. I should have five hundred dollars American and a passport good enough to get me across the border with Venezuela.' He lit another cigarette and inhaled deeply, starting off his cough again. When the cough had subsided he went on, 'I asked her where the money was coming from and she said that was the cream of it, her husband would pay.'

'Her husband?'

'That's what she said.'

'What happened then?'

'Happened? – nothing. I went back to my room.'

'You didn't give her a tumble to round off the evening?'

'No, she tried it on but I was in no mood for it. I'd been pretty low with bronchitis and – well, she just had to go without.'

'How did your prints come to be on the photograph in her handbag?'

'I've been thinking about that. I remember she asked me to get her handkerchief from her handbag. I saw the photo and asked her who it was.'

'Why did she carry it round?'

'Search me! She always had some man's photo in her bag, usually more than one.'

'Talking of photographs, did you notice one of her on her dressing table?'

Allen nodded. 'Yeh, in a frame, one she was fond of and carted everywhere with her.'

'When did you see her again?'

'I never did. Next day your blokes were swarming all over the place and as soon as I got the message I decided to beat it when I got the chance.'

'What were you doing in the Voodoo?'

'I had to keep off the streets and it was somewhere to go for the evening.'

'You're a liar!' Wycliffe spoke without heat. 'Do you think it was chance we picked you up as you came out?' He stood up and moved out of the sun, which was striking down exactly where he sat. 'You're not smart enough to be a crook, my lad! It would pay you to go straight. The girl arranged with the Masson-Smythes to have the thing set up for you and you thought you could go back to them and put the screw on a bit – "Look after me or else . . ."'

'That's not true!'

'Then why didn't you clear out altogether when you heard the girl had been murdered? Why hang about the town? You had twenty-four hours' start.'

'I was afraid of road checks.'

Wycliffe sighed. 'You make me tired! You're not even a good liar. What did you think when you heard that she'd been murdered?'

Allen looked at him, uncomprehending. 'I was scared – wouldn't you be? I mean, there was I on the spot, I'd been in her room and the police were already after me . . .'

Wycliffe was looking at him in detached appraisal, his stare was unnerving. In the end he made a little gesture. Impatience? Distaste? Helplessness? 'I'm going to send you back where you came from in the morning; you're no use to me. If it turns out that you did kill that girl . . .'

'I didn't kill her – why should I? I lost by it if anybody did!'

Wycliffe shook his head. 'For God's sake get him out of my sight!'

Allen sneered. 'That's the thanks you get – from cops!'

'Thanks for what?'

When they had taken him down Wycliffe stood for a long time looking out of the window and Gill found him there. 'Evening, Mr Wycliffe!'

Wycliffe did not turn round. 'I've just had a tête-à-tête with Allen. He seemed willing enough to talk about the girl but cagey on the subject of the Masson-Smythes. We want enough to put that pair inside so when Fehling comes in let him have another go at Allen – lean on him a bit.'

'I would enjoy leaning on that character myself . . .'

'No doubt, but you'll have to deprive yourself. I want you to ring the Yard, tell them we shall be returning Allen tomorrow. You can also tell them that you are coming up and that you'll need assistance.'

'To do what?'

'Contact the places she's worked at, get on to her former landlady and the neighbours in her new flat . . . Do the rounds, then ring me and tell me who did her in and why.'

Gill perched himself on the edge of Wycliffe's desk. 'When do I leave?'

'Tonight, there's a train around nine.'

'And how long have I got?'

Wycliffe turned to face him. 'Oh, don't hurry yourself, say twenty-four hours. Ring me tomorrow evening.'

Gill grinned. 'A cinch! Especially on a Sunday when London is like the Sahara desert.' He took out one of his cheroots and lit it. 'I haven't got Allen's story fitted in yet. If he's telling the truth, it was he who kept Millie awake in the next room. "Just voices", she said, "a man and a woman talking". Then she heard someone come out of the girl's room – that must have been Allen leaving. But Millie says next time she woke she heard a couple in there quarrelling and that the quarrel ended in lovemaking. We believe that the man who killed her was the man she made love with, so it couldn't have been Allen, he's the wrong blood group.' Gill broke off. 'Am I boring you, sir?'

'No, just confusing me, but carry on if you must.'

'Another visitor then. The man of the fire escape? If we believe Allen, that man could have been her husband come to deliver the money. If you ask me, it's a cock-up of a yarn. I mean, why kill your wife when you've just given her a thousand quid to help her get her lover out of the country?'

Wycliffe moved away from the window and sat at his desk. 'Get off my desk!'

Gill slid off the desk grinning. Wycliffe put his fingers together and stared at them thoughtfully. 'You have a way of making even the truth seem ridiculous, Jim. In any case, you haven't asked the most important question – how does one account for the restraint in killing and frenzied hatred suggested by the disfigurement?'

'I suppose it's possible that she was killed by one man and disfigured by another.'

'It's possible, certainly, but difficult to imagine a reason for it.'

A constable came in with a cup of tea on a tray. 'Sorry, sir, I'll fetch another cup, I didn't know the chief inspector was with you.'

'The chief inspector is leaving,' Wycliffe growled, and when the constable had gone, he went on, 'Run away, Jim. As a Dr Watson you're a dead loss and there isn't room for two Sherlocks.'

It was true, reasoned argument from Gill or from anyone else only confused him. Most of the time it hardly mattered but there came a stage in every case when it mattered a great deal. He seemed to have reached that stage now. He was like a man idly playing with a pack of cards, who finds that he has built or nearly built a clever little card house. Only two or three cards remain to be put in place and suddenly he values what he has contrived almost by accident and is afraid of spoiling it. In every difficult case in which he had eventually been successful, he had known such a time. Suddenly he would find himself in possession of a credible and convincing theory which seemed to need only a little more thought to work it out in compelling detail. It was then that he would pause, reluctant to discuss it, reluctant even to think about it.

Because his success seemed to be a matter of revelation rather than reason he had never developed any self confidence and set about every case with the feeling that this time he would be shown up at last. What an attitude of mind for a chief superintendent! He was humiliated by it and kept his self distrust a carefully guarded secret.

With Gill out of the way he felt better. He drank his tea and glanced through the reports in his tray. The Yard had sent someone to talk to the manager of Summit Theatrical Costumiers, the firm whose name appeared on the scrap of paper found in Allen's room with the address of the Marina scribbled on it. 'Yes, we have business dealings with Thelma Masson-Smythe at the Voodoo' . . . 'Yes, all the firm's letters are signed by me with the carbon in place.' Carbon copies of the correspondence with the Voodoo were produced and the fragment was found to match with the carbon copy of a letter dated 17th June regarding a disputed account. The carbon copy was being forwarded.

A bit of evidence linking the Masson-Smythes with Allen which might be useful if either or both persisted in denying the connection. It was obvious that the girl had sent him to the Voodoo and that he had been sent from there to the Marina.

Another of the reports also concerned the Masson-Smythes. They had been questioned about Allen's presence in the club and denied all knowledge of him. 'He is not a member, of course, but unfortunately it is all too easy for non-members to gate-crash . . . No, I've never seen him before.' Acting on instructions, the detective had seemed to accept this assurance without question. 'I hope he was convincing,' Wycliffe muttered. He wanted Allen's statement before he took any action against the Masson-Smythes and he thought that Fehling could be persuasive enough to make it good. He pushed the reports back into the tray and decided to spend the evening with his wife. He felt relaxed again.

He decided to walk, and not far from the station, by the Catholic Church, he almost collided with a woman coming out of the presbytery. She was vaguely familiar, tall and gaunt, wearing a severely tailored black costume and a black toque. Aunt Jane. He was sure that she had not recognized him, in fact, she had probably not even seen him and he could have sworn that her eyes were red with crying. He watched her stepping it out across the square. He wondered what secrets she had been whispering to her priest.

At the corner of Castle Hill a man selling newspapers, and a poster against the wall: *Moonlanding tonight?* He bought a paper and sharing the front page with the Apollo XI astronauts was a smudgy reproduction of Julie's photograph. The face looked back at him, the lips parted in a faint smile, the eyes wide and frank. Both Kathy and Piper had said that the photograph was 'like her' but that there was something not quite right about it. Could it be that the restoration gave her a look of innocence? It was his belief that satisfying sexual

275

experience leaves its mark on the face of a girl. He could not define it but he thought that he knew it when he saw it and he had once called it the Mona Lisa smirk.

'Good evening, superintendent!' It was the little redheaded reporter. 'So you know who she was.'

Wycliffe wagged the paper. 'It doesn't say so here.'

'I write the stuff, I don't read it. What I can't understand is why you've been so coy about publishing the photograph. I could have told you who she was quick enough and so could a good many others in this town.'

'We had a good reason.'

'I suppose I could try the dailies with that.'

'With what?'

'Detective Chief Superintendent Wycliffe told our reporter that the police had good reason for withholding publication of the dead girl's photograph! A nasty-minded editor might smell a rat and come to the conclusion that somebody was getting the blanket treatment.'

Wycliffe laughed. 'What's the time?'

Brown looked at his watch. 'Just gone six.'

'Come and have a drink.'

The pub in Castle Hill backed on to the harbour; in fact, the main bar was built out on stilts so that at high tide it seemed to be afloat. They were the only customers. Wycliffe ordered two beers and carried them to the window seat at the far end of the room. They were close to the quay where the pleasure boats unloaded and at this time the boats were nuzzling each other for positions close to the steps. The passengers from less aggressive ones had to climb over two or even three other boats to reach the steps, but it was all part of the fun. And it was all as stale to the reporter as it was novel to Wycliffe. Brown sipped his beer.

'Now, young man!' Wycliffe ruffled through the papers in his briefcase and came out with one of the photographs taken by the police photographer of the injuries to the dead girl's face. 'Would you have identified her from that?'

Brown gave the photograph one glance and turned away. 'Christ!'

'Exactly. That was all we had to go on.'

Brown was white and for a moment Wycliffe thought he was going to be sick. 'Are you all right?'

'I suppose so. But nobody ever said that . . .'

276

'No, we deliberately kept quiet about that but it doesn't matter now. I intend to make a statement to the press on Monday. But if you jump the gun . . . !'

'You can rely on me.'

'I hope so. Now, I want something from you. Tell me about the Collinses.'

The reporter was recovering his poise. 'It makes a change being interviewed.'

'You're not being interviewed, my lad, you're being interrogated and don't you forget it.'

'OK. Have it your way. You've met them?'

'I've met them.'

'Well, you know what they're like. Everybody thought that Willie would end up by marrying the woman who does the books . . .' He snapped his fingers in an effort to recall a name. 'Rogers – Iris Rogers. And she would have taken on where mother left off, if you see what I mean.'

Wycliffe nodded.

'People in the town used to say, "I wonder how much longer poor old Iris will have to wait" – of course they all knew that it would be until the old lady kicked the bucket.'

'The old lady is the boss?'

'You can say that again! Unless Willie was the product of a virgin birth, which wouldn't surprise me, there must have been a father round sometime but not in my day. Of course, the Collinses have got money – real money and it would be worth waiting for.'

'But he married Julie.'

Brown chuckled. 'It was a nine days' wonder – a kid of eighteen and a real doll at that! I mean, everybody wondered what he was going to do to her and what he was going to do it with . . .'

'You confine yourself to the facts, young man!'

'Sorry! I thought you wanted atmosphere, it must be the journalist in me. She was an orphan or something and as I remember it there was nobody at the wedding from her side except the foster mother.'

'Church?'

'You bet! With all the cake and trimmings, a real "do" for the town to gawp at and gossip about. Reception at the Royal.' He grinned. 'Even Aunt Jane was there.'

'Was that surprising?'

'I'll say! Aunt Jane is RC and she thinks the established church is the antichrist. They're a jolly family.'

'How long did Julie stay with them?'

'Six months, maybe. Even before that there was talk.'

'What sort of talk?'

Brown lit a cigarette and considered. 'After the excitement of the wedding had died down it all went quiet for a month or two, she was even helping in the shop and to everybody's surprise it looked as though it might work. Then she started living it up a bit; there's a country club on the Truro road and she was there most nights.'

'With her husband?'

'You must be joking! Anyway it wasn't long before she was involved in a car smash. She wasn't hurt but the driver was. It was Masson-Smythe, the chap at the Voodoo. I suppose he wanted to keep out of trouble with his wife so he said she'd thumbed a lift in the rain and he'd felt sorry for her. Could even have been true but it didn't make any difference to the gossip.'

'Anybody else?'

The reporter drained his glass. 'Have another?'

'No thanks. I asked you if there was anybody else?'

'There was plenty of talk but the only other name named, so to speak, was a chap called Byrne, a schoolteacher at the Greville Road Comprehensive.'

'Then she left him?'

Brown nodded. 'It was rumoured that she'd gone away with Byrne, I lost track of her, then at the beginning of last season she turned up doing her striptease at the Voodoo. I reckon she did it deliberately and it was bloody cruel. I mean, in this town . . .'

Wycliffe stood up. 'You'll keep quiet about all this?'

Brown grinned. 'You're the boss, but you'll owe me something for Wednesday's issue.'

'It will be all over by then.'

'You're serious?'

Almost to his own surprise Wycliffe decided that he was. They left the pub together. Outside Brown had a final go. 'You'll be seeing Willie tonight?'

Wycliffe looked at him poker-faced. 'The shop's closed for the week-end.'

★

278

'Madame is in the Television Lounge, superintendent.'

Since his identity had become known he had received VIP treatment at the hotel and he hated it. He didn't know how to behave; in his anxiety not to appear patronizing he thought that he was probably churlish. All the same, the man called after him, 'A moment, if you please, sir!' The porter was holding a little book. 'Perhaps you will be kind enough to sign my boy's autograph, sir?'

Wycliffe took the book and scrawled his signature.

'And write Detective Chief Superintendent, if you will, sir.'

He found Helen in the television room watching a report on the astronauts. The room was fairly full and all heads turned to look as he came in. 'They put on a photograph of the girl who was murdered and they had one of you on too – one I haven't seen before. You looked as though . . .'

He sat watching the television until dinner time and after dinner they took their coffee out on to the terrace where the light was fading into warm, intimate summer darkness. It was a time for mellowness and ease but he was restless. After he had lighted his pipe twice and put it out again, Helen asked, 'Why don't you ring the station?'

He pretended not to understand but after a while he said, 'I think I'll take a stroll before bed.'

'I'll expect you when I see you.'

9

He did not consciously direct his steps but without any clear idea in his mind about what he would do, he found himself outside the bookshop. Several of the shops in the street had their windows brilliantly lit, the florist's opposite, for example, had a window full of flowers cleverly lit from below and kept fresh by a fine spray which made rainbows in the light. But the bookshop was in total darkness, the old-fashioned blue canvas blinds were down. Looking up, he thought he could see a faint glimmer of light coming from the sitting room of the flat, one of the rooms which overlooked the street.

What were they doing? Was Willie in his room with his soldiers? Was he thinking of Julie? Wycliffe felt guilty; to confront him with the hideously mutilated features of his wife without warning was an act of cruelty. No wonder he had collapsed. In his own way he had deeply loved the schoolgirl to whom his mother had married him. At least he had loved the image he made of her.

What puzzled Wycliffe was his attitude afterwards. He had made no protest and seemed to bear no animosity against the superintendent, yet there had been a change in him not entirely explicable in terms of shock. At first Wycliffe could not make out what it was, then he decided that it was anger, cold anger, suppressed and dangerous. But against whom?

'I'm sorry that I had to submit you to that but it was necessary.'

No answer.

'You realize that your wife was dead before that was done to her?'

'Yes.'

'Have you any idea who could have done it?'

'No.'

'You are sure?'

'Quite sure!'

And that was all. Now he had to probe the wound.

He looked at his watch: a quarter to ten. Perhaps the two women were already in bed. When Julie was there they had played three-handed bridge. What did they do now?

He opened the door of the side passage which ran beside the shop. Almost at the far end there was a door in the left hand wall and a small light over a bell-push which shone on a printed card:

COLLINS. PRIVATE.

He rang the bell. Almost at once he was startled by a woman's voice from close at hand. A speak-box which he hadn't expected. He found the little metal grille and spoke into it.

'Come up, please.'

He opened the door and went up the carpeted stairs, past the green baize door to the bookroom and on up the next flight to the flat. The musty smell of the books pervaded everything. It was Miss Rogers who waited for him on the top landing – Iris, the reporter called her. She was tight lipped. 'You didn't waste much time getting here.'

'I beg your pardon?'

'It's barely ten minutes since Dr Rashleigh phoned you – or at least, he phoned the station.'

'What's the trouble?'

She looked surprised. 'Didn't he tell you?' She sniffed. 'As he was so anxious to drag in the police he'd better tell you himself. He's in the sitting room.'

In the dimly lit room where the brown velvet curtains met and overlapped across the window, Dr Rashleigh stood, elegant, yet restless and incongruous. He seemed relieved to see Wycliffe. 'So you've come yourself. I asked them to tell you but I didn't expect you to come. I don't want to make too much of this but I thought that in view of everything it would be better . . .'

'What exactly has happened?'

'She tried to poison herself it seems.'

'Who?'

Rashleigh looked impatient. 'Why, Aunt Jane, of course! Miss Collins.' Evidently the Collinses were such an established institution in the town that even this rather pompous doctor found it natural to speak of them with familiarity.

'What did she use?'

'Strychnine.'

'A pretty sure method.'

'As a rule, but not this time. She'll be up and about again tomorrow.'

'She's in hospital?'

'I thought it wiser for the night.'

Wycliffe sat down on one of the low armchairs and rested his head back against the embroidered runner. 'Tell me about it.' He got out his pipe and started to fill it. 'You said just now, "She tried to poison herself, it *seems*", – is there any doubt about it?'

Rashleigh looked distastefully at the other armchairs and chose instead a straight-backed dining chair. 'This *is* a depressing room, don't you think? Every time I come here . . .' His voice trailed off, then he added in a burst of confidence, 'I've been coming to this house for twenty-five years and in all that time I don't think they've moved so much as an ornament!'

It was obvious that he was talking himself into more relevant disclosures. He fiddled with the perfect crease in the fine herring-bone tweed of his trousers. It was difficult to credit that perhaps an hour earlier he was wrestling with a case of strychnine poisoning. 'I very much doubt if she intended to kill herself, superintendent. In fact, I strongly suspect that the effect of the strychnine she took was more than she'd bargained for, poor lady.'

'Then why did she take it at all?'

Rashleigh examined the long tapering fingers of a pale hand. 'Some people, especially women who are starved of . . . of affection, feel compelled to draw attention to themselves by some means, however drastic.'

Wycliffe felt like making a rude noise. 'You mean that she's tried it before?'

Rashleigh frowned. 'About three years ago; it was an overdose of a barbiturate which I had prescribed for her insomnia. On that occasion I persuaded her to enter a nursing home for a period.'

'A mental home?'

Rashleigh nodded unhappily. 'Yes.'

'Where did she get the strychnine?'

'Apparently it has been in the house for years, they had it for poisoning rats in the cellar. These old houses by the harbour . . .'

'Why did you send for me?'

Rashleigh bristled. 'I didn't *send* for you!'

'All right, why did you want me to be told?'

The doctor straightened his Greyhounds tie. 'One hears rumours. There must be few people in this town who have not heard that the girl murdered at the Marina was Collins's wife.'

Wycliffe had to acknowledge the truth of that. Kenny the Man, the Masson-Smythes, Sadie, the reporter, not to mention the Collinses themselves; somebody was bound to talk. But he was wilfully obtuse. 'You think that there may be a connection between the murder and this?'

'Certainly not!' Rashleigh was shocked. 'No direct connection that is. The emotional disturbance could well have been the trigger. With an unstable personality . . .'

'But do you discount entirely the possibility that Aunt Jane was poisoned by someone else?'

The doctor stood up to lend emphasis to his disclaimer. 'My dear superintendent! The very idea is unthinkable!'

'Who found her?'

Rashleigh smiled. 'You do not have to *find* someone suffering from strychnine poisoning. She was in her bedroom and her cries were heard by everyone in the flat – by Willie and his mother and by Iris Rogers.'

'What was *she* doing here?'

'You will be able to ask her that question yourself.'

It was odd, the more meticulous and precise the person he had to deal with the more abrupt and boorish his manner was apt to become. It was almost a reflex response. He invited snubs from such people and seemed oblivious of them. In fact, it was an aspect of his own sensitivity. In the presence of fastidiousness he felt that he and his job were being mutely criticized.

'I would like to see her bedroom.'

Rashleigh led the way. The room was next to the sitting room and, like it, overlooked the narrow street. It was large and sparsely furnished; an old-fashioned wooden single bed with slatted head and foot, a wardrobe, a chest of drawers and a table across the window which to judge from the few trinkets on it served as a dressing table. By the bed a small table held a reading lamp and several devotional books. Above the bed, a crucifix. The carpet was threadbare and the bedclothes lay on it in a twisted heap.

'She suffered convulsions, of course, but they were not excessively violent. I administered pentathol intravenously with success.'

283

Wycliffe looked round the room, bewildered at the perversity of human nature. Here was a woman, no more than middle aged, well-off, by no means stupid . . . He muttered to himself, 'It's masochistic!'

Rashleigh looked at him brightly. 'Isn't it?'

The tumbler was on the mantelpiece next to a plated alarm clock. Wycliffe picked it up; damp white crystals adhered to the sides and there was a similar sediment in the bottom. 'There must be enough here to kill an elephant!'

'There is, but it doesn't dissolve very easily in water, fortunately. She actually got very little down, I imagine.'

'But how do you know that she didn't intend . . .'

'I know my patient.'

'Where did you find the tumbler?'

'It had rolled under the bed.'

'How long after the call before you arrived here, doctor?'

'Not more than ten minutes. I was in my surgery as she well knew that I should be.'

Smug bastard! But he was probably right. 'She was conscious when you arrived?'

'Fully, but she said very little – just kept repeating the words, "God forgive me! God forgive me!" whenever the spasms allowed her to speak.'

'Where are the others?'

The doctor shrugged. 'Willie went to his room, I suppose that he is still there.'

'With his soldiers.'

A faint smile.

'And his mother?'

'Mrs Collins was somewhat excited. I gave her a sedative and she is sleeping.'

Wycliffe fiddled with the trinkets on the dressing table: a cameo brooch, a rosary, a locket . . . He sighed and became, abruptly, almost genial. He thanked the doctor for his cooperation and began to edge him out on to the landing.

'Good night, doctor! I expect that you can find your own way out.'

When Rashleigh had put on his hat and coat, collected his case and departed, Wycliffe stood in the passage outside Willie's door.

He had his hand on the knob. In any other household . . . Then he changed his mind and went on down the passage to the kitchen. The door was open and the light was on.

'Here I am, superintendent.' Iris was standing just inside the kitchen door. Had she been eavesdropping? If so she was entirely composed.

The kitchen had been modern in the thirties; a mottled enamel gas cooker and washboiler, a refrigerator with a lot of polished wood in its structure. But everything shone, and, as a bonus, the kitchen overlooked the harbour. The curtains were undrawn and he could see, vaguely, the outline of boats in the darkness.

'I thought you might want to talk to me.'

'Yes.'

'We could go to the sitting room.'

'I like kitchens,' Wycliffe said, which was true.

They sat on cane chairs placed on opposite sides of a large, square, scrubbed table, just like the one that had taken up most of the room in his mother's kitchen. Iris looked out of place in her severely cut two-piece and her no-nonsense blouse. She belonged to an office as surely as a typewriter or a filing cabinet. Wycliffe had known scores like her, hardworking, dependable, their one satisfaction in life being indispensable. She was not bad looking, big boned with a tendency to fleshiness, but her features were good. A slightly pinched look round the nostrils might mean a shrewish temper and when the light caught her at a certain angle it was possible to see golden hairs on her upper lip. Her hair was straw coloured and her skin freckled.

'I want you to know where I stand . . .' He could have forecast the opening. 'I've worked in this business for sixteen years.'

'A long time.'

She nodded. 'But there's more to it than that; if it hadn't been for that girl – Julie – I should have been married to him by now. I thought that it was better for you to hear it from me rather than from gossip.'

'Are you trying to tell me that you had a motive for the murder?' He couldn't resist provoking her.

She was contemptuous. 'Don't be absurd, I merely wanted you to have your facts right.'

'Thank you. Now, what do you know about this evening's business?'

She reached into her handbag, which lay open on the table, and drew out a silver cigarette case and a lighter to match. 'Smoke?' Wycliffe refused and she lit a cigarette but the hand holding the lighter trembled. Evidently she had less self possession than she liked to admit. 'If you think this affair tonight has anything to do with Julie's death then you're barking up the wrong tree. Aunt Jane is queer in the head – she's done this sort of thing before but she's no intention of killing herself.'

'Then why pretend? It's a hazardous business.'

Iris blew out a thin spiral of smoke and watched it rise. 'She did it to bring Willie to heel.'

'I don't understand.'

She looked at him doubtfully. 'Have you ever seen them together – Willie and his aunt?'

'I have.'

'Then you must have noticed. She dotes on him, it's pathological. To her, he's the son she's never had and the man she's never married.'

Wycliffe smiled faintly. He took out his half smoked pipe and asked permission to light it. 'What about tonight?'

She reached a saucer from the dresser to do duty as an ashtray. 'There was a row, I don't know what about. On Saturday nights I stay on late to square up the books for the week. I'd finished downstairs and when I came up to the flat as usual to tell Willie I was going, she was outside his door begging him to let her in. She was crying.'

'What happened?'

'When she saw me she went to her own room. I called to Willie to let me in and he did. He was obviously very upset but I couldn't get out of him what it was about. It was while I was with him that she started to scream.'

Wycliffe was watching her with a mild fixity of expression, almost as though his thoughts were elsewhere and when he spoke it was to say something not directly relevant. 'You would have married Mr Collins if . . . ?'

'If I'd had the chance – yes.' She stubbed out her cigarette in the saucer with a vigorous jab.

'The match he made seems to have been unfortunate.'

'Unfortunate! It was absurd and disastrous!'

'One would have thought that his mother and his aunt would have persuaded him . . .'

'They encouraged him! At least his mother did.'

'Indeed?'

'Yes. That seems odd to you, doesn't it? But she had a good reason – to stop him marrying me.'

'Mrs Collins disapproved of you?'

Her nostrils looked more pinched now and there were spots of colour in her cheeks. 'As a daughter-in-law, yes. She knew that once I was Willie's wife things would be different. I'm no teen-aged girl to dance to her tune. In her eyes, Willie's interest in Julie was an answer to a prayer, a young girl, an orphan, who could be brought up in the way she should go. With her, "Yes, Mrs Collins, No, Mrs Collins, It's very kind of you, Mrs Collins", the old lady thought that butter wouldn't melt in her mouth. For once, she was wrong!' Iris lit a second cigarette and smoked rapidly, making the tobacco glow and crackle and expelling the smoke in bursts. As Wycliffe watched her he was mildly perturbed at the antagonism he felt towards her. Surely she had the right to be resentful?

'How did he first meet the girl?'

'She used to come to the shop – into the secondhand department. At first she came with other girls and I think they did it for a lark, there used to be a lot of giggling, but the rest soon got tired of it and she came alone. She was at the grammar school doing "A" levels in history and English and, to give her her due, I think she had a genuine feeling for books. She soon got talking to Willie, who is more of a scholar than a business man, and he used to help her with her essays and advise her on her reading. Of course she was flattered by the attention of an older man and it was a novel experience for Willie to have a pretty young girl with auburn hair and violet eyes hanging on his every word. Of course, she saw her chance . . .'

'Are you saying that she set out to . . .'

'To seduce him – certainly she did!'

'A man double her age?'

She made a little contemptuous noise with her lips. 'You men are all the same, even policemen who should know better! You'll never believe that young girls can be truly wicked – certainly not the ones with a pretty face and nice legs. You should have seen this one go to work! "You make me feel so stupid! It's all crystal clear when you explain it. If you were a teacher . . . I feel so guilty, wasting your time like this . . ." And on another tack: "I suppose I've had a sad life, really . . . I often wonder . . . if my parents hadn't been killed. Daddy was a painter . . ." Actually daddy was a carpenter and they were taking their first holiday abroad – Majorca, I think it was, but she made it sound as though they took planes as we take buses.'

'She seems to have fooled Mrs Collins successfully, a difficult feat if I'm any judge.' Wycliffe was cool.

'She was taken in because she wanted to be!' Iris was more at her ease now. 'Of course you are writing off most of what I say on the grounds that I'm a frustrated old maid, a bit warped and more than a bit spiteful. Up to a point you may be right but there's more to it than that. As I said, I've worked in this business for sixteen years and without any false modesty I've saved it from the fate of most book-shops in towns of this size. I felt I had a stake in the place and I didn't see why I should be cheated of it by a scheming chit of a girl!'

Wycliffe looked at the chin, the set of the jaw and the pursed lips. 'The marriage lasted only a few months and it is two years since she left him – a year since she left the town altogether. During that time have you resumed your old relationship?'

She stubbed out her cigarette butt. 'Obviously we couldn't get married.'

'He had grounds for divorce.'

For some reason she flushed and shook her head. 'He wouldn't – at least . . .'

'What were you going to say?'

She hesitated. 'I was going to say that his attitude seemed to be changing in recent months. Given time I think he might have agreed, then she came back . . .'

Whether she realized it or not she was gilding the lily as far as motive went. She had reason enough to kill but surely not in the par-ticular way that Julie died?

'And now that she is dead?'

She looked up angrily and seemed on the point of protesting but changed her mind. 'I don't know. I don't know anything any more.'

Wycliffe smoked in silence for a while. 'Before he met his wife, were you engaged?'

'No, there was an understanding, I told you.'

'What does that mean?'

'I don't know what you're asking me.'

'Did you go to bed with him?'

Again the colour flooded her cheeks. 'Yes.'

'And now?'

Her reply was barely audible. 'Yes.' She made an angry movement. 'What does that make me?'

'I don't know. Compassionate or determined, it depends on your motive.'

She looked at him sharply but said nothing. Wycliffe sat with his elbows on the table and for at least two minutes the silence was unbroken except for the ticking of the kitchen clock. 'What has been the effect on Willie of his wife's death?'

She leaned back in her chair, more relaxed. 'I wish I knew. I can't understand him. I mean, he knew that she was dead on Wednesday and of course he was upset – desperately upset, but he was normal, if you know what I mean. He was just as you might expect him to be . . .'

'But now?'

'Since you were here yesterday he's changed. I can't explain it but it frightens me. I mean, he's doing all the usual things and when you speak to him he answers you quite sensibly, but you get the impression he isn't really there at all. He's like a man walking in his sleep but I can't find out what it is.'

'He won't discuss it with you?'

'No.'

'You know that I took him to identify his wife's body?'

'Yes, but seeing her shouldn't have affected him like that, surely?'

Wycliffe reached for his briefcase and took out the photograph of the dead girl's face. He placed it on the table within her reach. 'That may explain it.'

She took the photograph and glanced at it. 'My God! You let him see that!'

'The girl was murdered, that's all that matters to me – murdered and mutilated after death.'

'Whoever did that must be mad!' She shuddered involuntarily then went quiet, 'You don't think that he . . .'

'How do I know what to think?'

'But Willie couldn't! I mean violence of any sort appals him. He's gentle . . .' She stopped, looking at Wycliffe. 'Nothing I can say will make any difference, will it?'

He shrugged.

After a while she got up. 'I'd better go.'

'No.'

She looked at him in surprise but sat down again.

'Does the old lady suffer from heart trouble?'

'Why, yes . . .'

'Serious?'

'I suppose so, the doctor says any sudden shock might kill her. Actually I think she's shock proof except where Willie is concerned.'

'What about Aunt Jane?'

His manner was different, more relaxed. The way he said 'Aunt Jane' almost made her laugh. 'She's as strong as a horse.'

'Any insanity in the family?'

She became guarded once more. 'Well, you know about Aunt Jane – whether you call that insanity I don't know.'

'And?'

She fiddled with the clasp of her bag. 'Willie's father died in the asylum but that was before I started to work here.' She looked across at Wycliffe meeting his placid gaze. 'I know what you're thinking, but Willie is as sane as you or me.'

'When did you first hear that Julie had been murdered?'

She became obviously agitated. 'I heard about the murder Wednesday lunchtime but I didn't know that it was her.'

'Who told you that it was?'

She hesitated. 'I heard it from somebody yesterday – after you'd been.'

'You're a bad liar!'

She stood up, flushed and angry. 'I'm leaving!'

'No!' His manner startled her. 'I'm conducting a murder inquiry, Miss Rogers, and I will not listen to fairy tales. Please sit down and answer my questions truthfully. When did you first hear that Julie was back in town?'

'I don't know what you're talking about.'

He leaned forward in his chair and spoke confidentially. 'If you are frank now you may save yourself a great deal of embarrassment later. You have already told me – perhaps unwittingly – that Mr

Collins and, by implication, you also, knew on Wednesday that it was Julie who had been murdered. Now I want to know when it was you heard that she had come back?'

She gave in and sat down. 'I saw her just as she got off the coach on Sunday evening when I was on my way home from church.'

'Where do you live?'

She gestured vaguely. 'Up on the terraces, I have a flat.'

'Alone?'

'Yes.'

'Did Julie see you?'

'I'm sure she didn't; she was getting her luggage from the boot of the coach and talking to the driver.'

'But you had no doubt that it was she?'

'I'd know her anywhere.'

'How did you find out that she was staying at the Marina?'

'I followed her.'

'She took a taxi.'

'So did I – from the same rank.'

'Why?'

'Because I wanted to know where she was going. I've never made the mistake of underestimating her ability to cause trouble.'

'Didn't it strike you as odd that she should stay at a place like the Marina?'

'I couldn't understand it.'

'You told Willie you'd seen her?' It was inevitable that he would drop into the habit of calling them all by their intimate family names.

'I rang him as soon as I got home, it seemed the natural thing to do.'

'Of course, what was his reaction?'

She hesitated. 'It's difficult to say.'

'You mean that he seemed to know already?'

She looked steadily at the table top and said nothing. He could see that she was close to tears and tears did not come easily to her. He stood up and went to the window to give her a moment to recover. Not much to be seen, just the shadowy outlines of the moored craft and the shimmering paths of their riding lights. 'Did you expect Julie to leave him?'

He heard her stifle a sob. 'I didn't know at first, I wasn't sure what

291

she was prepared to give up. Then she started going out in the evenings and there were rumours about one or two men . . .'

'Masson-Smythe?'

'Smythe first, he runs the club where she went to work in the end, then there was a schoolteacher called Byrne.' She shook herself as though to rid her body of some cloying contact. 'Can you under-stand a girl like that? It was Byrne she went off with but it only lasted a week or two.' She laughed. 'Not even a long hot summer. Then she was back again.'

'You saw her go into the Marina on Sunday evening, was that the last you saw of her?'

'Yes.'

'Did you or Willie mention her again?'

'No.'

'Not even when you heard about the murder?'

'Well, yes. I heard about the murder from a customer. Willie had been at the printing works all the morning and when he came back, I said, "Was it her?" He was as white as death and he just said, "Yes".'

'Nothing more?'

She shook her head. 'He burst out crying.'

Wycliffe stood for a while, apparently lost in thought. Actually, though ideas chased each other through his mind they could hardly be said to have any pattern of rational consecutive thought. A mother's boy at thirty-six finds himself in love, probably for the first time in his life. The man on the fire escape – who was he? What did he see? Group AB? A question easily answered – too easily; he wasn't ready for that yet. He had once shocked a subordinate by saying, 'I like to have a theory before I get lumbered with too many facts!' Now the story was often told against him, but it was true. In this case he wanted to get the psychology right before he blundered into accusations of guilt. Could Willie have battered his dead wife's features into an unrecognizable tangle of skin and flesh and bone? Wycliffe felt sure that if he had killed his wife it was an unpremedi-tated crime – 'almost accidental' he had said to Gill. The restraint in the killing, the violence of the disfigurement – he kept coming back to it. Fear? Who else would need or want to disfigure the girl?

He was half surprised to find himself still in the kitchen with Iris sitting at the table watching him. The clock showed five minutes to eleven. It was beginning to rain, he could see the water beginning to run down the window panes, playing tricks with the harbour lights. 'Is there much cash kept in the flat or in the shop?'

The question surprised her. 'Some nights there may be as much as three or four hundred pounds in the safe in my office.'

'That money is in your charge?'

'Of course.' She added, 'Willie has a key.'

'Are cheques drawn on the business account signed by Willie alone?'

'They are not signed by Willie at all, the business belongs to his mother for her lifetime and she signs the cheques.'

'What about Aunt Jane?'

Iris bridled. 'It has nothing whatever to do with her!'

'But surely she must have shared in her father's will?'

'She was left certain investments which, by all accounts, have done very well for her.'

'Well, thank you Miss Rogers, you've been very helpful.'

'You're going?'

'Yes.'

'You're not seeing Willie?'

'Not tonight.'

She seemed reluctant to let him go. 'I hope that I haven't given you the impression . . .' She saw the look on his face and stopped. 'All right, I'm on the telephone at home as well as here. If you want me . . .'

'Yes.' He hesitated. 'Will the old lady be all right in the house with only Willie?'

Iris smiled. 'I've been thinking about that, perhaps I'd better stay here tonight.'

He decided to look in at the station on his way back to the hotel. To his surprise he found Fehling in the HQ room, his bulk squeezed into one of the bentwood armchairs, busy writing. 'Still here? Any progress with Allen?'

Fehling's satisfaction was unmistakable. 'He's made a fresh statement, sir.'

'Involving the Masson-Smythes?'

'Up to the neck! The girl sent him to the Masson-Smythes and they made the arrangements. This fellow Pellow is their go-between with the ships and he's done similar jobs before. Allen isn't very bright and when the girl was killed he panicked and went there.'

293

'Good!'

Wycliffe stood by the window watching the rain. A constable came in and began to collect dirty teacups from among the litter on the tables. Outside the rain was falling vertically, thin threads that gleamed in the light of the street lamps. The square was almost deserted, a single taxi on the rank, a man and a girl under one umbrella hurrying home. He turned to Fehling. 'It's time you got some sleep, Mr Fehling, but there are a couple of things I'd like you to lay on tomorrow. Pick up Dippy Pellow, quietly, without making a fuss. With Allen's statement and what you get from him, you should have enough to book him. Make sure the Voodoo is kept under observation but don't bring the Masson-Smythes in unless they try to make a bolt for it. One more thing, fix it so that Kathy Johnson can see Masson-Smythe without him knowing. I want to see if she recognizes him.'

'Anything else, Mr Wycliffe?'

Wycliffe was wandering aimlessly round the room as though loath to leave. 'What? Oh, no! Have a good night.'

He went down the stairs and out of the front door into the rain, his shoulders hunched, and by the time he reached his hotel he was soaked to the skin.

10

Wycliffe hoped that Sunday would prove uneventful and that he would have time to think. After breakfast – nine o'clock on Sundays – he went out on to the terrace to smoke his first pipe of the day. He was on his own – Helen had made friends with some local people who had a motor launch and she was going with them across the bay to explore a bit of Daphne du Maurier country. He could have gone with them but though he intended to have a lazy day his conscience would not allow him to break contact for eight or nine hours. In any case it was pleasant on the terrace. The sky was deep blue with fleecy white clouds and at dozens of moorings peppered all over the harbour boat owners were bailing out, scrubbing down, checking motors or rigging – whatever they were doing it seemed to be delectable employment to Wycliffe. Nearby a boy and a girl were cooking breakfast on a bottle-gas stove on the deck of a little sailing craft. They must have been hard put even to sleep in the tiny cabin. The boy wore shorts and the girl a bikini. Wycliffe secretly wished that he could have his youth over again in this permissive society on which so much is blamed. It looked good enough to him that morning.

He sat in one of the wicker chairs and read the two glossy Sundays, mostly about Apollo XI, until the church bells started ringing. One, close by, a cracked bell, tolled so rapidly that it imparted a sense of urgency to its message while across the water a more melodious cadence nicely countered its monotony. Sunday: there was something in the air at the same time relaxing and inhibiting. Because of his Methodist upbringing he associated it with the smell of pitch pine pews and hymn books. When the bar opened he had a drink brought to him on the terrace.

'Excuse me . . . Superintendent Wycliffe? . . . My name is Byrne . . .'

A stockily built young man, fair haired with a good-natured, not very intelligent face, and rugby player written all over him. 'It's about the photograph in the newspaper – I knew the girl . . .' He loomed over Wycliffe, standing first on one leg then on the other.

'Pull up a chair. Drink?'

'What? – No thank you . . . yes, I think I will, a beer if I may . . .'

Wycliffe signalled the waiter. The terrace was getting busy with people who wanted to get in some drinking time before lunch. They sat watching the harbour while they waited for the drinks. The young couple from the sailing boat were swimming now, chasing each other in the water and laughing. Byrne looked miserable, *la dolce vita* had landed him where he was now. The waiter came back with his beer and a whisky for Wycliffe.

'Cheers!'

'Cheers!'

Wycliffe put down his glass, his grey eyes on the young man. 'You went off with her, stayed with her about three weeks, then came back without her. Now let's have the details.'

Byrne looked relieved by this approach, he relaxed. 'I met her at a Rugby Club dance.'

'Are you married?'

'I am now but I wasn't then.' He hesitated. 'I want to keep my wife out of this if it can be managed. She's Welsh and just a bit . . .'

'Go on.'

'Well, I know it sounds odd but she made a bee line for me. You'd have thought I was the only man in the room.'

'She must like 'em stocky,' Wycliffe muttered, remembering Allen.

'Pardon?'

'Never mind!'

'Afterwards I wanted to take her home but she said that wasn't on.'

'Did you know who she was?'

'No, not then. Anyway, she asked me if I lived with my parents and I said I didn't, I had a flat. I must admit I was a bit taken aback when she said, "That's all right then, I'll take *you* home".' He looked out over the water. 'I suppose I was still a bit wet behind the ears but I couldn't make her out; I wondered if I'd picked up a pro without knowing it.'

'What happened?'

He turned his frank blue eyes on Wycliffe. 'I never knew a girl could be like that! And yet she was so small and so . . .' He fumbled for a word.

'Exquisite.'

He agreed at once. 'Yes, that's the word for her – exquisite and yet she was like . . . like . . . Well, I suppose every man has sort of sex fantasies. I mean he never expects them to come true, he never expects to find a woman who . . . But she *insisted* . . .' He broke off, at a loss for words to describe his relationship with the girl. The language of eroticism is limited and follows a tricky path between mere clinical description and obscenity.

'So you owe her something?'

He looked at the superintendent suspecting a joke but the grey eyes were serious. 'Owe her something?'

'For helping to make a man of you. You are probably a better husband because of her.'

He looked surprised. 'Yes, I suppose so, I'd never thought of it like that.'

Wycliffe emptied his glass. 'You continued to see her and finally took her away with you although, by then, you must have known that she was a married woman. Did you intend to go for good?'

Byrne felt that in some way the question was loaded against him and he bungled his answer. 'For good? I don't know, I suppose so, but I had my work to think of, hadn't I?' He paused, his brows creased in an effort to recall the past and to present it in a not too damaging light. 'During the few months from the time we met until we parted in Torquay it was as though I was permanently drunk. I mean, here was I, an ordinary chap to whom this tremendous thing had happened! That's how it seemed to me at the time – you understand?' He was pathetically anxious to be understood, like most people with a guilty conscience. '*Nothing* else mattered. If she'd been married to my own brother it wouldn't have made any difference.'

'And yet you walked out on her.'

The young couple were back on their boat. She was lying face downwards on the cabin roof, she had removed her bra and he was rubbing her back with sun lotion. Byrne was watching them, his mind in a whirl. He had rationalized and tidied up the whole episode with Julie months ago, before he got married, seeing himself, relatively, in a favourable light. At least he had had the sense to get away from a dangerous woman! Now here was this grave-faced policeman turning the whole thing topsy turvy, making it seem that he had been the prime mover, that he was in the girl's debt, that he had 'walked out on her'!

'Why did you leave her?'

He clasped his hands round one knee and rocked gently to and fro in his chair. 'I suppose I realized that there was no future in it.' It was not the answer he would have given ten minutes earlier.

'You came back together?'

'No, I left her in Torquay, I didn't even know that she had come back until I heard that she was appearing at the club.'

'Did you see her again?'

'No. About a year ago I heard that she had left the town. I got married shortly afterwards and I neither saw nor heard anything of her until last week.'

'Then?'

'I had a letter from her saying that she was coming back and that she might look me up for old times' sake.'

'You still have the letter?'

'No, I destroyed it in case Gwyn should come across it.'

'Did she tell you where to find her?'

'No.'

'Did you try to find her?'

He shook his head. 'No, I was terrified that she would come looking for me.'

'You didn't go to the Marina?'

'I swear I didn't. I might have done if I'd known, just to persuade her to let bygones be bygones.'

Wycliffe sat back in his chair. 'All right, Mr Byrne, thank you for coming, I'll get in touch if I need you again.'

'You'll remember about Gwyn – not knowing?' The eyes were pleading.

'I'll remember.' He almost added, 'Why don't you tell her before her friends do?' But his job was crime not marriage guidance. All the same he chuckled as he went in to his lonely lunch. 'I wonder if he's managed to teach Gwyn any of Julie's little tricks.'

He had just finished his lunch and was considering smoking a pipe on the terrace when he was paged by the loudspeakers, Fehling was on the telephone, obviously pleased with himself.

'Any luck?'

'Kathy Johnson identified Masson-Smythe as the man she found going through the register at the Marina. I found out that he patronizes the bar at the Royal on Sunday mornings so I sent DC Hartley along with Kathy to have a drink. She's positive he's the man.'

'Good!'

'And we've picked up Pellow. He was a bit truculent at first but once he realized we had it on him he was ready to cough fast enough. Actually he's not too sorry to get one in on the Masson-Smythes for getting mixed up with Allen. "A small time runt who'd grass on his own mother!" – Pellow's description.'

Wycliffe could almost sympathize. No professional would have loused up an organization like the Voodoo, if only because he might need it one day.

'He's admitted to three other cases in the past eighteen months, including Frank Ellison.'

'The Hatton Garden chap?'

'That's the man. Eighty thousand pounds' worth of uncut stones, never traced.'

'It will be a feather in your cap if you can get a line on that lot, Mr Fehling!' But to tell the truth, Wycliffe was not interested. 'Where is Pellow now?'

'In the cells.'

'And Allen?'

'We packed him off on the train this morning.'

'No news of Jim Gill yet?'

'He only arrived in London at six this morning, sir.'

'All right. You've done very well, Mr Fehling. Did you get any sleep last night?'

'A few hours, sir.'

'What about lunch?'

'I've had a canteen lunch, sir, but don't worry about me, if there's anything I can do . . .'

Fehling had the enthusiasm of a very young schoolboy. Wycliffe hesitated. 'I'll ring you back in a few minutes.' He dropped the receiver, looked up the number of the Voodoo and dialled.

'Masson-Smythe speaking.'

'Chief Superintendent Wycliffe.'

'Yes?' A blend of caution and habitual self confidence.

'I would like to see you as soon as possible.'

Thelma's voice in the background: 'Who is it?' And her husband too concerned to remember to cover the mouthpiece: 'Wycliffe.'

'Shall we say this afternoon at the police station?'

A momentary hesitation. 'I'm afraid that this afternoon will not be convenient, perhaps tomorrow at my office.'

Wycliffe recognized the professional, feeling out the ground. He was decisive. 'I think that it had better be this afternoon, here.'

'Very well, if you insist, though what more I can tell you . . .'

'Let us say at two thirty, then.'

A moment later Wycliffe was speaking to Fehling again. 'I've made an appointment with Masson-Smythe at the station for two thirty and I want you to keep it. Question him about his travel agency – lean on him, but keep off the girl and her death. I'll give you an hour, then I'll take over.'

Fehling was pleased.

The superintendent spent half an hour on the terrace. He then strolled through the deserted streets to the police station. It seemed that most of the population must be on the beach or out in boats and the square had been taken over by the pigeons, strutting up and down between the rows of parked cars. Outside the station, an E-type Jag, parked against the kerb. The wages of sin. From the desk he phoned Fehling, who came down a few minutes later.

'We've got him, sir. He's a slippery customer but he knows that he can't talk his way out of this one. We can slap half a dozen charges on him over the Allen business but it's going to be the devil of a job to get him on the others. It's Pellow's word against his.'

Wycliffe looked sympathetic but at heart he was only interested in Masson-Smythe in so far as he might shed light on Julie's murder. 'All right, I'll take over now and you can have another go later.'

Masson-Smythe was in Wycliffe's office, sitting in the chair by the desk. He looked changed; despite his natty summer suiting in fashionable cinnamon, he looked bedraggled. He was holding his glasses in his hand, leaving white circles round his eyes in contrast with his flushed features.

300

'Well, Mr Smythe, this man Allen seems to have caused both of us quite a lot of trouble.'

Masson-Smythe looked at him dully. Wycliffe beamed. 'Amateurs! Fortunately you and I are professionals and we know the score.'

Masson-Smythe said nothing but wiped his glasses and put them back on.

Wycliffe turned over the papers on his desk. 'You told me that you employed Julie Collins in your cabaret on the strength of a visit she made to your club on a rehearsal afternoon. You auditioned her and offered her a four month contract.'

'That is correct.'

'You did not tell me that for some time before you had, as the phrase goes, been on terms of intimacy with her.'

Masson-Smythe drew out a silver cigarette case. 'May I smoke?' He lit a Turkish cigarette and blew a cloud of pungent, silver grey smoke into the air. He was recovering confidence. 'I answered the questions you asked, superintendent.'

'I see. Would it be true to say, then, that you engaged her because she threatened to tell your wife of your relationship?'

'That would not be true. I offered her a contract because I thought she had the makings of a first-class cabaret artiste and events have proved me right.'

Wycliffe smiled. 'A club like yours, although it makes its money out of visitors, depends for its continued existence on the good will or at least the tolerance of influential locals. Knowing this, you employ the wife of one of the town's most respected business men simply because she's pretty good at taking her clothes off in public. Frankly, I don't believe it!' He brought out his half-smoked pipe and relit it, watching Masson-Smythe over the undulant flame of the match. 'But that is unimportant . . .' He broke off abruptly, looking across at DC Rees who sat in the corner taking notes. 'I suppose Mr Masson-Smythe has been formally cautioned? . . . Good! We must keep the record straight.'

The superintendent seemed to be in no hurry, he shuffled through the litter of papers on his desk and then, without looking up, 'What were you doing in the Marina on Monday evening?' Make your man comfortable, then kick the chair away.

301

Masson-Smythe stopped with his cigarette halfway to his lips. 'I don't know what you're talking about.'

Wycliffe was as bland as mother's milk. 'Oh, come, Mr Smythe! I have a statement here from a witness; not a shadow of doubt. In any case I can't see why you need be so coy. After all, we know that it was at Julie's instigation that you were arranging Allen's passage. Surely, that's what you've been talking to Mr Fehling about?'

Masson-Smythe leaned forward in his chair. 'All right, I went to the Marina to see her but she wasn't in.'

'So when did you see her?'

Now he was like a chess player, trying to foresee his opponent's next move. His hand went to his waistcoat pocket and his fingers searched for something they did not find. 'She telephoned me.'

'Saying what?' Wycliffe was intrigued by the movement of his right hand, he was passing his thumb over his fingers continuously in a rolling movement. A nervous idiosyncrasy, but an odd one.

'She telephoned to fix up details about Allen.'

'She must have had a considerable hold over you for you to take on that job. After all, Allen hadn't a penny and you must have known that he was no more than a petty thief. She was blackmailing you, wasn't she, Mr Smythe?'

Again the fruitless investigation of his waistcoat pocket and a resumption of the rolling movement of fingers and thumb.

'Think about your answer by all means. I have a colleague in London at this moment, searching her flat. I also have a witness who will state that Julie had a hold over both you and your wife while she was still under contract at the club. You were in a cleft stick over this man Allen. Far from turning him down or even making a little on the deal, you had to subsidize him. Julie had a thousand pounds in notes in her room when she died – when did you hand them over, Mr Smythe?'

'I gave her no money, I swear it!' Fingers and thumb were working overtime now, and suddenly their message was clear to Wycliffe. He put his hand into the pocket of his jacket and his fingers closed over a little steel ball-bearing, the one Fehling had found under the girl's bed.

'Do you think we could have the window open?' Masson-Smythe was sweating profusely, the perspiration running down his temples and filming his spectacles.

Wycliffe got up and opened the window himself, letting in the raucous screaming of gulls who were quarrelling over scraps thrown out from the canteen.

'I don't deny that I have given her money in the past. If your people have searched her flat they must have evidence that she was blackmailing me anyway.'

'How much and how often?'

'Perhaps five or six hundred over the past year.'

'Not bleeding you, then?'

'No, I had the impression that she thought I might be useful in other ways and, of course, I was right.'

'Her threat was exposure to the police?'

'She didn't threaten.' He lit another cigarette and inhaled deeply. He was silent for some time and Wycliffe let him be. The little clock on the mantelpiece dominated the room with its loud metallic tick. When he next spoke his whole manner seemed to have changed. 'I've knocked about the world since I was a boy of sixteen and there isn't much that can surprise me now. But that girl . . . ! I knew I was a damn fool to get mixed up with her. She was a shrewd, calculating bitch, but she had what it takes to hold a man. She was like a drug, you kept coming back though you knew she would finish you in the end. I was like a kid with his first girl.'

'How did she find out?'

He laughed. 'Pillow talk! Me! I wanted to impress her and she would lie there with her ears pinned back cooing away and then – Wham!' The suave tight-lipped mask had slipped to reveal a coarser, more violent personality underneath. His speech was different, even his postural reflexes seemed to have changed for he lounged in his chair where previously he had sat almost primly, conscious of his dignity. Now he looked out of place in his smart dandified clothes.

But he had stopped the rolling movement of his fingers and thumb, the tension had gone.

Wycliffe looked at the almost expressionless, almost immobile features and suddenly he understood. 'It was something more than your little racket which Julie held over you, wasn't it? It was not so much what you were doing as *who you were*.'

'There's no point in denying it now, is there, copper? I've known for eight years that I had only to get myself nicked once and it would

303

be all up.' He stroked his cheek. 'They can alter your face but they can't change your dabs.'

'Where did you break from?'

'The Moor.'

It had become a parlour guessing game with Smythe furnishing the clues and Wycliffe doing the guessing.

'Eight years ago . . . McClaren, the bank robber.' Wycliffe racked his memory. 'A bank in Holborn, you and three others, a bystander was shot and killed – shot when he tried to interfere. You got over the wall with . . .'

'Nick Crane but he was picked up.' Masson-Smythe seemed delighted to be remembered as though they were old friends meeting after a lapse of years.

Wycliffe remembered the case, not because he was involved, but because of the cold-blooded killing of a courageous young man who had tried to stop them getting away. 'You got fifteen years and you served two . . .'

'Three.'

'And they never recovered the money.'

'No.'

Young Rees had become so absorbed in the drama being played out before him that he had forgotten to take notes. Not that it mattered, Masson-Smythe, or McClaren, had gone beyond the point of no return. Wycliffe picked up the telephone. 'Ask Dr Rashleigh if he will kindly come to the station to do a blood test – a grouping test . . . Yes, as soon as possible, please.'

'What's that in aid of?'

'You'll see.'

'I didn't kill her.'

'No? You had ample motive and you've killed before.'

'That's not true. I didn't know there was a shooter in the outfit. Even the judge said there was no evidence to show which of us fired the shot.'

He was right, the gun had been left at the scene and it hadn't been possible to establish which of the three men had used it.

'Why did you go to the Marina on Tuesday night?'

'You mean Monday, surely?'

'Don't stall! It will do you no good as well you know! Why did you go to the girl on Tuesday night, the night she was killed?'

Smythe still hesitated and Wycliffe took the little steel ball from his pocket and lobbed it over. 'You left your calling card and you left the money – a thousand pounds in used notes.'

Smythe caught the steel ball, glanced at it and laid it on the desk in the ashtray. 'All right, I went there, but I didn't leave her any money.'

'Why did you go?'

'She insisted. As far as the money goes you can check my bank account . . .'

'A fat lot of good that would be. It would surprise me if you don't keep that amount of cash on hand. Anyway, if she didn't want money why did she tell you to come?'

He shook his head. 'I don't know but it was just like her. She could never resist cracking the whip. The point is, when I got there she was already dead.'

Wycliffe looked at him through narrowed eyes. 'You expect me to believe that?'

'It's straight up.'

'What time did you get there?'

'One o'clock was the time she gave me but I was early, say twenty or a quarter to.' He stopped to light a cigarette. 'The front door was unlocked as she told me it would be and I followed her directions. The bedroom door was a bit open and there was a light on. I think I called her name, but there was no answer and then I pushed the door wide open and went in . . .'

'Go on.'

'She was lying on the bed, naked. At first I thought that she was up to her games, then I thought she might be asleep and I touched her. She was warm but completely limp. I wondered if she was drugged but when I tried her heart and pulse there was nothing – not a dicky bird.'

'So?'

I scarpered. I got out of that place like a bat out of hell! I mean, what else could I do?'

'When you saw her on the bed how did she look?'

'Look? I've just told you, like she was sleeping though it seemed a bit odd to be sleeping naked with no bedclothes over her.'

'Did you see a door-stop in the room? A brass weight?'

'Was that what it was? I nearly tripped over the bloody thing in the middle of the floor.'

'Did you have intercourse with her?'

'Christ, no! What sort of bloody pervert do you take me for?'

'Did you search her room?'

Masson-Smythe leaned forward in his chair. 'Look, skip, do me a favour and get this straight: I went to the room, I found her lying there, I made sure she was dead and I scarpered. With my problems what else could I do?' He looked at Wycliffe intently, his eyes anxious. 'You do believe me?'

'There's no reason why I should.' Wycliffe picked up the telephone once more. 'I'm having you taken down. Later you'll be asked to make a formal statement.'

DC Rees went out with Masson-Smythe and Wycliffe remained in his chair, staring into space. Was Smythe telling the truth? Convicted of robbery with violence, an escaped convict with the strongest motive for killing the girl, was it likely that someone else had murdered her and that he had arrived, innocently, to find her dead? Yet it was too easy to pin the thing on him. And what about the disfigurement? If Masson-Smythe had found her dead, did he then set about destroying her features? And if so, why? A sudden flooding tide of anger? Most professionals were not like that, they seldom let their hearts rule their heads. But had he a motive for disfiguring her? Perhaps. An unidentified corpse found in a hotel bedroom doesn't worry anybody much but the police *as long as it remains unidentified*. But Julie Collins's corpse would soon bring the cops to his doorstep.

Wycliffe sighed and turned his thoughts to Julie herself. He knew quite a lot about her now, but the facts, put together, made a strange pattern – or no pattern at all. Although he knew well enough that human motives are always complex, that every man is a battleground of conflicting desires and emotions, he had still found it useful to try to pin-point a single dominant drive in accounting for any course of action. Greed, jealousy, love, ambition, lust . . . Single words, powerful words, and convenient shorthand with which to label the motives of a man – or of a woman. But Julie refused to be pigeonholed. His mental vision of her remained as enigmatic as his first actual sight of her, lying across her hotel bed, naked, in the posture of love.

Plenty of amateur psychologists would have little difficulty in explaining Julie. A neglected child, orphaned at an age when she needed a sense of security most – they would see in her ruthlessness, in the exercise of her power over men, a desire to hit back. And into her frenzied promiscuity they might read a continuing and unsatisfied yearning to identify herself with other human beings, to be accepted. Perhaps they would be right, but Wycliffe felt that such explanations were too facile, they were little better than his word labels. For one thing, neither Julie nor anyone else is simply a product of an environment. Nature, in his book, was at least as important as nurture. Look at Kathy Johnson. He got up from his chair, profoundly dissatisfied, and went into the HQ room.

It was empty but he could hear voices in the little office used by Fehling and Gill. He pushed open the door. Fehling heaved himself out of the chair behind the desk. 'Mr and Mrs Little, sir. Julie's foster parents.'

The Littles were in their late fifties. He was tall, his best suit hung loose on his bony frame and his face was creased with deep lines from nostrils to mouth. His domed head was bald and shining. A Geordie, he turned out to be, who had come south in the Depression and never gone back. His wife was local, plump, comfortable, with a mind of her own though ready enough to play second fiddle in deference to her belief in proper male dominance. They sat close, posed as though waiting for a picture to be taken. 'I only saw her photo in the paper after dinner when I settled down to have a read. It knocked us sideways and we thought we'd better come straight away . . .'

Mrs Little dabbed her eyes with a screwed-up handkerchief. 'I was telling this gentleman, nine years we had her, she was like our own flesh and blood.'

Under some pressure they admitted that Julie had not been an easy child. 'But we loved her none the less for that!' Mrs Little's features threatened to dissolve at any moment into uncontrollable weeping. 'Once we thought they might make us take her away from school.' She lowered her voice and murmured the dreaded word – 'Stealing! And no need for it, we'd always given her everything she wanted, hadn't we, Bert?'

Mr Little nodded and blinked. He had a habit of blinking nervously whenever he was addressed. 'And we had a bit of trouble with boys – not that I'm narrow, we didn't mind her having boy friends, but this was different. She got herself mixed up with a lot of young thugs. The things we found in her room! I mean it was obvious that she was going all the way and her not fifteen!' He broke off and sighed. 'But she was reasonable, she listened, which is more than some of them will.' He blinked furiously.

'And she was such a clever girl!' Mrs Little redressed the balance. 'You should see her school reports – everything "Excellent" – all her subjects, only at the bottom her headmaster would write something about her attitude and conduct being unsatisfactory.'

'What about her marriage?'

They looked at each other and tacitly agreed that it was mother's turn. 'We didn't know anything about it until young Collins came along and asked our permission. We was taken aback, I can tell you! At first we was all against it; for one thing she was too young to marry and he was a man of thirty-six . . .'

Mr Little, revolving his trilby hat in his lap, took up the tale: 'Of course it wasn't for us to decide really, it was up to the Children's Officer, but we talked it over and in the end we agreed it might be the best thing for her. She was set on it anyway.'

'It was a good chance,' Mrs Little said. 'The Collinses are a respected family in the town, she wouldn't want for anything. But it didn't work.'

'Have you heard from her since she went away?'

Mrs Little shook her head and her husband answered, 'Not so much as a Christmas card.'

'Did you know her parents?'

Mrs Little looked at her husband, her tiny mouth pursed in disapproval. He blinked and said, 'Yes, we knew them.'

'We used to feel sorry for the little girl, they neglected her, always gallivanting off and leaving her to fend for herself, poor little mite!'

'Her mother was on the stage before she married him – or said she was. She made up enough.'

'He was a carpenter, wasn't he?' Wycliffe asked.

Mr Little smiled. 'You could call him that, I suppose. He used to make old-fashioned chairs and tables in a shed behind the house. I suppose he must have sold them because they never seemed to be short of money.'

'He was all right in his way,' Mrs Little argued. 'It was her!'

'They lived near you?'

'Next door when we lived down on the Plain, before we moved to the estate. Julie used to spend most of her time in our place even then.'

11

It was after eight when Gill finally telephoned and Wycliffe had been sitting at his desk since six. From time to time he pretended to work on the reports but most of the time he dozed. His head would sag on his chest and he was asleep. It was a warm evening and he envied the people still messing about in boats in the harbour, the sea like glass on the evening flood. He even envied the people in church with the west doors open and the sun streaming down the nave. When the phone rang he woke with a start and it took him a moment to re-member where he was. 'Any luck?'

'Not so's you'd notice. It's no rest cure trying to find anybody in London on a fine Sunday. Anyway I had a word with the owner of the strip joints where she used to work and with her landlady of those days. Nothing much we don't know already. Then I ran down the manager of the night club where she's under contract – or was. I found him at a sort of pansies' *soirée* in Camden Town. He was a mite peeved at first . . .'

'Never mind the local colour, let's have the facts,' Wycliffe growled.

'Yes, sir! He's definitely cheesed off. Says he'll lose a mint through this. Apparently her act was a sensation. She used to come on all in white silk, down to her ankles, hair to her shoulders, innocent and virginal. Then she'd sing obscene little ditties in a husky contralto. All the time she'd never fetch a smile and look vaguely shocked when the audience laughed their heads off. The manager told me she's already made two records and was all set to be a money spinner.'

'There are easier ways of making a living than being a policeman.'

Gill cackled. 'You can say that again. You ought to see this chick's bankbook! Lovely figures all down one side – in black.'

'I gather you've been to her flat?'

'Eager Beaver – that's me! Nice place, nice neighbourhood.

People don't care what you do as long as you don't disturb them doing it. Her place, all white and oatmeal . . .'

'What? I thought you said oatmeal?'

'I did, it's a sort of beige . . .'

'Never mind. Any books?'

'Books? Hundreds! Place is like a public library. Some of them are quite interesting.'

'In what way?'

'Let's call them text books of sexual technology. She must have made a study of it.'

'I expect she did, it was her living one way or another.'

'She seems to have done a spot of blackmail as a sideline – nothing spectacular – chicken feed compared with what she got more or less legit. A little book with several addresses and against one or two of them sums of money at intervals. Amounts between fifty and three or four hundred. One of the providers is on our patch – our friend Masson-Smythe.'

'I've been talking to him this afternoon. Any evidence?'

'Evidence?'

'Don't be difficult, Jim! If she's blackmailing she must have something.'

'Not a thing!'

That was the irony of it. So many victims of blackmail are paying up on evidence long since destroyed.

'Anything else?'

'No, sir. Sufficient unto the day . . .'

'You'd better come home, my lad.'

Wycliffe put the telephone back on its rest, stretched and yawned. Sufficient unto the day . . . It was too late for dinner but he would be able to get cold meat and salad.

He had his cold meat and salad with half a bottle of Beaujolais, but only just. He was sitting back and thinking about lighting his pipe when the loudspeaker paged him. Helen, her hair bleached, her skin pink after a day on the water, looked at him with concern. 'You're dog tired.'

'Don't be silly, I've been sleeping most of the evening!'

It was Fehling, who had been given the job of getting a warrant and organizing the search of the Voodoo premises. 'I was beginning

311

to think that every magistrate had emigrated! Anyway, I made it in the end. I'm speaking from the club now.'

'Any luck?'

Fehling was hesitant. 'Of course we're not through yet, sir, but I've got a feeling this place is clean. There's nothing here which could incriminate a monk. They were ready for us!'

Wycliffe was not very interested but he tried to sound consoling. 'I shouldn't worry, we've got more than enough to cook Masson-Smythe's goose.'

'That's not the point, sir! I was counting on getting a lead on some of his pals – past and present.'

'Very frustrating!' Wycliffe couldn't get worked up over Fehling's yearning for promotion. 'Anything else?'

'Yes, the Masson-Smythe woman made a break for it just before I arrived. Not very clever! Apparently she phoned for a taxi and when it arrived just turned up on the step all ready for the off. Of course, DC Hartley, who was keeping obo, put paid to that! He's with me now, by the way, not much point in him going back on obo when . . .'

'None,' Wycliffe agreed. He saw no reason so far for stirring out of the hotel again. He wished that Fehling would dry up and he struggled to light his pipe with the receiver wedged between his cheek and his shoulder.

'There was one other thing, sir. In a drawer of Smythe's desk I found a silver framed photograph of the dead girl. I wondered . . .'

'The one from her dressing table?' Wycliffe was on the ball now. All that kerfuffle before coming to the point! Of course it might not *be* the point for Fehling.

'It could be, sir. We shall have to show it to the girl at the Marina.'

'Prints?'

'Only one or two smears, nothing identifiable.'

'I'll be down. Give me ten minutes.'

Thelma Masson-Smythe was composed and inclined to offence rather than defence. 'I don't know by what right . . .'

Wycliffe ignored her. She was lounging among the cushions of an overblown settee like some Hollywood *femme fatale* of the twenties. Her baggage, two suitcases, was still on the floor beside her.

'Open them up,' to Hartley who hovered in the background.

'They've been searched, sir, there's nothing . . .'

'Never mind, open them.'

Hartley lifted one of the cases on to a chair, snapped the catches and lifted the lid. Thelma Masson-Smythe sat up to get a better view. Her manner was indifferent, almost sardonic. The case was half empty, a few underclothes thrown in on two or three summer dresses neatly folded in polythene bags. Wycliffe lifted out a couple of slips, a brassiere and two pairs of briefs.

'You get a kick out of that?' As with her husband, the thin veneer was peeling off and the real woman beginning to show through, a hard-faced tart.

The second case held a coat and skirt, a nightdress and a few more items of underwear. Wycliffe closed the lid and turned to the woman. He was puzzled; sure that she had hoaxed them, but he could not see what she had achieved by doing it. 'You intended to travel light?' The first words he had spoken to her since his arrival.

She puffed cigarette smoke ceilingwards and watched it rise. 'I was in a hurry.' The plain orange dress she wore was sleeveless, tight, and so brief that it made Wycliffe slightly uneasy to look at her, embarrassed by the sheer bulk of naked pink flesh.

'No woman is in too much of a hurry to put in her toilet things.'

'I forgot.'

Wycliffe lit his pipe. 'You were told this afternoon that your husband had been arrested and that you would be able to talk to him if you came to the station.'

'I'm not responsible for his troubles!'

Wycliffe left her, still puzzled and disgruntled, and wandered about the premises, watching Fehling's men at work, searching every drawer, every cupboard. No stone unturned. But he agreed with the inspector, it was a waste of time. He looked at the silver framed photograph of the dead girl, a head and shoulders, a colour print like the stills outside cinemas.

'You think Masson-Smythe took it when he went to the Marina?' Fehling asked.

'It's possible.'

Fehling shook his massive head. 'I don't see why he should have unless he also battered her face in. I mean, if he wanted to destroy clues to her identity, there wouldn't be much point in taking the photo and leaving the girl . . .'

313

They were in Smythe's office and Wycliffe perched himself on the edge of the desk. 'Have you thought that it might have been a woman who did the battering?'

It was obvious that the idea had not occurred to Fehling, equally obvious that he was taken by it. 'Thelma?'

'I don't know.'

'She could have followed her husband . . .' He was getting enthusiastic. 'By all accounts she had reason enough to hate the girl.'

Wycliffe was still holding the photograph and he began to remove it from its frame. 'There, on the back in pencil: *Voodoo* and a serial number. That would be reason enough for Smythe to take it away with him, it was one of his publicity shots of the girl and he wouldn't want that found beside her body . . .'

'The same would apply to Thelma.'

'Of course!' He was chasing an elusive idea which had nothing to do with the photograph. 'Why did she call a taxi?'

Fehling looked surprised. 'To make a bolt for it, I suppose.'

'Nonsense! She's too wily a bird not to know that we had the place covered.'

'Then I don't follow . . .'

'She *wanted* to be stopped. She had no intention of taking that taxi.' He broke off. 'Send for Hartley.'

DC Hartley was a Wiltshireman and his voice would have been God's gift to a radio gardening programme. 'Sir?'

'Did anybody enter the premises during the evening before Mrs Masson-Smythe tried to leave?'

Hartley's expression was sufficient answer.

'All right, you forgot, what happened afterwards put it out of your mind . . .'

'I noted it, sir.' He brought out his notebook and flipped over the pages. 'Four thirty, sir. A girl, blonde, smallish, light blue summer dress and white handbag . . .'

'When did she come out?'

Hartley flushed. 'She didn't, sir.'

'Then she must be here now. Have you found her?' Nasty. Wycliffe didn't wait for a reply but turned to Fehling. 'That's where your evidence is gone. Now, Hartley, what did you do when you saw Mrs Masson-Smythe about to clear out in a taxi?'

'I went over and stopped her, sir.'

'Was she abusive?'

'Resigned, I would have said, sir. She didn't seem very surprised.'

'What did you do then?'

'Why, I went in with her to the lounge, I was about to phone through to the station and report when Inspector Fehling turned up . . .'

'And while you were escorting her indoors, the other young woman skipped out with a suitcase containing what Inspector Fehling is looking for.'

'And now,' said Fehling, ominously, 'we're looking for a smallish blonde who wears a light blue dress and carries a white handbag. Hartley!'

Wycliffe had found that the chance to play the great detective came rarely and when it did you had to avoid sounding smug. 'I should try 4a, Mount Zion, Hartley. Ask for Sadie Field.'

'The stripper?' Fehling was incredulous. 'I thought you said she was a decent sort of girl?'

'She is but she's also a bit dumb and scared of losing her job, just the sort Thelma would choose to do her dirty work. In any case, Sadie won't have heard yet that her employer has been nicked.'

'Well! What are you waiting for, Hartley?' Fehling was smarting a bit.

'Go easy on her!' Wycliffe ordered. 'She's more sinned against than sinning.'

He wandered out of the office and down the steps to the club. The lights were on, and two solemn dicks were shaking one of the giant polystyrene statues between them, to see if it rattled. It was too much for Wycliffe and he made his way back to the lounge.

Thelma seemed not to have moved but she was sipping a drink and there was a tray of drinks on a small table by the settee. 'Found what you're looking for, superintendent? If you would tell me what it is, perhaps I could help you?'

Wycliffe perched on the arm of a voluptuous black leather monster which seemed ready to engulf and perhaps digest anyone with the temerity to sit in it properly.

'Whisky, superintendent?' Her assurance was brittle and when he merely sat and stared at her without speaking he was gratified to see her shift her position slightly and make an ineffective effort to pull down the hem of her dress.

315

'I found an interesting photograph, a photograph of Julie Collins in a silver frame. It was last seen on the dressing table in her bedroom at the Marina.'

She stopped with her glass midway to her lips. 'That's not possible.'

'Oh, it's possible all right, your husband admits that he went to see the girl on the night she was murdered. He says, of course, that she was dead when he got there.'

She was off the settee in a flash, upsetting her drink down the front of her dress. 'You filthy, lying, stinking cop! You can't pin that on him!'

Wycliffe was unmoved. 'That remains to be seen, but what interests me at the moment is your share in the business.'

'Me?' Her surprise could have been genuine. Standing there with the gin soaking into the bodice of her dress, without shoes, her hair and eyes wild, it was hard to connect her with the woman in the blue gown whom Helen had described as 'striking', who moved about the club, suave and graceful, the experienced professional hostess.

'You haven't been told that Julie's face was destroyed by an attacker who battered her with a heavy brass weight.'

This stopped her. She went to the settee and sat on the edge, her legs apart, her hands drooping between them. 'Serves her bloody well right, she was a dirty whore!'

'You had reason to be jealous of her. Is it possible that you followed your husband that night . . . ?'

'Me? You think that I . . . ?'

'You hated the girl and you are obviously vicious.'

'You can't set me up, copper!' But there was no longer any punch behind the words. She was shaken, and she continued to sit in the same posture as before, for once unselfconscious, like a little girl, a little girl with a problem.

He drove back to his hotel. The town was deserted and as he passed through the square the town clock was doling out the strokes of midnight. The hotel garage was full so he left his car in the forecourt. The night porter admitted him. 'Developments, sir?' Wycliffe grunted. He had his foot on the carpeted stair, then he noticed that there was still light in the television lounge.

'They're down, sir.'

'Down?'

'The astronauts, they've touched down on the moon.'

He had forgotten and the fact unsettled him. But he did not go into the television lounge, instead he went through to the terrace. He lit his pipe and rested his arms on the balustrade, staring out over the harbour. It was very quiet, a noise of purring machinery from the docks, and that was all. He could make out the shape of the little sailing boat belonging to the young couple. There was a riding light at the masthead and he thought that he could distinguish a dim glow from the porthole of the tiny cabin.

Tonight men would walk on the moon. He tried to take it in, to grasp and hold the thought that this moment of time was shared with two men in their fragile capsule on the surface of the moon a quarter of a million miles away. He tried and failed. It was when he made an effort to think in a disciplined way about anything that he was most conscious of his shortcomings. And this reflection brought him back to the case. Not only did he find sustained logical thought difficult but he was always short of written data. He had the official reports but these were so full as to be almost useless. Any other detective would have a sheaf of private notes, but he rarely wrote anything down and if he did he either lost it or threw it away. Notes were repugnant to him. Even now he ought to be sitting at a desk with a notepad in front of him, jotting down his ideas, transposing and relating facts like a jig-saw.

Like hell!

But the price he paid was heavy, his thoughts went in circles.

Julie Collins had been strangled, then viciously assaulted. If Masson-Smythe spoke the truth, one did not immediately follow the other. Had the murderer been interrupted in his work? Had he retreated somewhere when he heard Smythe coming? The figure on the fire-escape? It seemed improbable. He could only have left the girl's room through the door, in which case Smythe would almost certainly have seen him. *Had* Smythe seen him? Unlikely but not impossible. But if the murderer had already gone when Masson-Smythe arrived, that presupposed that someone else had come after him and disfigured the girl.

Had the man on the fire-escape watched the murder, seen Smythe enter and leave, and *then* come in through the bathroom window to carry out his task? But why?

317

There was movement on the little yacht, a lithe figure climbing on to the cabin roof, standing by the mast; the glimmer of a cigarette.

And if Smythe was lying? It was possible though unlikely that the man who had intercourse with the girl was not her murderer. That let Smythe out, for according to Rashleigh he was Group O. But he could have been responsible for the disfigurement to make identification difficult and reduce the risk of being linked with the crime. Far fetched? But there had to be some explanation and if he had rejected every far fetched hypothesis in his cases a good many would have remained unsolved.

The girl had joined her lover, they were standing side by side now, he could see the glow of both cigarettes; from time to time one or the other would describe a small trajectory in the darkness.

As to suspects, he had plenty. Allen, Smythe, Collins, Byrne – though he could hardly take Byrne seriously. And if hate was the motive for the mutilation, who had better reason to hate her than the women?

He went inside.

'Not staying up for the walk, sir?'

'No.'

As he slid in beside his wife he could feel the glowing warmth from her sun-tanned skin. 'You'll be sore tomorrow,' he whispered.

12

He woke with his course of action clear in his mind and with the confidence that it would bring results. By the time he went to bed again the case would be over. A sanguine view considering his vague speculations of the previous night but it was a familiar pattern. Somehow the alchemy of sleep had once more cleared and ordered his thoughts. He could not explain it, he just knew, and because he knew he hummed a little tune in the bathroom. Helen, still in bed, called to him, 'You sound happy this morning!'

'I am! How are the shoulders?'

'Sore.'

'That'll teach you to go to sea decently clad.'

'The twins rang up last night.' The Wycliffes had twin children, a boy and a girl of nineteen and they had been camping in France.

'Oh, they're back are they?'

'They came back on somebody's yacht of all things – somebody they met in Cherbourg while they were waiting for the ferry.'

He couldn't help remembering his own youth when a day trip to Barmouth was something to look forward to and back on for weeks.

He was in the bedroom now, in his dressing gown. Out of the window he could see the little boat belonging to the young couple. They were swimming again, although it was raining. For some reason he felt a sudden pang of sadness and sighed.

'What's the matter?'

'Old age – what else?'

Before breakfast they watched a telerecording of the moon walk. 'That's one small step for man, one giant leap for mankind.' Neil Armstrong's words, they impressed him. He wondered why he felt that men who walked on the moon should have come from a better world.

When he arrived at the station there were half-a-dozen pressmen lounging round the enquiry desk, including Brown from the local paper.

'Good morning, lads!'

'Has Masson-Smythe been arrested?'

'What's he charged with?'

'Off the record . . .'

'Is the case over?'

Wycliffe lit his pipe. 'If you got all the answers you know very well you couldn't print 'em. Mr Masson-Smythe was with me yesterday afternoon . . .'

'. . . helping with enquiries!' they finished for him.

'Exactly! However, certain charges have been made but they have no direct connection with the murder.'

'What are the charges?'

'He will be coming up before the magistrates this morning.'

'What about Allen?'

'He is back in custody and, presumably, the law will proceed against him where it left off.'

'But he slugged you on Friday night at the club.'

'Did he? I shouldn't print that if I were you, he might have you for libel.'

One shrivelled little fellow who looked in need of a good meal but was, in fact, the most experienced of them, spoke for the first time. 'The super promised a statement and that's all we're going to get. Let's have it.'

'Good! Here it is: "For reasons connected with the inquiry, the police have not previously disclosed that the dead girl's features had been so mutilated after death as to make them unrecognizable."'

This silenced them and by the time they found fresh questions Wycliffe was half-way up the stairs to his office. Fehling was waiting for him. 'What about the Spaniard? He's due to sail at six this evening.'

'Let him!' Wycliffe growled. 'We've got enough crooks of our own.'

It was half past nine when he arrived at the bookshop. The little rat-faced man was scrubbing the steps but Wycliffe went to the side door. He did not ring, it was unlocked, so he climbed the carpeted stairs without invitation. At the top he called, 'Is anyone at home?' Aunt Jane came out of the kitchen at the end of the dimly lit corridor.

'I'm extremely sorry! I hope you don't mind me coming up but I think your bell must be out of order.'

'Superintendent!' She was all of a flutter but welcoming. 'Let me get out of this overall. Just step into the lounge, superintendent, I'll be with you in a moment.'

He found himself once more in the depressing room overlooking the street; nothing had changed. He stood by the window watching the traffic until she joined him. She was nervous, alternately patting her cropped hair and smoothing the creases from her blue linen dress. Except for a difference in length, it seemed to be a replica of a dress Wycliffe's grandmother had worn when he first remembered her. She made him sit down in one of the easy chairs and perched herself on one of the straightbacks.

'I'm glad to see you recovered, Miss Collins.'

'Oh, yes, I'm quite recovered, thank you, superintendent. They wanted me to spend a few days in a nursing home but I told them I have a few things to clear up here first. After that we shall see.'

Wycliffe scarcely knew where to begin.

'By all means smoke, superintendent! My father and my brother smoked a pipe and I like the smell of tobacco.'

It was something. He lit up.

'It was clever of you to come, superintendent.'

'Clever?'

'Of course! To realize that it was I who could tell you about Willie. Ada is his mother but she's never been *close* to him. Even when he was a little boy it was to me that he came with all his troubles and we would sit down together and work something out. He was such a sensitive child, superintendent, and Ada never really understood him. Willie is a Collins.'

'You've lived here for a long time, Miss Collins?'

'All my life, it's my home.' She looked down at her large bony hands, clasped in her lap. 'Ada always frustrated Willie; she still does. She seems to think it's a sin for people to do what they want, a sin not to be always *busy*. Yet we know our Lord's answer to Martha, don't we?' She spoke as though they shared a cosy but rather guilty secret. 'I can remember so well, when Willie was a little boy, she used to say, "You can play with your soldiers, Willie, but only until tea-time", "You can read *one* chapter of your book", or "You can go out for half-an-hour". Of course, she was just the same with his

321

father. I've always said he wouldn't have gone like he did if it hadn't been for her.'

'And Willie still comes to you with his troubles?'

She flashed him a quick, anxious look from her slightly protuberant eyes, and for some reason her lower lip trembled. He was afraid that she would cry but she recovered herself. 'He always confides in me.'

'Did he tell you that Julie had written to him to say that she was coming back?'

Her face hardened. 'Iris has been talking to you, I know. She's no right, she's only an employee!'

Wycliffe stood up. 'I could call him up and ask him now . . .'

'No!' Her reaction was so sharp that it startled him. 'No, I don't want him here.' She smoothed the material of her dress. 'He told me.'

'Did he think that she was coming back to him?'

'He hoped that she would.'

'And you?'

'I wanted what he wanted.'

He could see her mental conflict reflected in her face. 'She was a slut!' And she added, 'He would never have married her if it hadn't been for Ada's scheming.'

'When did you give him the money, Miss Collins?'

Her jaw set in a firm line. 'I don't know what you're talking about!'

He was gentle. 'I can get a court order in a case of this sort. Your bank would have to tell the truth.'

She gave in at once. 'Ada always kept him short! My brother never intended it to be like that. He left the business to Ada for her lifetime, just to protect her, but she's used the will to keep her son tied to her apron strings. The poor boy's never had any money of his own, just the pittance he draws as salary . . . It makes my blood boil!'

'So you gave him a thousand pounds in cash. What did he say it was for?'

'For Julie. He told me exactly what it was for, we don't have any secrets from each other. The money was for her.'

'Why, exactly, did she need a thousand pounds?'

'She said in her letter that she was in trouble with the police and that she needed the money to avoid going to prison. She hinted that if he helped her she would come back to him.'

'You believed all this?'

She gave him an odd look. 'Certainly not! But he did. It was very thinly disguised blackmail!'

'Yet you let him go through with it – gave him the money to go through with it.'

She laughed without humour. 'You don't keep people's love by telling them the truth, superintendent. You have to let them find that out for themselves – then be there waiting for them.'

Love should never repel but Wycliffe was repelled. The Marina seemed to him at that moment a haven of sanity and decency compared with this little bourgeois household. But what was the point in making such comparisons? Such judgements? People lived their lives and who was he to moralize? He had never had the Collinses for a family or Julie for a wife. If he had, who could say?

She sat watching him, a tentative smile on her lips. 'Anyhow, it will come right now.'

'Come right?'

'She's dead, isn't she?'

'Murdered.'

She shook her head.

'Julie was strangled, Miss Collins, there can be no doubt of that.'

But she continued to shake her head.

'Are you afraid that it was Willie who killed her? Perhaps you know that it was he – did he confide in you?'

The look she gave him sprang from a sudden flare of hatred. 'Don't be absurd! Willie wouldn't hurt a fly, you have only to look at him . . . Nobody but a fool would . . .'

'Then what are you afraid of?'

'That you will get things wrong.' She made an effort to control herself. 'After all, you don't know him as I do.'

Wycliffe looked at her for some time, his eyes steady and grave. At last she raised hers and their gaze met. They sat for a little longer in silence, then Wycliffe stood up. 'Well, Miss Collins, thank you for talking to me. I will go through the bookroom, if I may, to the shop.'

'You are going to see him?'

'There are one or two points.'

She would have liked to stop him but she realized that she was helpless. 'Very well! You know the way. But remember, super-intendent, he's not himself.'

He went down to the next landing while she stood at the top of the stairs watching. The only light in the corridor and down the stairs came from fanlights over the doors of the rooms. The atmosphere was oppressive, claustrophobic. He paused at the green baize door. 'To spend one's whole life in such a place!'

One old gentleman burrowed among the books but otherwise the secondhand department was deserted. Willie's mother's chair was empty though her knitting lay beside the till. He went down the spiral staircase. At the bottom, a door which he had noticed before was standing slightly ajar; he pushed it open without knocking and came upon a tableau which interested him. Iris, Willie and his mother in attitudes which they held as though petrified. The old lady had an unhealthy flush, Iris was pale, Willie looked sullen. The room was a little office and in contrast with the gloom of the flat which he had just left, it was gay with reflected sunlight, the ceiling and walls brilliant with dancing patterns of light from the waters of the harbour outside. He must have blinked foolishly in the doorway. The old lady was first to recover. 'You wished to speak to me, superintendent?' Precisely the right blend of courtesy and rebuke. He had to admit to a grudging admiration, and yet she had made a substantial contribution to the wrecking of two lives and, perhaps, to the premature ending of a third. But was it fair to blame her? No doubt she had told herself that she had to provide the drive which Willie lacked. No doubt she had said the same of his father. Perhaps she was right.

'I want to talk to your son, Mrs Collins.'

Willie seemed to awake from a trance. 'To me? Then we'd better go upstairs.' The old lady made a move but he added, 'No, mother!' He followed Wycliffe out, leaving the two women together.

Willie's room was as gay as the office. Wycliffe sat himself in a chair facing the window while Willie took the swivel chair by his work table. He had been busy, the table was covered by a large sheet of cardboard on which a large-scale map had been drawn and in one corner a legend: *Austerlitz: December 2nd. 1805*. Fragments of card in various shapes and sizes with evocative labels were pinned to the map. Willie had sought refuge from reality in the reconstruction of one of Napoleon's most famous victories.

'So the money came from your aunt.' Frontal attack.

'She told you!'

324

'She had no option. Now, Mr Collins, last time I was here you told me that you hadn't seen your wife since she left the town. Now you will have to tell a different story so make sure this one is the truth.'

Willie looked older and vaguer, it was impossible to know whether his attention had been gained, whether he understood the seriousness of his position. Wycliffe suspected that he was too withdrawn, too self absorbed.

'When did you give her the money?'

He looked as though he did not understand the question and made no attempt to answer.

'I have a witness who will say that your wife was expecting a visitor at midnight on the night of her death. He will also say that she was expecting to receive certain money from her husband – from you, Mr Collins.'

The words seemed to be lost on him. He passed his hand over his forehead and murmured, 'I want to know who did that to her; if only I could be sure!'

Wycliffe remembered times in his own life when he had seemed to lose contact with the world outside, to become aware of it only when it obtruded in some unwelcome fashion. At such times he might have voiced his thoughts aloud and been ashamed and irritated if someone overheard and tried to answer. But it was not for him to be sympathetic. 'It is my belief that on Tuesday night, just before midnight, you went to the Marina to give your wife the thousand pounds you had obtained from your aunt. You did this by arrangement with your wife, an arrangement made over the telephone or, perhaps, you discussed it when you met her outside the hotel on Tuesday morning. You were seen talking to her,' he added and Willie did not deny it.

Willie stood up and began moving restlessly about the room. Wycliffe was still not sure how far he had penetrated the depths of his introspection. 'Why did you kill her?'

The thick lenses flashed in the light but Willie said nothing.

'You made love to her, then you strangled her – why? Did she ridicule you? Did she tell you that she had fooled you again? That she had no intention of coming back to the life you could offer her?' There was no doubt now that he had riveted Willie's attention. 'Or did she make you intolerably jealous by taunting you with the affairs she had had with other men? Worse still, were you standing on the fire escape, watching, while she tried to persuade Allen to make love to her?'

He paused and though Willie said nothing his eyes never left Wycliffe's.

'You said yourself that there is a point beyond which the worm will turn. For everyone, according to you, there is a threshold of violence. Did Julie push you over that threshold?'

He was gambling on the assumption that in the five days since Julie's death Willie's guilt had become an insupportable burden, that he would find immeasurable relief in confession. For Wycliffe was satisfied that Willie had killed his wife and equally convinced that he had not mutilated her afterwards. The sight of her in the mortuary had overwhelmed him and Wycliffe believed that eventually the blend of guilt, bewilderment, horror and fear would be too much for him. All his life he had taken his troubles to someone, usually to Aunt Jane; the two of them would 'sit down and work something out together'. Had he gone to her and blurted out, 'I've killed Julie'? From Aunt Jane's manner Wycliffe was inclined to think not. Willie was carrying this, his greatest burden, alone – so far.

He was standing by the shelves where his soldiers were deployed, fiddling with them, shifting one here and another there, then putting them back to their original positions. His hand hovered over a troop of cavalry and he lifted one of the red-coated horsemen and held it, seeming to study the modelling intently. Wycliffe let him be and looked out of the window, watching three tugs fussing round a giant tanker like Lilliputians round a Gulliver.

'She said in her letter that I mustn't come to the hotel until she sent for me but I couldn't keep away. I walked past the place six or seven times on the Monday without catching sight of her, but on Tuesday morning I was lucky, I met her just as she was coming out of the gate . . .' His voice faltered and he stopped speaking. No doubt he was reliving the moment when he had first set eyes on her after months of separation. 'She seemed no different, it was just as though we had run into one another in the street as we sometimes did when she was . . . when we were living together. She said, "Oh, Willie! this will save me phoning", and she told me what she wanted me to do – to bring the money that night.'

'She had told you in her letter how much?'

He resented the interruption and dismissed it with a nod. 'She told me to come by the fire escape which goes up to the bathroom window at the back of the hotel. There's a footpath which runs along by the railway cutting round the backs of the houses . . .' His voice trailed off into silence. He put down his horseman and picked up another.

'Did you tell anyone of your appointment?'

He looked at Wycliffe for some time before answering, as though debating in his mind what to say, then, 'I told my aunt.' As he spoke, his hand closed on the little horseman and the delicate metal legs snapped. He opened his hand and looked blankly at the fragments then he allowed them to slide off his hand on to the carpet.

'Why did you kill her?'

No answer.

Wycliffe was conscious of the delicacy of his task, to exert enough pressure to make him talk without reducing him to hysterical incoherence. 'You loved her?'

'She was the only . . .' He broke off and after a moment said, simply, 'Yes.'

'Have you ever had a blood test, Mr Collins?'

'A blood test?' Surprise, but not apprehension.

'To determine your blood group.'

'Yes, I'm AB.'

'A rather rare group.'

'Yes.'

'The man who had intercourse with your wife immediately before her death was of that group.'

The sensitive mouth twitched but he said nothing.

'It is possible to tell from the semen.'

No response.

Wycliffe was beginning to be oppressed by a curious lethargy. The warm room, the dazzling light, Willie's answer drawn from him laboriously, flat and colourless. He lit his pipe. When he spoke again his manner was friendly. 'You are not the stuff of which criminals are made, Mr Collins. Sooner or later you will find it imperative to talk. Already you are torn apart by a conflict between your instinct for self preservation and an almost irresistible longing to discharge some measure of your guilt by confession and by explanation. To explain – to be able to say, "This is *why* I did it; this is how it happened!"

'Believe me, the conflict is spurious. You cannot, whatever you do, preserve yourself, you have already destroyed the person you were.'

Willie was still standing by the shelves but he was watching Wycliffe and listening. 'Confession, atonement, absolution – is that the formula?' Except for a tremor in his voice the question might have been part of a cosy academic discussion.

'No. Because in my view there is no atonement for murder.'

'A priest would do better.'

'But I am a policeman.' He knew that Willie was on the brink of decision, he knew too that silence would be his best advocate, but at that moment the door opened and Aunt Jane came in.

Wycliffe stood up. 'I think, Miss . . .'

But she turned on him, silencing him with a look. 'I wish to make a statement, superintendent.'

'About what, Miss Collins?'

'I killed Julie.' She spoke triumphantly, the slight smile which so often seemed to hover round her lips was more pronounced, and, as always, it was a smile of satisfaction. 'I killed her, there is no need to torture this poor boy any longer.'

Wycliffe was surprised less by the confession than by Willie's reaction. He gazed at his aunt and in his gaze there was nothing of incredulity or relief or bewilderment, only hatred, and hatred so intense that Wycliffe wondered if he might attack her.

'Well? Are you going to arrest me?'

'I shall need more than a simple assertion of guilt before I do that, Miss Collins.'

'All right! I'll tell you about it. Am I allowed to sit down?'

'Of course!' He gave her his own chair and perched himself on one corner of a built-in cabinet. She sat on the edge of the chair, bolt upright, bony hands clasped in her lap. Her grey eyes seemed more protuberant, her wispy hair more wild. 'I must caution you . . .'

She brushed aside his words. 'When Willie showed me her letter I knew that it would be useless to refuse to help or to argue with him but I was determined that he shouldn't be trapped by that creature a second time.'

Wycliffe glanced across at Willie but he had resumed his seat by the table and his head was bent over his reconstruction of the battle.

'When he told me that he was to see her on Tuesday night I decided to follow him.' She pursed her lips.

Wycliffe looked at the hard embittered features, the mean mouth, and wondered how the love of this woman differed from that of another. Why should it repel instead of attract? Why should it isolate rather than unite? Because it was selfish? Possessive, certainly, but hardly selfish . . .

'You followed your nephew to the hotel?'

She chose to think that he was doubting her and turned to Willie for confirmation. 'You know that I'm speaking the truth, don't you, Willie?'

But Willie continued to stare at the desk as though he had not heard.

'He came into my room next morning just as it was getting light and saw my wet things. It started to rain just before one o'clock when I was coming back and I got nearly wet through. When Willie opened my door I was awake and he was about to speak when he caught sight of my wet coat spread over the dressing table to dry. I could see by the look on his face that he understood.'

'Understood what, Miss Collins?'

She looked at him craftily. 'That I had followed him.'

Wycliffe waited, but no more came. 'Is this true, Mr Collins?'

Silence for a moment, then the single word, 'Yes.'

This confirmation seemed to be what she had waited for and she continued her story. 'As I said, I followed him when I heard him leave the house just before twelve on Tuesday night. There was nobody about and I had to stay well back for fear of being seen but I knew where he was going so it hardly mattered. I was surprised when he walked right past the Marina but he continued round the corner towards the railway and I understood. He took the narrow path that leads behind the houses on the edge of the cutting and at one of the back doors he stopped and let himself in. After a minute or two I followed. Luckily I waited by the door for a while for it was some time before I saw him on the fire escape; he seemed to be waiting but after a little while I heard a window opening and he disappeared inside. There was only one light on in the place and that was in the room next to the top of the escape.'

329

'What did you intend to do? What was the point of following your nephew?'

She gave the question thought, frowning as though in an effort to recall her exact state of mind. 'I'm not sure what I intended to do. I think I meant to wait until Willie had gone and then go in and talk to her . . . I don't know for certain because everything turned out differently. At any rate I climbed the escape and when I got level with the lighted window I could see that it had no blind and the curtains were not drawn so I could look right into the room.' She hesitated and for the first time seemed to have difficulty in going on.

'What did you see?'

She sighed. 'They were both there, Willie and the girl. Willie must have given her the money before I got there and they were talking. She was sitting on the bed in her dressing gown and Willie was standing over her. He seemed to be reasoning with her or arguing, then she started to laugh. She stood up and took off her dressing gown so that she was naked, then she . . . she began to . . .' She broke off and there were spots of colour in her cheeks. 'I never imagined that any woman could be so degraded!' She made a curious little noise, between a sob and a snort. 'We all know that men . . . She undressed him – literally and I had to watch while . . . And she was laughing all the time, that made it worse. She seemed to be taunting him and even while he . . . while he was under the spell of her lust, she continued to laugh at him and provoke him. I could see that he was angry because there were tears in his eyes and from a child he has always cried when he was angry and not when he was hurt. She was a devil and she deserved to die!' The telling of her story had excited her so that she was breathing rapidly and her hands twisted incessantly in her lap.

He looked at Willie, still slumped in his chair without a movement. Her gaze followed Wycliffe's and for a moment her features softened. Wycliffe looked from one to the other and felt sick. 'What happened?'

'Afterwards he got up and dressed himself . . .'

'Leaving Julie on the bed?'

A moment of hesitation, then, 'Yes, leaving her lying there, watching him.'

'Did she lie still?'

Her eyes narrowed. 'She wasn't dead if that's what you mean. She continued talking to him and laughing.'

'And what did he do?'

'He just dressed and left.'

'And she was alive when he left?'

'Certainly she was alive.'

'What did you do?'

'I was afraid for a moment that he would come out on to the fire escape and find me there but he didn't, he must have left by the front door. The window of the bathroom was still open and I climbed in. When I got to her she was still lying on the bed.'

'She must have been surprised to see you.'

'I suppose she was, I didn't give her much chance to think about it. I stood over her and told her what I thought of her.'

'What did she say?'

'She . . . she called me obscene names.'

'Then you strangled her?'

She looked at him curiously. 'I am a strong woman, superintendent, she had much less strength than I and it was surprisingly easy.'

'There must have been a struggle.'

'Hardly any.' She stopped for a moment, apparently to order her thoughts. 'I don't think I really meant to kill her. I didn't . . .'

'You were going to say?'

'Nothing.'

Wycliffe studied her gravely, his eyes steady and unblinking. 'Having strangled her, you then battered her face to make it unrecognizable.'

'No.' Again the crafty look. 'I did not. I heard the front door open and shut and footsteps on the stairs. I was frightened because I felt sure that whoever it was would come to her room. I don't know why I thought so but I was right.'

'So what did you do?'

Incredibly, in view of what had gone before, she looked embarrassed. 'I hid in the clothes cupboard.' She gave a self conscious little laugh. 'I hadn't more than got inside when a man came into the room. He called out, "Julie", in a loud whisper. Then he made some joking remark and walked over to where she was lying on the bed. I couldn't see what he was doing there but I heard him let out an oath.'

'Then?'

'Then he went. He went so quickly and quietly it took me a moment to realize that he had gone.' She sighed deeply. 'I came out of the cupboard . . .'

'Did you see the man?'

'Only his back and that not very clearly, I was afraid to open the door more than a crack.'

'Did the man search the room or take anything from it?'

'I told you, as soon as he found that she was dead he couldn't get away fast enough, but there was one thing, I'd forgotten it until now – he took away her photograph.'

'Her photograph?'

'Yes, one in a silver frame, I noticed it when I was looking in the window and when I came to look for it afterwards, it was gone. He must have taken it.'

'All right go on.'

'I knew what I had to do; if I could prevent that vile woman from causing any more wickedness, I would do it. First I searched the room for anything that would identify her or link her with Willie and . . .'

'But the man had already seen her, lying there – dead.'

She smiled unpleasantly. 'It was obvious that he wouldn't talk. Why didn't he rouse the house? In any case it was a risk I had to take.'

'When you searched the room did you find anything?'

She nodded with satisfaction. 'I found a book of poetry Willie had given her. Apart from the shop label there was an inscription on the fly-leaf in Willie's writing.' She looked across at her nephew, 'I have the book still.'

Willie gave no sign that he had heard.

'It was then that I missed the photograph and realized the man must have taken it.'

'You did not recover your money.'

Her look was enough to tell him that the money had no importance for her. 'I had other things to think about. I had to make her unrecognizable and I was afraid that I should make too much noise and wake the house.'

'What did you use? What weapon?'

'There was a heavy brass weight in the middle of the floor. I suppose they used it as a door stop. It was the weight which gave me the idea in the first place.' She glanced across at Willie and lowered her voice to a whisper, 'I *wanted* to destroy her, she had no right . . .'

'To do what?'

She looked at Willie and back to Wycliffe. 'To live.'

'And having done all this, you walked out. Did you use the fire escape?'

She nodded. 'I went the way I had come.'

'What time was this?'

'It was striking one when I passed the church, just when it started to rain. When I got back here I got out of my wet things and before going to bed I looked in Willie's room. His bed had not been slept in and he was not there. I heard him come in about an hour later.' She looked at Wycliffe challengingly. 'I have told you what happened, superintendent, now you can do what you have to do.'

Wycliffe sat staring at her for a long time but his eyes had lost focus. There was silence in the room except for the noises from the docks and the muffled sounds of traffic in the street. He could hardly believe in the reality of his experience, it was like one of those pointless but infinitely depressing dreams from which one knows there will be an awakening. He stirred himself. 'Mr Collins!'

No response.

His temper was wearing thin. 'Mr Collins! Kindly turn round and give me your attention!'

Willie obeyed and faced him with a blank stare.

'I want to know if you have been listening to what your aunt has told me?'

'I have been listening.'

Aunt Jane watched her nephew with a solicitude which was at once pathetic and nauseating. He avoided her eyes. Wycliffe concentrated all the force of his personality on getting Willie to look at him and to answer his question. 'To the best of your knowledge, is your aunt's account of what happened true?'

Willie stared at the superintendent and the silence lengthened. Aunt Jane made a small movement as though she would have stretched out her hand to touch him but a frown from Wycliffe stopped her.

'What my aunt has told you is true.'

'You say this, realizing the full implication of her story?'

Another interval. 'Yes.'

'Now, I suppose, you will arrest me,' from Aunt Jane.

'I shall ask you to come with me to the police station and to make a statement. After that we shall see.' He reached for the telephone on Willie's desk and dialled a number. Aunt Jane sat bolt upright on the edge of her chair, serene and content. Willie sat with his head in his hands staring at the carpet.

13

Wycliffe was back in his little office; the clock on the mantelpiece showed a quarter past three and outside the sun still shone. On his desk, two statements, neat little wads of typescript, one from William Reginald Collins, the other from his aunt, Jane Alicia Collins. The two statements corroborated each other in every detail for which corroboration was possible and on the strength of them Jane Alicia Collins had been charged with murder. Jim Gill, who had travelled down overnight, sat on the other side of the desk.

'So it's in the bag?'

Wycliffe was morose. 'You've read the statements?'

Gill nodded. 'I have and it seems watertight to me. What's the matter? Are you afraid they won't stand up in court?'

'I feel sure that they will.'

'Well then!'

Wycliffe stood up. 'She didn't do it, Jim.'

'Didn't do it? But she's made a perfectly reasoned and credible statement full of circumstantial details and Fehling found the weight, locked away in a drawer in her bedroom, with blood and hair still adhering to it . . .'

'And covered with her prints – I know all that, Jim. She battered the girl's face in, there's no doubt of that, but she didn't kill her. I've known from the start that the strangling and the mutilation were irreconcilable, the one came of too much loving, the other from passionate hatred and jealousy.'

Gill took out his cheroots and lit one. 'With all due respect, sir, that's just your reading of the case . . .'

Wycliffe was impatient. 'Read her statement again! It would have been better if you could have listened to her as I did. Circumstantial, as you say, until you come to the bit where she is lying, the bit where she claims to have strangled the girl. Apart from anything else, can you imagine a young and healthy girl being overwhelmed and strangled without one hell of a struggle?'

'You think Collins did it while he was making love to her?'

'I'm sure of it. I very much doubt if he meant to but she was provoking him beyond endurance and unwittingly she reached his threshold of violence.'

'Come again?'

'According to Collins, the point at which the worm turns. Of course, Aunt Jane saw it all through the window and when Willie had cleared out she went in and tidied things up in her own inimitable way.'

Gill studied the ash as it grew on his cheroot. 'If you thought like that, why did you have her charged?'

'What else could I do?'

Gill made a sudden movement which scattered the grey ash over his blue pinstripe. 'Give me ten minutes with Master Willie and I'll give you a confession to beat that one! Little runt, hiding behind a woman's bloody apron!'

Wycliffe smiled. 'He's done that all his life and he's too old to change now. But assuming you got him to talk, what good would it do? Julie's death would blight four other lives – Willie's, his mother's, his aunt's and probably Iris Rogers's too.'

Gill shook his head. 'You mustn't try to play God in this game, Mr Wycliffe.'

Wycliffe looked at him with great gravity. 'I'm not playing God, Jim, you've got the roles mixed, I'm cast as Pontius Pilate.'

That evening at a little after six, Wycliffe and his wife were sitting near the edge of the low cliff which juts out into the sea to form the main bastion of the harbour, a natural breakwater. The tide had turned but the ebb had not yet acquired strength and the flat calm of the evening flood imparted a stillness to everything encouraging a mood of nostalgic sadness.

'What shall we do tomorrow?'

She turned to him in surprise. 'What about the case?'

'It's all over, Gill and Fehling will deal with the paper work.'

She smiled. 'In that case . . .' She broke off. 'Look! There's a ship coming out.'

Creeping out of the harbour, a small vessel with gleaming white paint on her superstructure but the black hull gashed with ugly red splashes. The name on her bows was clearly visible: *SS Peruvia.*

'She's bound for Barranquilla, a port in Colombia, and her skipper is a Spaniard called Hortelano.'

'How on earth do you know that?'

'It's a long story!' He leaned towards her suddenly and kissed her.

'What was that for?'

'For being more or less normal.'

Wycliffe and the Guilt Edged Alibi

I

The estuary of the Treen River divides East from West Treen, but the two are linked by a car and passenger ferry, a floating platform with a ramp at each end and a hut-like superstructure on each side. The hut on one side houses the diesel engine and the one on the other provides shelter for foot passengers when it rains. The engine drives sprocket wheels which, as they rotate, pick up a pair of chains from the bed of the river and haul the craft from shore to shore and back again. Sailings are at half-hour intervals from June to August inclusive, but less frequent at other times. By the third week in September business was already slack, and at ten-thirty on Tuesday morning the skipper and his mate had made only two return trips, one for the workers at seven-thirty and one for the white-collars at eight-thirty. Now they were taking aboard the milk lorry on its way back to the factory after the morning collection from farms on the east side. Apart from the lorry there was a private car, a Cortina 1600, driven by a smooth-faced young fellow who probably sold soap. The lorry clanked up the ramp, rattling the timber treads, lurched along the length of the deck and came to a halt, its near-side wing almost touching the steel plates of the chain-chute and its radiator an inch or two from the safety gates. The driver, like all regulars, prided himself on occupying the minimum of space even though at this time of year he usually had the ferry to himself. The Cortina revved and skidded on the slimy ramp, ending up in the middle of the deck space where there should have been room for a dozen like him. The driver looked bored and lit a cigarette.

Dickie Bray, mate on the ferry for thirty-eight years, was a hunchback with spindly bowed legs, but agile as an ape so that the economy of his movement was a joy to watch. He did everything except drive the engine, which was the job of the skipper who rarely left his noisy, smelly little hut. Dickie closed the landward gates, operated the great spoked wheel which raised the ramp, then with a desultory wave of the hand, gave the skipper 'the off'. The ferry drew smoothly, almost imperceptibly away from the shore. Dickie collected a fare from the soap salesman then joined his friend the lorry driver at the seaward gates. The milk factory paid by the month. The two men filled and lit their pipes and stood, arms on the gates, staring at the silver grey water just ahead of where the chains broke surface. The tide was flowing strongly, eddying round the clumsy craft and pushing her broadside upstream against the chains. The shiny peak of Dickie's cap seemed to obscure his vision but he was the first to spot the body bobbing about in the track of the port chain. Often the chains disturbed mysterious debris on the bottom, sending it up for a few seconds of turbulent surface life, but this was different: a brown bundle of clothes, the material bellied out by water like a parachute. Dickie gave a screech like a startled gull, the signal for an emergency stop; the engine died at once and the chains ceased to rattle through the chute. The bundle bobbed alongside, kept there by the flow of the tide. Dickie went over the gate on to the ramp and began fishing with a boathook; the skipper came out of his cabin and lowered the ramp until it was awash and Dickie could land his catch. A smooth operation, all over in less than a minute. The soap salesman got out of his car and joined the little group around the bundle which proved to be the body of a woman.

She lay on the boards in a pool of water. Her posture was stiff though credibly life-like, but her face was pallid, gnawed and leprous. The salesman went quickly back to the deck leaving the other three staring down at her. The ferrymen had fished several out of the estuary, dead or alive but mostly dead, and the lorry driver had a strong stomach. It was impossible to tell from her face but her figure was that of a young woman, small and well proportioned. She wore a brown two-piece with what seemed to be a pink blouse. Her shoes were dainty and fashionable. Her hair was black like a Spaniard's but in whatever style she had worn it, now it splayed lankly on the timbers. There was a necklace of amber beads round her throat and she wore a wedding ring, half buried in the sodden flesh of her finger.

The skipper, a little man with shiny brown cheeks like a hazel-nut, was sparing of words. He looked at his mate and a silent message must have passed. Dickie nodded, 'I thought so too.'

The lorry driver looked at both of them. 'Who is she?'

Dickie straightened himself and glanced vaguely in the direction of the west bank where the other half of the town sprawled raggedly up the hillside. 'I reckon it's Mrs Bryce – Matt's wife.'

The lorry driver whistled.

Dickie took his pipe, half smoked, from his pocket, looked at it and put it away again. The skipper said unexpectedly, 'Death is no respecter of persons.' He was a chapel man.

Without another word, as though working to a well rehearsed drill, the skipper and Dickie lifted the body and carried it into the passenger hut where they laid it on the slatted wooden seat and covered it with a tarpaulin. Water dripped through the slats to form a pool on the floor. Then they got moving again and in a few minutes the ferry was nudging the cobbled slipway on the western side. Dickie lowered the ramp while the skipper went over to the soap salesman. 'You'd best wait . . .' He nodded towards the little hut where the body was. 'I expect they'll want a word . . .'

Dickie was off up over the cobbles on to the wharf, lolloping along close to the houses, like a chimpanzee. The lorry driver climbed back into his cab and re-lit his pipe.

The slipway cut into the wharf at a steep angle so that the ferry was largely hidden except to anyone actually passing by; but there was nobody about. A few yards upstream was the boatyard, dominated by a huge corrugated iron shed, rusting in attractive browns and oranges and reds, like encrusted lichens. Just downstream was the car-park, given over for the week to a fair with dodgems, roundabouts, booths and stalls. But at this time of day it was shrouded in striped canvas.

The sun shone out of a watery blue sky, the breeze was fresh and the tide lapped and chuckled round the ferry. A baker's van cruised slowly along the wharf but the driver appeared to notice nothing. The church clock chimed and struck eleven.

Another ten minutes went by before a small blue and white police car came down the slipway and pulled up just short of the ramp. A uniformed constable got out, followed by Dickie Bray. The constable came aboard, walked over to the entrance to the passenger hut, peered inside, then placed himself on guard at the door. Dickie joined the skipper in the engine room to share a flask of lukewarm black tea. 'The sergeant's fetching Dr Greenly.'

The skipper nodded.

It was a quarter of an hour later that Sergeant Penrose and Dr Greenly arrived and by that time a few quay loafers had gathered at the top of the slipway. Dr Greenly, the police surgeon, was self-important, red-haired, red-faced, and irritated by this interruption to his rounds. The sergeant came across to the engine house, leaving the doctor with the body. 'Just the bare facts; there'll be statements later.'

The salesman got out of his car and came over. 'Is it all right for me to shove off? I'm losing business.'

'That will be in order, sir. Just identify yourself to the constable and tell him where you can be reached.'

The lorry driver, too, was sent on his way.

When Dr Greenly came out of the passenger hut he seemed worried rather than irritated. 'You know who you've got in there?'

The sergeant nodded. 'Apparently it's Mrs Bryce.'

'It is.'

'The point is, Doctor . . .'

'The point is, Sergeant, that I'm not satisfied Mrs Bryce's death was due to drowning.'

'You don't think . . . ?'

Greenly cut him short. 'I don't think anything at the moment except that you should get in touch with your inspector. In cases of prolonged immersion speed is important if the cause of death is to be correctly determined.'

Pompous old fool! But Penrose knew the signs; this was going to be one of those cases where everybody is anxious to get out from under. The sister of a former cabinet minister and prominent front bench politician. 'I'll radio Information room at once, Doctor.'

He had to drive his car up on to the wharf before he could raise Information Room on his radio but when he succeeded their response was prompt. In five minutes he had his instructions. Inspector Harker of Divisional CID was on his way. He would notify relatives and make arrangements for formal identification. No room for blundering sergeants in this exercise! And a suitable vehicle would be sent to transport the body to the pathologist's laboratory at the county hospital. The goods to be delivered in a plain van.

All the same it was after midday before Detective Superintendent Wycliffe, head of Area CID, heard of the crime.

The Area Crime Squad is not housed in the hew police head-quarters on the outskirts of the city but tucked away in a Queen Anne house in a secluded crescent near the cathedral. The other houses in the crescent are used as offices by the diocesan authorities who, nearly thirty years ago, had leased one of their houses to the now extinct city force as temporary premises after the bombing. The chief superintendent's offices on the first floor include a large, finely proportioned room with a heavily decorated plaster ceiling which catches dust and houses spiders. The two tall sash-windows over-look a small public garden laid out round a fragment of the old city wall and, beyond that, a modern shopping precinct.

Wycliffe was sitting at his desk reading and making notes from a book entitled *Psychopathic Aggression* written by a gentleman with an unpronounceable Polish name. He had had time for such things recently for business was slack. The notes on his pad were cryptic but, as he would probably never look at them again, this scarcely mattered.

'The psychopath is never a depressive; his hatred is always untroubled by feelings of guilt . . .

   'The psychopath appears to be wholly indifferent to the opinions of others, even to their manifest and threatening hostility . . .'

The page was covered by his ragged and rather clumsy script and there were half-a-dozen such mutilated extracts. During every slack period he promised himself that he would catch up on his reading and he would accumulate a little sheaf of notes which would go into a drawer at the first telephone call and into the waste paper basket when he came across them a month later. The present lull had lasted longer than usual and it seemed that, with the tourist season over, crooks as well as landladies and hotel keepers had gone to Majorca for their holidays. But for him it ended with a call on his private line from headquarters. He picked up the telephone.

'Wycliffe.'

'Ah, Charles! I wondered if I might catch you.' It was Bellings, the assistant chief, suave and a master of double talk. No love lost between the two men. 'This is a delicate matter, Charles, probably a mare's nest but there has to be an investigation. We must try not to tread on anybody's toes.'

Wycliffe let him run on. It was the sort of situation Bellings enjoyed: at heart he was a politician rather than a policeman.

'You know Treen? A little watering place and a bit of a port . . . The Bryces are big people there, they own the harbour installations, the timber-yard, the canning factory, the coal-yard and half the town . . . Clement Morley, the former Minister of State, is a brother-in-law . . . You see . . . ? What?' A cultured laugh.

Wycliffe had not spoken a word; he was trying to light his pipe while holding the telephone to his ear with his shoulder.

'There's nobody with you?'

'No.'

'Good! His wife has been found drowned.'

'Whose wife? Morley's?'

'No, my dear chap, Bryce's. Actually there are three brothers and this is the wife of the eldest – Matthew, the head of the clan. She is Clement Morley's sister.'

'And it's a job for us?'

'Well, that's the point. The police surgeon isn't too happy and the body has been sent to Franks, the pathologist . . . We shall know better how to proceed when we have his report . . . On the other hand . . .' Bellings left the unfinished sentence hanging in the air. Unfinished sentences were part of his stock-in-trade. 'My wife and I have met the lady socially. Unstable, neurotic . . . One wouldn't be too surprised to hear that she had . . . You get my meaning . . . ? And Charles, there's quite a bit of gossip about another man, but we don't want to make too much of it unless it's strictly relevant . . .' Bellings' voice drifted away into silence but he hadn't yet made his point to his entire satisfaction. 'You appreciate, Charles, that she is Morley's sister, so we can't afford to have a . . . a cock-up.' The vulgarity was exquisitely enunciated. One had the impression that he had learned a certain number of such expressions for use in dealing with his social inferiors although, as Wycliffe knew, his father had been a taxi driver. 'The Chief feels that your experience and tact . . . This fellow Morley has a reputation as a head hunter . . .'

'I know him,' Wycliffe growled, and immediately regretted it.

'Socially?'

'You could say that.'

Bellings purred. 'Well, that's splendid! A weight off my mind. By the way, Charles, Treen is not a bad little place – book in at the Manor Park; they do you very well there . . .'

When Bellings rang off, Wycliffe asked to be put through to Franks, the County Pathologist. They had worked together before. But, as he expected, it was much too early for any news. Franks promised to ring the police station at Treen as soon as he was ready with a preliminary report. As there was no point in starting a full scale investigation without more to go on, Wycliffe felt justified in taking a look round on his own.

At one o'clock he was joining the west bound traffic out of the city at the start of his seventy mile drive to Treen. As though to mark the end of his inaction the weather had undergone an abrupt change. Blue-black clouds which had swiftly climbed up the sky from the south east now blotted out the sun, and it was raining. By the time he had cleared the suburbs he seemed to be in the middle of a cloudburst. All the cars had their lights on and they were swishing through a surface film of water which could not drain away fast enough, sending up bow waves of muddy spray. The windscreen wipers thudded monotonously and inadequately.

Wycliffe, a cautious, perhaps a nervous driver, knew that he would hate every mile of the journey. Although the first fury of the rain storm soon spent itself there was no sign of it stopping and it was almost three o'clock before he could leave the grey stream of lorries and cars on the main road for the eight miles of country lanes which led to Treen. The final approach to the town is down a one-in-six hill with cunning twists, except for the last quarter-of-a-mile which runs straight and steep between two rows of terraced houses propping each other up against the slope.

The principal shops of the town are grouped round a cobbled square with the war memorial in the middle, but the life of West Treen is on its waterfront, strung out along half-a-mile of the west bank of the estuary from the railway station to the harbour. The timber-yard, the coal-yard, the fish canning factory on the site of the old ice works, a boatyard, the ferry slipway, then the slipway, then the harbour with its pubs, cafés and souvenir shops. Beyond the harbour a few bungalows, then National Trust property to Trecarne Head.

Wycliffe parked in the square which was almost deserted. The rain had eased to a drizzle but the cobbles were still running with water and a drain at the lower side of the square was choked so that a pool of brown, muddy water had formed, covering the pavement and threatening nearby shops. A man, his head and shoulders draped with a sack, stood, up to his ankles in the water, prodding listlessly with a stick.

A short, narrow street opened on to the harbour and Wycliffe had his first view of the estuary. There was little colour in the scene but he liked the place on sight. Across the narrow strip of water, opposite where he stood, was the other half of the town, a huddle of grey, slate-roofed houses, but elsewhere the fields and little patches of woodland came almost down to the water, separated from it by a few feet of rocks and shingle. Away to his right, between the two head-lands, he could glimpse the distant horizon of the sea. Nearby most of the cafés and shops were closed, some of them boarded up for the winter. It was half-tide and three or four faded blue fishing boats neatly matched their reflections in the still waters of the basin. He came to a large, ugly house with several gables and pebble-dashed walls. It had a wooden verandah built out over the wharf with seats underneath where half-a-dozen men in blue jerseys and peaked caps smoked in silence. Gilded, cut-out letters, fixed to the verandah rail, read: 'Treen Hotel. Tourist and Commercial'.

A mile or so out of the town he had noticed an impressive drive entrance with an arched sign above it: 'Manor Park Hotel'. No doubt it adjoined the golf course and no doubt it was in or trying to get into the pages of *The Good Food Guide*. Wycliffe liked good food but he felt that the hotel on the wharf would be nearer to the realities of life in Treen. He pushed open the glass swing doors of the entrance and found himself in a dimly lit lobby, deserted but for a giant marma-lade cat curled up on the reception desk. The bell was answered by a girl who came out wiping her hands on a kitchen cloth. Wycliffe asked her for a room which opened on to the verandah and got one without difficulty. 'There is no-one almost, now that the season is over . . .' She was foreign, Swedish, he guessed, very fair and aggressively healthy, with rather too much bosom and self-confidence for the average English male.

'You want to eat tonight?'

He understood that the question referred to dinner and said that he did.

'Then it is mix grill or salad.'

He nodded, 'That will do.'

She frowned with impatience. 'Which?'

'Oh, the mixed grill.' He was a mug, always falling for the idea of lamb's liver, kidneys and mushrooms, when experience told him that he would get sausage and bacon with a slice or two of greasy tomato.

'Seven o'clock, then.'

'Is there any chance of something to eat now?'

'The kitchen is closed.'

'All right, I'll bring my car round.'

She prodded the air with her ball-point. 'After you have sign the register.'

Outside the rain had stopped and watery sunshine was transforming the field across the water from olive to lime green. He fetched his car from the square and drove it into the hotel yard between stacks of beer kegs waiting to be collected by the brewery. He left his case in the car and made his way back on to the wharf. An isolated, single-storeyed building, little more than a hut, had a faded signboard advertising snacks. It was better than nothing, but he was surprised on opening the door to find a dozen or more customers at plastic-topped tables. Like the men under the verandah, several of them wore blue jerseys and peaked caps. There were a couple of card games in progress with money on the tables and the place had the atmosphere of a club, so that they seemed to look at him with mild hostility. Strangers out of season are as welcome as winter blow-flies.

The man behind the bar looked up from reading his newspaper. He had the features and build of a heavyweight all-in wrestler, close-cropped black hair almost met his eyebrows over the low forehead, his nose was broad and flattened and he had heavy, stubbly jowls. He acknowledged Wycliffe curtly, Wycliffe ordered coffee and a ham sandwich.

'Only cheese.'

'All right, cheese.' He waited while the man drew his coffee and slapped two pieces of bread around a piece of rubbery cheese.

'Fifteen pence.'

Wycliffe took his food to an empty table near the bar and the wrestler returned to his paper. Wycliffe watched the card players playing amid a litter of tea cups; the air was pungent with the smoke

349

of strong tobacco. There was little conversation and what there was fragmentary and allusive; some of it might have referred to the dead woman but he could make little of it. Every now and then someone would break out into a ribald laugh. He was about to order another coffee when the door opened and a man walked up to the counter watched by all of them. He was in his early forties, lean and athletic, with strong features and straight, thin lips. Wycliffe thought that he must have paid more than a hundred guineas for his suit, which was tailored to emphasize his slim waist.

'Has Jewell been in?'

The wrestler was respectful, subservient. 'Not since this morning, Mr Bryce. If he comes in . . .'

'Tell him to get in touch with me at the office.'

The man caught sight of Wycliffe, gave him an appraising look, ran his eyes over the others and walked out, leaving the door open behind him. The men were looking after him and one of them got up and shut the door.

'Bryce? Is he one of the brothers?'

The wrestler folded his arms on the bar counter. 'That was Mr Sidney. As far as the business goes, he *is* the brothers.'

'I thought Matthew was the eldest.'

'He is, but Mr Matt has other interests, Sidney is the second one.'

Wycliffe waited for him to enlarge, but he was disappointed. 'Is the young one in the business?'

'George?' A short, humourless laugh, but no comment. One or two men from the tables were beginning to pay attention to the conversation.

'Boslow – where is it?'

The big man looked him over. 'Are you press?'

'No.'

'Up the river beyond the timber-yard. Follow the waterfront.' He turned away decisively.

After a second cup of coffee Wycliffe walked along the wharf, upstream. A fair, roundabouts, dodgems and a few stalls and booths occupied a broad stretch of tarmac which was probably a car-park at other times. Three or four caravans and a couple of lorries were parked against the high wall which separated the ground from the churchyard and the fair people were hanging out their washing on improvised lines. Wycliffe skirted the fair and reached the ferry

350

slipway. The weird contraption was in mid-stream, making for the western shore; he noticed that the great chains anchored on the slipway were motionless. He picked his way among the dinghies and small power boats drawn up on the wharf by the boatyard and came to the cannery. The cannery looked new: glass and concrete, with a glimpse of white tiles inside. A hiss of steam and a faint smell of fish. Treen Canneries Ltd.

Treen Coal Company was next door. A coaster was being unloaded by grab and telpher, bridging the wharf and dumping the coal directly into the yard. A buffer-stop marked the end (or the beginning) of the railway track.

The sky had cleared at last, baby blue with white cloud masses near the horizon, and the sun was warm. The tide was ebbing strongly. Wycliffe walked on the sleepers like a schoolboy. After the coal-yard, the timber-yard, surrounded by a high fence. Here the family declared itself: Bryce Brothers, Timber and Builders' Merchants. A circular saw screamed tormentedly. Beyond the timber-yard a well-maintained road cut off to his left, presumably returning to the town; the wharf petered out but the railway track continued, running under the trees by the river. On a bend, a quarter of a mile farther upstream, he could see the little station, the terminus for passenger traffic. The trees were part of an estate and a little way along the road Wycliffe could see impressive gate posts and a drive entrance. This must be Boslow.

Matthew Bryce's wife had been found in the river. Matthew had interests which absorbed him to the exclusion of the family business. Sidney was the man to be reckoned with there. And George, the youngest, was rather a sour joke. Wycliffe sighed. Sometimes he baffled himself. Any other detective would have been fully briefed on the family by now. Back in his office, simply by picking up the telephone, he could have learned a great deal from Harker of the Divisional CID. Even more if he had paid a call at the local nick instead of walking in the sunshine. Sometimes it seemed that he had an antipathy for facts.

He left the railway and walked along the road as far as the drive gates. If the place had been a remand home, a school, or a home for unmarried mothers, it would have been better cared for. The gravelled drive was weedy and the laurels and rhododendrons were rampant. All the same, Wycliffe, though a socialist by birth and

351

conviction, felt a pang of regret whenever he heard of an estate falling into the hands of some welfare organization or the municipal park keeper. Tree choppers, all of them! He walked up the drive. It was designed, of course, to make you wonder what you would find around the next bend, and there were several bends before the shrubs ended and he found himself looking across an acre or so of rough grass to a smallish Regency house with bow front and first floor verandah, washed out pink stucco and white woodwork. It reminded him of an iced cake.

Away to his right there was a lake which seemed to be half covered with water plants and beyond that, the fringe of trees by the railway track.

'Are you looking for someone?'

A girl, seventeen or eighteen, slim as a boy and almost as tall as he was. She had her jet black hair gathered into a pony-tail and she wore a faded checked shirt, blue jeans and flip-flop sandals. She must have walked on the grass or he would have heard her.

'Is this Boslow? I'm looking for Mr Bryce.'

'Which one?' She eyed him, it seemed, with suspicion, reluctant to give him information.

'Mr Matthew. Do all three brothers live here?'

She looked vague. 'It's my father you want; you'd better come up to the house.'

'So you are . . . ?'

'Grizelda Bryce.'

She was good-looking; an oval face with high cheekbones; warm, brown skin, freckled under the eyes. Her lips were surprisingly full and sensuous – the only sensuous thing about her. Her manner struck him as odd, not hostile, but detached; it seemed to him that he was only engaging part of her attention. They started to walk towards the house.

'I'm a detective – Chief Superintendent Wycliffe.'

'You've come about my mother?'

'I'm sorry about what has happened; it must be a terrible shock for you and your father.'

She said nothing. They did not cross the grass but followed the gravelled drive, a concession to elegance in the great sweeping detour which it made.

'They think it wasn't an accident, don't they?'

352

'That's what we've got to find out – how your mother came to be in the water.'

She looked at him, a sidelong glance. 'She did it herself!' Her manner was almost spiteful.

'What makes you think so?'

She shook her head.

He always felt at a disadvantage when questioning girls, especially respectable ones. His wife, Helen, said that it arose from childhood repression. 'You are still at school?'

'I've just left.' Listless.

'Boarding school?'

'No!' With emphasis.

'How old are you?'

'Eighteen.'

'Are you going to University?'

'That's their idea.'

'Who are they?'

'My mother, my uncle . . .'

'Not your father?'

She shrugged.

'And what about you?'

'I want to finish with it.'

'With what?'

'With studying.'

'To do what?'

Shutters down. 'I don't know.'

'Boy-friend?'

She seemed about to protest but changed her mind. 'No.'

Despite her apparent calmness and reserve she was very unsure of herself. Even physically she had not yet acquired the grace of movement which would come with the confidence of full maturity. Every posture, every step had in it an element of bravado, a trace of aggression.

'You didn't get on very well with your mother?'

'Who told you that?' Anger flared.

'You did.'

'Clever!' She was contemptuous.

They walked in silence for a dozen steps. 'When did you last see her?'

353

'Haven't they told you?'

'I want you to tell me.'

She stopped walking as though telling her story needed concentration. 'I saw her last Thursday evening – when we had supper. I had a headache and I went to bed early. Next morning my father told me that she had gone to stay with an aunt in St Ives.'

'On the spur of the moment?'

'It happens like that. Aunt Joyce is mother's sister and she's married to Francis Boon, the sculptor. She sometimes threatens to commit suicide and they ring up Mother to come and stay with her. It usually means that she thinks she is pregnant. Francis is a Catholic and she's frightened of having children.'

'How many have they got?'

'They haven't got any.' Her flat tone was a comment in itself.

'And your aunt rang up on Thursday evening?'

She frowned and looked very young. 'That's the funny part about it: she says that she didn't. In any case, Mother didn't go there.'

'But you and your father thought that she had?'

'Yes. It wasn't until yesterday – Monday – that Uncle Sidney rang up to speak to her and found that she wasn't there.'

'Have you any idea where she might have gone?'

'None.'

Wycliffe let it go. They entered the house. The hall was dominated by a staircase of white-painted iron which swept upwards in an opulent curve, but the paint was chipped and the ironwork was dusty. She led him to a door at the back of the hall and into a room with french windows opening on to a cobbled yard. She looked round as though expecting to see her father but the room was empty. 'Wait here; I'll go and fetch him.'

The room had once been the library of the house and there were still a great many books about, but much of the shelving was occupied by mechanical models, models of steam engines, pumps, pithead gear, hoisting engines and even sections of steam boilers. Every spare bit of wall space was crowded with faded photographs of machinery, foundry operations and mine workings. A large table placed between the windows was littered with prints depicting more machines. The whole place was musty, the books mildewed and the dust was everywhere.

Wycliffe was kept waiting only a couple of minutes before the girl returned with her father. Matthew was a bigger man than his brother with more flesh on him. He looked a good deal older, with sparse, grizzled hair, shaggy eyebrows and a looseness in the skin under his chin. One eye was bleached and glazed, partly covered by a permanently drooping lid, but the other was brown, sparkling and youthful. He evidently cared little for his appearance: his corduroy slacks were too large and almost threadbare and his polo-necked sweater had worn through at the elbows.

'Good of you to come!' A firm handshake. Bryce swept a few books from a chair on to the floor and Wycliffe sat down. 'Drink? . . . No, of course not – too early. Run along, Zel, there's a good girl.' A boisterous assured manner, but the glance of the good eye was restless, flitting everywhere, and there was not a scrap of repose in his whole body. Wycliffe thought that his nervousness was temperamental. Neuroses are supposed to go with the lean, hungry look but in Wycliffe's experience at least as many victims are well covered.

Wycliffe said something soothing and sympathetic and added, 'I understand that you have identified your wife's body, Mr Bryce?'

'The body? Oh, yes, I have been over with Inspector Harker. It's Caroline all right, no doubt about that, poor girl.' His manner was a detached kindliness as though he were speaking of a casual acquaintance, but he looked at Wycliffe anxiously. 'Have you decided that there is something suspicious about her death?' He sat in the swivel chair by his work table.

'The circumstances make an inquiry inevitable, sir.'

'By a detective chief superintendent?' He smiled. 'Or has my brother-in-law been pulling strings?' He raised his hand when Wycliffe would have answered. 'I'll be frank. If my attitude seems strange it's because there was no love lost between Caroline and me. We lived our separate lives and tried to see as little of each other as possible.' As he spoke he pivoted himself back and forth on the swivel-chair but his lively brown eye never left Wycliffe's face.

'Your daughter seems to think that her mother took her own life.'

'Is that what she said?' He stopped fidgeting, evidently surprised. 'I wonder why? There's no knowing what goes on in her head.'

'You don't agree?'

'That Caroline killed herself? Of course I don't, and Zel doesn't believe it either. You couldn't live in this house for a week without

355

realizing that the one person Caroline would never harm would be herself. Zel knows that as well as I do.' He broke off and looked at Wycliffe with the air of one who has been frank at some cost and is rather proud of it.

'Do you think that her death was accidental?'

Bryce placed his hands between his knees and clamped them there as though to restrain their activity. The damaged eye gave him a somewhat lugubrious expression but he seemed sincere enough. 'I find it difficult to imagine Caroline meeting with that kind of accident. A car smash, certainly – she drives like a fiend. But how could one drown in the estuary except when bathing or boating? And I can assure you that Caroline did neither.'

He produced a crumpled packet of cigarettes and after offering them to Wycliffe straightened one and lit it. His lips were an incongruous feature, delicate, thin and sensitive like a girl's, and the filter tip of the cigarette scarcely seemed to touch them. Wycliffe got out his pipe and lit it, puffing out little spurts of grey-blue smoke. 'Why should Zel tell me that she thought her mother had committed suicide if she thought no such thing?'

Bryce pondered. 'Zel is a very intelligent child. She has probably come to the same conclusion as I but carried her reasoning a step further.'

'What does that mean?'

The cigarette made Bryce cough. 'Zel evidently thinks that her mother was murdered and she's afraid that I did it.'

'She is protective where you are concerned?'

'Very. The poor child, she hasn't had much of a life.'

'You are being very frank.'

Bryce crushed out his half-smoked cigarette. 'I've no option. Plenty of people will tell you of the life Caroline and I led.'

'You saw your wife last on Thursday evening?'

'Yes.'

'When Zel went to bed with a headache?'

He made a small gesture of assent.

Out in the yard fat pigeons were strutting up and down, pecking between the cobbles. The yard was in shadow but the sun caught the lichen-covered roof of the old stables, making the colours glow.

Zel came in. 'You're wanted on the telephone.'

It was Franks, the pathologist, breezy as ever. 'I tried the nick but they hadn't seen you so putting two and two together . . .'

'What have you got?'

'Can I speak freely?'

'As far as I can see there's only this one phone.'

'Good! The woman certainly wasn't drowned: she collected a hefty crack on the base of her skull before she was put into the water. The blow killed her.'

'How long before she was put into the water?'

Franks sighed. 'You know as well as I do that it's impossible to tell with any certainty. At a guess I'd say not less than twenty-four hours; but I could be a hell of a lot wrong.'

'So it must be murder.'

'Seems like it, though I remember one case, not unlike this, where it turned out to be accidental death. A chap painting a bridge fell off, cracked his skull against a projecting bolt, spilling some of his brains, lodged on one of the bridge piers, then slid off into the water at least twenty-four hours later. His mates never missed him, his wife reported to the police when he didn't come home and his body was fished out of the drink three days later. Fortunately he left traces of his passage on the bolt and on the bridge pier.'

'But in this case . . .'

'In this case the skin wasn't broken. A neat job.'

'Not a very powerful blow.'

'No, though I'd say a fairly hefty weapon, something about an inch-and-a-half in diameter, round. A piece of iron or lead pipe would fit the bill.'

'In your opinion, how long has she been dead?'

Franks hedged. 'You know the score. Strictly off the record, I'd say one day before she was put in the water and perhaps three or four days since then.'

'She seems to have gone missing on Thursday evening.'

'That would fit. Incidentally she had a deeply incised post-mortem wound right round her left leg above the ankle.'

'A weight tied on?'

'Wired more likely. It must have broken loose.'

'That clinches it then. Even your bloke on the bridge didn't tie a weight round his ankle.'

The telephone was in a little room off the hall and Wycliffe could see most of the hall through the open door. Even so, he lowered his voice. 'You've examined the organs, of course?'

'I haven't had a chance yet. Anything special in mind?'

'Nothing more than the obvious.'

'OK. I suppose I shall be seeing you?'

'Probably.' Wycliffe said 'Goodbye' and rang off.

2

When Wycliffe rejoined Bryce the sun had moved round a little and the yard was filled with sunshine which even reached into the room, emphasizing its dust and shabbiness. Bryce was at his table, sorting papers.

Wycliffe's mood had changed: he was more relaxed, less official, as though he had established a right to be in the house. Instead of sitting down he stood, smoking his pipe and looking at the models and photographs. 'You are interested in the history of engineering?'

'I've been fascinated by machines ever since I was a boy.' Bryce came over and joined him. 'For forty years I've collected models, prints, photographs and every scrap of information I've been able to lay my hands on. I'm talking about real machines – with flywheels, cranks, cogs, belts and pulleys – not the newfangled things where you press a button and you hardly know whether the damn thing is going or not!' He was fiddling with his models, taking them off the shelves and putting them back again as though for the sheer pleasure of touching them. 'It's bred in the bone, I suppose. One of my ancestors – another Matthew, with his brother, Tobias, worked with William Murdock for the Boulton and Watt team. Then they broke away and set up a foundry on their own a bit farther up the river from here. They were the original Bryce Brothers. The foundry is gone but the house they built is still there. In 1860 the firm built a new foundry on the site of the present timber-yard and that con-tinued in production without a break until 1919.'

Outside in the sunshine Zel was scattering grain for the pigeons and from time to time she glanced into the room to see what was happening.

'As a matter of fact, I'm writing a book – *Machines of the Industrial Revolution* – written from the standpoint of the practical engineer.' The one good eye seemed to question Wycliffe, seeking his approval. 'I suppose you think this is a futile way to spend one's time?' He waved his hand vaguely to indicate the things around him.

Wycliffe mumbled something non-committal. He moved round examining the models and photographs with Bryce on his heels. On one of the shelves he found a different sort of photograph, a studio portrait of a girl in a tarnished silver frame. He took it down to examine it. The resemblance to Zel was unmistakable. But it was not Zel: this girl had escaped the thick lips and her features were more nearly perfect; her hair, dark and lustrous, fell almost to her shoulders.

'My wife, taken when we were married.'

'She looks very young.'

Bryce took the photograph and studied it broodingly. 'She was eighteen, and three months pregnant. I was thirty-seven.' His mouth screwed itself into a grimace. 'If I don't tell you somebody else will. I'm sure that it has become part of the family legend.'

'At what time did your wife leave here on Thursday night?'

'At about ten.'

'She told you that she was going to visit her sister?'

'Yes. She came in here and said that Joyce had phoned and that they were going to send a car for her.'

'Doesn't she drive herself?'

'I told you, like a madwoman; but at present she is under a two-year disqualification – *was*, I should say.'

'Did she tell you why she was going?'

'There was no need. Joyce is married to the sculptor, Francis Boon. They are both neurotic and they seem to move from one crisis to the next. Caroline acts as a sort of referee . . .'

'And the car came for her at ten?'

'She came in here at about that time and said, "The car is here; I'm going." She was wearing out-door clothes.'

'You didn't see her off?'

'No.'

They moved back to the chairs and Bryce lit another of his crumpled cigarettes.

'Zel had gone to bed when your wife left. Who else was in the house?'

'Only Irene.'

'Irene?'

360

'My cousin. She acts as housekeeper; in fact, she runs the place with the help of a daily maid.' He brushed ash from his cardigan on to the floor. 'On Thursdays Sidney spends the evening at the Golf Club and he's rarely in before midnight. He's Chairman or President or something.'

'He is unmarried?'

Bryce nodded. 'And likely to stay that way.'

'And what about your youngest brother?'

'George? What's he got to do with it?'

'Doesn't he live here?'

For some reason Bryce seemed to become cautious. 'No, he took a place of his own some years back.'

'What did you and your wife quarrel about on Thursday evening?'

Bryce paused to consider his answer but he did not deny the quarrel. Wycliffe's pipe had gone out and after looking into the nearly empty bowl disconsolately he put it into his pocket.

'It was about business,' Bryce said, 'not a personal thing at all.' He hesitated, then seemed to make up his mind. 'I suppose you'll have to know sooner or later.

'My brother Sidney, Caroline and I are directors of the family business and yesterday, Monday afternoon, we were supposed to meet with representatives of a large West of England firm to sign transfer documents.'

'A merger?'

'A sell-out! Under my father's will our family business was turned into a limited company with my brothers and I holding the shares. As the eldest son I received a controlling interest, but a few years back when we needed more capital for expansion, Caroline offered to put in a substantial sum of money she had received under her father's will. In return she was allocated shares amounting to about one sixth of the paper capital . . .'

'Enough to cost you your control of the company.'

'Exactly; though the fact hardly bothered me at the time. We are a prosperous concern, the profits have always been good and I saw no reason why there should be a difference of opinion on major policy. Neither was there until six months ago when we received an offer to buy us out. Sidney had meantime acquired George's shares and as he might reasonably expect a managing directorship on the new board he was strongly in favour. I was equally strongly against.' He broke off. 'You appreciate the position?'

Wycliffe grunted. 'It's not difficult; the decision rested with your wife.'

'Precisely, and she supported Sidney.'

'Because the offer was a good one or because she was opposing you?'

Bryce shook his head. 'For both reasons, I should think. I suppose that she might have been glad to frustrate me and at the same time, by obtaining cash or a holding in the new company, she would, no doubt, feel freer to go her own way.'

'If your wife had sold out her holding for cash, how much would she have received?'

'Around fifty thousand pounds for an original stake in the company of ten thousand. As I said, the offer was a good one.'

'Yet you opposed its acceptance – why?'

Bryce smiled. 'I suppose because I feel some obligation to a business which has sustained the family for a century and three-quarters and because I believe that a business which is too big for every employee to know the boss is a bad business.' He stopped and shrugged his massive shoulders. 'There are many reasons but they would bore you, I am an anachronism in modern business as Sidney never tires of telling me.'

Did this mild-mannered man realize that he had gone a long way towards making out a case against himself for murder?

'I understand that it was your brother who telephoned and discovered that Mrs Bryce was not with her sister?'

Bryce nodded. 'He rang from the office yesterday morning. He was worried about the meeting in the afternoon and wanted to make sure that Caroline would be there. When he found that she was not with Joyce he telephoned me here. At first I couldn't understand what he was talking about, he was so angry . . .'

'Angry?'

'He thought that I had played some trick on him – that I knew where Caroline was and that I had persuaded her not to come to the meeting.'

'And now?'

'I am afraid that I don't understand . . .'

'What does your brother think now?'

A quick smile. 'You will have to ask him that. Since the meeting yesterday we have scarcely spoken.'

'The deal fell through?'

'I refused to sign the transfer documents, naturally.'

Naturally.

'Were you surprised when you heard that your wife was not with your sister?'

'Of course I was surprised.'

'Worried?'

A curious look which Wycliffe could not interpret. 'I did not suppose that anything very terrible had happened to her.'

'What did you suppose?'

Bryce's manner was calm and grave; indeed he seemed more at ease now than when Wycliffe first arrived. 'I thought it very likely that Caroline had used a visit to her sister as a pretext.'

'For what?'

'Two or three days spent with another man – it wouldn't have been the first time.'

'Your wife was unfaithful to you?'

'Habitually.' The only sign of emotion was a restless movement of the right hand, ruffling the papers on the table.

Long years of police work had failed to inure Wycliffe to this intimate, probing surgery, but it had to be done. 'You know the man?'

Bryce nodded.

'His name?'

Bryce hesitated.

'It will not be difficult to find out.'

'My brother, George.'

'You accepted this situation?'

Bryce drew a hand across his forehead as though ridding himself of an invisible cobweb. 'I regarded it as one of the hazards of marrying a girl twenty years younger.'

'Detective Superintendent Wycliffe stated that the possibility of foul play had not been excluded.' That would be his press release; but it would be enough. Suspected murder of sister of one of Britain's most colourful politicians. They would have a field day. Bellings wouldn't like it. For Wycliffe it would probably mean a complicated, tedious and frustrating inquiry. For all those at all well acquainted with the dead woman it would mean irksome, persistent questions, an intrusion into their privacy, the airing of little vices and the exposure of protective lies. For Wycliffe's team it would mean hundreds of hours of unwanted overtime and reams of paper.

Now was the time to mobilize his team, to choose his operational HQ and get to work; but he was reluctant. He preferred to hang about this house, getting used to the feel of it, getting to know the people who lived in it. He got up, walked to one of the windows and stood staring out into the yard, trying to persuade himself that an hour one way or the other would make no difference.

'Who do you think killed your wife, Mr Bryce?'

Bryce ran his fingers over the ridged corduroy of his trousers, exploring the velvet feel. 'I don't know.'

'Do you and your wife have separate rooms?'

'Yes.'

'I would like to see your wife's room.'

'To see her room? Why yes, of course!' He led the way out into the hall and up the white staircase. In his slippers he had the flat-footed walk of an old man. The carpet on the stairs was dusty and threadbare, dangerous in places. At the top, a long corridor bisected the house lengthwise with rooms opening off on each side. Bryce went to the left and opened a door into one of the front rooms. He stood aside and allowed Wycliffe to go in first.

It was a large room, a sitting-room, and in contrast with what he had seen of the rest of the house, it was modern, uncluttered and scrupulously cared for. It could have been a set for a photograph to illustrate a Habitat catalogue; slatted wood furniture with bright orange cushions, adjustable pendant lamps with lustrous green shades, and shaggy, Scandinavian rugs on a polished, wood floor. There was a large nest of shelves against one wall housing some paper-backed books, a rack of records and a record player, a few pieces of Copenhagen pottery and a transistor radio. Wycliffe wandered round like a dog sniffing out the topography of an unfamiliar backyard. The records seemed to be exclusively 'pop' and the paper-backs included a fair sprinkling of sexy best sellers. All very adolescent.

'Does your daughter use this room?'

'Zel?' He looked surprised. 'No, she has a sort of den in one of the attics.' He added after a moment, 'If you want Caroline's bedroom, it's through there.' He pointed to a door set back in an alcove by the fireplace.

The bedroom was smaller than the sitting-room. Originally it had probably been a dressing-room but Caroline had made it into a luxurious and very feminine bedroom. Wycliffe sank to his insteps in a shell-pink carpet, the walls were ivory white and there were two geometrical abstracts mounted on plinths on the wall above the bed. The bed itself looked like a pink soufflé. It was double, but it seemed unlikely that it had ever been shared with Bryce. There were built-in floor-to-ceiling cupboards with ivory-white sliding doors and gilt fittings. Wycliffe slid back one of the doors. He knew little about women's clothes but enough to realize that here was what the well-dressed woman wore and plenty of it.

'I suppose you have no idea what clothes your wife took with her?' It was silly to ask; what would Bryce know of his wife's clothes? He was looking round her bedroom as though he had wandered unexpectedly into some rather embarrassing, exotic place.

'I've no idea.' He looked bewildered.

'Only a week-end case.' Zel was standing in the doorway of the bedroom, watching. She had changed into a washed-out blue linen frock and her hair, released from the pony-tail, reached to her shoulders, soft and lustrous like her mother's in the photograph.

'How can you possibly know?'

It was her father's question but she spoke to Wycliffe. 'There's only one case missing. I looked.' She went to the cupboards and slid back one of the doors. There were three white pigskin travelling cases standing in a row and room for a fourth.

'Do you know your mother's clothes well enough to tell me what is missing?'

She was so calm and matter-of-fact that it was difficult to remember that she was the dead woman's daughter. 'She must have had with her a knitted twin-set in a sort of cinnamon colour and a day dress. There's a white mack missing and a long summer coat, light fawn with brown wooden buttons. I expect she was wearing the twin-set and the mack . . .'

'You've checked her clothes?'

She looked him straight in the eyes. 'I wanted to be sure.'

'Of what?'

She shrugged. Then, to her father, 'Aunt Mellie rang up.'

'Mellie? What did she want?'

'She's only just heard about Mother.'

Bryce sighed. 'My sister, Melinda, Mr Wycliffe.'

It was the first Wycliffe had heard of a Bryce sister. 'Isn't she concerned with the firm?'

Bryce shook his head. 'She never got on with Father. In his will he left her a sum of money but she wouldn't accept it. She's married to a seaman and she has a small place up on the hill above East Treen.' He gestured vaguely across the estuary.

He was out of place and uncomfortable in these elegant, feminine surroundings. In any case, he wanted to get back to his engines. 'Do you want me any more, Superintendent?' He hesitated. 'Zel can show you anything you want to see and she can tell you as much as I can . . .' He escaped like a fish let off the hook.

Zel was eyeing Wycliffe appraisingly. 'You think that he doesn't care; but he's very upset.'

'And you?'

'Of course!'

He followed her back into the sitting-room and started to prowl around. It wasn't a systematic search; what he did was what a really inquisitive stranger might like to do to a room which interested him.

'Your mother had a car?' He had found a log-book in her name in one of the drawers of the bureau.

'A Mini. My father doesn't drive much; when he wants to go anywhere he has one of the works cars.'

'Can you drive?'

'No.'

'Where is the Mini now?'

'I don't know; it isn't in the garage.'

In one of the other drawers there were clippings from women's magazines, mainly beauty and health hints, and underneath, a slim book which he lifted out: *The Postures of Love.* (Thirty-five photographic plates. Send £3. Delivered in a plain wrapper.) He caught Zel's look of contempt, slipped the book back and shut the drawer.

'Do you want to see anything else?'

'I don't know – perhaps.'

Caroline Bryce was thirty-four, young enough to make a fresh start, old enough to feel threatened by time. Emotionally immature and chasing after something she wouldn't have recognized had she found it. And she had got herself murdered.

'Who runs the house, pays the bills – that sort of thing?'

'Cousin Irene. She's a sort of housekeeper and she's been here ever since I can remember.'

Getting an eighteen-year-old girl pregnant had probably been Bryce's one great sexual adventure. At thirty-seven. Then, at any rate, he must have known what it was to succumb to passion. But now? And what had happened in the intervening years? Wycliffe had learned long ago that few men live entirely without sex.

'At what time did you go to your room on Thursday evening?'

'About nine, as I told you. I didn't feel well, it was the first day of the curse.'

He was surprised by her bluntness, which seemed out of keeping with her general demeanour. 'Did you go straight to bed?'

'Almost.'

'You didn't hear anything from downstairs? Your mother telephoning, talking, quarrelling – anything?'

'I sleep in one of the attics.'

'Are you keeping something from me, Zel?'

Her soft black hair tended to slip forward, hiding part of her face, and from time to time she would sweep it back in a gesture which had become automatic. 'I don't know what you are talking about.'

'I think you know more than you have told me.'

She moved to one of the windows and stood looking out over the park. 'I saw her go if that's what you want me to say.'

'I want you to tell me the truth.'

'That is the truth, I saw her go from the window of my room.'

'I should like to see your room.'

She turned without a word and went to the door. He followed her into the passage and up narrow stairs, lit only by a murky skylight, to a long corridor carpeted with worn sisal matting. 'Don't think I couldn't have a proper room if I wanted one. I like it up here.' She unlocked and opened a green-painted plank door and stood aside for him to go in.

It was a large attic with a dormer window, furnished as a bed-sitter with odds and ends of furniture which looked as though they had been rescued from a lumber room; but the overall effect was pleasing. A table in front of the window had on it an aquarium, a

367

rectangular tank with glass sides. Graceful, feathery water-weeds kept the water fresh and several small greeny-brown fish swam amongst them. Two or three ram's horn snails scavenged over the glass.

'Are you interested in this sort of thing?'

She gestured vaguely, refusing to be humoured.

There were bookshelves covering most of one wall; school books and paper-backs stuffed in anyhow – a motley collection like the shelves one sees outside junk shops.

He went to the window. The attic was at the back of the house overlooking the cobbled yard and, beyond that, the back land and its junction with the inland road from the town to the station. There was a street lamp on the corner.

'You saw your mother from this window?'

'Yes.'

'At what time?'

'About ten o'clock, perhaps later.'

'Had you been looking out of the window for an hour?'

He saw the faint sneer on her lips. 'I had been to bed but I couldn't get to sleep.'

'So you got out of bed and looked out of the window?' He was trying to needle her into a show of spirit but her face went blank again and she answered flatly.

'I got out of bed to get some aspirin and as I passed the window I saw the light go on in the garage – it's switched on from the kitchen. Then I heard the back door open . . .'

'So you went to the window to see who it was?'

'Yes, and I saw her crossing the yard carrying one of her suit-cases.'

'She went to the garage?'

She nodded. 'The one where she keeps the Mini.' She pointed to the second of four garages which had once been stables.

'She drove off in the Mini?'

'Yes.'

'So no-one came to fetch her.'

'No.' She hesitated then added, 'I think she told Father someone was coming to fetch her because she knew he would make a fuss about her driving while she was disqualified.'

'You did not really believe that she had gone to visit her sister?'

'No.'

'What time did your Uncle Sidney come home on Thursday night?'

She looked at him, obviously surprised at the change of subject. 'I don't know, he's usually late on Thursdays because he spends the evening at the Golf Club.'

'Does he have his own rooms?'

'He has a bedroom, of course, and his own sitting-room, but he eats with us.' She was peering down into the aquarium tank as though the conversation had ceased to interest her. She picked up a glass pipette with a rubber bulb at one end and started to fish round the tank as though trying to capture some creature on the bottom.

'What are you doing?'

'I was trying to get this leech.' She allowed water to flow up into the pipette and withdrew it, holding it up for Wycliffe to see the tiny, worm-like creature writhing in the tube. 'They're pests: they attack the other animals.' She squirted the contents of the pipette into a saucer and returned to search the tank for other victims.

Wycliffe was at a loss: it was rare in his professional experience to be treated so casually. 'Seeing your mother go off like that you must have wondered where she was going?'

She was intent on the capture of another leech. 'I could guess.'

'What?'

'That she was going to a man.'

'But you didn't contradict the story which your father told you next morning – that she was staying with her sister?'

She emptied another pipette-full into the saucer. 'I got two that time!' She looked up at him with candid brown eyes. 'No, I didn't contradict him; there didn't seem to be much point.'

While she continued to poke about in her tank Wycliffe took stock of the room. Part of one wall was occupied by a large and faded poster about hippie flower power, mildly erotic; there were several pop star pin-ups and two framed pencil portraits, one of Zel and the other of a youth with serious eyes and sensitive features. They impressed him by their economy of line and a haunting delicacy almost impossible to describe.

'These are good!'

She looked over without much interest. 'They were done by a girl at school.'

'An odd sort of girl.'

'What?' He had more of her interest now. 'Why do you say that?'

'This portrait of a young man is certainly a self-portrait.'

'Clever you!'

'Boy-friend?'

'You could call him that.'

'A secret?'

'It was until she found out.'

'Your mother? What did she have to say about it?'

'You really want to know?'

'I asked.'

'She said, "Do you let him screw you? If you do you'd better go on the pill: I don't propose to have a squalling brat about the place!" Now I've shocked you, I suppose.'

'No, but was that your intention?'

She had her back to him, bent over the tank and she did now answer.

'Who is he?'

'That's my business.'

Wycliffe did not argue. 'Well, I must go; but I shall be back with more questions. If your father wants me he can telephone the local police station.'

'All right, I'll tell him. Can you find your own way down?'

He went down the attic stairs to the first floor landing. The house was utterly silent. Not even the ticking of a clock. He went along the broad corridor, passed the top of the stairs and opened a door at random. A bedroom, furnished with heavy mahogany pieces, a thick red and black carpet on the floor. The bed was a massive affair with scroll-work and bunches of fruit at the head and foot; it was covered with a real old patchwork quilt. The room reminded Wycliffe of his grandmother's bedroom and it had probably been the same when the Bryce parents slept there. For some reason which he could not explain to himself he knew that it was Sidney and not Matthew who slept there now.

A door off the bedroom opened into a small bathroom which looked like an exhibit from the showrooms of some specialist in sanitary ware. Of course, that would be part of the family business. Over the wash-basin a mirror-fronted cupboard contained a variety of toilet preparations, aftershave lotions, hair creams, hand creams, talcum powders and a few patent medicines.

The great double wardrobe in the bedroom held several suits, all of good quality, and there was a bow-fronted chest of drawers filled with shirts and underclothes, expensive and beautifully laundered. Sidney was a dandy.

Next door was the sitting-room, another large room, with leather armchairs, a mahogany desk with silver ink-stand and pen-tray and massive, glass-fronted bookcases with books on economics, company law, accounting and business management. It was less a sitting-room than an office but, again, Wycliffe had the impression of a stage set rather than a room where somebody lived and worked. It was a strange household; not, perhaps, a household at all – just a house in which people lived, each, it seemed, with a feverish desire to impress his or her personality on part of it. Matthew in the old library, Caroline in her aggressively modern suite, Sidney with his ponderous Edwardian elegance. And Zel – did she live in a real world?

He went over to the bookcases. A dull lot. Below the glass-fronted cases were cupboards and Wycliffe opened the doors. These cupboards too, were full of books which were more interesting. Romances by the score. As far as he could tell they seemed to be mainly stories of chivalry, the sort of thing most boys grow out of in their teens: fair damsels in dark towers rescued by fearless, spotless and apparently, castrated Sir Galahads. But at the end of one of the rows he found a nest of books which were quite different: *Girlhood, The Psychology of Female Adolescence, The Difficult Years, You are Sixteen* and *Sex and the Young Girl.* All were fairly new. They were objective, factual works with nothing pornographic about them; but strange reading, all the same, for a bachelor of forty-five. He shut the doors. When you lift a stone you never know what you will find underneath.

He let himself out into the corridor, closing the door silently behind him, and reached the top of the stairs in time to witness a little scene in the hall below. Bryce was there with a woman, a dumpy little grey-haired woman in her fifties, dressed for out-of-doors and carrying a loaded shopping bag. Her free hand rested on his arm and she was looking up at him with an expression of concern. Bryce stood, his back to Wycliffe, shoulders drooping, trousers sagging. The woman saw Wycliffe almost at once and drew away. Wycliffe went down to be introduced.

'Superintendent! I thought you'd gone. This is my cousin, Irene – Miss Bates. She keeps house for us. She's just come back from shopping.' He added, 'I'm afraid she's a little deaf.'

At first she reminded Wycliffe of the little painted figure of the farmer's wife which used to be included with toy boxes of farm animals. She was comfortably plump and motherly with rosy patches of colour on her cheeks; all she needed was a white apron to tie round her waist. But looking more closely he could see the moist eyes, the loose, wet lips; and the colour of her cheeks began to look more like an alcoholic flush than a sign of health.

'This is a dreadful business!' Her voice had that curious tone quality which comes after years of partial deafness.

'Just for the record, Miss Bates, where were you when Mrs Bryce left the house last Thursday evening?'

She looked at him blankly.

'You'll have to speak up,' Bryce said. 'She won't wear a hearing-aid. The superintendent wants to know where you were on Thursday evening when Caroline went out.'

Wycliffe was at a disadvantage. He wanted to ask cousin Irene a few questions – but not standing in the hall with Bryce acting as interpreter. 'Is there somewhere . . . ?'

'Take the superintendent up to your room.' She seemed reluctant, but Bryce held out his hand for the shopping bag: 'I'll drop that in the kitchen.'

'No!' She twitched the bag away from him and both men heard the clink of bottles.

Her sitting-room was on the first floor overlooking the yard. It was a comfortable-looking room, but shabby and in need of a good clean. It had an old-maid smell compounded, amongst other things, of stored linen, camphor balls and cats. A giant, doctored tabby slept in a saggy, chintz-covered armchair; he opened his green eyes momentarily, stretched, unsheathing his claws, then went back to sleep. There was an old-fashioned treadle sewing machine in the window and a television set by the fireplace. A second door opened into an adjoining bedroom and Wycliffe could see part of the foot of a brass bed and the corner of a white quilt.

'Were you here on Thursday evening, Miss Bates?'

She looked at him vaguely. 'I'll just go and take off my things.' She disappeared into the bedroom, taking her shopping bag with her. He could hear her moving about and, after a moment or two, the sound of something being poured into a glass. She was fortifying herself and, indeed, when she came back into the room a few minutes later she seemed more alert and her eyes had lost their moist, glazed look.

'The evening Mrs Bryce left . . .' Wycliffe reminded her.

She sat on the arm of the cat's chair. 'I'm here every evening from about nine o'clock after I've cleared away the supper things.'

'Do you remember last Thursday evening in particular?'

She stroked the cat's sleek body absent-mindedly but her eyes avoided Wycliffe's. 'I suppose it was just like any other evening.' Her glance fell on the machine in the window. 'I remember; I was sewing.'

'Did you look out of the window?' He had to repeat the question.

A decisive shake of the head. 'No, what would I look out of the window for?' She seemed to be following her own train of thought and Wycliffe's questions were an intrusion on it; yet she was frightened of him. Every now and then he would catch her stealing sly, wary glances but she never met his eyes directly. 'There's nothing to see out there, only the yard. In any case I was sewing.'

'So you didn't see Mr Bryce or Mrs Bryce?'

'No.'

'Or Zel?'

'I didn't see anyone!'

'And you didn't hear . . . ?' He broke off and apologized. 'Was there nothing that struck you as unusual that evening?'

'Nothing.'

'Were you surprised to learn next day that Mrs Bryce had gone to stay with her sister?'

She dabbed her lips with her handkerchief. 'Why should I be? She often went there.'

'Have you any idea who might have wanted to kill her?'

'No.' Then she added, 'Nobody in this house.'

'How can you be sure?'

She shrugged. 'I live here.'

'What about Zel?'

For once her eyes met his, anxious and scared. 'What do you mean by that?'

'What sort of girl is she?'

Her plump, ringed fingers were intertwined and she was alternately tightening and relaxing their grip. 'Like most young girls these
days, I suppose.'

'What does that mean?'

'Hard and selfish – spoiled.'

'Not by her mother?'

She gave him a quick, knowing look. 'You're right there! Her
mother understood her too well. Her father and her Uncle Sidney
made up for it though.'

He got out his pipe and asked permission to smoke. She watched
him fill and light it. 'My brother always smoked a pipe; I like to see a
man with a pipe . . .' The tension relaxed.

'This seems an odd sort of household. How long have you been
here?'

'Since I was . . . about fifteen years.'

'You came after Zel was born, then?'

'She was three. I'd been keeping house for my brother; he died of
a coronary and as they needed somebody here Matt asked me to
come. I've been here ever since.'

'How do you get on with the brothers?'

She took time to consider. 'Matt is kindness itself, gentle as a
lamb . . .' She put her hand to her mouth and did her best to suppress a belch. 'George was wild but, speak as you find, he was all
right with me.'

'And Sidney?'

She pursed her lips.

'You don't like him?'

'I like a man to be a man; he's more like a woman.'

'He seems very fond of his niece.'

'Too fond if you ask me!'

'What about Caroline Bryce? How did you get on with her?'

She pondered. 'I didn't approve of her way of life, of course, or of
the way she treated Matt, but outside of that I had no complaints.'

'Friendly?'

She looked at him briefly. 'She used to come and talk with me
sometimes. Now and then she would come up here of an evening
after supper and we'd have a good old gossip. She was lonely – like

374

me.' Cousin Irene looked bleakly from her TV set to her sewing machine.

'What sort of woman was she?'

'Not so bad as she was painted. She ought never to have married Matt and she knew it. She needed affection but Matt was incapable of giving it to her. And Zel . . .'

'What about Zel?'

'In my opinion she wasn't a natural daughter. Caroline used to say they'd poisoned the child's mind against her, but if you ask me that one never had much love for anybody but herself.' She sighed breathily. 'I shall miss Caroline.'

Wycliffe wondered if the two women had exchanged their confidences over a glass or two of gin. 'Somebody murdered her.'

She looked at him sharply. 'Why do you say it like that?'

'Because it's true and it's my job to find out who did it. It's your duty to help me but I think you're holding something back.'

He spoke kindly but her agitation returned. She got up and went over to the window, ostensibly to straighten the curtains. 'You've no right to say that! I've told you everything I know!' She turned to face him and he was astonished at the change in her: the colour had spread to the roots of her hair and she was flushed as though of a fever. He looked round the pathetic, spinsterish room and wondered what possible good he was doing by upsetting her.

'Don't upset yourself.'

'That's all very fine; you come here badgering me then you tell me I'm telling lies! You've no right to accuse me . . .'

Wycliffe stood up. 'I'm not accusing you of anything, Miss Bates. Thank you for being helpful.'

'You're going?' She watched him, tense, on the verge of tears.

He nodded. She crossed the room to stand beside him, looking up in what seemed to be an agony of apprehension. 'You won't . . . ?'

'I won't what?'

She shook her head. 'Nothing. Take no notice, I'm not well. Anybody will tell you I'm not well.'

He opened the door, certain that before it closed behind him she would be at the bottle.

At the bottom of the stairs he met Bryce. 'You're wanted on the telephone.'

He went into the little room off the hall.

'Wycliffe.'

'Mr Bellings for you, sir. Hold on, please.'

An interval, a click, then Bellings' voice. 'Is that you, Charles? . . . I've been trying to get you for the past hour! . . . I spoke to the local sergeant but he didn't even know you were in the town! In any case, I thought you were going to stay at the Manor Park?'

'Have you been ringing them too?' It was the first time Wycliffe had spoken.

'I didn't have to. Clement Morley did so then telephoned me when he couldn't locate you.' The PRO in Bellings was outraged. Crime left him unmoved unless it made an unsightly kink in his graphs, but anyone who made a balls-up of public relations was for the hot seat. 'I gather that there is some doubt?'

'About what?' As usual, Wycliffe's response to the stimulus of his immediate superior was a retreat into sullen taciturnity.

Bellings was reluctant to be more explicit. 'About the cause of death.'

'There's no doubt about that; she was murdered.' He was tempted to add, 'Unless she fell off a bridge backwards, hit her head in falling, landed on a buttress then slid off into the water two or three days later . . .' But Bellings was without humour.

'I see.' A moment of silence. 'The Chief is very concerned about this case, Charles . . . Do try to be a bit accommodating where Morley is concerned – it oils the wheels . . . Are you there?'

Wycliffe grunted.

'I hope that I have made the position clear?'

'As crystal!'

'The Chief . . .'

Wycliffe dropped the receiver, his lips moving in silent imprecation. He got out his pipe and lit it again before leaving the house.

3

The estuary looked even more attractive, calm and peaceful in the sunshine. Three dinghies, two with white sails and one with blue were weaving complex patterns between the mooring buoys off the town, and a tug, towing a mud-barge, pushed swiftly downstream for the open sea, raising a herring-bone pattern of swell which rocked the smaller craft. As he drew near the timber-yard a long drawn-out wail announced the end of the working day and by the time he reached the gates men were streaming out, some on bicycles, some on foot. Half-past five.

Wycliffe's acquaintance with Clement Morley dated back more than thirty years to when they had been schoolboys together. Morley's father, a tool-setter by trade, had started a small engineering works in 1939 and it had grown with the war and the post-war boom until, in the early sixties, the old man had sold out to one of the big boys for over a million. Young Clement had shown a taste for politics and after a year or two in local government, learning the trade, he put up for parliament. He had been an MP since 1954 and in 1959 he served for a few months in a junior ministerial post. He was noted for his speeches, delivered with almost Churchillian fire and eloquence, on any subject linked with his particular brand of morality, from bare bosoms on TV to full frontal nudity on the stage. A prime minister had once referred to him as 'Our Champion of the non-event', but Morley had a strong non-confirmist lobby behind him.

Before collecting his car from the yard Wycliffe went into the hotel and made a telephone call from the public box. As a result of the call several people had to change their plans for the evening. In particular, Chief Inspector Gill, Wycliffe's No. 2. The recent lull had made it possible for him and his wife to lead a more normal home life, and for this particular evening they had engaged a baby-sitter so that they could go out together and sample the swinging night life of the city. (Two tickets for the University Theatre followed by a nosh-up at the Chinese.) Instead, Gill would be travelling to Treen with three others of the squad, a detective sergeant and two constables, one a woman.

Detective Inspector Harker of Divisional CID who had taken Bryce to identify his wife's body, would be drawn back into the case with his sergeant and three constables from the uniformed branch. Finally, a police driver with a truck was detailed to tow one of the mobile HQ caravans to Treen to provide a base for Wycliffe and his team.

Having thrown these several stones into the private pools of other people's lives, he felt that he had made a start on the case. Soon it would begin to move out of his control, seeming to take on a life of its own.

He asked one of the hotel staff where Clement Morley lived.

'Up the hill out of the town; you can't miss it – there's two great gateposts with greyhounds on the top . . . On the right about a mile and a half out . . .'

He found the posts and followed a short drive which brought him on to a gravelled sweep in front of the house where a black Mercedes was parked. It was a terrace from which the ground fell away rapidly in grassy slopes ending in woodland. The slopes were so steep that he could see the distant blue of the sea above the trees. The house was squarely built of grey stone without a creeper to relieve its barrack-like severity. He parked his Zephyr by the Mercedes and rang the doorbell. A formidable female with a disturbing squint admitted him. 'I'll see,' she said.

Wycliffe was received by the ex-minister in his office, where he sat at a table littered with papers. A red-head, wearing a tight, black jumper suit hovered at his elbow and was dismissed with a nod as Wycliffe came in.

Morley was the same age as Wycliffe – forty-five – but his hair, which had been jet black, was now grey. He had been a tall, weedy youth and he was still thin and bony except for a well-developed paunch. He still wore large, circular spectacles which gave him an owl-like expression and made his features seem even leaner and more angular in contrast with his thick, protuberant lips. Those lips had fascinated and repelled Wycliffe as a boy and they did so still, their moist, pink fleshiness reminded him of entrails.

'Wycliffe? Wycliffe? That's an uncommon name. I went to school with a Wycliffe.' He was boisterously patronizing. 'You wouldn't be Charlie Wycliffe? – Charlie Wycliffe – that's it! Well, well!' He laughed. 'After all these years!'

Wycliffe refused a cigarette and listened to the ex-minister reminisce about their school days, memories so different from Wycliffe's own that he found it difficult to believe in their common origin. At any rate, the great man seemed little grieved by his sister's death.

'Half-sister. Caroline was my half-sister, you must remember . . .'

Wycliffe had forgotten that old man Morley had married twice; his first wife had died while Clement was a young child.

'Now, tell me about poor Caroline.' He took a cigarette from the box on the table, fitted it into a holder and made a ritual of lighting it. 'Did she take her own life?'

'She was murdered.' Wycliffe was blunt but Morley seemed unaffected. He nodded as though the news was no surprise.

'I see!' He made himself more comfortable in his upholstered swivel-chair. 'We've not been particularly close in recent years . . . To be frank, her conduct had been something of an embarrassment to me. All the same . . .' He looked at Wycliffe through a thin haze of cigarette smoke. 'I would be the last one to want anything hushed up – you quite understand, Wycliffe?' He gestured with his large, bony hands which had black hairs on the backs. 'You've no idea who did it?'

'Not yet.'

He shook his head. 'It all comes of marrying a man old enough to be her father and a fool at that! I warned her at the time but it was never any use talking to Caroline. Obstinate!' He chuckled briefly. 'She got that much from the Morleys anyway. My colleagues on the front bench . . . But that's another story.' He was silent for a while. 'At the same time I hope that you will be discreet. I sent for you to tell you how important it is to avoid unnecessary scandal, scandal which could do me and the party a great deal of harm and nobody any good . . .'

Wycliffe looked at him blandly. Morley was sitting with his back to the window and through the window Wycliffe could see the tops of the trees and the sea beyond. He was watching a ship creep almost imperceptibly along the distant horizon and remembering a visit he had once paid to the Morley home while they still lived in a council house. A leggy little girl of three or four had insisted on showing him her dolls; that little girl must have been Caroline. Another little girl, much younger, sat on her potty in the middle of the room to the intense embarrassment of Clement who kept trying to stand between her and Wycliffe.

Morley was beginning to look at him uneasily for he had scarcely spoken since coming into the room. Now he began to ask questions.

'Is this your permanent home, sir?'

'I come here whenever I can get away from London.'

'When did you arrive here last?'

'On Wednesday.'

'Any particular reason for this visit?'

Morley looked annoyed. 'I scarcely think . . .'

Wycliffe's expression was utterly blank but his eyes worried Morley.

'There was not too much on and I felt in need of a break. I get in a round or two of golf . . .'

'You are Chairman of the Building Trades Corporation?'

Morley was eyeing the chief superintendent with concern. 'I suppose Bryce told you?'

'About the take-over – yes.'

'That was the reason for my visit; it is a deal I have planned for some time.'

'I understand that Sidney Bryce was in favour of the sale?'

'Of course he was! He's a businessman and he knows on which side his bread is buttered. We've been friendly for years – even Caroline married into the family.'

'But Matthew opposed it?'

Clement Morley blew through his thick lips. 'Matt, as I said, is a fool! He lives in the past, and that, as my old father used to say, never filled anybody's belly!'

'Surely Bryce Brothers must be small beer to a firm like BTC?'

The coarse hands dissented. 'By no means! They have a large turnover and though they have fingers in too many pies, a pro-gramme of rationalization would . . .'

'And it all depended on your half-sister?'

'What?' Morley seemed, suddenly, nervous. 'I don't understand you.'

'Which way she voted.'

For some reason he was relieved. 'Oh, yes, that is quite true; it all depended on Caroline.'

'And she wanted the deal to go through?'

His manner was edgy. 'Certainly! She had very good reason – a handsome profit on her investment.'

'Matthew would have stood to gain more than his wife, yet he was opposed to the sale.'

Morley laughed. 'Matthew is a sentimentalist but there is . . . was no sentiment in Caroline where business was concerned.'

'When did you last see her?'

'Caroline? We saw little of each other. She made a good deal of unpleasantness when my father died and, in any case, her way of life was repugnant to me.'

'To your knowledge, did she have any enemies?'

'Enemies?'

'She was murdered; somebody must have killed her.'

Morley stubbed out his cigarette in a crystal ashtray. 'A woman in her position, living as she did . . .'

'What was her position?'

It was clear that Morley resented having his words challenged in this way. 'Surely it is obvious! A woman with a fair amount of money in her own right and with wealthy and influential connections . . .'

Wycliffe realized that Morley was anxious for him to place a certain interpretation on his half-sister's murder but he was by no means sure that he understood the reason for this anxiety. To proclaim to the world that she had been murdered by her lover would surely do no good to the Morley image?

Morley shuffled the papers on his desk and went through the ritual of positioning his blotter and pen-tray. 'Have you any knowledge of Caroline's private affairs? Her will, her business papers – that sort of thing?'

'Not yet.'

'I take it that you will . . .' He broke off.

'That I shall what?'

Morley was embarrassed. 'Go through her effects.'

'Certainly.' Wycliffe was cool. He wished that he could smoke but he did not want to establish the kind of relationship which would make it possible. He remained silent while the grandfather clock by the fireplace checked off the seconds with a heavy tick. Morley seemed to be absorbed in his private thoughts. Wycliffe looked round the gloomy, depressing room with its modern oak panelling, its heavy furnishings; a ponderous and pompous room like its owner. Over the mantelpiece were two photographs in ornate gilt frames, photographs which Wycliffe vaguely remembered from the Morley living-room of thirty years ago. The Morley parents. The old man – by no means old when the photograph was taken – a factory worker in his Sunday suit, butterfly collar, waistcoat and watch chain. A compelling face, thin-lipped and resolute. Morley's mother, a girl in her twenties, a flapper with crimped, bobbed hair, a bold face and thick, protuberant lips which she had handed on to her son.

'You did not get on well with your step-mother, did you?' The question, in its offensive irrelevance, arose from a sudden memory of the hard-faced blonde who had taken the first wife's place and dominated the little council house. He recalled vividly her manner of speaking to young Clement, the barbed words, uttered with barely concealed antagonism.

Morley was obviously put out but he answered with fairly good grace. 'She resented me as the child of the first marriage.'

'Is she still alive?'

'She died a year before my father.'

For a little while Morley seemed to have forgotten the deference due to him; now he remembered. 'Well, Wycliffe, if that is all, I'm a very busy man.' He stood up. 'I think we understand each other. I merely wanted to make it clear that, while I have nothing to hide, I should not enjoy having the family's linen washed in public' He nodded in dismissal but Wycliffe sat tight.

'I have one or two more questions.'

The ex-minister had already begun to sort through his papers and looked up in surprise. 'Indeed?' He glanced at the clock. 'I can give you another five minutes – what is it you wanted to know?'

'Some information about George Bryce.'

The thaw was immediate. 'George?'

'I gather that Matthew and he did not get on.'

Morley smiled. 'That is an understatement. Matt ordered him out of the house two years ago.'

'Not because he had sold his share in the business?'

Morley lit another cigarette and exhaled slowly. 'That may have had something to do with it but there was more.'

'Your half-sister?'

Morley growled something unintelligible.

'What sort of chap is he?'

'George? A rake and a wastrel with the years catching up on him.'

'Where does he live now?'

Morley jerked a thumb over his shoulder. 'A small place by the river, above the station. Actually it's the house the original Bryce brothers built for themselves – Foundry House, they call it.'

'Alone?'

Morley frowned. 'His is the only name on the voters' list.'

Wycliffe stood up.

'Is that all?'

'How does he make a living?'

Morley sneered. 'By his wits.'

'Was he never in the business?'

'No; when he left school he went, of all things, to study medicine. Even more surprising, he qualified . . .'

'So he's a doctor?'

'A doctor without patients. After he had completed his hospital training he decided that medicine was not for him – too much like work, I imagine. To the best of my knowledge he's never done a day's work since.'

It was clear that, at last, Wycliffe had given him the chance to say what he had been waiting to say all along.

'Well, thank you for your help, sir.'

Morley came with him to the door and saw him to his car. 'About George, you may be on to something. I've heard queer stories . . .'

Wycliffe drove back to his hotel and ate an indifferent meal, scarcely noticing the food. Only three tables were occupied, grouped round an electric heater; the rest had chairs stacked on top of them. A party of commercial travellers ate at one of the tables and at another a middle-aged couple in country tweeds looked like survivors from an era when people took walking holidays. The Swedish girl, whom the commercials called Nora, waited at table. When

Wycliffe baulked at a selection of tinned fruits swimming in custard she seemed to be so affronted that he ate them to avoid a scene.

Afterwards he went in search of the police station.

The late summer evening dusk filled the narrow streets of the little town with purple shadows. There was no-one about; even in the square only a black mongrel dog, making a tour of the perimeter, sniffing at the corners and cocking his leg. The fair was in full cry, and the racing canned music and the amplified bleat of some pop singer hung like a pall over the houses. Wycliffe found the police station in a little cobbled court off the square, a small granite building with a blue lamp and the date 1896 over the door.

In the office a little old lady, crisp and neat as a Meissen figure, was laying down the law to the sergeant behind the desk. 'I have no wish to cause unpleasantness, Sergeant, but one cannot stand by while children are permitted, perhaps encouraged, to commit theft.'

The sergeant's eyes were glazed in patient resignation but when he caught sight of Wycliffe he became brisk. 'We will certainly look into your complaint, Miss Allard, and thank you for reporting the incident.'

But the old lady had not yet made her point to her entire satisfaction. 'I am not one to interfere, but I ask you, Sergeant, what would young Billy be doing with a travelling case? It was a quality article and by no means worn, though a little mud-stained.'

'Exactly, Miss Allard; I have noted your description.'

'I mean, his mother has had plenty of time to report the find if she had any intention of doing so. Billy had it with him when he came from school . . .'

Her voice, a gentle sawing sound, like wind in the rushes, monotonous and soporific, seemed as though it might go on for ever but in the end the sergeant edged her to the door and eventually through it.

'I'm sorry about that, sir!' Then he added, 'I've been expecting you, sir. Mr Bellings telephoned.' A gentle, well-merited rebuke, for, whatever one's rank, it is unforgivable to prowl about on someone else's patch without a word.

'You know why I'm here?'

'Yes, sir.'

Wycliffe well remembered the day when the top brass used to ask him damn silly questions like that – but you have to say something.

'Do you know much about the Bryces?'

Penrose hesitated. 'A little, sir. Everybody speaks well of Mr Matthew though why, I'm not quite sure. He's hardly ever in the town and they never see him in the yards. All the same, the idea seems to have got round that he keeps Mr Sidney in check – stops him turning the time and motion boys in – that sort of thing. Sidney runs the business and he's got a bit of a reputation as a would-be slave-driver, out for every penny.'

'What about George?'

The sergeant frowned. 'He's nothing to do with the business as far as I know.'

'What's he like as a man?'

'He's got a temper: more than once he's come near to being in trouble with us when he's had a few drinks too many . . .'

'Women?'

'It seems so. They say he was kicked out of the house by his brother for having an affair with his sister-in-law. That was before my time, but I do know her car is parked on the waste ground by Foundry House often enough.'

'Has Sidney got any vices?'

'Not unless making money and playing golf are vices.' The sergeant smiled. 'He doesn't seem to have time for anything else.'

Wycliffe was staring out of the office window which was frosted halfway up. Just across the court, in a little sitting-room, three children were watching television, their intent faces lit by flickering light on the screen. He got out his pipe.

'What was that about a travelling case when I came in?'

The sergeant was young and anxious to make a good impression. 'One of our problem families, sir, the Jordans. Father is on the Assistance for nine months of the year, there are six kids, three under school age, and mother puts the older ones up to nick anything they can lay their hands on. Proper female Fagin she is, if you understand me, sir.'

'I have read *Oliver Twist*.'

'Of course, sir. Well, this old lady, Miss Allard, lives next door with her two sisters and they are always complaining about what goes on in the Jordans'.'

'What are you going to do about the travelling case?'

'I'll get one of my chaps to call in the morning.'

385

'Go there yourself – now. I'll look after the shop.'

'Sir?' He had been warned about Wycliffe's eccentricities.

'I'm interested in that case. Try and get hold of it before they've flogged whatever was in it.'

The sergeant put on his helmet and left. Wycliffe was alone in the little office. Light green paint peeling off the walls, the slightly greasy pitch-pine of the counter and the fly-blown face of the clock on the wall. Twenty years ago he had spent a few months as a sergeant in a little office almost the twin of this. He sat on the stool and put his elbows on the counter, smoking his pipe and wondering what he would do if he had a customer.

But, as always, he found it impossible to think logically, constructively. He supposed that there were people who could sit down and consider any problem which faced them, weigh the evidence and decide on a course of action. There must be such people, otherwise there would be no mathematicians, no philosophers, no scientists; but from a very early stage in his career he had realized that he was not one of them. At first he had worried about this defect, sometimes he still did, but the fact remained that whenever he decided to 'think things out' his mind became vague, filled with hazy pictures, half-remembered phrases, and with anxious reflections on his own conduct. Was he making a fool of himself? That was the question which constantly cut across any serious attempt at analytical thought.

The atmosphere of Boslow lingered with him, an old and beautiful house which should have left some impression of grace and elegance, however decayed. Instead it had depressed him. His dominant recollection was one of near squalor and tattiness despite the incongruous and rather tasteless luxury of Caroline's room and the heavy ostentation of Sidney's. The house was a shell, like a hermit crab's, not made for the life within it.

Fugitive images flitted through his mind. Matthew Bryce, nervous, intense and, somehow, not quite genuine. Wycliffe found it hard to put his finger on it, but he had the impression that Bryce had been playing a part. There were moments when he had caught that restless, intelligent eye upon him as though he were gauging an effect. Then there was Zel, curt, grave, with an air of matured sadness which seemed to have little to do with her mother's death. 'She did it herself!' had been Zel's first reaction. Then she told of seeing her mother leaving with a suitcase, driving off. And he could hear Bryce's voice, speaking of Caroline's inopportune pregnancy: 'I am sure that it must have become part of the family legend.' Had he said it with a sneer? For all his Robert Owen socialism he seemed to have a certain arrogance. And lastly, the pompous Morley, falling over himself to involve George. 'I've heard some queer stories . . .'

He got off the stool to stretch his legs and stood by the window. Across the court the sitting-room was in darkness: the children must have gone to bed or, perhaps, to the fair. He became aware again of the music which must have been a background to his thoughts all the time; it filtered through into the secluded court, muffled by the houses.

Jimmy Gill arrived with his detectives before the sergeant returned. Gill was young for a chief inspector, rugged and tough. While strangers were invariably surprised to learn that Wycliffe was a policeman, Gill would never raise any eyebrows on that score. Wycliffe liked him and the two men got on, largely because their temperaments were complementary.

He came into the little office, blinking in the light, for it was now quite dark outside.

'Where are the others?'

'Waiting in the car.'

'You'd better book them in at the hotel on the quay. That's where I am and there's plenty of room.'

Gill lit one of his little black cheroots which he smoked instead of cigarettes, hoping that they were less hazardous. 'The van will be here soon, I passed it about twenty miles back. Where shall we put it?'

Wycliffe had in mind a little patch of grass between the ferry slipway and the boatyard. He told himself that it was conveniently placed between Boslow and the town, but this was rationalization: he fancied that particular spot for his command post.

'I've been in touch with the electricity people and the telephone engineers. They will be here first thing.' Gill never forgot anything. The caravan had electric lighting run off batteries but the batteries had to be charged from the mains.

Wycliffe gave him a potted version of the case to date and when Sergeant Penrose returned with the travelling case his office was full of tobacco smoke. Chief Inspector Gill was perched on a stool like a gargoyle on its plinth and Chief Superintendent Wycliffe was sitting on the counter with his legs swinging.

'What's all this then?' Gill slid off the stool and took the case. 'Let's see what's in it.'

'It's locked, sir; they hadn't got round to opening it.'

Gill took a paper clip from the counter, straightened it, then put a small hook on one end. With this he attacked the locks on the case and in thirty seconds he was able to snap back both catches. He looked round for approval – it was his party piece – but Wycliffe was staring out of the window and the sergeant was too intimidated to say anything. Gill started to lift out the contents of the case, dropping the items one by one on the counter. Wycliffe turned to watch. The fawn coat with the wooden buttons was there, so was the dress; a spare set of underclothes, a nightgown, a bed-jacket, quilted dressing gown, toilet articles, a pair of mules, three paper-backed thrillers and a packet of indigestion tablets.

Gill said, 'Not my idea of the gear for a dirty week-end.' He picked up his half-smoked cheroot from the counter, where it was beginning to scorch the varnish. 'Where the hell was she going with that lot?'

Wycliffe turned to the sergeant. 'Where does the boy say he got the case?'

'He found it under Gummow's Bridge, sir. There's a stream . . .' He showed them on a wall map of the district. Gummow's Bridge carried the station road over a small stream which, later, ran through Boslow and emptied into the lake. It was not more than two hundred yards from the back door of Boslow.

It seemed incredible that the dead woman had carefully packed her case then thrown it into a stream two hundred yards from her home. But almost as incredible that she had been attacked within a few seconds of leaving the house. Even if she had been, why had her attacker been in such a hurry to throw out her belongings? It didn't make sense.

'You'd better see about getting your people booked in, Jimmy; then you can send them to fix up the van.'

The newcomers, divisional and area, disturbed the off-season peace of the Treen Hotel, but the proprietor, a youngish man with a magnificent growth of red moustache and sideboards, entered into the spirit of the thing, so that when Gill came up to the superintendent's room at a little after ten, every man and the police-woman had a bed to go to.

Wycliffe had the french window open and was standing on the balcony, leaning on the rail, smoking his pipe. The room was in darkness. 'There's a bottle of beer on the dressing table.'

'Thanks, but I had a couple with the landlord before coming up,' Gill said and joined Wycliffe outside.

The evening was mild and the waters of the estuary faithfully reflected every mast-head light and every street lamp on the wharf. Across the water Treen's other half looked remote and secretive with its pattern of lights and unaccountable patches of darkness.

'It doesn't make sense, Jimmy. She leaves home at around ten on Thursday evening. The girl, Zel, saw her go with her suitcase, and heard the car drive off. Two hundred yards away the suitcase is found under a bridge. I suppose she could have picked up somebody just outside the house . . .'

Gill was following his own thoughts. 'She must have had a hand-bag; we must search the stream tomorrow.'

'We've got to find the car.'

They smoked in silence for a while. Wycliffe was the first to speak. 'The things in her case . . . does anything strike you about them?'

'Except that they seem a pretty unglamorous collection, no.'

'Has your wife ever been in hospital?'

'Hospital? But the Bryce woman was due back for the take-over meeting on the Monday. In any case, ten o'clock at night is no time to be going into hospital unless you're an accident case or an emergency.'

'The night train for London leaves the junction at 10.45; the junction is seven miles away.'

'Are you suggesting that she was off to some plush pad in London for an abortion?'

'Franks wouldn't have missed that.'

'What then? I don't get it.'

'She could have been ill, or thought she was.'

'A couple of days under observation in some clinic – is that it?'

'It's possible. We must ask Franks to take a second look; the indigestion tablets may be a lead.'

Gill whistled. 'I'll get on to the railway; she would have booked a sleeper . . .'

'I have and she did.'

'Her doctor would know.'

'We shall have to find out who he was.'

'No time like the present!'

Wycliffe sighed. 'Sleep on it, Jimmy!'

All the same, for a long time after Gill had gone the chief super-intendent remained on the verandah, arms resting on the wooden rail, smoking his pipe.

Caroline Bryce had been murdered when she was setting out for London. Whether the hospital idea was right or wrong remained to be seen, but who had reason to kill her? Obviously Matthew Bryce – a double motive: her conduct as a wife and the fact that she would destroy the family business by which he set such store. If Bryce had killed her the fact that she intended to be away for a few days would give him a breathing space before people started to ask questions. But how to explain the travelling case? Only a fool would pitch the thing in a stream near the house unless it was intended to be found. And what about the car? Presumably it had been used to transport the body to a suitable spot from where it could be dumped in the river; but where was the car now? And if Zel was telling the truth her mother had left the house alive and alone.

His pipe had gone out and it was getting chilly. A damp mist was creeping up the estuary from the sea so that navigation lights now shone dimly and there was scarcely anything to be seen of the lights of East Treen. Wycliffe knocked out his pipe and returned to his room, closing the french window behind him.

As he was dozing off a phrase recurred to his memory with such clarity that, for a moment, he almost believed that the words had been spoken aloud. 'Nigger lips!' It was one of the unflattering epi-thets the boys had applied to Morley when he was at school. Wide awake, he fell to thinking about Morley's lips, those incongruous features which had come down to him from his mother. But why lose sleep over Morley's lips?

4

'Control to all mobiles: Keep look out for red Mini-Cooper saloon, Z, Bravo, Victor, One Five Nine, Johnny . . .'

House to house inquiries, Treen and district: 'Were you in the vicinity of Boslow House on Thursday evening?

'Have you seen a Mini-Cooper saloon, registration number ZBV 159J?

'Were you anywhere along the river bank above the town?

'Did you see anything unusual or suspicious?'

And so on. And so on.

The routine had begun. Already a uniformed constable was hammering away at a typewriter in the HQ room of the caravan while the smell of the night man's bacon and egg still lingered. Two plain-clothes constables were questioning the fair people, having to rouse them from their beds, for they were not early risers.

Wycliffe's office in the caravan was at one end, its window overlooking the estuary. It was small, but convenient. There was a sofa-seat which converted to a bunk, a desk-table, a few built-in drawers, a telephone and a couple of folding chairs for visitors. His visitor now was Jimmy Gill. Gill sat astride his chair, enveloping it, his arms resting on the back, his chin on his arms. He was ugly, with thick, rubbery skin set in deep lines and he had a chronic five o'clock shadow, but Wycliffe had heard that women found him irresistible.

'Franks says she'd been in the water three or four days before they fished her out and that there must have been a considerable interval between her death and the dumping of the body.'

'He only gives that as an opinion,' Wycliffe growled. He was never very enthusiastic about Jimmy Gill's excursions into speculation. At this stage it was enough to think about the people involved, to recall what they had said and done and their manner of saying or doing it. But Jimmy was not easily put off.

'When Franks gives an opinion it's good enough for me. So, if she was killed on Thursday night, the body was probably kept somewhere until Friday night . . .'

'Why?'

Gill shrugged. 'Probably because the murderer hadn't made up his mind what to do with it.'

'I don't believe that this crime was unpremeditated.'

'Whether it was or wasn't the body didn't go into the water right away and it's unlikely that anybody would try to do such a disposal job in broad daylight. Even at night the quays and wharfs are well lit.' He massaged the bristles on his chin. 'I've been having a natter with the harbour-master; I'd say she was ditched upstream, beyond the wharf. But in that case it would have to be done within an hour either side of high water, otherwise the body would have to be humped over deep mud.' He consulted his notes. He had arrived only the night before and, presumably, he had slept; but he was fully briefed. 'High water on Friday night was at 21.49 and sunset was at 19.16 so it's my guess that the body was put in the water between ten and eleven on Friday night . . .'

Wycliffe was unappreciative. 'I know how your mind works, Jimmy, but what we need at the moment is some nice, tangible evidence.'

'A red Mini, for instance.'

'That might help, certainly.'

As though to oblige them both, there was a tap on the door and the duty constable came in looking nervous. 'Message from Information Room, sir – about the red Mini . . .'

The car had been found in a disused quarry on the hill behind the town. Although there was a good enough track running in at the level of the quarry floor, somebody had driven the car over rough ground higher up and pitched it over the brink, to fall fifty feet on to a heap of discarded steel drums, old beds and rusty car bodies.

Wycliffe stood up.

'Are you going there, sir?'

'No, you are, my lad.'

When Gill had left, Wycliffe telephoned the pathologist.

'It's possible that she was due to go into hospital for a period of observation . . .

'I suppose there is no possibility that she was pregnant? . . . No,

392

just as I thought. Thanks. It could be the digestive tract, perhaps the stomach . . .'

He had decided to call on George Bryce and he set out alone, on foot. He followed the wharf upstream; MV *Alacrity* had finished discharging her coal and was waiting for the tide to put to sea. It was a fine day, blue overhead and cloudless, with nothing to disturb the stillness but the hum of machinery from the timber-yard. He reached the end of the wharf and the entrance to Boslow but he continued along the railway track which ran its course between the estate and the river. There was no proper boundary wall; only a bank under the elms, covered with moss and ferns, which must have been a paradise of primroses in the spring. On the river side the embankment sloped gently to a narrow beach of muddy shingle which would be covered at high water. It was here that, according to Gill, Caroline Bryce's body had been pushed into the water on Friday night. It would not have been difficult at high water.

He had to step off the track at one point while a diesel engine pulling a few trucks trundled down the line. A quarter of a mile on he came to the station, a single platform with a loop line, a signal box and no-one to be seen. Beyond the station the railway cut across the neck of a promontory which jutted out into the river. It was on this land, about two acres, that the Bryces had built their first foundry and their home – Foundry House. There was no sign of the foundry, but the house, four-square and built of brown stone, rose out of the wilderness of bracken and gorse. A few tall pine trees, stripped of all but their topmost branches, were grouped behind the house. The gorse was in its second flowering, filling the air with scent, and the bees were busy collecting their bonus offer. There seemed to be no direct way to the house, but a broad, muddy track fringed the river and Wycliffe followed it. He came to a stone-built boathouse and a blue Triumph parked in the cleared area round it. There were planks missing from the doors of the boathouse and through the gaps he could see the dull gleam of the water in the dock, but no boat. On the platform beside the dock there was room for a couple of cars so George Bryce probably used it as a garage.

In front of the boathouse some attempt had been made to counter the mud by putting down rubble, and a narrow path led off through the gorse in the direction of the house. He followed the path. There was no sound but the droning of the bees. This seemed to him a place after his own heart; the sunshine, the silence, the neglect and the general air of mouldering decay appealed to a streak of indolence in his nature about which he always felt guilty. He knew that his retirement, when it came, would be as crowded with activity as his working life, and for this, unreasonably, he blamed his wife, for whenever he mentioned his lotus-land dream she said, 'It wouldn't last twenty-four hours!'

In front of the house there was a small area of rough grass and on a rug oh the grass a red-headed girl was sunbathing in the nude. She sat up without embarrassment. He noticed that her freckles came down in a deep V between her breasts. She reached for a housecoat and slipped it on. He had the impression that he had seen her before somewhere.

'What do you want?'

'I'm looking for Mr Bryce – Mr George Bryce.'

'He's gone out.' Her manner was remote, disinterested, reminding Wycliffe to the distinguishing characteristic of the modern young, lack of curiosity.

'I'm Detective Chief Superintendent Wycliffe.'

'I know. You came to see my boss, Clement Morley.'

So that was it. Perhaps he was being unfair, but he found it difficult to imagine this girl being much use to a politician except, perhaps, in bed.

'I only work for him when he's down here – just his letters and any typing he wants done.'

'You live in Treen?'

'At the Golf Club – my father is the "pro". I'm Margaret Haynes.' She stood up, scratching her thigh unselfconsciously. 'George will be back soon; you'd better come in.' She picked up her sun-tan lotion and pulled on a pair of sandals. She was pretty but her features were a trifle pinched. Her mouth, in particular, had a mean look.

The sitting-room where she took him was high-ceilinged, with a dusty, plaster cornice and a monstrous ceiling-rose made ridiculous by a dangling electric flex and a bulb without any shade at the end. The furniture was 1930 vintage, imitation leather armchairs with sprung velvet cushions. A carpet-square, threadbare and dusty, made an oasis in a desert of stained floorboards. There was a pervasive smell of dust and damp.

'I'd better put something on.' She left him but returned in a few minutes wearing a sleeveless summer dress. 'Smoke?' She took a packet of cigarettes from the mantelpiece and offered it to him.

'No thanks; pipe.'

'Don't mind me.' She lit a cigarette.

'You do Mr Bryce's letters?'

She frowned. 'I don't think he has any. We're just friends.'

'I believe that Mrs Bryce – Mrs Matthew Bryce was also a friend of his.'

She looked at him coolly. 'He's a friendly man.'

'I suppose you know that she was murdered?'

'Mr Morley told me.' She flicked ash vaguely in the direction of the fireplace. 'Hard luck. But I don't know why you come after George: there's been nothing doing in that quarter for months.'

'They quarrelled?'

'I don't think so; he moved on.'

There were footsteps in the hall, then a voice, 'Maggie!'

She went to the door. 'You've got a visitor, a detective—' She turned to Wycliffe. 'What did you say your name was?'

George Bryce was thirty-four, trying to look ten years younger and almost succeeding; only the lines from his nostrils to his mouth betrayed him. He wore a dark-blue blazer and cavalry twill trousers. His jet black hair rippled back in tight rows of curls. Perhaps the Bryces came of Jewish stock?

'I'm investigating the death of your sister-in-law, Mr Bryce. You will understand that it is necessary for me to know as much as possible about her way of life; about her friends, and about her enemies. You may rely on me not to put a false construction on anything you may tell me; but it must be the truth.' Smooth talk. The dentist says, 'It won't hurt.'

Bryce sat on the arm of one of the leather chairs while the girl lit a cigarette and handed it to him. 'You'd better go.' His manner was brusque.

She looked at him, startled. 'Go? But . . .'

'Just go!'

She was like a little dog who had been kicked. She went as far as the door, then turned back, trying to retrieve something of her dignity. 'I'll see you tomorrow?'

'Perhaps.' Bryce had no thoughts for the girl. It was obvious that his concern was with Wycliffe. 'Well?'

'You were on friendly terms with your sister-in-law?'

'Yes.'

'Intimate terms?'

Bryce made an impatient movement. 'As though you didn't know!'

'Right up to her death?'

Bryce hesitated. 'No.'

'When did your relationship with her come to an end?' Sometimes Wycliffe listened to himself using the euphemistic jargon of his trade and squirmed.

'A couple of months ago.'

'Why?'

'I had been trying to break it off for some time.'

'Why?'

He did not answer.

'Was it because you had found someone younger?'

Bryce fingered his dark sideboards, brushing the soft, tiny ringlets the wrong way. 'No, Caroline was changing; she was becoming . . .' He hesitated for a word.

'Possessive?'

'Yes.'

'Women are apt to when they feel their youth slipping away.'

'I suppose so.'

'Where were you on Thursday night, Mr Bryce?'

'On Thursday? Was that when . . . ?'

'She was murdered on Thursday night, but, according to our expert, her body was not put into the water until later, probably twenty-four hours later.'

'Who's your expert – Franks?'

'Yes.'

'A good man. If he says that, ten chances to one he's right; but it's very odd.' He paused, seemingly engaged in some private calculations. 'I was here on Thursday night.'

'Alone?'

Was there a moment of hesitation? 'Yes.'

'Were you at home all the evening?'

'No, I . . .'

'What time did you return?'

Bryce fingered his sideboards. 'Latish; about half-one, I should think.'

Wycliffe brought out his notebook, which rarely saw the light of day. 'Who were you with?'

Bryce looked at the notebook and frowned. 'I don't want to involve . . .'

'It's your own involvement you need to worry about, Mr Bryce!'

'Very well. We made up a party, three chaps and three girls . . .'

'Names and addresses?'

'Nick Scoble, Paynter's Lane, Bodrifty . . . Alfred Miller, 15 St Clement's Terrace, Treen . . .'

'That will do for the moment. Was Miss Haynes one of the girls?'

'No.'

'When you returned here on Thursday night or Friday morning, was there anyone here waiting for you?'

'No, definitely not.'

Wycliffe was reflecting that at any time Bryce decided to go back to medical practice he would not be short of women patients.

'When did you last see your sister-in-law, Mr Bryce?'

His cigarette had burned down without him noticing and he discarded the stub with a little yelp of pain. 'On Tuesday.'

'Two days before she was murdered?'

'I suppose it must have been. She came here.' He seemed to make the admission reluctantly but Wycliffe was by no means sure that he was not playing a part, rather cleverly. He had placed himself between the Chief Superintendent and the window so that it was difficult to see his face clearly.

'I understood you to say that you had broken with her two months ago.'

'Yes, but she came here and took me by surprise; she wanted to consult me about something.'

'About what?'

'About her health – you know that I'm a doctor?'

'Was Mrs Bryce your patient?'

He shook his head. 'I don't take patients; but she wanted my advice about something which had been worrying her. She had been subject to more or less chronic indigestion and colonic pains.'

'Had she been to her own doctor?'

'She didn't have one. Like a good many women who worry about their health she had a horror of doctors.'

'She was worried?'

'Very.'

'With reason?'

Bryce became cagey. 'I doubt if she had reason for serious concern, though it's difficult to be sure without proper tests. I think the indigestion remedies she took made her colonic condition worse rather than better.'

'You advised her?'

'She refused to go to any of the local men, so I suggested that she booked in at a private clinic for a couple of days so that she could have the necessary tests.'

'She agreed?'

'She asked me to suggest somewhere and I told her of a place in town run by a chap who was at University with me . . .'

'This clinic . . .'

'The Harcourt Clinic, Cherrington Street – it's off Wimpole Street.'

'Did you make the arrangements for her?'

'There and then, by phone. She was booked in Friday to Sunday. She said she had to be back here for the meeting on Monday.'

'About the sale of the firm to BCT?'

'That's what she told me.'

'Had you heard of the proposed sale before that?'

He shook his head. 'It was nothing to do with me. I sold out years ago, more's the pity. She seemed to think she was on to a good thing.'

Facing the window, as he was, Wycliffe had a clear view of the area in front of the house and he had not seen Margaret Haynes leave. He felt pretty sure that she was listening at the door but it was of no concern to him.

'You and Mrs Bryce parted on good terms?'

'The best. She said that she was very grateful and she seemed to mean it.'

'Although you are a doctor, you do not practise. You live on your investments?'

Bryce lit another cigarette. 'You must be joking! You haven't been talking to the family without discovering that I'm broke. It's no secret; I've been that way for some time.'

'Did you receive money from your sister-in-law?'

'You know damn well I did. You must have found my IOUs – unless . . .'

'Unless what?'

'Unless she'd scrapped them.'

'Why should she?'

'As she was leaving on Tuesday after I'd fixed up the clinic for her, she said, "Thanks, Georgie. I might decide to do you a good turn; I'll think about it." I wondered then whether she meant that she . . .'

'Who do you think killed your sister-in-law, Mr Bryce?'

He frowned. 'I don't know; I can't imagine who would want to.'

'Her husband seems to have had motive.'

'Matt? You can't be serious! Matt wouldn't kill a mouse.'

Wycliffe changed the subject again. 'Your affair with Mrs Bryce seems to have lasted longer than most.'

'I suppose it did; we suited one another.'

'If your brother had divorced her would you have married?'

He seemed amused at the idea. 'You've got it all wrong. Caroline wouldn't have married me if I'd asked her. She wanted security.'

'And you? What did you want?'

He smoked for a while before answering. 'Freedom, I suppose. I still do.'

'Apart from Mrs Bryce, does anyone else from Boslow visit you here?'

He shook his head. 'Only Zel.'

'Zel?'

'She's a funny kid; she used to hang around here quite a bit at one time.'

'But not now?'

Bryce smiled. 'She still comes now and then; she turns up and slopes off as the mood takes her.'

'She doesn't hold your relationship with her mother against you?'

'If she does it's never stopped her coming here.'

Wycliffe seemed to be running out of questions; the silences became longer. 'How did you get on with your father?'

'Father? The old man was all right as long as you did what he wanted. As he had the purse strings, we mostly did – except Mellie. She wouldn't knuckle under to him.'

'I suppose you have somebody in to do the housework?' Wycliffe had not the least idea why he asked some of the questions, except that they helped him to build up a picture in his mind, to fit people into a context. Zoologists are told that it is unprofitable to study an animal divorced from its environment; Wycliffe thought that the same principle applied to suspects and witnesses.

Bryce was getting impatient with the constant changes of ground and he answered curtly. 'A woman comes in three days a week.'

'Which days?'

'Tuesdays, Fridays and Sundays. On Sundays she's supposed to cook me an evening meal but as I'm usually out, God knows what she does.'

Wycliffe stood up and prepared to leave. As he did so he saw Margaret Haynes run lightly across the grass and disappear along the path through the gorse. He lingered until he heard the car engine start. Bryce heard it too and looked startled but said nothing.

Bryce saw him to the door. 'I would run you back to town but I've rather a lot on at the moment . . .'

Wycliffe said that he would enjoy the walk along the river bank. As he was about to enter the path through the gorse he looked back, but Bryce had already gone inside. The house looked blind and empty, the windows, which seemed to have no curtains, were dark and unreflecting.

The blue Triumph was gone but an old MG sports, looking rakish and sly, was parked nearby. It evidently belonged to George. Wycliffe slid back the bolt of the wicket in the boathouse door and passed inside. He paused to allow his eyes to become accustomed to the dim light, for there were doors on the river side also, though there was a large gap below them to allow for the rise and fall of the tide. The building of the boathouse must have been a substantial undertaking for a channel had been scooped out and lined with stone to give access to the river at all states of the tide. At least, that had been the intention; but long since silt had built-up in the dock almost to the level of the mud outside.

The platform beside the dock was paved with stone but it had accumulated a layer of mud which clearly showed the marks of tyres. Wycliffe thought he could make out at least two sets. This was not surprising: evidently he used the place as a garage, and no doubt his visitors did too. He continued to prowl round but found nothing in the least suspicious. When he was about to give up he heard footsteps outside. A car door slammed and the engine spluttered into life. It seemed that George Bryce had given him just enough time to get clear before leaving himself.

He walked back the way he had come. The sun shone brilliantly out of a cloudless sky; red flowers of campion and white umbels of cow-parsnip seemed to wait, still and breathless in the heat. It was more like a day in July except that the leaves would have been a fresher green. He took off his coat and carried it over his arm. Somewhere across the water a clock struck twelve.

After more than twenty years as a policeman Wycliffe was rarely surprised by human behaviour but often puzzled and always intrigued. Matthew Bryce had married a girl young enough to be his daughter; he had turned his back on the business he seemed to love to devote himself to a nostalgic quest for something which was dead and gone. His brother George tried desperately to cling to youth, in order, so it seemed, to live out its sexual fantasies. Then there was the girl, Margaret Haynes. What did she want? Surely not the practised and blunted passions of a man like George? Presumably these people like most others wanted to be happy; consciously or unconsciously they sought after happiness, but what an extraordinary way to go about it!

Sententious thoughts of a middle-aged policeman walking in the sun. 'They grab!' he muttered. But to give him his due, he recognized in them his own humanity and that was what made him a good policeman.

As always he found it easier and pleasanter to reflect on the people he had met rather than to think analytically about the crime. It was obviously possible that George Bryce had killed his sister-in-law. A discarded mistress.

When he arrived back at the caravan he found Jimmy Gill dictating his report to a woman PC. The uniformed duty constable was still hammering away at his typewriter and an alarming quantity of typescript had accumulated in the wire tray at his side. Jimmy followed Wycliffe into his tiny private office.

'Did you get the car?'

'A breakdown truck is taking it to Division. Forensic can look at it in their garage.' Gill perched himself on the edge of the table and lit a cheroot. 'Incidentally I got hold of that kid who found the case – bent from the cradle, that lad – poor little bastard! That yarn about finding the case in the river was all balls. He found it in the car in the quarry but he wanted to keep that quiet so that he could go back and nick what else he fancied. That toffee-nosed sergeant wants his arse kicked . . .'

There was an elemental crudity about the chief inspector which sometimes irritated Wycliffe. 'Get off my table!'

Gill got off, grinning, and sat on the chair.

Wycliffe had come to a decision. 'I want the boat-house at Foundry House searched. Try not to scare George Bryce if you can help it, but I want the place gone over . . .'

'. . . with a fine-toothed comb.'

'Don't be infantile, Jimmy! And check on these characters; George says he was with them on Thursday night and early on Friday morning. If it's an alibi, see if it stands up.' He handed Gill his notebook with the addresses of George Bryce's friends.

'You think he needs an alibi?'

'I don't think anything; I just want information. Which reminds me, send Birkett to chat up the woman who does for George. She goes there on Tuesdays, Fridays and Sundays so she could have been there when Caroline Bryce visited on the Tuesday. See if you can find out how long she stopped and whether the old girl knows what it was all about.'

Gill stood up and picked a few memorandum slips from the tray on the table. 'There were several calls for you . . .'

'Clement Morley, Bellings and who else?'

'Sidney Bryce wants to know when it would be convenient, et cetera, et cetera . . . and the same from Mrs Joyce Boon.'

'Joyce Boon? Who the devil is she?'

'Wife of Francis Boon, sister of the deceased. They've come up from St Ives and they're staying at Boslow. Apparently they wanted to use Caroline's rooms and she was more than a mite peeved when our chaps told her they couldn't.'

There were two detectives at Boslow, searching Caroline's rooms and going through her papers with the Bryce lawyer.

Jimmy Gill stopped on his way out. 'There's one more thing – you'll see it in the reports. Our chaps have done the rounds of the fair people and they've turned up a chap called Brandt. His father was a German POW who married an English girl and got himself naturalized after the war. Brandt is a sort of general factotum and hanger-on at the fair.'

'What about him?'

'He's got form. Two convictions for GBH – once on a woman.'

'Don't be daft, Jimmy!'

Gill shrugged. 'You're the boss!'

Wycliffe lunched at the hotel where he was conscious of the surreptitious attention of three divisional men lunching at another table. He could never get used to the fact that most men who worked with him were scared of him, that he had a reputation. When he went into the bar for a drink after lunch they were there before him. He acknowledged them curtly. One, a detective constable with a face and figure like Harry Secombe, plucked up courage. 'Have one with us, sir.'

Wycliffe's bland, expressionless stare almost froze the poor man. 'Thank you – no.'

His response was reflex. If he had given himself time to think he would probably have acted otherwise; but it was always the same. He did not know why. Bellings would have accepted the drink and stood a round or two. 'At least I don't patronize them!' he growled to himself. But why could he never unbend? Was it because he was never sure of himself?

In the afternoon he drove out to Boslow, parked in the drive and rang the bell. The door stood open but nobody answered his ring so he went in. The hall was dim after the bright sunshine outside. Somebody opened a door at the back of the hall and he heard a woman's voice, harsh and discordant. 'You ruined my sister's life and now you've killed her! A young girl she was when you married her, and you, old enough to be her father!'

There was an interjection which he could not hear but it served to inflame her even more. 'You dare to say such a thing! You . . . !' Words failed her and she slammed the door.

Wycliffe had moved towards the scene and now saw that it had taken place in the doorway of Bryce's room. As she turned from the door she saw him and seemed annoyed rather than startled. 'Who are you?'

She had straight, black hair, but very short, and her long face with

403

high cheekbones gave her a masculine look. She was not very tall, thin and bony, and the flowered dress she was wearing hung from her shoulders in ample folds.

Wycliffe introduced himself and she became affable at once. Her recent anger had left no trace; she was neither flushed nor, apparently, ruffled. 'I'm Joyce Boon, Caroline's sister.'

Presumably the little girl he remembered sitting on her potty in the middle of the Morleys' living-room. He sighed inwardly, 'Thirty years!' She led the way across the hall to a room which Wycliffe had not been in before, a large and once elegant drawing-room. Now, however, the furniture was shrouded in dirty and torn loose covers, the carpet was dusty and almost worn through and the faded wallpaper showed great patches of damp around the chimney.

A little wisp of a man with a few straggling blond hairs on his chin was in the act of pouring himself a whisky. He was excessively pale – etiolated, like a plant grown in darkness. 'My husband, the sculptor.' It seemed that he could hardly have the strength to sculpt in anything more refractory than balsa wood.

Boon looked at him nervously, then at the drink in his hand. Wycliffe shook his head.

'Francis has been ill; he's convalescing.' Everything Joyce Boon said seemed to be spoken in capitals.

'Do sit down.' She looked at one of the easy chairs critically before sitting down herself. 'This place! One would think that the Bryces were paupers! I wanted to move into Caroline's rooms but your men would not allow it.' She raised her hands in an extravagant gesture to forestall an apology which Wycliffe had no intention of making. 'You don't have to apologize! My dear man, I'm not a fool! I realize that poor Caroline was murdered and that you have to investigate her death.' She stared at him with great gravity. 'I only hope that you are not too late.'

'Too late?'

She seemed surprised by his obtuseness. 'Don't you think it's very likely that you are? – too late to find any evidence, I mean. After all, Caroline died on Thursday evening and he had three days to cover his tracks. He's been very clever.' She added, having realized a possible explanation of his slowness, 'You realize that Matthew killed her, I suppose?'

Wycliffe was icily cold. 'Perhaps you and your husband will help me by answering some questions.' Without waiting for a reply he went on, 'Mr Bryce says that his wife told him she received a phone call from you on Thursday evening, asking her to come and stay with you.'

'It's a lie!'

'Possibly, but have there been occasions when such a thing did happen? Did you sometimes telephone your sister asking her to visit you at short notice?'

'Sometimes; I'm very highly-strung and Francis is an artist . . .' She spread her hands. 'We have our crises.'

'Is it possible that Mrs Bryce might have used such visits as an excuse to absent herself from the house for other reasons?'

Joyce looked at him wide eyed. 'My dear man! You don't have to mince words with me! Caroline had a man and she used to spend the odd day or two with him when her husband thought she was with me. Why not?'

'Why not, indeed?'

'Her husband could give her nothing – *nothing*. You understand? But she never did it without warning me – in case he phoned.'

Francis Boon had poured himself another whisky and was staring moodily into his glass.

'Did she never consider divorce?'

'Why should she?'

Wycliffe felt like Alice after an encounter with the White Queen. Joyce Boon's attention was temporarily distracted: she was staring at an unfaded patch of wall-paper above the fireplace. 'There used to be a Fragonard hanging there – What happened to it?'

'I've no idea.'

'You remember the Fragonard, Francis?'

Boon only shook his head vaguely.

'It was the only decent picture in the house. I suppose the fool has sold it or given it away . . . Anyway, coming back to Caroline, she *had* to lie to Matthew. I never lie to Francis because he understands me and if I want an affair all I have to do is say so and he understands – completely! It's the only possible basis for marriage.' She looked at her husband. 'As for Francis, if I were a possessive woman . . .'

Wycliffe happened to glance out of the window and saw Zel saunter past. He was reminded of a phrase of Lawrence Durrell's –

405

something about 'the sulking bodies of the young'. Joyce Boon had seen her too.

'And there's Zel – absolutely and completely spoiled by her father and her uncle. She should have been sent away to school, and that was what Caroline wanted, but no, she didn't want to go away from home!' She shook with irritation. 'And they've brought her up to hate her own mother! Somebody will have to take that girl in hand.'

Wycliffe was feeling the bowl of his pipe in his pocket and reflecting that there must be some profoundly depressing psychological reason for the fact that it gave him satisfaction. 'There are just two more questions, Mrs Boon. First, about your sister's estate: do you know anything of a will?'

She looked at him in surprise. 'Hasn't the lawyer told you?'

'I'm asking you.'

She shrugged. 'Well, that's it, isn't it? Years ago they made wills leaving everything to each other. Recently Caroline said that she intended to alter hers but she never did.'

'Would you have known?'

'Caroline told me everything; we had no secrets. In any case, if she had changed her will he would have had no reason to kill her.'

'But Mr Bryce is a rich man; the money could mean little to him.'

'Not the money, but his precious company. He's got his majority holding back, hasn't he?' She sat back in her chair with evident satisfaction. 'You said that there were two things. What was the other?'

'Who was her lover?'

'Why, George Bryce, of course. God knows why. You would have thought one of the family was enough . . .'

'There was no-one else?'

She was emphatic. 'No, there was no-one else.'

'You would have known?'

'I would have known.'

'She was a bitch!' It was Boon's first and only remark.

Joyce looked at him with a tolerant eye. 'Francis never liked her.'

Wycliffe sat staring out of the window. Joyce Boon pursed her lips and waited for him to speak.

'Did you know that your sister was ill?'

'Ill? Caroline was never ill. She never had a day's illness in her life.'

'On Thursday evening when she left here she was on her way to a London clinic for observation . . .'

'I don't believe it. She would have told me!'

Wycliffe said nothing.

'What was wrong with her?' She stood up and almost stamped her feet. 'My dear man! I've a right to know; I'm her sister!'

'She suffered from chronic indigestion and she was afraid that it might be something more serious . . .'

She looked at him suspiciously. 'Are you trying to tell me that she committed suicide? If so, I don't believe . . .'

'No, your sister was murdered.'

As he left the room he almost fell over Irene Bates in the passage. Impossible to believe that she had been eavesdropping so he assumed that she must be waiting to speak to him. 'You wanted to see me?'

She stared at him like a frightened child and her lower lip trembled as though with some sort of tic.

'Did you know that Caroline was ill?'

She looked less frightened. 'She worried about herself: she was terrified of cancer and every ache and pain . . .'

'When she left here on Thursday she was due to catch the night train to London where she was booked in at a clinic for observation.'

The news touched her and she dabbed her eyes with a screwed-up handkerchief. 'Poor girl!'

'I'm going to her rooms to talk to the lawyer; if you have something you want to tell me . . .'

She recoiled. 'I've told you! There's nothing!' She shuffled off towards the kitchen.

Inspector Wills had made a name for himself and a job as a specialist in accountancy, wills and probate. He had assisted Wycliffe before. Lean, dark and precise, he looked more like a company secretary than a policeman. He introduced Wycliffe to the Bryce lawyer, Mr Lambert, middle-aged, plump, bald and jovial.

'You acted for Mr Bryce and his wife?'

'And Sidney.' Lambert grinned. 'When relations became strained between Matthew and his wife I suggested to her that she might find somebody else but she laughed and said it was worth something

407

to have a foot in both camps. Actually we got on very well, poor woman!'

'Anything to tell me?'

'Not much, sir. Mr Lambert is being very cooperative.'

'No point in being anything else, is there?' Lambert reminded Wycliffe of one of Dickens' more amiable and ebullient lawyers. 'If you chaps don't get what you want one way you get it another.'

'Mrs Bryce's will leaves everything to her husband; it is dated fifteen years ago and Mr Lambert says there has been talk of changing it.'

'Only talk – nothing definite.'

Inspector Wills passed him a sheet covered with figures.

'This could mean something. According to her bank statements these sums have been paid into her account over a period of five years by quarterly instalments. It seems that she had this income of nearly two thousand five hundred a year apart from the return on her investment in the company and apart from what Bryce allowed her.'

'Unknown to me,' Lambert put in. 'Of course I can find out from the bank the source of the payments and I'll let you know unless . . .'

'Unless what?'

'Unless the information is prejudicial to the interests of one or other of my clients.' Lambert seemed to think this a great joke.

'No IOUs amongst her papers?'

'None that we've found.'

5

It occurred to Wycliffe that he was putting off meeting Sidney Bryce. He had an antipathy to businessmen, by which he meant people who put a price tag on everything and judge every issue in terms of economics. He had met businessmen who were not in the least like that but he insisted on regarding them as exceptions to a general rule. In any case he had already seen Sidney Bryce at the snack bar on the wharf and, if looks were anything to go by, he must be the type-specimen of the genus.

He told the duty constable to telephone Bryce Brothers and find out when Sidney would be in his office.

'Mr Bryce will be in his office until six o'clock and he will be expecting the chief superintendent.'

A clearer conscience. His puritan ancestry and upbringing prevented him from ever being entirely at peace with himself unless he was planning or doing something which he found disagreeable. Fortunately women are fundamentally amoral and thanks to his wife, Helen, he was learning to live with an uneasy conscience.

The clock on the shelf above his little table showed half-past three. It was hot. He wrestled with the mysterious mechanism of the caravan window and got it open. A faint, tangy breeze filled the room and rustled the papers on his table. The ferry was on its way over to the east side, carrying a bus and a couple of private cars. He must cross over sometime and explore the narrow streets which ran between the grey huddle of houses round the quay. He picked up a bundle of reports from his tray.

The name Brandt caught his eye. 'Frederick Brandt, 26. Fairground labourer . . . shares a caravan with Margery Cook, 19. On being questioned Brandt admitted that he had served two terms of imprisonment for causing GBH.' A lot more, totally irrelevant, then: 'Brandt stated that he left the caravan, alone, at seven o'clock and returned at eleven . . . He claims to have spent the whole evening at the Station Arms . . . In answer to the routine questions he stated that he remembered passing the walls of a "big house" but that he had noticed nothing. He had not, to the best of his recollection, seen a red Mini saloon . . . The witness was nervous and gave the impression that he was not being entirely truthful . . . Blah, Blah, Blah, W. H. Pascoe, Detective Sergeant.'

W. H. Pascoe, Detective Sergeant, had more to say on another sheet: 'John Trew, landlord of the Station Arms, confirmed that Brandt had been in his bar on Thursday evening but said that he had not stayed the whole evening. At about nine forty-five he had left in company with Lena Rowe, a known prostitute.'

Wycliffe decided to talk to Brandt himself; he would call in at the fairground on his way to see Sidney Bryce. As he was leaving he asked the duty constable, 'Any news of Mr Gill?'

'Not yet, sir.'

Wycliffe grumbled to himself. 'Why the hell can't he report in like anybody else?' In fact, Jimmy Gill suffered from the same complaint as his chief, a tendency to play a lone hand.

It was Wednesday, half-day closing for the shops, and, presumably for that reason, the fair had started early. Instead of skirting the ground, Wycliffe walked through it in search of Frederick Brandt. A fair in daylight is like a woman in curlers, but a few youths and girls were conscientiously trying to whoop it up without much success. The dodgems were doing business and so was a contrivance, new since Wycliffe's day, which swept rotating carloads of its victims at the ends of long poles through a seemingly unpredictable and hazardous trajectory. To judge from the screams it was money well spent.

But for Wycliffe the heart and the lungs of the fair were missing, the giant steam traction-engines and the steam organ. As a child it had been enough for him to stand looking up at the spinning fly-wheel of Lord Nelson or The Gladiator. He remembered the twisted brass supports for the canopy, like sticks of barley sugar; the gleaming cross-head darting to and fro; the oily, steamy, wash-day smell, and the ground under foot trembling to the rhythm of the monster. 'You see that round thing in front, driven by the belt; that's the dynamo – it supplies electricity to the whole fair.' His father was as captivated as he was, and they would stand together, spellbound. If

410

they tired, there was always the steam organ with its posturing cavaliers and pirouetting ladies, banks of brass trumpets and, above all, its drenching cascade of sound. All gone.

He made his way to the caravans which bordered the ground on two sides. Most of them seemed to be deserted, but a woman, sitting on the steps of one of them peeling potatoes, directed him. 'Brandt? The little white van. What's he done? The bogeys was in there this morning nearly an hour.'

Brandt's IQ must have been well down in the double figures; he had the build of a young gorilla and nothing to keep his hair from his eyebrows. The door of the caravan was open and Wycliffe found him lying on one of the bunks, turning the pages of an American comic. The caravan was filthy. He looked at Wycliffe, vaguely at first, then with dawning intelligence. 'Are you a scuffer?' He dropped the paper on the floor and sat up.

'Where is your girl-friend?'

'Marge? She's working – on the darts.'

'And you?'

'You what?' He looked uncomprehending.

Wycliffe sat himself on the opposite bunk. 'Why aren't you working?'

'Oh, I work when they shut down: cleaning up, that's my job – and helping Mr Oates with the maintenance.'

'So you go to the pub in the evenings on your own.'

He looked sheepish. 'You got to do something, and Marge don't mind, not if I . . .'

'But she would mind if she knew you'd picked up a trollop like Lena Rowe?'

He nodded. 'That's why I never said anything to your . . .' He broke off, confused. 'She was here.'

It was like taking money from a blind man, but this near-idiot had already put two people in hospital and himself in gaol, so what price freedom?

'Where did you take her? – Lena, I mean.'

It was rather a question of where she had taken him, but it amounted to the same thing.

'Not far from the boozer there's a big house with a wall and in the wall there's doors for garages . . .'

'Well?'

411

'There's a bus shelter; we went in there.'

'What time was this?'

He thought for a moment. 'I don't rightly know; it were after I left the boozer. She wanted me to be quick because she had another fella lined up she said.' He grinned. 'God! She was a scrubber! She wanted three quid – three bloody quid for . . .'

'When did you see the car?'

'The car?'

'The red Mini.'

'Oh, that. It come out of one of the garages an' drove off at a lick down the road.'

'Towards the town or away from it?'

'What?'

'Towards the pub or the other way?'

'Oh, the other way, away from the boozer. I said to the bird, "He's in more of a bleeding hurry than you are!" I said that to her.'

'He?'

'The driver.'

'There was a man driving the car?'

'Well, there would be, wouldn't there?'

'Not a woman?'

'Oh, I don't know about that; I couldn't see.'

'But you saw the red car.'

'Oh yes, I saw it pass under the light. It was a red Mini.'

'And that was all you saw?'

'I was busy.' He paused then added with concern, 'You won't tell Marge? She'd kill me.'

More likely that he would end up by killing her without meaning to. 'I won't tell her unless I have to; but you behave yourself.'

He was glad to escape into the air, to get away from the odour of stale sweat and burnt fat. At times like this he thanked God that he was not a parson, nor any of the species of social workers spawned in town halls. He had only to catch crooks, not to try to patch up lives.

So it looked as though Zel had told, at least, part of the truth. The red Mini had been driven from Boslow at about the time she said; but the question remained – by whom? If, as Zel said, her mother had driven the car away, why had she not gone to the station to catch her train? If Caroline really had left Boslow alive then this told strongly in favour of Matthew Bryce. Had she been stopped

412

by someone on her way to the station? By her murderer? So far it seemed that only George Bryce knew of her true destination that night; he had made the appointment.

Wycliffe was tempted to go back to his headquarters for news of Jimmy Gill, for it seemed that the cards were stacking against George; but he decided to see Sidney Bryce first.

Bryce Brothers' head office was in the square, above a large hardware shop which belonged to the firm. Sidney's office overlooked the square. It was a modern office, functional to the point of being spartan. No sign of the Edwardian banker here. He received Wycliffe with cordiality but without effusion and got right down to business. Against his will, Wycliffe was favourably impressed.

'I expect that you would prefer to ask me questions.'

Wycliffe found himself becoming genial. 'The obvious one, I'm afraid: have you any idea who killed your sister-in-law?'

'None.'

Wycliffe nodded. 'Do you think it possible that she was killed to prevent the sale of your firm to BTC?'

Sidney opened a cigar box and offered it across to the chief superintendent.

'No thanks; I prefer a pipe.'

Bryce nipped off the end of his cigar and lit it. 'The answer to your question is, "Definitely not". It is quite true that now Caroline is dead the deal will not go through; it is also true that my brother Matt was bitterly opposed to the sale. But Matt would never . . .' He broke off with an expressive gesture. 'Matt is totally incapable of violence.'

A soft buzzing came from the intercom on his desk and he flicked a button. 'No calls please, Mrs Grose.'

Wycliffe was filling his pipe. 'In my experience, even the most gentle of men may be goaded into violence; it is often a question of touching the tender spot. We all seem to have one.'

Sidney was thoughtful. 'The tender spot – yes, you may be right. But for Matt, despite all his concern for the business, that would not be it.'

'His wife's infidelity?'

Bryce shook his head vigorously. 'He was almost indifferent; he accepted the situation, which had been going on for years.'

It was refreshing not to have to spell everything out. Bryce

413

assumed that he had done his homework, that he was acquainted with the family skeletons.

'If Matt has a tender spot, as you call it, it is Zel. If someone harmed or threatened Zel . . .'

'But Zel's mother could hardly be in that category.' Wycliffe was bland.

'No-one would think so, certainly.' Sidney Bryce was toying with his cigar which had gone out. Wycliffe was sure that he wished to convey something without putting it into words. 'All the same . . .'

'Perhaps there was too little difference in their ages. A girl of sixteen or seventeen can be competition for a mother of thirty-four.'

Bryce made a curious gesture of distaste. 'A woman jealous of her own daughter! It seems incredible. But you are right: Caroline was jealous of Zel.' He looked at his dead cigar and dropped it into the ashtray. 'I am a bachelor and I know very little of these things; but I would have thought that any normal woman . . .'

Wycliffe wanted to say no more than would keep him talking.

'How did this . . . this jealousy show itself?'

'In a hundred ways. Of course, she was too clever to let Matt see. In any case, Matt is not very observant; sometimes he hardly sees what is going on under his very nose. I had never realized that a woman could be so unfeeling.' He held up his hands in a helpless gesture as though words failed him. 'She would allow Zel to plan something for days or even weeks – some trivial thing which would give the child pleasure, an outing, a school trip, a picnic – then the day before or even on the day she would pretend to know nothing about it. She would laugh and say, "But my dear girl, whatever gave you the idea that I would allow such a thing? Really! You are too absurd!"' He broke off, realizing that he was betraying himself. 'I'm sorry. You can see that I feel strongly on the subject.'

'That is quite natural,' Wycliffe said; but he wondered if it was. In the few minutes he had been in the room he seemed to have found Sidney's tender spot. Obviously he lived vicariously through the lives of his brother's family. A common enough phenomenon with maiden aunts – but bachelor uncles? Was it a more sinister situation?

'I can see that you disliked your sister-in-law.'

'That is an understatement.'

'Which makes it all the more strange that you entered into a business arrangement with her to frustrate your brother's wishes.'

414

'You mean, over the deal with BTC?' Bryce seemed surprised. 'That was quite a different matter. In any case there was no arrangement as you call it. I did not conspire with Matt's wife behind his back; it happened, for once, that we were in agreement.' He sat back in his chair and recovered his self-possession as his thoughts turned back to business. 'The point is that Matt's ideas are fifty years out of date. Our firm was built on two principles, diversification of investment and paternalism toward our employees – both perfectly valid in their time but now, dead as the dodo. Nowadays one has to specialize – to narrow the scope of one's business and concentrate on being more efficient than one's competitors; and in labour relations one has to recognize that there is no obvious identity of interest and use the machinery of collective bargaining. BTC would have done these things and the result would have been not only continued prosperity now, but an assurance for the future.' He stopped speaking, gazing at the blotter in front of him. 'One has a conscience in these matters.'

It was a new thought for Wycliffe.

'Your sister-in-law had no doubts about selling?'

'Doubts? On the contrary, she was delighted to be rid of her investment in the firm, particularly on such favourable terms.'

Wycliffe thought it was time for a lull. If you are fishing it is a mistake to be too eager. He smoked his pipe and looked out of the window. He could see over the grey slate roofs of the houses on the lower side of the square to the high ground above East Treen; a field of yellow stubble, where the corn had been harvested, caught the sun and glowed like Van Gogh sunflowers. Few people can sustain silence for long and Bryce was no exception.

'Perhaps I should tell you that if the deal had gone through, Caroline would have taken cash for her holding and left Boslow.'

'She told you?'

'Yes.'

A tap at the door and a grey-haired, motherly soul put her head round it. 'What is it, Mrs Grose?' Bryce was irritable.

'I know you don't want to be disturbed, Mr Sidney, but there's a call for the chief superintendent.'

It was Jimmy Gill. 'They told me you'd gone to see brother Sid. It's probably not wise to say much over the phone but I thought

415

you ought to know. It looks as though the car spent Thursday night there.'

'Is that all?'

'It's possible that we've got the weapon.'

'You want me to make a decision?'

'Among other things – yes.'

'I'll be right back.'

Wycliffe dropped the receiver. Bryce was studying some papers on his desk. 'A development?'

'Of a sort. I'm afraid that we shall have to postpone our conversation; but you have been most helpful.'

Mutual assurances of goodwill before parting. Bryce came downstairs to see him off. Lovely flannel to delight the heart of Mr Bellings.

'I'd better start with the cleaning woman, Gerty Pearce. According to Birkett, she's a regular Mrs Mop: on the right side of fifty, talkative but not malicious.' Jimmy Gill sat in Wycliffe's office, smoking one of his cheroots. Wycliffe had considered lighting a pipe but the air was thick already.

'She was there when Caroline Bryce came on Tuesday afternoon – early afternoon, she says it was. George took Caroline into the sitting-room and they talked for half-an-hour. The old girl heard nothing that was said but she doesn't think they could have been quarrelling.'

'Where did Caroline leave the car?'

'According to Gerty she always left it outside the boathouse, even when, as she put it, "they was going steady like". Before Caroline's visit on the Tuesday Gerty hadn't seen her for several weeks, though up till then "she'd been in and out like she lived here".'

'Has she any suggestion as to why that changed?'

'She thinks George got tired of her when he found the other. "Most men prefer lamb to mutton if they can get it" was Gerty's way of putting it.'

It was refreshing not to have to spell everything out.

'Anything else from Gerty?'

'Only that the girl, Zel, was always hanging about the place.'

'Doing what?'

'Gerty says she was spying on her mother.'

'What about the boathouse?'

Gill rubbed the bristles on his five-o'clock shadow with the flat of his hand. 'With one exception the tyre tracks are from one car, presumably George's MG.'

'And the exception?'

'The red Mini.'

'You seem sure of yourself.'

'Not me. Dr Bell of Forensic was at Divisional HQ so I asked him to come over. He had been working on the Mini and he is in no doubt that the track belongs to the off-side front wheel. He thinks somebody had tried to obliterate the marks but missed one. It's recent, and he says it could have been made on Thursday night.'

'So we conclude that the Mini spent Thursday night in George's boathouse, is that it?'

'It looks like it, but I suppose the question is where Caroline spent that night.'

'And whether she was dead or alive.'

'Franks thinks she was dead.'

'But Franks would be the first to admit that he couldn't sustain that in court; it's no more than an informed guess.' Wycliffe pushed the window wider to get rid of the smoke. 'I don't know what gives you the idea that those damn things are less dangerous than cigarettes; they nearly kill me.'

Chief Inspector Gill looked at his half-smoked cheroot in surprise. 'These? They're mild as mother's milk – they tell you that on the telly. But if they offend . . .' With a dramatic gesture he pitched the butt out of the window. 'Now, where were we?'

'I was on the point of asking you what George Bryce had to say about all this?'

'He couldn't say anything; he wasn't there. Apparently he hasn't been back since you saw him leave this morning.'

Wycliffe shrugged. 'I suppose he could have taken fright. Anyway, what was that you said about a weapon?'

'It's not certain; but lying in a corner of the boathouse there's a pile of scrap including some lengths of lead piping. One of the pieces, about eighteen inches long, has a ragged end and there were one or two hairs adhering to it. Forensic are going to let you have a report.'

Wycliffe nodded. 'Did you check on George's story – what he was supposed to have been doing on Thursday night?'

'Birkett saw the two chaps, Scoble and Miller. Both of them say he was with them until one in the morning on some sort of jag. They left him at Whitecross, about seven miles from Treen, and they were a bit worried about him driving home because he was high. Of course, they may be lying; Birkett is checking it out.'

'Anything else?'

'Nothing.' Gill looked at his chief with a sardonic grin. 'How long does Georgie have to absent himself before you put out a call?'

Wycliffe glowered. 'All right! I'm no more anxious than the next one to make a fool of myself.'

'What about a quick one before dinner?'

It was a quarter past six. Through the rear window of the van Wycliffe could see the estuary fringed with broad stretches of black mud. Low tide. Two concrete slipways reached out from opposite banks like fingers, making it possible for the ferry to continue running. He picked up a bundle of reports. 'Give me ten minutes with these and I'll join you.'

The reports summarized the results of house to house inquiries, but only one item interested Wycliffe.

A motor bike had been parked at the end of Station Road, a few yards from the back entrance to Boslow, between eleven and one on the night of the murder. The householder, a widow living alone, had noticed it when she put the cat out before going to bed and she had been awakened by someone trying to start it just after one o'clock. She remembered that the machine had a bright red petrol tank and this fact had enabled the owner to be traced; he was John Evans, an apprentice at the boatyard. He said that he had parked his bike there while he walked with his girlfriend on the river bank. Between eleven and one? It sounded thin.

He walked over to the hotel and joined Gill in the lounge bar of the hotel. A red-head in a white sweater with plenty of uplift and slim-fit black pants was perched on a bar stood sipping gin. Wycliffe did not recognize her until she spoke – Margaret Haynes. 'I thought I might see you here.'

She was chummy, Wycliffe was distant. 'You wanted to see me?'

She slid off the stool, her eyes on Jimmy Gill. 'It seemed like a good idea.'

Wycliffe bought drinks and they took them to a window seat away from the bar. Apart from the barman they had the place to themselves.

'I've been talking to Gerty Pearce, she's been telling me . . .' She was staring at her glass, running her index finger round the rim, determined to be interesting. 'Before you get any ideas about George you ought to know that I spent Thursday night with him.'

'At his place?'

'Of course.'

'You didn't think to tell me that this morning.'

'You didn't ask me.'

'Mr Bryce told me that he spent the night alone.'

She shrugged.

'Where is he now?' Gill put the question.

She gave him her full attention before answering. 'Isn't he back yet?'

'Back from where?'

'I've no idea. I know he was off somewhere. I expect it was about money; it usually is.'

'What time did you meet him on Thursday?'

'I went to his place in the evening, but he wasn't there so I decided to wait. I must have fallen asleep . . .'

'You have a key?'

'No need; it's never locked.'

'So you were there when Bryce came back?'

'Yes.'

'What time?'

'Midnight, one o'clock, I haven't a clue really.'

'So you must have seen Caroline Bryce?'

She looked suspicious. 'I don't get you.'

'You didn't see her?'

'No, of course I didn't!'

Wycliffe was unimpressed by the story. 'You will be required to make a statement.'

The blue eyes regarded him with practised candour. 'Why not?'

'What time did you leave Foundry House on Friday morning?'

She drained her glass and put it down with an expectant glance at Jimmy Gill. He got up. 'Same again?' She followed him with her eyes as he went to the bar but she answered Wycliffe's question.

'It must have been about six; there are no clocks that work there but I got home before Mum and Dad were about.'

Wycliffe wondered what Mum and Dad thought about their daughter and what they said. Probably it was too late to say anything. 'If you come to my HQ caravan first thing tomorrow morning one of my officers will take your statement.'

Gill came back with the drinks. 'I gather you work for Morley?'

'I type his letters for him when he's down here.'

Gill grimaced. 'Funny job for a sex-kitten like you. I thought the Right Hon was all against what comes naturally.'

She grinned; this was the kind of talk she understood. 'He doesn't come naturally or otherwise when I'm about; I just type his letters and mind my own business.' She laughed across at Wycliffe. 'Are all your policemen like him?'

Gill looked like a lecherous toad. 'He's not married, is he?'

'Not as far as I know.'

'And not interested?'

'If you're trying to say he's a queer, you may be right; but it's no good asking me.' She sipped her drink. 'Satisfied?'

'Perhaps. What does he think about your goings on with George Bryce?'

'I've never asked him; it's none of his business, is it?'

When she had finished her drink she got up. 'See you around!' She walked away from them, wiggling her bottom as she went.

Gill sighed. 'Like a victory roll! What a dolly!'

It was one of the chief inspector's assets that he could get answers to questions which few policemen would dare ask. He emptied his glass. 'Do you think she was telling the truth?'

'I doubt if she'd recognize truth if she saw it,' Wycliffe growled.

The gong sounded and they went in to dinner.

6

Thursday morning; forty-eight hours after the ferrymen had fished Caroline Bryce's body out of the water. It seemed to Wycliffe that he had been talking to and thinking about Bryces for much longer.

On his desk were two reports, one from Dr Bell, head of Forensic and the other from the pathologist, Dr Franks. Dr Bell confirmed that a few hairs taken from the lead piping found in the boathouse were human and that they matched the hair of the dead woman. Dried mud removed from the treads of the wrecked Mini had come from the floor of the boat-house. An examination of the clothing, especially of the shoes, taken from the body, suggested that immersion had lasted less than four days rather than more. In other words, Bell was of the opinion that the body had been placed in the water on Friday night and not Thursday, welcome confirmation of Franks' conclusion based on his study of the body itself. A longish section of the report dealt with finger-prints, but only one reference interested Wycliffe: an unidentified set of prints found on the underside of the steering wheel of the Mini. These prints were unknown to Criminal Records and they did not match those of anyone involved in the case so far. Dr Bell was prepared to say that the prints were 'quite recent'.

Wycliffe was growing concerned. There was still no news of George Bryce and almost hourly the case against him was being strengthened. The previous evening, reluctantly, he had circulated Bryce's description: 'Wanted for questioning . . .' Now it certainly looked as though he had done a bunk. Margaret Haynes' testimony was in his favour but, unsupported, it was not worth much. Her statement would be checked with great care but it might be impossible to confirm two vital points, the time he had returned to Foundry House and whether she had spent the night with him as she said. Which reminded Wycliffe that she had not arrived to make her statement. Probably she was still in bed. He reached for the tele-phone. 'Send a car to pick up Margaret Haynes; she's the daughter of the golf "pro" and lives at the Club. She has volunteered to make a statement and she may be on her way here; tell the driver to look out for a red-head, nineteen or twenty years old . . .'

He dropped the telephone. Through the window he saw a uniformed policeman go to one of the parked cars and drive off. His headquarters had grown: there were two caravans now and a temporary fence round them enclosing enough ground to park four or five vehicles. The fence was Jimmy Gill's answer to the over-inquisitiveness of the press. It was raining and the ground was becoming soggy with a chain of puddles spreading across it. He could sit and stare out of the window with an almost blank mind indefinitely. He forced his thoughts back to the case. It seemed that Caroline's Mini had spent Thursday night in George's boathouse. With or without his knowledge? And where was Caroline? Had she got cold feet about her London trip and driven to Foundry House instead of to the station? She would have found the house empty; perhaps she had decided to wait. It was just possible that she had met the Haynes girl there. Then George had returned, making a very incongruous threesome. Wycliffe sighed; it was not impossible. He would have to get the truth out of the Haynes girl.

Assume for the moment there had been a row and George had killed her. He had to dispose of the body but the tide was already well into the ebb and the river was the obvious place. He might reasonably have decided to wait until the next night . . .

He was not enthusiastic about the theory and more interesting thoughts jostled each other on the fringes of his mind: words, names, brief but vividly recollected incidents, odd disjointed phrases – scarcely thoughts at all. He found himself saying: 'It all started a long time ago; it is not a bit of use considering the events of a day or of a week and expecting to understand them. These people had been in Treen for a long time, they had grown up there, and their jealousies, their spites, their loves and their hates had grown with them.'

'So what?'

His telephone rang.

'There's a man on the line, sir; a Mr Eva, a grocer with a little shop on the outskirts of St Austell. He thinks he had George Bryce in his shop yesterday evening.'

'Put him through and listen in.'

Fortunately Mr Eva was lucid and sure of his ground. 'This man certainly answered the description in the paper . . . No, we didn't watch TV last night . . . No, I don't know Mr Bryce by sight. I know his brother, Mr Sidney, through Rotary . . .' He must have been speaking from the shop: Wycliffe could hear the noise of a cash register from time to time. 'Yes, he came into the shop just before closing time – about ten minutes to six . . . Quite a lot of stuff – about five pounds' worth, mostly canned goods and cigarettes . . . Yes, he was alone; of course there could have been somebody waiting for him in the car outside.' Mr Eva interrupted himself to tell someone that the large packet had gone up to four shillings. 'No, I didn't notice what sort of car it was . . . I don't know about nervous, but he seemed to be in a hurry . . . My place is on the A390 about a mile on the Treen side of the town . . . Yes, I'm pretty sure he was going towards the town.'

Wycliffe thanked him and said that he would send someone to take his statement. 'Looks as though he's holed up somewhere not too far away.' This to the duty constable who had listened in. 'Get on to Information Room and ask them to raise Chief Inspector Gill on his car radio. Pass on the message; he'll know what to do – and ask him to meet me here sometime before lunch. Got that?'

At this time of year there must be hundreds of untenanted furnished cottages and caravans within a radius of ten miles where a man could live comfortably if he had food. And at six o'clock the previous evening Bryce had been buying stocks of food a few miles away. The chances were that he had come back to Foundry House and spotted the police before they spotted him. Then he doubled back, bought provisions, and now would be sitting pretty until his supplies ran out. The only thing was a search of likely premises.

The constable who had been sent to bring in Margaret Haynes returned. 'Miss Haynes left home early this morning and her mother has no idea where she has gone.'

'What does she call early?'

'Before nine, sir. Mrs Haynes took her daughter a cup of tea at eight o'clock but when she went to her bedroom just before nine the girl was gone.'

'Gone? Had she taken anything with her?'

'Only the clothes she was wearing.'

'So it looks as though she intends to come back. If she was going to join Bryce she would have taken a change of clothes at least.'

Wycliffe was depressed; he felt that he was losing his grip on the case. The weather hardly helped; rain was sweeping up the estuary driven before a rising wind which buffeted the caravan so that it shuddered on its supports. He stared out at the dissolving landscape in a mood of gloomy petulance, feeling that he was overdue for a stroke of luck.

And luck of a sort came his way. A woman, a permanent resident on a caravan site a few miles down the coast, reported to the police a 'suspicious character' who had moved into one of the many unoccupied vans on the site.

The same rainstorm which helped to depress Wycliffe drove over the desolate caravan site, its teeth sharpened by sand blown from the beach. Two policemen in heavy blue raincoats, their collars turned up, stood by one of the vans; one knocked with his knuckles on the door. The curtains were drawn and the van seemed to be deserted. After an interval the policeman knocked again and this time there was a movement inside and a voice said, 'Who is it?'

'Police! Open up!'

And in due course the door was opened and George Bryce stood there gazing at them rather stupidly. He was bleary-eyed and un-shaven, in shirt sleeves and slippers; a very different figure from the dandified man-about-town Wycliffe had met at Foundry House.

'Is this your caravan, sir?'

'It's not actually mine, no.' He seemed to collect his wits. 'But the owner is a friend of mine.'

'And you have his permission to use it?'

The second policeman cut in. 'You're George Bryce!'

He made no attempt to deny it.

'We must ask you to accompany us to the nearest police station, sir.'

Bryce gazed at them with a puzzled frown as though he could not be sure they were real. 'Why?'

'To answer some questions.'

Wycliffe heard the news by telephone. 'He's at Division now, sir. Shall we send him along to you?'

Looking out of the window at the rain-soaked world he was on the point of saying 'Yes' when it occurred to him that there is always a risk of treating human beings like commodities once you have a little power over them. 'I'll come to Division.'

He was driven over and at Divisional Headquarters they found him a room and a stenographer. Bryce was brought in. He had shaved and smartened himself up but he looked older, less sleek, than when Wycliffe had seen him the previous day.

'Smoke if you want to.'

Bryce got out his cigarettes and lit one; but all the time his eyes were fixed, not on Wycliffe, but on the stenographer who happened to be a seventeen-stone constable. Perhaps he was afraid of physical violence.

'Would you like to get in touch with your lawyer?'

'I haven't got one.'

'You could get one.'

'No.'

Wycliffe cautioned him. The room was lit by a glaring fluorescent tube in the ceiling and the only window looked out on a blank wall across a narrow alley; the kind of room which would have driven Wycliffe mad had he been forced to work or live in it.

'Yesterday evening you visited a grocer's shop near St Austell where you bought a lot of tinned food?'

Bryce nodded.

'Earlier you had gone to your house, found the police there and cleared out – Why?'

Bryce shifted uncomfortably in his chair. 'I was afraid that I might be arrested.'

'Why should you be arrested?'

'I don't suppose you sent your men there for fun; you must have thought you had something against me.' His eyes were still on the constable who was writing everything down.

'But what was the point of running away? You must have realized that you would have been picked up sooner or later.'

'I thought you might find out you were wrong.'

'You thought that we might decide that someone else had killed your sister-in-law?'

'I suppose so – yes.'

'What about Margaret Haynes?'

425

Bryce stopped with a cigarette halfway to his lips. 'What about her?'

'When did you last see her?'

'Yesterday morning. You were there.'

'And when did you last speak to her – on the telephone perhaps?'

'I don't understand.'

'I think you do. When did you tell her to come to me with the tale that she spent Thursday night at Foundry House?'

Little drops of perspiration were running down Bryce's nose. 'I didn't tell her to do that; but it's the truth.'

'It's a lie, of course. If she was there she would have seen Caroline Bryce.'

George Bryce was badly scared and his eyes went from the constable to Wycliffe and back again, never still. 'I don't understand what you are getting at.'

'All right, I'll be more explicit. Caroline Bryce spent Thursday night and all day Friday in your boathouse, in her Mini; she was dead.'

Bryce would have interrupted but Wycliffe went on. 'On Friday night at high tide you put her dead body in the water having weighted it with something which you wired to her ankle; then you drove her car to the quarry above the town and pushed it over the edge of the scrap heap.' He paused and regarded Bryce with mild curiosity. 'If you didn't kill her, why did you go to all this trouble?'

Bryce's face was white and his voice was scarcely audible. 'You see how it is; I don't stand a chance.' He was silent for a moment then he added, 'I didn't kill her.'

'The weapon with which she was killed was found in your boathouse – one of the pieces of scrap lead piping which lie there. I am going to charge you, Mr Bryce. It is up to you whether the charge is murder or being an accessory . . .'

'I didn't kill her. I'll tell you what happened.'

'Very well; but I'll repeat the caution.'

Bryce took a grubby handkerchief from his pocket and wiped the sweat from his face. 'Christ! It's hot in here.'

'Take your time.'

'I came back on Thursday night – Friday morning, as I told you; I'd had a few drinks so I left the old bus outside the shed and padded off to bed. Next morning I got up when Gerty arrived, about eleven, with the father and mother of a hangover. I pottered about the house a bit. It was pouring with rain so I thought I might as well put the car under cover.' He stopped speaking and took a deep breath. 'When I opened the shed I saw her car. I thought it was bloody queer but it didn't bother me too much till I saw she was in it . . .'

'Was she in the passenger seat or the driver's?'

'The driver's. She was wearing the safety harness, all strapped in, and her head was bent forward on her chest.'

'What did you do?'

'Do? I got out, shut the doors and hared back to the house. I wanted to think.'

'Without finding out whether she was dead or not?'

He was silent for a moment, fiddling with his sideboards. 'She was dead all right; I made sure of that . . .'

'How long? You're a doctor; how long had she been dead?'

Bryce was obviously afraid of a trap: his eyes never left Wycliffe's face. 'I didn't examine her thoroughly; she was all slumped up. In any case the circumstances . . .'

'How long?'

'In my opinion – for what it is worth – about twelve to fifteen hours.'

'Say between nine and midnight the previous night?'

He nodded. 'About that.'

'Which lets you out.'

Bryce said nothing.

'Did you come to any conclusions as to the cause of death?'

'It seemed obvious: her head was bent forward and the hair had been parted at the base of the skull as though to display the injury.'

'Which was?'

'A depressed fracture of the occipital region of the skull.'

'Any blood?'

'No.'

'So you went back to the house. What did you do then?'

He dabbed his upper lip with his handkerchief. 'I had to think.'

'It didn't occur to you to inform the police?'

'Of course it did; but with my reputation in this place I'm a sitting duck for anybody who wants to set me up.'

'Who would want to do that?'

'I've no idea but, evidently, somebody did.'

'Your brother Matt?'

A quick look. 'Not a chance! Matt will open the window to let out a bloody wasp which has just stung him.'

'Why did you have to leave Boslow?'

Bryce shrugged.

'Was it because you were sleeping with Caroline?'

'That's what they say, isn't it?'

'But what do you say?'

Bryce was silent for a while. The muffled sound of traffic reached them in the claustrophobic little room like sounds from another world. 'I'm going to tell you the truth even though it could be twisted against me.'

'I'm not going to twist anything and you would certainly be wise to tell the truth.'

Bryce played with his sideboards, pulling at the soft hairs. 'Matt wasn't unduly bothered about Caroline and me. I'm not saying that it didn't go against the grain at first, but he got used to it. He knew he couldn't give her what she wanted – what she needed, and I'm not only talking about sex. Caroline needed affection, she needed people to like her and to show that they liked her; but Matt is incapable of any show of emotion even to people he really loves. You may not believe it but in the end it suited Matt to have me round – keep it in the family, so to speak.'

'Then why did he kick you out?'

'It was over Zel.'

'Zel?'

'He thought that I had seduced her.'

'And had you?'

'No, I bloody well hadn't! Barely nubile girls are not my line.'

'All right, go on.'

'The poor kid fell for me. You know how adolescent girls can get a thing about an older man without any encouragement. And Zel got no encouragement from me. Perhaps she was jealous of her mother and wanted to take her place. Psychology was never my strong suit, but whatever it was it was bloody embarrassing . . .'

'Well?'

Bryce made an irritable movement. 'Do I have to draw a bloody

428

picture? She made life complicated, always coming into my room in her little nylon nightie. Poor little bastard, it was pathetic. I tried to make her see sense, I reasoned with her; but it didn't work.'

'Did you try telling her mother?'

'Like hell. Caroline could be sadistic with the kid. I dared not risk it.'

'So what happened?'

'Matt got wind of it.'

'You explained?'

'I didn't get a lot of chance.'

'What about Zel?'

He hesitated. 'I'm not sure, but I think Zel told her father in the first place.'

'That you had made advances to her?'

He nodded. 'I suppose it was her way of getting her own back.' He lit another cigarette.

In the last half-hour he had succeeded in making Wycliffe more kindly disposed towards him.

'After you came to Foundry House she continued to visit you. Did she still try to get you to make love to her?'

'It wasn't the same.' He seemed to have difficulty in choosing his words. 'Her attitude to me was almost patronizing. I don't know how else to describe it. And she spied on me and on her mother. She still comes and goes as the whim takes her and one hardly knows when she's there and when she isn't; but one way and another there isn't much she doesn't know about what's gone on in my house over the past two years.'

'You don't discourage her visits?'

Bryce raised his hands in a gesture of helplessness. 'What good would it do?'

Wycliffe stood up and walked over to the window; by putting his face close to the pane of glass he could peer up at a narrow band of dun-coloured sky with clouds like smoke chasing each other across it. He filled his pipe and lit it, taking time over the ritual. Bryce sat in silence, his hands clasped round one knee.

'What about Clement Morley?'

'What about him?'

'See much of him?'

'Not more than I can help. I've no room for his sort and he hates my guts.'

'Why?'

'For one thing, I suppose, my affair with his half-sister would hardly do his Sunday school campaign any good.'

'But he would hardly have murdered Caroline to spite you.'

Bryce grimaced with distaste. 'I suppose not; but I could believe almost anything of that greasy bastard. Caroline had something on him.'

'On Morley?'

He nodded. 'She knew something.'

'You've no idea what?'

'Not a clue; she could be close when she wanted to be.'

'Do you think she was blackmailing him?'

Bryce hesitated. 'I think she probably threatened him from time to time. She loved to have something she could hold over you, and when she had she didn't let you forget it.'

'And what did she hold over you? Was it the fact that you owed her money?'

He did not argue. 'All right, I admit it. You can't say I'm not being straight with you.'

Wycliffe lit his pipe and waited until it was drawing nicely. 'Let's get back to Friday night, when you put her body in the river.'

'It was as you said: I had to wait for the top of the tide because of the mud . . .'

'And the car?'

'After I'd dealt with the body I drove the car up to the edge of the quarry and pushed it over.'

'There's a track in on the level of the quarry floor – why didn't you simply drive in?'

He fiddled with his sideboards. 'There's a cottage too near for comfort. In any case I had some idea of making the car less noticeable by smashing it on a pile of scrap.'

'And then you walked back?'

'Yes.'

'Meet anybody?'

'No.'

There was little more to be got out of Bryce. He repeated that it had been he who broke off the affair with Caroline; which was probably true, though a man like George Bryce would never admit to having received marching orders from a woman.

After he had signed his statement, Wycliffe had him charged and taken into custody.

It was after three when Wycliffe arrived back at his Treen headquarters, and it was still raining. Jimmy Gill was sitting in the gloomy little office going through reports.

'Any news of the girl?'

'Her mother rang up; she's getting worried.'

Wycliffe stood by the window, staring out over the grey waste of the estuary. 'She didn't go to join Bryce, that's certain.'

Gill tilted his chair at a dangerous angle. 'I wish she had.'

Wycliffe got out his pipe. 'There's no reason to think . . .'

And Gill interrupted, 'None at all; all the same I shall feel happier when we hear that she's back with Mum.'

'So shall I,' Wycliffe agreed.

'If she told somebody she was coming here to make a statement . . .' Gill broke off and allowed his chair to come back to a safer angle. 'Anyway, what did George have to say for himself?'

Wycliffe told him.

'You sound as though you believed him.'

Wycliffe nodded. 'I think I do.'

'Which leaves us with the other two brothers and with Morley. What about Matt?'

Wycliffe studied the bowl of his pipe. 'Everybody I've spoken to so far except Joyce Boon has been only too anxious to convince me that Matt wouldn't kill a cockroach. In any case, what motive did he have last week which he hasn't had for years?'

'It would have to be something to do with Zel.'

'But what? What has changed? The girl is growing up, legally she's an adult, certainly she's more capable of standing up for herself now than she has ever been.'

Gill nodded. 'I see that: all the same, Matt is a credible suspect – murderers are rarely logical. Matt had the opportunity. He could have killed his wife before she left Boslow, driven the car to Foundry House and left it in the boathouse with the body in it . . .'

Wycliffe sighed. 'Save it, Jimmy! You may be right but it doesn't get us anywhere. We need to know more about these people. They've got a long history here in Treen, they're well dug in.' He

431

came to a sudden decision. 'I'm going to see Margaret Haynes' parents.'

The girl's continued absence was troubling him. She had seemed ready enough to make a statement but she had not come.

7

Wycliffe drove to the Haynes' bungalow, a pleasant place on rising ground behind the club-house, backed by trees. From the terrace in front of the house it would have been possible to see the sea but for the steady rain like a grey curtain over the estuary. Mrs Haynes took him into the sitting-room, its once gay chintzes faded by the sun. She was a red-head like her daughter and still not much over forty. She wore a tight black skirt and a frilly white blouse with a plunging 'V'. She was at once concerned and petulant.

'I really can't understand her, Mr Wycliffe! She takes no notice of me; and if her father says a word she flares up. We sent her to a good school and when she said she wanted to do secretarial training we paid for her to go to a special college . . .

'Of course, she never kept a job for more than a month. It isn't that we mind about the money, but a girl should do something, don't you think? Then when Ricky – that's my husband – when Ricky put in a word for her with Mr Clement Morley and she got the job, things seemed to be better for a time. Of course, it's only when he's down here, but it's better than nothing.

'I mean, she's never home! I used to lie awake at nights listening for her to come in, but I had to stop it . . . Ricky said . . .'

'How old is your daughter, Mrs Haynes?'

'She was nineteen last month.'

'Does she ever stay out all night?'

'Sometimes she spends the night with friends but she always tells me if she is going to do that.'

'You have no idea where she might have gone?'

The rather stupid face wrinkled into lines of worry. 'Why, no! Apparently she was due to go to Mr Morley's at two o'clock. He telephoned at about half-past to ask where she was. That made it worse because she's never let him down before. I suppose I wouldn't have been bothered then if it hadn't been for your policeman coming here this morning. What do you want her for? I mean, she hasn't done anything . . . ?' Her manner was blended of fear and aggression.

Wycliffe tried to be reassuring. 'Nothing! She was going to help us with our inquiries into Mrs Bryce's death . . .'

'But how could she? She only went near the place once in a while.'

'She was a friend of George Bryce.'

'Not a friend; she just knew him.'

'Try to think back to last Thursday, Mrs Haynes. Did Margaret come home that night?'

'Come home? Of course she came home! What are you suggesting?'

'You said that she sometimes stayed with friends.'

She was mollified. 'Yes, but not Thursday . . .'

'You are quite sure?'

She pulled her skirt over her knees. 'I'm quite sure as it happens; that was the night Ricky was so ill. I had to get up to look after him and I happened to look into Margaret's room.'

'And she was there?'

'Of course she was there – fast asleep.'

'What time was that?'

She thought for a moment. 'Around two in the morning it must have been.'

Wycliffe fended off a large mongrel dog which had lolloped into the room and wanted to lick his face. 'She has a car, hasn't she?'

'Stop it, Ben! He's terribly affectionate . . . No, the car is ours but she uses it more than we do.'

'Did she go off in it this morning?'

'No, she couldn't have done. Ricky had a bit of an accident last night; he hit the hedge trying to avoid a cat and damaged the steering. It had to be towed to a garage.'

'So she must have been walking.'

'Unless she used her bike; she does sometimes when her father has the car.'

Wycliffe asked to see the girl's bedroom and was taken to a room at the back of the bungalow furnished as a bed-sitter. Everything for the room of a teen-aged daughter straight out of the pages of *Good Housekeeping*. It was all there including the record player, the transistor radio and the posters on the wall. What more could a girl want? Yet Wycliffe had the impression that these things were now no more than leftovers and that the room was merely a place to sleep.

'I'm afraid I haven't got round to tidying up – as you see, Margaret is not particular about her clothes.' As she spoke she was picking up from the floor the white jumper and black pants the girl had worn the previous night. The bed was unmade and her pyjamas, too, were lying in a little heap on the floor.

'You don't think anything has happened to her?' Tears glistened in her blue eyes and trickled down her freckled cheeks as she fitted the pants on to a hanger. 'I couldn't bear that; she's all we've got. I couldn't have any more, you see.'

'I shouldn't worry, Mrs Haynes. It's just that we're anxious to talk to her. After all, what could happen in broad daylight?'

She made a consciously brave effort to smile. 'No, I suppose I'm silly; but it's natural for a mother to worry, isn't it? Ricky gets annoyed with me, but it's different for men.'

Wycliffe asked her if she knew what clothes her daughter had been wearing and after she had searched in the wardrobe and a chest of drawers she decided on a blue knitted woollen dress, a brown mackintosh with gilt buttons, and brown, wet-look shoes with block heels and stub toes.

'I can't think where she's gone! I've telephoned round to all her friends . . .' She looked out of the window at the sodden grass and the rather gloomy background of trees. 'Such dreadful weather too!'

'Did she receive a telephone call last night? – after she came home?'

Mrs Haynes shook her head.

'Nor this morning, before she left?'

'No; I would have heard it ring.'

'Could she have made a call without you hearing? Say, this morning while you were in the kitchen getting the breakfast?'

Mrs Haynes hesitated. 'I suppose she could. From the kitchen you can hear the phone ring but you can't hear anybody speaking.'

Before he left Wycliffe confirmed that Margaret Haynes had taken her bicycle.

The girl was a complication he could well have done without. If she was off on some stunt of her own that was no more than a nuisance, but if . . . But why should anyone want to harm her? What had put the idea in his mind?

'I want this girl found.'

They were meeting in the largest compartment of his caravan, his 'operations room' as the press called it. There were ten of them tightly packed around the long table being briefed by Chief Inspector Gill with Wycliffe looking on.

'The last we know of her, she left her home between eight and nine this morning.' He passed round a photograph. 'One like that is being copied and will be circulated. Margaret Dorothy Haynes. Aged 19. Height: 5 feet 6 inches. Weight: 115 pounds. Red hair, blue eyes, freckled complexion . . .'

When Gill had finished, Wycliffe looked round the group at the faces trying to look earnest. 'Any questions?'

A sergeant from Division, mistakenly anxious to be noticed, risked a question. 'Is there any special reason for starting a search so soon, sir? I mean, in the normal way . . .' He broke off, silenced by the blank stare which Wycliffe turned on him. There was a moment while everybody wondered what was coming. Wycliffe shuffled the papers in front of him. 'If she's dead, it's too late.'

Afterwards he had a call from Clement Morley. What did Wycliffe think about Margaret Haynes' disappearance? Surely it must be a coincidence that she had decided to go off? He had heard that George Bryce had been charged with being an accomplice and he hoped that the criminal would not be allowed to slip through the fingers of the police.

Wycliffe said that he hoped so too.

A little later Bellings rang to say much the same thing and got the same reply.

'Bloody fools!' Wycliffe smoked moodily. Jimmy Gill sat opposite him in his little office. As usual the chief inspector was trying to work things out.

'In one way, the fact that she hasn't got a car should make it easier.'

Wycliffe took no notice; he was following his own train of thought. 'I want you to start chatting up the locals, Jimmy. Get all the gossip you can on the Bryce family over the past twenty years; the same for Clement Morley and the dead woman. Why did Morley move to this part of the world in the first place? What is the local version of his sex life? In what circumstances did Matthew marry Caroline? I know that she was pregnant but I want details. How long had they known each other? Was there someone else on the horizon?' Wycliffe broke off. 'You don't look enthusiastic.'

Gill rubbed his bristly chin. 'Surely our first job is to find the girl; we can write their biographies afterwards.'

Wycliffe made a gesture of impatience. 'We've got a small army looking for the girl, Jimmy; you've just briefed 'em. It's our job to keep the case moving.'

Gill got up, seeming to unroll his lean, ungainly length. 'You're the boss!'

Wycliffe's expression was bland. 'That's right.'

'Just one question: do you think Sidney is kinky?'

'Why do you ask?'

'The books on adolescent girls.'

'You mean, if we searched the place, would we find a drawer full of brassieres and briefs? Perhaps, but I doubt it. Probably Sidney sees Zel as the daughter he never had. He may have fantasies about her, but he's fond of her and wants to understand her better. The only way he can think of is to buy some books. It's logical, even sensible, I suppose. No doubt a Freudian psychologist would turn it into a phantasmagoria of eroticism, but he might do the same for you or me.'

Gill's sardonic grin almost split his face in two. 'You surprise me, sir!'

'I'm glad. Now get out and let me get on with some work.'

The pile of typescript on his desk had reached alarming dimensions; he had to skim through it on the off-chance that, buried in the pages of inanity, there might be a reply to a question, a casual observation which meant something. If there was he would probably miss it. At six o'clock he switched on the transistor radio and listened to the news. After a lengthy report on the transfer of certain footballers came an item on his murder. 'The murder of Mrs Caroline Bryce, sister of Mr Clement Morley, former Minister of State and prominent front-bencher, continues to baffle the police. The arrest of George Bryce, the dead woman's brother-in-law, is not thought to have brought the case any nearer solution.' Small earthquake in Chile. Few dead. Anti-news. He went across to the hotel for dinner. A stiff breeze blew up the estuary driving fine, cold rain before it. Rain by the sea is so much wetter; the very landscape seems to deliquesce. The fair had not bothered to open but there were lights on in the caravans and appetizing smells came from them. The wharf was deserted but for a couple of sea-gulls perched on the rail, heads to the wind.

He ate without relish and afterwards drank a glass of rum to put some warmth into him for the walk back. He wondered if he was hatching a cold.

When he arrived back at the caravan Jimmy Gill was waiting for him in the main office. Jimmy's chair was tilted back and he had his feet on the table. The duty constable typed conscientiously, eyeing the chief inspector from time to time and wishing that he would put his feet up somewhere else. When Wycliffe came in Jimmy carefully retrieved his feet and righted his chair.

'Anything new?'

Gill followed him into his private office. 'About the girl – Margaret Haynes – somebody saw her going in the direction of George's place on Thursday night, the night Caroline was murdered.'

'At what time?'

'A few minutes after ten.'

'Reliable witness?'

'I think so. He's a railwayman, works at the station, stationmaster, booking clerk, porter – Pooh-Bah of the whole works. He was on two till ten and he was walking back along the tracks to the town. She was walking on the tracks too – the other way.'

'He knew her?'

Gill nodded. 'Apparently she uses the track regularly as a short cut; George does it too when he walks. They're not supposed to, of course, but the railway blokes turn a blind eye.'

'Did he speak to her?'

'Said "Goodnight!" She answered him normally as far as he could tell.'

Wycliffe got out his pipe and started to fill it. The rain was driving against the window now – the wind must have backed a few points – and it was impossible to see anything through the curtain of water streaming down the glass. 'If she was going to Foundry House she would have got there about the same time as Caroline.'

Gill sat himself on one of the folding chairs, riding it. 'She must have gone there. Where else could she have been going?' He reached over and crushed the butt of his cheroot in Wycliffe's ashtray. 'Franks says Caroline was killed by a blow, not necessarily powerful but delivered with a heavy weapon. We've got the weapon and a woman could have used it.'

Wycliffe made an irritable movement. 'You're as full of red herrings as a kipper factory, Jimmy!'

'I'm only saying it's a possibility. After all she and Caroline were after the same man.'

Wycliffe grunted. 'It's possible that she *saw* the murderer.'

Gill whistled. 'And now she's missing!'

Wycliffe said nothing.

Gill waited but when nothing came he went on, 'There's another report. A postman saw the Haynes girl cycling down the hill to town between quarter and half-past eight this morning and the vicar saw her in Station Road a few minutes later.'

Wycliffe was going through the papers in his tray. 'Nothing since?'

'No.' Gill waited then added, 'Station Road is on the way to Boslow and Foundry House.'

'And to the station.' Wycliffe looked up and caught the flicker of a smile on Gill's lips.

'She didn't catch a train; we've checked.'

'Nor the ferry?'

'Nor the ferry.' Gill liked to do his thinking aloud, preferably to an audience; Wycliffe kept his thoughts to himself. Whenever they were alone Gill tried to start a discussion and Wycliffe to block it. It was a game in which both knew the rules.

'On Thursday night she was seen walking along the railway in the direction of Foundry House; this morning she is seen cycling along Foundry Road . . .'

'What about boy-friends? She's only been with Bryce about six months. There must have been somebody before that.'

Jimmy grinned. 'Half the eligible males in the town. She's a warm-hearted dolly it seems.' He ran the nail of his little finger between two of his front teeth and examined the fragment of food he managed to extract with approval.

Wycliffe watched him, fascinated. 'You have the most revolting habits, Jimmy.'

'A man of the people, that's me! As I was saying, since she left school she seems to have had most of the boys in the town chasing after her and a fair proportion probably homed on target. But there doesn't seem to be much in it from our point of view – no heart-broken, jealous calf wanting to save her from herself.' Jimmy Gill had the knack of making the most human and laudable ambitions sound like the pipe-dreams of an idiot. 'As far as the lads go, it seems to have been a brief chase, a quick tumble and "ta ta, Dolly"!'

'Perhaps that's why she turned to George.'

'Could be, poor little bitch.'

Wycliffe continued to go through his papers. 'I see you sent a man to talk to the sister – Melinda Bryce. Any good?'

Gill shook his head. 'Tabb went there. Apparently she walked out on the family at eighteen and married a merchant seaman. He did very well for himself and now he's the skipper of one of the big tankers.' Gill's expressive hands sketched in the air a tremendous bulk.

'What about her?'

'Tabb says she seems a very decent sort; inclined to have a quiet laugh at the family but not malicious – nor very informative.'

'I imagine it depends on what she is asked.'

Wycliffe worked on his papers for another hour; then he went to the hotel bar and spent the rest of the evening there.

He drank more than was good for him and when he went up to bed his head felt too big for his skull. Before undressing he opened the french window and went out on to the balcony. It had stopped raining, the sky was speckled with stars and away to the south-east he could see every now and then the beam of the lighthouse sweep-ing out a sector of the sky.

His sleep was disturbed, shot through by vivid, senseless dreams in one of which he was being tried by an Assize Court with Bellings on the Bench. Bellings was saying to him, 'My dear Charles, I charge *you* with being an accessory . . .'

He woke at last, surprised to find the room full of sunshine. The air was chilly, washed clean and tangy with the smell of fresh fish. The sky was blue with billowing white clouds sailing across it. He felt better. Not that he had reached any conclusion about the case – only about himself: he had decided that he was trying too hard. Not far from the window a fishing vessel was unloading her catch with gulls

440

screaming, swooping, soaring and getting very little out of it. He could sympathize.

He felt almost in a holiday mood. What should he do? The answer was to get away somewhere, away from reports, away from Jimmy Gill and, most of all, away from the end of a telephone. All these, at a certain stage of a case, had an inhibiting effect on him. In the Midlands city where he had made his name as a detective he might, when he needed to get away, spend a couple of hours wandering round the covered market or he might sit in a park watching the mothers out with their children, or just walk in the streets.

He called at the caravans. No news of the missing girl. Constable Edwards, a red-faced country youth, was cooking breakfast, boiled eggs for himself and the sergeant.

'Put in a couple for me.' He had not waited for breakfast at the hotel and it was still short of eight o'clock. He ate his two eggs with wedges of brown bread spread with butter and thought that he had never tasted anything more delicious.

Constable Edwards was the sort to flourish in a desert. 'The farmer looks after us . . . none of your shop stuff.'

Two cups of strong tea and he was ready to go. 'Tell Mr Gill that I've been in.'

'Where can Mr Gill get in touch with you, sir?'

The blank stare he received from the chief superintendent reminded him of the tip he had been given: 'Never ask him where he is going.'

He followed the wharf upstream, past the various Bryce enterprises, the boatyard, the cannery, the coal-yard and the timber-yard. It seemed much longer than three days since he had first taken this walk. Was he making for Foundry House or for Boslow? Neither: he was just walking and it was a pleasant day. Without thinking he found himself walking on the railway track, adjusting his stride to the distance between the sleepers. He reached the point where the road doubled back to the town, past the gates of Boslow, but he continued along the track. His mind was almost blank but it occurred to him that Margaret Haynes had walked the same path on the night Caroline had been murdered. The railwayman had not, apparently, been asked whether he had seen her before or after Boslow turn. Gill had assumed that she was on her way to Foundry House but it was possible . . . Thought for the day: Why should she go to Boslow?

441

He had the estate on his left now, its boundary marked by the bank and by the fringe of trees. Plenty of places where a bicycle and a body could lay hidden. Presumably Jimmy Gill's men had search-ed; but their search could hardly have been more than cursory. If the girl did not turn up today they would have to get more men on it.

At one point there was a break in the almost continuous line of the bank and a single granite slab, crusted with moss, spanned the stream and led into the woodland. The stream must carry the overflow from the lake and, somewhere, find its way under the rail-way and out into the river. Wycliffe crossed the bridge and entered the wood. There was plenty of evidence of the passage of heavy feet through the undergrowth, crossing and re-crossing; they had made a thorough search here at any rate. He ploughed through in his turn, traversed the narrow strip of woodland and came out on to a paved area by the lake. The stone slabs of the paving were moss-covered; brambles, springing from between the slabs, formed a tangled web on the surface and here and there gave rise to bushes bearing large, succulent blackberries – the best, he thought, that he had ever tasted.

The lake was larger than he had supposed, and a little way from the shore a sculptured monstrosity formed a small artificial island with granite steps leading up to a group of frolicsome boys and bemused dolphins, inseparable companions in such situations. Away to the right, set back a little from the lake, there was a classical summer-house, its façade pock-marked by peeling stucco. It was only as he went towards it that he saw a punt across the lake with two men in it, previously hidden by the island. Several more men stood in a group on the shore and a police truck was parked nearby. He thought he could spot Jimmy Gill. They were going to drag the lake, and he sat on the steps of the summer-house to watch.

He had scarcely settled himself when he heard a movement from inside the summer-house followed by a stifled cough. He took no notice but continued to watch the activities of Jimmy Gill's team. It was nine-thirty.

At ten-thirty he was still there, immovable as the petrified youths on their island perch. He held his pipe between his teeth but it had long since gone out. There was a sudden movement behind him and Zel came out of the summer-house. She appeared to be sur-prised to find him there and he pretended to equal astonishment.

She had forgotten to button her blouse down the front and exposed her midriff. 'Do you want something?'

He shook his head. 'No.'

Her gaze was on the far side of the lake. 'They've searched the copse; now they're going to drag the lake.'

He noticed that her jeans had little triangular rents in the material showing white skin underneath. 'Won't you sit down?'

She seemed about to refuse, but changed her mind and sat on the step beside him.

'You look as though you've been doing some searching on your own account.'

She glanced down at her jeans. 'I know the place better than they do.' She had glimpsed her unbuttoned blouse and was trying, unobtrusively, to button it.

'But you found nothing?'

'No.'

Across the lake the shore party were paying out rope to the men in the punt.

'Do you know Margaret Haynes?'

'Of course.'

'Well?'

'She was no particular friend.' Her manner towards him had changed since their last meeting. She was no longer indifferent, but antagonistic, perhaps nervous.

'She can't be more than a few months older than you.'

'Six months, actually.' She picked at loose threads in her torn jeans. 'You speak of her as though she were alive, but you know that she is dead, don't you?'

'I know nothing of the kind, there is not a scrap of evidence . . .'

She gestured impatiently. 'It's obvious!'

He got out his pouch and started to fill his pipe. 'You mustn't let your imagination run away with you. Does she ever come here – to the house?'

'Not often. Mother always insisted on me having a stupid party at Christmas and on my birthday; she only did it because she knew how much I hated it. "You should mix more," she used to say.'

'And Margaret came to your parties?'

'Always until this year.'

'And why not this year?'

'I think that she had other things to do.' Her poise was unnerving.

'What sort of girl was she?'

'You know the sort of girl she was.' She was staring out over the lake, her eyes a little wide, her hands clasped round her knees.

'Men?'

She nodded.

'You know that your Uncle George has been arrested?'

She nodded.

'As an accessory; that does not mean that he killed your mother . . .'

'I know what it means.'

'Tell me what happened on Thursday evening, the evening your mother left.'

'I've told you.'

'Tell me again.' He had only a vague idea in questioning her; had he been completely honest he would have had to admit that he wanted to strike some spark of emotion from her, to disturb her poise.

She repeated her story without hesitation and when she came to the part where she saw her mother leaving, carrying the suitcase, he interrupted. 'Now, tell me *exactly* what happened from then on – She crossed the yard and . . .'

She looked at him, frowning, like a child reciting a lesson anxious to get it right. 'She opened the little back-door of the garage – the one where we keep the Mini . . .'

'Did she have to unlock the door?'

'There is no lock. She went in . . .'

'Did she shut the door behind her? Could you hear her? Did she have difficulty opening the big double doors?' He forced her to tell every detail and she did so without faltering until it came to a question of whether or not her mother had closed the big doors after taking the car out of the garage.

'Listen! You heard her open the big doors, then there was a short interval while she came back into the garage and got into the car. Do you remember hearing the car door slam?'

'Yes, I think so.'

'Only once?'

'Yes.'

'Then you heard the car engine start and she drove out of the garage?'

'Yes.'

'Right! She drove out of the garage; now, did she stop, get out, come back and shut the big doors or did she drive straight off?'

'She drove straight off.'

'So that the doors were open in the morning?'

For some reason the question disturbed her. 'I don't know; you're confusing me. I don't see that it matters anyway.'

He was dissatisfied. What she had told him did not ring true to his practised ear. Years of listening to prevarication, half-truths and downright lies had given him the perception of a connoisseur where truth was concerned. But why should she lie? Only, presumably, to protect her father. But had she knowledge or mere suspicion?

'I must get back to the house.' She stood up.

'How are your Aunt Joyce and Uncle Francis?'

She looked down at him in surprise, perhaps because of the abrupt change of subject, perhaps because of his familiar use of family names. 'They've gone. Father told them they had to go last night and they left this morning.'

Which meant that there had been a row.

'I'd better get back . . .' Either she wanted or expected him to come with her, but he merely looked at her with a bland smile and nodded.

'I'll go then.'

He watched her stroll with exaggerated nonchalance along the edge of the lake without once looking back.

If she was lying, Caroline could have been killed before she left Boslow, then she could have been driven to Foundry House and the car, with the body in it, left in the boathouse for George to find. The only thing against this reading of the facts was that George said he had found her in the driver's seat. Could it be that Caroline had been murdered by her husband and that he had deliberately set out to incriminate his brother?

The police truck was cruising slowly beside the lake and seemed to be towing the shoreward end of the drag line. Trust Jimmy Gill to think up something complicated!

'You'd better come out now.' Wycliffe seemed to be talking to himself. He continued, 'I'm getting tired of sitting here and you must be tired of being holed up in there.'

There was a movement in the summer-house and after a moment a youth came out, blinking in the sunlight and brushing dust from the seat of his trousers. He was the boy of the self-portrait in Zel's room: the finely-drawn, almost feminine features were unmistakable.

'Sit down and tell me about it.'

'About what?'

'First of all, who you are.'

The boy sat on the step nervously, as though poised to run.

'What is your name?'

'Evans, sir; John Evans.'

'Evans?' The name troubled Wycliffe: he thought he had heard it before in connection with the case. Then he remembered. 'You're the boy with the motor bike.'

Evans flushed but said nothing.

'Are you still at school?'

'No sir, I'm an apprentice in the boatyard.'

'You like the work?'

'Oh yes; I want to be a designer.'

'But you're not working today?'

'I'm having my fortnight's holiday.'

'You are a friend of Zel?'

'Yes.'

'In love with her?'

He flushed like a shy girl. 'Yes.'

'You meet in there?' He jerked a thumb in the direction of the summer-house.

'Sometimes.'

'On the night of the murder?'

'I was there but she didn't come; she was not well.'

'You left your bike in Station Road – why?'

He shrugged. 'It seemed safer; in any case you can't bring a motor bike along the railway track.'

'Why try to keep your relationship with Zel a secret?'

He hesitated, trying to find words which would not offend. 'It's Zel's people: they wouldn't approve – they would expect her to find somebody better.'

'Her mother knew.'

446

He seemed genuinely surprised. 'She did? Zel didn't tell me.'

'In any case, good boat-designers make a lot of money.'

He brightened. 'Yes, some do!' But gloom returned. 'It's not as simple as that.' His fists clenched in response to some inner frustration.

'Zel is a very attractive girl.'

'Yes.' The boy gazed across the lake, dully.

'I have a daughter not much older.'

'Oh?' A not very successful attempt to seem interested.

'I think I have a snap of her here.' Wycliffe got out his wallet and handed the boy a coloured snapshot of his twin son and daughter. He handed it wrong side up and the boy took it clumsily, turning it over.

'They're twins.'

'Very nice.'

Wycliffe took back the photograph and replaced it in his wallet.

'I'd better be going: my mother will be expecting me. I promised to do some shopping.' He stood up, hesitated, then made off.

Wycliffe felt restless. At the back of his mind he had the germ of an idea. He could not say exactly when it had occurred to him; perhaps it had been already there when he had talked about filling in the family backgrounds of Morley and the Bryces. He needed to talk to someone who knew them well but could be objective about them. A remark of Jimmy Gill's recurred to him: 'She is inclined to have a quiet laugh at the family – not malicious . . .' Melinda Bryce. If he was right there wouldn't be much to laugh at, but perhaps she would be able to answer some of the questions he wanted to ask. Gill had said that she lived on the other side, above East Treen.

The ferry was at the slipway, silent and deserted. He went aboard and sat on one of the slatted seats, smoking his pipe, for almost half an hour. The pace of life appealed to him: from where he sat he could see nothing that moved but the clouds and the water. Then a furniture pantechnicon came slowly along the wharf and nosed down the slipway. The driver, unaccustomed to such hazards, edged his van gingerly into position, switched off his engine and climbed down from his cab with an air of modest triumph. His arrival seemed to be a signal, for almost at once the two crew members turned up from nowhere, the engine was started, the shoreward gates closed and they were away.

Treen's other half had quite a different character: the hill rose even more steeply and the level ground by the water was scarcely wider than a single street. The houses were in terraces and their little gardens clung to the slope. There were fewer shops and the whole aspect of the place was less prosperous; one had the impression that it had lost any reason for its existence fifty years ago and carried on with a dwindling momentum. It was very warm for late September. Wycliffe looked at his watch but it had only just gone a quarter to twelve. Too early for a drink. One day our permissive society will really get the bit between its teeth and allow a man to have a drink when he feels like one, though we may have to shoot a few brewers and publicans first.

'Zion House?'

An old man sitting on a seat outside the pub directed him. 'Up the hill and the first turning on your left beyond the houses. Just a lane it is – leads to the old mine.'

The pantechnicon passed him and started the long uphill grind to wherever it was going. There was a *Marie Celeste* atmosphere about the place, as though everybody had abruptly evacuated the place for no discernible reason. The houses straggled for a quarter-of-a-mile up the hill then gave way to fields. Wycifffe found the lane, a stony, rutted track between high hedges. Some way ahead a jagged finger of masonry, the broken chimney of the mine, jutted skywards.

Zion House was two-storeyed, square and built of lichen-covered stone roofed with delabole slate and it stood in a walled garden laid out with shrubs and borders which must have required hours of devoted care. A gravelled path led to the front door which stood open. He rang the bell without result so he tried again. A little girl of four or five came round the corner of the house and stood staring at him with solemn black eyes.

'Will you tell Mummy I'm here?'

No answer; but after a further inspection the little girl went off the way she had come and returned a few moments later with her mother. It was only then that Wycliffe realized that he did not know Melinda Bryce's married name.

8

'Trelease.' She peeled off a pair of gardening gloves to shake hands.

Melinda Trelease, née Bryce, was the sort of woman Wycliffe admired: frank, open features, a ready smile and a manner with men which was not sexless but said neither 'Come aboard' nor 'Lay off'. She was dark, as all the Bryces seemed to be, and she had her share of good looks, but what impressed him most was her obvious vitality.

'You've come to ask me about Caroline, I suppose. I've had one of your men here already.' She led him into a large, comfortable sitting-room with a bow window which faced down the estuary towards the sea.

'John, my husband, is a merchant navy skipper – he's away nine months of the year; my son, Philip, is at University and I see very little of him even in the vacations. Young people seem to be very busy these days. So Judy and I have to keep each other company.'

The little girl sat on the settee beside her mother, never taking her eyes off Wycliffe.

'I've not been very intimately mixed up with the family since I was married at eighteen, so I doubt if I can tell you much that you don't know already.'

Wycliffe noticed a rack of pipes by the fireplace and, subconsciously, his hand went to his pocket.

'Do smoke if you want to.'

'Your father disapproved of your marriage?'

She laughed. 'And cut me off without a shilling – no, it wasn't as bad as that. I didn't fit in at home and marrying John was just symptomatic. Father was old-fashioned in his ideas, but it wasn't that either. It was just that they all seemed to be obsessed with the firm. From infancy I was brought up with the idea that the world would come to an end if the firm had a bad year. It was like a religion with them.'

'Even with George?'

'George was only fourteen when I left home so he didn't really count. Everything one said or did, every friend one made and every quarrel one had was scrupulously and ponderously examined to decide what effect it might have on our business relations. It was ludicrous – mad!' Although she obviously meant what she said, she spoke without heat and certainly without malice. 'Father was a bit of an autocrat, but I wouldn't have held that against him if he hadn't always used the threat of cutting us out of the business. To him it was a fate worse than excommunication – and Matt and Sidney went along with him. I don't blame them, but I just couldn't! And Father couldn't understand a Bryce who thought of the firm merely as a way of earning a living.' She brushed a wisp of hair back from her forehead. 'Luckily I met John, we married and the problem as far as I was concerned was solved.' She smiled at him and put her hand over the little girl's. 'No regrets!'

'You broke off all connection with your family?'

She seemed surprised. 'Good heavens, no! Nothing so dramatic. I visited regularly and I still do, but I've always refused to get *involved*, that's all.'

'Even to the extent of refusing your legacy?'

'That was no great sacrifice. John and I have never been short.'

'Your father died two years after your marriage?'

'In nineteen-fifty-three, yes.'

'And your brother married Caroline Morley shortly afterwards.'

She frowned. 'You're suggesting that there was a connection – yes, I think there was. I don't say that Father stopped the boys from meeting girls or anything of that sort, but he was so damned possessive . . .' She hesitated as though at a loss for words. 'I know it sounds silly but he so filled their lives that they never seemed to have time for anything else.' She grinned, ruefully. 'God defend me from ever doing that to one of mine!'

Wycliffe took time to get his pipe drawing nicely. It was astonishing the extent to which the room expressed the personality of the woman of the house. Its serenity was almost tangible. Trelease must begrudge every day he spent on his oil tanker. She was watching him with a faint smile as though she guessed his thoughts.

'You have been to Boslow and seen what it is like?'

He nodded. 'Your brother Matt's marriage was sudden. Had he known his future wife long?'

'A few months. Clement Morley bought a house in West Treen just before my father died – not the one he has now but a smaller place out towards the headland. Caroline, of course, was his half-sister and she used to come down to stay with him. She was the sort of girl to get herself talked about and she got Morley talked about too for a while. I think she came to Boslow with him two or three times, but when Matt said that he was going to marry her everybody was astounded. Of course, when it turned out that she was pregnant, people thought they understood.'

'Thought?'

She frowned. 'I ought to – tell you that I disliked Caroline, so I'm bound to be prejudiced.'

'But?'

She grinned. 'I thought at the time that Matt had been caught, and I've had no reason to think otherwise since. Matt wasn't the sort to sweep a young girl off her feet: he wouldn't have known how to begin. His shyness and nervousness with women were a standing joke. The alternative is to suppose that she made a dead set at him – but why? A man twenty years older, set in his ways, timid and gauche with women . . . I know a girl will sometimes fall for the handsome-mature-man-greying-at-the-temples, but Matt was no film star even in those days.'

'You think that she saw him as a suitable father for someone else's child?'

'I think it's possible. She was the daughter of old Morley's second marriage and he made no secret of the fact that she couldn't expect much under his will. Matthew could give her money and a certain position and Boslow provided a pretty good base for operations.'

'You certainly didn't like her!'

'I told you.'

He stood up and walked round the room with the freedom of an old friend. There were two good pictures and several prints on the walls. One of the pictures was a Fragonard, a saucy boudoir scene.

'Do you like it? Matt gave it me. It used to hang in the drawing-room at Boslow, but nobody appreciates painting there and I loved it so much that I overcame my scruples . . .' She laughed. 'John thinks it might give our visitors the wrong idea.'

'You are on good terms with Matt?'

'Why not?'

Wycliffe went to the window and stared out. From this angle the two headlands at the entrance to the estuary presented a 'V' with the sea between. To say that he was thinking would have been too precise a description of the vague notions which were passing through his mind. 'Do you think that Matthew knew or suspected that he had been cheated?'

'I'm certain that he did not.'

'And does not?' He turned to face her.

For the first time she was put out by a question. 'I don't know.'

'If he discovered that Zel was not his daughter . . .'

'But how could he unless Caroline told him; and why should she do that after all these years?'

'Spite?'

She shook her head. 'But Matt would never . . . There's not a scrap of violence in his nature; he is the most gentle creature alive.' However she was disturbed. 'Judy, go and see what's happened to Trotsky.' She turned to Wycliffe 'Trotsky is our cat – a Russian blue as you probably guessed.'

She stood up and brushed the hair from her forehead as though she would rid herself of a tangle of thoughts at the same time. 'I suppose anybody might be provoked; but whoever killed Caroline tried to involve George – isn't that right?'

'It seems so.'

Her face cleared. 'Then you can put Matt right out of your mind! A fit of anger is one thing, but a calculated scheme to shift the blame . . . I'm his sister, Mr Wycliffe, and I know that Matt would be totally incapable of doing such a thing.'

They were both standing now; the serenity of the room was broken. 'Matthew had good reason to dislike his younger brother.'

She made a gesture of impatience. 'He sent him packing from Boslow, but he gave him Foundry House to live in. Is that the action of a vindictive man?' She looked at Wycliffe's face, now a mask of professional reserve. 'I can see that I'm wasting my time; but you will find out for yourself.' She smiled suddenly. 'For God's sake let's sit down; this is absurd! 'Would you like a drink?'

'Very much.'

'Sherry, gin, beer – and I believe I could find a little whisky . . . ?'

'Beer, please.'

She went to fetch it.

If Matthew was not Zel's father, who was? A question which Melinda avoided. Of course it could have been someone who had long since faded from the scene.

She came in with a tray and glasses, an unopened bottle of beer, a bottle of gin and some orange juice. 'Help yourself.' She poured herself a small gin, flushed it with orange and sipped. He poured his beer and took an unmannerly gulp.

'I needed that!'

'Good!'

'What do you think of Zel?'

She placed her glass on the tray. 'I'm sorry for her. She's a strange child – and no wonder, the way she has been brought up.'

'She seems to get plenty of affection from her father and from her uncle.'

'Sidney? Bless his heart! He used to buy books to find out how she should be brought up! They say some women want children without a husband; poor Sidney certainly wanted children without a wife!'

'Do you see much of Zel?'

'Very little. I've tried. Several times recently I've asked her up here – pressed her to come, but she never has.' She frowned. 'I thought I might have helped her. To find her feet in the world a girl needs a woman behind her. Caroline couldn't be bothered so she was left to the well-meaning bumbling of Matt and Sidney.' She brushed a wisp of hair from her eyes and patted it back in place. 'It's a pity she can't find a boy-friend.'

'She has. I was talking to him this morning.' Wycliffe told her of the encounter by the summer-house.

'Evans? I know the boy. I can understand them wanting to keep it quiet. Matt and Sidney would go through the roof.'

'Is there something wrong with the boy?'

'Not that I know of. It's his mother: she has quite a reputation in the town. She's a widow who never seems to have had a husband, and with no obvious means of support.'

Judy came in carrying her rather elegant cat. Her chubby little hands gripped him under the armpits allowing his heavy body to dangle unbecomingly. 'I found him. He was asleep on the water tank.'

Poor Trotsky!

'Why did Matthew throw George out?'

Melinda's brown eyes met his. 'According to Matthew it was because of his affair with Caroline.'

'You believe that?'

She shook her head.

'George says that Matthew accused him of trying to seduce Zel.'

'That sounds a more likely reason.'

'George says that Zel made it up, that she pursued him.'

She shrugged. 'I could believe that.'

'On evidence?'

'Zel is an odd child.'

'She is no longer a child.'

'No.'

Wycliffe looked at his watch. 'I must be off: I'm stopping you from getting your lunch.'

'It won't take much getting and if you care to stay you'll be very welcome.'

He was under the spell of the golden light and the personality of this woman. She seemed to have mastered the difficult art of being female without being either aggressive or coy. They had lunch in the dining-room with trench windows open on to the garden. Cold beef and salad with tomatoes, basil and chives with a hint of lemon and garlic; apple pie and cream to follow.

'If you are right about Zel, have you thought who her real father might be?'

'I've thought, of course, but not to much purpose.'

She saw him to the gate and stood with Judy clutching her hand to watch him make his way along the lane until he was out of sight.

Matthew Bryce must have led a lonely, introspective life, trying to recapture with pathetic enthusiasm a time that had passed, trying to preserve methods and traditions of the steam age in the world of the computer and the shop-steward. In his emotional life he had made a late bid for romance and had landed himself with Caroline. But Zel was his consolation, his daughter, that mysterious, alluring enigma – a girl. She was his, the more so in that her mother was antagonistic towards her. Caroline had intrigued with his brother under his roof and he had reacted mildly. Caroline had carried on her affair outside and he had not reacted at all. Events and his relatives were

454

conspiring to take his business away from him but he could take refuge with his models, his prints and his books. He still had Zel.

But what if after eighteen years Caroline had decided to disillusion him? Would he have believed her? Could she have given proof? What sort of proof? Had she named Zel's real father?

'. . . a calculated scheme to shift the blame . . . I *know* that Matt would be incapable of such a thing!' But suppose Caroline had told him that George was Zel's father? When Caroline was eighteen, George would have been sixteen; it was not impossible.

He was back on the water-front, waiting for the ferry, watched by the same old man sitting outside the pub.

'She won't be over for a bit; they'm gone to their dinners.'

He walked by the river towards the sea and his thoughts depressed him. The road soon gave way to a footpath and he found himself skirting fields of stubble, separated from the estuary only by gorse bushes growing on the edge of a low cliff. Such a walk should have restored his good humour, but not now. He sat on a stile, brooding, until he saw the ferry leave the other side; then he walked back to the slipway.

On the way across he stood by the hunch-back. Both of them leaned on the gates, smoking.

'So they ain't found t'other.'

'T'other?'

Dicky took his pipe from his mouth and regarded him. 'The Haynes girl: they bin searching for her over to Boslow all the morning.' He pointed with his pipe-stem to the water swirling past. 'I reckon she'll be turning up one of these days like t'other. They'm wasting their time if you ask me.'

At least they were doing something. What the hell had he been doing? Strolling round like a summer tourist and lunching with an attractive woman.

Dicky spat a brown bolus into the water. 'A nasty business whichever way you look at it!'

True.

Wycliffe walked rapidly and abstractedly along the wharf back to his caravan and did not notice three or four pressmen lolling against the railings until they called to him.

'Anything new, Mr Wycliffe? Why did you have the lake dragged? Do you think the girl has been murdered? Do you expect . . . ?'

'Why don't you boys go home?' As well ask the lions to stop eating Christians.

He pushed open the door of his caravan. 'Is Mr Gill back?'

'Not yet, sir. I think they've moved upstream to Foundry House.'

'Any message?'

'Mr Bellings wants you to telephone him . . .'

Wycliffe handed the sergeant the photograph of the twins which he had shown to the boy, John Evans. 'Handle it carefully and see that it goes at once to Fingerprints.'

Afterwards he continued walking upstream, past the cannery, the coal-yard and the timber-yard, familiar ground now. Beyond Boslow turn he came upon a constable wearing thigh boots and standing guard over a pile of implements and three pairs of shoes with socks pushed in them. 'What goes on?'

'Mr Gill and Constable Edwards are searching the bed of the stream, sir. It's the overflow from the lake and it enters the river, after passing under the railway, further down. The rest of the search party are covering the area round Foundry House, sir.'

Standing on the edge of the bank Wycliffe could see Jimmy Gill and the constable about a hundred yards downstream. Their heads did not reach the level of the banks.

'What size are your boots?'

'Nines, sir.'

Wycliffe took eights but they fitted reasonably: a little long in the legs, but he turned the tops down. When he was comfortable he slid down the steep bank into the stream and started to pick his way after the others. The bottom was gravel without any boulders and the water scarcely came over his ankles except where the stream had scooped out miniature whirlpools. It would be a different story after a few hours' rain. It was a strangely different world between the steep, fern-covered banks; the air was saturated with moisture and with the acrid smell of sodden earth and rotting vegetation. A fish shot away from his feet and a cloud of gnats maintained station round his head.

The other two were taking their time and he soon caught them up. Gill greeted him with a cynical smile. 'As you see, sir, we are leaving no stone unturned.'

Wycliffe did not answer.

'We dragged the lake this morning.'

456

'I know.' Wycliffe stumbled as one foot went into a pool which was deeper than most. Gill grabbed him. 'Hey up! At least it's quiet down here – far from the madding crowd and all that. It could catch on as a new sport – stream-walking.'

'For God's sake don't tell the BBC. They'll have an outside broadcast team on it before you can blink.'

They covered another hundred yards and the stream turned to the left and into a culvert under the railway. Arched over with granite blocks it was high enough to stand up in. The old Great Western never skimped or botched a job.

'This is where the stream goes through to the river.'

'So I had imagined.'

As they entered the culvert, Jimmy Gill, who was leading, stopped them. 'We've found her.'

A moment for his eyes to become accustomed to the gloom and Wycliffe could see the figure of a girl lying in the stream, one leg doubled beneath her. She was wearing a brown raincoat with gilt buttons, and now the wet-look shoes with their block heels were really wet. Beyond he could see the gleaming chromium of her bicycle.

At that moment they were startled by a sound like approaching thunder and it was overhead before any of them realized that it was a train of waggons on the way to West Treen. Wycliffe waited for the rumbling to pass, then turned to the constable. 'Get out where you can use your personal radio, tell them the news and ask them to get busy. I would like Dr Franks to join me here as soon as he can.'

When he had gone Jimmy Gill shone his pocket torch on to the girl's head. She was lying face down in the water, her red hair streaming forward in the gentle current. The base of her skull was a mass of hair and clotted blood. 'Not such a clean job this time,' Gill said. 'I reckon he must have had two or three goes.'

Wycliffe was silent.

'She was last seen on Thursday morning, cycling along Station Road. It's now Friday afternoon.' Gill made his calculation. 'She can't have been here more than thirty hours.'

'So?'

'I don't know. Most of yesterday it was pissing down with rain; I was wondering whether there could have been enough water in the stream to carry her down from further up.'

'And her bike? No, somebody slung the bike in and dragged her in

457

after it.' Wycliffe was still gazing down at the girl's body. 'Let's get out of here!'

They walked a little way upstream and climbed the bank. The sunshine was an indecency and Wycliffe could not help thinking of his own daughter who was near enough to the same age as the dead girl in the culvert.

Jimmy Gill lit a cheroot and puffed vigorously, as though the acrid smoke was a breath of fresh cleansing air. 'It begins to look bad for your friend Matthew.'

'He's no friend of mine, but I find it difficult to see him as a murderer. All the same . . .'

'If he killed his wife he must have done it before driving her over to Foundry House; and Zel saw or heard enough to know what had happened. When he got there he drove the car into the boathouse, transferred the body to the driving seat and strapped it in. It must have been a premeditated crime because she was killed with a piece of lead pipe like the scrap in the corner of the boathouse and he left his weapon there. In any case he must have known that George would be out or he wouldn't have dared.' Gill smoked in silence for a while. 'It fits. The Haynes girl was on her way to see George on Thursday night. She didn't know he wasn't there, or she was prepared to wait until he came back. As she arrived in the clearing she saw Matthew come out of the boathouse. She kept out of the way until he had gone, then she took a look in the boathouse to see what he had been up to . . .'

'Plucky girl!' Wycliffe was satirical.

'All right! Perhaps she didn't go into the boathouse. When she heard that Caroline had been found there she would put two and two together . . .'

'And?'

'Well, one possibility is that she tried a spot of blackmail on Matthew.'

'Are you saying that, yesterday morning, Margaret Haynes went to Boslow, rang the front doorbell, accused Matthew of murdering his wife and was then lured here, killed and pushed into the culvert?'

Gill grinned. 'You've got the knack of making reasonable ideas sound bloody silly if you don't like them.'

'That idea is bloody silly.'

But Gill was not put off. 'All the same, I think we should put the screw on Matthew.'

Wycliffe did not answer and the chief inspector went on: 'What bothers me is the question of motive. I would like to feel that we were on firmer ground there. As you said yourself it's difficult to understand why a man should suddenly murder his wife after putting up with her for nearly twenty years. There must have been a crisis.'

Wycliffe sat on a weathered granite block of which there were several between the railway and the stream, vestiges of some forgotten enterprise. He got out his pipe. 'I had lunch with Melinda Bryce.'

Gill was sour. 'Good for you. I'm still waiting for mine.'

'She thinks Zel is not Matthew's daughter.'

'Then whose?'

'That's a question. But if Melinda is right and if Matthew only recently discovered the fact . . .'

'We have our crisis and our motive! She could have blurted it out in a row from sheer spite!'

'We still have to prove it,' Wycliffe grunted.

9

The naked body of the girl, once Margaret Haynes, lay face downwards on the dissecting table. Dr Franks, in his white overall and
wearing surgical gloves, stood on one side, Wycliffe on the other.
Her red hair had been gathered into a top-knot and held by a surgical
clip; the base of her skull around the damaged area had been shaved.

Franks, pink and chubby like a healthy baby, was intently examining the girl's feet. 'The fact that she has been lying in running water
means that all the post-mortem changes are retarded . . . Also there
is a certain amount of rigor remaining . . .'

Wycliffe shifted impatiently. 'Save all that for your students. How
long has she been dead?'

Even with twenty years of experience behind him Wycliffe was
never at ease in the presence of death. Franks, on the other hand,
had acquired a cheerful, cynical indifference and a ghoulish sense
of humour which jarred on the detective. The only flaw in a professional relationship which had ripened into friendship. Franks
approached a post-mortem with a gusto and relish which might be
admirable in a craftsman of another sort.

'You're always in a hurry, Wycliffe; you should relax more – your
arteries are probably beginning to tell a tale. Take notice – I do.'

His fingers, short but tapering, like musician's, were running over
the limbs as he spoke.

'Thirty to thirty-six hours at a guess, but I may have reason to
think again . . .'

'Yesterday morning at eight-thirty she was seen alive near where
we found her.'

'Then it looks as though I've hit the jack-pot again.' He bent over
the girl's head, probing gently round the damage. 'It seems as
though she was hit at least twice and probably three times. One of
the blows was more violent than the others and, as you can see, she

lost some blood – more than you'd think from the look of this. Some of it was probably washed away.'

'So you think she was put in the stream immediately after receiving the blows?'

'There is some damage to the top of her head and lacerations of the face; these would be consistent with her having been struck down while she was on the bank and falling into the stream. It's a messier job than the other.'

'The same sort of weapon?'

Franks looked at him in mild reproof. 'How the hell do I know until I've made a proper examination? There's no reason why not: the Bryce woman might have been in a more favourable position from the murderer's point of view – bending down, say.'

'Is Caroline Bryce's body still here?'

Franks shook his head. 'The undertaker fetched it away this morning; they're having the funeral tomorrow. The coroner issued a certificate . . .'

'Nobody tells me.'

Franks chuckled. 'Your office has certainly been notified but you're never there to know one way or the other.'

'Cremation?'

'Nope! Burial in the churchyard; all nice and respectable.' He looked at Wycliffe with sudden concern. 'Why? You're not suggesting . . .'

'I suppose you've still got your copies of the photographs?'

Franks was more puzzled: 'What the hell are you getting at? I get a set, but so do you . . .'

'Show me yours, there's a good chap!'

Franks hesitated but gave in. 'OK! I suppose this will keep for another ten minutes.' He motioned to one of his assistants to draw a sheet over the body.

He peeled off his gloves and led the way through a tiled corridor to an office which looked out on to a little garden. He unlocked a filing cabinet and drew out an envelope. 'Here it is. Now, for Christ's sake tell me what you're after!'

The envelope was bulky and contained upwards of thirty full-plate photographs of the dead woman, taken from every angle, with clothes and without. Wycliffe shuffled through them. 'Don't say . . .' He broke off. 'Ah! Here we are.' He held out a photograph of Caroline's

461

head and neck taken in profile; the black hair was drawn back from the eroded features exposing one ear – the left. He pointed to the ear. 'Is that an attached lobe?'

Franks took the picture. 'You can see for yourself.'

'Never mind what I can see. I'm asking you as an expert.'

'Well, of course it's attached – why?'

'Put it in a supplementary report; we may need it.'

'I suppose it's no good asking . . . ?'

'Am I right in thinking that it is impossible for a couple, both with attached ear lobes, to have a child whose lobes are free?'

Franks, like all experts, shied from the categorical reply. 'If we are right about the genetics of the thing – yes. The attached or adherent lobe is inherited as a recessive so that it would be impossible for parents with attached lobes to hand on the dominant, free-lobed condition to their children – why?'

'Because Caroline and Matthew Bryce both have attached lobes and the girl, Zel, has not.'

'Ergo, the girl is a bastard. You do have fun!'

'It may not be so funny as you think.' All the same Wycliffe seemed, suddenly, to be in a better humour. 'Have a good evening. I'm off.'

He drove at his usual sedate pace back to the caravans and arrived there after the sun had set and the whole estuary was filled with purple mist. The water was glassy, lambent and mysterious. He now rated sufficient importance for the hotel to lay on a special meal for him whenever he arrived, but he had no enthusiasm for a tough steak with potatoes and carrots out of tins. WPC Rowse happened to be on duty in the caravan.

'Can you cook?'

'I can do you a bacon and cheese omelette, sir.'

After his meal he telephoned Clement Morley and asked to see him. Morley was reluctant and haggled, but without much conviction. 'It's late and I still have a great deal of work in front of me . . . Yes, I heard about the finding of Margaret Haynes' body, on the News. Very sad; terrible, in fact. I suppose you know that she worked for me part-time doing shorthand and typing . . .'

Wycliffe was silent.

'All the same, I don't see how I can help you.'

'That's for me to judge, sir.'

'Very well, you'd better come along. Say in half-an-hour.' He sounded subdued and worried.

Wycliffe parked his car in front of the house as the church clock was counting out the strokes of ten. The weather was on the change and a cold, damp breeze off the sea played tricks with the sound, whisking it away, then tossing it back with startling clarity. The squint-eyed old spinster who should have been a housekeeper in a presbytery showed him to Morley's study without a word. Morley received him with a certain deference. He looked ill; his pallid skin showed a dark flush under the eyes. 'A terrible business, Wycliffe. On top of the other it has quite unnerved me.'

Wycliffe seated himself opposite Morley with the desk between them; the ex-minister matched his bony fingers and studied them. 'I came to know the girl through her father who is the golf "pro". She seemed to be drifting as so many young people do these days and I thought it would be a kindness to offer her a job.'

Wycliffe cut in without ceremony. 'It was not about Margaret Haynes that I wanted to talk to you, Mr Morley. At the moment I am more concerned with Mrs Bryce.'

The brown eyes rested on Wycliffe's for a moment then flitted nervously away. Something had knocked the stuffing out of Clement. 'Caroline? What can I tell you that you don't already know?'

Wycliffe's manner was calm, placid, disquietingly so. He seemed in no hurry to come to the point.

'Would you like a drink?'

'No, thank you.'

'Smoke if you wish.'

'I am going to ask you some questions, Mr Morley, and I should tell you that I am in a position to satisfy myself as to the truth of your answers.'

'That is an insulting remark!' A flash of the old Morley.

But Wycliffe seemed not to hear. 'When you first came to Treen, nineteen years ago, you had a smaller house, near the headland?'

'While I looked round for a more suitable place, yes.'

'Your half-sister came to stay with you?'

Morley had unclasped his hands and he was looking at his up-turned palms with curious concentration. 'Once or twice. She took a fancy to Treen as I had done.'

'It was during one of these visits that she met and married her husband?'

'It was.' Morley put his palms together again and rubbed them gently. 'I was invited to Boslow and I took Caroline with me on two or three occasions.'

'Did she seem interested in Matthew or attracted by him?'

Morley hesitated. 'Not especially.'

'So that you were surprised when she said that she intended to marry him?'

'I was more than surprised. Like everyone else, I was astounded!'

'And you did your best to discourage her?'

'I had no influence over Caroline but I pointed out how unsuitable the match would be.'

'You did not know at the time that she was pregnant?'

'I did not!' He raised a hand to his eyes as though to brush away a source of irritation. 'Look here, Wycliffe! I can see no point in raking over the past.' If it was an attempt to recover the initiative it was still-born; it hardly got off the ground.

Wycliffe's bland stare did not waver. 'Very well, let us come to recent events. When I was here on Tuesday you seemed anxious to know if the police had been through your half-sister's papers and personal effects – why?'

'Surely it is natural that I should want to know whether there was anything that might shed light on her death?' He reached into a cupboard under his desk and brought out a decanter and glasses.

'Would it surprise you to know that there was?'

Morley's hand was unsteady as he poured himself a drink. 'Are you sure that you won't join me?'

'Please answer my question.'

'I don't see how I can unless I know the nature of the . . . the evidence.'

'Do you know that Matthew is not Zel's father?'

Morley's quick, nervous glance had a wild quality like that of a trapped animal. 'Rubbish! Who has been retailing such wicked gossip?' All the same he could sit no longer. He stood up, glass in hand, and moved to the window. The curtains had not been drawn and he stood with his back to Wycliffe, staring out into the darkness. 'Really, Wycliffe!'

But Wycliffe was unmoved. He sat in his chair, seemingly calm

464

and impassive, but his mind was furiously alive. A great many things, including, perhaps, his career, depended on how he played his cards now. 'I have proof that Zel is not Matthew's daughter.'

'Proof! I can't believe it!' Morley's face was invisible but his voice was tremulous and he seemed to have lost control of its pitch.

'Proof that would stand up in court. It was a well-kept secret until last week when Caroline chose to tell her husband.'

A silence which lengthened. It was one of Wycliffe's less obvious assets that he knew how to endure silence. Few people do. The ticking of Morley's grandfather clock became suddenly audible, then intrusive and, finally, dominant. Morley continued to stand with his back to the room, motionless. The ticking of the clock imposed a rhythm on the silence, adding to the tension. An aeroplane throbbed in the distance, came nearer, then its sound died away.

Morley turned. He looked composed but he groped for his chair like a blind man and sat down.

Wycliffe spoke. 'You have not asked me who her father is.'

Morley made a tiny gesture of helplessness. 'You know?'

'Yes.'

The ex-minister seemed to have aged; his cheeks sagged and he was suddenly thinner, poorer. 'It would have finished me.'

Wycliffe's gaze was unfocused; he might have been absorbed in his private thoughts or half asleep.

'All my life I have hated certain things . . . I have fought against them – *fought!*'

Wycliffe had a sudden, vivid memory of a group of boys exchanging dirty stories behind the lavatories in the school yard and of one boy, standing apart, his ears cocked, trying to catch the forbidden words.

'I'm not a hypocrite; I've really believed in what I've tried to do.'

Three days ago Wycliffe had come near to hating this man, his pomposity, his offensive patronage, his assumption that he was entitled to special treatment. He would have anticipated with satisfaction the chance to deflate him, to expose him as a fraud. But not now.

'I was twenty-eight, she was eighteen. I had seen very little of her since leaving home six or seven years earlier. She was almost a stranger.' He smoothed his blotting pad with the palm of his hand. 'She was lovely. I could not think of her as a relative . . . she seemed a different kind of being.' He looked away, across the room. 'I had never had a woman . . .'

Wycliffe waited.

'Even so I would never have . . . She teased me, taunted me for the way I lived, laughed at my . . . my restraint . . . It was only the once, just the one time.

'Then, after a while, she told me that she was pregnant. I had no experience; I was green. But I knew enough to know that with money these things could be put right. It was simply a question of making the right contacts. Believe me, I had a struggle with my conscience, but the alternative was unthinkable . . . I had just been elected to Parliament and already I had begun to establish some reputation as one who stood for the old values of decency and reticence . . . and here I was with my half-sister!

'But she would not hear of an abortion. For weeks she kept me in an agony of suspense then, one morning at breakfast, she said, "Clem, your troubles are over – for the moment." I thought that her . . . that she meant the whole thing had been a mistake on her part but, after a little while, she added, "I'm going to marry Matt Bryce; he thinks it's his." She seemed to look on the whole thing as a huge joke. "We are going to get married in a Registry Office so that it won't look too bad." What could I do?'

With the absurd deliberation of a man who is either drunk or undergoing great mental stress, Morley arranged the items on his desk, placing them with such care that his life might have depended on their symmetry.

'As the years went by I came to believe that it had all worked out for the best. Although Caroline was now living in Treen I saw very little of her and when we did meet there was never any reference to what there was between us. I heard talk of her affair with George Bryce but Matt did not seem to mind and it was none of my business although I suffered indirectly through being related to her. Then, five years ago, when my father died, there was a change. Caroline and my other half-sister, Joyce, did not get what they thought they were entitled to, and Caroline blamed me.'

'She blackmailed you.'

Morley stroked his cheeks with his fingers then looked at his hand uneasily as though he expected something to have rubbed off. 'It wasn't blackmail. I made her certain regular payments.'

'Quite large sums.'

'The payments were made openly, by cheque. There was nothing underhand on my side.'

'But she threatened you.'

He would not meet Wycliffe's eyes. 'From time to time she reminded me of what was rarely out of my mind and pointed out how damaging it would be if people got to know . . .'

There was silence again except for the ticking of the clock. Once more Wycliffe forced Morley to break it. His voice sounded harsh and unnatural. 'I did not kill her.'

Wycliffe did not even look at him.

'Why should I want to kill her? I could afford to pay what she asked and, in a way, it helped to . . . to . . .'

'To ease your conscience?'

'Yes.'

Wycliffe got out his pipe and started to fill it. The position was so different now; almost, it seemed that Morley would need to ask the detective's permission before he poured himself another drink or lit a cigarette. The human peck-order is far more subtle than that of the hen-house.

'I didn't kill her.'

'Perhaps your half-sister decided that she was no longer satisfied with money.' Wycliffe spoke between puffs at his pipe, causing the flame of the match to undulate over the bowl. 'It is possible that, being a vindictive woman, she might get more satisfaction from exposing you.'

Morley gestured helplessly. 'I can't *prove* anything, but I tell you I didn't kill her!'

Wycliffe did not answer directly. 'Evidently Margaret Haynes knew too much and she had to be silenced.'

'You can't think . . .'

Wycliffe stood up.

'You're going?'

'I'll find my own way out.'

'But . . .'

'You were going to say?'

'Nothing.'

Wycliffe was at the door and he did not turn back. Morley

467

followed him into the hall but he was too late: the front door slammed.

It had started to rain, just a fine drizzle, and as Wycliffe drove back to the town the street lamps were haloed.

Next morning Wycliffe went to the funeral. It was fine, with a blue sky and powder-puff clouds, but the air was moist, threatening rain. There were more people about than usual, perhaps because it was Saturday and the women were doing their week-end shopping. In the square there were stalls around the war memorial, selling fruit and vegetables, cheap clothing, hardware and second-hand ornaments. Women gossiped in little groups and Wycliffe thought that they eyed him with some hostility as he passed. He was not surprised. One murder in a small town is exciting, something new to talk about. Two are a different matter; people begin to feel that somebody has slipped up, their security is threatened and they naturally hold it against those who are there to protect them.

Wycliffe joined the funeral party in the church. Family and close friends occupied the front pews; then there was a large gap separating them from a score or so townspeople who sat at the back. Wycliffe took a position in no-man's-land.

The family was there in force, all except George. Matthew wore an ancient black suit which was too big for him; Sidney was immaculate in clerical grey. Zel was between them, wearing a bottle-green winter coat with fur trimmings; she sat bolt upright, staring in front of her. Joyce and Francis Boon were in the front pew on the other side of the aisle. Joyce had a chic, black two-piece while Francis wore a dark overcoat probably hiding something wildly unsuitable underneath. He looked unnaturally pale and stared round the church as though trying to remember why he was there. Clement Morley sat next to Francis and kept turning towards him as though irritated by something he was doing. Melinda Trelease sat with Cousin Irene behind the brothers; she must have found somebody to look after Judy. The church was heavy with the rather oppressive scent of the flowers heaped on the coffin and disposed round the altar.

They filed into the churchyard. Like most of Treen it was on a steep slope and the bearers had to carry the coffin up a path broken at intervals by short flights of steps. The old part of the churchyard was sheltered by pines but the new part had only recently been taken in from the surrounding fields and Caroline's grave was dug through rough grass. Wycliffe had expected a family vault. As they gathered at the graveside, Morley caught his eye and looked quickly away. He was still very pale with dark rings under his eyes. Zel, too, was pale; she stood at the edge of the grave as they lowered the coffin into it but never once looked down, Matthew, on the other hand, never took his eyes off it. It was impossible to divine his thoughts; almost certainly he was looking back over nineteen years during which there must have been some moments of happiness. Joyce Boon held a little handkerchief and dabbed her eyes; Cousin Irene, in black from head to foot, wept unashamedly.

'Forasmuch as it has pleased Almighty God in his great mercy to take unto himself the soul of our dear sister here departed, we therefore commit her body to the ground . . .'

Gulls suddenly screamed overhead in a running dog-fight, drowning the voice of the priest. Wycliffe was aware of little groups of sight-seers dotted about the churchyard. What did they expect to see? An avenging spirit rise from the grave of the murdered woman?

At last it was over and they trooped down the hill with the vicar holding Zel's arm and speaking soothing words. At the gate she deserted the vicar abruptly and came over to Wycliffe. She was secretive and intense. 'I must talk to you, it's urgent!'

The car for the chief mourners drew level and stopped. Matthew and Sidney stood to one side, waiting for Zel.

'I shall be at Boslow later today.'

This did not satisfy her and she would have argued, but Joyce Boon, with Francis in tow, stopped to speak to the chief super-intendent. 'It was good of you to come; the family appreciate it very much.' She seemed to be a self-constituted master of ceremonies but her eyes were red. Perhaps she had really been weeping for her sister. Zel got into the car reluctantly and was driven away.

Clement Morley made a point of not seeing Wycliffe; he was picked up by his own car, the black Mercedes with a chauffeur at the wheel. Wycliffe walked back through the town to the water-front and to his headquarters. Chief Inspector Gill was waiting for him.

'Good funeral?'

Wycliffe went through into his office and sat down. Gill followed him. 'Are you going to see Matthew?'

Wycliffe nodded. He was thinking about Caroline, about the funeral and the motives which had drawn the family together in this strangely moving ritual centred on a dead woman who was certainly not loved by most of them.

Gill took up his favourite position, astride one of the chairs. 'What's all this about ear lobes? I don't get it.' He had been reading some notes Wycliffe had dictated for the record.

Outside the estuary was grey, swept by a sudden shower. Saturday morning. Nine days ago Caroline Bryce was still alive. What had happened in the last ten or twelve hours of her life? It seemed to Wycliffe that he had made remarkably little effort to find out; he had been content to nibble round the edges. Meanwhile Margaret Haynes had also died. Last Saturday at this time she had still four days to go . . .

He recollected himself and realized that Jimmy Gill was watching him with a malicious grin deepening the lines of his ugly, intriguing features. 'Ear lobes.'

Wycliffe gathered his wits. 'It's a question of inheritance. A couple whose ear lobes are attached cannot have a child with free lobes. Matthew and Caroline both have attached lobes and Zel's are free.'

'So we have proof?'

'Yes.'

'But no proof that she is Morley's.'

'Only his admission.'

Gill rubbed his bristly chin. 'I don't see why he should have admitted it. He has everything to lose.'

'Morley thought that Caroline had left some evidence that he was Zel's father and when I told him I had proof that Matt was not, he assumed the worst.'

'Self-incrimination by a trick.' Gill was facetious.

'Morley isn't accused of any crime.'

'That's right, he isn't – not yet.'

Wycliffe detested Gill's probing. He hated having to explain himself, not because he was modest but because he was ashamed of the vagueness of his mental processes. Some of his colleagues were only too anxious to expose the rational processes by which they had reached certain (correct) conclusions but Wycliffe had never indulged himself. Often after he had arrived at some decision he found himself trying to rationalize it to satisfy others. Gill might well ask, 'What made you pick on Morley as the girl's father?' He hardly knew himself. To start with he remembered looking at Zel and thinking, 'There's very little Bryce in you.' Then he had heard that Morley had made regular payments to his half-sister and somebody, George probably, had said that Caroline 'had something on Morley'. And only the previous morning Melinda Bryce had told him that Caroline had been the sort of girl to get herself talked about and 'for a while she got Morley talked about too'. It was only afterwards that he had seen the possible significance of the remark. But, perhaps, the idea had first been seeded while he was looking at the photograph of Morley's mother which hung in his study. He had been struck by her thick lips which she had handed on to her son. Zel had them too, in less degree. It was only the previous afternoon while he was talking to Dr Franks in his dissecting room that the obvious had occurred to him: *Morley's mother was not Caroline's*. How then could Zel . . . ? So a fact here, a fact there, collected in the rag-bag of his memory would suddenly fall into a pattern. But how could such a random and fortuitous process be explained?

'I'm going to lunch.'

Just as he was leaving a telephone message came for him.

'The prints on the photograph you sent us include a fresh set which match those on the steering wheel of the vehicle abandoned . . .'

'What the hell is all this?' Gill demanded.

'He's Zel's boy-friend and I think it very likely that he drove the car with Caroline's body in it from the Boslow garage to Foundry House.'

'You mean the girl got him to do it in order to save her father?'

'How should I know?' Wycliffe was suddenly ill-tempered. He gave instructions for Evans to be brought in.

10

Wycliffe lunched at the hotel, where there were more people than he had yet seen. Farmers who had brought their wives Saturday-shopping came to the hotel for lunch. It was a regular feature of the off-season life of the little town; everyone seemed to be on first name terms with everyone else and the manager spoke of them collectively as his 'Saturday Regulars'. Despite the heavy and frequent showers the fair had started early and its canned music blared insistently creating a holiday atmosphere.

The superintendent came in for a lot of surreptitious attention; people pointed him out and whispered. One man who had spent too long at the bar explained loudly to his embarrassed companions why the Area CID was bound to be less efficient than the Yard.

After lunch he went back to his headquarters. In the big room of his caravan Constable Edwards was typing reports while John Evans sat opposite, across the table. Sitting by Evans was Matthew Bryce. They sat there, the boy and the man, looking for all the world as though they were waiting for the dentist. Wycliffe greeted Bryce curtly and ignored the boy. He went through to his own office and Constable Edwards followed him.

'What's Bryce doing here?'

'He arrived about half an hour ago, sir. He wants to see you and he insisted on waiting. I couldn't get out of him what it's about.'

'Have they spoken to each other – Bryce and the boy?'

'Not a word, sir.'

Bryce probably had not the least idea why Evans was there. Evans would certainly know Bryce and he must be very worried, wondering why he was there with Zel's father and how much Wycliffe knew. No wonder he was white and tense.

'Send him in.'

'Mr Bryce, sir?'

'The boy.' Wycliffe got out his pipe. 'Bryce can wait if he wants to.'

'He's soaked to the skin; he must have walked from Boslow and he hasn't even got a raincoat . . .'

Wycliffe paused in the act of lighting his pipe. 'The boy! And take Bryce over to the other van; I don't want him eavesdropping.'

'These partitions are almost sound-proof, sir.'

'Do as I say!' Occasionally Wycliffe indulged himself in a fit of deliberate bad temper, deriving a certain satisfaction from the concern and discomfort he created around him. He had the wit to realize that these fits came when he was least sure of himself and they helped to restore his self-confidence.

John Evans came in and stood nervous and gangling near the door of the little office, looking at Wycliffe.

'Sit down. How long have you been waiting?'

'About an hour, sir.'

Wycliffe stared at him with a gloomy expression. 'Good! I hope it was long enough to make you decide to tell the truth.'

The boy flushed. He sat nervously on the edge of one of the collapsible chairs pulling his fingers so that occasionally a joint cracked.

'Don't do that!'

'Sorry.'

They sat in silence while Wycliffe turned the pages of a report.

'How old are you?'

'Eighteen and a half, sir.'

'A responsible adult!' Wycliffe raised his eyes from the report and looked at him. 'Can you drive a car as well as a motor bike?' The boy hesitated. 'It's a simple matter to find out.'

'Yes, I can drive a car.'

'Good! Now, I'm going to caution you, then I shall ask you to tell me what you did on the night Mrs Bryce was murdered – last Thursday week.'

The pale blue eyes flitted round the room as though seeking escape. 'I don't know what you mean.' But the denial was only half-hearted.

'Your fingerprints were on the steering wheel of Mrs Bryce's Mini and your motor bike was seen, parked at the end of Station Road, after eleven o'clock on that night.'

'Oh God!' The words, little more than a sigh, were also a surrender.

'Zel came for you, didn't she?'

'Yes.'

'Tell me about it.'

'I go to art class on Thursday nights and I had just got back. I got off the bike and I was going to push it into the court where we live when I saw her coming down the street.'

'What did she say?'

He licked his lips. 'She was very upset; she said something had happened to her mother and she wanted me to come back with her. I took her on the pillion and we drove to Boslow. She made me stop at the end of Station Road.'

'Then?'

'We went in the back way and in to the garage where they keep the Mini . . .' He broke off and Wycliffe waited for him to go on. 'Zel's mother was lying there on the floor between the car and the double doors of the garage. She was dead.' His gaze was fixed on the ground as though he could still see the dead woman lying there.

'What did you do?'

'I was afraid . . .'

'Of what?'

He moistened his lips. 'I could see that she had been . . . that she had been killed.'

'And you were afraid that Zel had done it?'

He nodded. 'I asked her and she told me not to be a fool. She wanted me to help her to get . . . to get the body to her uncle's house. At first I wouldn't do it but she . . .' He broke off and hid his face in his hands. When he looked up his eyes were full of tears.

'She told you that if you refused to help her to save her father from arrest you couldn't really love her and that it would be all over between you. Is that it?' Wycliffe reeled off the words as though repeating a formula and they had a curiously bracing effect on the boy.

'She told you?'

Wycliffe said nothing.

'Anyway I did what she wanted. We got the body into the passenger seat of the car and I drove it to Foundry House. We put

474

the car in the boathouse and shifted the body to the driving seat and strapped it in.' He shuddered. 'It was horrible!'

'Then?'

'We walked back to Boslow. I hardly knew what I was doing. I tried to persuade Zel to go to the police. I think I threatened to go myself.'

'But you didn't.'

He shook his head, miserably.

'From the time you drove away from Boslow until you got back, did you see anyone?'

'No.'

'Think!'

'We saw nobody; it was late . . .'

'Did you know Margaret Haynes?'

'Yes.'

'Well?'

'Well enough to speak to her if we met in the street.'

'Have you ever had intercourse with her?'

The boy flushed. 'No.'

'Apparently she went with a number of young men?'

'So they say.'

'You know that she has been murdered too?'

'Yes.'

'We think she was killed because she knew something about Mrs Bryce's death. Now, are you quite certain that you did not see her that night?'

The boy's eyes were riveted to the chief superintendent's. 'Certain.'

'One more question, equally important. Between the Thursday on which Mrs Bryce died and the following Thursday when Margaret Haynes disappeared, did she make any contact with you?'

'No.'

'With Zel?'

'Not as far as I know, and I think Zel would have told me if she had.'

Gill came in and stood in the doorway, sizing up the situation. Wycliffe nodded. 'This is John Evans; he is going to make a statement.'

The boy looked from Wycliffe to Gill and back again with fresh apprehension.

'Constable Edwards will take your statement next door.'

Evans stood up. 'Are you going . . . Shall I be allowed to go home after . . . ?'

Wycliffe softened and spoke kindly. 'We'll see. I think we'd better find you a lawyer.'

'Poor little bastard!' Gill said when the boy had gone. 'That's what comes of listening to a woman!'

Wycliffe was looking out of the window of the caravan. The rain had stopped again and there was a pale, golden light over the estuary as the sun struggled through. Gill took his usual seat on one of the collapsible chairs.

'It looks bad for Matthew. The girl must think he did it – or she must know that he did.' He lit one of his cheroots. 'I suppose the next move is to Boslow?'

'No need: Bryce is here, in the other van, waiting.'

'You sent for him?'

'He came of his own accord.'

'To give himself up?'

'How should I know? You'd better bring him over.'

When he came in, Bryce looked frail and ill. There were dark patches of damp on his shoulders and sleeves and on the knees of his trousers.

'I thought I'd wait until after the funeral.' He sat on one of the chairs, his hands resting listlessly in his lap.

'Before doing what?'

He looked up in surprise. 'Giving myself up. I thought you understood.'

Wycliffe's expression was utterly blank. 'No.'

'I killed my wife.'

'And Margaret Haynes?' The question came sharply from Gill.

Bryce nodded.

'You wish to make a statement?'

Bryce stirred like a man required to make an effort beyond his strength. 'If that is what I have to do.'

'I must caution you . . .'

'Do you mind if I smoke?' He took out a packet of cigarettes which were crushed and damp.

476

They moved to the larger room and Wycliffe sent for WPC Rowse to take shorthand. The interrogation began. Wycliffe and Gill sat at one side of the long narrow table and Bryce at the other. WPC Rowse made herself inconspicuous on a chair by the door.

'She told me that she was going to stay with her sister, Joyce . . .'

'Did you believe her?'

Bryce glanced up in reproof. 'Does it matter?' He was so tired that any interruption to his train of thought made it difficult for him to go on. 'I knew that whatever she said she would take the car. She has been disqualified before and it made no difference. I went out to the garage to wait for her. I can't say how long I waited but, at last, I heard her footsteps as she crossed the yard. I had the light on and when she came into the garage she found me going through some nuts and bolts I keep there. She muttered something and passed round on the other side of the car to open the big double doors. I got there first and stooped down, pretending to have trouble with the lower bolt. She was impatient as usual. "Let me do it!" she said. "I'm in a hurry." So I let her take my place and as she bent down I hit her with a piece of lead pipe across the base of the skull.' He paused for a long time. 'She collapsed without a sound; I couldn't believe that it was all over.'

The room was full of smoke. Bryce was taking short, deep inhalations from his cigarette. Gill had his cheroot going and Wycliffe gripped his unlit pipe between his teeth. Gill was watching Bryce with ferocious intensity. 'How did you intend to dispose of the body?'

Bryce noticed the accumulated ash on his cigarette and knocked it off in the common ashtray. 'I hadn't any clear idea . . .'

'You must have thought about it.'

Bryce shook his head. 'I don't think so. I couldn't see beyond the actual . . .' He hesitated for a word.

'Killing – is that what you are trying to say?'

'I suppose so, yes.' He seemed dissatisfied and after a moment added, 'I don't think that I expected to avoid the consequence of what I had done. After a while I went indoors, to my room. I didn't go to bed that night.'

'And next day?'

'Next day I put off going into the garage and when I did, I thought I must be losing my reason. The body was gone and so was the car!

477

For a moment I wondered if it had all been a dream. Had I really murdered Caroline?'

Wycliffe watched Jimmy Gill grind out the stub of his cheroot. 'Did it occur to you that you might not have killed her, that she might have got up and driven away?'

He shuddered. 'Good God, no! There was no question of that!'

The vigour of his denial surprised Wycliffe.

'All right, go on.'

The gaze of his good eye wandered vaguely over the table-top never lifting to the eyes of his questioners. 'You can imagine the state in which I spent the next days, not knowing what had happened to her body . . . When, on Tuesday, it was taken from the estuary, I was in no better shape.' He stopped to light a fresh cigarette from the butt of the old. The afternoon sun was streaming in through the windows and it seemed that the rain had gone for good. Bryce blinked in the sunlight.

'Would you like the curtains drawn?'

'What? No, I'm all right. I was saying, on Tuesday they found her body and in the afternoon you came. Then, on Thursday, I heard that her car . . . that George was mixed up in it. It was un-believable!' He stopped speaking, as though living again in his mind the events of which he told. 'That morning I met the girl, Margaret Haynes . . .'

'By arrangement?'

'What? No, certainly not. By chance. I was out for my morning walk and I met her on the far side of the lake near the summer-house. She seemed to want to speak to me . . .'

'You knew her?'

'Of course! She had stayed at the house several times for Zel's parties.'

'Do you take a walk every morning?'

'I rarely miss.'

'Always the same walk?'

'I suppose so – yes.'

'So that Margaret Haynes might have counted on meeting you there?'

Bryce looked surprised as though the idea was new to him. 'Yes, I suppose she might; I hadn't thought of that.'

Gill was doing the questioning now, Wycliffe seemed to have lost interest. He had started to fill his pipe and appeared to be absorbed in his own thoughts.

'Anyway, what did she say to you?'

'She asked me if I knew who had killed my wife and I said that I did not. I wondered what she was after and thought it might be something George had put her up to. Then the shock came. She told me that she was at Foundry House on the night Caroline died and that she had seen Caroline's Mini driven into the boathouse. A few minutes later Zel and a boy had come out . . .' Bryce's voice faltered and he broke off.

'You believed her?'

'Of course I believed her! Why should she make up such a story? In any case it explained what had happened.' He focused his good eye on Gill. 'It also meant that Zel was in grave danger; that was the thought uppermost in my mind. You must believe that. I asked her whether she had told anyone what she had seen and she said that she had not. I didn't stop to think, to reason out a course of action. It seemed to me then that I had no other course. I struck her across the base of the skull with the heavy ash stick which I carry when I am walking and the poor girl went down like a log.' He shifted his position in his chair and his right hand smoothed the table-top as though to remove unseen irregularities.

'You hit her only once?'

'I don't know. It is possible that I did more. For a few moments I must have been insane.'

'It is important.'

His good eye wavered in its gaze. 'I can't be sure. As I said, I think I was mad.'

'What did you do then?'

'Do?'

Wycliffe stirred himself. 'You had a body on your hands; did you just leave it there in the hope that somebody would come along and dispose of it for you a second time?'

Gill looked at Wycliffe, surprised by the irony. Bryce seemed not to notice. 'No, it was broad daylight so I had to do something. I carried her into the undergrowth and hid her as well as I could; then I hid the bicycle – she had been wheeling a bicycle – in the same way.'

'She was not found in the undergrowth.'

479

'I know. That night I went out and . ...'

'Why did you kill your wife?' Wycliffe cut in across his words and surprised even the WPC who looked up from her book to see what was happening.

'I . . .' Bryce made a helpless gesture and was silent. Wycliffe smoked placidly. Gill, obviously puzzled by the line Wycliffe was taking, chose to keep quiet. The WPC studied her shorthand notes. Wycliffe's bland stare never left Bryce's face.

'Was it because she had told you that Zel was not your daughter?'

Bryce winced as though from a blow. For a moment he said nothing; then, in a voice that was scarcely audible he murmured, 'So you know.'

Wycliffe was still watching him. Not a muscle of the chief super-intendent's face moved. The silence lengthened. When it seemed that it might never end, Bryce went on in a more controlled voice. 'She knew that Zel was the only human being in the world I cared for, and she had to destroy . . . to destroy the legitimate basis for that affection.'

'You were having a row?'

He nodded. 'During supper that night, Zel went up to her room . . .'

'You believed what your wife told you?'

He was staring at his hands, spread out on the table-top. 'She made sure of that; she told me to ask Morley.' He turned to Gill as though seeking support. 'Can you believe that a woman . . . ?'

But Wycliffe, utterly impassive, interrupted him again. 'So you killed her to keep the truth from Zel?'

He shook his head. 'No, I had no right to keep the truth from Zel. I killed her because she was not fit to live.'

Abruptly, Wycliffe stood up. 'All right, Mr Bryce. Your statement will be typed and then, if you wish, you may sign it.' His brisk, almost cheerful manner seemed out of place. Gill was puzzled.

'And after I've signed?' Bryce stood up, wearily.

'One thing at a time.' He called a constable. 'Take Mr Bryce to the other van and stay with him until his statement has been typed; then let him read it and sign it.'

Bryce went out, followed by the constable. Wycliffe watched him cross the grass to the other caravan; his tread was heavy. WPC

480

Rowse uncovered the typewriter. Gill followed Wycliffe into his private office and sat down. 'So that's that, then?'

'You think so?'

Gill grimaced. 'I suppose it makes sense. I couldn't really believe that the old boy killed the Haynes girl to protect himself. But to save Zel – that's a horse of a different colour.'

'But he hasn't saved her.'

'No.'

Wycliffe was looking out of the window. The ferry was grinding its way across to the east bank, apparently empty. Bryce kills his wife, Zel and her boy-friend thoughtfully plant the body on his brother who disposes of it for them. Bryce then murders the girl, Margaret Haynes, because she saw something of the part Zel played in the business. Wycliffe shook his head.

Gill, for once, was watching him in silence. 'When he's signed his statement you'll have him charged?'

Wycliffe did not answer.

It was almost six when they told him that Bryce had signed his statement. He crossed the grass with Gill at his heels to the other van. Bryce was still seated at the table with his signed statement in front of him. His signature, in a bold flourish, would have looked more in keeping at the foot of a painstakingly engrossed Victorian lease.

Wycliffe picked up the statement, weighing the little wad of typescript in his hand. 'You came here of your own accord, Mr Bryce, and made this statement voluntarily. Are you willing to go on helping us?'

Gill looked at him as though he had taken leave of his senses; even Bryce seemed surprised.

'Aren't you going to charge me?'

'You can't be charged here; we shall take you over to Divisional Headquarters where you may be asked some more questions. I'm sure you will understand that there are several points to be cleared up. Of course, you are entitled to have your solicitor present.'

'No.'

'As you wish.' Wycliffe's manner was kindly but indifferent. Motioning Gill to follow him he went out and they walked a few paces on the wet grass.

'I don't get it!' Gill said.

'I want him stalled and I want you to go to Division with him to make sure they understand the position. He can be questioned, he can make another statement if he wants to, he can see anybody he wishes or he can spend a quiet night in a cell, but he's to be kept out of circulation – helping us with our inquiries.'

Gill was on the point of arguing but changed his mind.

Wycliffe had been tense and ill-at-ease, but when Gill and Bryce were driven off in the police car he seemed to relax. He walked over to his own van and stood in the central office staring out of the window into the early dusk.

'Can I help you, sir?' The duty constable watched him with concern.

Wycliffe turned as though surprised to find that he was not alone. 'What? No.' He filled his pipe and lit it. 'I'm going out.'

'Sir?'

Wycliffe looked at his watch. 'Ring Boslow and ask for Mr Sidney Bryce. Tell him that his brother, Matthew, has been here, that he has made a statement and that he is continuing to help us with our inquiries; he will not be home tonight.'

The constable scribbled rapidly.

'Got that?'

'Anything else, sir?'

'You can tell him, also, that I am on my way to see him,' Wycliffe went into his office and came out wearing a shabby fawn raincoat.

'I'll get you a car, sir.'

'No, I shall walk. You get on with your telephoning.'

He stood on the steps of the caravan in the drizzling rain, his coat collar turned up, his hands deep in the pockets. He set out, following the wharf upstream. The fair was hard at it, the bright lights mistily diffused. The ferry was at the slipway, its navigation lights burning. Wycliffe walked with head bent, a preoccupied, shabbily-dressed, middle-aged man in a hurry.

When he reached the beginning of the railway track he took to it and paced the sleepers with no apparent awareness of his surroundings. He left the line near the entrance to Boslow and walked up the drive between the dripping laurels.

There were no lights showing in the front of the house but when he rang, the door was opened almost at once by Sidney, looking

strained and anxious. 'I had just got in when your man telephoned . . .'

Wycliffe became aware for the first time that his mackintosh was
wet: it was dripping pools of water onto the floor.

'Let me take your coat . . .' Sidney held the mackintosh at arm's
length. 'What sort of statement has Matthew made?'

'A confession.'

'To murder?'

'To the killing of his wife and of Margaret Haynes.'

Sidney was distraught. 'I can't believe it! I must see him – where is
he?'

'He is at Divisional Headquarters. I was going to suggest that you
go over with Zel.'

'You think that Zel should go?'

'I think so, yes. Where is she?'

Bryce looked embarrassed. 'She's with Cousin Irene – Miss Bates,
our housekeeper.'

'Good! I want to see Miss Bates.'

'I hardly think that is possible. Apparently Matt told Irene something of what he intended to do and she's very upset; she's made
herself ill.'

'You mean that she's drunk.' There were times when Wycliffe
could be brutal.

'The worse for drink, certainly.'

'I still want to see her.'

'I don't think . . .' But Wycliffe was halfway up the stairs.

Irene's room was almost in darkness. Zel came from the direction
of the bedroom and whispered: 'She's asleep.' Wycliffe went to the
bedroom door, opened it and peered in. The room was very small
with a latticed window high in the wall. A brass-railed single bed, a
chest of drawers and a fireplace with a gas fire, a bamboo table near
the bed with a night-light already burning. The room stank of gin.
Wycliffe crept in and stood looking down at Irene. She was breathing heavily and she looked like an old woman. Her dentures were in a
glass on the table and without them her lips were pursed together as
though in a self-satisfied smile. He went back to her sitting-room
closing the bedroom door behind him. Zel was standing by the
window looking down into the yard.

'He told her?'

'So it seems. She took it badly.'

'And you?'

She turned to face him; in the near darkness her face was a pale blur. 'I want to talk to you; I wanted to this morning.'

'Is anything wrong?' Sidney was standing in the doorway. His futile question remained unanswered. Wycliffe went and switched on the light. Irene's cat jumped down from its chair, stretched, clawed the carpet, then padded out into the passage.

'I lied to you about what I saw on Thursday evening, the night my mother . . .'

'I know.'

He had never seen her in a dress before; it was of a green, silky material, patterned with black arabesques, and it made her a woman. She sat in one of the easy chairs, pulling her dress down over her long, straight thighs. She was pale with dark areas beneath her eyes.

Sidney hovered nervously. 'I don't think you should say anything to the chief superintendent, Zel . . . It's not that we have anything to hide but I am sure that we should consult . . .'

Wycliffe was standing by the window now, lighting his pipe. Sidney's protest died away and neither of them took the slightest notice.

'Your mother did not leave here alive on Thursday night, did she?'

'Is that what he told you?'

'Is it the truth?'

She nodded. 'Yes.'

Wycliffe puffed at his pipe to get it going. 'Before you say any more I should tell you that I know John Evans drove the car with your mother's body in it to Foundry House. I know also that it was your idea and that you went with him.'

The girl merely murmured, 'I see.' Complete acceptance.

Sidney was scandalized. 'But Wycliffe! You really can't . . . !'

'I must caution you . . .'

She listened to the formula with indifference.

'If all this is true, she did it to protect her father!' Sidney Bryce had interposed himself between Wycliffe and the girl as though to ward off a physical threat.

'Be quiet!' She might have been speaking to a child and Sidney looked at her in astonishment as though he were seeing her for the first time. She had her hands clasped round her knees and she was looking down into her lap as though she were ashamed. 'I want to tell you the truth. Everything happened as I told you up to the point when I saw my mother cross the yard and go into the garage.' She looked up quickly to meet Wycliffe's bland stare. 'I stood by the window. I suppose I was waiting to hear her open the big doors, start the car and drive away; but nothing happened. I waited for what seemed a long time . . . and still nothing. I was puzzled . . .'

'What did you do?'

'I couldn't think what she could be doing in there so I put on my dressing-gown and went downstairs to find out.' She stopped speaking.

'Well?'

'I went out to the garage and I found her lying on the floor between the car and the doors. She was dead. I could see . . . I could see where she had been hit and there was a piece of pipe lying beside her.'

'During the time you were looking out of the window you did not see your father?'

'No.'

'Nor afterwards?'

'No.'

'The main doors of the garage were still shut?'

'Yes.'

'Can they be opened from outside?'

'No: there is a bar across which holds both doors.' She was answering his questions in a low but distinct voice and she seemed composed.

'Go on.'

'I was distracted. I didn't know what to do.'

'You thought that your father had killed her?'

'You shouldn't answer that, Zel!'

She looked at her uncle as though surprised to find him still there, but she answered Wycliffe. 'It seemed the only explanation; they had been having rows.'

'What did you do?'

'I got dressed, then I ran down to John's place. Luckily I caught him just as he was coming back from Evening Class. I got him to come back with me.'

'To do what?'

She pressed her hands between her knees and hunched her shoulders. 'I hardly knew; I couldn't think clearly. All I wanted was to get her away from the house. John wouldn't help at first but I persuaded him . . . We got the body into the car and while we were doing it I thought of George's boathouse. Don't ask me why; I wasn't being logical – it just seemed a good idea . . .'

'You knew that your uncle would not be at home?'

'It wouldn't have mattered if he was; the boathouse is too far from the house. In any case he isn't usually home until very late.'

'So you persuaded John Evans to drive there and you went with him?'

'Of course; he wouldn't have known what to do otherwise. When we got there I made him help to get her body into the driver's seat, then we strapped her in and left.' She paused, staring at the floor for a long time. Wycliffe said nothing and she went on at last, 'You see, I thought she would be found there and they would think she had driven over to see George and somebody had attacked her.'

'You walked back to Boslow?'

'Yes. John was in a terrible state and I wasn't sure he wouldn't go to the police, so we stayed together a good while.'

'What about the piece of pipe?'

'The pipe? Oh, I wanted to get rid of that so I took it with me in the car and dropped it on a pile of scrap in a corner of the boat-house.'

Outside a rising wind blew rain against the windows. Sidney Bryce stood, shocked and bewildered, not knowing what to say or do.

'You did all this to protect your father?'

'Yes.'

'Then why tell me about it now?'

'Because it's useless now and last night he told me something that changed everything.' She seemed to expect a question but none came.

'Last night he told me that I am not his daughter. He thought that he had better tell me before someone else did.'

'Zel! My poor child!' Sidney's voice was anguished and he moved to the girl's side and put his arm round her protectively. She shook him off.

'Leave me alone, for God's sake!'

Poor Sidney; his world was crumbling. And yet, it seemed, he could be no more than a spectator.

Wycliffe was standing by the window holding his pipe which had gone out. She looked up at him, her voice brittle. 'Do you like riddles? I'm not my father's daughter, so who am I?'

Despite himself he was touched. 'I'm sorry.' The words seemed to have been forced from him.

She was picking at a loose thread in the hem of her dress. 'Sorry? Why? Because I am the result of dirty games between my mother and her half-brother? I expect that sort of thing happens all the time.'

This was too much for Sidney. He confronted Wycliffe. 'Half-brother? Does this mean that Morley . . . ?'

'Is my father – yes, he is,' Zel answered him. She turned to Wycliffe. 'You don't seem surprised.'

Wycliffe's blank stare never faltered. 'I knew.'

'How could you possibly know?'

'It's a long story.'

'Not as long as mine; it took me eighteen years.'

The house was silent. It seemed to be quite dark outside: the window of which the curtains remained undrawn was a rectangle of blackness. Wycliffe was oppressed by a sense of unreality: the girl herself, the events she described, the room with its depressing reminders of a woman who drank herself into a stupor because she was superfluous, and an awareness of other rooms in the house, rooms which were no more than refuges.

'Your father is at our Divisional Headquarters. Do you want to see him?'

'No.'

'I think you should.'

She looked at him and seemed to read something in his expression which made her change her mind. 'All right.'

'Your uncle will take you over.' He turned to Sidney, addressing him directly for the first time since they had come into the room. 'If you prefer it I will send for a police car.'

Sidney seemed to come alive abruptly. 'No, I'll take my own car.'

'I'll wait for you downstairs.' Wycliffe went slowly down the white staircase into the dimly-lit, cavernous hall. At the bottom of the stairs he turned towards Matthew's workroom, opened the door and switched on the light; the musty smell was overpowering. The room had undergone a transformation since the last time he had been in it and it was evident that Matthew had not expected to come back. The shelves had been stripped and the books sorted into heaps, there were large cardboard boxes labelled with lists of their contents and, on the table by the window, there was a large envelope addressed to Sidney and boldly endorsed: 'Instructions for the disposal of my books, models and papers.'

Wycliffe gave all this scant attention. He crossed the room to the french windows. They were secured by a bolt and a spring lock; then he left the room, switched off the light and shut the door behind him.

A minute or two later he was joined in the hall by Zel. 'He's gone to fetch his car.' She was wearing the green coat she had worn to the funeral and carrying a lizard-skin handbag.

'Will Miss Bates be all right on her own?'

'I suppose she'll sleep it off as usual.'

Sidney Bryce brought his car round to the front of the house. He made a great business of locking the front door while they waited on the gravel. Then he got into his car with Zel beside him. 'Can we give you a lift back to town?'

'Thanks, I'll walk.'

The rain had stopped and the rising wind stirred the branches of the elms so that crisp, papery leaves fluttered down like pale moths.

11

When the tail-lights of Sidney's car had disappeared he went to the back of the house and let himself in through the french window to Matthew's room. Once inside he made for the kitchen. It was a barn of a place which had not been modernized or even thoroughly cleaned in thirty years. He looked in the refrigerator, a monster of white enamelled metal and varnished wood. It was empty except for the remains of a ham and a bottle of white wine which had been opened. He cut himself some ham, found a loaf of bread in the larder, and ate the ham with dry bread, sitting on a corner of the kitchen table. Probably because he had not eaten for several hours, he enjoyed it. He thought of Bellings and smiled to himself. He considered making tea or coffee. There was a kettle on the gas cooker but when he tried to light the ring he found that the gas had been turned off at the main. He washed down his food with the white wine, over-chilled and almost tasteless.

He was in for a long vigil, but the prospect did not depress him. In earlier days he had kept observation on countless occasions, often for seven or eight hours at a stretch and once for seventeen hours without relief. He rather liked the long periods of enforced inactivity coupled with the need to remain alert. One noticed things which normally escaped attention, sounds, smells, the shapes of buildings, the profile of roofs. One became aware of subtle rhythms in the progress of a night and of a unique succession in every dawn. There was time to think.

Sidney Bryce and Zel must have reached Divisional Head-quarters. Wycliffe wondered what they had said to each other on the way. Probably very little. Sidney would have made several attempts, but Zel had almost certainly rebuffed him, brusquely, even cruelly. Would her interview with Matthew take place with Sidney looking on? Probably; they would need his presence to guard their tongues. Their only true communication would be through looks, small gestures and words which did not mean what they seemed to say.

He was moving round the house with a freedom which could only come from the certain knowledge that he would not be disturbed. He had plenty of time. He was tempted to light his pipe, but he knew that for the non-smoker fresh tobacco smoke is as salutary as a shout. First he went to Cousin Irene's room. He crept through the sitting-room and in to her almost airless little bedroom. She was still deeply asleep but her breathing was quieter. The yellow light seemed to blanch her features.

Opposite her sitting-rooms across the passage, was a linen cupboard. He opened the door and swept the interior with the beam of his pocket torch. There was a kitchen chair, probably used to get linen down from the higher shelves. It might be useful later. He worked his way along the main corridor, looking in all the rooms, and found Matthew's bedroom. It was small and looked over the yard. There was a single bed, a bookcase, a chair and sisal matting on the floor. He opened the window and put his head out; he could smell the sea and hear the music of the fairground carried on the wind.

It was after midnight when he heard Sidney's car. It stopped by the garages at the back and, listening, he could follow the business of putting the car away and shutting the garage doors. He heard footsteps in the yard but no voices; then the back door was unlocked and they were in the kitchen. A moment or two later they came out into the hall, the staircase lights were switched on and Wycliffe retreated down the passage to his linen cupboard.

'He didn't seem too upset.' Sidney's voice.

There was no reply.

'Try not to dwell on it, Zel.'

Still no answer.

'Would you like one of my tablets to help you sleep?'

'No.'

'Goodnight, Zel.'

'Goodnight.'

He heard Zel go up the stairs to her attic and the lights were switched off. The darkness seemed absolute. He sat on his chair with the door of the cupboard open and it was not long before he could make out the foreshortened rectangle of the door and then, beyond it, the gleam of the glass knob on Irene's door across the way. He settled down to wait.

There were vague, indefinable sounds of movement; a lavatory was flushed and for some time after that water gurgled through the plumbing. Then there was silence. As the darkness had seemed absolute at first, so did the silence, but it was not long before the house seemed to be full of sounds, minute crepitations, creaks and even small thuds and squeaks. Rats? More than once he was almost convinced that someone was creeping stealthily down the corridor but nobody passed between him and the dimly reflective knob on Irene's door. Then something brushed silently against his legs and he barely suppressed an exclamation. Irene's cat. It mewed plaintively then moved off.

He would have given a great deal for a smoke but otherwise he was content. It seemed that the wind had dropped again; probably it was raining. He looked at the luminous dial of his watch: one o'clock. He shifted into a more comfortable position and the chair creaked horribly. His eyes remained fixed on the door across the passage, almost hypnotized by the dull gleam of the glass knob. The knob seemed, suddenly, to change its position; it appeared to be staring down at him like a malevolent eye. He must have lost his sense of orientation in the instant of dozing off and he pulled himself together with a convulsive start. It was then that he caught the first whiff of gas. At first he thought that he had been mistaken; then he smelt it again, insidious and persistent. In a single movement he was across the passage and in Irene's sitting-room. He switched on the light, not caring now. The smell of gas was definitely stronger – the gas-fire in her bedroom! Yet no-one could have got into her room without him seeing. Or could they? He blundered into the bedroom and there the smell was much stronger, though still not overpowering. He could hear the gentle hiss of escaping gas. He stooped, turned off the tap on the fire and the hissing ceased.

He went to the window, struggled with it for a moment, then got it open so that the chilly night air flooded the little box of a room. Cousin Irene stirred and made some inarticulate sound. He went to the bed and hoisted her on to his shoulder, carried her into the next room and lowered her into one of the armchairs, then threw open the big window until the sashes met. When he turned back to Irene she

491

was blinking at him, dazzled by the light. He went back to her bedroom, gathered up an armful of bedding and tucked her up in the chair. Then he extracted an arm from the bundle and took her pulse. It was slow but not, he thought, dangerously so. All the same . . .

He went down the passage, knocked on Sidney's door, opened it and went into his sitting-room.

'What is it?' Sidney stood in the doorway of his bedroom, pulling on a dressing-gown over silk pyjamas. 'Wycliffe! What are you doing here?'

Wycliffe told him what had happened. He was like a man who wonders from what direction the next blow will come.

'Will she . . . ?'

'She'll be all right. I want you to stay with her while I telephone.'

He went downstairs to the telephone and spoke to the duty officer telling him to send the police surgeon and a WPC. 'And let Mr Gill know.'

When he returned to Irene's room she was vomiting into a basin held in Sidney's trembling hands. Zel arrived and stood in the doorway. 'What's happened? What's the matter with her?'

Wycliffe told her. 'The doctor will be here soon.'

'Will she be all right?'

'She'll probably have nothing worse than a hangover in the morning, and she must be used to that.' He turned to Sidney and asked him to fill a hot-water bottle.

'Zel will do that.'

'I need her here.'

Sidney went.

Zel helped him to get Cousin Irene back to bed and to tuck her in. The gas had cleared and they were able to shut the windows.

'She must have tried to kill herself.'

Wycliffe said nothing. Sidney came back with a hot-water bottle. 'She'll be all right now until the doctor comes.'

As they stood by her bed Irene opened her eyes and looked at them. The vacant stare resolved itself into fright and she tried to sit up, shouting, 'No, no, I won't!' Wycliffe was able to calm her and soon she was sleeping again.

'I'll stay with her,' Zel said.

'No, I want to talk to you.' Wycliffe took her arm and led her into her mother's sitting-room. Sidney followed, hesitantly, as though he

492

half expected to be sent away. It was chilly and Wycliffe switched on the electric fire. 'Sit down.'

She sat in one of the low chairs with orange cushions and pulled her dressing-gown over her knees. She looked very young. 'I knew she was upset but I never thought she would try to kill herself.'

'When you came in with your uncle, why did you turn the gas on at the main?'

Sidney was standing behind Zel's chair, his hands gripping the back. 'What are you talking about? I don't understand how you came to be here. Obviously it's fortunate that you were, but I still think you owe us an explanation . . .'

Wycliffe ignored him.

She swept the soft black hair back from her face. 'I turned the gas off; we always turn it off at night.'

'The gas was already off. You turned it on.'

She frowned. 'I see what you're getting at. I suppose it's possible I made a mistake. If it was off already and she'd left her fire turned on . . .'

'My God, Wycliffe, even if that's what happened, you can't blame the poor child for that – not after all she's been through!'

Wycliffe was standing on the hearth-rug, looking down at the girl. He did not even look up at Sidney's interruption. 'It was no mistake. Before you left with your uncle you had turned the gas off at the main and the tap on in Miss Bates' bedroom; then, when you came back, you turned on the main before going to bed.'

'Why should I do that?' She asked the question in a level voice without a trace of emotion or fear.

'Because you wanted to kill Irene Bates.'

'What?' Sidney bleated.

'You were afraid that she was ready to tell me what she had seen from her window on the night your mother was killed. Fortunately, in the morning, she will still be able to do so.'

She was perfectly calm; in fact he noticed that her hands, which had been clenched in her lap, now relaxed.

They heard the drone of a car engine in the distance, then the sound of a car in the drive and the screech of wheels braked on gravel.

'They've arrived,' Wycliffe said.

★

493

He was driven to Divisional Headquarters in a police car. Gill sat in front with the driver. Wycliffe and WPC Rowse were in the back with Zel between them. They were expected. An office was put at Wycliffe's disposal and he had arranged to talk to Matthew Bryce before taking the case any further.

He sat with Gill in his office, smoking and waiting. The clock on the wall, with Roman numerals under its fly-blown glass, showed five minutes past three. The internal telephone rang and Gill answered it.

'Is he dead? . . . Have you sent for a doctor?' A longish interval, then, 'You've got good reason to be!' He slammed down the receiver. 'That was Clark, the duty officer. Matthew Bryce has killed himself – slashed his wrists. When they went to fetch him they found him on the floor of his cell – dead.'

'They've got a doctor?'

'Apparently the police surgeon was in the building on a drunk-in-charge case. Bryce is dead all right. Incompetent bastards! Clark says he's worried; I told him, he's got reason to be.'

'Bryce wasn't a prisoner; he was here voluntarily.'

'A fat lot of good that will do us in the bloody press. In any case, you'd think they'd have kept an eye on him. A man doesn't die that way in five minutes.'

They went downstairs to the cells, a short, tiled passage with two cubicles opening off and security doors. On the floor of one of them Matthew Bryce lay in a pool of his own blood. A young man in a raincoat stood by with Inspector Clark, the duty officer. Clark was near retirement, a copper of the old school, with close-cropped hair and a reassuringly massive bulk. 'Chief Detective Superintendent Wycliffe, Dr Oates, our police surgeon.'

Wycliffe looked down at the dead man. 'How long do you think, doctor?'

'Since he did it? Quite a while. At a guess, I should say three or four hours.'

'His brother and his daughter must have been here at eleven. How long since he was last seen?'

Inspector Clark spoke as though he were giving evidence. 'His visitors left at 11.15, sir. He then said that he would like to settle down for the night. A constable got him a glass of hot milk from the canteen and he was brought down here. It was explained to him that

494

he was here of his own accord and that he was not under any form of restraint. The door of the cell was not locked.' The inspector's anxiety to cover himself irritated Wycliffe, but with an inevitable inquiry ahead, who could blame him?

'So your men saw nothing of him from, say, 11.30 until – until when?'

Clark hesitated. 'Until ten minutes ago, sir, when the sergeant went to tell him you wanted to talk to him.'

Wycliffe looked at the dead man. Although he had known him for such a short time he felt a bond of sympathy. He wished that the doctor had closed the eyes. The good one, staring upwards, was more disquieting than the damaged one, which looked much as it had done in life.

'He left this.' The inspector held out a sheet of paper torn from a pocket diary. It must have been found on the floor for it was stained with blood. On it a message written in pencil:

'I am too much of a coward to face the consequences.'

'What did he use to cut his wrists?'

'Razor blade, sir. We had no right to search him.'

'Save the excuses, Inspector!' Wycliffe snapped.

'Reasons, sir, not excuses.'

'There was no-one in the other cell?'

'No, these are new. There's a drunk in the old block; that was why we put him in here.'

So Matthew Bryce had not lived long enough to know that his self-sacrifice would go for nothing. Wycliffe turned away. 'Send the girl upstairs to me.'

She came accompanied by a policewoman. She was pale but composed. Her face looked a little thinner, her eyes a little larger; like the rest of them she must be very tired. She glanced at Gill and Wycliffe in turn and took her seat. The policewoman stood by the door.

'I have bad news for you, Zel.'

She gave no sign that she had heard.

'Your father – Matthew Bryce . . .'

'What about him?'

'He has taken his own life; he left this note.'

She took the note, read it, and handed it back with no visible sign of emotion.

Wycliffe waited for her to speak but she said nothing. She had presumably noticed that the paper was stained with blood, but she did not even ask how he had died.

'I'm sorry. If you go with the policewoman she will see that you have a chance to get some sleep.'

'Won't you question me?'

'That can wait.'

'No.'

'You want to make a statement?'

'If that's what you call it.'

Wycliffe cautioned her.

'I killed my mother and Margaret Haynes. I tried to kill Cousin Irene.'

It is strange that more and more of the drama of our lives seems to be played out in dingy offices in front of officials.

'You want to tell me about it?'

'Yes.'

At a sign from Wycliffe the policewoman came to the table and prepared to take notes.

'Why are you so anxious to tell me now? You tried to kill Miss Bates because you thought that she might give you away.'

She shrugged. 'But you found out. I knew that you would, sooner or later; it was only a question of time.'

Gill lit one of his cheroots. 'You expected to be found out?'

'I'm not a fool.'

'Then why . . . ?'

She shifted irritably in her chair. 'I wanted to make them suffer – all of them.'

'All right, go on.'

The institutional cream paint on the walls was peeling in places; the lamp, suspended by a long flex, cast only a small circle of bright light, so that much of the room was in shadow. Outside the streets of the town were silent and deserted; only occasionally a car sounded a long way off, drew nearer, then seemed to rush past the police station. WPC Rowse recorded the girl's statement, her head bent over her book, her blonde hair shining in the light.

'It was Monday when I decided what I would do. We were having supper and they had started to quarrel. I got up and walked out.

496

They must have thought I had gone to my room; but I listened outside the door.'

Wycliffe had the picture in his mind. The gloomy dining-room, the only common ground in the house, no-man's-land. Sidney could not have been there; they would not have quarrelled in front of him. But Irene was there, a nonentity, of no more account than the furniture.

'She was shouting at him, as usual; he said nothing or almost nothing. She was practically screaming with temper. "You've given me nothing! Nothing! Do you understand? Even your precious Zel is another man's bastard!"' She repeated her mother's words in a dry voice more effective than emotion would have been.

'He said something I couldn't hear and she laughed. "If you don't believe me, ask Clement; he's been trying to forget for nearly twenty years that he fathered that kid, but he hasn't succeeded yet."' She broke off, then added, 'She knew how to hurt him.' But there was no compassion in her voice. She coughed and put her hand to her neck. 'My throat is dry.'

'Would you like something to drink?'

She nodded.

'Coffee?'

'If you like.'

Wycliffe picked up the telephone and asked for coffee to be sent up from the canteen.

In twenty-five years of police work he had never felt so inadequate or so reluctant to follow a case through to its conclusion. On the way over in the police car she had spoken once.

'When will it be?'

'When will what be?'

'My trial.'

She had asked the question almost as though it were some treat that she was looking forward to and he had answered her harshly. 'You haven't been charged with any crime yet!' She seemed indifferent to her fate; perhaps, more accurately, unaware that she was seriously threatened. He was worried and puzzled by her attitude.

He was looking at her with his professional, blank expression, reluctant to admit, even to himself, that he felt guiltily protective towards her, this girl who had killed two people and tried to kill a third. He would not have felt the same about a man. In this he was unlike Gill. Apart from a passing regret that she was not available to sleep with, the chief inspector's attitude was probably the same as it would have been to anyone else about to be charged with murder, old or young, male or female, pretty or plain. Gill's utilitarian attitude to women made it easier for him. Wycliffe was a romantic; Gill was the better policeman.

A constable arrived with coffee and biscuits.

Wycliffe continued to watch her while she sipped her coffee and nibbled a biscuit, her features calm and, apparently, unconcerned. Had she any idea of what lay before her? The inescapable humiliations of prison life? Her fellow prisoners – would they disgust her? Probably; until with the passage of years she was no longer capable of experiencing disgust or humiliation. Then, when they let her out, still a young woman, would she be like certain other women Wycliffe had known – women broken in spirit, with grey minds, slow-speaking, slow-moving, emotionally castrated.

He thought not. She was made of sterner stuff. For her, prison might be a stage on which she could dramatize herself to impress her fellow prisoners, less intelligent than she. She might tell them her story, but not all at once, letting it drop, little by little, embroidering the theme and so creating her own legend.

Gill waited for Wycliffe to resume the questioning and, when he did not, carried on himself. 'Was that why you killed your mother – because of what you overheard?'

Once more she brushed her hair clear of her face. 'What did it matter to me which of them was my father? She was still my mother.'

'But I don't understand why you had to kill her. At eighteen you are an adult; you can do as you like and your father and uncle would have seen that you wanted for nothing.'

Her dark eyes regarded him. 'You don't understand a thing. I wanted to get back at them almost as much as at her.' For the first time there was anger in her voice.

'Why?'

She made a contemptuous gesture. 'You've seen them! You've seen what they're like!' She looked from Gill to Wycliffe and back again. Never once did her eyes rest on the girl who was writing her words in a book.

By painstaking questions Gill took her through the events of Thursday night. She answered his questions glibly, mostly with indifference, occasionally with impatience. Her answers filled several pages of the policewoman's notebook. Wycliffe sat through it all without a word. His silent presence was beginning to generate a new tension, and from time to time Gill glanced at him, giving him the chance, inviting him to take over. Wycliffe seemed not to notice. He continued to sit, slumped in his chair, staring at the girl with eyes which never wavered. Several times Zel looked at him; she must have wondered why he looked at her with such an unremitting gaze yet never spoke.

He was still thinking about what might happen to her. It was possible that she would not be sent to prison; her lawyers, with the help of their headshrinkers, would put up a fight. Perhaps they would be right.

His mind went back to the morning when he had first heard of the Bryces. Four, nearly five days ago. It seemed much longer. He had been reading a book on psychopathology and he had made some notes.

'The psychopath appears to be wholly indifferent to the opinions of others, even to their manifest and threatening hostility . . .'

Gill ploughed on. 'When did you realize that Irene Bates had been watching from her window and that she had seen you and not your father go into the garage before your mother?'

She was casual. 'I suppose I ought to have known it all along; she sits in that room with the curtains back, sewing, and she never misses a thing. You get so used to her spying that you forget.'

Forget that she is not part of the furniture.

'After she heard about Margaret Haynes she started looking at me in a queer sort of way. I could tell that she was frightened of me, then I knew.'

'What did you do?'

'Nothing. I knew she wouldn't do anything unless my . . .' She broke off.

'Unless your father was involved?'

'Yes.'

'She was very fond of your father?'

'I suppose so.'

'And when he made his statement to us you knew you had to do something. Time was short – you were almost too late – but, luckily for you, when Mr Wycliffe came to question her she was too drunk.'

499

She did not speak.

'So you made your impromptu plan and if all had gone well, by the morning, this morning, Cousin Irene would have been dead. There would have been an inquest and the coroner would have dribbled on about your aunt being depressed because of the family tragedy – sympathy with the relatives and a nice tidy funeral.'

She was indifferent. 'I suppose so.' She was playing with the spoon in her coffee cup, moving the handle round the rim with the tip of one finger. Gill watched her for a while.

'What about Margaret Haynes?'

'What about her?'

'She was a friend of yours, wasn't she?'

'No.' She continued to play with her spoon and did not raise her eyes. 'She rang me early that morning and asked me to meet her somewhere. I could tell she knew something . . .'

'What did she want?'

'She wanted to tell me that she had seen me coming out of the boathouse with John Evans – that she knew.'

'Was that all?'

'She said that she was going to make a statement to the police and that she would tell them what she had seen.'

'Unless what?'

She was slow in answering, staring down at her empty cup. 'She wanted to make sure that George was kept out of it; she seemed to think the police believed he had killed my mother.'

'She was warning you?'

'You could call it that.'

'And you killed her.'

She had resumed playing with her spoon, rotating it round and round so that it made a monotonous grating sound. 'She asked for it.'

'You hit her more than once?'

'I had to. It didn't work like the first time; she just lay there groaning.' She looked up suddenly, facing Gill. 'I had some loose change in the pocket of my coat with a handkerchief. I pulled out the handkerchief so that the money was scattered on the ground. She stooped to help pick it up and I hit her with the piece of pipe. I suppose I didn't hit hard enough.'

'You had brought the pipe with you?'

500

'In my sleeve.'

'You killed her because she threatened you, is that it?'

She made an irritable movement which knocked over her cup so that the dregs spilled into the saucer. 'I've told you!'

Wycliffe stood up, flexing his knees to rid them of stiffness. The others looked at him expectantly, but he said nothing and moved away from the table, out of the circle of light, to stand by the window.

It was not raining but the wind swept through the town in sudden gusts, rocking the sign-boards and sending litter scurrying before it. The street lamps on their high swan-necks swayed slightly, changing the pattern of shadows on the shop-fronts and on the road. Wycliffe lit his pipe. Gill, no doubt casting uneasy glances over his shoulder, went on with the questioning; the policewoman wrote it all in her book.

The clock on the wall showed ten minutes after four.

'He is blind to the consequences, even to himself, of his own aggression . . . unable to grasp the idea that his violence may recoil . . . He is totally unable to identify himself with any other person . . .'

Wycliffe tried to understand. Violence always shocked him, though it was so often the raw material of his work, but cold violence aroused in him a revulsion which he found difficult to control. He did not want to believe that it was possible for this girl . . . Zel was about the same age as his daughter, Ruth. Without returning to the table, cutting across her answer to one of Jimmy Gill's questions, he asked, 'Did you have sex with John Evans?'

'What has that got to do with it?'

'He says that you did not.'

'He should know.'

Gill looked at him in surprise. The little policewoman, her blonde head bent over her book, wrote down questions and answers.

'Are you a virgin?'

'No.'

'Who, then? George?'

'Perhaps.'

Wycliffe came back to the table and seated himself once more opposite the girl. He took his time and during that time nobody else seemed to move a muscle. 'Look at me.'

She raised her eyes and looked at him without flinching, but it was evident that she was aware of the new element of stress. Wycliffe looked into her eyes, even leaning across the table as though to make closer contact.

'Why did you tell your father that George had tried to seduce you?'

'Because it was true.'

'It was a lie!'

'Why should I lie?'

'I suppose it was flattering to your pride to pretend that a man of the world like George was attracted to you. In any case you were jealous of your mother. It is not unusual.'

She mustered some indignation. 'Are you saying . . . ?'

Wycliffe went on as though she had not spoken. 'Although George Bryce did his best to let you down lightly, your pride was hurt – and he wasn't going to get away with that; he had to go.' Wycliffe stopped to relight his pipe but he continued to watch her over the flame of the match. 'The psychiatrists will spend a lot of time and a lot of somebody's money trying to find out what they will call your *real* reasons for what you did. They will probably decide that you are emotionally retarded.' He spoke between puffs at his pipe. 'That sounds innocent enough, but three people have died.' He blew out the match and dropped it into the tin lid which served as an ashtray. 'You are going to be the centre of attraction for a long time, Zel. You will enjoy that. Nobody will spare a thought for the silly woman who had the misfortune to become your mother and who died thirty or forty years too soon. Nobody – or nobody who matters – will trouble themselves about the girl – the girl of your own age whom you clubbed to death because she had the impudence to get into bed with a man who wouldn't have you . . .'

He stopped speaking and sat back in his chair. She was drawing her forefinger repeatedly across the shiny table-top and studying the slight smears which it made.

'Of course, in the end, they will put you away for quite a long time and people will forget about you.'

She did not look up.

'Take her away.'

The policewoman sprang to life. Zel looked up in surprise. 'Have you finished?'

'*The psychopath is never a depressive; his hatred is always outwardly*

502

directed . . . He has no problem of self-justification and is untroubled by feelings of guilt . . .'

It was broad daylight when Wycliffe arrived back at his hotel. A damp breeze ruffled the surface of the estuary and overhead grey clouds scurried inland. He felt sick at heart. The hotel was not yet awake and he let himself in with the pass-key they had given him. On an impulse he went into the telephone booth in the lobby and dialled his home number. After a brief interval his wife's voice came sleepily. 'My husband is away . . .'

'I know.'

'Charles! Is something wrong?'

'Nothing. Is Ruth there?' Ruth was his daughter.

'Of course! She's in bed asleep; it's only six o'clock.'

Of course.

'What's the matter, Charles?'

What could he say?

The girl was a mental case; there could be no other explanation . . .

Wycliffe and Death in a Salubrious Place

To David Dearlove
in appreciation of his kindness
in allowing me to use
one of his songs

1

Sylvie died without knowing why. In the instant when she had realized his intention and before the blow fell, when it was already too late to make the smallest effort to escape, she had experienced not only a paralysing fear but profound astonishment. It is said of some who die by violence that their features express neither horror nor fear but only intense surprise. Had it been possible to discern any expression on the battered face of the girl it might well have been one of blank incredulity. She died because she had not listened, because she was indifferent.

For twenty minutes the man had walked beside her when, above all else, she wanted to be alone. With the masochistic self-indulgence of deeply injured pride she wanted only to relive the moment, probe the wound, extract the last scrap of pain and humiliation from the experience. But she had not wanted to die. Even in the depths of her misery a small voice whispered that it would pass. A tiny part of her mind was beginning to make healing adjustments; even, perhaps, to skirmish with the practical problems which would now confront her. At heart, she was a realist.

It was late. Overhead, in a cloudless sky, the stars were brilliant points of cold light. Nearer the horizon they twinkled through thickening mists. The landscape in the starlight was pale, almost bleached.

They had climbed the slope out of the valley. Salubrious Place was behind them, two or three lights, orange rectangles, tawdry compared with the pure light of the stars. Without thinking about it she saw him stoop and pick up a sort of bar with a loop at one end. The area around the quarry was littered with odds and ends of scrap from the machinery which had once been used to work it. He liked to have something in his hand when he walked over the downs. Usually it was a stick and he would cut and slash at the brambles bordering the path like a destructive small boy.

509

They walked, picking their way round the big stones, avoiding the pot-holes but they saw almost nothing, their consciousness was not involved. His voice punctuated the silence. Intense, soft, sometimes stung to anger by her failure to respond. To her, with her present preoccupation, it was no more demanding of attention than the sound of waves breaking lazily on the beach or the mournful tolling of the bell-buoy out to sea.

Then, suddenly, her attention was arrested, but it was too late, she did not even raise a hand to ward off the blow. She crumpled. It is possible that he delivered another blow while she lay on the ground but afterwards he could not remember. Perhaps he stood over her for a time, certainly he was stunned. Then he heard voices and laughter, for a moment he could not remember where he was or what had happened, it was like waking from a vivid dream. But memory came flooding back and he realized that he still held the iron bar with its looped end. He threw it away from him with all the energy he could muster and heard it clatter, metal against metal; perhaps it had fallen into the quarry, striking one of the rusting, broken trucks which were strewn over the quarry floor among the boulders. So much the better. He rubbed his hand vigorously against his jacket.

The voices were getting closer; they had finished their session at the Barn and were on their way home. In a couple of minutes they would be with him. He stooped and lifted Sylvie's body. It was a struggle. Her weight surprised and dismayed him. For a moment he swayed and almost fell with her but he managed to stumble away from the track through a gap in the brambles and gorse. In a small clearing he rested, trying to control his breathing and the beating of his heart. They were level with him now, shouting, laughing absurdly, jostling each other. Ten yards away but more remote than the mountains of the moon. Their footsteps and their voices died away at last.

He had another ten or fifteen yards to go. For the first time he noticed the mist drifting in from the sea, eddying, swirling, dispersing. He must try again. He put out his hand and touched a warm stickiness which made him want to vomit. He had been careful not to look at her head and face, now, accidentally, he had touched. He rubbed his hand on the short turf. He had carried her so that her head was well away from his clothing but it was still possible . . . He

510

took off his jacket and placed it carefully on the ground then he bent to lift her once more. He would have dragged her body to the quarry but already his instinct for self-preservation was at work. If he could get her to the quarry without leaving too many traces her death might be put down to accident. He knew the weather in the islands, this mist would thicken to fog in a short while and it might then be supposed that she had lost her way.

Another effort which taxed his strength to the limit and he had her body more or less securely over his shoulder. He tottered the distance to the quarry edge, dropped her to the ground for fear of being carried over with her. He had a dread of heights. With his foot, he gently propelled her body to the very edge then kicked vigorously. It seemed a long time before he heard a splash and a muffled thud. She had fallen in the water and soft mud which lay at the foot of the quarry face.

He walked back to where he had left his jacket but before putting it on he took off his shirt and rolled it inside out, just in case. His jacket felt cold and damp against his naked body. He was trembling and shivering at the same time.

All through the summer night the islands had been blanketed in sea fog and measured bleats of the signals on Temple Rock and on Ship Island had punctuated the moist silence, blending in a complex rhythm. Now it was full daylight, a diffused opalescent brilliance from no apparent source revealing a tiny world of gorse and bracken.

'She'll clear directly.'

Two men in reefer jackets and sea boots trudged along a stony track.

'We're wasting our time, Matt, until she clears a bit.' He spoke almost pleadingly but the other man seemed not to hear.

The two men represented contrasted island types: Matthew Eva, thickset, powerful, blond, with thinning, curly hair and a ruddy complexion; Jack Bishop, thin, small-boned, dark and sallow. The lion and the jackal.

'There's nothing can have happened to her, Matt. She'll have lost her way in the fog and decided to sit it out somewhere. Your Sylvie's a sensible girl, got her head screwed on. She'll be on her way home by now.'

'You reckon?' Matt was cynical, not consoled.

Moisture stood out in little beads on their jackets and glistened on their features like sweat.

Suddenly, magically, the curtain of mist lifted and their range of vision increased from a few yards to a mile or more. They could see the rough moorland sloping away to the sea on their left and to their right, Carngluze, a rugged outcrop of granite, the highest point in the islands, emerged spectrally from the mist and was lost again.

'There!' Jack Bishop said as though he had contrived the miracle himself.

For more than an hour they quartered the rough ground. The mist still hid the carn and there was a grey, impenetrable wall not far offshore. There was no sign of Morvyl or Biddock nor any hint of the Western Rocks. From time to time they stopped and shouted, their voices small, 'Sylvie! Sylvie!'

'We'd best get back and if she isn't home we can get together a party and make a proper search . . .'

'I'm going to look in the quarry.'

'The quarry? She wouldn't have had any call to go near the quarry.'

But Matt was already ploughing through a thicket of gorse.

The quarry had been cut and blasted out of the side of the carn to provide material for almost all the buildings on the island which antedated the era of the concrete block. Now it was deserted with the rusty stanchions of a derrick, a giant winch and the corroding shell of a steam boiler, as monuments to an age that was gone.

The two men stood on the lip of the quarry with the granite face dropping sheer for thirty or forty feet below them. At the bottom brambles grew among the rusting bogies of overturned tram-trucks and, nearer the face, there was a pool of grey-green water fringed with some kind of rush.

'There she is.' Matt spoke seemingly without surprise or emotion as though he had only found what he expected to find.

A girl in a red wet-look mackintosh, her body curiously twisted, was lying in the rushes, her face in the water, her blonde hair floating like weeds. 'My God!' Jack Bishop whispered.

They followed round the edge of the quarry to where a tram-track ran down a steep slope to the floor. Their sea boots slipped and slithered on loose gravel and once they were down they had to scramble over the bramble-covered debris of granite blocks and scrap iron which littered the ground. When they bent over the girl they were standing in several inches of soft grey mud. They lifted her and carried her clear of the rushes then laid her on a granite slab which was more or less flat.

Matthew Eva looked down at his daughter, his china-blue eyes hard and cold. There could be no possible doubt that she was dead, the frontal bones of the skull and her facial bones had been splintered inwards like the cracked shell of an egg.

It was not the first time the two men had encountered violent death; wrecks, drownings and cliff falls marked the calendar of the islands. All the same . . .

She was blond, like her father, and her skin, where it was undamaged, was delicate and translucent. Under her mackintosh she wore a white blouse and a tartan pinafore dress. Jack Bishop looked from her to the rim of the quarry and back again finding no words for the emotion he felt. All he could say was, 'She must've mistook her way in the fog and just walked over . . .'

'Don't give me that!' The intensity of anger in Matt's voice frightened him. 'You fetch Freddie Jordan, I'm stopping here.' Freddie Jordan was a sergeant of police, the law in the islands.

The sun was winning the battle overhead and by the time Bishop got to the top of the ramp he was sweating. He glanced back once and saw that Matt had covered his daughter's body with his coat. It was two miles to the town and when he reached the slopes above the bay the church bell was tolling for Holy Communion. Eight o'clock. Sunday morning.

A perfect crescent of sand stretched for a mile beyond the town, white in the sun; the sprawl of grey houses and the patchwork of lichen-covered roofs reached up the hill towards him.

By the time Sylvie's body had been brought in and laid in the mortuary the church bells were pealing for the ten-thirty service and the pleasure boats were loading with trippers for the off-islands.

The little grey, granite police station was on the waterfront and Sergeant Jordan lived in the house next door. With the help of two constables he policed the islands under the direction of a sub-divisional headquarters on the mainland. He was an islander and, on the whole, he had a soft billet. A spot of illicit salvage, a few domestics, petty thieving, and the occasional punch-up on the quay.

'My girl was murdered.'

Jordan ran his hand over his thinning and greying hair. 'You can't say that, Matt, you heard what Dr Ross . . .'

'To hell with Ross!' Matthew Eva leaned across the sergeant's desk to make his point. 'Did you see my girl's face and head?'

Jordan nodded.

'Forty feet at most that quarry is, from top to bottom, and a quagmire to fall on, soft as a feather bed . . .' He broke off as a new thought struck him, his voice fell. 'You saw my wife when they picked her up?'

Jordan nodded once more. 'I saw her.'

'Ninety feet off Cligga Head and solid rock below. Did she look like Sylvie?'

'No, Matt, she didn't, but you know as well as I do no two cases are alike. We've seen a few falls between us . . .'

'Apart from anything else,' Eva went on, ignoring the sergeant, 'is it likely that the same accident would happen to two members of the same family – mother and daughter, inside two years?' His voice had become husky with fresh grief and the sergeant spoke sympathetically.

'Believe me, Matt, you have the sympathy of everybody in the islands and from nobody more than me. There will be a full investigation. I've reported to my bosses and they'll see to that, but there's nothing more I can do.'

Eva wore no jacket and his shirt sleeves were rolled up; his massive freckled arms, covered with golden hairs, rested on the desk. He tapped the desk with a broad forefinger. 'You know as well as I do that Sylvie was murdered and that Peters killed her. If you don't do something about that, I will.'

The sergeant was provoked, he stood up. 'If I were you, Matt, I should guard my tongue; that sort of talk will do you no good and it won't bring Sylvie back. As to threats, don't force my hand. If you put a foot out of line I shall have to run you in.' His voice softened. 'Don't be a fool! We've got to do our job according to the book but that doesn't mean that it won't be done.'

Matt Eva stood up also and the two men faced each other across the desk. Eva was a head shorter than the sergeant but his was the more impressive figure. 'If that's how you want it . . .'

Jordan remained cool. 'That's how it's going to be, Matt.'

Eva snatched up his coat from a chair, slung it over his shoulder and stalked through the outer office on to the quay, leaving the door open. He stood for a moment, hesitating in the sunshine, then made off along the wharf. Once he had an idea in his head there was no shifting it. A stubborn man, a good friend and a bad enemy, liable to fits of violent temper.

The pleasure boats were on their various ways to the off-islands. A few tourists strolled in the sun, family groups trudged along with their packed lunches in the direction of the beach. M. V. *Islander* was at her berth unloading mixed cargo with her own derricks. Like any other fine Sunday in summer.

And, as on other off-duty Sundays, at twelve o'clock Matthew went into the Seymour Arms, though today he stole in furtively, feeling that what had happened should have separated him from his routine, but unable to face the aching loneliness of his empty house.

Somehow, over the years, the locals had kept the public bar of the Seymour for themselves. Through the small archway behind the bar it was possible to catch a glimpse of floral dresses and shirts, of red, peeling faces and shoulders in the saloon. And laughter and shouting provided a clamorous background to the decorous silences in the public.

Jack Bishop was playing cribbage with Charlie Martin and half a dozen other men sat on the wooden benches round the walls. They looked up as Matthew came in and acknowledged him without a word. He went to the bar, collected his drink, and took his usual seat by the window. They all knew, of course, but it would be some time before the subject was broached.

Charlie Martin was a power in the islands, he was chairman of the boat syndicate and he owned a lot of property in the island and on Morvyl. He was seventy-five, turned the scales at two hundred and fifty pounds and had the silky white hair and flowing moustaches of a biblical patriarch as well as the manner to go with them. He studied his cards through heavily lidded eyes under bushy brows. 'Four.'

'Ten.'

'Fifteen.' Charlie heaved his bulk forward to peg up two points on the board.

Jack Bishop fumbled his cards nervously, one eye on Matthew. 'Twenty.'

'That's a four, not a five!' Charlie Martin's voice was a gravelly

515

bass. 'What's the matter with you, boy? You're like a woman with a beetle in her drawers.' He put down a ten. 'Twenty-nine.'

'Go.' Another point for Charlie.

The game came to an end, Charlie emptied his glass and signalled to the barman to refill it. Nobody expected him to move from his chair.

'I heard about your girl, Matt, a bad business, I'm sorry.' The old man had his back to Eva and he did not turn round. 'I understand that she lost her way in the fog last night and walked into the quarry.'

'That's what they are trying to say.' Matthew was surly, like a rebellious child.

'It is an easy thing to do.' When Charlie Martin was speaking seriously he enunciated each syllable very precisely, like a Highlander.

The atmosphere in the little bar was remarkable as though everyone knew that more was being said than just the words which were spoken.

'I suppose that she was on her way back from Peters' place?'

'She had been there.'

'There must have been others, also on their way home?'

'She didn't leave at the same time. They say she left alone but . . .'

'A pity.' Charlie Martin studied his huge signet ring, twisting it round on his finger. 'That young man is not wanted in the islands.'

There was a murmur of approval.

'He murdered Sylvie.'

'That is a foolish thing to say unless you can prove it.' The old man took a sip from the tankard which the barman had set on the table by his hand. 'All the same, there can be no doubt that he has been a very bad influence on our young people.'

It was almost as though a formal resolution had been tabled and approved. Matthew Eva got up to go but Charlie, still without turning round stopped him with a raised hand. 'You will have no-one at home to cook you a meal?'

'No, but . . .'

'You will come home with me.'

At two o'clock when Sergeant Jordan wanted to speak to Matthew he had no difficulty in finding him. There were hardly any of the locals who did not know that Charlie Martin had taken him home to Sunday dinner. Jordan found them in the sitting-room of the big house under the fort. A bow window commanded an uninterrupted view of the bay, the walls were covered with photographs, mainly of ships and wrecks but some were of people dressed in the fashion of an earlier time, people, for the most part, now dead and gone.

'A drop of brandy, sergeant?' The old man and Matthew were drinking brandy out of balloon glasses.

'What I have to say to Matt is rather private, Mr Martin.'

Matthew's high colour was heightened still further by food and drink and his speech was a little slurred. 'I've nothing to hide, Freddie Jordan, what is it?'

Jordan shrugged. 'Dr Ross is unwilling to commit himself to a definite statement but he is of the opinion that Sylvie's injuries could be accounted for by the fall . . .'

Eva turned to Charlie Martin. 'What did I . . . ?'

But the old man spoke soothingly. 'Listen to the sergeant, Matt, give the man a chance.'

'According to Dr Ross, Sylvie's skull was remarkably thin and this would make her far more liable to the kind of injuries she suffered than a person with a normal skull.'

Charlie Martin nodded. 'An egg-shell skull, I came across it once – first mate on the old *Cecilia* . . . But never mind, go on, sergeant.'

'It seems that in addition to head and facial injuries she also had fractures of the left femur and tibia and a fractured pelvis.' He looked at Eva sympathetically. 'I'm sorry, Matt, but I said I would keep you informed.'

Eva was staring unseeingly at the pattern on the carpet. 'Is that all?'

'No, there's something else – two things in fact. Ross says there were no signs of sexual assault but . . .'

Eva looked up, 'But what?'

'Sylvie was four months pregnant.'

'Pregnant!' He was shocked.

'She hadn't told you?'

'Of course she hadn't told me! What sort of a damn fool do you take me for?'

Charlie swirled his brandy round the glass and sniffed. 'Had she been to see Ross?'

'A fortnight ago. She wouldn't tell him who the father was but she said she wanted to have the baby.'

'He should have told me!' Matt's chin jutted out in fresh aggression.

'He wanted to but she wouldn't let him.'

Matthew placed his glass carefully on an ornate Burmese ebony table. 'That settles it!'

Charlie Martin spoke quietly. 'Don't be stupid, Matthew, it settles nothing, it poses a question.'

'A question to which we all know the answer!' Eva rounded on the sergeant. 'Have you seen Peters?'

'I've talked to him.'

'Since you heard from Ross?'

'Yes. He says that as far as he knew Sylvie left with the others last night.'

'That's not what they say.'

'No. About the baby he said that he had no idea she was pregnant and he denied that the baby was his.'

'And you believe him?'

'I've no reason not to at the moment.'

Eva stood up, menacing. 'Are you saying . . . ?'

'The sergeant is just giving you the facts as he sees them, Matt, calm down!' Charlie Martin turned to Jordan. 'What happens next?'

Jordan was cautious. 'That will be up to the coroner and my bosses. With Dr Ross unwilling to commit himself firmly one way or the other I should think they would bring in a pathologist.'

Charlie nodded. 'Obviously the best thing, sergeant; the best thing for everybody.'

Chief Superintendent Wycliffe caught his first glimpse of the islands as the helicopter crossed the coastline of the mainland. Against the sun they appeared as low, dark silhouettes on the sea, like ships in convoy. Twenty minutes later he was looking down on the little archipelago and he was reminded of maps on the flyleaves of books about treasure voyages which he had read as a boy. Although he was now forty-six he felt the same sense of anticipation he had known as he turned over the title page and started to read at Chapter One.

It was incredibly peaceful and calm. They were flying over a small town at the end of a long, white beach. He could see boats in the harbour and people strolling along the wharf. Then they were looking down on a chequer-board of tiny fields and they had ceased to move but hovered in space like a kestrel with fluttering wings. The descent was gentle and they touched down in a field near a hut which looked like a bus station but had HELIPORT painted in big white letters on its sloping roof.

Sergeant Jordan was there, his massive form bulging in his uniform, moon-faced and slightly apprehensive. Wycliffe found it difficult to behave normally. If he had taken the four-hour sea passage it might have been easier but by this science-fiction machine the transition was too rapid, it had the quality of a magical experience. He felt as Alice must have done when she stepped through the looking glass. Jordan insisted on carrying his case.

'I've got a car outside.'

'A car?'

'It's nearly two miles.'

The air was balmy and sweet with no tang of salt, which surprised him. 'Isn't it peaceful?'

The sergeant gave him a sidelong look. 'Your first visit to the islands, sir?'

'Yes.'

'It's not always like this.'

Outside a little blue and white police car was waiting; for the other passengers on the helicopter there was a minibus. Jordan put the chief superintendent's case in the boot.

'The hotels and boarding houses are pretty full, sir, I didn't think you'd want to be with a crowd so I've fixed you up at my place – just until you have a chance to look round.'

'Thanks.'

'I hope it will suit you, sir.'

Wycliffe hoped so too.

Everything but the sea and the sky seemed to have been scaled down, tiny fields, tiny houses, roads in which it was impossible for two vehicles to pass except in a few prescribed places. They arrived on the wharf and the sergeant pulled up outside the police station. The wharf was almost deserted; the island's fleet of boats rode at moorings, white and red and blue hulls reflected in the pale green water.

'They're having their evening meals, it'll liven up directly.' Jordan seemed anxious to forestall any possible criticism of his island but Wycliffe had still not recovered his poise.

The sergeant's house, next to the police station, fronted directly on to the wharf and his wife was waiting for them at the front door. She was a good-looking woman, with clear, smooth skin, grey hairs which she did nothing to hide and frank blue eyes which were still girlish. 'I'll show you to your room.'

His bedroom looked out on the wharf and the harbour, a bright, plainly furnished room with white walls, polished wood floor and mats. A double bed with a white, honeycomb quilt.

'I hope you haven't turned out of your room . . .'

'No, we sleep in the back, it's quieter.'

She had a meal ready by the time he had unpacked and washed, grilled mackerel with a white sauce and potatoes and carrots. When the meal was over Jordan said, 'I expect you are waiting to hear all about it.'

But Wycliffe wanted nothing more than to walk round the harbour in the gathering dusk and to drop into a pub for a beer. 'Perhaps we could go for a walk?'

'Walk? Where to?'

'Just a stroll, you could tell me what I ought to know on the way . . .'

'If you like.'

Jordan had been right; the wharf was now alive with people, people walking arm in arm or standing in little groups gossiping or sitting on the piles of timber which were stacked at intervals. The darkness was warm and soft, navigation lights on the moored craft cast ribbons of light over the water and the people in the houses along the wharf had their windows and doors open making their lives part of the life of the wharf.

'He's a keeper on the Temple Rock.'

'What?'

'Eva, the girl's father, is a keeper on the Temple Rock light. They do four weeks on and two off, he's just started his spell ashore.'

'I see.'

'He's a widower, his wife died nearly two years back and since then the girl has looked after him. She was coming up for twenty . . . It's very odd and tragic, his wife died by falling off a cliff.'

'Any suggestion of foul play there?'

'None. Poor old Matt was off on the light, it was a terrible shock for him.'

'How does . . . How did the girl manage when her father was away?'

'She stayed on in the house.'

'Alone?'

'Why not? This isn't London and there's an aunt a few doors away.'

'What sort of a girl was she? A tart?'

'By no means, she always seemed a very pleasant girl. Of course, like the rest, she got mixed up with Peters.'

'Tell me about Peters.'

Wycliffe was only half listening. A boat was coming into harbour, her red and green lights and the white light at her masthead glided between the breakwaters; he could just hear the slow throb of her engine.

'Vince Peters, I suppose you know he's the pop singer . . .'

'I've a daughter. He packed it in a year or two back, didn't he?'

'Yes, just over two years. I suppose he's made his bit and decided to pull out while the going was still good. I don't blame him but I wish he'd gone somewhere else.'

'I suppose he yearned for the simple life.'

'Don't we all? Of course the establishment here keeps a close watch on anybody trying to buy land in the islands and they wouldn't have sold Vince Peters enough to bury himself.'

'Well?'

'His lawyers worked through a front man – a respectable, retired naval officer. There were red faces when Peters turned up one morning with his guitar and his mistress.'

'Now he holds court for the island's youth – is that it?'

'You could say that.'

They had reached the Seymour Arms, the door of the saloon bar was open on to the wharf and people were sitting outside drinking. Inside it looked like a rugby scrum.

'Pity!' Wycliffe said. 'I could do with a drink.'

'I'll get it from the public. Beer for you?'

The sergeant disappeared up an alley by the pub and returned a few minutes later with a pint in each hand. They found a seat on a pile of galvanized pipes recently unloaded from the *Islander*.

'Cheers!'

'Kids here haven't got much to amuse them. An old film on

Saturday night, a youth club run by the vicar and a dance in the church hall once a month.' Jordan paused to gulp his beer and wiped his mouth. 'Peters put an old barn at their disposal, fixed them up with stereo and stacks of records and throws in, as a bonus, guitar lessons for anybody who wants them. Of course he's got them eating out of his hand.'

'No harm in that.'

'There are plenty in the islands who wouldn't agree.'

'And you?'

The sergeant watched while a young couple strolled by, absorbed in each other and mesmerised by the warm darkness. 'I don't know. Sometimes I think they're right; that he's a bad influence.'

'In what way?'

'It's difficult to pinpoint. You know what kids are, once you've got their loyalty, they can be dominated . . .'

'Do you think he killed Sylvie?'

'No. Sylvie lost her way in the fog and walked over the edge of the quarry.'

'Then why am I here?'

'With due respect, sir, that's none of my doing.'

'It's a direct result of your report to your divisional HQ. They referred it to Area and here I am.'

Jordan finished his beer. 'We islanders form a tight community.' He gestured widely with his empty tankard. 'These people, the tourists, make no real impact, life goes on apart from them . . .'

'So?'

'It doesn't take much to stir up trouble. We're like a big family, always bickering amongst ourselves but ready enough to combine against any stranger who steps out of line. With Matthew Eva shooting his mouth off about Peters it could turn ugly.'

'You mean they might take the law into their own hands?'

'It wouldn't be the first time.'

Wycliffe got out his pouch and started to fill his pipe. 'I'm not the riot squad.'

'No, but you're well known and you've no axe to grind. If, after an investigation, you say that she hasn't been murdered, they will take your word for it.'

'I'm not the coroner either.'

Jordan was unperturbed. 'All the same, I think you understand me, sir.'

Wycliffe put a match to his pipe. 'I do, too well.'

Bellings, the deputy chief, had said to him, 'It's really a diplomatic mission, Charles. The chief had a word with the Lord Warden of the Isles . . . It would be better if we at least go through the motions of an investigation into the girl's death. We don't want trouble . . .' And trouble, in the deputy chief's vocabulary, meant anything that might upset influential people. 'Look upon it as a holiday, Charles . . .' Wycliffe got up from his rather uncomfortable seat on the iron pipes. 'Dr Franks is flying over tomorrow.'

'The pathologist?'

'Yes. If we're going to play games we'll do it properly.'

Back at the Jordans' house Mrs Jordan brought in three cups of cocoa. 'I'm not very keen on cocoa,' Wycliffe said.

Mrs Jordan was brisk. 'Drink it up! It will make you sleep.'

Something did. In bed he listened for a time to footsteps on the cobbles and to snatches of conversation from people passing just below his window. A bell-buoy rocked by a slow and gentle swell clanged monotonously, then he slept.

2

When he woke the sun was shining and the ceiling of his room was bright with dancing reflections from the waters of the harbour. His watch had stopped because he had forgotten to wind it. He got up and looked out of the window. Most of the craft in the harbour had been moved from their moorings and were lying alongside the quay. A small tanker-waggon was filling their fuel tanks by means of a long flexible hose. A very stout man in a blue jersey, with white hair and moustaches like God-the-father, seemed to be in charge. Wycliffe washed, dressed and went downstairs. It was seven o'clock but the Jordans were early risers and they were both at their breakfasts in a little kitchen at the back of the house. Jordan was like a schoolboy at the start of a holiday.

'Where do we begin, sir?'

'Begin?'

'What's the programme?'

Wycliffe looked vaguely out of the little window to the rising ground behind the house where Jordan had a vegetable patch and kept a few hens. 'I haven't got a programme.'

'Will you want to see Matthew Eva?'

'Perhaps, I don't know.'

Jordan's kindly moon-face looked hurt, he thought he had been snubbed. In fact Wycliffe had spoken the literal truth.

He was smoking his after-breakfast pipe, Mrs Jordan was washing up in their little lean-to scullery. 'Have you got a map of the islands?'

'I'll get one from the office.' He was back in a moment with an inch-to-the-mile Ordnance and spread it on the breakfast table. 'We are here.' His index finger blotted out the harbour.

'And the Peters' place?'

'Here. It's almost in the middle of the island, a quarter of a mile beyond the quarry. Salubrious Place, it's called, lying in a dip of the downs. It used to be a farm but Peters let off most of the land to a neighbouring farmer and kept the house and outbuildings.'

'I'll borrow this.' Wycliffe folded the map and slipped it into his pocket. 'Tell Mrs Jordan I'll be back for lunch.'

'What about Dr Franks?'

'He'll have to see the body and I expect he'll want to take a look at the quarry. Is there a cliff rescue team or something of that sort?'

'Of course, they're part of the volunteer service for fire and rescue in the islands.'

'Then you'd better alert them, Franks may need their help.'

'What shall I tell him, sir?'

'Tell him? Nothing, he's the expert, it's up to him to tell us.'

Jordan was disappointed in his desire to show off his island to the chief superintendent but a little flattered that he was being left to receive the pathologist.

Wycliffe stood with the sergeant at the doorway of the police station, taking in the scene. Refuelling was complete, the tanker-waggon had gone but the old man remained; he was sitting on a bollard making entries in a book with black, shiny covers.

'Who's that?'

'Charlie Martin.' The sergeant told him about Charlie Martin.

Wycliffe walked over and stood beside the old man. 'Good morning, Mr Martin.'

Charlie totted up a column of figures and entered a total. 'Good morning, Mr Wycliffe.' Evenly matched. He turned to a fresh section of the book and began another addition. Wycliffe waited.

'I suppose you know that I'm here to find out how Sylvie Eva died?'

'There will be plenty here anxious to tell you.'

'Why should Peters kill her?'

'I didn't say that he did.'

'What do you think?'

'She was pregnant.'

'That would be no reason to kill her.'

The old man shifted impatiently. 'This is not the mainland.'

'The islanders want to be rid of him, is that it?'

'We shall be glad to see him go.'

'Why?'

'Because he corrupts our young people.'

525

'In what way?'

The old man shrugged. He resumed his additions and it was obvious that there was no more to be got from him.

Wycliffe climbed the hill from the town and came out on to a rough moorland, yellow with gorse. The road petered out into a track good enough for a Land-Rover, heavy going for a car. Away to his left there was an island which seemed no more than a stone's throw across the water. According to his map it was Morvyl and the channel was nearly a mile wide. There were no houses to be seen, only little square fields, green and brown, moulded to the contours of the land. Beyond Morvyl he could see the double hump of Biddock which was uninhabited and beyond Biddock, the Western Ledges with Temple Rock lighthouse rising out of the sea like a slender white finger. Calm as it was, there was a lace of foam round the base of the tower.

He followed the track for about a mile and a half until it forked. The right-hand fork was tougher and strewn with boulders but it seemed to skirt the towering granite mass of Carngluze so he followed it and came to the quarry. He stood on the lip of the quarry, looking down. The drop was sheer, a granite face with crevices from which a few tufts of sea pinks grew. At the bottom there was a shallow pool with rushes round the margin and he thought he could see the depression left by Sylvie's body.

According to his map, by continuing on his present path he would rejoin the main track not far from Salubrious Place and he would be following, in the opposite direction, the path which Sylvie must have taken to her death. In a very few minutes he was looking down into a shallow valley with a stream running through it and on the far side a copse of pines. Near the copse a stone house with outbuildings formed three sides of a courtyard, the fourth side was walled with a broad gateway, its posts surmounted by stone figures of indeterminate form. The grey slate roofs and the walls were covered with lichens and seemed to be as much part of the landscape as the granite outcrops which dotted the moor. Apart from the stream it was silent and, apparently, deserted.

Wycliffe walked down the steep track, crossed a bridge over the stream and entered the cobbled courtyard. Three or four cats lazed in the shade of an old contorted pine tree but there was no other sign of life. The house was on his left and the other two sides of the rectangle were occupied by anonymous farm buildings in a good state of repair. One of these buildings had been plastered over the stone and whitewashed providing an ideal surface for a painted inscription in letters two feet high: 'GO HOME MURDERER!' Underneath another, less expert hand, had added a sentence containing similar advice in cruder terms. Evidently the islanders had fired their opening shots.

The front door of the house stood open to a hall with stone paving partly covered by Persian rugs. He rang the doorbell and heard it jangle somewhere inside the house but nobody came. Then he heard a rhythmic thumping sound coming from one of the outhouses and made in that direction. The sound seemed to come from behind a door at the far end of the courtyard. He pushed open the door and found himself in a large whitewashed room with shelves against the wall supporting rows of greyish clay pots arranged according to shape and size. The room was L-shaped and in the angled portion a girl was working at a potter's wheel. He watched while she moulded and drew up the spinning clay into a rather elegant, round-bellied pot with a flanged rim.

'Are you looking for someone?' She continued her work.

'Mr Peters.'

'In the house.'

'I've tried but there's no answer.'

She took a wire and removed the pot from the wheel. 'Hold on.'

She was seventeen or eighteen, a pretty, plump girl with sturdy legs. Ordinary. Was she Peters' mistress? He had expected Kings Road with beads and tassels but this girl could have been doing her 'A' levels at school. She put the new pot on a shelf with others to dry.

Wycliffe introduced himself but she showed little interest. 'You've come about Sylvie?' She led him back to the house, through the hall to a large kitchen at the back where Peters was stirring something in a saucepan on the stove.

'For you, Vince. Why can't you answer the door when somebody rings?'

The kitchen window looked out across a small green meadow to the sombre pines. There was a row of beehives just short of the trees. The sun was in the front of the house and though the kitchen window was large the room seemed inadequately lit.

'Detective Chief Superintendent Wycliffe.'

Peters continued to stir whatever it was in the saucepan. The smell was appetizing.

'Mr Peters?'

'That's me.'

He was tall and very thin, round-shouldered and hollow chested but he looked younger, less dissipated than the photographs Wycliffe had seen as pin-ups and on record sleeves. The haggard, tortured look was 'in' with the kids. He had a great mop of frizzy red hair and there were carefully cultivated tufts on his cheek bones and a triangular growth on his chin but his upper lip was bare. He wore a green singlet tucked into faded blue jeans and no shoes or stockings.

'Wasn't it an accident?'

'Why do you ask?'

'Do they usually send a chief super to sort out an accident?'

'Some of the islanders are saying that she was murdered.'

'And that I murdered her?'

He held his left arm tightly against his body, slightly flexed at the elbow as though he had injured it in some way.

'Was she here on Saturday evening?'

'She was here most evenings when there was a session in the Barn. As you probably know the kids have a sort of club in the Barn.' He stopped stirring, turned down the gas and came over to the table. 'You'd better sit down.'

The kitchen had been modernized, eye-level units, laminated plastic, and old-fashioned sweet bottles, exotic with gilt labels, for stores. There was only a stool to sit on, an angular thing with chrome legs. Wycliffe perched on it uncertainly. Peters sat on the corner of the table.

'Did she always stay after the others had left?'

'No.'

'But she did on Saturday evening.'

'No.'

'The others say that she did.'

Peters shrugged.

'Did you have any conversation with her that evening?'

'We chatted for a bit.'

'What about?'

'What do people talk about?'

528

'Was there something special about your relationship with Sylvie – different from the others?'

'Not special – no.'

'But she was pregnant.'

'Pregnant.' Expressionless.

Wycliffe got out his pipe and started to fill it. He was trying to control his exasperation. Peters might have been in a soundproof glass box for all the communication there was between them.

'I'd like to look round.'

'Help yourself.'

'I want you to show me.'

'What?'

'The Barn for a start.'

Peters went across to the stove to see how his cooking was going, lifted the lid, sniffed and covered the saucepan once more.

'You enjoy cooking?'

'I enjoy cooking.'

'You must find life here a change from what you've been used to.'

'I get along.'

'The appeal of the simple life?'

It was like trying to scratch glass with a pencil.

As they were crossing the courtyard Wycliffe noticed that he limped. One leg – the left, dragged slightly.

Wycliffe pointed to the inscriptions. 'When were these done?'

'During the night.'

The original barn door had been remounted and had a wicket cut in it. The wood had been stripped of paint, polished and varnished to a perfect surface but the whole of the lower part of the door was blackened and blistered by a recent fire.

'This too?'

'They started a fire with shavings and paraffin.'

'You saw them?'

'It was about three in the morning; believe it or not, I was asleep.' He pointed to one of the windows. 'It was when they smashed that I woke up.'

'What did you do?'

Peters shrugged. 'We got up and put the fire out which, I suppose, was what they intended.'

'You think they smashed the window to draw your attention?

529

'I imagine so. They wouldn't want to burn the place down at this stage. Just a broad hint.'

'You take this very calmly, Mr Peters.'

'It's a way they have with strangers, I'm making no complaint.'

'I think you are wrong.'

'You wanted to see the Barn.'

They moved into a lofty room open to the roof trusses, cool and dimly lit. The walls were covered with evocative posters and blow-ups of pop stars, larger than life. At one end there was a platform with all the electronic gadgetry which has made the pop scene what it is and behind this, an enormous photograph of the late Jimi Hendrix in one of his orgasmic experiences with a guitar. Wycliffe was reminded of a church with its holy pictures.

'It seems that Sylvie fell into the quarry.'

Peters said nothing.

'Her skull and face were smashed in and she had a fractured pelvis and thigh.'

'Nasty!'

'Who runs the pottery?'

'It was Clarissa's idea – the girl I live with – and she runs it.'

'The girl I met when I arrived?'

'No, that's Brenda Luke, she comes in part-time to help.'

'You sell the pottery?'

'We don't give it away.'

'Where is Clarissa?'

'Gone to the farm for milk.'

'The two of you live here alone?'

'A woman comes in from the village a few hours each day.'

Wycliffe wandered round the Barn, looking at the posters, wondering what to do next. Peters watched him in silence for a while then he laughed. 'This is a fun place, man!'

'How old are you Mr Peters?'

'Twenty-eight.'

Wycliffe nodded. 'Getting beyond it.' He had the impression that Peters was uneasy, that he was putting on a not very convincing act to cover his concern.

Peters went to stand in the doorway, looking out into the court-yard. Was he sulking?

'Do you open the Barn every night?'

'Four nights a week. Mondays, Wednesdays, Saturdays and Sundays.'

'How many youngsters come each night?'

'It varies; there are between thirty and forty members and most nights about twenty turn up.'

'Only members?'

'Each member can bring a friend and during the season, like now, some of them do but not many, they like to keep it to themselves.'

'How many were here on Saturday?'

'About the usual, you can look in the book.' He turned to point to a table near the platform. 'It's in the drawer.'

The book was an ordinary club register and seemed to have been well kept. Wycliffe counted twenty-five signatures on the Saturday night, only three of whom were non-members.

'I said. The kids are exclusive.'

Turning back through the book Sylvie seemed to be one of the club's most regular attenders.

'Did Sylvie have any close friends?'

'Not that I know of.'

'What's the membership subscription?'

'There isn't one.'

'So what do you get out of it?'

'I do it for love, man.'

Ask a silly question.

'I want a list of these boys and girls.'

'Help yourself.'

Wycliffe wrote the names in his notebook.

When he had finished he came out into the still, silent courtyard drenched in blinding sunlight. The cats were lying just within the narrow strip of shade afforded by the buildings.

A girl came through the gateway carrying an enamel milk can in one hand and a basket of vegetables in the other. Wycliffe glimpsed a rather sallow face framed in straight black hair, shoulder length. She wore faded blue, bib-and-brace overalls and her figure was as slim as a boy's. She must have seen them but she gave no sign and went into the house. The cats stirred themselves, stretched and followed her.

Wycliffe puffed at his pipe, half-drugged by the sunshine and the silence. 'Clarissa – is she Italian?'

'Corsican.'

There was no point in hanging around; he had made his duty call, shown the flag. No more was required of him unless Sylvie really had been murdered except to put a stop to the islanders' schoolboy escapades. He looked at his watch. Half-past ten.

'I shall arrange for a man to keep an eye on your premises at night for the time being.'

'Suit yourself.'

Peters stood in the middle of the courtyard and watched him go. But a change had come over the ex-pop idol. It was as though the act he had put on for the superintendent had utterly exhausted him and he seemed to sag in body and spirit. Wearily, he turned and went indoors. Clarissa was in the kitchen putting away vegetables she had brought from the farm. He stood, watching her work. The unselfconscious movement of her body had always been a joy to him. Unhurried, unhesitating, never seeming to change her mind. Smooth, elegant, precise. But now he watched her with a new attention, as though seeing her about her household chores had a special significance, as though, perhaps, he did not expect to have many more opportunities.

'Police?' She continued working without looking at him.

'Yes.'

'What did he say?'

'That she was pregnant.'

'Pregnant?' She turned to face him, her dark eyes wide with surprise.

Peters sat on the corner of the table. 'I knew about it, she told me.'

She came over and stood looking up at him her small pale hands resting lightly on his thighs. 'Jackie Martin?'

He shook his head, took her face between his hands and kissed her. 'She thought that she could take your place.'

'You mean that she deliberately . . .'

'Yes.'

'Poor child!' She frowned. 'Is that why she killed herself, Vince?'

'The police think that she was murdered.'

Her dark eyes searched his face with anxious concern. 'You talked to her on Saturday?'

He nodded. 'She wanted to talk so we went for a walk. She told me about the baby and she seemed to think all she had to do was to go for the nearest parson.'

532

'Then?'

'Then nothing. I tried to explain but it was obviously a hell of a shock.'

Clarissa's features were set in an expression of infinite tenderness. She lifted one hand and her thin, white fingers traced the line of his arm, the arm which seemed to be immobilized against his body. His features trembled, he held her close to him with his good arm and his whole frame was shaken by deep, dry sobs. 'Help me, Clarissa!' he whispered.

Neither of them had heard Nellie Martin come in but suddenly they were aware of her standing in the doorway of the kitchen, watching, a thin little smile of contempt on her hard, lined face. She stood her ground for a moment then muttered something and a little later they could hear her moving about upstairs.

Just over the bridge Wycliffe had passed a middle-aged woman, shabbily dressed. He had wished her good morning and she had acknowledged him only by the smallest movement of her lips but when he looked back, she had stopped to stare after him. Presumably she was the Peters' daily help.

Once on the moor he made a detour back to the town, following the coastal path in its devious course round small promontories and inlets, skirting tiny coves of white sand which dazzled the eyes. He arrived back past little houses with gardens in which there were gay clumps of mesembryanthemums and tall, exotic, perennial echiums like cartoon plants from a Disney film.

Dr Franks, the pathologist, plump and chubby as an overweight baby, was waiting for him at the police station with Sergeant Jordan. In a fawn linen suit, silk shirt with a colourful cravat and sandals, the doctor looked like a rather elegant tourist of the thirties.

'You've been to the mortuary?'

'I've just come from there.'

'Well?' The two men had known each other for too long to stand on ceremony.

'Her skull bones are certainly very thin, the whole of the head is delicately structured.' Franks studied his beautifully manicured hands, the plump, pink fingers and the nails with their half-moons perfectly displayed. 'In a fall one would expect such a subject to suffer considerable bone damage.'

'The question is, did she sustain *all* her injuries in the fall?'

Franks shook his head. 'I can't answer that. I haven't seen the quarry yet. Jordan is taking me there this afternoon with a couple of chaps from the cliff-rescue service.'

'What will you be looking for?'

'From the position of the body when she was found it seems that she fell feet first with her left leg doubled under her; that would account for the pelvic and limb fractures.'

'And the rest?'

'If she died as a result of accident or if she was simply pushed over alive, they must have been inflicted by her striking the rocks as she fell.'

'And you are going to look for traces.'

'Exactly.'

'I wish you joy!'

The conversation became general. 'You've found somewhere to stay?'

'The sergeant got me in at the Atlantic, I think he had to bribe the receptionist.'

They chatted until it was time for Franks to go to his hotel for lunch. He was enthusiastic about a newly conceived project in which he planned to use the harbour as a base for cruising in the islands in his recently purchased cabin cruiser.

Wycliffe looked out at the blue untroubled waters. 'I don't suppose it's always like this.'

'Oh, we're not scared of a bit of a blow, she's a good sea boat.'

The look on Jordan's face caused Wycliffe to change the subject once more. 'There's nothing more you can tell me about the girl?'

Franks shook his head. 'Not really. It's just that the skull and facial damage seems excessive, even allowing for the fragile bone structure.'

Wycliffe lunched with the Jordans off a steak pie which was delicious but lay heavily on the stomach. At two o'clock he stood in the doorway of their little house watching the visitors crowding to the boats for the afternoon trips. Charlie Martin was there and raised his hand in enigmatic salutation. Jordan came out of the house on his way to pick up Franks. He glanced up at the cloudless blue sky, then at the scores of lightly clad trippers. 'They're going to get wet.'

'Matthew Eva – where can I find him?'

Jordan considered. 'Unless he's giving a hand on the boats he'll most likely be at home. He lives at 6, Bethel Street, sir, it's up the alley by the Seymour Arms.'

A few minutes later Wycliffe set off along the quay in the direction of the Seymour Arms. A narrow cobbled lane ran steeply upwards past the side of the pub. Neat little houses were stepped against one another on both sides, built by men who had enough of wind and weather, earning their daily bread. A little metal sign, white letters on a blue ground, Bethel Street. The door of number six stood open. Wycliffe knocked. He was almost inside a dimly lit sitting-room which had a chiffonier, a table in the middle with a potted plant, and walls covered with photographs. A door at the other side of the room opened making a rectangle of sunlight and a thickset man in a seaman's jersey came forward to meet him.

'Mr Eva?'

'That's me.'

'Wycliffe. Detective Chief Superintendent.'

'I know.' His manner was distant but not aggressive. 'You'd better come in.'

They went through the dismal little sitting-room which was probably never used into a bright, tidy kitchen with a shiny electric cooker and a large plastic-topped table on which there were the remnants of a meal.

'I just finished my dinner.' Eva gestured vaguely at the dirty dishes. 'Not had time to clear away.'

Otherwise the place was meticulously clean and orderly like a well-run ship's galley. Outside the window a yard, a little garden beyond with fruit trees and a few greens.

Wycliffe offered his sympathy. Eva got out his tobacco pouch and pushed it over. 'Smoke?' Wycliffe started to fill his pipe.

'I'll miss her, there's no denying that.'

'You are a widower?'

'Two years. Sylvie kept house since then. A good girl. I'm a keeper on the Temple Light – away a month at a time and she looked after the place . . .' The blue eyes glistened.

'You think that she was murdered?'

'I know she was, mister, no two ways about that!' His aggression flared, but he controlled it. He took back his pouch and started to fill his own pipe. 'Sylvie knew this island like the back of her hand. Since she was old enough to go out by herself she's wandered over it till she got to know it better than I do myself.' He paused in the act of pressing down the tobacco in his pipe to look Wycliffe straight in the eyes. 'She *couldn't* have lost herself!'

'I understand that there was a dense fog . . .'

'Fog? It was no more than a bit of mist then but even if she'd been blindfold she couldn't have walked into that quarry by no accident.'

'What if she did it on purpose?'

'You mean suicide?'

'It's possible.' Wycliffe looked at the shining window panes, the bright paintwork and the polished linoleum to remind himself that he was talking about a real person, a girl who would have made a good wife and mother and would probably have known as much happiness as most. 'She was pregnant; even in these days there are still girls who can't bring themselves to face . . .'

Eva nodded. 'I know what you're getting at. It's true Sylvie was strictly brought up according to how things are these days but if she wanted to do away with herself she wouldn't have done it that way.'

Wycliffe spoke gently. 'Why not?'

'I tell you she wouldn't!' He almost shouted.

Wycliffe smoked in silence. A cat leapt on to the window ledge outside and Eva went to open the door.

'It was the way her mother went.'

'Suicide?' Wycliffe was taken off-guard.

'No!' Eva was like a rumbling volcano, ready at any moment to erupt into violence but who could blame him? 'They were out for a walk along the cliffs – like sisters they was rather than mother and daughter. It was rough, blowing a gale – October. Sylvie turned to speak to her mother and she wasn't there . . . They found her that evening. I was on the rock and it was three days before they could get a boat off to fetch me.'

'What a terrible thing for both of you!'

Eva sat stroking the blond hairs on his wrist. 'She took it bad. For a week she scarcely spoke but she come to terms in the end like we all have to.'

The cat, a magnificent black and white tom, was mewing plaintively and rubbing round the table leg. Eva got up to pour milk into a saucer on the floor.

'I suppose Sylvie had boy friends?'

Eva looked up angrily but changed his mind. 'At the time her

536

mother died she was going out with a young man. Jackie Martin, he's a year or two older than Sylvie but none the worse for that. He's an island boy – been away to college and come back to teach in the school.'

'Any relation to Charlie Martin?'

Eva laughed shortly. 'All the Martins are related. Originally there was really only three families in the islands, the Martins, the Jordans and the Evas but we don't take much count of relationships beyond second cousins.' He paused to collect his thoughts. 'Anyway, as I was saying, they took up together and her mother and me was content. He wasn't what we would have chosen for Sylvie but he seemed a quiet, decent lad and one of us.' He smoked in silence for a while. 'Mother's boy – that's his trouble but it takes all sorts. I thought that as soon as Sylvie got over the first shock the two of them would have made a match of it. But it wasn't to be . . .'

Eva was staring at his cat who had finished the milk and was now stretched out on the mat in a patch of sunlight, washing himself. 'By the time she got round to going out again Peters had opened his club and all the youngsters was off there every chance. She went there a few times with Jackie but it wasn't his style – nor mine from what I hear.'

'What do you hear?'

He shrugged angrily. 'It's easy to see what he gets out of it! Anyway, I told Sylvie she wasn't to go there but what can you do with a girl of nearly twenty?' He gestured helplessly with his large hands.

'When I came home on my next shore leave I could see that it was all over between her and Jackie. She was off to Peters' place most every night and there was nothing I could do to stop it. I must admit it took her out of herself a bit but I didn't like it – not one bit!'

'When did you come home on your present leave, Mr Eva?'

He had to think, time had acquired a different meaning for him recently. 'Thursday – Thursday afternoon, it must have been.'

'Did you notice any change in Sylvie?'

He hesitated. 'Yes I did. She seemed excited – full of something.'

'Happy?'

'Not happy exactly.'

'Worried?'

'Not worried either – just excited, keyed up. I must admit I didn't

537

think much about it, you know what girls are. I asked her if there was anything up and she pretended not to know what I was talking about – said she was no different to usual, that it was my imagination.'

Wycliffe smoked, staring out of the window at the blackcurrant bushes. The sky was no longer blue, it was smoky-grey and he remembered Sergeant Jordan's prophecy – 'They'll get wet.'

'It looks as though it's going to rain.'

Eva did not bother to look out of the window. 'Aye.'

Without being aware of when the change had taken place Wycliffe realized that he no longer thought of the investigation as a sham. He was thinking and behaving as though Sylvie's death had not been an accident.

The sky was darkening rapidly and the kitchen, which a few minutes earlier had been full of sunshine, was dimly lit as though with the approach of night.

'Storm coming up?'

'The glass has been dropping since first thing this morning but it won't last long.'

'I would like to take a look at Sylvie's room.'

Eva nodded and led the way up steep, narrow stairs to a tiny landing off which two doors opened. 'There's only two bedrooms, this is Sylvie's.'

It was a small room with a sloping ceiling and a dormer window overlooking the back garden. The walls were white and the divan bed had a white quilt. There was a tiny wardrobe, a chest of drawers and a table under the window with a record player on it and a small stack of records. On the chest of drawers, apart from a swing mirror and a few toilet articles there was a framed photograph of a grave faced, attractive woman of about forty.

'My wife,' Eva said from the landing.

Wycliffe made a vague gesture at the drawers. 'Have you . . . ?'

Eva shook his head dumbly. The drawers were lined with white paper and scrupulously tidy. One contained her underclothes, one was full of back numbers of a girl's magazine. One of the two top drawers had in it a couple of handbags, three or four belts and a box with a few bits of cheap jewellery. Eva was watching him. 'It's not much, is it?' Wycliffe knew what he meant.

The other top drawer held handkerchiefs and scarves but underneath them there were two albums and a diary. One of the albums contained family photographs with Sylvie herself figuring in most of them at all stages of her growing up. The other album was a scrap book devoted exclusively to Vince Peters. There were pictures and clippings from newspapers but there were also originals which he must have given her and, in pride of place, a studio portrait of him inscribed: 'To Sylvie with love from Vince 1971.' The diary had most of its pages blank but from time to time there were cryptic entries usually involving initials. On the 15th April she had written in bold print '280 days!' and on the 20th July there was an entry 'It's definite'.

'I'm afraid that I shall have to send someone to make a proper search.'

Eva shrugged and said nothing.

'I'll be seeing you again, Mr Eva, meantime . . .'

Eva saw him to the door and stood watching as he hurried down the cobbled alley to the quay. As he reached the quay fat raindrops were beginning to fall out of a leaden sky making large, circular wet patches on the tarmac.

3

The worst of the rain had spent itself within the hour but the wind which sprang up behind it blew steadily, raising a choppy sea and giving the trippers a bonus thrill. The boats returned early, while it was still raining, and Wycliffe, standing in the front room of Jordan's house, watched the passengers coming ashore, wet but cheerful, with spray on their faces and the tang of salt on their lips. Charlie Martin was there, standing aloof but with an eye for everything. In his oilskins and sou'wester he seemed as indifferent to the weather as the Temple Rock itself.

It was after six when Sergeant Jordan returned with Franks. Fortunately Jordan had insisted on them being prepared for rain and they were none the worse.

'I managed to get a good look at the face before the rain came.' The tubby little doctor was pleased with himself, having shown the cliff-rescue people that he could make good use of a bo'sun's chair. 'There are no signs I can find that she hit the rock on the way down. The face isn't as sheer or as smooth as it looks, there are bosses and ridges where a falling body might strike but I don't think she did. As far as I can tell she fell clear.'

They were sitting in Jordan's front room, drinking tea out of. willow-patterned cups. Franks added a second spoonful of sugar to his tea and stirred absently.

'So?' Wycliffe was impatient.

The doctor considered his words. He liked to make a good story. 'In my opinion she fell feet first and her landing was responsible for the fractured limb bones and pelvis.'

'What about the damage to her skull?'

Franks was staring out of the little window at people passing by. 'I don't see how that could have been caused by the fall.'

'But the head injuries killed her?'

540

'Without doubt.'

'So it's murder.'

'She obviously didn't do it herself.'

Wycliffe got out his pipe and started to fill it. 'Presumably she was attacked, battered about the head, then her body was pushed into the quarry.'

Franks nodded. 'That would fit the facts as I know them.'

'What about the weapon?'

'Weapon?'

'Whoever did it couldn't have used his bare hands.'

Franks ran his fingers through thinning hair. 'As usual, you want me to do your job for you. The very extent of the injuries makes it difficult to come to any conclusion about the nature of the weapon but if I must say something, it's this – with her skull the weapon need not have been heavy or the blow powerful. It's really quite remarkable that she got through her life so far without some sort of skull fracture. A severe bump on the head would have been enough, the sort most kids get some time or other.'

'How many blows – two, three – many?'

Franks grinned. 'Your confidence is touching. The answer is that I don't know. I should have thought more than one blow from a weapon with a relatively small surface but a single blow from a weapon with a large surface of contact would have been enough.'

Before his evening meal Wycliffe spoke on the telephone with Chief Inspector Gill, his Number Two at the Crime Squad.

'You want me to come over?'

'Yes, get the first flight in the morning.'

'What's the weather like?'

'Don't bother with your suntan lotion.'

'We can call on divisional assistance as we need it but you'd better bring a team – who's free?'

Arrangements made, Wycliffe had his meal. Sergeant Jordan was subdued and Wycliffe preoccupied. 'We shall need a headquarters. In view of the accommodation problem we shall have to make arrangements for our chaps to sleep and eat there. A church hall – something of the sort.'

'The school is shut for the holidays, there's a canteen . . .'

'Good! See what you can do.'

'I'll see the headmaster in the morning.'

'Tonight.' Wycliffe was a changed man, gone was the rather sleepy benevolence which had puzzled the sergeant.

All the same, after his meal and while Jordan was trying to get authority to use the school as a headquarters, Wycliffe was on his way to the Seymour Arms. There were not many people about, partly because it was the time of the evening meal in hotels and boarding houses, but also because the strong wind was sweeping rain squalls across the island. Overhead smoky clouds chased each other and above them the sky was dun coloured giving no sign of where the sun might be. Wycliffe turned up the collar of his coat and kept close in under the houses.

There were few customers in the public bar of the Seymour. Charlie Martin was in his usual place, reading a newspaper. Three men were playing darts. The landlord, not yet needed in the saloon, had been chatting to Martin. His attitude to Wycliffe was civil but distant. Wycliffe took his drink to a seat near the bar from where he had a good view of the whole room. Charlie, after a curt nod, went back to his newspaper. For the darts players it seemed that Wycliffe did not exist.

One of them was dark and stocky with a red face and a big paunch from too much beer-drinking. His appearance was not improved by a cast in his sight. The second man was taller and in better shape; he was fair, with sideboards and tracts of hair across his cheeks which linked with a luxuriant, silky moustache. The third man was older and very tall. His face was fleshy with thick lips, he had a stubbly beard and spiky white hair. Wycliffe was struck by his eyes which, when they were not focused on anything in particular, had a wild look, like the eyes of an animal. The others seemed to humour him and they paid for his drinks.

More customers arrived, ordered their drinks and disposed themselves round the room, taking seats which through long usage they had come to regard as their own. Nobody seemed to notice Wycliffe. Four of the men settled down to a game of whist while two others got out a chequer-board. They were following a well-established routine and there was no need to say much. Wycliffe sipped his drink and watched. A pall of blue smoke grew and floated just below the raftered ceiling.

The darts game finished and the players came over to the bar to replenish their glasses. The man with the red face turned to Wycliffe.

'Was she murdered or wasn't she?'

'It seems very likely that she was.'

The red-faced man opened his mouth to say something but Charlie Martin cut in. 'Will you be making an arrest?'

Wycliffe shook his head. 'It's far too early to be talking about an arrest. To do that we need evidence – evidence pointing to a single person.'

There was a derisory laugh from the company and the old man frowned. 'But there will be a full police inquiry?'

'Of course.'

'Good!' After taking a mouthful of beer and carefully wiping his moustache with a red and white pocket handkerchief, he got up, went to a wall cupboard and came back with a cribbage board and a pack of cards. 'You will play a game with me, Mr Wycliffe?' It was the accolade of acceptance. Everybody in the bar was paying attention.

'I'm sorry, cribbage is not one of my games.'

'Pity!' Martin looked round the room in the manner of an officer choosing a subordinate for a mission. 'Henry! Give me a game if you please.'

A middle-aged, black-bearded man in a reefer jacket with brass buttons, joined the old man at his table. 'Our harbour master, Mr Wycliffe – Captain Osborne.' Wycliffe acknowledged the introduction and the two men settled to their play.

Wycliffe was disappointed, he had hoped that the atmosphere of the bar would have loosened tongues but it seemed that they all took their cue from the old man.

The darts players were still standing at the bar and one of them, the white-haired chap with the thick lips, caught Wycliffe's eye and gave a significant jerk of his head in the direction of the door. A few minutes later he drank up his beer and left. Wycliffe waited for a while, then, after a word with Charlie Martin and the harbour master, he followed.

The quay was almost deserted. A hardy couple, determined to make the most of their holiday, plodded along heads down to the wind, but there was no-one else in sight. Beyond the breakwater there were white flecks on the sea and in the harbour smaller craft tossed uneasily at their moorings. It was a very different scene from the one which had greeted him on his arrival when Jordan had said, 'It's not always like this.'

As he was passing the boatmen's shelter his name was called and he turned to see the white-haired man with the wild eyes standing in the doorway.

He followed him into the little hut which was just big enough for a table with a bench on either side. There was a strong smell of paraffin but it was cosy enough; the whitewashed stone must have seen generations of fishermen come and go before tourists set foot in the island.

'You said you wanted evidence.' The man towered over Wycliffe. His manner was both aggressive and nervous; he shifted from one foot to the other and darted quick glances round the hut, almost as though he were looking for a way of escape.

'Who are you?'

'Marsden – Nick Marsden. I just wanted to . . .'

'Where do you live?'

'Quincey Cove – down the valley from Peters' place.'

'Well?'

'I was on me way home and I saw him . . .'

'Who?'

'Peters.'

'When was this?'

'The night he knocked off Sylvie Eva. He was with her.'

'Where?'

'I saw 'em come out of his place together.'

'Where did they go? What direction?'

'Up the valley. They walked up the valley by the stream.'

'Towards the farm?'

He nodded. 'They was falling out.'

'What about?'

He shook his head vaguely and the wild look came into his eyes. 'I couldn't hear what they was saying.'

'But you knew they were quarrelling.'

'Yes, I knew, you could tell.'

'Did you follow them?'

A sheepish look. 'A bit.'

'Where did they go?'

'They must've gone to the quarry.' Sly.

'By following the stream? Don't try to be clever. You stopped following them – why?'

'He's a bastard.'

'But why did you stop following them?'

'He turned round and saw me.'

'Well?'

'He told me to bugger off.' He passed his hand over his head where the hair stood up in white bristles like a clothes brush. 'He was real mad at her – shouting.'

Marsden was not drunk but he had had enough to drink. His thick lips were moist and he breathed through them making a sort of bubbling noise as he did so.

'What have you got against Peters?'

'He's a bastard.'

'You said. But what have you got against him?'

'He killed Sylvie, didn't he?' An aggressive thrust of the stubbly chin.

'Remember that it's a very serious offence to try to mislead the police in a murder inquiry.'

'I ain't misleading you, I only told you what I saw.'

'All right! If you are of the same mind in the morning you can come to my headquarters and make a statement.' Wycliffe turned to go.

'Bloody coppers!'

'By the way, why couldn't you have told me this in the pub?'

Marsden looked aggrieved. 'Well I couldn't could I? That was Peters' brother I was with.'

'The chap with a moustache?'

'Aye.'

Wycliffe stepped out on to the quay and Marsden followed him. After a few yards Wycliffe looked round, Marsden was padding back to the Seymour.

Now that he seemed to have a case to work on Wycliffe was anxious to get started; he chafed at the inevitable delay before he would have a headquarters properly organized and his men deployed. Chief Inspector Gill would be the driving force and he could not arrive in the islands for another twelve hours. It was impossible to sit still and wait. The rain had gone, the wind had dropped and the sky was clearing. Away to the west broken clouds were reddened by the setting sun.

He decided that he would take another look at Salubrious Place; at least he would find out whether Sylvie's death had put a stop to the nightly sessions there. He climbed the hill out of the town and came up on to the moor in gathering darkness. The beam of Temple Rock light swept the sky every twenty seconds, dimmed by the rapidly fading twilight. On this, his second trip, it seemed a much shorter distance to the point where he could look down into the valley. There were lights in the house and in the outbuildings but what caught and held him was the fountain of sound which seemed to well up out of the valley: raucous, metallic and underscored by a powerful, throbbing pulse which could be felt rather than heard. It was uncanny in this deserted place. He descended the steep stony track, crossed the bridge and entered the courtyard.

The single window of the Barn cast a rectangular kaleidoscopic pattern of flickering and flashing colours on the cobbles. Evidently they had all the psychedelic props. Wycliffe stood at the window and looked in. Under the darting, dancing and stabbing lights ten or a dozen couples gyrated, writhed, wriggled and jerked in serpentine ecstasy to the monstrous rhythm of drums and guitars, amplified to the level of stupefaction.

Near the window a girl with small, pale features, wearing a red, sheath mini-dress, danced with closed eyes, lost to everything but the rhythm, even to her pimply-faced partner. Peters was there, wearing black tight trousers and a black turtle-necked sweater. He was not dancing but moving slowly among the dancers, watching. They seemed unaware of him – unaware of everything but the rhythm. The foreign girl – Clarissa – was there also, dancing opposite a hefty blond youth with a broken nose. Wycliffe went inside and stood at the end of the hall waiting for a break in the barrage of sound. It came at last; abruptly, without warning, so that the senses reeled under the impact of silence. The couples stopped dancing, seemed to emerge briskly from their trances and began to chatter. Peters came over to the chief superintendent with a sardonic grin on his face but his eyes were grave.

'Come to dance, man?'

Wycliffe was grim. 'Sylvie Eva was murdered.'

'Well! That really is a drag, man.' If Peters was putting on an act to incense Wycliffe he succeeded.

Wycliffe wandered round the hall feeling slightly ridiculous, expecting to see derisive grins, but modern youth are so practised in the acceptance of the bizarre that a middle-aged detective invading their private stamping ground is unlikely to cause the turning of a single head.

'Were you here on Saturday evening?'

'Me?' The youth addressed, pimply and inoffensive, looked surprised.

'Yes, you!' Wycliffe was unnecessarily brusque.

'Saturday? Yes, I was here.'

'What time did you leave?'

The youth shrugged. 'Half-eleven, give or take five minutes.'

'With the others?'

'Yeh – we went together as always.'

'But not with Sylvie Eva?'

'I can't hear you.'

The comparative silence had been split apart by a banshee howl as a canned singer launched into his number.

'Let's go outside,' Wycliffe suggested.

The young man looked across at a mousey little girl in jeans and a suede jacket who stood watching them. 'It's Georgina – she's my girl.'

'Then bring her with you.'

Outside in the courtyard it was fresh, the air clean and sharp with the tang of the sea.

'What's your name?'

'Nance – Jeremy Nance.'

'And yours?'

'Georgina Keys.'

'How old are you?'

'Sixteen – both of us.'

'You enjoy coming here?'

The boy was enthusiastic. 'It's great, isn't it, Georgie?'

'Yeh – great!' She was plain and skinny, her features were a little pinched but the boy seemed to defer to her in everything.

They moved over to the metal chairs under the pine tree and sat down; it was chilly but it was possible to talk. The mood had changed in the Barn and somebody with an engaging, throaty baritone voice was singing to a guitar accompaniment—

'Hear the news and the weather
Though they're always the same;
Read the cereal packet
For the novelty game;
Then have a go at a crossword
Till you're stuck for a clue;
　　And while you think you're killing time,
　　It's time that's killing you,
　　It's time that's killing you.'

'That's Vince – isn't he great?'

Georgie listened, entranced. 'That's special, we can't get him to sing very often . . . Isn't he super?'

'On Saturday night Sylvie did not leave at the same time as the rest of you?'

'What? – Oh, no, she didn't.'

'Did she usually go home with you?'

'Sometimes she stayed on.'

'Why?'

It was light enough to see the boy's embarrassed shrug. Georgie had no such inhibitions. 'She had a thing about Vince, she was always round his neck.'

'Did she go to bed with him?'

'What do you think?'

'Was Peters specially keen on Sylvie?'

The girl laughed. 'You must be joking! Vince can always take or leave it and as for Sylvie, I know she's dead but let's face it, she was a bit of a drag.'

'Oh, I wouldn't say that; Sylvie was OK.' Jerry tried to be fair.

'Didn't she come with a boy friend?'

'She came sometimes with Jackie Martin, the schoolteacher, but that was a while ago. He stopped coming, I think he was too old,' Jerry said.

'I don't know about that, Sylvie was quite old – anyway she stopped bringing him and she hasn't come with anybody else. Jackie Martin still hung around to take her home some nights.'

'And Sylvie got mad about it.'

Georgie sneered. 'Sylvie pretended to get mad.'

Peters' voice came over again, they must have been dancing in between—

> 'Watch some more television
> Like the evening before;
> Test your wit and your knowledge,
> Disagree with the score,
> So go to bed with a novel
> To find out what real lovers do:
>> And while you think you're killing time,
>> It's time that's killing you,
>> It's time that's killing you.'

'Tell me about Saturday night – when did you first miss Sylvie?'

'Got a ciggie, Jerry?'

The boy handed her a packet of cigarettes and a box of matches. 'We didn't *miss* her like that, she just wasn't with us on the way home.'

'Nobody mentioned the fact?'

Georgie fumbled with her cigarette, choking on the smoke. 'One of the girls said something about it being Sylvie's turn.'

'Her turn?'

'With Vince, some of the girls get a kick out of him.'

'Not Georgie, we're going steady, aren't we, Georgie?'

'That's what you say.' She pulled her skimpy suede jacket more tightly round her and shivered. 'It's cold!'

'I won't keep you long. Was it foggy?'

'A bit, not bad; you could see all right.'

'I think it got worse later.'

'Do you know Nick Marsden?'

Georgie giggled. 'Nick? He's crackers.'

'He spies on us,' the boy said, 'but nobody takes any notice of him.'

'Did Sylvie have girl friends?'

Georgie hesitated. 'She didn't have many friends: her only special friend was Sally Rowse.'

'Is Sally here tonight?'

'No, I don't think her mother would let her come.'

Wycliffe stood up. 'Well, thank you both for your help. I may want you to make a statement tomorrow.'

'Did somebody kill Sylvie?'

'We've got to find out.'

Peters was ending his song—

> 'Don't see people but shadows
> Don't have wishes but dreams
> Don't know things but their pictures
> Not what is but what seems;
> Rather have a stained-glass window
> Than one you can really see through;
> > And while you think you're killing time,
> > It's time that's killing you,
> > It's time that's killing you.'

The applause was flattering.

'We'll get back, he might do an encore.'

Two things occurred to him. One was that despite the fuss they were making few of the islanders really believed that Sylvie had been murdered. Had they believed it there would not have been a score of youngsters at the Peters' place two nights later. The other was that the youth of the island had a good deal in common with their mainland brothers and sisters.

The two youngsters had gone back inside but Wycliffe lit his pipe and strolled round the courtyard, smoking. The clouds had gone and the indigo sky was full of stars; the mood in the Barn had changed too, beat and protest had given place to ballads, sentimental and easier on the eardrums. During the quieter passages he thought that he could hear the surf on the beaches though the nearest sea must have been more than a mile away.

Sylvie Eva had been murdered; Sylvie Eva had been pregnant. The two facts might have been added up quite simply once, but not now, not even on the island. But, on the face of it, it seemed that Peters had gone in for murder. What motive could he have had? Passion? Not with half the girls on the island anxious to jump into bed with him. Fear? Of what? Wycliffe shrugged, it was too soon to look for conclusions.

At last the music stopped, the flashing lights were switched off and the youngsters started to leave. ' 'Night, Vince . . . 'Night, Clarissa . . . See you Wednesday . . .' All very conventional and respectable. A few minutes after they had gone Clarissa came out and crossed the courtyard with a light, quick step. Lights sprang up in the house. He could still hear voices and laughter from the other side of the valley as the kids made their way home. They were not oppressed by Sylvie's death. When Peters came out Wycliffe intercepted him.

'I would like a word with you, Mr Peters.'

'Still here, superintendent? The night is young – come in.'

'You may not want Miss . . .'

'Clarissa and I have no secrets.'

He was shown into a large sitting-room at the back of the house. One wall was made up of floor to ceiling curtains, presumably because the stonework had been replaced by glass. The room had been furnished out of the modern-furnishings department of Harrods and it looked like a studio set for a stockbroker's drawing-room. Peters seemed older, more serious, worried. Perhaps he was tired.

Wycliffe had to sit on a monstrous black leather settee.

'Drink? Whisky? Vodka? Gin?'

'Whisky.'

'Does that mean that I'm not suspected?'

'It means that I can do with a drink.'

The walls were painted dove grey, and there were several modern paintings on plinths. Wycliffe recognized a Piper and two Bratbys. Peters poured out whisky for Wycliffe and orange juice for himself.

'Here's to the Scene!'

'I am told that you were having an affair with the dead girl.'

Peters grinned. 'Is that what they say?'

'And with several of the other girls who come here.'

'It's not illegal, is it?'

'Not if the girls are over the age of consent.'

Peters was silky. 'I'm always very careful about that.'

'Giving the local dollies a treat – is that the angle?'

Peters was reproving. 'That's not quite nice, Mr Wycliffe.'

'It's a hazardous game in a place like this.'

'But it was not I who was murdered.'

The door opened and Clarissa came in carrying a tray with two steaming pottery mugs on it. She had changed into a black, silk trouser suit which clung to her body. She was obviously surprised to find Wycliffe there. 'I'm sorry, Vince, I did not know . . . I made the cocoa . . .' She spoke with clipped precision.

Wycliffe had difficulty in covering his amusement. It must mean something that Vince Peters, ex-pop idol and notorious sex symbol, went to bed on cocoa.

Clarissa put the tray down on a low table and looked questioningly at Peters.

'Ma'moiselle Loiseau, Detective Chief Superintendent Wycliffe.' Peters made the introductions with a flourish. 'Mr Wycliffe thinks that I murdered Sylvie.'

'That is foolish!' The dark eyes rested on Wycliffe in quick appraisal. She was small, fragile, exquisite, an exhibition piece too precious one might think for everyday use, but there was strength in the set of her jaw and fire in her eye.

'Somebody killed her,' Wycliffe said. 'Somebody beat her over the head and face then pushed her body into the quarry.'

'That is terrible but it was not Vince – he could not harm anybody. I know what the islanders say and sometimes he is foolish but . . .'

'. . . underneath there beats a heart of gold. The superintendent doesn't believe it.'

Wycliffe sipped his whisky. 'You told me this morning that Sylvie had no close friends . . .'

'I told you that I didn't know of any.'

'But what about Jackie?' Clarissa pronounced the name in two quite distinct syllables.

'The schoolteacher?' Wycliffe asked. 'I thought that had been broken off . . .'

'It has.'

'Pooh! A lovers' . . . How do you say? A small quarrel. When he is here he talks to me – I can tell. He is in love, that boy.'

'He comes here?'

'But certainly! Not to the Barn, you understand, that he does not like, but he is a friend of Vince . . .'

Peters was not pleased. 'He comes here to see me because we are both interested in the same thing.'

'And what is that?'

'Flies!' To Clarissa it was obviously an inconceivable pre-occupation. 'They are – how do you say – Dipters – is that right?'

'Dipterists.'

'Yes, they collect flies!' She squirmed deliciously. 'Vince does not like me to tell people.'

'Which doesn't stop you.'

Wycliffe noted that since they had come into the house Peters had not once addressed him as 'man'.

'You also told me that Sylvie did not stay behind on Saturday night after the others had gone.'

'That's right, she didn't.'

'No, she did not! Sometimes . . . but not on Saturday; on Saturday it was just like now, the two of us.'

'The other youngsters say that she was not with them.'

'I can't say about that.' Peters sipped his cocoa.

'A witness states that you were seen with Sylvie Eva walking in the direction of the farm.'

'What witness? As you must know by now some of the islanders would say anything they thought would shop me.'

Wycliffe was content not to press the point for the moment. Softly walkee . . . 'You will be required to make a statement, Mr Peters.'

'Any time.'

Wycliffe walked home in the starlight. Not far from Salubrious Place he met Nick Marsden shambling along the track, on his way home. He was too far gone to bother with Wycliffe.

Jordan was waiting up for him, the clock on the mantelshelf showed half an hour after midnight and Jordan was mildly reproachful, 'Mr Bellings, the deputy chief has been trying to get you on the telephone, sir.'

'I don't doubt it.'

'And several newspapers . . .'

'What about the school?'

'That's fixed. The chairman of the Education Committee was on to me earlier; apparently Chief Inspector Gill telephoned him direct.'

'Good old Jimmy!' Wycliffe was glad that he would be seeing him in the morning. 'Anything else?'

'Dr Franks left a message for you to ring him at his hotel.' Jordan consulted a scrap of paper. 'The number is 221.'

Franks answered from his bed. 'I'd given you up.' He sounded weary. 'I'll send you my report but I tell you now there will be very little new in it. I'm satisfied that her injuries cannot be wholly attributed to the fall. The skull damage must have been inflicted before her body was pushed into the quarry and it was the skull damage which killed her.'

'Anything more on the weapon?'

Franks seemed to hesitate. 'Next to nothing, I searched the wounds very thoroughly for foreign matter.'

'Well?'

'I found a few fragments of rust – tiny red flakes.'

'An iron bar of some sort.'

'It looks like it. Not the sort of thing your well-dressed gent carried about with him.'

'No, but there's plenty of scrap lying about out there.' Wycliffe considered. 'It would be worth a search, he's not likely to have taken the thing home with him.'

'The trouble will be to recognize it when you find it.'

'You confirmed the pregnancy?'

'No doubt about that.'

'Blood groups?'

'The mother was group O and the baby A.'

Wycliffe made a considerable effort of recollection. 'So the father must be group A or AB – is that right?'

'Quite right.'

'Thanks, it's better than nothing.'

'Our motto is service.'

'Good night.'

Wycliffe was thoughtful. The investigation had started to silence local gossip but it was now certain that the gossip had been well founded. Sylvie had been murdered and that is what had been claimed. Now, looking for a number one suspect, who filled the bill but Peters? And they had said that too.

Wycliffe believed that, over the years, he had acquired the ability to exclude at will, certain topics from his mind. If he worried about his cases at all it was at the subconscious level or because he chose to worry in the hope that some constructive idea might emerge. Now he went to bed and to sleep, dreaming that he was on a rocky shore facing an incoming tide with a wall of high cliffs behind him. Only when the water was lapping round his ankles and he was clawing at the smooth rock face with his fingers, did he wake, his heart racing, his nails digging into his palms.

Vince Peters lay awake far into the night but that was nothing new. He had sleeping tablets but his doctor had told him that his insomnia was voluntary. Which was true, up to a point. He was greedy for life, each night he was reluctant to snap the last thin thread of consciousness. In any case he liked to take stock of himself, to strike a balance for the day. This morning he had had pins and needles in his left leg. But there seemed to be some easing of the rigidity in his arm . . . And what about his mind? Who could tell?

Sometimes he could look at himself objectively, as a case for treatment. But for him there was no treatment. It came on like the tide, advancing, retreating and again advancing, gaining a little each time.

Then there was the business of the girl. He felt sorry for her, poor little cow. But one way and another she had been asking for it. The doe-eyed copper had seemed suspicious and he and his mates would probably ferret out the truth in the end. Bully for them! Why should he care? But he did. He thought of Jackie Martin and grinned to himself. Probably Jackie had made his statement to the police already and wet his trousers in the process.

He sighed and turned over. Clarissa stirred in her sleep.

4

Next day the routine of a murder investigation was getting under way. Chief Inspector Gill arrived with four crime squad detectives and a uniformed sergeant with three constables from Division. They moved into the school, a fairly new building, glass and concrete with shiny parquet floors on which it was difficult to stand up. Two classrooms became dormitories with beds and blankets supplied by the island's emergency service. The headmaster's office became Wycliffe's and Gill was given the office of the deputy head. A telephone engineer was busy draping temporary cables round the building to provide extra telephones and a switchboard was set up in the main hall which was to be the control room. A police radio mechanic was installing a two-way radio-control panel to handle messages through the personal radios of the men and in the canteen two local women were preparing meals.

Wycliffe brought Chief Inspector Gill up to date on the case then he wandered round the school getting the feel of it, like a dog in a new home. Gill sat on a table in the hall, directing operations and smoking his black cheroots. Already three detectives were taking statements from the young people who had been at the Barn on Saturday night. Jeremy Nance was there with his girl friend, looking very important. Nick Marsden was there, sitting on a form by himself looking lost.

Finally Wycliffe seated himself behind the headmaster's desk and, almost immediately, Jimmy Gill came in with a small sheaf of type-script – the first reports. He looked round the office and his ugly, rubbery face wrinkled expressively.

'Schools give me the creeps.'

'You've got a guilty conscience, my lad!'

Gill slid the papers into Wycliffe's tray.

'Anything there?'

'This might interest you.' Gill extracted a typewritten sheet from the pile and started to quote from it. 'Vincent Steven Peters, born 22nd April 1944 . . . 4 Mill Lane, Bolton, Lanes . . . Educated Falls Road Junior, Bolton Grammar and Birmingham University . . . He didn't stay the course – packed in at the end of the first year to join a folk group called The Mariners. Later they went in for pop and changed their name to The Sockets. During a European tour with the group in 1970 he met Clarissa Loisseau, a Corsican girl who was living in Paris. They lived together and continued to do so after he left the group.'

'I suppose it would have been bad for his image to get married. Anything else?'

'Only that when he left The Sockets it's estimated that he must have been worth half-a-million.'

'Anything from CRO?'

'Nothing against him.'

Wycliffe sighed. 'It's a funny world.'

'More peculiar than funny, I'd say,' Gill remarked.

'Any news of the inquest?'

'It's fixed for this afternoon. The coroner will take evidence of identification and adjourn. Jordan will be there, of course.'

'You'd better go.'

Wycliffe told him what little Franks had been able to discover about the weapon. 'It's worth a try, Jimmy. Get some men out there and search. After all there can't be all that many bits of iron lying around which are easily portable and suitable as a weapon.'

'Needles in haystacks are our speciality,' Gill said.

Very little emerged from the morning's work. One of the girls said that far from staying on after the others, Sylvie had left early on the night she died. Wycliffe spoke to the girl himself. A tall, well-made teenager with blonde hair to her shoulders, straight and sleek as a waterfall.

'You are Sally Rowse?'

'Yes.' She held herself upright in her chair, hands clenched.

'I believe that you were one of Sylvie's closest friends?'

She nodded, not far from tears.

'Tell me what you told the sergeant about Saturday night.'

'About Sylvie leaving early?'

'Yes.'

557

'Well, there's a cloakroom at the Barn. I was just coming out of the loo and there was Sylvie putting her coat on. I said something like, "Had enough?" and she said, "You could say that". It didn't mean anything – just chat.'

'What time was this?'

'Before ten, say a quarter-to.'

'Did she seem worried or depressed?'

The girl hesitated. 'No, I don't think so. She wasn't exactly swinging but Sylvie was always a bit moody. I thought, perhaps, she had to go home early because of her dad.'

'When you went back to the Barn was Peters there?'

'I don't know.' The translucent skin of her forehead wrinkled into a frown. 'I don't think he was.'

'Did you see him again that evening?'

She shook her head. 'It's no good, I don't think so but I'm not sure.'

'Never mind. What about Clarissa?'

'No, Clarissa wasn't there definitely. She didn't come in at all on Saturday evening.'

'Was that unusual?'

'No, she often doesn't come in and when she does she doesn't stay long. I don't think she cares for it all that much.'

'Have you any idea where Sylvie was going when she left?'

'No, I told you, I thought she was going home.'

'Could she have arranged to meet someone?'

'But who?'

'Wasn't she friendly with Jackie Martin, the schoolteacher?'

Sally shook her head with decision. 'She wouldn't have been going to meet Jackie, that was ancient history.'

Wycliffe was smoking his pipe, the atmosphere was becoming more relaxed, the girl had got over her nervousness and was starting to talk naturally. 'Of course, she couldn't quite shake him off, he kept hanging around. Sometimes he would wait for her when she was at the Barn.'

'And she objected?'

'Well, he was a bit of a pest. All the same I felt sorry for him. Sylvie didn't mince words.'

'But he persisted?'

'Yes.'

'He must have been very fond of her.'

She nodded gravely. 'Yes, I think Sylvie was the only girl who ever took any notice of him and when she ditched him . . .'

'Jackie isn't very popular with girls?'

She grinned briefly. 'He hasn't got a clue! I don't know what it is about him really but he's so *serious* . . . He puts you off.'

'Would it be right to say that Sylvie broke it off with Jackie because she became attached to Peters?'

She considered this. 'I suppose it would. She fell for Vince in a big way, there's no doubt about that.'

'And she wasn't the only one, apparently.'

'That's true. Apart from all the glamour – him being who he is and all that – he's still quite a nice bloke to be with. He can make you *feel* somebody when he puts his mind to it . . .'

'Is it true that he has sex with several of the girls?'

Again the frown. 'I know that's what they say but I think all that talk is exaggerated.'

'By whom?'

She looked surprised. 'Why, by the girls. It's the thing to say.'

'A sort of status symbol?'

'Something like that.'

'What about Sylvie?'

She thought for some time before answering. 'In Sylvie's case I think there was something in it. Vince treated her a bit different from the others. Of course, I don't *know* anything. Sylvie wasn't the sort to talk.'

And that was all. Trinity House were able to confirm that the fog did not really thicken until after midnight. The signals on Temple Rock and Ship Island were logged at 01.07 and 01.11 respectively. In his mind's eye Wycliffe could see the young people setting off home in the moist darkness, shouting to each other, laughing. Where was Sylvie then?

Wycliffe and Gill interviewed Jackie Martin together. He was a tall, thin, studious-looking youth with glasses and he walked with a stoop as though to minimize his height. He looked pale and ill and his movements were jerky – unpredictable.

'Not the first time you've been in this room, Mr Martin?'

'What?' He looked round vaguely.

'You teach in the school, don't you?'

'Oh, yes, I see what you mean.'

'What do you teach?'

'Biology.'

'Sylvie's death must have come as a great shock to you.'

He nodded, dumbly.

'Did you know she was pregnant?'

He shook his head decisively. 'No, I didn't know – not until her father told me yesterday.'

'Is it possible that you were the child's father?'

He flushed. 'Me? No! We . . . Sylvie and I never . . .'

'Have you any idea whose child it might be?'

'No, none.'

'Are you saying that Sylvie would go with anybody?'

'No! I'm not saying that.' He picked at a loose thread in the seam of his trousers. 'I suppose it must have been Peters' child.'

'You are a friend of his?'

'Not a friend.'

'But you visit him.'

'We have a common interest but I don't like him very much. At least I don't like some of the things he does . . .'

'Such as?'

He shifted uneasily in his chair, apparently in an agony of discomfort. 'He had sexual relations with several of the girls.'

'With Sylvie too?'

'Yes.'

'Was that why you and Sylvie broke it off?'

He blushed again. 'When she met Peters she didn't want me any more.' His humility was embarrassing.

'What is your common interest with Peters?'

'We are both interested in the Diptera – the two-winged flies.'

Gill, who had not so far spoken, stretched his legs and asked lazily, 'Don't all flies have two wings?'

'True flies do but there are many insects loosely called flies which have four wings.'

'Well I'm damned!' Gill said without a smile.

'What do you do with these flies?'

'We collect and study them – there are five thousand species in Great Britain and eighty thousand in the whole world . . .'

'And Peters is interested in these insects?'

560

'Oh, yes. He studied zoology at University and he was going to specialize in entomology but he got mixed up in this pop music . . .'

'Did you go to University, Mr Martin?'

'No, I wasn't good enough. I trained to teach at a College of Education.'

Gill leaned forward as though much interested. 'Although Peters took your girl away from you, you still visit him?'

Martin looked surprised. 'I told you, we are both interested in flies.'

'Where were you on Saturday evening?'

'Why do you ask me that?'

Wycliffe was reassuring. 'We ask every witness that question and later today we shall start to ask everyone in the island.'

'Oh, I see. I was at home.'

'All the evening?'

'Yes.'

'Anyone to confirm that?'

'My mother, I suppose.'

'You and your mother live alone?' Wycliffe was convinced that the boy's mother would turn out to be a widow. He was wrong.

'My father is there too but he's an invalid, almost helpless.'

Wycliffe thought he could sense the claustrophobic atmosphere of the home which had produced this sensitive, slightly effeminate and pedantic young man.

'Even after your relationship with Sylvie ended you sometimes waited for her when she was at the Barn?'

It was painful to watch him. His hands gripped his knees, the knuckles showing white. 'That's my business!'

'Yes. But did you meet her on Saturday night?'

'No, I did not!' He almost shouted. 'I told you, I was home all the evening.' He stood up, looking round the room wildly as though he could not remember where the exit was. 'Oh, God! Why do you have to keep on and on?' He burst into tears and rushed out of the room.

'Let him go!'

'Bloody little drip!' Gill said.

Wycliffe sighed. 'We can't all have heads and hides like rugby footballs, Jimmy.'

Wycliffe was interested in going through the reports to come

561

across Marsden's statement. Nicholas Jason Marsden, aged sixty-one of Quay Cottages, Quincey Cove. Occupation: Fisherman. The statement merely confirmed what he had told Wycliffe the previous night. Wycliffe asked Jordan about him.

'The Marsden family is our cross, sir. They've lived out to Quincey Cove for a hundred and fifty years and now there's five generations of them, living. Old Emily must be knocking on for the century and there's Moira who's fifteen so it won't be long before we've got six generations to contend with. Nick is the oldest living male – the women always outlive the men by twenty years at least.'

'What do they all do for a living – fish?'

Jordan scratched his ear. 'A good question. Of course, they've got their pots . . .'

'Pots?'

'Crab and lobster, sir. They do a bit of long lining too but that's not the half of it. Where there's pickings, there you'll find a Marsden and what they can't get any other way, they'll nick.'

'Has he got form?'

'Not half what he should have – bound over in sixty-three, three months in sixty-five and a year in seventy.'

'He seems to hang around the youngsters who go to the Barn.'

'I agree he's a bit of a Peeping Tom but I think he's harmless from that point of view.'

'I hope you're right! So you wouldn't look on him as a good witness?'

Jordan laughed. 'I wouldn't believe him if he told me the time. Lying comes more natural than the truth from the Marsdens. They're all alike.'

'Has he any special reason to have it in for Peters?'

'I'll say! Peters owns all the land down the valley to the cove and he's trying to get the Marsdens out.'

'Seems a bit hard after a hundred and fifty years.'

Jordan hesitated, torn between local loyalties and sweet reason. 'It is hard but Peters has a point. He never gets any rent – not that he seems to care about that, but he's keen to have the cove tidied up. It's a pretty spot and Marsden's place is surrounded by all the junk in creation, piles of drift-wood, scrap, staved-in boats, oil drums, beds, mattresses – you name it, he's got it. Peters gave him six months to get it tidied up and when nothing happened he applied for a possession order. It comes up in a fortnight's time.'

'Marsden seems to get on well enough with Peters' brother.'

'Oh, he does that all right and it's not so surprising as it sounds. If you ask me the Peters brothers don't hit it off. Roger stays at a café on the quay when he's in the islands and I don't think he sees much of his brother.'

Deputy Chief Constable Bellings telephoned.

'So it's murder, Charles.'

'It looks like it.' Wycliffe was always at his most boorish with the suave, politically-minded Bellings.

'What does the Lord Warden have to say about that?'

'I've no idea, I haven't asked him.'

'You mean you haven't made contact? You should, Charles, you really should. Sir John's influence isn't confined to the islands, he's a man to be reckoned with. What about this fellow Peters?'

'What about him?'

'He's evidently a thorn in the flesh of the locals.'

'But that doesn't make him a murderer.'

'No, of course not. Anyway, don't neglect Sir John, the Chief would be most upset if he thought . . .'

Being a detective has its dramatic moments but mostly it is boring routine; asking dull questions and getting dull answers, making and reading endless reports, talking to people who are frightened and suspicious or cunning and deceitful. And after all that you have to keep your superiors happy, the worst chore of all.

The midday boat brought a police Land-Rover and a number of reinforcements, a mixed bag, drawn from several divisions, in the charge of an inspector. After a meal they were put to work on house-to-house enquiries. 'Where were you on Saturday evening between seven-thirty and midnight? Did you know Sylvia Eva? When did you last see her? Have you seen her recently in company with a man? Have you seen . . . ? Do you know . . . ? Will you let us know if . . . ?' The answers were laboriously written down and some of them were afterwards typed with carbon copies to swell the files.

Wycliffe had a canteen meal with Chief Inspector Gill and the newly arrived Inspector Golly. Golly had a protruding Adam's apple and a jet black military moustache; he wore bandbox uniform and held himself like a guardsman. Wycliffe felt an irrational dislike. The meal was depressing – fish cooked in batter with tinned peas and pulpy tomatoes.

'I am at your disposal, sir.'

Wycliffe looked at him blandly and said nothing.

'If you will give me your instructions, sir.'

'I am going to put you in charge of paper, Mr Golly. It will be up to you to collect it, read what is on it and decide what to do with it.'

'You want me to be a collator for the case, sir.'

'You have an apt turn of phrase, Mr Golly,' Wycliffe said gravely.

In the afternoon Inspector Golly came to see Wycliffe; he stood in the office, waiting to be addressed. Although it was stickily hot he was still wearing full uniform.

'Mr Golly?'

'I thought you should see this, sir.' He placed two sheets of notepaper on the desk – a letter, beautifully written in italic script. 'It's young Martin's writing, sir, I checked.'

The letter was undated and bore no address. It read:

My dearest Sylvie,

I am forced to write to you because you will never let me see you alone. I have tried to accept that all is over between us and to resign myself to seeing you give yourself to someone else; someone who, in the long run, is sure to hurt you. I think I could bear losing you if it meant your happiness but you know in your heart that it does not, that you are to him only what others have been and will be.

I do not ask you to love me, only that you will let me see you sometimes. I will do anything you say, accept any conditions you make if you will only give me a little hope. If you will not, I do not think that I shall be able to carry on living. During the precious time that we were together you became so much a part of me that I cannot now truly exist without you. I lie awake at night, I cannot eat and I cannot work, for you are always in my mind and your dear face is always before my eyes. If you have any kindness left for me let me talk to you, my darling. I will wait for you tomorrow night as so many times before but this time in the hope that you will take pity on me.

Counting the hours and the minutes, my love.

J.

As Wycliffe finished reading Gill came in, just back from the inquest.

'How did it go?'

'Very businesslike. Evidence of the finding of the body, identification and adjournment. No messing. The funeral is tomorrow.'

Wycliffe passed him the letter. Gill read it and dropped it on the desk with an amused leer on his face. He had never needed to beg of any woman; his ugly, expressive features and his blatant sexuality seemed to be irresistible. 'Martin?'

Wycliffe nodded.

'Well, I've told you what I think of him. Where did it come from anyway?'

'Sergeant Scales found it in the girl's bedroom, in a pocket of one of her coats. I brought it along to Mr Wycliffe at once.'

As a matter of routine, Wycliffe had given instructions for Sylvie's bedroom to be searched.

'No date,' Gill said.

'But there's an envelope with a postmark.' Inspector Golly produced the envelope like a conjurer.

Gill took it. 'Is this a bloody lucky dip? What are we supposed to do next? Guess what you've got in the other pocket?'

Golly stiffened but said nothing. Wycliffe was having trouble keeping his pipe alight. Gill put the envelope on the desk.

'It's postmarked six o'clock Friday evening so she got it on Saturday morning. That boy conned us, she left early to meet him.'

'Or not to,' Wycliffe said.

'I don't get it.'

'I'm saying that it's equally possible she left early to avoid him.'

Gill slumped on to one of the chairs by Wycliffe's desk. 'You may be right at that! Either way the lad's got some talking to do. We'd better have him in.'

'See him at home first.' In Wycliffe's experience there was much to be gained from seeing a man in his normal surroundings. There might come a time when it would be good psychology to bring him into the neutral or even hostile context of an interview room but it was a mistake to start there. It was for this reason – at least, with this excuse, that he insisted on going out and seeing for himself. 'Where does he live?'

'The Tower House on the quay, sir.' Golly had only been in the islands a few hours but he had taken the trouble to brief himself from the case records.

'Thank you, Mr Golly.'

Gill's face was one broad, sardonic grin.

Wycliffe went down the steep slope from the school to the quay. At the peak of the season the *Islander* brought day trippers from the mainland; eight hours on the water, four on the island. She was lying at her berth and her returning passengers were straggling up the gangway. Charlie Martin was sitting on his bollard, smoking his pipe. He looked at Wycliffe, his serene blue eyes, speculative, appraising.

'No arrest yet, Mr Wycliffe?'

'Not yet, Mr Martin.'

The old man studied the bowl of his pipe thoughtfully then raised his eyes to Wycliffe's. 'I suppose it's possible that the lass had an accident after all?' He asked the question with disarming naïvety.

Wycliffe was puzzled. 'If so it was a very odd sort of accident.'

Martin nodded. 'It's odd how people fall. I remember a case when I was a young man – fifty years ago . . .' And he launched into a tedious anecdote about a mate of his who had fallen from the crosstrees to the deck of a wind-jammer. Such loquacity was uncharacteristic and obviously had a motive though Wycliffe was not sure what the motive was. He excused himself at last and continued along the quay.

The Tower House was the folly of a well-to-do oddity who had settled on the island in the 1830s when the islanders scraped a living out of a traditional blend of primitive cultivation, equally primitive fishing and better organized smuggling. The house stood apart from others along the quay; it was four storeys high, octagonal in shape and surmounted by a cupola of sheet lead turned almost white by the weather and bird droppings. The tower was neglected, with stucco peeling off the walls and the woodwork destitute of any sign of paint.

Wycliffe knocked on the door which opened on to the street. After a short while his knock was answered by a woman in her late forties. She was thin, wiry and tough with the look of one who has survived more than her fair share of adversity. She was wiping rough, reddened hands on a white towel.

'Yes?'

'Mrs Martin?'

'What do you want?'

Wycliffe introduced himself although he was sure that she knew him and said that he had come to talk to her son.

'About the Eva girl?'

'About Sylvie, yes.'

She sniffed. 'I don't know why you have to keep pestering my son, he's upset enough already.'

'Is he at home?'

She hesitated then bowed to the inevitable. 'Yes, he is. You had better come in.'

If the outside of the house was neglected the inside was spartan but scrupulously clean. The little hall was floored with red quarry tiles, worn but shining and the wooden, spiral staircase was covered with polished linoleum held in place by gleaming, brass stair-rods. A single door off the hall stood partly open into the living-room and Wycliffe glimpsed an old-fashioned range and, seated beside it in a slatted wooden armchair, an incredibly thin old man with paper-white features and lifeless, staring eyes which seemed dispro-portionately large. She pulled the door to quickly, shutting out the image.

'My son's room is on the top floor, I'll take you up.'

Wycliffe protested that he could find his own way and after a moment of doubt she agreed. 'A remarkable house you have, Mrs Martin.'

'It's cheap.'

It was not until he had turned the spiral, out of sight of the hall, that he heard her open the living-room door and her dry, aggressive voice saying, 'It's nothing, don't excite yourself. Just somebody to see Jackie.'

One room on each floor. The doors set deeply in the thick walls, each in a Gothic arch like the doors in a church. Although Martin must have heard him climbing the stairs he gave no sign until Wycliffe knocked at the door of his room.

'Come in.'

The landing and stairs had been cut off in such a way that the room had seven sides, three of them had windows and the others were lined with bookshelves and cupboards. As Wycliffe entered, Martin got up from a table near the middle of the room where he must have been sitting, brooding for there was nothing on the table. He looked even more pale and pinched than he had done in the morning and his eyes behind the glasses were red rimmed.

'I'm sorry about this morning, I couldn't help it.'

Wycliffe was drawn, irresistibly, to the windows and stood, with his back to the room, staring out over the harbour, the shallow bay and the open sea beyond. 'What a view!'

'What? Oh, yes, I suppose it is pretty impressive if you're not used to it.'

Wycliffe continued to stand by the window and the silence lengthened. Martin fidgeted until he could stand it no longer and burst out, 'What do you want? Why have you come here?'

Wycliffe did not answer immediately but after a little while he said, quietly, 'You know that Sylvie was murdered?'

Martin laughed, almost hysterically. 'You believe that?'

'I know it to be a fact.' He turned to face the young man.

'They said that to make trouble for Peters.' He was standing, gripping the edge of the table with both hands. 'They want to get him off the island.'

'It's not a question of what anybody said. Somebody killed Sylvie by beating her across the head and face with a weapon of some sort; then, and not until then, her body was pushed into the quarry.'

He thought Martin was going to faint and guided him to a chair. The boy collapsed into it and sat with his eyes closed. Wycliffe drew up the only other chair and sat near him.

'You were very much in love with Sylvie weren't you?'

The eyelids flickered but there was no other response. Wycliffe knew enough of human nature to recognize that his collapse was half genuine, half a protective sham. The boy was near the end of his tether but he was prepared to make himself appear worse than he was in order to avoid questions.

As Wycliffe took the letter from his pocket Martin's eyes opened.

'From you to Sylvie, written the day before she was murdered and arranging to meet her on Saturday evening when she left the Barn . . .'

'You have no right!' His anger flared and died.

Wycliffe leaned forward in his chair and spoke with great gravity. 'Sooner or later you will have to tell me what happened on Saturday night.'

'Nothing happened. I told you, I was here all the evening.'

'You did not keep the appointment you made?'

'No!' Defiant.

'That is a lie!'

Martin sat motionless and was silent. The windows were open and the noises of the waterfront drifted up to them. The *Islander* gave a short blast on her siren to warn latecomers, gulls shrieked, the engine of a motor launch spluttered into life. It was even possible to hear the words of two tourists discussing whether or not they would go on an evening cruise round the island.

'What do you want me to say?'

'I want you to tell me the truth about Saturday night.'

'You won't believe me.'

Wycliffe said nothing.

'Sylvie usually left the Barn at about eleven o'clock, sometimes later.'

'Well?'

'I left home about ten and I got there by half-past.'

'Where?'

'Where I had waited for her before, at the top of the slope above the valley.'

'Near the quarry?'

'Fairly near, I suppose.'

'What happened?'

He shook his head. 'Nothing happened. I waited there until they broke up and they all came up the hill together. Sylvie wasn't with them.'

'How could you know? It was dark.'

'I would have recognized her.'

'Did any of them see you?'

'I don't think so.'

'What did you do?'

Another long silence.

'Well?'

'I went down to the house. The Barn was in darkness but there was a light in the living-room at the back of the house. The curtains were drawn and I couldn't see anything.'

'Then?'

'Nothing. I thought she must be with Peters so I came home.'

It was so fatuous that it had the ring of truth. 'Is that the truth?'

'I swear it!'

'What time did you get home?'

'A quarter-to-one or a little after.'

'How long did it take you?'

'A bit longer than usual because of the fog – about three-quarters of an hour.'

Fact or fiction? By leaning on the boy a bit harder he might find out but it was too early. When he put pressure on a suspect he liked to have most of the cards already in his hand.

He pottered about the room trying to get the measure of its owner. A fairly catholic collection of books. Natural history, entomology, evolution and genetics. A few books on archaeology and history, some popular works on psychology and shelf after shelf of historical romances from Dumas to du Maurier. Martin's insect collection was housed in a stack of cork-lined boxes and he had an old-fashioned binocular microscope with a brass tube.

Wycliffe had sensed the claustrophobic atmosphere in which Martin lived, now he was struck by the introverted character of the room. It was a severely circumscribed world, a cell, a cocoon, almost complete in itself – almost but not quite. Martin had to venture out, not only to earn his living but to give substance to his romantic dream. That had been Sylvie's role and she had let him down.

'While you were waiting for Sylvie did you see anyone?'

'No, well, only Nick Marsden. He was mooning about as usual. I didn't take much notice.'

'I would like you to come back with me to make a statement.'

He looked at Wycliffe with frightened eyes. 'Shall I be free to go afterwards?'

'Why not?'

As Wycliffe went out on to the landing he saw Mrs Martin disappearing round the bend of the stairs but when they reached the ground floor the living-room door was closed. Martin hesitated. 'I'd better tell her . . .'

He went into the living-room, closing the door behind him but he was only gone for a short time. They walked along the quay and up the slope to the school. Martin walked self-consciously in company with the chief superintendent as though all eyes were on him. Charlie Martin saw them pass but he gave no sign.

'Has your father been an invalid for long?'

'Eleven years. Of course, he's a lot older than mother, he'll be seventy-two next month if he lives that long. I don't know how she . . .'

'You were saying?'

'Nothing.'

They reached the school entrance and as they passed through the swing-doors Wycliffe said, 'By the way, Mr Martin, do you happen to know your blood group?'

Martin seemed surprised by the question. 'Group O – why?'

Wycliffe was saved explanation by several pressmen waiting for him in the foyer.

Jackie Martin spent the evening in his room. He tried to work on his insects, then he tried to read but he found himself going over and over the same lines. He looked out of the window and saw in the eastern sky a pale reflection of the sunset. As usual on a fine summer evening the quay was crowded with people and their voices reached him – normal, cheerful voices, the voices of people quietly enjoying themselves. Boys arm in arm with scantily clad girls. He watched, half yearning, half contemptuous. Sometimes he felt that he would give ten years of his life to change places with any one of them.

Not for the first time he thought about suicide. His memory was well stocked with literary and historical suicides but when it came to the point he found himself ignorant. How to set about it? He could not face pain, nor could he contemplate those awful moments which must come to a drowning man when he begins to suffocate . . . The immediate response must be to breathe . . . In his imagination he lived through such moments and groaned aloud. He told himself that he was not afraid of death, death seemed almost friendly but dying . . .

He had to talk to somebody or he would go mad. Not his mother. He could not face another confrontation which would end, inevitably, with them wallowing in each other's emotions. Afterwards he would feel drained – physically and mentally.

He put on his jacket and crept downstairs but as he reached the little hall the door of the living-room opened.

'Where are you going?'

'Out.'

She looked at him for a moment in silence as though trying to make up her mind then she kissed him on the cheek and let him go. 'Be careful!'

For once it was better outside.

He walked up the hill and out of the town on to the moor. It was dusk and growing dark. He hurried as though he had a pressing appointment and only slowed when he came in sight of Salubrious Place. There was nobody in the Barn and the house showed only a single light. His courage all but failed him, he almost turned back.

When he rang it was not long before a light went on in the hall and Clarissa answered the door.

'Jackie!' She sounded surprised but not unwelcoming. 'Come into the living-room.'

Vince was sitting at a table on which playing cards were laid out. The big room was lit only by a standard lamp near the table and the curtains had not been drawn over the great wall of glass which separated the room from the meadow. The last vestiges of daylight were fading from a cloudless sky.

'We are playing Bezique and I am winning so Vince will be glad to stop.'

Vince's greeting was cool.

'Don't let me stop the game.'

'Don't be silly! We will play three-handed bridge,' Clarissa said.

And they did. For a time Jackie came near to feeling normal. Until he noticed the way Vince was looking at him. There was no mistaking that look, he had been on the receiving end too often. Later, Clarissa switched on the lights, drew the curtains and brought in tea and little pâté sandwiches. Then he had to go. Vince saw him to the door. In the hall Vince gave him a deliberate, detached, speculative look. 'You haven't got the guts to go through with it, have you?'

It was after midnight when he let himself into the Tower House. The door creaked but he shut it quickly behind him almost as though he were afraid that he had been followed. After the soft, balmy night air the cold, close and humid darkness in the little stone hallway might have repelled him but now it seemed like a welcome. He crept up the stairs. The door on the first landing where his father and mother slept was a little open and the pale yellow beam of the nightlight reached out across the red tiles. He could hear the shallow, wheezy, tremulous breathing of his sleeping father. How often had he listened to it wishing that it would stop for ever? His father's senile petulance, his slobbering habits, his incontinence, frightened and sickened him. They were a persistent, intrusive nastiness too close to the core of his life. But now he had other things on his mind.

He continued up the steps to his own room. He did not switch on the light but sat in a chair by one of the windows. The night was full of stars and the room was full of shadows with pale highlights like reflections in a mirror. All his life he had been a victim. As a schoolboy he had been the butt of other boys, the one who always tried not to be noticed and rarely succeeded. To please his mother he had become, of all things, a schoolteacher and narrowly avoided being the victim of his pupils by ingratiating himself with them at the expense of work and true discipline. Slowly and painfully he had acquired, layer by layer, a protective skin; now it had been stripped away and he was vulnerable as never before.

He could still see the look on Peters' face.

His eyes filled with the burning tears of self-pity and he began to sob helplessly. His mother came in. She stood over his chair and cushioned his head against her breast, stroking his hair and murmuring consolation. 'Oh my boy! Oh my boy!'

5

Wednesday was another fine day. Wycliffe woke early to the now familiar pattern of dancing wavelets reflected on the ceiling. Charlie Martin was in his usual place with his little black book and the tanker waggon was refuelling the boats. A few visitors were about, taking a walk before breakfast, trying to glimpse something of the real life of the island as one goes back-stage at a theatre.

When he went downstairs the Jordans were already at breakfast – grilled mackerel, caught that morning.

'You were talking about Peters' brother last night, sir.'

'I saw him in the bar with Nick Marsden – what about him?'

Jordan wiped his lips with an outsized table napkin. 'He's an odd sort of chap, spends a lot of time on the island. God knows what he does for a living.'

Wycliffe waited while Mrs Jordan slipped another freshly grilled fish on her husband's plate. 'The point is, as I told you, he doesn't live at Salubrious Place, he lodges with Wendy Hicks, the widow woman who runs the Quay Café.'

Mrs Jordan made a curious, disapproving noise and Jordan laughed. 'You can see what the women think of her but she seems to be the attraction. But apart from all that the brother seems a decent enough chap and he gets on well with most of the locals – the men, anyway.'

Wycliffe was having difficulty in removing the bones from his fish and he made no reply.

By the time he set out for his headquarters the quay was busy. He went into the shop for some tobacco and queued with the tourists who wanted their morning papers. He was conscious of being pointed out by the knowledgeable to the uninformed. News of the murder had reached the tourists mainly through the London dailies for the islanders were disinclined to discuss their domestic affairs with foreigners. The little man behind the counter reached past two customers in front of Wycliffe to hand him his tobacco. 'The usual, Chief Superintendent!' Wycliffe growled unpleasantly.

The improvised headquarters was running smoothly thanks to Gill. Wycliffe had no organizing flair but to Gill organization came as naturally as breathing. The atmosphere was businesslike, everyone busy, nobody flustered; tables and desks were uncluttered and files in constant use were housed on trolleys which had been borrowed from the canteen. All of which was surprising when one looked at Gill himself; ungainly, slovenly in dress, he never stood if he could sit or sat if he could sprawl.

Wycliffe spent half an hour going through the reports. Nothing much. The constable who had been on watch at Salubrious Place reported seeing Jackie Martin leaving the house at 11.30 the previous night. The constable's turn of duty had started at 10.00 so that Jackie must have arrived before then.

After going through the reports he held a conference in his office; Chief Inspector Gill and Inspector Golly. The three principals had identical files. Wycliffe lit his pipe, Gill was smoking a cheroot. Golly sat upright in his chair and waited to be addressed.

'You first, Jimmy.'

'I don't suppose you want statistics of the house to house reports and the circulars?'

'Not really.'

Gill grinned and turned over several pages of his file. 'Mr Golly has had them all nicely typed out.' He flicked the long ash from his cheroot vaguely in the direction of the ashtray on Wycliffe's desk. 'Half the males in the island, tourists and locals alike, seem unable to give a precise and/or substantiated account of their whereabouts and activities on Saturday night.'

'Get on with it, Jimmy!'

Gill stretched out his long legs. 'It comes to this: it's possible that we have some sort of kink loose on the island who gets his kicks from knocking off girls after dark. If it's one of those we shall soon know, but I don't think so and neither do you.'

'No, I agree, it hasn't got the marks. Mr Golly?'

Golly seemed startled by the implied question. 'I don't know, sir. I wouldn't like to give an opinion at this stage.'

Gill opened his mouth to say something scathing but, catching

Wycliffe's eye, changed his mind. 'The crime we've got on our hands probably runs true to type. The kid got herself slugged because she was involved in an emotional mess. She was probably the cause of it, she probably enjoyed being in it, but she didn't think anybody was going to take it seriously enough to slug her if she stirred it up a bit more. Silly little bitch! They ask for it!' Gill, though apparently happily married, never missed a chance to preach his gospel against womankind, or, at least, against emotional involvement with women. He turned to Golly with a ferocious grin. 'Sometimes I think you're better off with a nice, clean-living young man.'

The inspector smiled doubtfully.

Gill went on, 'Where does that get us? As far as we know the two chaps she was involved with were Peters and Martin. Neither of them can give a satisfactory account of himself for the relevant times on Saturday night. Let's start with Peters. In his statement he says that he left the Barn at a little before ten. He had a headache and he went for a walk. Down the valley to the sea, up on to the cliffs and back over the moor by the usual path to the house. When he got back the kids had gone. Apparently it was nothing unusual for them to be left to pack up. One of them would lock the Barn door and hang the key on a hook just inside the front door of the house. Ma'moiselle Loiseau says that her lord and master came in at five minutes after midnight.' Gill looked from Wycliffe to Golly and back again. 'Walking for two bloody hours over rough country in the dark! It's so bloody stupid it might even be true but, of course, there's not a scrap of corroboration.' He rifled through a few more pages of the file.

'And here is Master Martin's contribution. He left home to meet his girl friend at five minutes to ten. He reached the appointed spot at about half-past and hung about there until the party in the Barn broke up and the kids went home. Mark you, he didn't trouble himself to ask one of them what had happened to Sylvie. He assumed that she was with Peters and he went down to the house. According to him he loitered around the back of the house for some time, then he got tired and went home, reaching there at a quarter to one.' Gill slapped the file shut. 'Marvellous, isn't it? And not a shred of evidence to support that load of crap either.'

Wycliffe had listened without comment and without much

apparent interest. Now he turned to Inspector Golly, 'Anything to say about that, Mr Golly?'

The inspector braced himself. 'Two things strike me, sir. First, if the dead girl was having an affair with Peters she could have aroused the jealousy of Peters' mistress . . .'

'You think so?' Gill was ironic.

Golly ignored him. 'According to Peters' story, the Loiseau girl must have been alone for the whole evening. Peters was at the Barn until ten and after that he was walking on the moor until midnight.'

'The point being?'

'That Miss Loiseau had, not only a credible motive, but also an opportunity to commit the crime.' Golly felt the need to define his position more clearly. 'I am not saying that the young lady is a murderess, only that even when we limit the choice of culprit to those emotionally involved with the dead girl she cannot be excluded.'

'I think you put that rather well, Mr Golly.'

'Now for my second point. I believe that Dr Ross put the time of death at between eleven and twelve – not earlier.'

'Well?'

'Martin admits to having been in the vicinity of the quarry from half-past ten until the young people left the Barn at half-past eleven. Peters, whether or not he took the walk he describes, could have been there at the relevant time and, if he is telling the truth, he *must* have been there at some time shortly before midnight.'

'You are saying that both of them could . . .' But Golly would not allow himself to be interrupted.

'I am saying more than that, Mr Gill, if you will allow me to finish. After half-past eleven Martin says that he walked down to the house, loitered round the back for a while then walked home, arriving there around a quarter to one having taken three-quarters of an hour on the way. Surely it is remarkable that Martin and Peters do not appear to have met?'

'You've got a point!' Gill admitted generously. 'A good point.'

'In other words,' Wycliffe said, 'it seems that they can't both be telling the truth and that's always something.'

'In my opinion all we need do is to lean on 'em a bit. The two of them together don't add up to one good man.'

Wycliffe knocked out his pipe into the ashtray. 'They won't run away, Jimmy, and before we commit ourselves I'd like to feel a good deal surer of my ground.'

'You're worried about motive?'

'Partly, yes.'

The chief inspector lit another cheroot and puffed lazily. 'My money is on Martin and he seems to have had motive enough. I don't think he planned to kill the girl but when he met her it's more than likely that her attitude brought his jealousy and frustration to flash point. As far as Peters is concerned . . .'

The telephone rang and Wycliffe answered it. The Lord Warden would be grateful if Mr Wycliffe could find time to lunch with him. A launch would be at the Seymour Steps at 12.00 noon.

A Royal Command. Wycliffe grumbled. He had no social aspirations and he had never been a golf-and-country-club copper. That was why he would remain stuck at his present rank and why he thought himself lucky to have got so far. He had no grievance. He was a Jack and he wanted to stay that way. Nowadays it was difficult above the rank of detective inspector but by being bloody minded, good at his job, and by carefully cultivating a reputation for eccentricity, he had managed it – more or less. If you wanted 'in' at the administrative level you had to mix with the administrators. That was reasonable. He didn't.

'What's he called?'

Inspector Golly looked mildly surprised and reproving. 'Sir John Gordon – quite a notability. He had a distinguished career in the Diplomatic Service before he succeeded his father here. Everybody was surprised when he gave it up on his father's death. The post of Lord Warden is hereditary but there is no obligation to reside here . . .'

'Really! Thank you Mr Golly.' Another aspiring chief constable.

Wycliffe stood up. 'Getting back to the case, we need more facts. Follow up the time angle. Somebody must have seen young Martin leave to keep his appointment, just possibly somebody saw him coming back. God knows what goes on after dark in this place. It seems that Nick Marsden was out on the moor – was anybody else? Somebody might have seen Peters. The place seems to be plagued by naturalists – don't any of them keep the silent watches of the night?'

Gill knew if Golly did not that there would be no more discussion.

It was rare for Wycliffe to take part in more than a brief exchange of views. He had said more than once that other people's ideas only confused him.

Inspector Golly ventured, 'The house-to-house and the questionnaire both appear to have covered the ground pretty well, sir . . .'

'No doubt, Mr Golly, no doubt, but look into it. Mr Gill will put you on the right lines. Thank you.'

Golly, who thought that he had made a good first impression, now began to wonder.

Perhaps it was because Jimmy Gill's view of the case came so close to his own that he had refused to hear any more. He had, as often before, the feeling that it was too soon to jump to any conclusion but he would have found it difficult to offer any logical objection to action if he had allowed the discussion to develop. He was restless and the very atmosphere of routine efficiency in his headquarters oppressed him. It is easy to be superbly efficient in gathering, classifying and filing damn-all. Most offices specialize in it.

He washed behind his ears, combed his hair and stole guiltily out of the building and escaped down on to the quay. There were not many people about. The pleasure boats had already left for the off-islands and the *Islander* had not yet arrived with its day-trippers. Half-a-dozen men with a council lorry were erecting scaffold poles in barrels of sand at intervals along the quay. Carnival Week was due to start that evening with a grand procession.

Uncertain of the licensing hours or whether the islands were troubled by such things, he walked in the direction of the Seymour Arms and found the bars open. In the public one of the boatmen was drinking with Nick Marsden. The landlord was reading a newspaper spread out on the bar. Marsden acknowledged Wycliffe with a diffident glance and a few moments later he and his companion drank up and left.

The landlord was patronizing. 'Making progress, sir?'

'Of a sort.'

'It's difficult for an outsider. Impossible, I'd say.'

Wycliffe ordered a pint. 'Have one with me.' He lit his pipe. 'That was Nick Marsden wasn't it? He seems quite a character.'

'He's clever.'

'Clever?'

The landlord drew a pint and placed it on the counter. 'How do you make your living, Mr Wycliffe?'

'Work for it, I suppose.'

The landlord nodded. 'So do I. Nick Marsden hasn't done a week's work in forty years but he doesn't go short of his beer or his baccy and his belly is never empty.'

'I see what you mean. It must be a knack.'

'If it is, all the Marsdens must have it, they're born scroungers.' The landlord drew a second pint. 'There's a whole clan of 'em over to Quincey Cove. Nick and me went to school together and I know the breed. Cheers!' He blew the froth off his beer and drank half of it.

'Apart from his scrounging, what sort of chap is he?'

The landlord gave him a sly look. 'I know what you're thinking but all I can say is I've never known Nick to be violent, he isn't that sort. As a boy you might say he was a bit of a coward. He used to get teased a lot because of the way he dressed but though he was big I never knew him to do anything about it . . . Of course, as a young man he was a great one for the women.' He took another gulp of beer and laughed. 'There's respectable grandmothers in this town today who couldn't lift their skirts fast enough for Nick when he was in his prime.'

'And now?'

The landlord made a gesture of contempt. 'Now he's just a dirty old man who gets his kicks watching the kids.'

'As long as he only watches.'

The landlord shrugged. 'She wasn't sexually assaulted, was she?'

There was silence for a time. When Wycliffe spoke again he changed the subject. 'It seems odd to me, the islanders have the reputation for not looking kindly on strangers and Vince Peters is a case in point. But Peters' brother isn't doing so badly from what I hear.'

The landlord gave him an appraising look. 'You've been getting around!' He finished his beer and wiped his lips. 'In this island, Mr Wycliffe, there's plenty of room at the bottom; you're only in trouble if you try to muscle in at the top.' He pushed his empty glass to one side and rested his arms on the bar. 'I wouldn't say this to anybody, Mr Wycliffe, but . . .' He got no further; his expression, which had been confiding, changed to one of professional geniality. 'Morning, Mr Martin.'

Charlie Martin had come in and was taking his usual seat. He looked depressed and his acknowledgement of Wycliffe's greeting was perfunctory.

When he had finished his drink Wycliffe went outside and stood with his arms resting on the rail staring into the harbour. He was trying to decide what colour the water was. Blue? Green? Blue-green? It was shot with gold – or yellow and the tip of each tiny ripple was silvered. If you added to that a certain indefinable trans-lucency . . . He wondered too, why he had ever become a policeman and why a detective? He hadn't a clue what to do next.

He watched the *Islander* glide between the pier-heads and pass snugly into her berth. He watched the day-trippers stream off and immediately lay siege to the few shops on the quay. What came ye out into the wilderness to see?

A black launch with gleaming brasswork and white, coiled rope on the foc'sle slid into the harbour. There were two people in the well, the young man at the tiller in blue jersey and peaked cap and a dark girl in a flowered shirt and shorts. The helmsman cut back his motor, brought the launch round so that she glided to the steps and, as she did so, the girl stepped on to the gunnel and ashore in a single movement. She was up the steps on to the quay almost before the launch had come to rest.

'Superintendent Wycliffe?' The boatman held the launch to the steps with a boathook while he stepped aboard then, with a swirling wake, they were away across the harbour.

'I'm John Jenkins.'

Wycliffe had had nothing to do with the sea until he took up his west-country appointment four or five years previously and he had never ceased to be impressed by the skill and craft of those who lived by it.

'Who was the young lady?'

'Miss Gordon.'

The usual cagey, taciturn reception accorded to a stranger. This young man had an air of self-confidence, of true self-possession which he might have looked for in vain among the factory workers of his old manor. Perhaps he was romanticising but it seemed to him that our modern industrial society fails to provide the challenge which enables a man to find himself.

The town faces east, on one side of a narrow neck of land which juts out from the main body of the island. Morvyl lies away to the west and so they had to double Cligga Head at the northern tip of the promontory. As the launch came through the pierheads John Jenkins opened the throttle and she charged into a surprisingly choppy sea, throwing up clouds of spray. The young man grinned, reached into the stern locker and handed him an oilskin coat. 'You'll get wet.'

They were running parallel with the coast and he could see the string of sandy coves, the low cliffs rising to the moor and the granite mass of Carngluze topping the lot and looking like an enchanted castle from a story book. As they approached the headland the cliffs became higher and steeper. Cligga itself rose sheer for ninety feet – not very high but impressive against the Lilliputian landscapes of the island. It was from Cligga that Sylvie's mother had fallen to her death and he could see the low platform of rock at the base which must be covered at high tide.

Off the headland there were cross currents which tumbled them a bit, then they were running into the sound which separates the island from Morvyl. The cliffs on either side were low and gentle with gorse and heather coming down almost to the tidemark. They made a broad sweep – to avoid a reef, John Jenkins said – then they crossed the sound and entered a tiny harbour with a few cottages backed by trees, a rare sight in the islands. They nosed their way through a clutter of small craft to the steps of a jetty. Wycliffe tried to step ashore with nonchalance if not with grace; for him the trip had not been long enough.

'You can't miss it, through the big gates and up the drive.'

The quay was almost deserted. Two old men on a seat seemed to be asleep and apart from them there was only a donkey in the shafts of a cart piled high with seaweed.

The gates at the end of the waterfront stood open between high granite pillars surmounted by carved beasts. He set off up the drive between masses of rhododendron and laurel. What impressed him was the silence. To the best of his recollection he had heard nothing but his own footfalls since John Jenkins had cut the engine. He saw little of the famous gardens for the drive ended suddenly in a gravelled area before the house. The house was nothing special, a gabled affair covered in creeper, which could have been built at any time in the fifty years before the first war. Wycliffe, who had a feeling for architecture, wondered what had been torn down to make way for it.

Everything went well enough. Sir John turned out, predictably, to be sixtyish, lean, bronzed, effortlessly courteous but not obtrusively Eton and New College. There was no sign of a Lady Gordon and they were only three to lunch, the third member of the party, a Dr Swann, an Oxford zoologist.

Wycliffe enjoyed his lunch, lentil soup flavoured with orange and coriander, a chicken salad and fruit. They drank a light, dry hock which had a faint bouquet of wild flowers. Gordon did the talking and he talked well, telling of his early years in the service which he had spent in Nanking when, despite Chiang Kai-shek's republic, the old China was still much in evidence. Wycliffe found himself thinking of Lamancha, Hannay and Sandy, the cult figures of the British hegemony. As a good socialist, Wycliffe disapproved but enjoyed himself all the same.

Afterwards they went out on to a terrace at the back of the house overlooking a small, formal garden. For the first time conversation turned to Sylvie's death.

'A tragic affair! . . . When I asked your chief for his help I had no idea it would turn out to be murder . . . This Peters fellow . . .'

Sir John spoke somewhat disjointedly with long pauses so that his hearers had plenty of time to match their own detail to his evocative outlines. It amounted to a rather skilful justification for the party line on Peters. 'We all want to preserve the beauty and character of the islands . . . They are so small . . .' With a sly twinkle in Swann's direction, 'It is a rather delicate exercise in conservation, you cannot risk the random importation of new, exotic species . . .'

A little more of the same and Sir John seemed to be hinting at what a happy solution it would be if it turned out that Peters had murdered Sylvie. 'Such an intractable young man! Not, perhaps, the best influence on our young people either . . . There have been times, I must confess, when I have had misgivings about my own daughter . . .'

Wycliffe pricked up his ears but nothing came of it. He began to wonder whether there was going to be any milk in the coconut. Perhaps it was only a social occasion. But it came.

'Actually, Dr Swann has something to tell you which you may think important . . .'

Swann was no conversationalist, he had contributed almost nothing to the talk so far. Wycliffe knew the type. A naturalist, happiest when human contacts could be cut to a minimum. He rather liked what he had seen of Swann but he was piqued at the way he had been lured into hearing evidence in a social context. Why couldn't the man have come to his headquarters like anybody else? There was a simple answer to that one – he was a friend of the Lord Warden. Wycliffe became terse and official.

'You are a naturalist?'

'Small mammals – rodent and shrews mainly. I'm doing a count among other things.'

'A count?'

'A census if you like. Population density in relation to habitat – that sort of thing. You won't want the details but it involves setting traps – live traps of course, and I make a point of inspecting my traps every six hours.'

'You work alone?'

'Always. I see enough of people during term time. My base is here, on Morvyl. I have a room with Ernie Stoffles and his wife. Ernie puts me ashore on the island of my choice with a little tent and enough food. I tell him to come back for me in three or four days – up to a week, depending on the size of the island and the variety of habitats which it offers.'

'And last week?'

'Last week I was camping near Salubrious Place, a little way up the valley above the house. I was there from Monday to Sunday. Ernie took me off from Quincey Cove at about eight on Sunday morning. He was late because of the fog but by lunch-time I was on Menhegy.'

'You have something to tell me about Saturday night?' Wycliffe caught Gordon's eye. A very faint smile. He had got the message but it would make no difference. Paternalism is the kindest word for it and it may not be such a bad thing.

Swann was diffident. 'I doubt if it's important – only a snatch of conversation I happened to overhear – but I thought you had better be the judge. It was the girl's name – Sylvie – which made me wonder . . .' He uncrossed his legs and bent forward in his chair. 'I

584

had set up my tent in a small clearing in the bracken about two hundred yards upstream from the bridge which leads to Salubrious Place. There's a path which runs by the stream up to the farm and, of course, it was a convenient spot for me, sheltered, plenty of water, and milk and eggs from the farm. After dark I usually settle down to get what sleep I can between visits to my traps. It was a little after ten and I was already in my sleeping-bag. I think that I was vaguely listening to the music from the pop club or whatever it is they have in the Barn when I heard voices close at hand. I looked through the tent flap and saw a man and a girl walking along the track in the direction of the farm.

'The man said, "I'd have to be still wet behind the ears to fall for that one, it's the oldest trick in the book!"

'Then the girl spoke for some time but more quietly so that I could not hear what she said.

'When the man answered he sounded more reasonable. He said, "That's up to you, Sylvie. If it's a question of money . . ." But the girl interrupted, angrily. She said something about not wanting his money and she sounded as though she were crying.

'The man spoke to her soothingly. "Surely, Sylvie, you must have known the score?"' Swann broke off. 'I didn't hear any more. I'm sure I've got the sense right in what I've told you but I couldn't swear to the exact words. I hope I haven't wasted your time.'

Wycliffe thanked him and told him that it would be necessary for him to put all that he had said into a formal statement. 'It might help us a great deal.' He hoped that he meant help, not confuse.

Sir John was still the perfect host. He even accompanied Wycliffe to the gates and stood, watching, while he walked the length of the quay to the steps. John Jenkins was there. So were the old men but the donkey had gone.

'Have you been waiting all this time?'

'No, Sir John told me when to pick you up.'

A well organized exercise! Wycliffe was piqued but his mood failed to survive the trip back. After all, he now had firm evidence that Peters had been with Sylvie an hour or so before she died.

It was as they were entering the harbour that he remembered with a twinge of conscience that it was the day of Sylvie's funeral. He had remarked on the number of boats at their moorings and John Jenkins had told him that afternoon trips had been cancelled because of the funeral. As the launch glided almost silently between the maze of craft he could see the hearse emerging from Bethel Street on to the quay.

In the islands funerals are still public occasions for the expression of communal concern and responsibility. There is no question of hustling the corpse off at thirty or forty miles an hour to the grave yard or the crematorium. It is paraded in stately progress through the streets with half the population following.

Wycliffe reached the top of the steps and mingled with the groups of tourists who, deprived of their planned enjoyment, were prepared to make do with what offered. Some of them were taking photographs. After all, it was the funeral of the murdered girl. As with all island funerals it was a men-only occasion and though they walked in threes behind the hearse, the procession stretched almost the length of the quay. Many of the men were in the clothes of their trade – blue jerseys and caps – with the addition of a black armband. The middle man of each group of three carried a wreath.

Charlie Martin was right up in front with the girl's father and, to Wycliffe's surprise, so was Jackie. He wore a dark suit and he looked so pale it seemed doubtful if he could complete the course. Jordan was well up in the procession with his two colleagues and so was the squint-eyed Ernie. But Peters had, presumably, decided that discretion was the better part or, maybe, funerals were not his thing.

It was strange and touching to see the solemn procession passing under the flowered arches which had been put up for the carnival events. Wycliffe wondered a little that they had not been cancelled for the night of the funeral but in this he showed lack of understanding for in a properly integrated society there is a time and place for everything.

After the procession had passed he climbed the slope to the school. Gill was there and he had had the good sense to send a wreath.

When Gill heard the new evidence he chuckled. 'Like the man said, it's the oldest trick in the book. The little dolly can't get her man any other way so she fixes it so that he puts her in the club. Somebody should have told her that it don't work any more in this wicked world.'

Wycliffe wondered what Sir John would have made of Gill.

'At least it proves Peters was lying and, incidentally, that Marsden wasn't.'

Wycliffe nodded. 'But I doubt if it gets us anywhere.'

Inspector Golly, who had listened with attention, preened his moustache with a careful forefinger. 'In spite of what Mr Gill says I would have thought that the girl's pregnancy gave Peters quite a strong motive.'

'How come?' From Gill.

'Because if the girl made a . . .'

'Stink?' Gill suggested.

'. . . a fuss, Peters' position on the island would have become untenable. He would have had to leave.'

They were interrupted by the telephone ringing. Wycliffe spoke to the duty-officer.

'DC Norris has just come in, sir. He thinks he's found the weapon.'

'I'll come out.'

The three men went out into the hall. Detective Constable Norris, a young, blond giant, was standing over his find which lay in a polythene bag on the duty-officer's desk. It was a five eighth diameter ring-bolt, that is to say, an iron rod, five eighths of an inch in diameter, with a ring at one end and threaded for a nut at the other. It was approximately eighteen inches long and heavily corroded. Scores of rust fragments lay loose in the bag.

'You can't see through the polythene very well, sir, but the ring end is encrusted with what looks like blood and other matter. There are also two tiny threads of material caught in a particularly rusty patch about halfway along the shank.'

Wycliffe turned to Gill. 'Have Scales examine it for prints – not that he will find any on that. After he's finished, send it to Franks. Then find out what Martin and Peters wore on Saturday night and get their outside clothing. Be as diplomatic as you like but get it and send it to forensic. Norris's threads may check or there may be fragments of rust or rust marks. It's worth a try.'

The constable had found the bolt on the quarry floor, twenty feet beyond where Sylvie's body was found. It was almost under a derelict tip-waggon, beyond the water which covered part of the quarry floor and largely sheltered from the rain by the waggon.

'He must have pitched it away, sir.'

Wycliffe agreed. 'Well, he wouldn't want to take it home with him, would he? I think I'll have another chat with Mr Peters.'

Usually Vince looked forward to Clarissa's shopping expeditions to the mainland. He could persuade himself that it would be pleasant to have the place to himself; a change, a holiday. There was another reason, he depended on her so completely that he felt the need, from time to time, to prove to himself that he could manage without her. But the truth always caught up with him before she had been gone more than a couple of hours. At first he would enjoy a refreshing sense of freedom, like a small boy let out of school, he would potter about, feed the cats, fetch the milk from the farm, plan his lunch and set about getting it. But by eleven or half-past he would be wondering about her, then worrying. If that damned helicopter came down into the sea . . . That would be the ultimate irony, then he would be left alone. It was absurd, of course, but it made him nervous. He would be sure to listen to the lunch-time news.

It was as though he were separated from a part of himself. Did that mean that he loved her? Did need equal love? He supposed that it was a kind of love, the love of a child for its mother, of an old woman for her dutiful daughter, selfish and born of necessity. That morning, when she was leaving, while she was raising her lips to him to be kissed, she was feeling in the pocket of his jacket to make sure that he had his tablets. The right pocket, he could no longer use the other. His left arm was rigid and useless, locked at the elbow, slightly bent.

'You'll be all right? You're sure?' There was a new intensity in her concern.

A mother rather than a mistress. And when he had other women she showed no jealousy, only concern – concern for him. Her every act seemed to be tailored to his needs, even, he suspected, these periodic visits to the mainland when he could be alone for a little while and feel independent. It was good for him.

He took trouble over preparing his lunch then dawdled over eating it – killing time. Afterwards he allowed himself a thimbleful of brandy. At two o'clock he washed up and put the dishes away. It was very odd. On other days, when Clarissa was at home he could shut himself in his room for hours at a time, working on his flies, forgetful of himself. With Clarissa away he seemed to be fighting a running battle to keep his mind from introspection and self-pity.

Half past two. An hour before Roger was due. He wished that he had asked him to come earlier. He was tempted to go for a walk but refused to give way to weakness. He went upstairs to his room. His heart thumped unpleasantly as he climbed the stairs. Perhaps that was the brandy. He sat at his desk. The perpetual calendar said Wednesday 25 August. Clarissa had changed it that morning as she always did. In three days he would be twenty-nine years old.

Barbellion had lived to be thirty.

A year ago his doctor had recommended him to read Barbellion's *Journal of a Disappointed Man.* It had become his bible. He could recite long passages and often did so when he needed something to bolster his spirits. Barbellion had not conquered illness and death, he had civilized them and transformed them into a literary experience.

'I suppose the truth is I am at last broken in to the idea of death. Once it terrified me and once I hated it. But now it only annoys me . . . What embitters me is the humiliation of having to die . . . To think that the women I have loved will be marrying and forget, and that the men I have hated will continue on their way and forget I ever hated them – the ignominy of being dead!'

But Barbellion had been untroubled by guilt. Resentment, bitterness and frustration, but not guilt.

Recently he had been conscious of a growing sense of guilt, something which had not troubled him since adolescence. He supposed that it might be a morbid effect of his complaint but that did not help. He had reason to feel guilty.

He was troubled by an increasing desire to put himself right with the world. There were reparations which could be made and others which could not. He was glad that he had asked Roger to come.

Roger and Clarissa. But what about Sylvie?

And Jackie Martin. Last night he had been able to watch him with an interested detachment. There was something fundamentally childish about Jackie. The Peter Pan syndrome. A tragedy masquerading as a fairy tale.

He had once known and become close friends with a dwarf. At first it had been disconcerting, embarrassing, to hear him talking, expressing the opinions and sentiments of a mature man yet looking like a precocious child. He had similar feelings when he was with Jackie but for opposite reasons. He wondered what Jackie would do – probably nothing.

He heard a noise downstairs. Roger must be early.

So, in the late afternoon, Wycliffe walked under the flowered arches by the harbour. Now elaborately decorated floats were parked in a long line. All the lorries in the island, carts towed by tractors, and a great variety of handcarts, prams, barrows and trolleys were all carrying large, unstable superstructures the skeletal elements of which were smothered with bunting, leaves and flowers. In the interests of business, carnival week started on a Wednesday so that its benefits were spread over two weeks' ration of visitors instead of one. Tonight the grand procession would be headed by the Lord Warden himself.

Wycliffe made his way up the hill out of the town. He had no special reason for going to see Peters himself, but he was attracted to the valley. Its mysterious isolation at the still centre of the island appealed to him.

It was hot in the afternoon sun. The pleasure boats had been to collect the trippers they had taken to the off-islands in the morning and they were on their way back, creeping across the great expanse of sea, each leaving a thin line of white wake, converging on the harbour. In the hotels and boarding houses they were preparing the evening meal but the beaches were still dotted with picnicking groups and children still shouted, screamed and splashed in the shal-lows. But the valley, when he came to the top of the steep slope, was deserted, the one place in the island where it was possible to forget that it *was* an island. Not, of course, what the tourist paid for.

Wycliffe walked down the stony path, crossed the bridge and entered the courtyard where the cats lay in the dappled shade of the pine tree. The air was heavy with its resinous scent.

A girl came running out of the house and collided with him. He caught and held her arms and she looked up at him with wide, frightened eyes. It was the girl from the pottery and the fear changed to relief as she recognized him. 'It's Vince, I think he must be dead!'

He followed her into the house but she stopped short in the hall. 'Upstairs.'

Wycliffe went upstairs. On the landing there were several doors but one stood open into a room furnished as an office or study. Peters was seated at a desk by the window, his body slumped forward. The glass of the lower window pane was shattered. There were a few slivers of glass on the desk but most of it must have fallen outside.

There could be no doubt that Peters was dead. A neat, round hole just forward of the left temple marked the entry of the bullet and, by bending over the body, he could see the ragged wound of exit behind the right ear, almost hidden by the position of the head on the desk. There was a little but not much blood.

Automatically his mind reconstructed the trajectory of the bullet. It seemed that the line of fire had been at a downward angle passing through the head from the left temple to the right tympanic bulla and out through the glass of the window. Passage through the bones of the skull must have given it sufficient wobble to shatter rather than pierce the glass.

The room was at the back of the house, overlooking the meadow with its pine trees and the row of beehives. Through a gap in the trees he could trace the course of the valley to a triangle of sea which glittered brilliantly in the sunshine.

The girl was waiting for him in the hall. She was nervous but not hysterical. 'He's dead, isn't he?'

'Yes. Where is Clarissa?'

She was dulled by the shock and it took her a moment to grasp the question. 'She's not back yet.'

'Back from where?'

She swept her hair from her face as though in an effort to clear her mind. 'Clarissa caught the morning flight to do some shopping on the mainland and she's due back at nine o'clock.' Her features wrinkled and she might have cried but she controlled herself. 'Some-body will have to tell her.'

Wycliffe was at the telephone which stood on a small table in the hall. He wiggled the receiver rest to attract the attention of the oper-ator. 'Two-three-two, please.' It was the number allocated to his temporary headquarters. He was connected promptly and the duty-officer put him through to Chief Inspector Gill.

'Jimmy? I want you out here with the team . . . Yes, Peters . . . Shot. You might find out if Franks is still on the island, if not he'll have to come back. If you can't get hold of Franks, Ross is the local man.'

While they waited he asked the girl questions to keep her mind off the body upstairs. He realized that he did not even know her name.

'Luke – Brenda Luke.'

'Where do you live?'

'The Terrace.'

'With your parents?'

'With my mother. She's a widow.'

'What time did you arrive here?'

She glanced at her watch. 'About half-past four.'

'Did you see anybody?'

'No.'

'You went straight to the pottery?'

'I always do.'

'What made you come to the house just now?'

'The loo . . .'

'The front door was open?'

'Yes, it usually is in fine weather.' Her expression changed.

'What's the matter?'

'I've just remembered something.' She looked puzzled. 'When I came through the front door I heard somebody in the kitchen. I thought it was Vince and I called out as usual, "It's only me!" There was no answer but I didn't take any notice because they often don't hear or don't bother to answer.'

'But you are sure that you heard someone there?'

'Quite sure.'

Wycliffe left her to make a quick tour of the back of the house – kitchen, dining-room, sitting-room; there was no-one. The rooms were scrupulously tidy, nothing had been disturbed. He returned to the girl. 'What made you think that the noise you heard came from the kitchen?'

She frowned. 'I don't know – yes I do! It was running water – a tap turned on and I think I heard the clink of glass as though somebody was washing up.'

'What about the woman who comes to do the cleaning?'

'Wednesday is her day off.'

Wycliffe went to the telephone once more and gave instructions for as many men as could be spared to cover the ground between the town and Salubrious Place, identifying everyone they met. There would be very few, the odd walker, birdwatcher or botanist, perhaps a couple looking for a quiet spot. It was a slim chance but one he dared not neglect.

The girl looked surprised and it seemed to worry her. 'Why did you do that?'

'We ought to find out who was about the place oughtn't we?'

She agreed, dubiously. 'I suppose so.'

Wycliffe changed the subject. 'Isn't it odd that Clarissa chose to go shopping on the woman's day off?'

Brenda smiled faintly. 'It was the only day Vince would let her go, he couldn't stand Nellie.'

'Nellie?'

'Nellie Martin – the daily help. She's all right really but Vince has got a thing about her.' Her face clouded. 'I keep talking about him as though he were still alive.'

'Nellie Martin – any relation to the other Martins I know?'

She looked surprised. Always having to remind herself that he knew nothing of her island. 'She's Jackie's mother!'

Another link.

They moved out of the hall and into the courtyard. She looked back at the square, grey-stone house, stark and sombre even in the sunshine. 'I didn't think he would really do it.'

'Do what?'

She was impatient. 'Kill himself. Clarissa thought he might, I know. Sometimes she was afraid to leave him alone and I used to tease her about it. But she was right, wasn't she?'

'What made her worry?' Wycliffe did not want to tell her at this stage that Peters had been murdered. 'Did he threaten to kill himself?'

She frowned. 'No, I don't think so but he got very depressed sometimes. It used to come over him suddenly and he would shut himself up in his room for hours at a time.' Brenda was coming to terms with the new tragedy and shock in the way most of us do, by discussing, explaining, rationalizing.

And Wycliffe encouraged her. 'What made him so depressed?'

She looked at him almost challengingly. 'People will say that he killed himself because he murdered Sylvie.'

'Is that what you think?'

'No. Vince had his faults, he was selfish but he wasn't like that. He wouldn't hurt anybody – not physically. In any case he had these fits of depression from the time he first came here. I think he was worried about something – something he wouldn't talk about. Sometimes, when he was talking to you, you would see a sudden change in him . . .'

'A change?'

She nodded. 'As though he had remembered something he was trying hard to forget.'

They were interrupted by the sound of a car engine. The police Land-Rover came into view at the top of the slope across the valley. The unsurfaced track was like a scree and the police driver took it with extreme caution.

'Did Peters have a gun?'

She shook her head. 'I don't know but I suppose he must have had.'

6

The truck came to a halt on the far side of the bridge and Chief Inspector Gill got out, followed by Franks, two detectives and a constable in uniform. Franks crossed the bridge, beaming.

'Well, what have you got for me this time?' Nothing could daunt the chubby little doctor. He accepted death as others accept bills, unpleasant but inevitable. 'The first qualification for medicine,' he was fond of saying, 'is a total lack of imagination.'

Wycliffe greeted Gill while Detective Sergeant Smith, the squad's photographer, unloaded his equipment from the truck and draped it round the constable. Smith was a prematurely wizened dyspeptic who sucked soda mints most of the time. He scowled at Wycliffe and shambled off to the house followed by the constable. Roger Scales, whose speciality was fingerprints, came across the bridge carrying his little leather case. In contrast to Smith, with his little toothbrush moustache and his natty, gent's suiting he looked more like a prosperous accountant than a detective. But they were two of the hand-picked men in Wycliffe's squad and they had worked with him ever since his arrival in the West Country.

An hour and a half later Smith had added a score of photographs of Peters dead to the thousands which must exist of Peters living. He had also photographed the room from every angle and in painstaking detail. Scales was at work on prints, many of them were photographed by Smith directly, others which were inaccessible to the camera had to be 'lifted' on tape, a tedious and highly skilled operation. Routine – and most of it, perhaps all of it, would prove to be a waste of time. But detectives, like archaeologists, rarely have a second chance to gather their data.

Franks had made a preliminary examination of the body, all he could do until it had been moved to the mortuary. Down in the hall four men smoked and chatted round the 'shell' which would be

Peters' temporary coffin. They were waiting for Wycliffe to give the word for him to be moved. Franks made a final note in his tiny, gilt-edged notebook and snapped it shut.

'Ready, if you are.'

Wycliffe went to the top of the stairs and called to the men below. 'All right, boys!' He stood with Franks on the landing while the body was removed.

Franks was thoughtful. 'What do you make of it?'

'Why ask me?'

'You saw the powder marks?'

'I saw them.'

There had been scarcely any blackening of the skin but close examination had shown the presence of a scattering of colourless grains around the wound of entry. This meant that the shot had probably been fired from a distance of not more than two feet.

'You would have expected him to get up or something, not to just sit there, waiting for it. Perhaps he thought it was a joke.'

'Evidently, it wasn't.'

'It must have been somebody he knew pretty well.'

'I agree, it's not common to be shot by a complete stranger.' Wycliffe was being deliberately uncommunicative – not because he wanted to snub Franks but in self defence. Talking tended to crystallize ideas and he wanted his thoughts to remain fluid. 'What we have to do is to find the gun.'

They followed the coffin downstairs and in the hall they were joined by Gill. The three of them went out into the sunshine. Wycliffe put a match to a half-smoked pipe, Jimmy Gill lit one of his cheroots which he hoped were less lethal than cigarettes. Franks mopped his bald head with a whiter-than-white handkerchief.

They walked across to the shade of the pine tree and Gill sat himself astride one of the metal chairs. 'Three of the divisional boys turned up – said they'd been told to cover the ground between here and town . . .'

'That's right. Did they meet anybody?'

'An octogenarian bird-watcher and a couple of teenagers who wanted to be alone. What's it about?'

Wycliffe was snappish. 'Never mind that now, Jimmy, you can find them something useful to do.'

Gill blew a cloud of smoke up into the pine tree. 'I have, they're gardening.'

'Gardening?'

'Looking for the bullet in the back meadow.'

Wycliffe sat on one of the chairs and Franks, after flicking his handkerchief over another, sat down gingerly. 'This is a very nice place. One could do a lot worse than retire to a property like this. I wonder what he gave for it . . .'

'His life, by the look of it,' Gill said. He looked round disparagingly. 'It would give me the screaming abdabs in a week.'

'In my view,' Franks said, pedantically, 'it must have been somebody he knew and trusted, not someone he would expect to shoot him.'

'I don't expect anybody to shoot me,' Wycliffe remarked, reasonably.

'But you know what I mean. To allow somebody to point a gun at you from a couple of feet and simply sit and wait for it . . .'

This line of thought had to be explained to Gill who was leaning back in his chair trying to blow smoke-rings.

'What bothers me is that he didn't leave the gun behind.'

'I don't see why that should bother you, he probably slung it away to make sure it couldn't be found and traced.'

'If I could be sure of that I'd feel a lot happier,' Wycliffe said.

'Me too!'

Franks looked from one to the other, mystified. Jimmy Gill explained. 'Nobody holds on to a hot gun unless they intend to use it again.'

'How long has he been dead?' Wycliffe demanded.

Franks considered, fingering the creases in his fine, herring-bone tweed. 'You know it's damn' difficult to give a straight answer. There were signs which bothered me. I don't want to say too much until I've had the chance . . .'

'An informed guess.'

Franks continued to prevaricate. 'Fully clothed, in a warm room . . . heat loss would be slow . . . The corneae were opaque but the lids being open . . .'

'Skip the pathology lesson, for God's sake!'

Franks grinned. 'On the evidence, so far, I'd say he died between half past three and four but I might have to revise that significantly. Anyway, not later than half past four.'

Wycliffe frowned. 'The girl who found him at a few minutes after five says she heard somebody in the kitchen . . .'

'Then if that somebody was the killer he must have hung round for at least half an hour after committing his crime.'

'What sort of idiot would do that?' Gill demanded.

'Perhaps he was looking for something,' Franks suggested.

'There were no signs of the place having been turned over.'

Wycliffe was staring absently into the bowl of his pipe which had gone out. 'The point is that we've got two murders on our hands. Are we to regard them as two cases or one?'

Gill, his long body contorted on the tiny chair, shifted impatiently. 'They must be one case. On an island this size you don't get two un-related killings in a single week! In any case, whether he killed the girl or not, Peters was closely involved with her.'

Wycliffe nodded. 'I agree, so the question becomes, are we look-ing for two murderers or one?'

Ants were dropping from the branches of the pine tree and Franks was picking them off his suit with apparent concentration but he was following the discussion. 'Surely, if there are two murderers there must be two cases?'

'No, I get Mr Wycliffe's point. If Peters murdered the girl then someone – her father, for example, might have decided to settle accounts with Peters himself. After all, it was to deal with the pos-sibility of such a vendetta situation that you were called in, wasn't it?'

Wycliffe knocked out his pipe on the heel of his shoe and started to refill it. 'I suppose you could put it that way though nobody anticipated murder. There are some big fish interested in this little pond and authority is very sensitive to public opinion in the islands. My inquiry was to be prophylactic rather than remedial. Nobody wanted a regular campaign to oust Peters. It would have got into the papers.'

Gill succeeded in blowing a smoke-ring and watched it rise in the still air until it disappeared in the branches of the tree. 'All the same, Sylvie was murdered, and now Peters.'

Wycliffe stood up, his hands thrust deep into his coat pockets. He said, almost apologetically, 'Peters died because Sylvie died, but why?'

598

It was a rhetorical question or, rather, it was a question that he was asking himself. He stood, apparently undecided what to do. 'Sylvie's funeral was this afternoon.'

'So?' Gill looked at him with curiosity.

'There must be quite a few people with alibis for this. I got back at half past two and the funeral was then on its way to the cemetery. I imagine there was some sort of do afterwards – or wasn't there?'

Gill nodded, thoughtfully. 'There was, at Charlie's place. I'll look into it.'

Wycliffe still stood, irresolute. 'I think I'll take a look round.' He set off across the courtyard in the direction of the house but after a few steps he turned round. 'What happened to Brenda Luke?'

'I sent her home with Jordan. I told her we would talk to her later.'

Wycliffe said nothing and continued on his way to the house, head bent, shoulders drooping.

Franks looked after him with concern. 'What's the matter with him? He doesn't seem to be his usual self.'

Gill grimaced. 'He feels responsible for Peters.' He threw the butt-end of his cheroot in the direction of a sleeping cat and missed. 'I'd rather have an ulcer than a bloody conscience.'

In the hall Wycliffe met Sergeant Scales, his fingerprint man. Scales was the sort to get through a lot of work without flapping. 'We've finished his room, sir, and we've started down here. Peters' own prints, of course, are all over the place upstairs. And there are two female sets which occur several times; I assume they belong to his mistress and the cleaning woman. Then there is a single set – all four fingers of the right hand – a man's, quite clear and definite and fresh. They are on the side of the filing cabinet, near the top edge, as though somebody had rested against the cabinet, his arm on the top, his fingers bent over the edge.'

'Made today?'

'I think so. I would be surprised if they were older but I could be wrong.'

'What about the gun?'

'No sign of it yet but one of the divisional men found an unopened box of .38 revolver ammunition in that drawer.' He pointed to one of the top drawers of a chest of drawers which stood in the hall.

'Unopened?'

'That's right, sir. Makes you think doesn't it?'

'It does indeed. Anybody upstairs?'

'Not at the moment, sir. Andrews and Cole will be starting their inventory directly.'

Wycliffe went upstairs and shut himself in the dead man's room. He closed the door with a satisfaction he would have found difficult to explain. He wanted to immerse himself in the world of the dead man, to exclude comment, suggestion and discussion. Above all he did not want to be watched.

Although Scales and Smith had gone over the room with meticulous thoroughness he knew that they would have been scrupulously careful to put everything back as they had found it. Apart from any changes the murderer had made the room was as it had been when Peters sat in his chair that afternoon . . . doing what? The desktop was bare except for a telephone, a pen tray, a blank scribbling pad and a calendar. The pen tray held an expensive ballpoint and a gold fountain pen engraved 'V.P.'.

When does a man sit at his desk with nothing in front of him? When he is bored, when he wants to think. Wycliffe started to pry into the desk drawers. Soon two detectives would be busy making a detailed inventory of everything in the room and, eventually, he would be presented with several pages of typescript itemizing the contents of every drawer and cupboard. All the same he couldn't resist poking about for himself. There was nothing of interest in the desk – stationery, a few bills, a couple of snapshots of Clarissa and the usual collection of rubbish most people hoard in drawers. Several keys without identification labels.

Wycliffe got up and started to prowl about the room. The insect cabinet consisted of a score of glass-topped, cork-lined drawers, each drawer contained hundreds of flies and each fly was spread-eagled on a pin with a little white card giving coded information about it. On the top of the cabinet a card index file contained the records in Peters' spidery hand.

There were sounds of heavy footsteps on the stairs, a peremptory knock and a head round the door. 'If it's convenient to start the inventory, sir . . .'

'It isn't, laddie! Go away.'

The big filing cabinet was divided into two parts, one part held correspondence, mainly, it seemed, with his accountant and various agents; the rest of the cabinet – nine or ten drawers – was filled with press cuttings, photographs, hand-outs and hundreds of record sleeves from recording companies all over the world.

The book shelves held mainly works on entomology, flies in particular, but there were a number of books on medical subjects, a few of them professional texts, most of the 'health for all' variety. Was Peters a hypochondriac?

The built-in cupboard contained an expensive looking binocular microscope, a few bits of scientific apparatus which Wycliffe could not identify and a deed-box which was locked. He found the key among those in the desk drawer.

The box contained a bundle of manilla folders, each one labelled with the title of a song. Wycliffe recognized several of Peters' hits. Each folder held in its pocket a small tape, presumably a recording of the song, and a lyric, written in a neat schoolboy hand and corrected with scratchings out and interpolations. Altogether they made an unpretentious little bundle but the contents of the box had made several fortunes.

He re-locked the box and put the key back in the desk drawer.

Although he would never admit it, Wycliffe rather liked poking about in somebody else's room. It was all part of his intense interest in people. Some men spend their days watching birds or badgers or red deer, Wycliffe watched people. His interest was usually sympathetic, never malicious, and what he learned, not only helped him with his job but helped him to come to terms with himself. He went back to the chair by the window, the chair in which Peters had died, and sat, staring out into the meadow. After a little while his mind was almost a total blank. Was this how Peters had been when his killer arrived? Had he been slow to react because he was deep in a mindless reverie?

This room probably had more in it of the man Peters than any other place. Wycliffe was sitting in Peters' chair, surrounded by Peters' belongings. Apart from the chalk circles marking prints the room was as Peters had made it, as he had lived in it.

But it did not help him to form a clear picture of the man. Peters remained an enigma. A clever boy, son of a working-class family. 'O' levels, 'A' levels, University. But he throws up a promising academic career for the 'Scene'. Nothing remarkable about that. More remarkable, he had made it to the top. Fame and fortune, girls and girls.

Then he chucks it in. Why? Disgust? Disillusionment? If so, would he have treasured all these mementoes of those years? Here in this room were the props of Vince, the Pop Idol, cheek by jowl with the trappings of Peters, the student. There seemed to be a fundamental ambivalence at the core of his life.

Wycliffe got up from his chair and went out on to the landing where Andrews and Cole were waiting to start their inventory. 'It's all yours.'

He was uneasy. He felt that he had achieved nothing but that he had come close to making a real step forward. He had missed something obvious, perhaps failed to interpret evidence which had been presented to him.

Preoccupied and morose he was driven back to town by a uniformed constable.

The quay was alive with people, the carnival procession had formed up, the band was playing and they were about to move off on their tour of the town. He told his driver to drop him at the Tower House and to take the car back through the side streets. He felt sure that Nellie Martin would not be watching the procession.

She answered his knock. 'You again! What is it now? My son is out.'

'I wanted to talk to you, Mrs Martin.'

Reluctantly she stood aside and after she had closed the door she followed him into their living-room which was also the kitchen. The old man was seated in his chair by the stove, his head lolled back, his eyes were closed and a weak, bubbling sound came from his open mouth. Wycliffe had never seen a living person so white, even his lips were no more than a pinkish margin to the mouth.

'You haven't been to the Peters' place today?'

'It's my day off.'

'I'm afraid I have some bad news for you. Mr Peters is dead.'

A kettle on the stove had started to boil and she moved it away from the heat. She had not asked him to sit down but he did so, on a heavy, dining chair with a fretted back and upholstered seat. There was not a scrap of comfort anywhere in the room.

'He was shot.'

'You mean he committed suicide?'

'He was murdered.'

She gave no sign of surprise or interest.

'Do you know if Peters owned a gun?'

'He had a gun – yes.'

'How do you know?'

'I clean the place, don't I? Anyway he made no secret of it, he kept it in one of the drawers of the chest in the hall.'

'Has he ever mentioned it to you?'

'When I first went there to work he used it once or twice to fire at a target in the meadow but he gave that up.'

'Why?'

She shrugged. 'How should I know?'

The band was passing outside the window and conversation became impossible but the old man slept on undisturbed. The window was tight shut and with the stove burning the heat in the room was unbearable.

'Was there ammunition in the drawer with the gun?'

'There was a box, I suppose it was ammunition, I didn't take much notice.'

'One box or two?'

She shook her head. 'I couldn't say. I've got other things to think about.'

'Working in the house as you did you must know something of his affairs. Would you say that there was anybody with whom he was on particularly bad terms?'

A bitter little smile. 'Just about everybody on the island.'

'You know exactly what I mean, Mrs Martin.'

She was brushing ash out of the fender. She seemed quite incapable of standing still and most of the time she had her back to him. Now she turned on him. 'And what if I do? It's none of my business!'

'Murder is everybody's business.' The hoary old platitude but he had to say something.

Through the lace blinds he could see vague outlines of the decorated floats passing by and there was frequent clapping and mild cheering. They could even hear the money boxes of the collectors being rattled under the noses of the spectators.

'There was his brother.'

'Roger?'

She nodded. 'Always falling out over money. No love lost between them two.' It was obvious that she had more to tell but by pressing her he might get less than by letting her go her own way. In due course it came.

'I heard him on the telephone yesterday.'

'To Roger?'

'They had an appointment for this afternoon – he asked him to come to the house. Between half past three and four, he said.'

'You are sure of that?'

'I said it, didn't I?'

'Are you willing to put what you have said into a statement and sign it?'

'If I have to.'

As he was leaving she volunteered one more piece of information. 'You know where to find him I suppose?'

'I understand that he lodges at the Quay Café.'

'You could call it that.'

He was glad to get out on to the quay in the fresh air. There was nobody about but he could hear the band playing somewhere in the town. He noticed that the set pieces for the night's firework display had been erected on rafts in the harbour.

Back at his headquarters Inspector Golly was waiting for him and followed him into his office. 'After the funeral . . .'

'One moment, Mr Golly. Who's on duty?'

'Sergeant Scales and one of the local men, PC Trembath.'

Wycliffe picked up the telephone and asked for Trembath to be sent in. The young man arrived promptly, anxious to make a good impression.

'You know Roger Peters?'

'Yes, sir.'

'I want you to write out his description, give it to Mr Golly and he will see that it is circulated to all our men.'

'You want him brought in, sir?' Golly enquired.

'I do. For questioning. And Trembath – I want you, after you've written the description, to go home and change into plain clothes. Then go to the Quay Café and if Peters is not there wait for him. Don't leave until you are relieved or until you bring Peters in.'

When Trembath had gone Wycliffe turned to Golly. 'Now, about the funeral . . .'

Golly had a list of those who had returned to Charlie Martin's house after the funeral. There were between thirty and forty names and among them Wycliffe noted Sylvie's father and Jackie Martin.

'As far as can be ascertained, sir, all these men were there until at least four o'clock.'

'Which makes a pretty good alibi for quite a few. I want this list checked and cross-checked, Mr Golly. And don't forget, nobody is going to be anxious to help.'

A quarter past eight. Time to pick up Brenda Luke and take her to the airport. He had had nothing to eat since lunchtime but he was anxious to see for himself how Clarissa received the news of Peters' death.

In Jordan's little car he drove through the town and up a steep hill to The Terrace where the Lukes lived. The streets were clear for the carnival procession had reached the recreation ground from where they would disperse after judging.

Mrs Luke was outsize and addicted to floral voile dresses worn with ropes of imitation pearls draped over her bosom. Her hair, tinted with a mauve rinse, was set in unnatural waves and her heavily made-up lips were almost lost in the folds of fat which encroached from either side. 'I don't want to be rude but I was just going out again, another minute and you would have missed me altogether!' Her manner was arch, as though they shared a salacious secret. 'Never mind! It's Brenda you've come to see, isn't it?'

Wycliffe was shown into a tiny sitting-room in which there was scarcely space for the three-piece suite.

'Brenda!'

Brenda came in looking pale.

'Now, you must tell her, Mr Wycliffe, not to worry. She's a great one for taking other people's troubles on her shoulders.' She looked at her daughter critically. 'Look at her! She looks quite peaky – you're not sickening for something are you?'

'She's had a shock, Mrs Luke, it's only natural that she should be upset – two of her friends in a few days . . .'

'Not friends exactly – acquaintances, you might say. I know it's sad, a tragedy really, but you can't live other people's lives for them – that's what I always say.' She looked from her daughter to Wycliffe and back again. 'Well, if that's all it is, I'll leave you to it.' She was on her way out into the passage when she turned back. 'Oh, Bren, I forgot. You're too late to see the carnival but Mrs Paul asked me to come to their place to watch the fireworks. Why don't you come down later – when Mr Wycliffe has finished with you? It would cheer you up.'

'I'll think about it, mother.'

After a moment or two the front door slammed. Wycliffe wondered if Mr Luke had died in self defence. The girl looked at him with a vaguely apologetic look.

'I thought you might like to come to the airport with me to meet Clarissa. She has to be told.'

'You want me to tell her?'

'It might be better.'

She nodded. 'I think you're right.' She was a kindly, sensible girl.

'I've got a car outside.'

She fetched her coat and they got into the little blue and white Morris. Wycliffe drove inexpertly but slowly through the narrow lanes to the heliport. Brenda sat with her knees together, her skirt pulled down as far as it would go but still not far enough to cover her plump thighs. She seemed anxious to talk.

'I got to know Clarissa soon after they came here . . . I felt sorry for her really. I know Vince is dead but he wasn't fair to her.' She swept back the hair from her face in a quick movement. 'He was selfish – always thinking of himself . . . Anyway, she started the pottery. I think she wanted to feel a bit independent. I'd done some pottery at school and she said I had a flair . . . I started to help out when she got busy, then we came to an arrangement – commission. Another season and I'd probably have given up my job and gone to work there full time.'

'You have another job?'

She seemed surprised by his ignorance. 'I work for the Boat Syndicate, for Charlie Martin. Of course there isn't much to do in the winter but they're very good – always full pay. But it isn't much of a job – boring.' The ultimate condemnation.

All she needed was a gentle prod now and then to keep her going. 'Clarissa is sweet.'

'Did they quarrel?'

She shook her head. 'You couldn't quarrel with Clarissa – nobody could. As far as Vince was concerned, she just took what he dished out. No, he didn't ill-treat her – not hit her or anything like that. He just took notice of her when it suited him and ignored her at other times.'

Evidently she had not fallen for Peters like the others, or, if she had, disillusionment had followed.

'Did they have many visitors?'

'Visitors? Not very often. Apart from the kids, that is. And Jackie Martin, if you count him. Once in a while his accountant or his agent would come over, then, of course, there was his brother – Roger.'

'What about Roger?'

'He's older than Vince, some sort of salesman, I think, though he can't do very much work.'

'Does he come often?'

'He seems to spend most of his time on the island and he visits Vince pretty often. He seems to be short of money and I think he sponges on Vince.'

'When did you last see him at the house?'

She considered. 'Friday, I think it was – no, Thursday. They had a row.'

They had arrived at the heliport. Wycliffe parked his car and they walked through the little waiting-room on to the grass landing field. The sun was dipping into the sea, that sad, solemn moment of a summer day when everything is suffused with golden light. Wycliffe recalled his youth. Chapel on Sunday evenings with the sun filtered through cheap stained glass. The sound of a brass band reached them from the town.

'They quarrelled?'

'Yes. Clarissa and I were working in the pottery and we went over to the house to get a drink. Roger was there and Vince was telling him off. He seemed quite worked up. Of course he stopped when we arrived and I didn't quite gather what it was about but afterwards Clarissa said, "I'm glad Vince is putting his foot down. Roger is very weak and he will live off Vince if he can." It was the most I've ever heard Clarissa say against anybody.'

She stared out over the glassy sea. 'I can see the helicopter.'

Then Wycliffe spotted it, a black dot creeping almost imperceptibly nearer. 'Is Roger married?'

'Separated.'

'Apparently he doesn't stay with Vince when he's here.'

She gave a quick, faint smile. 'No, he lodges at the café on the quay.'

'So?'

'The café is run by a widow woman – Wendy Hicks. The gossip is that Roger Peters is her lover.'

'Are there any other relatives?'

'No, Clarissa says both parents are dead and there were no other children.'

A moment while they watched the helicopter drawing nearer, seeming to move crabwise across the sky.

'Brenda, there's something I must tell you before Clarissa comes. Vince did not kill himself, he was murdered.'

She did not seem to be surprised. 'I wondered. When I thought it over it seemed odd that you were so anxious to find out who it was in the kitchen. Do you think it could have been . . . ?'

The beat of the rotor blades was suddenly very close, then over-head. The machine hovered like an angry mosquito then dropped quickly and smoothly to the ground. The engine cut and the blades came to rest.

'There she is.'

Wycliffe saw the slim, dark figure at the top of the steps, her arms full of parcels. She saw Brenda and tried to wave. Brenda went to meet her. He saw them meet and then he saw the vivacity die from Clarissa's face and a frightening blankness take its place. She released her parcels to Brenda mechanically and, mechanically, she allowed herself to be guided towards him.

'Oh, yes, the police.' Complete acceptance.

She sat beside him in the little car, her hands resting listlessly in her lap, her eyes looking straight ahead. He had to tell her that she could not go to Salubrious Place until his men had finished there. 'You'll be able to use at least part of the house tonight but wouldn't it be better if you stayed in the town?'

'I want to go home as soon as possible.' Tonelessly.

'I'll come with you, Clarissa, keep you company.'

'Thank you.'

'Meantime you must come home with me.'

Wycliffe was impressed by her grief. No demonstration. Many people are surprised and hurt when misfortune strikes home, others are always aware that it could happen. The world is divided into those who say, 'Not to me!' and the others who ask, 'Why not?'

'There are one or two questions I must ask you now,' Wycliffe said. 'The rest can wait.'

'I want to help.'

'Did Mr Peters own a gun?'

A faint, sad smile. 'Please call him Vince, never was he called Mr Peters. Yes, he had a gun. I do not know why. I think he bought it in America for fun. Once or twice, a long time ago, he played with it in the meadow – shooting at bottles, but I did not like that.'

'Where did he keep it?'

'In one of the drawers of the chest in the hall. I did not want it in the house but when I say that he just laugh at me.'

'Was there ammunition with the gun?'

'Yes, there were two boxes but one was not full – some had been used.'

'Who else knew of the gun?'

She frowned. 'I do not know. I do not think he told anyone and I did not. I would think no-one knew that it was there.'

'The cleaning woman?'

'Oh, yes, she would know, I suppose.'

'His brother?'

'Roger?' She hesitated. 'Roger might know that Vince had a gun but I do not think he would know where it was kept.'

'Jackie Martin?'

She hesitated again. 'I do not think Jackie Martin would know unless his mother told him.'

Wycliffe thanked her. 'I won't trouble you any more tonight.' He promised that he would arrange transport for them to Salubrious Place when his men had finished. 'It may be late.'

Then he drove them in silence to the little terraced house above the town. The streets were mysterious in a purple summer dusk.

The town was empty, everybody was gathered on the quay to watch the fireworks. He threaded through narrow alleys to avoid the harbour and came out at the foot of the steep slope up to the school. As he parked the car in the playground there was a powerful hissing sound, a trail of fire across the sky, a loud report and a shower of stars crackling overhead. The first rocket.

The duty-officer sat by the radio panel. A detective was writing his report, it was quiet as a church. He went through to his office. Jimmy Gill was supervising the search at Salubrious Place.

Searching a house takes a long time when you have no idea what you are looking for and very little idea of what may turn out to be important when you find it.

Wycliffe filled his pipe, taking his time, lit it and puffed contentment. The firework display was reaching a climax. From his chair he could look down on the harbour. A set piece was spluttering and spitting fire on its floating raft. 'Welcome to the Islands', reflected faithfully in the oily black water. Peters might have doubted the sincerity of the greeting. For a guilty moment Wycliffe wished himself young again, a girl on his arm, embracing, kissing, whispering and losing identity in the crowd which was as good-natured as the warm darkness.

He sat a while watching the fireworks without switching on the lights. Then he reached for the telephone and asked to be connected to the hospital where the mortuary was and where Franks was conducting the post-mortem. He had to wait some time before they could get Franks on the line and when he came he sounded tired.

'I thought you would be watching the fireworks.'

'I am. Have you finished?'

'All I can do tonight.'

'One question – was Peters in good health?'

Franks laughed shortly. 'You noticed? I thought I had news for you.'

Wycliffe had noticed nothing physical to lead him to the conclusion that Peters was seriously ill. He had deduced illness from seemingly irreconcilable aspects of the young man's life.

'I wondered this afternoon,' Franks went on. 'His left arm was rigid. Of course, that could have been due to local injury, but it wasn't.'

'What was wrong with him?'

'Disseminated or multiple sclerosis. Small areas of the nervous system become sclerotized and these areas may be anywhere in the brain or spinal cord. The disease is progressive . . .'

'It's a death sentence, isn't it?'

'Not necessarily, by any means. Its progress may be so slow that the expectation of life is scarcely affected.'

'But with Peters?'

'I've had a word with Ross who was his GP – a good chap. Ross was worried, there was no sign of a let-up.'

'How long would he have had?'

'Impossible to say, but if there was no slowing down it could hardly have been more than two or three years.'

So Peters had been under sentence.

'Did he know?'

'In general terms – yes. Ross said he took it very well. Usually people suffering from the disease are encouraged to carry on with their jobs but in his case . . . Well, co-ordination was the essence of it and that tends to suffer in the early stages.'

It helped to resolve the enigma and put a tragedy in its place.

A fusillade of rockets shot into the air, diverged and fell in cascades of crepitating stars.

'Would his mind have been affected?'

'How the hell would I know? It depends on the distribution of sclerotized areas.'

'What about his blood group?'

'Group "A".'

'So he could have been the child's father?'

'Yes.'

'Anything else for me?'

'Not much, the track of the bullet was just as it seemed to be – nothing fancy.'

'Time of death?'

'I've found nothing to make me change my mind. Probably between three-thirty and four-thirty. I can't be more definite.'

'What about his clothing?'

'I didn't get anything from it but I've had it packed up ready for your people to collect. I suppose it will have to go to forensic?'

'I suppose so, but there's not much point. I don't suppose you've had a chance to do anything with that ring bolt I sent you?'

Franks was smug. 'I made time. It's the weapon all right. Blood, a small amount of hair and tissue . . . It's her blood group and her hair.'

'How many blows with a thing like that?'

'Perhaps one, more likely two.'

'Thanks. Good night.'

Down at the harbour, another set piece. Catherine wheels, red, green and white, whirling in a frenzied pattern.

Multiple sclerosis. It explained a lot.

Wycliffe's thoughts ranged over the day which had started with his tentative, almost half-hearted investigation into the death of a young girl. Her death had been made to look like suicide – or accident. If it hadn't been for the islanders there would have been no awkward questions. She had been clubbed to death. Peters had been shot. Had they died by the same hand? Wycliffe's training would tell him that they had not. Case histories show that multiple killers stick to one method. They are poisoners, or stranglers, or knife men, or they bludgeon their victims to death. But the motives for such killings are usually pathological, that is to say, they are not 'reasonable' to the ordinary man. Is it likely that someone more rationally motivated might be less hidebound? More opportunist in his approach? Wycliffe was inclined to think so and for that reason he was unwilling to discount the possibility that there had been only one killer. On the other hand, he must consider the alternative.

Like every investigator, detective or scientist, Wycliffe had learned that the key to success lies in asking the right questions and the selection of the 'right' questions seems to be an intuitive process. At least he had never come across a set of rules for doing it.

Now he felt that the right question was 'Why?' not 'Who?' Why had Sylvie been bludgeoned? Why had Peters been shot? He was sure that the answers would be linked.

He resisted the temptation to try to answer his questions now. He had found it best not to strain too hard after truth. Better to let impressions, facts, ideas and incidents accumulate, mix and blend and crystallize in the slow chemistry of the mind.

7

He was restless. He telephoned Jimmy Gill who had no news for him. He arranged for one of Jimmy's team to fetch Clarissa from the Lukes' and bring her home. 'I expect that she will come back with the Luke girl. Let them carry on as normally as possible.'

Twenty minutes past ten. If he went back to the Jordans' he could hardly ask them to cook him a meal and he had no appetite for what he could expect from the canteen. He walked down the corridor to the operations room. The duty-officer was reading a newspaper, a cup of tea at his elbow. One of the divisional men was typing his report. More paper. Always more paper. It was a disease – Parkinson's disease. He chuckled at the bad pun.

'Good night, sergeant.'

'Good night, sir.'

And the same to you.

He strolled through the playground and down the slope to the quay. The fireworks were over and chains of fairy lights had been switched on. Scores of couples were shuffling round the wharf to waltz tunes played by the brass band who must have been almost blown out.

The Quay Café was one of the granite fronted houses facing the harbour. It had a shop front but the windows were covered with net curtains which made it difficult to see inside. He pushed open the door. Trembath was there and spotted him at once. A moment later they were resting with their arms on the quay wall, looking out over the harbour.

'So he's not turned up?'

'No, sir. At first she pretended she hadn't seen him since Monday but I wouldn't wear that and in the end she said he was out pollacking with the Rowses.'

'Is that likely?'

'Quite likely, sir. I know he often goes out with the Rowse brothers and there's plenty of pollack about at the moment.'

'Which means what?'

'That he might not be back until two or three in the morning.'

'What's the food like in there?'

'The food? All right, I suppose. Chips with everything.'

'You get along home. I expect you've got a wife waiting for you.'

'Yes, sir, but . . .'

'Scoot, laddie!'

He went across to the café.

A dozen marble-topped tables, a black and white tiled floor, a counter with tea and coffee machines and shelves with cakes and sandwiches on paper doilies. An ABC tearoom, 1892 vintage. But on the wall behind the counter there was a large mirror with the menu written on it in white water paint. As Trembath had said, chips with everything. A door in the back wall stood open and through it he could see the kitchen beyond and hear the voices of two women.

At one of the tables a boatman in his blue jersey and still wearing his cap, was eating forkfuls of beans and sausages washed down by gulps of strong tea. At another table a young couple sat with empty coffee cups in front of them. Wycliffe sensed that they were in the silent stage of a quarrel, looking at each other surreptitiously and wondering if it would be possible to make it up before they had to separate for the night.

One of the women came through from the kitchen. Thirty-four or five, not bad looking, plump, comfortable, but her face over-made-up. Her lips were slashes of crimson and her eyelids the colour of a ripe bruise. Her see-through blouse was well filled. She wiped the counter with a damp cloth and asked him what he wanted.

'Mrs Hicks?'

She nodded.

'Roger in?'

She was contemptuous. 'You know the answer to that one. I wasn't born yesterday.'

'I'll wait.'

She paused, as though considering. 'You'll have to wait a long time.'

'Until when?'

'Maybe all night.'

'Then I shall need something to eat. Say, eggs and sausages. No chips. And I'll start with some coffee.'

She nodded towards one of the tables. 'I'll bring it.'

A long wait.

It had been half past ten when he settled down to his meal. Soon afterwards the dancing on the quay had stopped and there was an influx of customers, mostly young people, presumably with good digestions. The widow and her unseen helper in the kitchen were kept busy. After his meal Wycliffe smoked his pipe and listened to the chatter at the tables. He heard no mention of Peters. Most of the customers seemed to be visitors and the news hadn't got round to them. He went out on to the wharf and sat on a bollard from where he could keep an eye on the café. The fairy lights made multi-coloured streamers on the water. Along the quay, the Seymour Arms was a blaze of light and the noise of people all talking and shouting at once reached him as a pleasant murmur.

By half past eleven people were leaving the café and there were no new customers. He went back inside, the widow was putting chairs on some of the tables and there were only two customers left. She looked at him wearily. 'I thought you'd gone.'

He sat at his former table, now laden with dirty dishes. The two remaining customers paid their bill and left.

'I'm closing.'

He did not answer and she went over to the shop door and reversed the 'open' card.

'What do you want him for?'

'Just a few questions.'

She had finished putting up the chairs on the cleared tables, now she came and sat near him. 'God! I'm all in.' She put her feet on a second chair and leaned forward to massage her ankles.

Wycliffe smoked his pipe. 'Does he come here often?'

'Pretty often.'

'As a lodger?'

'You could say that.'

'You mean that he's more than a lodger?'

She lit a cigarette and puffed luxuriously. 'I mean that he doesn't pay his rent.' She grinned and added, 'All the same, he's good company and it's nice to have a man about the place again. I won't deny it.'

She seemed a decent body, the sort Wycliffe could get on with. A realist. She had life taped.

'Why don't you marry him?'

She looked at him speculatively. 'You're an odd sort of copper. As to marriage, I've got the café, what's he got?'

'A job, I suppose, and a brother with money.'

She laughed. 'His job doesn't amount to much. He's a freelance salesman working on commission and most weeks he doesn't make enough to live on. Poor old Rog couldn't sell nuts to a squirrel. As to his brother's money, if Roger ever got his hands on that I wouldn't see him for dust. I've got no illusions about Master Roger but beggars can't be choosers and I know where I am with him.'

'Where does he live when he's not here?'

'He's got a room in Plymouth – Frobisher Terrace.'

Wycliffe smoked placidly. The clock on the glass shelf above the sandwiches showed a quarter to twelve. A little old woman wearing a shabby brown coat down to her ankles came through the door from the kitchen. She clutched a paper carrier bag.

'I'll take the sandwiches.'

The widow sighed. 'You do that, Elsie, they won't be much by tomorrow.'

The old woman reached down the sandwiches, wrapped them in a couple of paper doilies and put them in her carrier bag. 'I'm off, then. I've finished most of the washing up but I'll do the rest in the morning.'

'All right, Elsie, thanks.'

The old woman trotted over to the door and let herself out. 'Good night, then!'

The widow watched her go. 'Poor old soul, she's got nobody. She comes here as much as anything for the company.' She got up and went behind the counter; when she came back she was carrying two bottles of ale and glasses. 'Drink?'

'Thanks.'

They sat opposite each other, drinking their beer.

'If you ask me, it's the chance of getting hold of his brother's money that ruined Roger.'

'Not much of a chance, surely.'

She wiped her lips with the back of her hand. 'I don't know about that. Vince could pop off at any time.'

'How do you know that?'

'Rog told me, he's got something wrong with his nerves. That's why he packed it in with the pop business.'

'Even so, there's no certainty that Roger would benefit, is there?'

'I don't know, but blood is thicker than water – at least, that's what they say.'

'Vince is dead.'

'Dead?' She put down her glass which had been halfway to her lips. 'Is that why you're here? What's it got to do with the police?'

'He was shot.'

'You mean that he shot himself?'

'He was murdered.'

She kneaded her left breast unselfconsciously. 'You think Roger did it?'

'It's just one possibility.'

She did not argue. 'When did it happen?'

'This afternoon.'

'Then it couldn't have been Roger, he was over to Morvyl with Billy Rowse. The Rowses are mechanics and Billy had to go over to see to Sam Tripp's wind pump.'

'When did he get back?'

'About seven, I think it was.'

'And where is he now?'

She looked pained. 'I told Eddie Trembath, he's out pollacking with the Rowses.'

'On carnival night?'

She smiled wearily. 'That sort of thing doesn't mean much to the islanders, it's for the trade. When there's pollack about and the weather is fair you won't catch many of the menfolk gawping at processions and fireworks. A gallon of beer in the bottom of the boat and they're away.'

Wycliffe could sympathize.

She added, 'As I told you, he could be away all night, you'd much better leave it till morning.'

Wycliffe shook his head.

'All right, suit yourself.' She finished her beer and gathered up the empties and the glasses. 'I must get on.'

617

Wycliffe felt drowsy. For a time he was dimly aware of the widow woman moving around, clearing up, then there were gaps. He must have dozed fitfully. Two or three times he woke with a start to find her still carrying dishes into the kitchen or putting chairs on to tables, then, the next time, the café was empty, everything had been cleared away and the clock on the glass shelf showed a quarter past one.

He felt foolish and he had a headache. The kitchen was in darkness and he called out, 'Mrs Hicks!' Then he found the switch for the kitchen lights. 'Mrs Hicks! Are you there?' He found the stairs at the back of the kitchen and went up, wondering what he would do if she had gone to bed. A small landing with three doors opening off. He tried them all, flicking switches. Two bedrooms, unoccupied, and a long sitting-room at the front, overlooking the harbour.

For the first time he noticed that it was raining, streaming down the windows and he could hear water chuckling in the downpipe. He went back downstairs feeling a fool. As he entered the café, the shop door opened and the widow came in. She stood there, her plastic mackintosh dripping on to the floor, and she looked at him diffidently, a little frightened, like a naughty child who expects to be smacked. She opened her mouth to speak but he brushed past her, out into the rain.

'Take the umbrella! You'll get soaked!'

But his pride would not let him hear. Although he was not far from Jordan's house he was wet through before he got there. But he was beginning to recover his good humour, even to see the funny side. Although Peters had been tipped off by his widow woman, it was unlikely that he could get away from the islands.

From Jordan's office, with his clothes dripping on to the floor and forming a pool on the linoleum, he phoned his headquarters at the school and arranged for a watch to be kept on the café. Then he crept up to his room. From across the landing, Jordan's snoring continued without interruption.

Next morning it was still raining, the waterfront was deserted, the boats were still at their moorings and it looked as though they would stay there. He stopped at the shop to buy tobacco and a newspaper. From the rack, the tabloids bleated in heavy, black type:

POP STAR FOUND DEAD

Wycliffe bought a *Guardian*; its pale-pink literacy appealed to him. No banner headlines; a three-column spread on the economic situation, but they still found space on the front page for a decorous headline in twenty-four-point:

MYSTERY DEATH OF FORMER POP STAR

The facts, as Wycliffe had made them known, were followed by a potted biography of Peters and, 'The police are treating Peters' death as murder. Detective Superintendent Wycliffe is investigating a possibility that Peters' death may be linked with that of a nineteen-year-old girl whose body was found in a disused quarry on the island last Sunday . . .'

Sylvie's death had made scarcely a ripple in Fleet Street but linked with the Peters shooting it would do better.

When he reached the school there had been no news of Roger Peters. The Rowse brothers had been summoned and were being questioned by Detective Sergeant Gifford, one of the divisional men. Wycliffe went along to the classroom where they were being interviewed. They were twins, impossible for a stranger to tell them apart, cheerful, round-faced and with complexions like the shell of a hazelnut.

They said they had put Roger Peters ashore on the quay at one o'clock in the morning. They had not seen anybody waiting for him but it had been raining hard and they had other things to think about. The one who admitted to being Billy said that he had taken Roger with him the previous afternoon when he had gone to Morvyl to do a repair job on Sam Tripp's wind-pump.

'We left about half past two and got back round seven.'

'Was Peters with you the whole time?'

'No, he stayed with the boat, mostly.'

Wycliffe got him to point out on the map where Sam Tripp's place was and noted that it lay just across the sound from Quincey Cove.

'Apart from yourselves, did Roger have any friends on the islands?'

The brothers looked at each other. 'Most of us was on good terms with Roger.' Billy added, after a moment's thought, 'I'm not sure if I know what you're after, Mr Wycliffe, but if I do, you can forget it. Roger wouldn't harm anybody.'

His brother, Henry, nodded, 'Nobody.'

Wycliffe spent the next hour on routine work with Gill. They asked the Plymouth police for information about Roger's lodgings and about his contacts in Plymouth.

Sergeant Scales reported having found prints of two fingers on the stainless-steel sink in the kitchen at Salubrious Place and the prints matched those on the filing cabinet in Vince Peters' room.

The telephone rang. It was the duty-officer to say that Peters' lawyer had arrived and wanted to see the chief superintendent. Wycliffe had a professional dislike of lawyers but this one was by no means true to type. Wycliffe thought that he must have been a 'one-off'. Young, with straggling blond hair, he wore a hipped-up version of a shooting jacket, light-brown cords and suede shoes.

'Tim Wells. I got your message about poor old Vince. Any ideas?'

Wycliffe waved him to a chair. 'No, Mr Wells, have you?'

'Me? Not a clue! We handled Vince's business but he was always close about his private life. All the same, there are one or two things you ought to know. First, there's big money involved, so his will is important.'

Wycliffe looked at the candid blue eyes and wondered if there was hope of a new breed of lawyer. 'You are willing to tell me about it?'

'Why the hell not? That's why I'm here. The will is simple enough, taken by itself. Two hundred thousand and the house to his dolly girl and the residue to his brother.'

'You said, "taken by itself" . . .'

Wells nodded. 'I did. Most wills can be changed, some of our clients in the pop world, especially the women, change their wills as often as their hair styles. It's good for trade, but confusing.'

'But this will?'

'Was different.' The lawyer got out his cigarette case, offered round and lit up. 'Vince couldn't change it – at least, not the provision for his brother, that was the subject of an agreement.'

'Agreement? But in an agreement there must surely be some sort of quid pro quo?'

'There is, but it's vague – "in consideration of services rendered to the performing group known as . . ." blah, blah, blah.'

'Will it stand up?'

'It doesn't have to, the will is good. If Vince had changed his will it might have been a different matter but we took counsel's opinion.'

'When was that?'

'When the group wound up.'

'What does the residue amount to?'

Wells pursed his lips. 'Royalties, the residue of his capital . . . say, an income of twenty or thirty thousand a year.'

Wycliffe whistled. 'That's a great deal of money.'

'It's not peanuts.' Wells blew a thin thread of smoke ceiling-wards. 'This brother – where is he?'

Wycliffe was cautious. 'I understand that he is in the islands and we expect to contact him today.'

'When you do . . .'

'Of course. I'm grateful to you for your cooperation, Mr Wells. About the agreement you spoke of – what were its terms?'

'That Roger should receive not less than a half-share in the net value of the estate and Vince was precluded from making any deed of gift without the consent of his brother.'

'Extraordinary!'

'You're telling me!' Wells stood up. 'I suppose I'd better look in on the place. Is Clarissa there?'

Wycliffe offered him transport and the lawyer accepted. 'I'm not really the outdoor type. However, if you want me during the next day or so, I'm staying at The Garrison.' And Mr Wells drifted out.

When he had gone, Gill uncoiled himself from his chair. 'Like the man said, twenty or thirty thousand a year is more than peanuts, it's motive for murder.'

Wycliffe was drumming out a tattoo with his fingers on the desk top. 'And Sylvie?'

'There are a few things we don't know yet.'

Wycliffe grinned. 'Like the man said, "You're telling me!"' He got out his pipe and lit it. 'I'm worried about that gun. There's no doubt in my mind that the killer didn't just ditch it. If he was going to do that there would have been no point in taking the ammunition.'

Gill, for once, was serious. Policemen usually are when the talk is of guns. 'It worries me too but if we're right it alters the whole character of the case. It means we're due for another killing.'

Wycliffe stood up and walked over to the window. Rain was

621

streaming down the glass, distorting his view. 'Not necessarily, it could be that he's the sort who feels safer with a gun and that he won't use it unless it comes to a showdown.'

'I don't know that that makes me feel any better.'

'Nor me.'

'In any case, there isn't much we can do about it.'

Wycliffe stared down at the deserted quay. 'We must warn our chaps to be careful; that goes for you, too.'

Jimmy Gill lit a cheroot and flicked the match in the general direction of the ashtray. 'Jackie Martin's alibi doesn't look so good by daylight, does it?'

It was true. Inspector Golly had organized a careful check on the times various people had left Charlie Martin's house after the funeral and, so far as Jackie Martin was concerned, there was conflicting testimony. It was possible that he had left as early as three o'clock, in which case he was still in the running. 'I can't see that boy with a gun,' Wycliffe said, 'but funnier things have happened.'

'He's kinky,' Gill said, spilling ash down the front of his suit.

The telephone rang. 'Brenda Luke is here, sir. She says she wants to add something to the statement she made – something she has remembered.'

'Bring her in.'

She came in, looking self-possessed and good enough to eat. Wet-look mac and shoes in red with a waterproof hat to match, her hair glistening with rain drops. She smiled at Gill but addressed herself to Wycliffe.

'Since I made my statement I remembered something. I can't really understand why I didn't think of it before.'

Wycliffe drew up a chair for her.

'I can't stay long. There's nothing doing in the ticket office this morning and I want to get back to Clarissa.

'It's just that your detective asked me if I'd seen anybody when I was on my way to the house yesterday afternoon. I said I hadn't but that wasn't true . . .'

'Well?'

'I saw Nick Marsden. You get so used to him hanging about, you don't take any notice.'

'Where, exactly, did you see him?'

'As I was crossing the bridge I saw him further down the valley. I suppose he was on his way home.'

'How far away?'

'It's difficult to say, I suppose a couple of hundred yards.'

'But you didn't see him while you were walking down the track from the moor?'

She shook her head. 'No, I didn't, that's what worries me.'

'Could he have come from the house?'

'If he'd come from the courtyard I would have seen him but he could have come from the back of the house, through the meadow.'

It might mean anything or nothing. There was no accounting for the movements of a man like Marsden.

She frowned. 'I'm a bit worried, I don't want to get him into trouble, but he was there . . .'

'I quite understand. Did he seem to be in a hurry?'

A pause. 'No, just like usual. He always looks as though he's going to fall over his feet the next step he takes.'

Wycliffe thanked her and arranged for her statement to be amended. When she had gone, Gill said, 'Marsden and Roger Peters were drinking buddies, don't you think we ought to bring Marsden in?'

Wycliffe shrugged. 'Maybe you're right.'

Gill sent Jordan to find him. The search did not take long. Marsden was propping up the bar of the Seymour. Despite the rain he had walked in with no more protection than his seaman's jersey. The public was unusually crowded because of the rain. None of the boats had gone out and most of the boatmen were there. The room was full of noise and smoke and the smell of wet wool. Charlie Martin was playing cribbage with the harbour master, the dominoes were out and others were playing whist.

Jordan had to push his way through to the bar. Charlie Martin followed him with his eyes. Marsden was drinking with Jack Bishop. The landlord was in the other bar for the visitors had nothing to do either. It was his daughter who greeted Jordan. 'The usual, Mr Jordan?'

'No, thanks, Clara, I wanted a word with Nick.'

Marsden was, as usual, not drunk but he had had quite a few. His skin, like his lips, was moist, he seemed to sweat beer and one had the impression that it might be squeezed out of him as from a sponge.

'You want me, Mr Jordan?'

He followed Jordan out, like a dog, and asked no questions until they reached the quay.

'Mr Gill will tell you what you need to know.'

In build and features there were resemblances between Marsden and Jimmy Gill. The huge frame, the rubbery features, thick lips and spiky hair, but the Chief Inspector was twenty-five years younger and in better shape.

Gill made him sit on a small, folding chair and sat himself on another, not two feet away. 'You know the score, Marsden, I'm not going to beat about the bush with you. Do you smoke?'

'Cigarettes.'

'You'll have to make do with one of these,' and he thrust one of his cheroots under the man's nose.

Marsden accepted the cheroot and lit it from Jimmy's lighter.

'I've just been speaking on the telephone to Peters' dolly-bird.'

'You mean, Miss Clarissa, I expect, Mr Gill.'

Gill gave him a dirty look and let it go. 'She told me that when they first went there, you used to do odd jobs about the place.'

Marsden was wary. 'I used to help out, neighbourly like.'

'Neighbourly, my arse! You used to make a few bob for yourself doing odd jobs and take the chance to nick what you could until Peters found you out.'

Marsden's protest was half-hearted.

'I don't care if you nicked the whole bloody outfit.' Gill thrust his stubbly chin forward and came a bit closer. 'I gather that one of the jobs you helped with was bringing a certain chest of drawers from one of the rooms upstairs down into the hall . . .'

'It's a long time ago . . .'

'Shut up! I'm not asking you, I'm telling you. In carrying the drawers down, you saw that there was a gun in one of them . . .'

'I never nicked no gun!'

'I didn't say that you nicked it, I said that you saw it.'

'I don't remember a gun.'

'You don't have to.'

Ash dropped down Marsden's cheroot on to the floor and Gill snapped, 'Don't make a bloody mess or you'll have to clear it up!' He allowed a small pause during which he pretended to consult some papers he held in his hand. Keep 'em guessing! 'Yesterday, a few minutes after Peters is known to have been shot, you were seen leaving the house. Everybody knows you hated his guts – and why. So!' Gill sat back with a dramatic gesture. 'What have we got?'

Marsden was gathering his wits and beginning to formulate some sort of reply but Gill interrupted. 'Don't say anything, you'd be wiser not to. We've got you, with motive, means and opportunity. Better men than you have found themselves in the topping shed for less, Marsden.'

The thick, moist lips hung loosely and Marsden looked at his interrogator with frightened eyes. 'You don't think . . .'

'Where's Roger Peters?'

It took a moment for Marsden to reorientate his thoughts. 'Roger?'

'Yes, where is he? He stood to gain a fortune by his brother's death. What was it? A deal between the two of you? What are you supposed to get out of it?'

Marsden shook his head in consternation. 'I don't know where he is, Mr Gill, straight up, I don't. As for any deal . . .'

Gill's voice was venomous. 'If you're covering up for him, Marsden, you're a bigger bloody fool . . .'

'Christ! I can't afford to cover up for anybody in the spot I'm in! What is it you want me to do, Mr Gill?' He was sweating profusely and the beery smell, mixed with the odour of sodden wool, filled the room.

'I want your version of exactly what happened yesterday afternoon.'

It came fast enough. According to Marsden he had been on his way home. He'd left the Seymour at about two o'clock and by the time he reached Peters' place he was finding the heat a bit too much for him so he decided to have a kip in the bracken.

'Which side of the stream? This side or the house side?'

'This side, just below the bridge.'

'How long did you sleep?'

Marsden contorted his features into a semblance of contrition. 'I'd tell you if I knew, Mr Gill, but I ain't all that good on time, especially when I've had one or two.'

'All right. Then you woke up – what happened?'

625

'Something woke me. I thought it was a shot and there was what sounded like breaking glass. I said to meself it must be one of the boys trying to put the wind up Peters. Somebody putting a few shot-gun pellets through one of his windows, I thought.'

'What did you do?'

Marsden wiped his forehead with a filthy rag. 'I sat up and took a gander but I couldn't see nobody so I went over. There was nobody in the yard and I couldn't see any broken window so I went round the back – into that bit of meadow . . .'

'Well?'

Marsden was getting increasingly agitated. 'I said I'd tell you the truth, Mr Gill . . .'

'You'd better!'

'Well, I soon spotted there was a broken window in the up-stairs . . .'

'And?'

Marsden looked at the chief inspector as though trying to guess how far he was tying a noose round his own neck, then he decided to take the risk. 'I saw Peters slumped across the table – or desk, whatever it is by the window in that upstairs room.'

'But you didn't report what you had seen, you didn't even tell the officer who questioned you in the house-to-house.'

Marsden seemed to be appealing for reason. 'Well, I ask you, Mr Gill, I didn't want to find meself at the dirty end, did I?'

'Well, you're there now!' Gill snapped. 'I'm holding you for further questioning.' He lit another cheroot and gave it to Marsden.

'After that, I suppose, you went home?'

'I went home, Mr Gill. Yes, I did.'

'Did you meet anybody?'

Marsden choked on the smoke and had a lengthy fit of coughing. When he had recovered he said, 'No, I didn't meet anybody.'

'And are you quite sure you've no idea what time it was?'

The concentration was painful. 'I just thought of something. Not long after I came out of the meadow I heard the siren of the old *Islander*.'

'What time would that be?'

Marsden scratched his head. 'When she's doing these day trips she'll cast off at half past four and she always gives a blast five minutes before to hurry 'em up.'

'Would that be ten minutes or longer after you heard the shot?'

'After I woke up? More like a quarter of an hour I should think but I never was much good on time.'

'And you saw nobody until you got home?'

'No, Mr Gill, I'd swear to that.'

'Nobody on the beach?'

He shook his head. 'No, but come to think, the Rowses' boat was drawn up on the shingle but there was nobody there.'

'Did you see anybody return to the boat later?'

'No, sir. I was all shook up and I went to bed. When I come down an hour or so later she were gone and I never thought any more about it.'

'Why should Peters' death shake you up?'

Marsden looked surprised. 'Why, it's obvious! As you said yourself, everybody knew I'd no good blood for Peters and there I was, on the spot, when he got it.'

'I'm very glad you appreciate your position,' Gill said. 'By the way, was what you told Mr Wycliffe true?'

'Gospel truth, Mr Gill! I'd swear it on my mother's head.'

Gill sniffed. 'Don't you ever wash?'

Marsden grinned. 'I must admit I'm not over fond of water, Mr Gill.'

Wycliffe was uneasy. He was sure that Peters' death must be linked with Sylvie's, yet the evidence, so far, seemed to point the other way. Roger Peters had a strong motive for killing his brother but what possible reason could he have had for murdering Sylvie? None of the mass of reports so painstakingly prepared gave any hint of a connection between them. The fact that Vince Peters had been murdered did not, of course, clear him of possible guilt for Sylvie's death, but it was inconceivable that the motives for the two crimes were unconnected. The obvious link between the killings was Jackie Martin, yet Roger Peters seemed to be doing his best to look like a guilty man. In any case, was it likely that Jackie Martin had shot Peters?

Jackie Martin. The boy intrigued him. Wycliffe was no psychologist but it would have been difficult not to see him as a textbook case. He had made a belated attempt to break out of the magic circle of possessive motherhood and failed . . . Given the talent, he might

627

have found release for his pent-up frustrations in creative work, he might have grown into a Stendahl or a Lawrence. His books and his studious habits seemed to hint that he was dimly aware of the possibility of escape along that road. Given common-or-garden guts he might have persevered and stretched the silver cord until it snapped. In the event, it looked as though his frustration had exploded in a fit of juvenile rage in which he had knocked Humpty Dumpty for six.

And his mother. Some people seemed dogged by misfortune, ground down by circumstance. They are scarcely figures of tragedy for in tragedy there is an element of dignity. The Nellie Martins of this world live out their lives in drab misery, struggling against the odds, intensely jealous, possessive, bitterly resentful and worshipping the little grey god of respectability.

He was intrigued and repelled by the strange menage at the Tower House, and he sensed that only in their relationships would he find the explanations he sought.

It was still raining though less heavily. On the quay, a few visitors in raincoats and carrying umbrellas found the rain preferable to the anonymous drawing-rooms of their boarding houses. Although it was midday the lights were on in the saloon bar of the Seymour as he passed and they seemed to be doing good business.

Jackie, in his shirt sleeves, was seated at the table with a plate of stew in front of him and an open book beside his plate. The old man, in his chair beside the cooking range, was feeding himself with a spoon from a bowl supported on a board which rested across the arms of his chair. It seemed a miracle that his frail, trembling hand should ever guide the spoon to his mouth, but he managed.

Nellie Martin stood by the stove, one hand resting on the brass rod which ran just below the mantelshelf. It was her customary place at mealtimes. Supervising. Waiting to offer somewhat belligerent service to her son and her husband. She would eat a mouthful herself between clearing away and washing up.

The windows were tight-shut. Water streamed down the panes behind the lace blinds and the atmosphere in the room was hot and humid.

Jackie never lifted his eyes from his book but neither did he turn the page.

When Wycliffe knocked on the front door, his mother went to one of the windows and lifted the blind aside then she turned to her son and nodded.

'I'll go upstairs,' Jackie said, getting up.

'No!'

She went to the door. 'What is it now?' Weary and aggressive at the same time.

'I want to talk to your son, Mrs Martin.'

'We're having our meal.'

Without waiting to be invited he took off the oilskin coat he was wearing and hung it on one of the pegs in the hall where it dripped on to the red-tiled floor. He came into the kitchen and sat on a chair by the windows. Jackie acknowledged him with a glance then looked down at his book. His mother went over to her place by the stove. Nobody spoke. The old man looked at Wycliffe from time to time with eyes which had long since ceased to question. An alarm clock ticked loudly on the mantelshelf and the stove crackled. The old man let his spoon fall into the fender. His wife picked it up and gave it to him. For the second time she asked, 'What is it now?'

She might well ask, he hardly knew himself.

'Don't you go to the Peters place any more, Mrs Martin?'

'Is there any reason why I shouldn't?'

Wycliffe shrugged.

'I don't go there until the afternoon on Thursdays.'

Jackie was scarcely touching his food and his eyes never left his book.

'When were you last at the house, Mr Martin?'

'Me?' Jackie looked up, startled.

'He was there on Tuesday night.' Tight-lipped.

'Not yesterday?'

'Yesterday he went to the funeral.'

'And afterwards?'

'He went to his uncle's, most of the mourners did.'

'What time did you leave your uncle's, Mr Martin?'

This time he was allowed to answer for himself. 'I can't say exactly but it must have been about four.'

'He came in here at twenty past four. I noticed because I was cooking a few buns and that was when they were due to come out.'

'Did you know that Peters had a gun?'

'No, I didn't, I swear!'

It was remarkable. Through all this the old man went on with his meal. Now his plate was empty and he started to wave his spoon about in an agitated fashion. His wife took the plate and put in its place a bowl containing some sort of milk pudding. The ritual of feeding continued.

'Why did you go to see Peters on Tuesday night?'

'I often go there.'

'I know, you told me. But Sylvie was murdered on Saturday night. On Tuesday when I talked to you, you were deeply distressed . . .'

'That's natural enough!' Tartly, from his mother.

'Quite natural. What surprises me is to hear that you were paying a social call the same evening.'

'I had to talk to Peters.'

'About Sylvie?'

Jackie stared down at his plate with unfocused eyes.

His mother intervened. 'He couldn't just do nothing!'

'Did you accuse Peters?'

'No, when I got there he and Clarissa were playing cards and I couldn't see him alone.'

'So what did you do?'

His reply was all but inaudible. 'I played cards with them.'

Wycliffe had heard that Jackie's clothes, which had been sent to forensic, had been collected when his mother was out. He doubted if Jackie had told his mother.

'Well, that's all for the moment. If all goes well, we shall be returning your clothes in a day or two.'

'What clothes?'

Jackie was silent.

'What clothes?' She moved closer to the table.

'My fawn trousers and sports jacket.'

'You said you'd sent them to the cleaners.'

'I didn't want to worry you, mother.'

She turned to Wycliffe. 'Why did you take his clothes?'

'For routine examination. Your son's are not the only clothes which are being examined.'

She looked from Wycliffe to Jackie and back again, trying to assess this new threat. Wycliffe felt more than a twinge of compassion but he had a job to do.

After lunch the rain eased, then stopped. Wycliffe and Gill were driven in the Land-Rover to Salubrious Place. The downs were like a green sponge and brown water oozed out of the soil and trickled across the track collecting in the ruts and potholes. In the valley the bridge was barely clear of the stream which had turned into a brown torrent.

Wycliffe, who hated keeping people waiting about, sent the Land-Rover back. 'I'll call if I need you.' He was keeping an appointment with Clarissa but Gill was on his way to Quincey Cove. The only way was to walk down the valley – unless you had a boat.

Clarissa was cordial, she seemed genuinely glad to see him. She took him into the large, opulent sitting-room which had one wall entirely of glass and made Wycliffe feel like a goldfish. Water was still trickling down the glass and the meadow appeared as kaleidoscopic patterns of greens. The cats prowled restlessly, jumping up on to the furniture and down again. 'They are not happy indoors but they do not like getting their paws wet.'

She wore a black jumper and skirt with a gold chain round er neck and a small cross at her breast. She was almost certainly a Catholic which must have added to her problems. She was pale and her beautiful eyes were puffed with much crying. But her manner now was perfectly controlled. She thanked Wycliffe for being considerate. 'Brenda is staying with me – she is gone to the farm at the moment, but she has been much help.' Her precise enunciation and the vagaries of her syntax made her, somehow, more pathetic, more appealing.

'There are a few questions.'

'Of course!' She perched herself on the edge of one of the huge, black armchairs and waited like an obedient schoolgirl.

Wycliffe was feeling the bowl of his pipe in his pocket. When he could not smoke it was his consolation.

'Light your pipe, Mr Wycliffe, I am sure you will feel much at home.'

He accepted gratefully. 'I believe you had a visit from Mr Wells, this morning?'

She nodded. 'Vince's lawyer, yes, he was here.'

'I expect he told you about the will?'

'Yes.' Her manner was casual as though it was a matter of no importance. 'But I already knew, Vince told me that was what he

631

would do.' She blinked rapidly and dabbed her eyes with her hand-kerchief. 'You will excuse me, please.'

'You also knew of the provision for Roger?'

She shook her head. 'No, I did not know that but I am not surprised. Vince was very good to his brother, always giving him money.'

Wycliffe was staring at an aggressive, abstract painting in flaring reds. 'Have you ever thought that Roger might have had some hold over his brother?'

She looked at him quickly. 'Yes, I have thought that sometimes. Is it true?'

It was Wycliffe's turn to shake his head. 'I don't know.' But he was beginning to have the germ of an idea. The possible significance of what he had seen in Peters' room dawned on him. He smoked his pipe in silence for a while.

Clarissa became uneasy as the silence lengthened. Outside, al-though it was no longer raining, the sky was overcast and, despite the huge windows and the fact that it was the middle of a summer afternoon, the room was only dimly lit. Clarissa shivered, got up and went over to the switches by the door. The two ceiling lights sprang to life. 'It is like winter,' she said, nervously.

Wycliffe agreed that it was but his thoughts had moved on. 'When did you decide to go shopping on the mainland?'

She was surprised by the question. 'I do not know. I go about once a month and it is not a thing to plan very much . . .'

'Except that it has to be on Nellie's day off.'

For an instant her face lit up with a smile. 'That is right. I expect Brenda told you, Vince did not like Nellie.'

'Why not?'

Her forehead wrinkled in a deep frown. 'She disapproved of him. She is – how do you say – narrow-minded. Is that right? Vince say she is like his mother was and it makes him feel uncomfortable.' She smiled again. 'Vince was silly about such things, he took too much notice. All the same he would provoke her by pretending to be very bad when he is not.'

'Why didn't he sack her?'

She shook her head. 'I cannot explain, he was like that. Some things he feel he must put up with. Also she is a very good worker and she had a very hard life.'

632

Wycliffe had turned the interrogation into a conversation and that was what he usually aimed to do. 'I should have thought that with Jackie single, earning quite good money as a schoolteacher, she would not have needed to go out to work.'

Clarissa shrugged. 'She is very independent and will not accept what she calls charity from her son. Also, Jackie is an only child and a little selfish so I do not think he will try very hard to persuade her.'

Wycliffe nodded. He was gradually getting to know these people so that what they did and said no longer surprised him. It was like doing a complicated jigsaw puzzle: at first there is very little logic in the procedure, then the pattern begins to emerge and finally a stage is reached when it is possible to predict what will eventually fill the blank spaces. He had not reached that stage yet but he was making progress.

'Is it possible that Vince had an appointment yesterday and wanted the house to himself?'

She took him up quickly. 'You mean a woman? If so, you do not understand. Vince did not hide such things from me, he did not have to. His life as a great pop star . . .' She spread her hands in an expressive gesture. 'Of course he had many women, it was part of the life – you understand?'

'And now – recently?'

Her face clouded. 'You know that Vince was very sick?'

Wycliffe nodded.

'It affected his heart and it was no longer wise . . .' Another telling gesture. 'He was advised by the doctor . . . All the same, there is lung cancer and I do not see the tobacco shops close their doors.' Again she was very near to tears.

Wycliffe was gentle. 'You do not have to tell me.'

'But I must! You will find out who it is that killed him. There were not many affairs of late but the silly girls . . . some of them.'

'Sylvie?'

'Especially Sylvie. For her I felt sorry, I think she loved him, for the others, he was a symbol – you understand?'

'You know that Sylvie was going to have a child?'

'Yes, I know. Vince told me. Poor girl!' She was silent for a time. 'How foolish! If only she had known. We wondered if she had killed herself because . . .'

'She was murdered.'

'I know that now.' She raised her eyes to his. 'You cannot think that Vince . . . ?'

'Do you?'

'Oh, no! It is not possible. If you knew him, you would not think so. Vince could be cruel, but in words or by his silence . . . I have never known him do anything violent – never! It was not in his nature.'

Another long silence while Wycliffe smoked. The windows were clearer and brighter, the clouds must be thinning.

'When I suggested that he might have had an appointment, I was not thinking of a woman.'

She frowned. 'I see. It is possible but I do not think so. I cannot think of anything Vince would try to hide from me. Some things he did not tell me but he would not try to stop me knowing.'

It was strange to hear her speak of Peters as she saw him through the eyes of love. His self-centred indifference became almost a virtue.

'He was very lucky to meet you when he did.'

She accepted his statement as an English girl would not, without any false modesty. 'Yes, it was at the right time – the psychological moment, as you say. Already there were signs of his illness, he would fumble the fingering of his guitar and sometimes he would have the double vision. It was in Paris that he realized he could not go on.' She looked at him with grave, sad eyes. 'You can imagine the effect on him, it was lucky I was there.'

'I understand that Roger was his manager?'

'That was what he was called but I did not see him do much.'

'From what I have heard, I wouldn't have thought him a very good business man.'

She smiled. 'You are right! Roger was like a child in business and Vince had to do all the real work.' She shifted a little irritably in her chair. 'That is why I become a little angry when he is here all the time asking for money . . .'

They talked for a while longer but Wycliffe learned nothing new. When he stepped into the courtyard there were patches of hazy blue in the sky, the clouds were breaking up. He decided to walk back.

8

Now that the rain had stopped the level of the stream fell rapidly which was as well for in places the path was broken away and there were gravelly, rocky stretches which had been submerged by the stream in flood. As Gill left Salubrious Place behind him the valley became more desolate and the sides steeper, with outcrops of granite sparsely covered with grey lichens. Fescue grass and clumps of sea-pinks covered the valley floor which was strewn with great grey boulders.

The clouds had melted away on the horizon but overhead they were still heavy and lowering. Despite this it was very warm. He began to sweat and took off his jacket. Nowhere could he see any-thing recognizable as the handiwork of man and landscapes without figures were, for him, a dead waste of space. Not for him, the wind on the heath, brother, nor the lonely sea and the sky. A few blocks of flats within easy reach of the local and a good supermarket was the landscape of his choice. But the scenery on the island consisted of landscapes in miniature and soon the valley became broader and shallower once more, the stream fanned out over gravel and finally lost itself in a broad beach of sharp, white sand. He was at Quincey Cove.

On his right and near at hand, a row of three stark little cottages stared blankly out to sea. The area in front of them was littered with junk of every description, some of it housed in decayed, make-shift sheds, most of it in jumbled heaps. To his left, across a narrow stretch of calm water, the southern tip of Morvyl was just in view. A low, rocky promontory, a tiny, white cove with a boat drawn up on the sand and, inland, three or four whitewashed buildings in a group and a slender, iron-framed tower with a windmill on the top. Pre-sumably, Sam Tripp's wind pump.

Three children were playing on the rough ground between the

mounds of junk and Gill went over to them. The eldest, a girl of seven or eight, immediately scurried into the nearest house like a frightened rabbit, the other two, boys of five or six, continued inexplicable labours on a go-kart made from a fish-box and pram wheels. Gill waited by the open door through which the little girl had disappeared. A dirty, green-painted screen prevented him from seeing into the room but he could hear low voices. Then an older girl, who looked eighteen but was probably younger, came round the screen. She was plump and stocky, a V-necked flowery dress, in need of washing, showed most of her bosom which had never known Playtex control. She was black-eyed with a mop of dark hair which looked as though she combed it with her fingers. She looked at him with a mixture of aggression and apprehension. She had an earthy, animal vitality which was not lost on Gill.

'Police.'

'What we supposed to 've done now?'

'Nothing. It's what other people have done.'

'Not our business!'

'Who is it, Moira?' A cracked old voice.

'I'll tell you in a minute – be quiet!' She added, under her breath, 'Silly ol' cow!'

'Your grandmother?'

'She's me great-great-grandmother – ninety-eight she is.'

'You are Moira Marsden?'

'If it's any concern of yours.' But her aggression had gone with her apprehension and she was merely being flirtatious.

Gill smiled his great rubbery smile, a real baby-frightener, but it went down well with the girls.

'I suppose you see most of what goes on round here?'

She looked at the empty beach and the empty sea. 'Job not to.'

'Do you know Roger Peters?'

'Sort of.'

'Ever see him about here?'

'Now and then.'

'When was the last time?'

She sniffed. 'Yesterday it must've bin. He come across from Morvyl in the Rowses' boat.'

'By himself?'

She nodded. 'He pulled the boat up on the shingle an' stuck the kedge in the sand.' She grinned. 'If he'd been gone much longer he'd had to swim for it. Tide come up the beach pretty fast.'

'What time was this?'

She looked vague. 'Round teatime when he come back, I reckon.'

'When's that?'

'Between five an' six.'

'How long was he gone?'

She was getting tired of his sustained interest in someone else. There were more important things. 'How do I know? What do it matter, anyway?'

'How long?'

'Might 've bin an hour or an hour an' a half. I tell you I didn't take that much notice.'

'But you know he came from Morvyl?'

'I saw him, didn't I? He put Billy Rowse ashore on the point, he hung about there for a bit, then he come over here, like I said. What you on about?'

'Did your father come home while Roger Peters was away up the valley?'

'He'd 've had a job, he bin dead five year an' more. Fell overboard when he was drunk.'

'I'm sorry.'

'I ain't, he was a bastard.'

'I was talking about Nick Marsden.'

'Oh, he's me grandfather. Yeh, he did come home.'

'Did he mention having seen either of the Peters brothers?'

'He never mentioned nothing, he was drunk like usual an' he went to bed.'

Gill turned on the charm. 'Thanks, Moira.'

She looked at him big-eyed. 'I could fancy you.'

'I'll be around.'

He left her, standing in the doorway, looking after him.

On his way back from Salubrious Place Wycliffe met the widow woman from the café, doing her shopping along the quay. She smiled at him, ruefully, but he thought he saw a glint of mischief in her eye. He had a soft spot for her and wondered why she had stayed unmarried. Perhaps she had found a way to get the best of both worlds but he doubted it. Not with Roger Peters.

637

He climbed the steep slope to the school, thinking. In the operations room he stopped to speak to Jordan who was duty-officer. 'Any news of Peters?'

'Nothing, sir. It's a bit of a puzzle really, we've got half our strength on it but so far we've drawn a blank. To be frank, I don't think any islander would risk a harbouring charge for Roger Peters. It's one thing to have a drink with a man or go fishing but it's quite another to fall foul of the police in a murder case.' Jordan scratched his ear. 'It's my belief that he must be sleeping rough somewhere. There's plenty of places where a man could lie up for days if he had a bit of food with him. But it's only a matter of time . . .'

'What about the widow woman?'

'What about her?'

'Wouldn't she risk a harbouring charge?'

Jordan looked puzzled. 'She might, but he can't be there. We've had the place watched since you left last night.'

'Not exactly.' Wycliffe lowered his voice so that a young detective working near by could not hear what he said. 'Send a couple of chaps along there to bring him in.'

'You mean . . . ?'

'I mean I've been taken for a sucker again. While I was walking from the café to your place last night, Peters nipped in and by the time our man went on obo that precious couple were tucked up in bed.' He chuckled. 'And she had the cheek to offer me her umbrella!'

In his office he found a new crop of typescript which had sprouted in his tray. Among the rest, a memorandum from the Plymouth CID which they had telephoned in reply to his enquiry about Roger Peters. Obviously it had been compiled by some Jack with a nice feeling for atmosphere, which pleased Wycliffe.

'Subject occupies a rented room at 14, Frobisher Place. Frobisher Place comprises three large houses once occupied by high-ranking naval personnel, now cheap lodging houses . . .' (A note of satisfaction there, surely?) 'According to his landlady, Peters' tenancy began six months ago. He is away from home a great deal and has told her that he is a travelling salesman. To her knowledge, he has no visitors but he receives a certain amount of mail, mainly business letters to judge from the envelopes. She says that he is "a nice man, keeps himself to himself and pays his rent regular". Our officer had the impression that there may be a more intimate relationship between

Peters and his landlady.' Peters must have a considerable talent for obtaining free digs.

'The landlady had a key to his room and allowed our man to inspect it. The room was shabby and not too clean. A minimum of battered furniture which went with the room was supplemented by items belonging to Peters. These included a good upright piano, a studio couch, a record player with a stack of records, a tape recorder and two guitars. In the clothes cupboard there were two good suits and three or four silk shirts along with other shirts and underclothes bought at a department store. There were few papers in the room but a box-file contained several letters about electrical goods for which he appears to have an agency.

'Further inquiries established that he frequents the Barbican area of the city and that he is on friendly terms with several of the boatmen. He is a customer at the betting-shop in that area and is believed to be in debt there . . .'

While he was going through the report Gill came in and they brought each other up to date.

'You really think he's at the café?'

'We shall soon know.' Wycliffe got up and went over to the window. The sun was shining now from a clear, rain-washed sky but it had come too late for the boats were still riding at their moorings. No doubt there would be evening trips. The quay was unusually crowded for the time of day with visitors parading up and down. The *Islander* was at her berth embarking day-trippers for the return crossing but there were very few because of the morning's rain.

The case against Roger Peters was beginning to take shape. He was forced to consider, very seriously, the possibility that Sylvie's death and the shooting of Vince Peters were two unconnected crimes. According to Nellie Martin, Vince had asked his brother to come to the house between half past three and four on the day of his death. Now, Gill had firm evidence that Roger had kept the appointment, and, more significantly, Marsden claimed to have heard a shot at about ten minutes past four. As Marsden did not meet Roger on his way to the cove there were reasonable grounds for believing that Roger must have been in the house when the shot was fired. It was by no means a cast-iron case but the circumstantial evidence was strong and men had been convicted on no more.

Gill was seated by his desk, browsing through reports. 'You think he did it?'

'He had motive, means and opportunity.'

'But do you think he did it?'

Wycliffe did not answer directly. He moved away from the window. 'They've found him, he's on his way up.'

The siren of the *Islander* blared, warning all laggards.

Five minutes later Peters was brought in. He looked pale under his tan, and worried. He might have spent part of the night in the widow's bed but it was obvious that he had not slept. Wycliffe waved him to a chair. 'Would you object to having your fingerprints taken, Mr Peters?'

'Would it make any difference if I did?'

Gill leered. 'It might – at this stage.'

Peters shrugged and Wycliffe picked up the telephone. 'Is Sergeant Scales in? Ask him to come here with his gear.'

Scales came in with his case, the prints were taken and Peters was given cleaning tissues to remove the ink from his fingers. When Scales had finished he glanced at Wycliffe and Wycliffe gave a small sign. Scales left with his case. The operation had taken less than five minutes. Gill shifted his chair so that he was on Wycliffe's side of the desk.

'Why did you hide away?'

He looked at Wycliffe through tired, blue eyes. 'How can you say I was hiding? You know I live there when I'm in the islands.'

Wycliffe was patient. 'You knew the police wanted to interview you and you deliberately evaded them.'

'I heard that Vince was dead – that he had been murdered, and I was scared.'

'Why?'

'Wendy said you seemed all set to latch it on me and I was the obvious one anyway.'

'Because of the will?'

Peters said nothing.

'You know about your brother's will?'

A momentary hesitation. 'Yes.'

'You couldn't have expected to stay out of circulation for long.'

Peters stared at the floor. 'No, but I thought it might be long enough for you to find out who did it.'

'So you deny shooting your brother?'

'Of course I deny it! I didn't do it.' He was fingering his moustache with nervous fingers.

'Did you know that your brother possessed a gun?'

Peters, staring down at the parquet flooring, was mumbling his answers so that they were scarcely audible. 'I knew that he bought one, it was while we were in the States in '68.'

'Did he feel threatened?'

'What?' Peters looked up. It was as though he were preoccupied, trying to make up his mind about something and Wycliffe's questions intruded on his thoughts. 'No, it wasn't that he felt threatened, he just bought it for kicks.'

'Do you know where he kept it?'

'I didn't know that he still had it.'

There was little family resemblance. Roger was of a stockier build than his brother and his hair was fair with only a trace of auburn. Although he had sideboards and a Gerald Nabarro moustache he had no beard to hide his weak chin.

'When did you last visit your brother?'

'Thursday, I think it was – yes, last Thursday, a week ago today.'

'That was when you quarrelled?'

Peters looked up sharply. 'We had an argument.'

'About money?'

He nodded. 'I suppose Clarissa told you.'

'Yesterday, Wednesday, where were you?'

'When?'

Wycliffe made an irritable movement. 'Any time – all day.'

There was a small silence while he thought over his answer, either to recollect or invent. 'I got up late and did a few chores for Wendy to keep the peace, then I went along to the Seymour for a jar.'

'Then?'

'Well, when I was coming out I met Billy Rowse and he said he had to go over to Morvyl in the afternoon to do a job on Sam Tripp's water pump so I said I would tag along.'

'Time?'

'I had my lunch first and we got to Morvyl about half-two.'

'And you left – when?'

'Just after six.'

'Were you with Rowse the whole time?'

641

'No, we went ashore at Penhallick Cove and I stayed with the boat. The cove is close to Sam's place.'

'You stayed with the boat for more than three hours?'

'I must have done.'

'Did you see anyone during that time?'

Peters frowned. 'I don't think so, it's a quiet spot.'

Wycliffe grunted. 'It must be.' The telephone rang and Wycliffe answered it. 'Wycliffe.'

It was Sergeant Scales. 'I'll speak quietly, sir. His prints match those we found on the cabinet in Peters' room and on the sink in the kitchen.'

'No possible doubt?'

'No, sir.'

Wycliffe dropped the receiver and turned to Peters. He looked at him in silence for a while. Peters met his eye and seemed, suddenly, to become aware that a new element had entered into the interrogation.

'I don't want to trap you into further lies, Mr Peters, so I will caution you, then I will tell you exactly what we know about your movements on the afternoon your brother was shot.'

Peters listened to the caution but said nothing.

'We know that you had an appointment with your brother yesterday afternoon. We also know that you used the Rowses' boat to cross the sound from Morvyl to Quincey Cove. At approximately ten minutes past four Nick Marsden heard a shot fired in your brother's house, he saw the broken window and he also saw your brother slumped over his desk. He then walked down the valley to his cottage at Quincey Cove; he did not meet you but when he got to the cove the Rowses' boat was drawn up on the beach.'

Peters sat staring at the floor, his hands clasped tightly round his knees, saying nothing.

'There is one other piece of evidence. Your fingerprints – fresh prints – were found on the filing cabinet in your brother's room and on the sink in the kitchen.'

For a time Peters gave no sign, then he relaxed and sat back in his chair staring straight at Wycliffe. 'I knew it would be like this!'

'You admit that you shot your brother?' From Gill.

He shook his head listlessly. 'No, but how can I prove that I didn't against all that?'

'You don't have to. All you have to do is to explain the facts as they affect you. Do you wish to make a statement?'

After a moment of hesitation Peters nodded.

'Before you do, are you willing to answer some further questions?'

'I suppose so.'

'Do you admit visiting your brother on the afternoon he died?'

'Yes, but he was dead when I got there.' Wycliffe said nothing and, after a while, Peters continued. 'Like you said, Vince phoned me and asked me to come to see him. He didn't say what it was about but I knew that it was about money. When I heard that Billy Rowse was going to Sam's place on Morvyl I thought it would be easier to slip across from there with the boat rather than walk all the way from the town.'

'You weren't bothered about being seen by the Marsdens?'

'No – why should I be? I didn't know I was going to find him shot, did I?' He seemed surprised and pleased to find this point in his favour.

'Were you in the house when the shot was fired?'

'No, I wasn't. I know it looks bad but the reason Nick Marsden didn't see me was because I saw him first, stumbling along beside the stream, more than half-pissed as usual. Nick can be a bloody nuisance when he's drunk – maudlin, so I dodged him. Actually I got to the house at half past four.'

'What happened when you got there?'

'Nothing happened. I went in by the back door and through into the hall. I called but nobody answered so I went up to his room where he spends most of his time . . . Of course, I found him.'

'What did you do?'

He shook his head. 'I was knocked sideways. Vince and I have been pretty close through the best part of our lives . . .'

'Did you touch him?'

He nodded again. 'I wanted to be sure.'

'How do you account for your fingerprints on the cabinet?'

'I don't know but it's quite likely I rested against it – I had quite a job to stop myself from fainting.'

'What did you do then?'

He seemed to be in the grip of considerable emotion and there was an interval before he started to speak again. 'I went back downstairs, I don't know what I would have done but when I was in the

643

hall I noticed that my right hand felt sticky . . . When I looked I saw that it had blood and stuff . . . I don't know how it got there, I must have touched . . .' He shuddered. 'I went into the kitchen to wash it off and while I was there the girl came in at the front door and called out.' He looked at Wycliffe. 'I have never been so frightened in my life.' His eyes had become wild at the recollection. 'I just went out of the back door and ran until I couldn't run any more.'

'Down the valley?'

'Down the valley to the boat.' He added, after a moment, choking over the words, 'It's no good, I can't explain it.'

In the silence they could hear noises from the quay, even the sound of voices. Gill took out his cheroots and offered one to Peters. Peters refused.

'Do you believe me?'

'You were your brother's business manager, is that right?' Gill asked the question while he was lighting his cheroot.

'Yes.'

Gill took his time. 'There was an agreement, wasn't there? Between you and your brother, an agreement in which he undertook to leave you the bulk of his estate.'

Peters nodded.

'What did he get out of it?'

Peters answered with what dignity he could muster. 'My services, I suppose.'

'As his business manager? You must be joking!'

Wycliffe was almost sorry for the man. He said, quite casually, 'Your brother never wrote a song in his life, did he?'

This was a blow he had not expected and he reacted slowly. 'I don't know what you mean.'

'I think you do.'

Wycliffe and Gill watched him while he considered the new threat. At last he reached a decision and seemed to resign himself. His manner was more relaxed as though he had got rid of a burden.

'In the beginning it was a question of tactics I suppose. For years, while Vince was at school and I was working as an assistant in a music shop, I tried my hand at song-writing. I never came within a mile of success. Then, when Vince was at University, he started to make a name for himself as a singer, first it was no more than a student thing, then he started to enter for talent contests and after that the clubs got interested. His trouble was to find good, new songs and one day I suggested he should try one of mine . . . It was Kalamazoo Baby . . . Through a mistake, I suppose it was, everybody thought he had written it himself and we decided it would be best to leave it at that – to concentrate on building him up.' He stopped talking, reached in his pocket for a packet of cigarettes and lit one before going on.

'Vince and I got on well together. Even working like we did – for years – in the pop racket, I can't remember a single real row. When things started to go big I was nominally his manager but Gus Clayton and Vince did most of the business side between them. Everybody thought I was a passenger, a poor relation. Well, it didn't hurt me and it was all good for the Vince image. One day Vince said he thought we ought to have an agreement – in case anything happened to him. He told me that he'd made a will. It was more a joke than anything else but in the end we drew up a sort of agreement. I didn't take it seriously and things went on as before . . . Until Paris, two years ago.' He broke off. 'You know that Vince was very ill?'

Wycliffe nodded.

'When he realized that he wasn't going to get better he changed.'

'Not surprising, really.'

Peters was anxious to be clearly understood. 'No, I don't suppose it was, he had to give up singing, the kind of life he was leading would have killed him in three months, the doctors said . . . His complaint had affected his heart or he had a weak heart as well. You could have understood it if he was damn near suicidal, but he wasn't. He took it all very calmly, he bought this place down here and settled down, more or less. But he'd changed, his character had changed. I couldn't get near him any more. And he got mean. I don't want to sound greedy but he was rolling in it and I had a claim to a good slice of the royalties, at least, but he wouldn't see it. You would think I was asking for charity. All he would say was, "Don't be in such a hurry, you'll be all right when I'm gone."' Peters stopped and seemed to want his point to sink in. 'Well, it wasn't good enough and I threatened to blow the gaff. I didn't want to. For one thing it would probably have had a bad effect on sales and, in any case, the last thing I really wanted was to hurt Vince. I don't think I would have done it when it came to the point.'

'What happened?'

'Vince said I was being unreasonable. He showed me letters which had passed between him and his lawyer about his will but he wouldn't give in . . .'

'This was the row you had a week before he died?'

Peters nodded. 'And I heard nothing more from him until he telephoned for me to come and see him.'

'You are willing to put all this into a statement?'

'Yes.'

Wycliffe signed to Gill and Gill took him out.

At the door he turned. 'You believe me, don't you?'

Wycliffe made a noncommittal gesture.

Did he believe Peters? He had to admit that he had been favourably impressed by his apparent frankness. But the frankness had followed an absurd attempt to hide and patent lies. He was weak, there was no question about that, but weakness is no testament to innocence. In Wycliffe's experience, violent crime was more often than not the work of weak, usually stupid people. And in some ways Peters was stupid, at any rate, limited.

But what about Sylvie? It always came back to the same question and he seemed as far as ever from getting an answer. He found himself saying aloud, 'There is not a shred of evidence to connect Roger Peters with Sylvie's death.'

There was no evidence to connect Peters with Sylvie's death but, all the same, he was still convinced that the second death had followed the first as part of the same criminal act.

'The press and TV people are here, they want to know if you are holding Peters.'

Since the morning the islanders had been intrigued, flattered and irritated by the antics of a TV reporter and camera team.

He made a statement, standing in front of the school, his fine, sandy hair blowing in the wind. On the 'News' that evening, they would be saying, 'Two men were at the Murder Headquarters of Detective Chief Superintendent Wycliffe today, helping with inquiries. Both made statements and later left. Chief Superintendent Wycliffe, Head of Area Crime Squad, spoke to our reporter:

'Are you satisfied with the progress of your inquiries, Mr Wycliffe?'

'I am not satisfied – no. I shall only be satisfied when an arrest has been made, but we are making progress.'

'Do you expect to make an arrest in the near future?'

'I hope that an arrest may be made shortly.'

'Would you care to comment on statements that Vince Peters' death could have been the result of an island vendetta against him?'

'I know of no vendetta.'

'Is it true that the islanders have resented your presence and that they have made your task more difficult?'

'No, it is not true. Oh the contrary, we have received a great deal of cooperation from the islanders.'

'Do you consider that the Vince Peters' shooting and the death of Sylvie Eva are connected?'

'I do not want to comment on that point at this stage.'

When the circus had gone his thoughts reverted to their original theme. If Roger Peters did not shoot his brother, who did? He had ideas on the subject but ideas are not proof. Back in his office he made notes on a memo pad, a thing he rarely did.

Nick Marsden heard the shot at 4.10.

Marsden hung about the house until 4.20.

Brenda Luke arrived at about 4.30 and went to the pottery.

Roger Peters arrived at the back of the house through the meadow also at about 4.30.

He regarded what he had written with distaste. It seemed most likely that the murderer had left the house between 4.20 and 4.30 but Roger Peters, coming up the valley, had seen only Marsden. Brenda Luke, coming from town, had also seen Marsden and no-one else.

Presumably the murderer had taken all possible steps not to be seen. All the same . . .

Wycliffe went to the Jordans for his evening meal. Fish pie followed by junket and cream. Jordan was on duty so Wycliffe ate his meal in the little kitchen with Mrs Jordan hovering round him.

After a while she said, 'I suppose you heard about the fuss on the quay this afternoon?'

'No.'

'The chap from the TV – he caught Jack Bishop coming out of the Seymour and started asking him questions about what the islanders thought of Peters. Was there a vendetta – that sort of carry on. Jack had had enough to drink and he was ready to talk, but just then, along comes Charlie Martin.'

'What happened?'

A short laugh. 'He stood in front of the camera and told them if they didn't move he would throw them and their camera in the harbour. I was out shopping. It made quite a stir.'

After his meal Wycliffe walked along the quay. Another warm, peaceful evening with a mackerel sky high over the sea. The tide was at full flood and the boats in the harbour were almost level with the quay. There was to be dancing later and the town band was already in position, warming up.

In the public bar of the Seymour, Charlie Martin was talking very seriously with Matthew Eva who looked old and drawn. Neither of them accorded him more than a bare acknowledgment. Wycliffe ordered a beer and took a seat near the counter. It was, presumably, like any other summer evening in the Seymour. Two hands of whist, a game of chequers and three or four men sitting round, sipping their beer and saying little. Yet Wycliffe was aware of an atmosphere of tension. Everyone in the bar seemed to be waiting, marking time. Rightly or wrongly, he felt that they were waiting for him. Waiting for him to point the accusing finger – and go! Get it over!

It was not long before Matthew finished his drink and left. Charlie Martin, who had his back to the bar, twisted round in his seat until he could see Wycliffe.

'Will you be so kind as to join me, Mr Wycliffe?'

Wycliffe took his drink to the old man's table. The eyes of everyone in the bar were on him.

Charlie Martin's huge, freckled hands rested on the table and his fingers beat out a gentle tattoo. 'Have you made up your mind, Mr Wycliffe?'

Wycliffe smoked his pipe in silence for a while. 'I have made up my mind but I still need evidence.'

The old man nodded as though it was the reply he had expected. 'We are not murderers, Mr Wycliffe, neither do we condone murder.'

'I am glad to hear it.'

'Peters alive was one thing, Peters dead – shot, is another.'

Wycliffe's bland expression did not change. When it came to Arab tea parties he could hold his own.

'One of your young men has questioned me twice about what happened after the girl's funeral; in particular he wanted to know when my nephew left the house after it was over. I told him that the boy was with me until four o'clock and that was the truth.'

'I have no doubt of it.'

The old man's blue eyes rested for a moment on Wycliffe's in shrewd appraisal. 'The boy was distressed – in a bad way. Once or twice while we were following the hearse and again during the committal, I thought that he would collapse.'

Wycliffe said nothing. Martin's ringed finger rapped on the table-top. 'Let's have something a bit stronger than this cat's piss, Mr Wycliffe. Two brandies, if you please, Jonathan – large ones.'

The barman brought the drinks and the two men did not speak until they were about to sip the brandy. 'Your health!'

For once the old man was uncertain how to play his hand and Wycliffe would not help him. 'Mother love can be a terrible thing, Mr Wycliffe – a crippling thing. The boy is more to be pitied than blamed.' He took out a large red handkerchief with white spots and patted his moustache. 'Love is only one side of the coin, Mr Wycliffe; hate is the other.'

The silence in the bar was impressive. Wycliffe had not heard a single word spoken by the other occupants of the bar since he had moved to Martin's table.

'In a small community like ours it is necessary that we stand together, there must be loyalty. But, as I said, we do not condone murder.'

Outside, on the quay, the band was playing and they were dancing.

'Jackie's father is my half-brother, he was the son of a second wife. I would have helped. A full-time nurse – day and night if necessary, or a nursing home. But Nellie was too proud, she made a virtue out of pride and it twisted her.' He paused to take another sip of brandy and put down his glass with seeming concentration. It was clear that he was approaching a climax in what he had to say. 'She was a Jenkins before she married.'

'A Jenkins?'

'Sister to Amos Jenkins who farms up the valley from the Peters' place.'

'Do they keep in touch?'

The old man's eyes expressed unmistakable satisfaction. 'Oh, yes. They are a tightly-knit clan, the Jenkinses. She visits every week on her free day. I've never known her miss.'

It was a small piece, not vital, perhaps, but it fitted.

Martin got to his feet and walked heavily to the door without another word. Wycliffe sat on for a few minutes longer and the silence in the bar was unbroken. Outside the dancers were applauding.

He had difficulty in making his way through the crowd, back to the school. The door of the café was open and the widow woman was standing on the step, taking the air. She pretended not to see him.

9

It was getting to be a habit, strolling along the quay on his way to the school. A scrawled poster outside the newsagent read:

ISLAND MURDERS
ARREST IMMINENT

That was how the press had translated his guarded statement. He bought his tobacco and thought that the shopkeeper looked at him with an apprehensive air. He was a thorn in the flesh; something to be got rid of as soon as possible, even though the removal might be painful.

Friday. He had been on the island since the previous Sunday night. Charlie Martin, standing outside his ticket office, acknowledged him curtly.

They all seemed to be telling him, 'Get it over!'

When he arrived at the school Jimmy Gill was there. 'You'll want to see this, it's just come through from forensic by phone.'

It was a preliminary report on the clothing which had been submitted for examination. Vince Peters' saxe-blue corduroy coat and trousers, Jackie Martin's Harris tweed jacket and Crimplene trousers. Nothing of note on the corduroys. Martin's trousers had been snagged in two places on the right leg and one of the snags yielded a minute fragment of red rust. There were also traces of powdered rust adhering to the material just below the pocket, also on the right side. Two fragments of rust had been recovered from the jacket, one from the pocket flap and one from inside the pocket itself. Faint traces of blood had been detected on the lining of the jacket in two places and the blood had been identified as human and belonging to group O.

'That clinches it so far as the girl is concerned,' Gill said.

Wycliffe was obstinately silent and sullen.

But Gill would never forget the next two hours and, as far as the squad was concerned, the events of those two hours would pass into legend. It began with a telephone call which Wycliffe made to Dr Ross. Gill did not hear what was said but he was in Wycliffe's office when the doctor rang back and he heard one side of that conversation. Wycliffe's manner was subdued, not to say grim.

'Thank you, doctor. I'm most grateful. You understand that I don't want the ambulance to arrive until . . . No, exactly. We want to make it as easy as possible . . . As you say, a tragedy.'

Wycliffe dropped the receiver onto its rest.

'What's on?'

'I've arranged for Jackie's father to be taken into hospital.'

'Does that mean . . . ?'

'Yes.'

'Who are you sending?'

'I'm going myself.'

'Then I'll go with you.'

'No, I'm taking Jordan, it will be . . .' He was going to say, kinder, but changed his mind and substituted, 'I want you here.'

He looked at his watch. 'Time I was going. I want you to send a car in half an hour.'

Down below, on the wharf, a queue was forming at the ticket office for boat trips. Brenda Luke would be there, pulling in the money for Charlie Martin and his syndicate. Charlie was in his usual place for this time of day, sitting on his particular bollard, keeping an eye on things. The boats were clustered round the steps waiting for their quotas. It was a fresh morning with puffy white clouds sailing in a blue sky before a stiff north-westerly breeze. It was calm enough in the harbour but outside the trippers would get their money's worth.

Jordan was waiting for him in the control room, dressed in plain clothes. He looked down at the grey worsted. 'I thought it might be better if . . .'

'Of course, you're quite right.'

Together they walked down the slope from the school on to the quay. Only Charlie Martin took any notice and he followed them with his eyes. As they drew level he made a slight movement of his shoulders which could have been interpreted as resignation.

'I feel sorry for the old man,' Jordan said. 'It'll be a terrible shock to him.'

'He knows.'

'You think so?'

'I'm sure of it.'

Jordan looked at him doubtfully but said nothing.

Wycliffe recognized two reporters outside the post office and they acknowledged him cheerfully. 'Anything for us, superintendent?'

He shook his head.

They arrived at the Tower House. Wycliffe paused on the step, he seemed to be hesitating about some course of action. At last he said, 'In spite of everything, I want you to stay here.'

'But the whole idea . . . It would come better from me . . .'

'Do as you're told!' Wycliffe knocked on the door and there was a considerable delay before it was opened.

Nellie Martin stood in the little hall, dressed in her old tweed coat. She seemed to have gone even thinner and her face was drawn and white. 'I was just going out.' But she stood aside for Wycliffe to come in and closed the door behind him. He followed her into the kitchen where the old man's chair was empty and the stove had not been lit.

'Your husband not down yet?'

'He's not well this morning, worse than usual.'

'I'm sorry.'

She was moving about the kitchen doing apparently pointless things, picking up a cup and putting it down again, pushing a chair a bit further under the table, straightening a mat with her foot . . . But Wycliffe noticed that she kept one hand in the pocket of her old coat.

'Jackie?'

She looked at him sharply. 'Up in his room.'

A pause during which they could hear people talking as they passed by outside.

'What are you here for?'

'I think you know.'

'You haven't brought his clothes?'

'No.'

She said nothing for a while but went on with her restless

prowling, then she turned on him suddenly. 'I don't care for myself.' And she added after a moment, 'You know that, don't you?'

'Yes, I know.'

Another lengthy silence.

'What I've had I shall never miss.'

'No.'

'It's only the boy I care about.' Her voice faltered and he thought that she would break down. It would have been for the best, but she got control of herself again. 'It was his clothes?'

'Yes.'

The silence this time lasted longer. Through the lace blinds Wycliffe could see people walking past. A faint call from somewhere upstairs and she jerked her head upwards. 'It's him,' and gave a contemptuous little twist to her lips. 'He can wait.'

It was obvious that she had not made up her mind what she would do and the smallest gesture or word out of place might precipitate a crisis. He was glad that he had kept Jordan outside. It was his responsibility.

'You wouldn't lie to me – not about something like that?' Her expression was almost pleading.

'No.'

She stared at him as though trying to see into his mind. 'No.'

She stopped by one of the windows. Tourists were trooping past on their way to the boats. 'You've got Freddie Jordan out there.'

'He's out there, yes.'

She continued to peer through the blind. 'There are two kinds in this world, aren't there?'

'Two kinds?'

'The ones who suffer and the ones who make others suffer. Look at them out there!' She turned away from the window. 'He would never have let the boy alone. He *knew*.'

'Vince Peters?'

She did not bother to answer that. 'I asked him what he was going to do and he said, "Jackie must tell them himself".'

'So you shot him.'

She nodded. 'I shot him.' She put her hand to her forehead in a curious gesture as though to brush away a fly or some other source of irritation.

'You went to see him on the way to visit your brother, is that it?'

654

'I took the gun out of the drawer and loaded it, then I went up to his room.' She was staring at nothing with unblinking eyes. 'The funny thing was he didn't seem to mind – he just sat there. I couldn't understand it . . .'

'He was suffering too – an incurable disease.'

She glanced at him sharply for a moment then the glazed look came over her eyes once more. 'So much the better for him.'

Another weak cry from upstairs.

'Shouldn't you go to your husband?'

She shook her head.

'He'll be looked after.'

'Do you think I care about him? He's nothing to me. He's never been a man, even before he was took sick . . .' Her eyes came alive again. 'You know he's not Jackie's father?'

'No, I didn't know.'

She nodded. 'Nobody knows. I kept the secret but if it hadn't been for the harm it would have done to the boy I would have shouted it from the housetops. Do you understand?'

'Yes.'

She laughed bitterly. 'You think you do.'

The letterbox rattled and the postman dropped something through which plopped on to the mat.

'Do you know Nicky Marsden?'

Wycliffe nodded. 'I know him.'

'A drunken sot who tried to show himself to young girls. He was Jackie's father.' She turned on him so abruptly that he was startled. 'Now do you understand?'

'I think so.'

'I'm guilty *because of what it did to Jackie.* For more than twenty years I've tried to pay the price but it was never enough.' She jerked her head upwards. 'Why do you think I've looked after him all these years? But you can't wipe out a living sin.'

She was back at the window, looking out. 'Don't they ever cheat or lie? Don't they ever *sin*? Don't those women out there . . . ?' She broke off and turned towards him again. 'But they don't have to pay, do they?'

She resumed her restless perambulation round the room but as she came close to the door, and before he could stop her, she slipped out into the hall. By the time he got there she was two or three steps up the stairs and she had the gun in her hand, pointed at him. 'Stay where you are! If you come any nearer . . . You know that I can.'

He was frightened but he managed to keep fear from his voice. 'How did you learn to use a gun?'

She laughed. 'Nicky Marsden taught me. He got hold of a gun from a Yankee officer and used to show off to the girls. I only tried it once or twice but I remembered.'

He tried to sound calm, reasonable. 'You will only make matters very much worse. Jackie can be helped.'

'Jackie can only be helped by me. It's always been the same.'

'That's not true!'

She shrugged as though the point was not worth discussion and then took another step backwards up the stairs. He moved towards her and she fired. He felt a sudden, numbing pain in his arm and put his hand to the spot. Already the blood had soaked through his thin jacket. He kept his feet but she had disappeared up the stairs. Jordan burst in. Wycliffe made to follow but at that moment there was a crash somewhere upstairs followed by what sounded like a muted explosion. Jordan, white faced, was looking at the blood running from Wycliffe's arm and trickling down on to the floor. Whatever his intention he had come between Wycliffe and the stairs.

'After her, you fool! I'm all right!'

But though Jordan tried he was too late. Already the flames could be heard and the walls were lit by an ugly, flickering glow. 'That stairs is like a chimney – there's not a hope.' And, indeed, the flames were roaring now, drowning other sounds. Then came a shot, an interval, then another.

'The old man!' Wycliffe shouted. 'She hasn't bothered with him!'

With his good arm he wrenched open the front door. They heard the joyous whoosh of flame due to the added draught and slammed the door behind them. At that moment Gill arrived with two men in a police car.

'A ladder for the first floor!' Wycliffe shouted but Jordan was off like a sprinter to his house which was no more than a hundred yards away. 'Help him! Don't just stand there!' A constable went after Jordan.

By a miracle they got the old man out alive. The fire which had started on the first landing had licked up through the staircase before starting to eat its way through the woodwork into the rooms. So he was put into the ambulance after all.

Wycliffe refused to go to the hospital and was bandaged by the ambulance men on the spot, strapped up like a chicken ready for the oven.

The Tower House continued to burn. A great pillar of smoke rose up from it and was whisked away by the wind over the harbour and out to sea. There was nothing anybody could do. The fire brigade played their hoses to no effect and the police kept back the crowds who preferred this to the boats or the beach. Then the lead cupola started to melt and hot metal bullets showered down, spattering on the ground like hailstones and forcing the fire brigade back as well.

Wycliffe and Gill sat in the headmaster's room at the school. Wycliffe was trying to light his pipe with one hand and Gill knew better than to offer help. From the window he could see the boats gathered round the steps for afternoon trips and the tourists being helped aboard. Charlie Martin was sitting on his bollard. From a distance even the Tower House looked much as usual except that its cupola was missing. The firemen were still there.

Gill said, 'She took a five gallon drum to the shop yesterday and had it filled with paraffin. The boy who works there carried it home for her on a trolley.'

Wycliffe did not answer. He had managed to light his pipe and he puffed away, staring at nothing.

'Apparently she uses quite a lot of paraffin and the shopkeeper didn't think anything of it . . . She must have had it on the first landing – ready.'

Wycliffe still did not speak. He had decided to go home by sea that afternoon. He would leave Jimmy Gill to tie up the loose ends. He could not rid himself of the thought that had he handled the case differently Jackie Martin and his mother might still be alive.

When, at 4.25, the *Islander* gave a warning blast on her siren, he was halfway down the slope to the quay. Jordan was with him, carrying his bag. At the bottom of the gangway Charlie Martin was waiting. He pressed a bottle-shaped package under Wycliffe's good arm. 'Look after it, Mr Wycliffe, it's a drop of the good stuff. Come back and spend a holiday – you'll be very welcome.'

He stood on deck while they cast off and watched while the

Islander passed through the pier heads and started to pitch gently in the swell. Soon the island grew smaller and he could no longer distinguish the harbour entrance. He knew then that he would never go back.

Wycliffe and Death in Stanley Street

1

Stanley Street is a cul-de-sac, blocked at the far end by iron railings which separate it from the railway embankment. The houses are cheap because of the trains but they are convenient for the shops. Prince's Street, the main thoroughfare between the docks and the city centre, is only a block away and the muffled roar of its traffic fills the gaps between the trains so that there is little risk of silence except at odd times in the small hours and on Sunday mornings.

Most of the shops in Prince's Street are real shops, not department stores or supermarkets, and most of them spill over on to the pavements. There are bakers who bake crusty bread, butchers who sell undyed meat (not in plastic bags), grocers, greengrocers, delicatessens, wine shops, tobacconists, stationers and ironmongers. And there is at least one pub every two hundred yards.

There are twenty-two houses in Stanley Street, most of them are dilapidated, but three or four have been converted into flats: two flats to each house with a shared front door. The flats are occupied by single girls who spend most of their days in bed and start work after the shops in Prince's Street have closed. A base in Stanley Street is convenient for pick-ups who dislike having to walk far. Most nights there are plenty of pick-ups: seamen from the docks, a few students sampling life in the raw and several middle-aged husbands and fathers from the suburbs. Each girl has her beat which includes at least one pub.

'Hullo, darling!'

Brenda was standing in the side entrance to a newsagent's. The barman at The Joiners had warned her off because the cops were taking an interest in the place. It was a nuisance but it would pass, it always did. The police were not interested in her, they were after pushers and somebody had tipped them off about The Joiners.

661

Good luck to them, she didn't like pushers either but she couldn't afford to stick her neck out.

'Hullo, darling, want to come home?'

It was drizzling rain, not many people about, just cars and the occasional lorry swishing through. Four days to Christmas and business was always bad at holiday time, especially Christmas. She was on the point of turning it in for the night, she was cold and the damp seemed to penetrate right through her. She walked a little way down the pavement to stand under the shelter of the railway bridge.

'Hullo, darling.'

A little fellow, his mackintosh buttoned to the neck; in his fifties or older. He stopped to look at her with hungry, timorous eyes.

'I'll give you a nice time. Number 9 Stanley Street, just round the corner. Go in and right up the stairs.'

The patter came automatically then she turned and walked off, leaving him standing. She didn't care a damn whether he followed her or not, she'd had enough. She turned the corner into Wellington Road, fifty yards along then another corner into Stanley Street. The houses were on one side only, facing the wall of a wholesale grocery warehouse. Most of the houses retained their little pocket-hand-kerchief gardens with hedges of jaded privet. The door of number nine was unlocked and there was a light in the hall. Another girl, Lily Painter, occupied the ground floor flat. The door of her front room was shut which meant that she was at home and engaged with a client. Probably 'Daddy', Brenda thought vaguely, it was his night.

She called, 'It's me, Lily,' and went on up the stairs.

They got on well together. Lily was twenty-six, five years younger. She was vivacious, pretty too, with a figure which took years off the old men and she was so popular that her clients came by appointment. Brenda felt no jealousy, you had to be realistic and it was a question of supply and demand. All the same, she sometimes wondered.

At the top of the stairs, two rooms with a tiny kitchen and an even tinier bathroom and loo. One of the rooms was her bedroom, the other a sitting-room which she kept private; no client was ever admitted. To make sure, it was always locked. She hung her wet mackintosh on a hanger and put it to drip over the bath. In the bedroom she turned up the gas fire, kicked off her shoes and unzipped her dress. For a moment she stood, in briefs and brassière, looking at herself in the dressing-table mirror. She was painfully thin, her ribs showed under her small breasts; her skin was white, bleached looking. She knew that most of her customers were disappointed when they saw her naked. She was thirty-two and she had no need of a clairvoyant to tell her that it would not be long before she began to look haggard. Her mother had lost what looks she ever had while she was in her thirties. Brenda put on her red dressing-gown of brushed nylon. She liked red, it seemed to go with her jet black hair and it made her thin, pale face look interesting.

In the kitchen she took a bottle of brandy from a cupboard and poured herself a tot. She drank it off and it warmed her, she felt better. She had forgotten about the man until she heard his slow footsteps on the stairs. She met him on the landing and took his wet coat. He came into the bedroom in a daze. She noticed that he was lame, trailing his left foot.

'I'll take it now, love – the money.'

He fumbled in his wallet and produced a couple of notes; she smiled and slipped them into a drawer of the bedside table.

'Aren't you going to take your clothes off?'

She lay on top of the bed and opened her dressing gown. He tried to kiss her but she told him not to, which put him off.

'I'm sorry.'

'No need to apologize, dear, but we got to be careful else we'd catch everything that was going.'

'Yes of course, I didn't think.'

She felt sorry for this sad little man and tried to help him. 'You married?'

'Sort of.'

It was soon over.

'The bathroom is at the top of the stairs.'

He went off, carrying his jacket and trousers. A few minutes later he put his head round the door, 'Thank you'. She helped him on with his wet coat and heard him clip-clop down the stairs, making heavy weather of it with his game leg.

A few minutes in the bathroom. Half past nine, too early to go to bed. She unlocked the door of her sitting-room. A cosy little room, suburban, with a three-piece suite, a fitted carpet, television and a picture of elephants trumpeting through African dust over the mantelpiece. She switched on the fire and the telly. No cigarettes.

She went to the top of the stairs to see if Lily was still engaged. Daddy must have left for Lily's door was slightly ajar; she would be tidying up. A three-and-a-half litre Rover or a Mercedes parked two or three streets away and in a few minutes Daddy would be back in his detached residence in Edgington or Farley and Mrs Daddy would say that he looked tired and offer him dry sherry.

She flip-flopped downstairs in her slippers and as she reached the hall the telephone rang. '70862. This is Bren – OK. See you next week then. Don't do anything I wouldn't.'

One of her few regulars calling off for the week.

She dropped the receiver back on its rest and went into Lily's sitting-room. It was very different from hers, more elegant and part of the business. There was a glass fronted cabinet with drinks for the clients, before, after or in between. Your feet sank into coffee coloured pile and there were erotic pictures on the wall: a series depicting sculptural reliefs from the temple of Khajuraho. Unassailable as works of art but effective as a mild stimulant for the jaded client without the implied insult of merely dirty pictures.

To Brenda's surprise the room was only lit by light coming through the open door of the bedroom.

'Lily, are you there?' For some reason she was nervous and her voice cracked.

Apart from being attractive Lily was educated and this went down well with a certain type of client. Intelligent conversation added a redeeming gloss to what might otherwise appear a sordid encounter. Of course, they paid for it.

'Lily?'

From the bedroom a door opened into a well-appointed bathroom all in shades of pink. Lily's bed was pink too and frilly, surrounded by wall mirrors. Lily was lying on the bed, on her back, her feet just touching the carpet, and she was naked, her small, girlish breasts wide apart. She was dead, her face contorted and frightful. Her reflection in the wall mirrors added another dimension in the grotesque.

Brenda did not scream or panic but she felt a sudden constriction in her stomach which made her want to vomit. She fought it down.

999 – She dialled.

'Which service do you require?'

'Police.'

A click. 'Police.'

She began incoherently.

'Please state your name, where you are speaking from and the number of your telephone.'

She managed it.

'Have you called a doctor?'

'She's dead! I keep telling you.'

'All the same . . . Please wait where you are and touch nothing. One of our cars will be with you in a few minutes.'

They seemed to take it as though it were an everyday event – so bloody calm. But for her it was Lily, one of the few people she could call a friend. For three years they had lived in the same house.

She opened the front door and stood on the step, she could not bear it inside. It was raining hard now. She heard the siren of a police car coming down Prince's Street. It turned into Wellington Road and the tyres screeched on the streaming tarmac as it made a second sharp turn into Stanley Street. The siren wailed to silence and two young coppers got out.

'Where is she, love?'

One of them went in to see while the other stayed with her. He was gentle. 'Brenda, isn't it?' She remembered him. He was fair haired and red faced, a regular country boy. He had booked her once for too blatantly soliciting, she had been going through a bad patch. 'Is there somewhere we can talk?'

The other came out of Lily's flat, grim faced, nodded to his mate and went out to the car. 'I'll report back.'

Upstairs in the kitchen, a policeman's cap on the plastic-topped table, his notebook open beside it. She could hear voices downstairs, probably the doctor had arrived.

'Lily Painter,' the young man wrote in his book. 'Any relatives you know of?'

'She never mentioned anybody. She told me once that her parents were both dead.' It was true, although they were friendly Lily said very little about herself or her family.

'You found her?'

'I went down to cadge a cigarette.'

'And just found her lying there – is that it?' He was looking at her with earnest blue eyes, trying to do his job without upsetting her.

Suddenly her heart seemed to stop. 'It must have been him!'

'Who, love?'

'The man who killed her – Daddy she calls him, he's one of her regulars and tonight was his night.'

'Who is he?'

She looked at him blankly. 'I've no idea, but it must have been him mustn't it? I mean, he must have been with her when I came in.' She shivered at the thought.

'Have you ever seen him?'

'Not to say seen him, just glimpsed him, coming in or going out.'

'Can you describe him?'

'Not really, he's oldish.'

'How old?'

She shrugged. 'Fifty? I don't know, do I? I only set eyes on him two or three times and that was in the hall where there isn't much light. Besides, they don't like being stared at.'

Another siren, getting nearer.

'The Brass.'

'He's been coming regular for a long time, she used to laugh about him—'

'Try to remember.'

She frowned. 'He was not very tall – on the small side. I think he was dark but I'm not sure. Perhaps he was grey – oh! and he wore a grey, herring-bone tweed overcoat, I remember that.'

'No hat?'

'No.'

'A bit posh?'

'I suppose he was – he would need to be to go to Lily.'

'Did you ever speak to him?'

She shook her head.

'Never mind, make yourself a cup of tea, love, you'll have visitors in a minute.'

She could hear them downstairs, and yet another siren. The telephone rang in the hall.

'Don't bother, they'll answer it.'

Detective Chief Inspector Gill was very tall, very thin, he stooped as a matter of habit. A large face with rubbery features and a permanent five-o'clock shadow. She had had customers like him, they left you sore inside and bruised out. He had a girl with him, a female dick in a turtle-necked sweater and a mini-skirt. Brenda had

666

had dealings with her sort, too. They were supposed to comfort you and catch you off balance at the same time.

The young constable handed his notebook to the big man who glanced at it, snapped it shut and tucked it into the constable's tunic pocket.

'Give it to Sergeant Scales downstairs and tell him to have the description put out. As for you, lad, back on watch!' His eyes came round to Brenda. 'What's this then? Making tea? Sue can do that, it's one of her few talents. Where are we?' He was opening doors off the landing. 'This'll do, in here.'

She followed him into her sitting-room where the gas fire seemed welcoming and the television was on showing the inevitable football match.

'Sit down.' He stood over the television set, watching. 'Christ! You'd think some of 'em had two left feet and creeping bloody paralysis.' He switched the set off and turned to her. 'Not working tonight?'

She did not answer and he grinned. He sat in the easy chair opposite her and lit a long, black cheroot. 'Now tell uncle all about it.'

She did and he questioned her minutely.

'This chap she called Daddy; what did she tell you about him?'

'Nothing much, just that he was kinky and she used to laugh at him. A lot of the old ones have kinky tricks.'

'What sort of tricks did he have?'

'He likes doing himself up in leather straps and he brings pictures.'

'Pictures?'

'To look at. Some of them are really past it.'

'Is that all?'

She shrugged. 'All she told me.'

From time to time trains passed at the end of the road, the house shook and the windows rattled.

'Now, what about this description, you can do better than that.'

The policewoman brought in tea but Brenda's went cold before she could drink it.

'You haven't got a ponce have you?'

'No.'

'Did she?'

A faint smile. 'I can't see any man getting money out of Lily.'

He clicked his tongue. 'Greedy, both of you. You need somebody to look after you in this game.' He flicked ash into the gas fire. 'No maid?'

'No.'

'You two in the house alone?'

'Yes.'

'Bloody asking for it.' He stood up and glanced round the little room. 'Nice if you can keep it. Anyway, I'm off. You can start telling Sue all about it.'

'But I've told you.'

He grinned, his greasy rubbery grin which showed all his teeth. 'You haven't started to tell anything yet, girlie.' At the door he turned, 'And Sue, get her to give you a description of that chap she had with her—'

'He doesn't know anything.'

'Let him tell it.' He went out, closing the door.

'His bark is worse than his bite, don't let it get you down.'

She felt constrained to put on a front. 'His sort don't worry me, I've seen too many.'

The WPC was a homely sort of girl after all. She was plump and not bad looking. She sat in the chair her boss had vacated.

'You didn't get your tea, I'll make you another pot.'

'No, I will, I'd feel better doing something.'

'Let's do it together.'

Both in the kitchen. Something like it was with Lily. Often they would muck in together and usually, for some reason, it was in Brenda's kitchen. 'More homely than my place,' Lily used to say.

'You were fond of her?'

'In a way.'

'Tough.'

It wasn't long before they were chatting like any two young women. Relaxed. They boiled a couple of eggs and ate them seated at the kitchen table. 'A funny sort of job, yours,' Brenda said, thoughtfully.

The girl looked at her and laughed. 'You should talk!'

What was the difference between them? Five or six years and four or five 'O' levels? More than that. Something fundamental.

'Now, about this chap you were with . . .'

At one o'clock the policewoman said, 'I'd get some sleep if I were you, the circus will start again tomorrow.'

She yawned. 'I think I'll give it a try.'

'I can stay the night if you like?'

'No thanks, I'll be OK.'

'Have you got any tablets to make you sleep?'

Downstairs they were still at work. Lily's flat seemed to be full of men and there were cables everywhere for camera lights. Sergeant Smith, the squad's photographer, cursed steadily. 'Not room to stand sideways in this bloody place, you need a sodding sky-hook.' But in the end the girl's body had been photographed from every possible angle and removed for the autopsy. Then came photographs of the rooms and after that Sergeant Scales, the finger-print expert, moved in. He needed Smith's help to photograph prints which were accessible to the camera, those which were not had to be 'taken off' on tape and photographed later. Finally, a meticulous search undertaken by Scales and an assistant in which they all but took the flat apart.

But there was nothing surprising in what they found, more in what they did not find. No letters, not a single photograph, no papers, nothing which helped to put her in the context of a family, almost nothing to relate her to any life outside the flat. There was an engagement book in which appointments were recorded by initials, sometimes only a single letter. The entry for that evening was J.H.

Stanley Street had not seen such activity since the war when all the houses on the opposite side of the street had been destroyed. Police cars and motor cycles were coming and going continuously and detectives went from house to house asking questions and collecting varied and unhelpful answers.

'Well, it's no surprise really, is it? I mean, if you go on like that what can you expect?'

'The men! Beastly, I call it. No, I haven't seen anybody tonight; I mean, I don't take that much notice and it was dark anyway. It's when they come in the afternoon, as bold as brass . . .'

'I thought it was illegal . . .'

'I keep myself to myself, what other people do . . .'

A lot of it got written down.

At two o'clock in the morning CID headquarters were still a blaze

669

of light and Chief Superintendent Wycliffe was at his desk. Type-writers were clacking and telephones ringing all over the place. Organized chaos. Chief Inspector Gill was lolling in a swivel chair opposite his chief. The two men could hardly have been less alike. Wycliffe, barely regulation height, looking more like a lean and kindly monk than a policeman; Gill, six feet four in his socks, a face like a rubber mould, extroverted and often coarse.

'We shall have to keep tags on all the whores in town, these cases are never one-off.'

Wycliffe did not answer, he was scraping out the bowl of his pipe into an ash-tray. At the beginning of a case he liked to avoid dis-cussion but thinking aloud seemed to be essential to Gill's mental processes. He tried again.

'Who's doing the PM?'

'Franks, he promised to look in on his way home.'

A messenger came in with a sheaf of photographs of the girl and Wycliffe flicked through them impatiently. 'I asked for something we could give the newspapers.'

'Sergeant Smith is working on it, sir. He says it will take him another hour.'

Gill chuckled. 'What did he really say?'

'Sir?'

Smith was a morose dyspeptic who declared most things he was asked to do to be impossible but did them just the same.

Wycliffe asked the messenger, 'Will three o'clock be time enough?'

'For the city edition of *The News*, yes, sir.'

Gill was curious. 'You seem to think there's going to be some trouble over identification.'

Wycliffe shrugged. 'I shall be surprised if there isn't. A girl on the game who makes a point of having no papers about her.'

Gill blew out a cloud of blue-grey smoke. 'I can't see that it mat-ters, except technically; her killer didn't care a damn who she was.'

'We don't know that.'

'I'd take a bet.'

Wycliffe lit his pipe, puffing hard to get it going. 'Lily Painter – it sounds a bit phoney, don't you think?'

'I don't see why, there must be scores of Painters in the phone book and plenty of girls are called Lily, even these days.'

'Maybe you're right.' But Wycliffe was not convinced. Lily Painter – the painter of lilies, gilder of lilies? Too fanciful for Gill, perhaps too fanciful for common sense.

Elsewhere in the building a circular was being prepared for tailors and outfitters about herring-bone tweed overcoats. A questionnaire was being drafted in preparation for a more exhaustive house-to-house. It asked for information about cars parked nearby and for news of anyone out and about in the area at the time of the crime. Detectives were going through the Voters' lists for initials which corresponded with those in Lily's engagement book. Lily, herself, was not on the Voters' lists.

A few respected citizens were going to feel a cold draught for a day or two and certain abused wives might get a fresh hold on their husbands.

Wycliffe was shuffling through Smith's photographs of the dead girl's body and of the room. He picked up one and passed it to Gill.

'What do you make of the damage to her neck? It looks as though the skin was broken just below the larynx.'

'It was.'

'What did he use?'

'His hands, the marks of his fingers are clear on the back of her neck. The injury in front was caused by a clasp or brooch. She was wearing a high-necked dress with a stand-up collar held together in front by this brooch. His thumbs must have been on the brooch, there's blood on the inside of the dress collar – not much, but enough.'

Wycliffe looked at Gill in surprise. 'So she was dressed when she was strangled?'

'It certainly looks like it.'

'But naked when she was found; so, presumably, the strangler stripped her body after death. Why would he do that?'

Gill was finding himself on the defensive without quite knowing how he got there. 'Because he was kinky, I suppose.'

Both men knew the usual pattern of sex crimes only too well.

'Where were her clothes?'

Gill got up and shuffled through the preliminary reports on Wycliffe's desk. 'There you are: a Paisley patterned dress, a nylon slip, brassière, briefs and tights, all lying on a sort of upholstered chest at the bottom of the bed.'

'Thrown or placed there, would you say?'

Gill reflected. 'Placed.'

'Just as a reasonably careful woman might do if she undressed herself?'

'I suppose so, but I don't see—'

Wycliffe was studying another of Smith's photographs. 'Look at this one. It shows the body on the bed and, as far as I can see, there's been very little disturbance, the bedding is scarcely rumpled.'

'That's right, it wasn't.' Gill scattered ash on the carpet. 'I take your point, we've got a very careful, methodical killer but I don't see where it gets us. What does it matter?'

Wycliffe scooped the photographs into a pile. 'All I'm saying is that it's an unusual sex crime.'

'A kink who lingered over his work.'

'Perhaps, but isn't it equally possible that he was trying to make his crime look like a sex killing?'

Gill stubbed out the butt of his cheroot. 'I suppose you've got a point there. We shall soon know. If he runs true to form there'll be another killing before long.'

'You sent the clothing to Forensic?'

'Of course.'

'And the brooch?'

'That's gone too. Scales checked it for prints but there was no surface to take them.'

'Handbag?'

'She had a handbag – tissues, compact, lipstick, a few pounds in cash, no keys.'

'You found no keys at all?'

Gill shook his head. 'No, it's odd. The tart upstairs says she had a key-ring with several keys on it and a charm.'

At half past two Dr Franks, the pathologist, arrived. As bouncy as ever, he looked as though he had just come from his morning shower, all talcum and aftershave. He had worked with Wycliffe so often that he regarded himself as one of the team.

'Not much for you, gentlemen. She was strangled, of course.'

'Big deal!' from Gill.

'Strangled with bare hands but the pressure below the larynx was applied through a brooch or something of that sort. The killer must have been facing her. I gather that she was wearing a high-necked dress with a brooch that would fit the facts, his thumbs must have been on that.'

'Any sign of a struggle?'

'No other marks on the body except for two bruises inside the thighs, and they were not recent.'

'What about intercourse before or after death?'

The chubby doctor shook his head. 'No evidence but that doesn't mean a great deal.'

'She was on the pill,' Gill said.

'Even so, most of these girls want another kind of protection with strangers.'

'Perhaps he wasn't a stranger.'

'In my view that's more than likely,' Wycliffe said.

Franks looked puzzled and Gill explained. 'The chief thinks it might not be the usual thing – not a sex crime.'

Franks shrugged. 'I can't see that it makes any difference at this stage.'

'It makes a great deal of difference. In the one case, we are looking for someone who is pathologically disturbed, who might kill any available woman; in the other, we are after a man who had, what seemed to him, a good reason to kill this particular girl.' Wycliffe made a gesture of impatience and changed the subject. 'What about the time of death?'

'As near as I can put it between half past eight and nine.'

Wycliffe referred to his notes. 'The girl from the top flat arrived back about a quarter to nine when she says the door into the dead girl's room was closed. It was nine-thirty-five when she rang 999 but before that she had stopped to answer the telephone in the hall. The door was then a little open. If she is right the killer probably left between eight-forty-five and nine-thirty.'

'Which fits,' Franks said.

Wycliffe stood up. 'I'm for bed.'

He drove home through deserted streets. He had been in the city for a month. In a political deal Area Police Headquarters had been transferred there and CID had followed. He wasn't sorry, the sprawling, bustling port pleased him better than the rather inward looking cathedral city from which he had come. On the debit side he had exchanged offices in a Queen Anne crescent for one floor in a wing of the new Area HQ. On the credit side he had bought a substantial granite-built house in half an acre of ground overlooking the estuary, and an endless panorama of ships steamed through the narrows at the bottom of his garden. For weeks Helen had been organizing workmen who would, one day, expect to be paid. He had never known her so content; so much so that she had scarcely noticed her fortieth birthday.

It troubled his socialist conscience sometimes. He felt that he had betrayed something, perhaps himself. Charlie Wycliffe, copper and Helen Wills, typist, buying beauty and privacy in this overcrowded island.

Bah! He worked hard.

Anyway, it was a good feeling as he turned off the road down a gravelled track which led only to his own property. A white, five-barred gate. WATCH HOUSE in white letters on a varnished plaque. Away to his right he could look down on the water gleaming dimly in the near-darkness. Navigation lights, some steady, some winking. It seemed a long way from prostitutes and sex crimes and police reports; but away to the north the lights of the city still flared in the night sky.

2

Stanley Street looked drab in the light of a grey morning. Wycliffe drove slowly down it and stopped at number nine. Opposite, one of the steel shutters of the grocery warehouse had been raised and a van had backed in to load with tinned soups, cornflakes and baked beans (3p off). No sign of the excitement of the previous night. 9 Stanley Street was now 'on file', its essence distilled into a few sheets of typescript, three or four scale drawings and a score of photographs. But Wycliffe was seeing it for the first time. There was no need for him to see it now. His job was to delegate and to co-ordinate, sitting in his nice new office but, as more than one of his subordinates had remarked, 'There's no show without Punch'.

The house was better cared for than most of the houses, the woodwork was fresh with apple-green paint, otherwise it was like the rest, like thousands built before the first war. A porch over the front door was supported on wooden pillars and next to the front door there was a big bay-window. The window of number nine was curtained with fine net.

Wycliffe's ring was answered by a constable who had been left on watch, though what he was supposed to watch nobody had told him.

'Busy?'

'No, sir, not exactly.'

'No, you wouldn't be, my boy, not in here, all the villains are out there.'

The constable had heard stories, there was a veritable folk-lore surrounding the superintendent, now he had a story of his own.

'Is she up yet?' Wycliffe jerked his thumb in the direction of the stairs.

'I haven't heard her moving about yet, sir.'

'All right, off you go.'

Wycliffe broke the seal on the door leading into the dead girl's flat.

The room was almost in darkness; heavy velvet curtains inside the net, screened the window. He whisked them back and let in the cold steely light. The morning after. Stale cigarette smoke mixed with the stink of flash-bulbs and faint, clinging perfume. Muddy footmarks on the carpet and tobacco ash left by his policemen, none of them house trained. He heard the front door slam behind the constable and his spirits rose. Apart from the girl upstairs he had the place to himself.

He looked at the pictures on the walls, poked about in the drinks cupboard where there were several bottles unopened: whisky, rum, gin, brandy and several sherries, even a Madeira. All tastes catered for, no expense spared. The glasses hadn't come out of a chain store either. Evidently she had a discerning clientèle. Odd that she chose to do it in a shabby back street. Odd, until you remembered that her customers could feel anonymous here, it was neutral ground. In any case a well-off neighbourhood wouldn't have stood for her line of business.

Not much furniture. The room was on the small side but what there was had style; a long settee upholstered in creamy-white leather and armchairs to match, a couple of low tables on castors and a bench with a stereo record player and a record rack underneath. There was a record on the turntable – Beethoven's Sonata in F for violin and piano. Wycliffe set it going. Cheerful, almost frivolous. Her taste or her customer's? Wycliffe let it play while he went into the bedroom.

Coffee and cream in the reception, pink in the bedroom. The other room had not looked like a brothel, this did. The carpet was pink, so were the bedclothes, all of them. The bed took up most of the space but there was a small dressing-table and a built-in wardrobe in white. Pink and white. It reminded Wycliffe of sugar covered biscuits he had been expected to like as a child and it made him feel slightly sick as they had done. Everything was confusingly duplicated in the wall mirrors. There were two doors with mirror panels, one into the pink bathroom and the other into a white, thank God, kitchen.

He rooted about in the drawers of the dressing-table. Cosmetics and toilet articles, a few bits of jewellery in a little teakwood box. The wardrobe was small and held a trouser suit, three rather severe looking woollen dresses and a varied collection of housecoats-cum-dressing-gowns. There were trays holding tights and brassières and a rack with three pairs of shoes. There were slippers (pink) on the floor.

'Who are you?'

He had not heard her until she spoke because of the music. She stood in the doorway of the bedroom, thin, pale, her black hair hanging lank and straight to her shoulders. She wore a red dressing-gown of brushed nylon which probably made her look paler than she was.

Wycliffe introduced himself. 'Are you Brenda?'

'I heard the music.'

'She didn't really live here, did she?'

'I don't know what you mean.'

'Any coffee upstairs?'

'If you like.'

He followed her up the stairs. In the kitchen she filled an electric kettle and switched it on.

'It's only instant.'

'Do you mind if I look round?'

'Help yourself.' Resigned.

He looked into the sitting-room with its picture of stampeding elephants over the fireplace. The mantelshelf was crowded with little china and glass animals and in one corner there was a glass-fronted cabinet with a lot more. He looked into the bedroom which was like a demonstration room in a chain-store showroom, all plastic and veneer, but he liked it better than the one downstairs.

'Your coffee's made.'

The kitchen window looked out over a concrete yard with the backs of Prince's Street beyond; but she had fitted red and white checked curtains which made the outlook seem almost gay.

'I said that she didn't *live* in that flat downstairs. You live here, anybody can see that.'

'It's true she was away a lot. Most nights she didn't sleep there and she was hardly ever there in the afternoons or all day on Sundays.'

'Where did she spend the rest of her time?'

Brenda shrugged. 'She never gave much away and I've found it best not to ask questions. Sugar?'

'No thanks.' He stirred his coffee. 'We didn't find any keys.'

She frowned. 'No, they told me. She had a key-ring with three or four keys on it including one of the front door downstairs.'

'You'd better get the lock changed.'

Wycliffe had a copy of the photograph which had appeared in the paper. Sergeant Smith had done him proud. Nobody would have suspected that the photograph had been taken after death, least of all after death by strangulation.

'What do you think of this?' He put the photograph on the table among the coffee cups.

'Where did you get that? I've never seen a photo of her before.'

'Is it like her?'

'Of course it's like her, it is her.' She seemed to hesitate.

'Well?'

'It's just that she looks different, sort of blank.'

'Last night you told Mr Gill that she was educated. What did you mean?'

'Well, she had lots of "O" levels and "A" levels, that sort of thing.' She brought out a packet of cigarettes from the pocket of her dressing-gown and offered it to Wycliffe. 'Cigarette?'

'No thanks – pipe.' He got out his pouch and started to fill it. 'Did she go to school here in the city?'

'I suppose so, she never mentioned anywhere else.' Brenda was not bright and she seemed to be almost totally lacking in curiosity.

'You think that she was a local girl?'

'Oh, yes, I think so.' She lit a cigarette, inhaled and coughed.

'Why?'

Brenda looked vague. She got up to brush the fragments of Wycliffe's tobacco into an ashtray. The kitchen, like the rest of the flat, was spotless.

'When did you first meet her?'

The smooth, sallow skin of her brow wrinkled. 'Two – three years ago. She had a beat then, like me. She said she was learning the job and asked me if I would share a house with her. She told me she was going to rent this place in Stanley Street.'

'You paid her the rent for this flat?'

'Yes.'

'Did she sting you?'

The tired, dark eyes widened. 'Not really. It's a job to get a place where the landlord or the neighbours don't complain. I was lucky.'

She was thirty-one or two and she looked older. An interesting face, thin but not sharp, a good, straight nose and rather fine, dark eyes. She could have been sitting across the breakfast table from her husband. Why wasn't she? Was it fear? Or an odd sort of courage? She wasn't happy but she was not alone in that.

'What sort of girl was Lily?'

Again the puzzled frown. The question was too much for her but she made the effort. 'She was queer. You never knew with her. She would say things.'

Wycliffe was smoking peaceably. 'What things?'

'Half the time I didn't know what she was getting at. She used to look at me and say things like, "You don't hate them, do you, Bren?" Another time it would be, "You're a bloody fool. You let them screw you but I screw them – and bloody how."' She looked at Wycliffe almost shyly as though she hoped that he might explain.

'Anything else?'

'She used to ask me about my family, especially about my father, whether he was a bastard and all that.'

'Was he?'

She pursed her lips. 'I've never really thought about it. I mean, you don't, do you?'

'Did she ever tell you about her father or her family?'

'Never.'

They sat in silence for a while and when she got up she took the dishes to the sink and started washing them. 'I suppose I shall have to find somewhere else.'

'I shouldn't be in a hurry, this is going to take some sorting out.'

She turned to him with a faint smile, the first he had seen on her pale solemn face. 'You're a funny sort of cop.'

Bellings, his immediate superior, would have said 'Amen' to that.

Wycliffe drove back to his headquarters through heavy traffic in the mid-morning rush. He was more than ever convinced that Lily Painter of 9 Stanley Street had had another address, another identity. It was important to know about her life away from Stanley Street and this must be his first priority.

On the way down the corridor to his office he stopped at Administration.

'Who's free?'

The constable in charge of work schedules was a young man with

679

aspirations and the sense to see that a modern police force runs on paper. He consulted his records. 'DCs Dixon, Fowler, and Shaw, sir.'

'Send Dixon and Fowler to my office. Enquiries concerning the murdered girl.'

Wycliffe had not yet settled down in his new office, he doubted if he ever would. The wood panelling 'it's real, not vinyl or laminate', the sectional bookcases with law books and police reports he would never open, one of those great square desks which looked as though it had been spawned in congress between a teak tree and a plastics factory and the horrid, ornamented grille spewing out tepid, de-oxygenated air with controls offering a choice between suffocation and frost bite.

Another innovation was a young woman in an office next to his, WPC Saxton. She was blonde with aristocratic features and she looked as though she had just emerged from the proverbial band box. She regarded him, so he claimed, with a mixture of tolerance and contempt which made him uncomfortable. She was there to look after him and she was conscientious.

On his desk, among the reports, there was an abstract of the Voters' lists giving the names of certain men whose initials matched those in Lily's engagement book. The searchers had confined their attention to areas of the city where better-off people lived, for the others would not have been able to afford Lily. There had been four entries in her diary with two initials and two with only a single letter to identify the client. Wycliffe's men had concentrated on those with two initials but, even so, the list ran to more than two hundred names. Now it was a question of going to work diplomatically, and patiently trying to eliminate the non-starters. A dozen men would be kept busy but it had to be done. Delicate, too. Touch one tender spot and the whole thing would blow up in his face.

Detective Constable Dixon arrived, he was a new member of the squad, seconded on trial from the local force. He was the same age as the girl who had been murdered.

'Did you go to a local school, Dixon?'

'No, sir, I went to school in Exeter.'

'Did you make the sixth form?'

'One year, sir, I wasn't up to "A" levels.'

'I've got a job for you, visiting some of the schools.' Dixon did his best to express keen attention from his curly blond hair to his shining toe caps. Although he was in plain clothes he still wore regulation shoes.

'I've been looking at the Education Year Book. There are seven comprehensive schools in the city, four of which were once grammar schools. There are also two direct-grant schools with sixth forms. I want you to take along a photograph of the dead girl and find out which school she attended; also, what her name was.'

'Her name, sir?'

'Unless I'm mistaken, it wasn't Lily Painter.'

'No, sir, I understand.'

'Remember, girls change a lot in nine years, between seventeen and twenty-six. It might help you to know that she had a good crop of "O" and "A" levels.'

'University?'

'Probably not.'

DC Fowler was an older man, forty-five. He had remained a DC because he had consistently failed the examination for sergeant but he was a good jack of the old breed, slow and dogged. His briefing was simpler. To find the owner of 9 Stanley Street. 'I don't want you to approach him, just find out who he is and anything else you can without creating a fuss.'

At the council offices Fowler found that the rates on 9 Stanley Street were paid by a firm of estate agents, Farley, Roscoe and Bates, on behalf of the owners; and the owners were given as the City Property Trust. Farley, Roscoe and Bates had a reputation for shady deals but they had never yet faced criminal proceedings.

Fowler satisfied himself that the City Property Trust did not appear in the telephone directory then he went along to the offices of the estate agents.

The usual shop window full of cards and photographs advertising properties for sale. An outer office with a languid blonde who had difficulty in summoning enough interest to find out what he wanted, but in the end he was shown into Mr Bates' private office.

Bates was a tubby little man in a blue pin-striped suit that was too small for him. He had a cold and spoke with a paper tissue held to his nose. 'No, Mr Fowler, we are not the City Property Trust, we merely act for them as we do for other clients – rents, rates, repairs, tenancy agreements and so forth.'

'Who is the tenant of 9 Stanley Street?'

Bates looked a little shocked. 'Really, Mr Fowler, you cannot expect me to—'

'She was strangled last night, as I expect you saw in this morning's paper.'

Bates removed the paper tissue long enough to sneeze. 'Dear me. Strangled. In that case you must surely know who she is.'

'We would like your confirmation.'

Bates stood up, though his legs were so short it made little difference, and went to a filing cabinet. He extracted a thickish file with his free hand, put it on the desk and riffled through the pages. 'Here we are, 9 Stanley Street, a tenancy agreement between Miss Lily Painter and the Trust entered into three years ago. I'm sorry that she has . . .' He seemed to find difficulty in ending the sentence and gave up.

'You knew her?'

'Oh, no, I never met the lady but she was a good tenant. A money order on the nail, the first day of every month.'

'A money order?'

'Always. Some people are funny like that, especially the ladies, they don't like cheques.'

'How much?'

Bates sniffed loudly. 'I beg your pardon?'

'The rent – how much?'

'I certainly cannot disclose such information about a client.'

'Don't strain yourself.' Fowler's stare was contemplative rather than aggressive. 'I'll just assume the rent was enough to tell you the place was being used as a brothel.'

'A *brothel?*'

'Premises where two or more prostitutes follow their trade. Your tenant was a prostitute and she sub-let to another.'

Bates took time off to search for a fresh tissue and to dispose of the old one. 'If what you say is true it is a matter for the owners, I am merely their agent.'

'So we had better get to the owners. The City Property Trust do not appear in the telephone book.'

'I could give you their address.'

'Good.' Fowler waited with his pencil poised.

'They have an office at 24 Middle Street.'

'And an ex-directory telephone number, I expect. What is it?'

'As far as I know they have no telephone. Our only contact with them is through the post.'

'What other rents do you collect for them?'

Bates looked scandalized. 'Now you really are going outside your brief, Mr Fowler.'

'All right. Any other properties in Stanley Street?'

Bates hesitated, then decided to accept the compromise. 'Numbers fifteen and twenty-two.'

'Both converted into flats?'

Bates was distinctly unhappy but he answered. 'Number fifteen has been converted but twenty-two is occupied by an elderly couple.'

'Who just won't die or get out – annoying for you. What do you do? Put fireworks through their letter-box or pay young thugs to break their windows?'

Bates stood up. 'Mr Fowler! You have no right to insinuate anything of the kind. I shall—'

'The rents you receive on behalf of the Trust – where do you bank them?'

'We don't. The money is sent to the Middle Street office.'

'Including cheques?'

'Including cheques.'

'Thank you, Mr Bates, we shall be in touch again.'

Fowler went back to his car and reported over the radio. After a brief wait he received instructions to take a look at the Middle Street premises. 'Mr Gill says you're to use your discretion, don't stir anything.'

'Which means,' Fowler interpreted, 'whatever happens I'm left holding the sticky end.'

Middle Street was a street of small shops not far from the city centre. It had largely escaped the wartime bombing and, until now, the devastation of the planners. But it was obviously ripe: two or three shops were boarded up having fallen into the hands of speculators who were biding their time. Fowler could dimly remember this street before the war. On Saturdays it had been closed to traffic and market stalls ran the length of the roadway. On Saturday nights it was like a fairground with cheap-jacks, quack doctors and buskers competing for the hard earned sixpences and shillings of their customers. All in the glare of spitting arc lamps.

Number twenty-four was a tobacconist's but there was a side door with a large letter-box labelled, City Property Trust. No bell. Fowler went into the shop where a fat man stood with his elbows on the counter reading a newspaper.

'City Property Trust?'

The fat man shook his head without looking up. 'Nothing to do with me.'

'There's no bell.'

'That's right. It wouldn't be much use if there was – there's nobody there most of the time.' His attention was still on the newspaper.

Fowler produced his warrant card. 'I want to get in touch with whoever runs it – when are they there?'

The tobacconist straightened up. He was a man of few words. 'They come and go.'

'When?'

'Afternoons mostly, of course, I wouldn't know about evenings and Sundays.'

'Who are they?'

'Search me.'

'You must have seen them.'

He shook his head. 'No, they come in the back way and I don't have a back entrance.' He kicked the door behind him which opened into his stockroom. 'You can see for yourself.'

Fowler saw. At the back of the stockroom a window fitted with fluted glass and, behind it, the blurred outline of a staircase like a fire-escape going diagonally across the window.

'I think it's a woman mostly – light footsteps, but sometimes there's more than one and I've heard a man's voice.' He showed a first sign of curiosity. 'What they done?'

'Nothing as far as I know, we want to get in touch with them about one of their tenants.'

'Then your best plan is to go to the agents, Farley, Roscoe and Bates, that's where I pay my rent.'

As Fowler was leaving he added, in a burst of confidence, 'Three or four times when I've come here late of an evening I've heard somebody moving about upstairs.'

'Thanks.'

Fowler again reported over his car radio.

'Which gets us no further,' Wycliffe said when the news was passed on to him. He was standing in the big window of his office looking out over the garden which had been contrived in a vain attempt to make the crudity of the new buildings acceptable. Grass, geometrical beds and unlikely rockeries – not a tree. Public officials have tree phobia. Beyond the sparse oasis a main highway ran north out of the city. The rain was falling vertically out of a leaden sky.

He turned to Gill who was sprawled in the customer's chair, smoking. 'Anything else?'

'Records have matched one set of prints found in the Stanley Street flat. They belong to Martin Arthur Salt, a former bookmaker, of 3 Lavington Place, sent down for fraud in '67. He served twenty-seven months of a three year sentence. I've got his file here.' Gill passed a folder across the desk and Wycliffe leafed through it idly.

The usual photograph which would make the archangel Gabriel look like an old lag. A thin face, deep-set eyes and a twisted nose. Thinning hair. Date of birth 27.2.30. Addresses of betting shops in the city and neighbouring towns which formed his empire. A list of pubs he frequented and one club. According to the file he had been suspected of running a protection racket with the help of two strong-arm boys but the fraud charge was all they could make stick.

Wycliffe closed the file with a sigh. 'Where is he now?'

Gill heaved his bulk forward to stub out a butt end. 'He's back at Lavington Place doing very nicely.'

'On what?'

'On the money stashed away in his wife's name before he was nobbled. I wouldn't mind doing bird for a couple if it meant I could live easy for the rest of my natural.' Gill maintained that crime paid and never missed a chance to underline his point.

'What about the muscle boys?'

'They were never charged but they both had form. Edward Short – he seems to have pushed off on to somebody else's patch; but the other chap, Peter "Dicey" Perrins, is still around. He seems to have kept his nose clean.

'I'm sending a crime car to bring in Salt.'

685

Wycliffe returned to his chair and started to fill his pipe. 'That's reasonable, Jimmy, but don't forget our first job is to find out who this girl was.'

Constable Dixon spent the morning and part of the afternoon going from school to school. Anxious to make a good impression he did not stop for lunch but contented himself with coffee and a sandwich in a snack bar. If he had imagined that getting out of uniform into the CID would give him status, he was disappointed. In only one school did he succeed in reaching the headmaster, in the others he received cursory attention from one of the secretaries between more urgent tasks.

'What did you say her name was? But if you're not sure of her name how can we help you? You can look at the school photographs if you like – they're hanging in the hall.'

' "A" level results for '64? The teacher responsible for examinations is with a class. If you'd like to wait for the bell you might catch him. In about fifteen minutes.'

He struck oil at last in one of the direct-grant schools. A plump, motherly, grey haired woman in the office looked at his photograph of the dead girl with interest. 'That face is familiar. '64, you say? Nine years ago. Hold on.'

She went away and came back with a ledger-like book. She flicked through the pages. 'Here we are – 1964 "A" level results. Abbott, Joyce; Barker, Gwendoline; Bonnington, Celia; Cave, Dawn – Goodness! How it takes you back. We had a good lot of girls that year.' She ran rapidly down the alphabet. 'Christine Powell – that's her.' She followed along the columns with a stubby finger. 'History, English, French and Art – all with A-grades. She was a very clever girl, there's no doubt about that – but wild—'

'She didn't go to university?'

'No, I'm sure she didn't, though with those grades she could have walked in. Wait a minute . . .' She went through to another room and came back with a file. 'Here we are, July '64 leavers.' Once more a long list of names. '. . . Paley, Parker, Powell. She went to the School of Art and Architecture, here in the city, to study art and design, though I doubt if she stayed the course.'

Dixon spread out the newspaper for her to read.

'Got herself murdered – well, I can't say I'm all that surprised. But what a waste. Boy mad she was, even in the third form. Well, poor girl, I suppose she paid for it.'

Dixon asked if the school had her address.

'We shall have her address at the time she left but as far as I know we've had no contact since.'

This time, the Admissions Register. 'Christine Powell, admitted September 1957, left July 1964. Address: 4 Conniston Gardens.'

'Conniston Gardens. They must have had money.'

'Oh, they did. If I remember rightly he was a big noise in the docks. He came in once or twice when the head had occasion to complain of one of Christine's more outrageous escapades. Of course he blamed the school. Not a pleasant man.'

Dixon reported over his car radio. 'Do I follow up at Conniston Gardens?'

After a brief wait he was told to report back.

Assuming the identification of the photograph to be correct, Wycliffe now knew the dead girl's name and could find out about her family. He questioned one of the local men, a sergeant who had nearly thirty years service behind him.

'Conniston Gardens? That would be Sir George Powell, sir. He was chairman of the Docks Board. He and his wife were killed in a road accident six or seven years back.' The sergeant passed a hand over his balding skull. 'Quite a character Sir George, they don't come like him any more. He was chairman of the Watch Committee back in the days of the old city force. A great Methodist with two bees in his bonnet: drink and sex.' The sergeant frowned. 'I can't recall a daughter but there was a son, all set to follow in father's footsteps. I don't know what happened to him.'

Well, it shouldn't be difficult to find out. Wycliffe had an odd feeling about the case. He was convinced that it was not a sex crime. But what? Did it mean anything that she had had a good education and wealthy parents? Why should it? She was a whore like any other.

A genteel tap on the door and the deputy chief came in. Hugh Annesley Bellings, the next chief constable, if diplomacy and friends meant anything.

'There you are, Charles.' Bellings always made his greeting sound as though he had run his quarry to earth after a long and tiresome chase. 'May I?'

He parked his slim bottom on the customer's chair, crossed his elegant legs and placed long, thin fingers tip to tip. One major snag in the recent move was having Bellings down the corridor instead of half-way across town.

'This murder, Charles, I find it very disturbing.'

'All murders disturb me.' Wycliffe came away from the window and sat in his chair.

'Of course, but the implications of this one are particularly unpleasant. It could well be the start of a series. This type of crime—'

Wycliffe felt like asking 'What type of crime?' but held his peace.

'Lily Painter, wasn't it?'

'Her real name was Powell, she was using a false name.'

'Indeed.'

'Christine Powell, she was the daughter of a chap killed in a road accident, a former chairman of the Docks Board.'

'But I gathered from the reports that she was a—'

'A common prostitute – she was.'

Bellings looked shocked and Wycliffe smoked his pipe in silence.

'But this is incredible. George Powell – well, I won't say that he was a friend but we met socially. He was chairman of the Watch Committee. As a matter of fact I'm still in touch with his son. I've never come across the girl but I do remember hearing some distasteful rumours. What a tragedy. The family seems to be dogged by misfortune – calamity one might say.'

'You mentioned the son.'

'Jonathan, what about him?'

'I need to get in touch, I must confirm the identity of the corpse if nothing else.'

Bellings forced his attention back to the police aspects of the case. 'Yes, of course.'

'Is he still here?'

'Oh, no. When his parents were killed he sold the place in Conniston Gardens and moved to London.'

'How does he earn his living?'

Bellings pursed his lips before answering. 'He's connected with a large property syndicate. George Powell died a rich man and Jonathan is no fool. From what I hear he hasn't been losing money over the past few years.'

Bellings reflected on a fate which was no respecter of persons. 'I'll telephone him. The poor fellow will be distrait.'

'I think I'd better do that.'

'What? Oh, yes, I suppose so. But do be careful, Charles.' He smiled. 'We really are in the big league with this one.'

'His address?'

'I'll phone it through.'

'Is he married?'

'Jonathan? No, he's a bachelor, confirmed I should say.'

When Bellings had gone Wycliffe telephoned the School of Art and Architecture. Although term had ended the principal was still there and agreed to see him.

The school was housed in a Victorian building with a stucco front and pillared entrance opposite the city polytechnic, a mushroom growth of glass and concrete approaching skyscraper proportions. The poly made the old building look squat, shabby and apologetic, like an elderly poor relation.

He was received in an office that had been carefully planned in every detail of furnishing and decoration to suggest a middle-of-the-road establishment that kept, nevertheless, an intelligent eye on the future. A couple of framed paintings were 'early modern' in conception, there were framed architectural drawings of un-exceptionable taste and a little bronze confection on a plinth with lots of spikes to point the way ahead. Too little or too much and the purse strings might tighten. There was no notice saying 'No pot here' but the point was being made. No polythene fun tents either.

'Mr Slater?'

They shook hands. The principal had a regulation haircut except for sideburns and he wore a corduroy jacket.

'As you know, I would like to hear what you can tell me about Christine Powell, the girl who was murdered.'

Mr Slater consulted a folder which lay on his desk. 'She came to us in 1964 to study Art and Design – at that time, a two year course intended to prepare students for work in industry. There was a choice of specializations in the second year.'

'You remember Christine?'

'Of course.'

'What sort of girl was she?'

'As a student she showed unusual ability . . .'

'As a person?'

The manicured fingers stroked a carefully shaven chin. 'There were problems.'

'Such as?' Wycliffe shifted irritably in his chair. 'I am not asking you for a testimonial, Mr Slater. The girl was brutally murdered and I have to find out everything I can about her that might have a bearing on her death.'

Slater decided to force himself. 'She was a very difficult girl to deal with; she resented every attempt to bring her into any degree of conformity.'

'To what was she expected to conform?'

Slater looked disapproving. 'To reasonable standards of conduct.' Wycliffe's silence forced him to continue. 'Her behaviour was often outrageous and she lost no opportunity of rendering herself conspicuous. Had it not been for her father's influence I am sure that my governors would have expelled her during her first term.'

'Did she complete the course?'

'She did not.'

'What happened?'

Slater looked faintly embarrassed. 'She was expelled.'

'Despite her father?'

'As a matter of fact the final outrage occurred after the crash in which he was killed.'

'What was this outrage?'

'She attended a founder's lecture, a semi-public occasion, in the nude.' Perhaps Wycliffe did not look suitably shocked for Slater added with asperity, 'These things matter in an institution which depends on public funds.'

'I'm sure they do. Why did she do it?'

'Why did she do it? Why do exhibitionists exhibit themselves? The excuse was that she did it for a bet.' Mr Slater placed the folder in a drawer of his desk. 'A great pity, she was very talented.'

'Had she any special friends?'

'There were a good many who enjoyed her notoriety at second hand. Towards the end of her stay here she did make one friend, a young man called Morris – Paul Morris. He was studying architecture and he was one of the most able pupils we have ever had. He was a retiring young man, introspective and shy, so their association was really quite remarkable and, to me, inexplicable.'

'What happened to him?'

'He qualified, of course, and he now works for Lloyd and Winter, here in the city. I've no doubt that he will go far.'

Back in his office Wycliffe telephoned Jonathan Powell at the number Bellings had given him. There was no reply and he gave instructions for the operator to keep trying. Then he telephoned Lloyd and Winter and asked to speak to Paul Morris. He was put through without difficulty.

Morris sounded abrupt and distant. If he was going to translate imagination and skill on the drawing board into commercial success he would have to do something about his manner on the telephone. But he readily agreed to come to the police headquarters in the afternoon.

'At two o'clock, Mr Morris, thank you.'

Morris had not asked why his attendance was required.

Half past twelve. Sixteen hours since Lily Painter or Christine Powell had been strangled. She had not been killed by a psychopathic nut on the loose. The evidence was against it. The missing keys, the methodical stripping of the body after death and the orderly placing of the girl's clothes. The murderer had tried, clumsily, to cover his tracks by simulating the trappings of a sex crime.

The commoner motives for murder are greed or fear or both. It seemed unlikely that anyone would profit financially from the death of Lily Painter though the possibility could not be ruled out. There was certainly money in the Powell family. Did someone fear her enough to kill her? Prostitutes, especially high class ones, are often in a position to blackmail, and relentless blackmail can be a powerful spur to violence though, in practice, it rarely follows.

Wycliffe sighed and lit his pipe. WPC Saxton opened the door of his office. 'It's time for my lunch, sir.'

'What? Yes, of course, you run along.'

She hesitated. 'Aren't you—?' But she broke off in mid-sentence and closed the door quickly. Strange girl.

There was a complication. Who had been murdered? Lily Painter or Christine Powell? The girl had led a double life and he knew little of one and nothing of the other. Yet it was one of his maxims; 'Know your victim'. He must practise it now. But which one had been killed? Which one?

Wycliffe soon tired of speculative thought, his ideas clouded and

691

his mind became confused, he would find himself repeating a particular word or phrase over and over again like a record caught in a groove. He knocked out his pipe and went down the corridor in search of Gill.

He found him with Martin Salt the ex-bookmaker and con-man whose prints had been found in the dead girl's flat. Salt was sandy haired and balding, freckled with a wispy moustache. His nose looked as though it had collected more than one well-directed punch.

'You know why you are here, Mr Salt?'

'Mr Gill has been telling me.'

'Well?'

'What do you expect me to say? That my wife doesn't understand me?'

'If she did she probably wouldn't pay the bills.'

Salt was not in the least put out. 'You're hard on me, Mr Gill. As you know, I'm unemployed.'

Wycliffe took time over lighting his pipe. 'Apart from the obvious what was your relationship with the dead girl?'

Salt sighed. 'I know better than to fence with you chaps so let's get this straight. I visited Lily once a week; she was accommodating and there it ended. She was a nice kid, I liked her.'

'You called her Lily?'

'What do you think I call a girl I'm in bed with? Miss Painter?'

'Her real name was Christine Powell.'

'So? The chick wore a phoney label. I don't blame her in that racket. Perhaps her family didn't care for it, some people are funny that way.'

'She was George Powell's daughter, the chap who was chairman of the Docks Board.'

Salt seemed to find this highly amusing. 'The holy docker? Christ! he would have gone for that.'

'You didn't know?'

'I'll say I didn't, but it's bloody funny. He was a regular Bible basher. Hot on vice too.' He laughed loudly. 'It's bloody funny to think of it, isn't it?'

'Very funny but I wouldn't laugh too soon.'

'You've got nothing on me, Mr Wycliffe.'

Wycliffe smiled. 'Do you know anything of the City Property Trust?'

Salt took a cigarette from his case and lit it. 'I've heard of them but I know nothing about the set-up.'

'Do you know who runs it?'

'Surprise me.'

'You don't happen to be involved yourself?'

'Me? I've no money as you should know.'

'Your wife, then?'

Salt blew a perfect smoke ring and watched it rise. 'I doubt it, but Mavis plays her cards pretty close to her chest these days – if you'll forgive the expression.'

Gill came to stand by Salt. 'You've got form.'

'Don't I know it.'

'Just remember, anything we find out that you haven't told us . . . You get the message?'

'Oh, I got the message in the first place, Mr Gill. When it's an open field you lean on anybody you can. Can I go now?'

Wycliffe intervened. 'Don't be impatient, Mr Salt. Do you know any of the other regulars at Stanley Street?'

'Sorry.'

'When were you last there?'

'Friday, that's my day.'

'So, if somebody said they saw you coming away from the flat on Wednesday evening, they would be lying?'

'*If* somebody said so. I've got a twenty-two carat alibi for Wednesday evening.'

'Save it, you may need it,' Wycliffe said grimly.

Salt looked put out. 'What's that supposed to mean?'

Wycliffe ignored the question. 'A regular visitor at Stanley Street with the initials J.H.'

Salt was about to deny any knowledge but changed his mind. 'J.H., you say, it's possible . . .'

'What is?'

'That your J.H. could be Jimmy Harkness.'

'Who is he?'

'He's a surveyor and valuer in a fairly big way of business.' Salt passed a hand over his thinning hair. 'I don't know, of course, but

693

I've heard that he's always willing to give a helping hand to a working girl.'

'Have you ever seen him there?'

'Sorry.'

'Has Christine Powell ever mentioned him?'

Salt shook his head. 'Never.'

'Then what have you got against him?'

Salt looked pained. 'You asked for a name, Mr Wycliffe. I've got nothing against Jimmy Harkness but I don't owe him either. If he was mixed up in this business I'd just as soon he didn't get away with it.' Self-righteous. 'Can I go now?'

'If you like.'

As Salt reached the door Wycliffe said, 'If you see Dicey Perrins around, give him my regards. We are old acquaintances.'

Salt turned to face the superintendent. He was about to say something but changed his mind and went out.

'We didn't get a lot out of him.'

Gill lit a cheroot. 'There's more to come, I'll screw him next time. What did you make of the bit about this chap Harkness?'

'He's got a grudge obviously but there could be something in it. Discreet enquiries.'

3

Among the reports which had come in as a result of house-to-house enquiries in the Stanley Street area was one from a woman who lived in Waterloo Place, a quiet street of small houses often lined with parked cars. She had gone up to her bedroom to fetch something and had happened to look out of the window. She had seen, some way down the street, a man in a grey overcoat trying to unlock the door of a parked car. She had noticed him because he seemed to be having difficulty and twice he had dropped his keys into the gutter.

'You hear so much about cars being stolen these days, I wondered. But as far as I could see from that distance, he looked a respectable body so I thought he must be just plain clumsy.'

'What sort of car?'

'Oh, it was a Mini.' She laughed. 'The only kind of car I can recognize. I can't tell you the colour exactly because the light from those street lamps is so queer but I think it was blue.'

'New or old?'

'How would I know? It seemed to go all right.'

'You saw him drive away?'

'Oh, yes. He went off down the street. He seemed a bit careless.'

'Careless?'

'As though he couldn't steer straight or something. I remember wondering if he was drunk.'

'What about the man himself? tall? short? young?'

'Well, I couldn't see very well and I wasn't paying that much attention; I mean, you don't, do you? But he wasn't short. I suppose he must have been tall because he had to stoop quite a bit to fit the key in the lock of the car door. As to his age, well, he wasn't old – not really old, but I can't say more than that.'

'Shabby or smart?'

She shook her head. 'The overcoat looked all right but that's all I can say. He was slim, I'd swear to that'

Brenda had spoken of Daddy as wearing a grey overcoat.

Another list. The owners of all blue or green Minis registered in the city and the county. Of course the car could have been registered anywhere in the country but one had to start somewhere. According to the traffic department the list was likely to run to four or five hundred names and it would certainly take a long time to prepare.

The enquiries among tailors and outfitters had been unproductive. Grey tweed overcoats seemed to have been purchased by half the male population of the city. Even the bespoke tailors had long lists. Still, it had to be done. Turn every stone. That's detection.

At two o'clock Wycliffe had gone out for a snack lunch and the architect, Paul Morris, was shown into Gill's office. He was tall, almost as tall as Gill, thin, pale, with black hair cut short and he was sombrely dressed in pepper-and-salt gent's suiting. 'On sale or return from a seminary,' was Gill's unspoken comment.

'Sorry to drag you up here, Mr Morris, wasting good drinking time.'

Morris sat where he was bidden but he did not smile. 'I was told that you thought I might be able to help with a certain enquiry.'

'That's right, any idea which?'

Morris was finding it difficult to keep his voice steady. 'I suppose you are investigating the death of the girl whose photograph appeared in the paper.'

Gill nodded, grinning. 'Right first time. She was murdered actually – strangled. Somebody got their hands round her neck and squeezed the life out of her – literally. A brooch she was wearing was forced into her neck until it brought blood. Nasty.'

Morris said nothing.

Gill lit a cheroot. 'You knew her?'

The young man was holding himself in with difficulty, his hands were clasped tightly between his knees. 'The newspaper did not give her right name.'

'Oh? What was she called then?'

'Her name was Powell – Christine Powell.'

'But you recognized her photograph in spite of the wrong name?'

He stared at the floor and spoke in a low voice. 'I tried to persuade myself that it was someone else.'

'But now you're convinced that it wasn't. That's something. How well did you know her?'

'Quite well.'

'How well is quite? Well enough to go to bed with her?'

'I did not go to bed with her.'

Gill looked surprised. 'Why not? Everybody else did. You queer or something?'

Morris coloured. 'You have no right to say such a thing. I—'

'When did you last see her? Was it yesterday evening?'

'No, I didn't see her yesterday evening. The last time—'

'What were you doing yesterday evening, Mr Morris?'

'I was at the office until six then I had a meal and after that I spent the evening at Andrew Jarvis's – the Old Custom House. I left there about ten.'

'No home to go to?' When Morris did not answer he went on, 'Who's this Andrew Jarvis? You'll have to spell everything out for an ignorant copper.'

'You know the Old Custom House?'

'A great barn of a place in Bear Street, some sort of second-hand bookshop.'

'Actually it's an antiquarian bookshop run by Jarvis. He has his own bindery and he does a lot of restoration work for libraries and museums.'

'Good for him. Where do you fit in?'

Morris took out his handkerchief and blew his nose. Afterwards he continued to hold the handkerchief in his hand, rolled up in a ball. 'Jarvis has turned one of the attics into a studio and I go there to paint.'

'Why?'

'Why? Because I have no facilities at home.'

'What does he get out of it?'

Morris made a grimace of distaste. 'He gets nothing out of it, he likes to help people who, in his opinion, have some talent. He sells pictures painted by local artists at a small commission.'

'So you spent yesterday evening there painting. I thought you chaps only worked in daylight?'

'I have to paint when I can.'

'Do you spend much time there?'

'Two or three evenings a week.'

697

'And week-ends?'

'Very often – yes.'

'And the chick – did she ever go there with you?'

'Sometimes, she is interested in painting.'

'Was.'

'I beg your pardon?'

'She *was* interested, she's dead – remember? Where and when did you meet her?'

'We met at an Arts Society meeting several months ago. She isn't a regular member but she came to hear a particular speaker.'

Gill studied the boy closely. 'You married?'

'No, I live with my mother who is a widow.'

'Anybody to support your story?'

'What story?'

'That you spent yesterday evening painting pictures. Was there anybody in the studio with you?'

'No, Andrew was there when I arrived but he had to go out and I was alone after that but it's absurd to think—'

'I don't think anything but I've got a different version of how you came to meet the girl.'

'A different version? I don't understand—'

'That you met her when you were both at the School of Art together – years ago.'

'But that's true. The point is we met again after not seeing each other for years.'

'Is it true that she got herself expelled?'

'In a way.'

'For coming to a lecture starkers?'

'It was a rag.'

Gill shook his head in mock solemnity, 'She doesn't sound your sort of girl to me.'

Morris was needled. 'I don't see how you can possibly know what "my sort" of girl is.'

Gill grinned ferociously. 'No but we've plenty of time to get better acquainted.' He stared at the young man and puffed smoke across the desk. 'Did she ever take you home?'

'Home?'

'To Stanley Street.'

'I didn't know she had a flat there until I saw the paper.'

Gill thought this might even be true. 'She ran a very profitable business from the flat in Stanley Street, she was a sort of high class call girl.'

Morris flushed. 'You can't expect me to believe that.'

'Suit yourself. When did you last see her?'

'On Sunday at Jarvis's.'

Gill crushed out his cheroot and sat back in his chair. 'So you were at Jarvis's studio from, say seven-thirty until about ten, last night – is that right?'

'Yes.'

'You spoke to Jarvis before he went out, was he back when you left?'

'No.'

'What about locking up?'

Morris looked surprised. 'I forgot – Derek was in the house all the time, I told him when I was going and, incidentally, he looked in for a word during the evening.'

'Derek?'

'Derek Robson, he's Jarvis's assistant and he lives on the premises.'

'You say he looked in to see you – when?'

'Not long after Andrew left, say a bit before eight.'

They sat in silence while the hand of the wall clock jerked forward three or four times, each time making a little click. When Gill spoke again his manner had changed, he was ingratiating, inviting confidences. 'What sort of girl did you *think* she was?'

'I don't know what you mean.'

Gently. 'Of course you do. Would you have married her if you'd had the chance?'

'There was no question of that.'

'Why not? Did you ask her?'

Morris stared dumbly at the top of the desk. There was no need for him to speak; the fact that the girl had noticed him had been enough, he had never aspired to more than that. Occasionally he had been allowed the privilege of her company. Gill, who assumed that all women would dance to his tune, made an involuntary grimace of distaste which was not lost on Morris.

'What did you like about her?'

Morris was silent for a while but he answered at last, 'She was very intelligent, very talented—', then he saw the look on Gill's face and stopped.

'Have you got a car, Mr Morris?'

'Yes, why?'

'A blue Mini?'

Morris looked concerned. 'Yes, why?'

'Did you have it at Jarvis's place last night?'

'Yes . . .'

'A man, tall, thin, wearing a grey overcoat and driving a blue Mini was seen near the Stanley Street flat at about the time of the crime. Have you got a grey overcoat?'

'Yes but there must be scores—'

'Hundreds.' Gill scowled grotesquely. 'Don't go away without letting us know, Mr Morris. Happy Christmas.'

Morris did not answer but he got up from his chair looking dazed.

'I expect you can find your own way out.'

When Wycliffe returned from his lunch Gill told him of his interview with Morris. 'Innocents like that are dangerous when they get away from mother – nobody to tell them right from wrong.'

Wycliffe was amused to hear that Morris was a regular visitor at the Old Custom House. 'You probably don't know this chap Jarvis; apart from running the antiquarian bookshop, he sells pictures painted by favoured local painters. Unless I'm mistaken he's an old queen. Helen and I were there a few weeks back looking at his paintings and we bought one for the new house. I think I might renew his acquaintance.'

With the visit in mind, Wycliffe collected his car from the car park and drove through the city centre in the direction of his home. About half-a-mile beyond the centre he turned left off the main road, parked his car on a meter, and walked down a narrow cobbled alley which took him to what had once been the maritime heart of the city. Now it was a picturesque backwater mummified for tourists. The sunshine was deceptive, the air was crisp and cold, there would certainly be a heavy frost before nightfall.

Three or four fishing boats still made a living out of the harbour, a few pleasure craft plied for hire in the summer and a score of shops along the waterfront sold antiques, pictures, Scandinavian rugs and furniture, way-out kitchen equipment and 'gifts'.

Perhaps the fishing boats had been out all night and had long since landed their catch, perhaps the owners of the pleasure craft were pursuing their winter occupations elsewhere, perhaps if he had not come in the slack of a week-day afternoon the shops would have been teeming with discerning customers clamant for a Redouté chopping board or a tea towel with a recipe for mead printed on it in Gothic characters. Perhaps. But now the harbour was dead. One man in blue overalls and a peaked cap was leaning on the quay rail smoking his pipe while a dog sniffed hopefully round the bollards.

Wycliffe strolled along by the shops until he reached the little square which was used as a car park but even here there was only a single car in the score of spaces which had been marked out. Fronting on the square and facing the harbour was the Old Custom House while to the left, Bear Street pursued its narrow and devious way back to the modern city. The Custom House was two storeys high with attics above and the upper storey jutted out over the pavement supported on pillars. A painted board slung between two of the pillars read: The Jarvis Book Shop – Antiquarian Books a Speciality.

There was no proper shop window but through high sash-windows under the arches made by the pillars it was possible to see rows of books in the dimly lit interior. A sign hung inside the glass panel of the door: Back Shortly. Wycliffe tried the handle of the door but it was locked.

On his earlier visit Wycliffe had been intrigued but repelled by Jarvis. Helen, his wife, like most women, had a soft spot for queers. After an hour spent in looking at books and pictures Jarvis had been calling Helen, 'Helen' and addressing Wycliffe as 'dear boy'.

Wycliffe made another circuit of the harbour and was diverted for a while by a few herring gulls fighting over an anonymous scrap of carrion. By the time it was over he saw Jarvis unlocking his shop door from the outside. Jarvis was a spruce and agile sixty, medium height, spare, with a smooth skin the uniform colour of old parchment. He wore a fawn, cavalry twill suit, a pearl-grey silk shirt with a red tie and sandals. His hair, elegantly silvered at the temples, contrasted too sharply with his chestnut-brown toupée.

'My dear boy!'

Wycliffe was made much of, taken through the shop between dusty shelves crammed with old books into an office where there was a roll-top desk, a swivel chair and more books in piles on the floor.

The place smelt, unpleasantly, of mouldering paper and glue. A coffee pot simmered very gently on a gas ring.

'I do hope I haven't kept you, dear boy. I lunch at a little place round the corner in Bear Street and I'm afraid I stopped talking.' He produced two cups and saucers from a cupboard and poured coffee. 'The food is passable but I can't stand their coffee. Milk? Sugar? No, I never take them myself.' He looked down at his belly flat as a boy's. 'One fights a rearguard action against the battle of the bulge.'

'You live on the premises?'

'Of course, dear boy.'

'Alone?'

'Except for my assistant, Derek.'

'I'm here on police business about the girl who was murdered.'

'Murdered? What girl?' Jarvis paused with his cup halfway to his lips.

'Don't you read the newspapers or listen to the News?'

'Neither, dear boy, I find them too depressing.' He sipped his coffee with an eye on the superintendent. 'Who was she? Someone I know?'

Jarvis was adopting a pose, carefully choosing his line, he was a born actor and it was second nature to him to dramatize every situation. On the other hand, Wycliffe thought he detected a certain uneasiness.

'A girl called Christine Powell, I think she came here from time to time.'

Jarvis looked solemn, he put down his cup to emphasize that Wycliffe had his undivided attention. 'She did, dear boy. You are right. Young Morris brought her. He was infatuated, poor lad.'

'You didn't like her?'

Jarvis smiled as though caught out in a minor fault. 'Am I so transparent? The truth is, dear boy, she was a whore but our Paul did not know it, he is too inexperienced to read the signs. Why she got her claws in him I've no idea; but women are naturally cruel, don't you think?'

He did not expect an answer and went on, 'Paul has the makings of a painter and I am anxious that he should make the most of his talent.'

'You allow him to use your studio?'

'It's not a question of allowing him, I *persuaded* him to do so. For several years I have usually had one or two young painters under my wing. At the moment, Paul is the only one but probably the most talented I have ever had. You see, dear boy, I have no creative ability myself but I recognize it in others—'

'In what circumstances did he bring the girl here?'

Jarvis drank off the rest of his coffee and poured another. 'For you, dear boy? Sure? Paul leads a lonely life and he has come to regard this place as his second home, he spents most of his free time here. His mother is a widow and though he has never said as much I suspect that she is not easy to live with. Anyway, he met this girl at one of our Arts Society meetings and a week or two later he brought her here.'

'Why?'

Jarvis's eyes widened in exaggerated surprise. 'Why? To show her off, dear boy. He was proud of her. It was touching but not a little embarrassing.'

'Embarrassing?'

'Of course. Distressingly so. How does one feel when a friend proudly displays the gem of his collection and one already knows it to be a fake?'

'I see, difficult for you.'

'Very.' He broke off to look at Wycliffe with birdlike curiosity. 'You don't think he killed her?'

'Do you?'

Jarvis chose to take the question at its face value. 'It's possible. It's possible. Paul is a complex personality, the circumstances of his up-bringing – no father and a possessive mother, almost certainly his development was impeded. One might say that he is just reaching intellectual and spiritual maturity – coming into flower, so to speak.'

'And that makes him more likely to murder someone?' Wycliffe could scarcely restrain a smile.

Jarvis was piqued. 'You are teasing me, dear boy. But the answer to your question is probably yes. Disillusionment in adolescence is always dangerous and from many points of view Paul is an adolescent.'

'Was he here yesterday evening?'

'Yesterday? Yes, he was.' Jarvis fiddled with the silvery hair at his temples. 'He dropped in just as I was going out so I left him to it.'

'You left him here alone?'

'Of course, dear boy, he wanted to work.'

'How much time does he spend here in the run of a week?'

'Three or four evenings, usually.'

'Week-ends?'

'As a rule, yes.'

'What time did you go out?'

'Just after seven-thirty. There was a Russian film on at the Arts Society which I wanted to see.'

'And he was not here when you returned?'

'No, I was late, after eleven.'

'Was your assistant on the premises?'

'Derek? Probably, I don't think he went out.'

On the face of it Jarvis was answering his questions openly and with welcome objectivity yet Wycliffe felt sure that he was holding something back. Most people have secrets to hide, at least a sensitive area which they do their best to guard. A detective is conditioned to sniff out secrets as a pig hunts truffles, but he can waste a lot of time uncovering petty subterfuges and evasions which have nothing to do with his case. He must exercise judgement.

'Did you know that the girl was Sir George Powell's daughter?'

'The Docks Board chap? You surprise me, dear boy.' But he did not sound very surprised.

'I'd like a word with your assistant; Derek Robson, isn't it?'

'That's right, I'll see if I can find him.'

'Looking for me?' He had probably been listening outside the door but he came in without a trace of embarrassment. A man in his early thirties; slim, tall, too self-consciously elegant in his movements. He wore a black, turtle necked sweater and black slacks. 'I gather we have the law on the premises, I suppose it's about Christine?'

'So you've heard what happened.'

'On the radio this morning. I gather Andy said that he hadn't; it may be true but I sometimes suspect him of saying things just to be interesting.'

Jarvis smiled weakly.

'I understand that you were here all yesterday evening, Mr Robson?'

He nodded. 'I was.'

704

'And that you looked in on Paul Morris who was working in the studio?'

'That's right, I did.' There was a Welsh rhythm in his voice and the merest trace of an accent although he did not look Welsh. 'To save you the trouble of asking, that was at twenty minutes to eight, I'd left my pen in the studio and I went to collect it. Does all this mean that poor old Paul is for the hot seat? Could he have done it? I mean, he came to my room just before ten—'

Wyclifie was bland. 'I've no idea who committed the crime, Mr Robson. I'm collecting facts. What was Mr Morris doing when you went into the studio?'

'He was painting – working on that city centre thing.'

'As Christine Powell was a regular visitor here, I suppose you knew her reasonably well?'

A faint smile. 'Oh, you could say that – definitely.' He stooped to a cupboard where Jarvis kept a stock of crockery and came up with a cup and saucer. He poured himself coffee from the pot which must have been almost cold. 'Paul, Christine and me, you could say that we were all good friends. In his more sentimental moments Andy would call us his children.'

'Can you suggest any reason why somebody might want to kill Christine Powell?'

Robson twisted his face into a comical expression. 'If you'll excuse me saying so, that's a damn fool question about a girl who lived as she did. Some Freudian nut, I suppose.'

'So you knew about Stanley Street?'

'She made no secret of it to me.'

'And to Morris?'

'Ah, there you have a real question. I doubt if she was as frank with Paul. Paul had most of his illusions intact and, for some reason, she was anxious to keep it that way.'

'Where did Morris park his car last night?'

'He usually left it in the square.'

'Just one more question, as far as you know, did Christine Powell live in Stanley Street or did she have another place?'

'As far as I know she lived there, didn't she?'

Wycliffe thanked him and got up. Jarvis walked with him to the shop door. Outside Wycliffe stood, looking up at the frontage. 'A fine old building, you are fortunate.'

'Not really, I have it on a lease with only two years to run.'

Wycliffe started off along the quay and Jarvis called after him. 'Remember me to your charming wife. Tell her that I am expecting some more pictures and I shall want her to look them over . . .'

The sun was still shining and the harbour deserted. At the top of the cobbled alley where he had left his car was a different world. A stream of cars, lorries and red buses taking harassed people to places they did not really want to go. Wycliffe manoeuvred his car out of the parking space and joined them.

4

On his return to the office Wycliffe spent an hour going through reports. Among others, information about James Harkness, the surveyor. As yet no official enquiry had been started, a random accusation by a man like Salt is not to be taken too seriously and, apart from that, there was only one thing against him, he had the initials J.H., the initials which had appeared in the dead girl's engagement book for Wednesday evening. Was Harkness Daddy? It was certainly possible. According to the report Harkness was in his early fifties, head of a very successful firm of valuers, married but without children and gossip had it that his wife led him by the nose. 'A weedy little man,' Gill called him, 'and his wife would make a good stand-in for Dracula's mother-in-law. She stalks around with two bloody great hounds on a leash, "Down, Major. Heel, Boy."'

Well, Harkness would keep.

He was on the point of leaving for home when the switchboard rang to say they had succeeded in getting through to Jonathan Powell's London home. Wycliffe told them to connect him.

A self-consciously refined voice. 'I'm afraid Mr Powell is not at home.'

'When do you expect him back?'

A pause for thought. Evidently Powell discouraged discussion of his movements. 'Mr Powell is away on business.'

Wycliffe became brusque and official and after some hesitation he was given an address of an hotel in the city.

'You mean that he's *here*, staying at the Royal Clarence?'

This was an unexpected development. If Powell had been in the city when his sister was murdered it could be coincidence but it could be something else.

The Royal Clarence was probably the oldest and certainly the most discreet of the city's hotels. It had been the town house of a distinguished 18th-century admiral and though the interior had been remodelled and the building extended, its frontage of mellow red brick with beautifully proportioned sash-windows had not been touched. It stood in a secluded backwater near the boundary of the old city, on the edge of a small public park which had once been the garden of the house.

Wycliffe left his car in the cobbled court next to a lethal looking Aston Martin and entered the dimly lit foyer. An elderly uniformed porter looked at him over steel-rimmed spectacles and asked his business.

'Detective Chief Superintendent Wycliffe. Is Mr Powell in his room?'

'He went up twenty minutes ago, sir, I'll telephone.'

'Don't bother. What number?'

'One-o-three, sir, but—'

But Wycliffe was already half-way up the stairs. The door of one-o-three was slightly ajar and Wycliffe heard a woman's voice. 'We shall be late, Johnny, it's seven o'clock already.'

Wycliffe tapped at the door.

'Just a moment.'

A brief interval and the door was opened by a tall, dark girl wearing a blue silk quilted dressing-gown.

Wycliffe introduced himself and asked to speak to Powell.

'He's in his bath.'

'I'm not, I'm dressing. Who is it?'

The girl shrugged and smiled indulgently. 'You'd better come in. Cigarette? Drink?' She pointed to a table which carried a fair selection of drinks. Evidently Powell did not practise the self-denial his father had preached. And he had good taste in women. This girl, in her middle twenties, was an aristocrat of her sex, her features were good but her beauty lay as much in a serenity of expression and demeanour. Wycliffe was reminded of what he had read of the well trained *geisha*.

'Do sit down, he won't be long.'

Powell came through from the adjoining room wearing dress trousers and a shirt, but collarless. He was stocky, muscular and heavy featured. All his movements seemed to be unnecessarily vigorous as though he chafed under some barely tolerable restraint. No doubt some journalist had called him a human dynamo. Wycliffe

708

had checked his age, he was thirty-eight, but he looked older. His curly hair was streaked with grey and his eyebrows had lost their sleekness and were becoming bushy. He looked at Wycliffe. 'Did you say police?'

'Detective Chief Superintendent Wycliffe.'

'What's it about?'

Wycliffe glanced at the girl.

'You can say what you have to say.' His manner was blunt without being deliberately offensive. 'Whisky?'

'No, thank you.'

'I think I will.' He poured himself three fingers and splashed a thimbleful of soda.

'Have you seen the papers today, Mr Powell?'

'No, have I missed something?'

Wycliffe produced a print of the photograph which Smith had taken of the dead girl. 'Do you recognize this girl, Mr Powell?'

Powell's manner changed. He took the photograph and examined it under the central light. When he turned to Wycliffe his aggression had gone and he seemed worried, tentative. 'That's my sister. What has she been doing?'

'I'm afraid that I have bad news for you, she was found dead in her flat last night.'

Powell stared at the superintendent, his face expressionless. 'In what circumstances?'

Wycliffe told him. 'I'm afraid that you will have to come to the mortuary to make a formal identification.'

Powell looked down at his shirt and trousers. 'I'd better get out of this. Sonia!'

The girl had gone into the next room, now she came back. She looked at him and said, 'I heard, I'm very sorry, Johnny.'

'You'd better go on by yourself, take a taxi.'

She put a hand on his arm. 'No, I'd rather stay here.'

'As you like.' He finished his whisky in a single gulp and went back to the bedroom.

The girl looked at Wycliffe and seemed about to say something but changed her mind. Powell came back a few minutes later wearing a grey lounge suit with a fine stripe. 'We will go in my car and I will bring you back here.'

Wycliffe was firm. 'No, we will use mine.'

'Take your coat, Johnny, it is bitterly cold.'

Powell ignored her and stalked out leaving Wycliffe to follow. In the foyer he stopped at the desk and scribbled a number on a pad. 'Ring this number and apologize for Miss Adams and me.'

'Certainly, Mr Powell, at once.'

'We were going out,' he told Wycliffe as they passed through the swing doors.

They drove to the mortuary in silence and Powell went through the ordeal without apparent emotion.

'Are you prepared to make a firm identification?'

'Yes, I am.' His eyes wandered over the other drawers in the white room.

Back in his car Wycliffe said, 'I'm afraid I must trouble you to come to my headquarters to make a statement.'

'Tonight? Won't the morning do?'

'Tonight.'

Powell was silent for a while as they drove through rain swept streets. Then he said, 'I suppose you're a pretty good policeman?'

Wycliffe did not answer.

'What makes you do it? What do you get out of it?'

'What makes you buy and sell property?'

Powell laughed shortly. 'That's easy, the money.'

'As an end in itself?'

'No, partly for what it will buy – house, car, boats, good food, service – and freedom, I suppose. Though it's a queer kind of freedom, I work harder than most.'

'You said, partly.'

'So I did. Money means power, the chance to manipulate people and situations. I enjoy that, so did my father though he wouldn't admit it. He had to find a moral justification for self indulgence – not me.'

Most of the headquarters building was in darkness but lights burned on Wycliffe's floor. He parked his car and the two men went upstairs together. Powell looked round the chief super-intendent's office, taking everything in. 'They do you pretty well.'

Wycliffe was secretly annoyed with himself for resenting Powell's rather casual, almost patronizing attitude. And he lost the initiative. Powell settled himself in the customer's chair, offered his cigarettes to Wycliffe and said, 'You told me she was found dead in her flat – what flat?'

'In Stanley Street, off Prince's Street. Didn't you know?'

Powell looked vague and did not answer directly. 'I have had very little contact with Christine since our parents died.'

'You quarrelled?'

'No, there were differences of interest and outlook, also twelve years.'

'When did you last see her?' Wycliffe's manner was curt because Powell irritated him.

Powell ran a finger round the inside of his collar. 'God! It's hot in here.' He was stalling and it was obvious, but suddenly he reached a decision. 'I might as well come straight out with it, I saw her yesterday afternoon.'

'At the Stanley Street flat?'

He nodded.

'Then why did you imply just now that you didn't know of it?'

Powell made a gesture of impatience. 'Does it matter? I suppose I was feeling my way. In any case, I think she's got another place, another flat, perhaps.'

'Where?'

'I've no idea. That will be your business to find out.'

Wycliffe sat at his desk, his clasped hands resting on the blotter, he scarcely moved. Powell was restless; he seemed to be holding himself in, simmering and likely to come to the boil at any moment. Presumably he had suffered a shock but Wycliffe had the impression that he lived most of his life under stress. Release for such a man was usually physical, squash or sex or both.

'I'd better explain. I came down specially to see her. My company has plans for the redevelopment of an area in the city, an area which was scarcely touched by the war. Over the past few years we have been buying everything in that area as it comes on the market – not openly, of course, but through agents. Otherwise the price would have risen against us. We now own about seventy per cent of the properties and all but one of the really key premises. That one we were expecting to come on the market soon and we were ready with a realistic bid; but it was snapped up under our noses.'

'Tiresome for you.'

'And expensive. I suspected a leakage of information and I was right.' Powell took time off to inhale deeply on his cigarette. 'Four days ago I received a letter from my sister offering me the property at a greatly inflated price.'

'Diamond cuts diamond.'

Powell grinned. 'Or dog eats dog. She'd got more of the old man in her than I'd thought. But you can see the fix I was in. A leakage of information is an occupational hazard, but a leakage to my own sister . . .' He made an expressive gesture with the hand that held his cigarette. 'I don't say that my fellow directors would think that I had double-crossed them but they would certainly assume that I had been indiscreet.'

Wycliffe was listening with an expressionless face. He was wondering if Powell ever stood aside to take a good look at himself. 'So you tried to persuade your sister to back down?'

Powell grinned, wryly. 'I'm not in the habit of wasting my breath. No, I told her that my company would buy the property at valuation and that I would make up the difference out of my own pocket.' He shrugged. 'That way I would be off the hook and as far as the money was concerned, well, it would still be in the family.'

'What did she say?'

'She accepted, of course, she is a realist.'

'Your father left you most of his money?'

'All of it. I know what you are thinking and you may be right. Father had no time for Chris, she was a late arrival and a mistake and father took a poor view of mistakes, especially his own. But Chris got several thousand under her mother's will so she wasn't destitute.'

'You mentioned your belief that she had another place . . .'

Powell tapped ash into the tray on Wycliffe's desk. 'You know the flat in Stanley Street? Of course, you must do. Well, in conversation with Chris it became obvious that she was running quite a business in property and one look at Stanley Street makes it obvious that she wasn't doing it from there. I said as much and she laughed, "This is just a listening post, Johnny boy." '

'A listening post?'

'That's what she said.'

'And what do you suppose she meant?'

Powell stubbed out his cigarette. 'Your guess is as good as mine, but I imagine pillow talk from the right people could be profitable as well as interesting.'

He must have been twelve when his sister was born and they must have shared the same house through most of her childhood, yet he had just come from identifying her body and seemed unmoved.

'Which property did she buy against you?'

He hesitated then shrugged. 'The cat is out of the bag anyway now, I suppose. It was the Old Custom House which fronts on the harbour at the end of Bear Lane. Our scheme is to develop the whole of that area behind the harbour – a mixed development: shops, flats, a garage – nothing ostentatious, no tower blocks; keep the scale of the place.'

'I thought the whole of the harbour came under a preservation order?'

Powell shook his head. 'Only the houses on the wharf.'

Wycliffe stood up to close the interview. 'One more thing, Mr Powell; where were you yesterday evening?'

He was clearly surprised by the question. 'Am I under suspicion?'

Wycliffe's face was bland and blank. 'Well over half the murders investigated turn out to be the work of relatives or very close associates.'

'And I stand to gain, I suppose.' A reluctant grin. 'I spent the evening with friends.'

'With Miss—'

'Miss Adams, Sonia Adams, yes, she was with me.'

'Where?'

'At the Establishment Club, it's—'

'I know where it is. Thank you, Mr Powell.' He walked with Powell to the top of the stairs. 'Let me know when you intend to leave the Royal Clarence.'

Powell went down the stairs three at a time. Wycliffe looked after him with mixed feelings. He frequently asked himself what he was doing with his life, now a good deal more than half gone. It puzzled and worried him that for people like Powell the question either did not seem to arise or was not urgent. Perhaps he misjudged the man. He returned to his office vaguely depressed.

Now was as good a time as any to talk to Bates, the estate agent. Bates almost certainly knew a good deal more than he had told. Wycliffe asked the switchboard operator to get Bates at his home number and a few minutes later he was put through. A woman took the call, she sounded brusque and prepared to be aggressive.

'Mrs Bates?'

'I'm Mr Bates' housekeeper.'

Bates was not at home, she had no idea when he would be back. He had gone out just after lunch. Often he did not come home until very late.

Wycliffe put on his mackintosh and, careful ratepayer that he was, switched off his office lights. The headlamps of cars on the highway chased fantastic patterns across his walls. It was ten o'clock. He walked down an empty corridor, its peace disturbed by the clacking of a single typewriter inexpertly used.

His way home took him through the city centre within a couple of blocks of Middle Street. What Powell had said had made him wonder whether it might have been Christine Powell who came and went so mysteriously at the offices of the City Property Trust. According to the tobacconist it was a woman. He parked his car and walked through drizzling rain. Middle Street was narrow and poorly lit, none of the shops kept their window lights on after closing time but there was a fish and chip shop half-way along, a blaze of white light. Wycliffe was almost seduced by the smell which brought back vivid, bitter-sweet memories of the midland town where he had spent his green years as a policeman. Only a growing respect for the subtleties of his digestive processes restrained him.

He looked up at the window over the tobacconist's and in the light from the chip shop he could see that they were curtained with some sort of drab stuff. Without any particular reason he walked along the street until he came to a narrow alley which led to a service road between the backs of Middle Street and the goods reception areas of some of the big stores which fronted on the city centre. The Middle Street premises had retained their back gardens and he found the door of number twenty-four. Unlike the others it had been freshly painted and it opened easily on well oiled hinges. The garden area had been paved and a brick path led to the foot of an iron staircase to the first floor where one of the windows had been replaced by a glass panelled door. He climbed the stairs; the glass door was uncurtained and with the help of his pocket torch he could see into a small but modern kitchen with white units against green walls. He pressed the bell-push and heard a bell ringing somewhere in the flat but there was no other response. A black and white cat came padding up the stairs and rubbed round his legs, mewing plaintively. By leaning over the rail of the little balcony where he stood he could just see into the room next to the kitchen. The beam of his torch picked out an elegant looking bed-head and above it a large picture or mural. He went back down the stairs and through the garden, carefully closing the back door behind him.

He returned to his car and started for home but he was uneasy in his mind. There was good reason to connect the City Property Trust with the dead girl, especially since his conversation with Powell, but he needed something more definite before going for a search warrant. In the morning he would probably be able to get his information, discreetly, from whichever of the banks handled the Trust's accounts. Meantime . . . He was tempted to radio a message for a watch to be kept on the premises but there was little real justification for such a use of manpower. He compromised by giving instructions for the Panda patrols to keep an eye on the place.

A newspaper bill-board in a shop doorway caught his eye, its message streaked by rain, CITY MURDER – LATEST. He wondered what they had found to say, the news that the dead girl had been the daughter of the celebrated Sir George Powell had not been released in time for the final edition.

When he reached home Helen was curled up on the sofa reading a gardening book. The red velvet curtains of the big window were drawn and the record player dispensed a discreetly muted *Lohengrin*. Helen, coming late to the pleasures of music, was now addicted to Wagner and the early operas of Richard Strauss.

'You look all in, darling. Have you eaten? There's cold chicken and I can easily cook vegetables or make a salad.'

He said no, but changed his mind after a sherry.

Before going to bed he telephoned Bates' house but the estate agent had not returned. From the housekeeper's manner he suspected that his call had got her out of bed. He dropped the receiver then lifted it again and dialled his headquarters. 'I want the Bates house watched, discreetly. Bates is not there at the moment but I want to know when he returns.'

He fell asleep as soon as he got into bed and was not awakened by the bedside telephone when it rang. Helen leaned over him to answer it and when he took the receiver from her he was still fumbling his way out of a confused dream.

'Wycliffe.'

It was an apologetic duty officer. 'I wouldn't have called you, sir, but you did leave word for us to keep an eye on the premises in Middle Street—'

Wycliffe propped himself up, one elbow digging into his pillow. 'Well?'

'There's a fire, Panda three spotted it – smoke coming from between the roofing tiles. Now it seems that the whole upper floor is alight. The brigade is there and so is Sergeant Barber.'

'What time is it?'

'Just after four. Panda three reported it at 0340 hours, sir.' So they had thought twice about ringing him.

'I'll be along.'

He got out of bed and put on his dressing-gown. Helen looked at him sleepily. 'Are you going out?'

He was honest enough not to say, 'I must'. Barber would have handled it and he would have had a full report in the morning but it was not the same.

'Shall I make you some coffee?'

'I'll make my own, would you like a cup?'

'To be honest, I'd rather go back to sleep.'

He did not make any coffee, instead he took a nip of whisky which tasted like vinegar but took care of the hollowness inside.

The rain had stopped and a pale half-moon sailed above broken cloud. It had turned colder.

He drove to the end of Middle Street, parked his car and walked down. The street was cordoned off and he was challenged by a uniformed constable. He had not been in the city long enough to be known to the whole force.

Flames were coming out of the windows above the tobacconist's shop and licking back over the roof; smoke and sparks rose high into the sky. Hoses were directed on to the flames and on to adjoining roofs. Firemen were helping owners of neighbouring houses with the removal of their goods. Pusey, the chief fire officer, was there in faultless uniform, standing by one of the pumps. He nodded to Wycliffe, they had met at a recent civic bunfight.

'What brings you out?' Pusey shouted above the noise of the engines.

'Curiosity. Nobody inside?'

Pusey shook his head. He had a weighty, portentous manner. 'I hope not. It was well alight when our chaps got here. I've got two appliances in the access road between this and the city centre so we are attacking from both sides. I can't afford to take risks in a high density area like this.'

They were interrupted by the fat tobacconist. 'I could have got half my bloody stock out while you've been here arsing about.'

His shop, so far, seemed untouched by the fire but thousands of gallons of water must have streamed down through and it was running in a miniature river out of the front door.

'Don't be absurd! You couldn't possibly go in there. Apart from anything else there is a risk of total collapse.'

'Bullshit. Give you chaps a bit of braid and you think you're the bloody army.'

'A dissatisfied customer,' Wycliffe said as the tobacconist lumbered off.

'Surly oaf,' Pusey grumbled.

Although it was four o'clock in the morning the police had their hands full keeping spectators out of the street. Men and women wearing overcoats or mackintoshes over their night clothes, some with children, stood staring, their faces blank.

'They can't all live round here,' Wycliffe said.

Pusey was disdainful. 'It's a free show.'

Sergeant Barber came to report to Wycliffe. 'Sorry, sir, I've only just heard that you were here.'

The fire had taken hold in the roof timbers and tiles were splitting with gun-shot cracks showering fragments down into the street; but the great quantity of water being poured into the building was beginning to have its effect – there was less flame though more smoke and steam. It rose in a lurid column to spread out in a black pall held by the quiet air.

'You seem to be winning,' Wycliffe said.

'Appearances may be deceptive.' And as though to justify Pusey's words there was a sudden rending of timber as the floors of the upstairs front rooms collapsed into the shop below.

The glass in the shop windows seemed to explode outwards spraying the street with thousands of tinkling fragments. The fire, freshly supplied with air and an abundance of fuel leapt joyfully into renewed life. The heat at this lower level drove the firemen back and even the appliances had to be moved.

In the instant when the floors collapsed Wycliffe had glimpsed two firemen seen through a doorway into one of the upstairs back rooms. Pusey had seen them too and he was both concerned and frightened. Wycliffe suspected that he might go to pieces in a crisis. 'Bond should have pulled his men out before this. If anything had happened—'

Wycliffe followed him through the alley into the access road. The contrast was surprising. The back of number twenty-four was still intact, the roof, apparently, little damaged. They picked their way over a tangle of hoses to where Station Officer Bond was standing by his communications van, talking to the man on radio watch.

'Well, are all your men out?'

Bond turned to Pusey – 'All out, sir, no casualties.'

Pusey's relief was obvious. 'You ran it fine.'

'Barnes and Pearson were the last two out, sir. They say they saw a body.'

'A body?'

'Barnes is here, sir, he can tell you himself.'

A fireman, his face blackened with soot, his voice hoarse with smoke. 'We didn't see him until just before the floors went. There was a sort of alcove in the front room which we couldn't see into. As the joists went and the collapse began he came sliding out, what was left of him. Weird. And, of course, down he went.'

'A man or a woman?' Pusey demanded.

Barnes reflected. 'I couldn't say, sir. I know I said "he" but that was a manner of speaking. There was not much to go by. You know what they're like after a blaze like this.'

Pusey was looking at Wycliffe with hostility. 'You expected something of the sort.' His manner was an accusation.

'No.'

'You still haven't told me why you are here.'

Wycliffe smiled. 'Do I have to?'

Pusey, a rather dull if conscientious official, was worried. He waved his hand in the direction of the fire. 'You expected this?'

'Certainly not.'

But Pusey was not satisfied. 'The head of CID doesn't turn out for fires, even in the city centre.'

Wycliffe was half irritated, half amused. 'I was interested in the premises because of a possible link with a case, but I certainly did not expect that someone would try to burn it down.'

'You are saying that this is arson?'

Wycliffe controlled himself. 'Are you saying that it is not?'

Pusey hesitated then said, 'Come with me.' He led the way across the road to a red van parked in the loading bay of the supermarket. With a key he unlocked the back doors, opened them and shone his torch inside. There was a strong smell of paraffin. The beam of the torch was directed on to a plastic bucket which had a candle inside. The candle was stuck to a square piece of ply-wood and though its wick showed signs of having been lit it could not have burned for more than a few seconds.

Pusey explained. 'An old dodge for starting a fire long after the fire raiser has quit. The ply-wood floats on the surface of the paraffin and when the candle burns down to it – POOF!' He gestured dramatically. 'This one was found in the back bedroom by my men and the candle had probably blown out in the draught caused when the fire raiser opened the back door. I was not first on the scene here but the officer who came with the first appliance told me that there were two distinct centres of combustion in the front of the building, so I conclude that there must have been two more of these. In this one a pair of kitchen steps had been placed astride the bucket and draped with inflammable material. No doubt the others had been treated in a somewhat similar way.'

Wycliffe was recalling his visit of the previous evening at about ten-fifteen. The fire had been spotted by one of his Panda-car men about five hours later. How long did these candles take to burn? It seemed probable that two of the three candles had been burning then. And someone was in the flat, dead or alive.

The collapse of the floors had given no more than a temporary boost to the fire and by the time Wycliffe returned to the front of the premises there were only occasional spurts of flame from the ruins of the shop. The fire was as good as out but it would be hours before it would be possible to search for the body. After he had arranged with Sergeant Barber to set a watch he went to his car. The spectators had thinned and though it was still dark there were already people on their way to work and the streets were coming alive with traffic.

When he arrived at the Watch House he could just see the silvery grey waters of the estuary in a landscape which was still shadowy and mysterious. He left the car in the drive and entered the house by the back door as quietly as possible. In the kitchen he set the percolator going and while it was going through its repertoire he telephoned his headquarters.

'Bates? No, sir, Fowler is watching the place and he reported in half an hour ago.'

So Bates had not returned home during the night and the body of an unknown lay under the smouldering remains of the fire.

He poured his coffee and was perched on the edge of the kitchen table drinking it when Helen came downstairs in her dressing-gown, her eyes puffed with sleep. In twenty years he had never once managed to enter the house without waking her.

5

He had a bath and breakfast. Helen saw that he had what he wanted and kept out of the way. In the early stages of a case he was usually taciturn and, apparently, irritable. In fact, he merely withdrew into himself, cultivating a feeling of detachment and rather enjoying the experience. He listened to the nine o'clock news on the radio. The fact that the dead girl had been the daughter of Sir George Powell had headline rating. The editorial boys had dug up some biographical titbits about the man who, in his lifetime, had always been good for mordant, quotable off-the-cuffs about every aspect of manners and morals. Older journalists were inclined to linger over his memory with nostalgic relish. The fire in Middle Street was not mentioned. Why should it have been? Few people knew that a body lay under the debris, fewer still, perhaps only Wycliffe himself, that the pyrotechnics had any connection with the Stanley Street murder. Did he know that they had? He was sure of it anyway.

'I know it's a silly question but have you any idea when you are likely to be home?'

He shrugged without answering. He was watching a tug towing two mud barges through the narrows out to sea. The sea sparkled in the sunshine, the sky was blue with puffy white clouds and the slopes across the estuary were fresh green. The whole tiling looked rather like an extravagant water-colour, the choice of colours naïve, childish. One day, when they had time, he and Helen would cross over and explore that headland, follow the coast . . .

He went to the telephone and dialled his headquarters.

'Bates? Yes, sir. He turned up at his house just after eight. DC Fowler saw him go in. Yes, he was driving a Rover 2000 which he left in the street outside his house. Fowler has been relieved by young Dixon. He's been told to keep in the background.'

So it was not the estate agent's body which had been burned in the fire; but the estate agent had been out all night.

'One more thing, is Inspector Wills there?' Bob Wills was knowledgeable on the subjects of accountancy and business, he spoke the language and he had the advantage of looking like a bank manager.

'Bob? – When the banks open I want you to make the rounds until you find where the City Property Trust banked. The place has been burned down in very suspicious circumstances so you've plenty of grounds. I want to know who signed cheques for the Trust and anything else you can find out about them.'

He got out his car and drove towards the city. In the sunshine the city centre looked like a film set for a Western done in bricks and concrete, low buildings spaced along wide streets, about as cosy as the Gobi desert. He turned off to Middle Street.

Two fire pumps were still there but they were idle and firemen were sweeping muddy water into the gutters. The air was acrid with the smell of charred timber. The ruins of number twenty-four steamed and smoked behind a temporary screen which had been erected to shut out the over-curious. The street remained closed to vehicles but most of the shops were open and loitering pedestrians were being moved on by a constable. Wycliffe went through a wicket in the temporary fence. Sergeant Barber, who must have been almost dropping on his feet, was standing with one of Pusey's men, surveying the ruins.

'They reckon it will be afternoon before we can start, sir.'

Wycliffe looked up to the first floor. Amazingly, the back rooms seemed to be more or less intact. 'Is it safe to go up there?'

The fire officer shook his head. 'Not yet. We are going to shore it up so that it doesn't collapse on us while we clear this lot but what's left of the roof is sagging and it won't be exactly safe even then.'

Wycliffe walked round to the back by way of the alley. The fire appliances had gone from the access road and a huge, articulated lorry had backed into the supermarket loading bay. From a distance the back of number twenty-four looked much the same as it had done before the fire, but in closer view he could see that the door at the top of the steps had been smashed in and that the sashes were missing from the windows. A seagull had chosen that particular roof on which to perch, probably because of the warmth rising from the débris of the fire. It moved crabwise along the ridge, pausing now and then to preen itself or to peer down into the street.

Wycliffe was trying to fit the new developments into some sort of pattern, without much success. If Morris had killed the girl in a frenzy of disillusionment, then what about the fire and the body buried under the rubble? Christine Powell's death would probably have precipitated all sorts of crises among her associates and a prudent man among them might want to remove from the Middle Street flat anything which could damage or incriminate him. He might even set the place alight. Bates, Wycliffe thought, was such a man and Bates had been out all night; but the funeral pyre had not been for him.

The firemen were certain that the flat had been locked, back and front, when they arrived; and Christine Powell's keys were missing when her body was found. How had the man (or woman) in the flat died? Had he perished in the fire of his own contriving? It seemed unlikely that he could have been trapped just twelve feet above street level. Suicide was a possibility, perhaps he had killed himself after setting fire to the place. It was equally possible that the dead man had been murdered. Only the post-mortem could give his speculations any substance. Until then—

He was standing in the middle of the narrow access road looking up at the seagull on the roof. The driver of the big articulated lorry shouted at him, 'You thinking to settle there, mate?' He stepped aside and the great shuddering monster, belching diesel smoke, snaked past him. He walked back to his car and drove slowly through the city centre to his headquarters. His driving was always contemplative and, even on motorways, he rarely exceeded fifty.

Back in his office he telephoned Lloyd and Winter, the architects, and asked to speak to Paul Morris. He was put through to Mr Winter.

'Mr Morris is not in today. No, we have had no message. I assume that he is unwell. Chief Superintendent, may I say that I am a little concerned? This is the second time you have been in touch with the office concerning Mr Morris, naturally I am anxious. As a witness, yes, I quite understand. Yes, of course. No, I am afraid that he is not on the telephone at his home.'

Wycliffe gave instructions for a crime car to call at Morris's house

723

and to report back. Then he made a second telephone call, this time to Jarvis at the bookshop.

'I'm sorry to pester you, Mr Jarvis, but I would like to know who leased your premises to you?'

Jaryis was obviously surprised but he made no bones about answering. 'It's no secret. My agreement was with the bookmaker, Martin Salt. That was thirteen years ago, later he transferred his interest to his wife. After that I think he was in trouble with your people.'

'Would it surprise you to know that the reversion of your lease was purchased by Christine Powell shortly before her death?'

'You astonish me, dear boy.' And he sounded as though he meant it. 'Even so, I can't see what it could have to do with—'

'Probably nothing.'

As he put the receiver back on its rest the intercom buzzed. Inspector Wills had made his round of the banks. The City Property Trust banked with the London and Provincial. All transactions were in the name of Christine Powell. One more loose end garnered in. The manager had said, that to the best of his recollection, Miss Powell had never visited the bank.

A shaft of sunlight had crept round until it was falling across his desk and, for the first time, he noticed a vase of bronze chrysanthemums near the intercom and, as WPC Saxton came in to go through the post, he pointed to them, 'I doubt if the auditor will allow those as a legitimate expense.'

'He won't have to, sir, I brought them.'

He was so surprised he forgot to thank her.

'My father grows them, they are a late flowering variety he developed himself.'

Late flowering. Perhaps WPC Saxton would bloom one day.

Jimmy Gill came in looking, as usual, as though he had slept in his clothes. 'Good morning, sir.' He started the day thus, formally, then felt that he had staked his claim to freedom of speech for the next twenty-four hours. WPC Saxton, knowing that the post would have to wait, retreated and Gill watched her go. He looked her up and down as though he were mentally undressing her, as he was. 'She's not bad, really, pity her hormones don't work.' He sat down in the customer's chair and lit a cheroot. 'So you're having Bates watched?'

'It seemed a reasonable precaution. We don't know where he spent last night.'

'We could ask him.'

'Give him time and he might want to tell us.'

Gill tried a new approach. 'Young Dixon who is keeping obo there reported a few minutes ago over his car radio. He says Bates has been trying to get someone on the telephone for the past hour.'

'How does he know?'

'The main room downstairs runs the full length of the house with a window at each end and Dixon can see in. Every few minutes Bates picks up the telephone, dials, listens for a while then drops it again.'

'I hope Dixon isn't being too clever.'

He brought Gill up to date. When he heard that it was Salt who had leased the Custom House to Jarvis, Gill was intrigued. 'I'll flay that bastard until I get something.' But he admitted that he doubted whether Salt had killed the girl. 'Burning the place down in Middle Street would be more in his line.'

They were interrupted by the telephone. PC Boyd in a crime car had reported over his car radio on his visit to the Morris home.

'Boyd says that Morris did not come home last night.'

'What does his mother say?'

'According to Boyd she's a near nutcase. She seems to have no idea where he is but she's convinced that he's staying away just to upset her.'

'When did she last see him?'

'Yesterday morning when he went to work.'

Wycliffe remembered the graphic words of the young fireman – 'he just came sliding out, what was left of him – weird. Of course, down he went.'

'I want his movements traced from the time he left home yesterday morning. Let me know if you need extra help. Try to get a photograph without upsetting his mother, we may need to circulate it.'

Gill was inclined to give a good deal of weight to Morris's disappearance. 'You must admit that there could be a case against Morris. You didn't see the boy, uptight and jumpy as a doe rabbit on heat. He never expected any girl to give him a second look then a real dolly gives him the come-on and he doesn't know what hit him or where. Sir Galahad and the pro'.' Gill's gestures had poetry in them even if his words did not. 'For a few weeks it's Stardust and Danny Boy all the way then he comes out of his trance long enough to realize that his holy grail has a few chips out of it. In other words the dolly does and says a few things that aren't in the script and he's worried.' Gill's face wrinkled in sympathy. 'If at that time some busybody passed him the dirt from Stanley Street, all done up in a plain wrapper, then, Bingo! the cork would come out.'

Gill stopped to relight his cheroot which had gone out and Wycliffe watched, mesmerized by the flow of words. 'We've no evidence that he knew anything about Stanley Street until you told him.'

Gill puffed on his cheroot until it was drawing again. 'And no evidence that he didn't.'

'In any case, what about the fire?'

'Suicide.' Gill was rarely at a loss to provide an impromptu explanation of anything. Wycliffe usually discouraged him for, as he said, Gill's ideas contained enough of the truth to confuse the issue.

'You may be right, but we shall know better when they get the body out, what's left of it.' He changed the subject. 'Anything fresh from you?'

'We've picked up another of the girl's customers. A chap called Purvis – Councillor Richard Purvis, he's managing director of Rootes Purvis Constructions. They've got their offices in that bloody great cube of concrete in the city centre.'

'How did you get on to him?'

'I took a chance and had a friendly word with Harkness. He's the chap who likes to be done up in leather straps so I just asked him how he managed about the buckles. You should have seen him. He went green. He's Daddy all right; he admits to visiting the flat every Wednesday evening.'

'What about last Wednesday?'

'He says the chick called him at his office and put him off. He's scared stiff that his wife is going to get wind of his adventures and he's willing to do the dirt on anybody. Purvis put him on to the girl in the first place.'

'Do you believe him when he says that he was not at the flat on Wednesday evening?'

Gill shrugged. 'He hasn't got the guts to step on a worm.'

'What about Purvis?'

Gill gestured broadly. 'I had a word. A different proposition altogether. He doesn't scare. He's already threatening to complain to his friend, Mr Bellings. Can't have snotty nosed coppers flat footing into his private affairs.'

'What sort of chap is he?'

'He started as a builder's labourer and he's proud of it – says he's still got dirt under his fingernails to prove it. You wouldn't notice, I'd say his backside fitted the boss's chair very well.'

'No Mrs Purvis?'

Gill's hands sketched something small and fragile. 'A little grey cooing dove. They live in a bloody great house in Conniston Gardens, near where the Powells used to live. She married Purvis when he had his foot on the bottom rung and, by all accounts, she would have been happier if he'd stayed there.'

Wycliffe sighed. 'Everywhere you turn in this case you come across property – buying, selling, surveying, building.'

Gill flicked ash on the carpet. 'I reckon our Chris was working a nice little racket; but, somehow, I can't believe that was why she got clobbered.'

Wycliffe cut short another exposition and Gill got up to go. 'I think I'll have another go at Salt, even if he isn't directly mixed up in all this there's not much goes on under the counter that he doesn't know about.'

Wycliffe got out a bulky file and settled down to work. He was drawing up a report for the chief constable on the re-organization of the whole CID in the police area. Re-organization, as well as being addictive, attracts favourable notice in the press and in committees. No administrator worth his salt will allow the dust to settle on one totally unnecessary and time-consuming general post before starting another. Wycliffe had set himself the difficult task of proposing seemingly revolutionary changes which would, in fact, alter very little. This he hoped to achieve by the simple expedient of changing the names of offices and procedures without changing the work of the people concerned. He worked for half an hour before boredom got the better of him. His office oppressed him, he felt deadened by it, muted. Even if he stamped his foot the carpet absorbed the sound. Double glazing shut out the real world including the friendly and capricious draughts which had been such a feature of his old office. He lit his pipe and sat back in his chair.

Morris.

Whatever one thought of Gill's flights of fancy there could be no doubt that Morris had become a central figure in the case. Either it was his body which lay under the ruins in Middle Street or . . . Or what? He had given instructions for the boy's movements to be traced but he needed to know more about him. By all accounts his mother lived in a grey world on the fringe of reality and Morris had built his life round his work and round his painting; he seemed to spend most of his free time at the Old Custom House.

Wycliffe pressed a button on his intercom. 'Miss Saxton? I'm going out.' He knew that the poor girl had been waiting patiently for him to call her in with the post. Why did it give him a perverse satisfaction to frustrate her?

He drove to the same spot at the top of the cobbled alley and parked on a meter. The harbour and the waterfront still basked in sunshine, an enclave of peace surrounded and all but engulfed by the sprawling bustling city. The car park in front of the Old Custom House was empty. Why had he not parked there? He would have had difficulty in explaining. Perhaps he wanted to make his contribution to keeping the place apart. It was a place where one should walk.

The bookshop had not changed either, the same notice hung inside the glass of the door, Back Shortly. Last time Jarvis had been lunching at a restaurant in Bear Street. It was now a quarter to twelve, perhaps he started early and finished late.

The houses in Bear Street were early 19th-century town cottages, a row each side, their front doors opening off the street A few of them had been converted into shops but most were still lived in. The restaurant was immediately behind the Old Custom House. There was a shop window through which he could see old fashioned marble-topped tables, a counter with an *espresso* machine and, behind the counter, an auburn haired girl. On an impulse he went in, the door bell pinged.

'Could I have a black coffee, please?'

A cheerful girl, freckled, with a large, generous mouth and a broad, flattish nose. She was refilling plastic salt pots.

'Quiet, isn't it?'

'It always is until we start serving lunches at one o'clock, then it's busy enough for an hour or so.' She was Irish.

He sat at a table near the counter and she brought him his coffee. A man in a chef's apron, red faced and stocky, stood for a moment in a doorway at the back of the shop then withdrew.

'I was looking for Mr Jarvis from the bookshop.'

'He doesn't come in until one.'

'The shop is shut.'

She grinned. 'He always goes for a walk before lunch if the weather is fine, his constitutional, he calls it.'

'What about Mr Robson?'

'What about him?'

'Does he have his lunch here?'

'Sometimes, it depends how he feels.' She went back to replenishing the salt pots.

'Two bachelors living alone, I don't suppose they do a lot of cooking.'

'None, as far as I know. We don't open in the evening but Dad cooks for them when he cooks for us and I take it in.'

'Take it in?'

'Through the back.' She indicated the back premises with a vague gesture. 'Our back opens into their yard.' She continued for a while, filling her salt pots. 'You're asking a lot of questions.'

'Do you know Paul Morris?'

'I know him, he spends a lot of time next door; what about him?' She wrinkled her forehead in a frown. 'Are you from the police? Is it about the girl who was murdered?'

He had really captured her attention now. 'You knew her?'

'Of course I knew her, she used to come next door. I didn't know what she was then, but it wouldn't have been difficult to guess.'

He had finished his coffee, now he paid for it and left. She came with him to the door. 'You don't think Paul Morris did it, do you?'

'I may come back to talk to you again.' Despite the frank, open manner he had the uncomfortable impression that she was acting a part for his benefit. The Irish are born actors. The trouble is, if you are a policeman long enough you come to suspect innocence itself.

Jarvis was back, standing in his shop doorway, presumably waiting for one o'clock. 'My dear boy. Another visit?' He did not sound pleased.

'I want to talk to Mr Robson.'

'To Derek? I'm afraid he's not here. He's a young man with a life of his own and business is slack just now. It seemed a good chance for him to have a few days off.'

'Where has he gone?'

Jarvis looked pained by the lack of good manners. 'I didn't ask him, dear boy. I imagine that he wanted to spend Christmas with friends, but I have no idea where.'

'I would like to see the studio where Morris paints if you have no objection.'

'Objection? Why should I object?' But it was obvious that he was not happy.

A wide passage lit by a large skylight led off the shop and it was here that Jarvis displayed paintings by favoured members of the Arts Society. They showed a range of talent from laboured picture-postcard scenes to self-confident landscapes and portraits. There were two doors off the corridor, both open. One led into the kitchen, tall and narrow and gloomy, the other into a sitting-room full of dusty furniture which was, obviously, scarcely ever used. But a french window opened on to a courtyard dominated by a magnificent cedar. At the end of the passage, stairs led up to the first floor and the smells of glue and mouldering paper began to blend with the odour of oil-paint and turpentine. Neither the stairs nor the first floor passage had any floor covering and the planks were worn unevenly. Narrower, twisting stairs continued up to the attics.

'Derek has his rooms on this floor, would you like to see?'

Wycliffe wondered why he was being given the chance.

In contrast to the ground floor the passage was brilliantly lit by the sun flooding through windows along its entire length. They were evidently in the part of the building which was built out on the pillars; the tall windows looked down on the empty square and, beyond, to the harbour which seemed incredibly blue in the winter sunshine.

'Bedroom.' Jarvis opened a door briefly, disclosing a small room with a single bed, neat and tidy but otherwise unremarkable. Was Jarvis using the occasion to show that his relationship with his assistant was respectable? 'And this is his sitting-room.'

A large, comfortable-looking room with a monster settee or divan and a couple of reasonable looking armchairs upholstered in pale

brown leather. The window overlooked the courtyard and the cedar
tree. Over the mantelpiece there was a framed, obvious self-portrait
of Christine Powell, a head and shoulders. It seemed to Wycliffe
cruelly satirical. Painted in different shades of green on an olive-
green background, the face emerged, lime green with near white
highlights. The eyes had been cleverly elongated and slanted to make
them sinister yet they were still the eyes of the photograph Smith had
taken and they seemed to follow Wycliffe disturbingly as he moved
about the room.

Jarvis saw his interest. 'That's the sort of girl she was.'

'She gave the painting to Robson?'

'She painted it for him.'

Wycliffe realized that he was being told something. Having failed
to get rid of him Jarvis was giving him information.

'She came pretty often with Paul, then, latterly, she came on her
own.'

'To see Robson?'

Jarvis smiled. 'Not to see me, dear boy. She was a trollop and Paul
is an innocent. Derek isn't above taking advantage of a situation like
that; in fact, I sometimes think he has a cruel streak in his nature.'

'Does Morris know?'

Jarvis pursed his thin lips. 'I doubt if Derek advertised the fact, but
it would have been quite in character for the girl to tell him herself.'

'I assume that Morris and Robson were not on good terms?'

'On the contrary, dear boy, they are the best of friends. Derek has
charm and sophistication which Paul sadly lacks and I am quite sure
that the boy admires and envies him.'

Wycliffe walked over to the window and stood looking down into
the courtyard. Beyond the cedar someone had parked a red E-type
and beyond that there was a black van with lettering on the side
which he could not read. 'Is that your car?'

'Derek's.'

'There must be money in the book business.'

Jarvis answered stiffly. 'We do well enough.'

'What exactly does Robson do, Mr Jarvis?'

'He's our buyer, that's his main job.'

'Buyer?'

Jarvis was straightening the cushions on the settee. 'We sell books
of antiquarian interest and importance, these books have to be

bought, dear boy. You can't just put in an order for ten gross assorted.'

'How do you set about it?'

'We specialize in foreign books, mainly French. Three or four times a year Derek takes the van across on the ferry and makes the rounds of the French dealers. We have a connection, built up over the years. Before Derek came I did the buying myself.'

'So Derek buys the books and brings them over in the van?'

'Yes.' Jarvis looked puzzled, wondering what the chief superintendent was getting at. Wycliffe did not know himself. 'Derek also travels in this country, buying from dealers and attending sales.'

'I suppose you sell mainly to collectors?'

'Collectors, museums, libraries, universities – we have every sort of customer.'

Wycliffe took out his pipe. 'May I?'

Jarvis made an expansive gesture. 'Liberty Hall, dear boy.'

Wycliffe was undergoing an experience which he had known many times before. In the course of an investigation, after a seemingly endless series of interrogations, interviews and reports, when his ideas were confused and contradictory, his mind would suddenly clear and the salient facts would stand out in sharp relief as though a lens had suddenly brought them into proper focus. At this stage he would not necessarily distinguish any pattern in the facts but he would, from then on, be able to classify and relate them so that a pattern would eventually emerge. Oddly enough this usually happened to him when he was talking, as now, at random – 'fishing'. And he had just learned at least one new fact; the association between the dead girl and Derek Robson could have made two people intensely, perhaps dangerously jealous. Andrew Jarvis who almost certainly had more than a professional interest in his assistant, and Paul Morris who seemed to have discovered the agonies of calf love at twenty-eight.

Wycliffe's eyes kept coming back to the portrait over the mantelpiece. Will the real Christine Powell, please stand up? Experience had taught him that things were never that simple. Even the most uncomplicated human beings do not fit into pigeon holes, and Christine Powell had been tantalizingly complex. Whore, business woman, probable blackmailer, Sunday painter. She might have been all these and more and it would probably be wrong to think of one label as being truer than another. If the painting were evidence, her estimate of herself was anything but flattering.

'I would like to see the studio.'

'Of course.'

The stairs were narrow, twisted and steep. The passage at the top was lit only by a small and dirty skylight. There were three attics, two small and one much larger. One of the small rooms was Jarvis's bindery. There was a bench with the tools of the trade and a number of old books in different stages of restoration from sewn sections to the all but finished article with its leather binding and gilded spine. Jarvis displayed his work with pride. 'It's a hobby more than anything else, I enjoy working with my hands.'

The second of the small rooms was a book store with slatted shelves round the walls and the books laid out in batches. 'Our last consignment,' Jarvis said, 'we haven't had a chance to sort them yet.'

The studio was large, lit by two dormer windows and, like the other attics, it was open to the roof trusses. There were shelves occupying the whole of both end walls and these were laden with large books and portfolios. An old fashioned slow-combustion stove stood in the centre of the room and its iron smoke pipe disappeared through the roof. A red mica window glowed pleasantly and waves of gentle warmth radiated in all directions.

'I try to keep the room warm and well ventilated to avoid mildew, dear boy.' He waved his hand in the direction of the bookshelves. 'I collect prints and illustrated books, some of them are quite valuable.'

There was a large easel near one of the windows, its back to Wycliffe, and a table with a palette, a jar of brushes and tubes of oil-paint.

'That's where he works.'

Wycliffe was pleased with the room, it was just such a room as he would have liked himself, but what would he do in it? As always when entering a room for the first time he was drawn to the window. Through the branches of the cedar which topped the building he could look down into the backyards of the little houses in Bear Street where women were hanging out their washing, taking advantage of the sun.

'Do you mind if I look round?'

Jarvis shrugged with unassumed indifference. 'Help yourself, dear boy.'

If he had stopped to think Wycliffe might have asked himself why he was showing such an interest in the place and he would have had difficulty in finding an answer. He had what amounted to a super-stition about coincidences and there were certainly coincidences connected with the Old Custom House. It was a key property in Powell's development scheme and his sister had held him to ransom for it; it was also the place where Paul Morris had spent most of his free time, some of it with the dead girl. Finally it was where he had claimed to be when she was murdered.

Wycliffe wandered round the room with apparent aimlessness. He looked at everything. The large portfolios were labelled with the names of famous wood engravers and print makers, including a few Japanese. The books were arranged according to the illustrator and not the author. In another section there were books on the tech-niques of wood engraving and of print making. At last Wycliffe reached the easel and stood looking at the picture which, pre-sumably, Morris had worked at on the night of the murder. It seemed complete, a large painting, over four feet high. Jarvis joined him.

'What do you think of that?'

The painting was a view of the city centre as it might appear from a low flying helicopter. The effect was remarkable, partly because the picture lacked any consistent perspective; each building seemed to have been drawn from a unique point of view but its architecture, though simplified, had not been distorted. Through the apposition of several such images the picture achieved an effect of controlled craziness. And the colours helped, flat and innocent of gradation, they presented a faceted whole which had a restrained gaiety.

'What do you think of it?' Jarvis repeated.

Wycliffe, who found it impossible to lie about such things, said, 'I don't know.'

Jarvis was clearly disappointed. 'But, my dear boy, anyone could see with half an eye that there is talent there, quite exceptional talent.'

Wycliffe was affable. 'I expect you are right, but to me there was more obvious talent in the self-portrait downstairs.'

But Jarvis scouted the idea. 'Exhibitionism, dear boy. All of a piece with the rest of her. I won't deny that she had a certain technique but . . .' He went over to a stack of canvases placed against the wall and selected one which he placed on the easel. It was a head and shoulders portrait of a young man. 'That's another of hers, a portrait of Paul, and bloody cruel it is. The silly boy brought it here to show me.'

Wycliffe had not met Paul Morris but he could believe that the portrait was less than charitable. The lantern jaw, the prominent adam's apple, the solemn, dark eyes exaggerated by the lenses of powerful spectacles, the uncertain expression of the thin lips and the black hair fitting like a priest's skull-cap. Wycliffe had the impression of brittle strength.

'There's more in that picture of her than of him and that's not what painting is about. This is pure self-indulgence . . .' Jarvis was on a hobby horse and Wycliffe had no desire to listen to a dissertation on the integrity of art. He continued to prowl while Jarvis talked.

There were two drawers in the little painting table but they held nothing of interest. Charcoal sticks, pencils, rubbers, a couple of palette knives and a sketch book with nothing in it. What had he hoped or expected to find?

There were two long grey linen coats hanging on a hook near the easel, one was covered with paint stains. 'Do these belong to Morris?'

'The paint stained one, the other is mine.'

Wycliffe lifted the jacket down and felt in the pockets. Jarvis watched him, frowning. 'You really do suspect the boy?'

Wycliffe was laying out the contents of the pockets on the table. A handkerchief, a pencil, a 'Bic', a soda-mint and a screwed up paper tissue. From the other pocket he removed a piece of white chalk and three envelopes. The envelopes were all addressed to Morris, one at his office, the others at the Old Custom House.

'He has post sent here?'

'Sometimes. He buys his paints and canvas from a London firm and that comes here.'

The envelope addressed to Morris's office was empty but it had evidently been used as a memo for there was a list of colours scribbled on the back. The second envelope contained an invoice for canvas but it was the contents of the third envelope which seemed to put a new complexion on the whole case. Morris's name and the Old

Custom House address had been printed neatly on the envelope and inside, written in the same manner, was a short note unsigned:

YOUR GIRL FRIEND IS A WHORE. IF YOU DON'T
BELIEVE ME YOU CAN FIND OUT FOR YOURSELF ANY
EVENING 9 STANLEY STREET. BOTTOM FLAT.

Wycliffe held the note for Jarvis to read. 'You must see whatever comes here for Morris?'

Jarvis fiddled with the silver curls at his temples. 'Not always, sometimes Derek takes in the post.'

'This seems to have come by hand, you don't remember this particular envelope?'

'No, dear boy, I don't.'

'What do you do with post which comes for him?'

'One of us would put it on his table here.'

'So that this might have been waiting for him when he arrived here on Wednesday evening?'

'It's quite possible, dear boy.' Jarvis seemed upset. 'I suppose you see this as giving him a stronger motive?'

'May I use your telephone?'

'What? Of course, dear boy. Downstairs in my office.'

'I'm taking this jacket and the contents, I'll give you a receipt.'

He telephoned his headquarters from Jarvis's office and gave instructions for Paul Morris's description to be circulated. '. . . to be brought in for questioning in connection with the murder of Christine Powell.'

Jarvis was standing at his elbow, he seemed to find it difficult to believe what was happening. The day before, when asked if he thought Morris might be guilty, he had said, 'It's possible'. But that was talk, this was real. 'I can't believe that the boy . . .'

6

Number three Lavington Place is one of a terrace of Regency houses with ornate, cast-iron verandahs on the first floor. The terrace had been given the Civic Trust treatment with icing pink stucco and white windows and doors. Even if Salt had no taste himself he had allowed the experts to have their way. Gill was received in the drawing-room where the Civic Trust had not penetrated and the Salts had gone a little off the rails with a huge, chromium plated gas fire, 'antique dogs', and wall-to-wall carpeting which created spots before the eyes. Mrs Salt, a little brown mouse of a woman, smiled and looked glad to see him.

'You're lucky to catch us in, Mr Gill, we've just come back from doing our Christmas shopping, haven't we, Martin?'

'Whisky, Mr Gill? Or is it too early?' Salt went across to a miniature bar. 'Would you rather Mavis stayed or went, it's all the same to us, isn't it, Mavis?'

Mrs Salt agreed.

Gill was smooth. 'I suppose as it's a question of ownership of property, it's Mrs Salt I should talk to.' He grinned like a cannibal presented with a tender missionary. 'But I've no doubt that you are in her confidence.'

Mrs Salt got up and went but she cast a slightly nervous glance at her husband as she turned to shut the door.

'This is good whisky.'

'It should be, the price I pay for it.'

Gill was making himself comfortable in an armchair upholstered in cherry coloured velvet. 'I'll stop arsing about and come to the point. It seems more than likely that Christine Powell died intestate so that her little lot should go to big brother Jonathan.' He chuckled. 'I may as well admit that I rather fancy the idea of him coming into a thriving little business in prostitution. But it means, if only for the look of the thing, he'll fall over backwards to be helpful to us. His lawyers will dissect the estate and offer each little bit for inspection under the microscope before getting shot of it.' Gill leered at Salt. 'You get my point?'

Salt stared at the glass in his hand. 'I don't doubt you're right, Mr Gill, but I can't see what it's got to do with me.'

'No? Everything will come out – everything, including the building in Bear Street which Powell will inherit from his sister. Don't tell me you haven't had a finger in that pie.'

Salt took time to consider. His moustache glistened with droplets of whisky which he had been too preoccupied to wipe off. 'There's really no secret about that, Mr Gill. The place belonged to me – to Mavis that is, long before I had that little spot of bother with the law. I bought it off a chap called Fitzy Simmonds who conned me into it. I was young then and Fitzy could have flogged Buck House to the Duke. I had some crazy idea of doing a conversion job – flats – down-town pads for young executives, that sort of crap. It was only after, I realized that young executives don't have any money. In any case you couldn't convert that barracks into a mausoleum.' He smiled disarmingly. 'I've learnt a lot since them days, Mr Gill.'

Gill was unimpressed. 'Too much. Now cut the biography and get on with it.'

'Well, to cut a long story short, I rented the place on a lease to Andrew Jarvis and that lease falls in in two years.'

'Where did the Powell girl come in?' Gill put down his glass, took a packet of cheroots from his pocket and lit one.

Salt thought while a gilded clock, let into a mirror over the mantelpiece, ticked fifteen seconds away. Then he ran his fingers through his thin sandy hair. 'I hope this is all off the record, Mr Gill?'

'I don't see anybody with a notebook, do you?'

'Not that I've anything to hide. As I told you, I used to go to Chris for—'

Gill raised an enormous hand. 'So it's Chris now, is it? Yesterday you thought her name was Lily and you were bowled over by the news that she was George Powell's daughter.'

Salt spread his hands expansively. 'Well, Mr Gill, that's understandable, isn't it? I mean, when a man's got form, like me, it don't pay to know too much too soon.'

'Your trouble is more likely to be knowing too much too late, Salt.'

'Well, as I was saying, I went to Chris for a bit off the ration. She was quite a girl and not only for what you might think, she had a head on her, a good business head.'

'You should know.'

'I do know, Mr Gill. We saw eye to eye about a lot of things. Anyway, one evening about six months ago she asked me if I wanted to sell the Old Custom House. I said I would consider a proposition and nothing more was said then. A day or two later she spoke to me on the blower and asked me how long Jarvis's lease had to run. I told her two years and then she made me an offer – a very good offer. After a bit of haggling for form's sake we made a deal.'

'You knew why she wanted the place?'

Salt grinned, almost with affection. 'She didn't give much away but I had a shrewd suspicion.'

'And you mean to say you parted with the place without trying to screw Powell yourself?'

Salt looked smug. 'I reckon I owed her, Mr Gill.'

'Since when has a thing like that bothered you? What did she have on you, Salt?'

'Nothing, Mr Gill! Nothing, as God's my witness!'

Gill relaxed, glancing round the room and studying the furniture. 'Somebody did you a good turn last night, Salt.'

'Me? That don't happen very often, Mr Gill, what was it?'

'Somebody set alight to twenty-four Middle Street, the office of the City Property Trust.'

Salt shook his head. 'I heard about it this morning but it don't affect me, Mr Gill. I remember Mr Wycliffe asked me about the Trust.'

'He did. Now I'm asking you and if I were you I'd do some remembering. You were hand-in-glove with the dead girl, you sold her the reversion of the lease on the Old Custom House, so don't tell me it comes as a surprise to you that she *was* the City Property Trust.'

Salt poured himself another whisky without asking Gill to join him. 'I'd like to know why you're pushing me so hard, Mr Gill.'

'Because you're a crook and because you served about a fifth of the time you should have served if there was any justice in this world. Now, what about this City Property Trust?'

Salt sipped his whisky before replying. 'Well, it's true she did some of her business in the name of this Trust—'

'Did you ever go to Middle Street?'

'A couple of times, three or four maybe.'

'Last night?'

'I swear—'

'Don't bother. She lived in the Middle Street flat, didn't she?'

'She seemed to spend a fair bit of time there – most nights, I think.'

'So if she had the dirt on somebody that's where she would keep it?'

Salt shook his head vigorously. 'I don't know anything about that, Mr Gill. All I know, she had nothing on me.'

Gill lit another of his cheroots. 'Going back to the property you sold her, was the sale completed?'

'Three weeks ago.'

'So what happens now?'

Salt frowned. 'Search me, Mr Gill. All I can say is, brotherly love apart, things seem to have turned out pretty well for Powell.' There was a moment of silence then he added, hopefully, 'Satisfied, Mr Gill?'

'No, but I'll look into it.'

Salt was peevish. 'What I've told you is straight up and you can see for yourself I had no reason to do her in. Anyway, I was soft on her.'

'Did she ever tell you anything about herself? Anything which might suggest somebody was putting the frighteners on her?'

Salt looked serious. 'No, she never talked much about herself anyway. It was only after we started doing a bit of business together that I found out who she was.'

'You've no ideas, then?'

'No, Mr Gill, I wish I had. Of course, she wasn't exactly what you'd call a good insurance risk, the way she went on.'

Gill was half inclined to believe him. 'One more question, this Jarvis chap, what's his racket?'

'Has he got one?'

'I'm asking.'

Salt shook his head. 'As far as I know he buys and sells books.'

740

Gill stood up. 'That's all for the moment, but be around, I'm sure we shall need you.'

At the door Gill stopped to look at a garish oil-painting of a nude girl seen through a gauze veil. 'Pretty.'

'That's a genuine oil-painting, Mr Gill, none of your reproduction rubbish. I paid good money for that and I'll give it you if I don't lose out over all this.'

Mrs Salt came out to see him off, treating him as though he had been a welcome guest 'A happy Christmas, Mr Gill.'

As he drove back to headquarters Gill thought things over. The odds were that Salt had told him the truth. Only one nagging doubt remained. It was conceivable that Salt had seen, or thought he had seen, a chance to get his hands in the Powell till. And if that had somehow gone wrong . . .

Wycliffe did not feel at home anywhere until he had established a routine. When a case took him to a new area for a while he would try to give his days some sort of pattern, even if it amounted to no more than having a drink in the same bar at about the same time or buying a paper at the same shop. The recent transfer of his headquarters had wiped the slate clean and he was in the process of sketching a new design. His lunch routine had been settled from the first day. By chance he had found Teague's eating house and from the moment he had entered the place he knew that he was destined to eat a great many meals there.

Teague's was wedged between a supermarket and a bank, its frontage was small but it ran back, little more than a passage, for fifty yards or more. There were two lines of old fashioned booths with a matted walk between. Each booth accommodated two people and there was a hook on which to hang hats and coats. The table was covered with a white damask cloth and there was a plated cruet stand with glass bottles. It was not cheap and there was a set meal each day, but the quality of the food and its preparation ensured that there were few empty booths.

Wycliffe took Gill to lunch there.

'Cosy.'

The set meal was soup or tomato juice followed by roast beef with a choice of vegetables and topped off by a soufflé.

'Drink?'

'Beer.'

'They do a very good lager here which I haven't come across anywhere else.'

It came, pale gold with a delicate lacy foam and nicely chilled. Gill took a gulp and said nothing.

'Like it?'

Gill shrugged. 'Give me a draught bitter any day.'

The main course arrived.

Wycliffe told Gill of the anonymous note he had found in the pocket of Morris's painting coat. 'As you so elegantly put it, "the dirt from Stanley Street in a plain wrapper".'

Gill smiled. 'I told you.'

Wycliffe helped himself to horseradish. 'I've put out a call for Morris and I've sent the note to forensic.' He spoke almost defensively. 'We shall look silly if it turns out to be his body in the fire.'

Gill looked at him curiously. 'I don't see why; it wouldn't mean that he hadn't killed the girl.' Gill was a master of the double negative. He patted his lips with his table napkin. 'I know what's bothering you – even if Morris did kill the girl, why would he want to start that particular bonfire? It would have been more logical, more understandable, at least, if it had been the place in Stanley Street. Obliterate the scene of her degradation and all that crap. Sow it with salt. I agree, but there are plenty of others who might feel relieved to hear that the Middle Street flat had gone up in smoke taking their dirty little secrets with it. Any one of them might have decided to go in for a spot of arson.'

'And the body?'

'One thing at a time. We shall know more when Franks is able to take a look.' An onlooker might have suspected that Gill was trying to be reassuring. He changed the subject: across the gangway a waitress was bending over one of the tables making out a bill and showing a neat little behind sheathed in black tights.

'I've often wondered why brunettes have more shapely backsides than blondes . . .'

They had decided against the soufflé and ordered coffee. The regulars seemed much at home; after their meal they lingered to do *The Times* or the *Telegraph* crossword, some even played chess with travellers' chess sets, resuming a game where it had been broken off the day before. Wycliffe looked round with satisfaction.

After lunch he did not go back to his office. As Gill had seen, he was restless and ill-at-ease because he could not formulate in his mind any coherent view of the case. He was floundering. He could not believe that Christine Powell had been murdered because of her shady deals in property, he did not believe either that she had died because she was blackmailing her customers. There was no proof that she had blackmailed anybody but, even if she had, the victims of blackmail rarely turn to murder. Had Morris killed the girl in a frenzy of disillusionment and anger? As Gill had said, it was plausible but the sequel, if sequel it proved to be, was not. The fire in Middle Street did not fit.

He was walking through the city centre, jostled by men and girls returning to offices and shops after the lunchtime break. A surprising number of them were carrying bottles for office parties after work. A news-vendor's bill caught his eye. It had two captions:

POWELL MURDER
BROTHER AT POLICE H.Q.

and

BODY IN CITY BLAZE
FOUL PLAY SUSPECTED.

Evidently the press had not seen any connection but later editions would almost certainly carry the news that the City Property Trust and Christine Powell were one and the same. The scope for journalistic speculation would spoil Mr Bellings's Christmas.

He was walking up Middle Street where a fire tender was still parked. The smell of charred timber was overpowering. A section of the temporary screen had been removed and a lorry had backed over the pavement to begin the removal of the rubbish. A constable, there to ward off sightseers, saluted. He had nothing to do, for the dust and the urgency of Christmas shopping were keeping people away.

Wycliffe was surprised at the transformation which had been achieved in a short time. The back part of the building had been shored up with a network of steel tubes and there was a ladder up to the first floor. The mass of rubble had been reduced and, unless the two firemen had been seeing visions, the uncovering of the body must be imminent. Five or six men, wearing heat-proof gloves and boots, were working under the joint supervision of Sergeant Scales, and the young fire officer Wycliffe had seen in the morning. Sergeant Smith, the photographer, was standing apart, morose as usual, his hands thrust deep into the pockets of his overcoat. He acknowledged Wycliffe with a barely perceptible nod.

'The rubble is being taken to a tip, sir, but the rest – everything that looks like anything – is being taken to an empty garage at headquarters.'

Wycliffe chatted for a moment then asked if it was safe to go up to the first floor. The fire officer was cautious. 'It's not safe, sir, the roof is very dodgy and the joists in the passage are not much more than charcoal, but if you're careful . . .'

Wycliffe picked his way over the rubble and climbed the ladder. He could have gone round the back and up the iron staircase but that would have brought him to the kitchen and he would still have had to make the difficult traverse to the bedroom where he wanted to go.

There had been a passage running parallel with the street, between the front and back rooms. The wall of this passage nearest the street had largely disintegrated, pulverized by the heat, but the further wall was still intact though stripped of plaster and badly cracked.

'Look out for those joists, sir,' the nervous young fireman called to him. The floor of the passage had gone and the joists were partially carbonized but it was not too difficult to step across into the doorway of the room in which he had glimpsed a bed when he had reconnoitred the previous evening. The room was a remarkable sight, he was reminded of the freak effects he had seen during the blitz. The back wall of the house seemed undisturbed except where the window had been demolished by the firemen. Even the blue, brocade curtains were still hanging. To the left of the window there was a large wardrobe, ivory white with gilt fittings, to the right, the pale blue textured wallpaper seemed undamaged.

The bed, against the wall at right angles to the window, had been pushed aside but the bed-head lamp and the picture above were still in place. The bed and the blue carpet were sodden with water and soot had been trodden in, but the only fire damage was on the wall against the passage where the plaster had crumbled, exposing the brickwork, and the carpet was scorched in a broad band. Apart from the bed and the wardrobe there was a dressing-table with a cracked mirror which hung drunkenly in its clips.

He was intrigued by the picture over the bed which was, obviously, another Paul Morris. This time his unique vision had been directed at the docks. Interest was created by soaring cranes, gantries and masts, squat warehouses and intersecting railway lines, each royally indifferent to its neighbour in the matter of perspective but contriving, none the less to achieve a unity which defied analysis.

So, whatever she thought of Morris, she had thought enough of his work to hang a picture over her bed.

He opened the wardrobe, expecting it to be crammed with clothes but there were relatively few. A couple of winter coats, half-a-dozen dresses, some blouses and three or four skirts, a couple of pairs of slacks and an anorak. There were two handbags on a shelf and a rack of shoes including a pair of heavy walking shoes. He knew little about women's clothes but he thought that these might be described as 'quiet', almost dowdy. The unlikely adjective 'demure' occurred to him – for the wardrobe of a tart.

He went through the handbags and through the pockets of all the garments which had pockets but his haul was unimpressive. One item only seemed to link her with Morris, a ticket for a concert by the Bournemouth Symphony Orchestra in the Central Hall. Clipped to it was a slip of paper on which was written in faultless italic script, 'I hope you can use this. All my love, P.' The ticket had been for the previous evening.

The dressing-table, which incorporated a set of drawers, told him little. She had been restrained in her use of make-up and her underclothes were plain and unglamorous like those he had seen in the Stanley Street flat. It was difficult to imagine the girl who had worn them using her body to trap men. There remained the little bed-side unit which consisted of a small cupboard with a couple of shelves and a drawer. The cupboard was empty except for a box of paper tissues while the drawer contained two books and a bottle of sleeping tablets. One of the books, well thumbed, was a translation of the *Journal of Marie Bashkirtseff* and the other was a paper-backed edition of Anthony Storr's *Human Aggression*.

There was a noise of someone scrambling over the joists and Sergeant Scales came in. The best dressed man in the squad, he was examining his overcoat to see if he had picked up any soot on the way.

'They've uncovered the body, sir. Not enough to move it yet but they won't be long. At the moment Sergeant Smith is taking photographs.'

'Have you told Franks?'

'I've sent a message through the duty room, sir, and I've asked them to send the van.'

Scales was looking round with interest. 'She seems to have had good taste. From the bits we've found and this, it looks as though she had a nice flat.' Scales was an authority on flats; his wife was a university lecturer and the two of them lived a Box-and-Cox life in a very elegant flat on the outskirts of the city. 'I like the picture . . .'

For the next forty minutes Wycliffe stood watching while the men worked to free the body and at each stage of the process Sergeant Smith took photographs. By a fortunate chance two beams had fallen across one another and helped to keep the weight of rubble clear of the body which, otherwise, must have been crushed. But the beams were several feet long so that removing them was a slow business. After a little while Franks arrived and they stood together in silence, watching. In another hour it would be dark but the work of clearing the site would continue under flood lights already rigged from neighbouring buildings.

It is notoriously difficult to predict what fire will do to a human body and how long it will take to do it. A great deal depends on the clothing, on the flammability of neighbouring objects and, of course, on the temperature attained. In this case the body was a blackened mass with calcined bone showing over part of the skull and at the knees; vestiges of shoes remained on the feet.

Franks looked at the body with distaste. 'I hate burnings, I always have.'

When they had got a sheet under the body and started to lift it Wycliffe left. He was driven back to headquarters in a Panda car. It was almost dark, the street lamps were on and the shop windows blazed with light. The air was clear and crisp so that everything seemed miraculously sharp and clean. People were out window shopping. Multi-coloured neon stars were suspended at intervals over the main shopping streets and snatches of carols churned out by loudspeakers reached him as his driver snaked through the traffic. 'Peace on earth and mercy mild. God and sinners reconciled.' But not yet.

WPC Saxton was hammering away at her typewriter. The bronze chrysanthemums were looking as fresh as ever.

After he had glanced at the additions to his 'In' tray he walked down the corridor to a room at the back of the building where Sergeant Bourne, surrounded by paper and filing cabinets, looked after collation and did whatever other jobs came his way. Bourne was twenty-six, a graduate, sharp of feature and of mind. Up and coming. He had a thick, dark moustache very slightly turned down at the ends, modern without being trendy.

Wycliffe walked to the window and stood looking out. Bourne's room overlooked the headquarters car park, now lit up. Beyond, unseen in the darkness, trees and fields stretched away to the horizon needing only outline planning permission to turn them into a developer's paradise.

'Can I help you, sir?'

Wycliffe glanced round the room which seemed bare and bright, a place to work. 'Nice room you've got here.'

'Sir?'

'I said you've got a nice room.'

Bourne was cautious. 'Quite nice, sir.'

'No carpet.' Wycliffe stamped his foot on the linoleum.

Bourne frowned. 'No, no carpet, sir.' He was worried, you never knew when you were being tested, or why.

'You are a graduate in English?'

Bourne brightened. 'Yes, sir. Had I known that I would enter the police I would have studied Law.'

'Are you on good terms with the City Librarian?'

'I know him, sir.'

'Do you also know Andrew Jarvis at the Old Custom House?'

'The bookseller — yes, indeed, sir.'

'Good! I've got a job for you. I want you to find out what you can about Jarvis's standing as a dealer. I understand that he specializes in foreign antiquarian books, mainly French. What sort of reputation does he have and what sort of business does he do?'

Bourne would have spoken but Wycliffe stopped him. 'At the same time, see what you can find out about Jarvis as a man. He seems to be a collector on his own account – prints and illustrated books. How well is he known? What does he spend?'

'I doubt if the City Librarian will—'

'So do I, but he should be able to put you on to the right people. Use your initiative but be discreet.'

Bourne glanced at the papers on his table. 'I've got one or two things—'

'They can wait.'

'If you say so, sir.'

'And Bourne—'

'Sir?' The brown eyes were anxious to please but cautious.

'Never mind.' If chief constables had batons there would be one in Bourne's haversack. What need had he also of good advice?

Back in his office Wycliffe dictated a memo to CRO asking for any information they might have on Andrew Jarvis and Derek Robson.

7

Wycliffe felt heavy and depressed. The body he had seen, charred and unrecognizable, had almost certainly been alive twenty-four hours earlier. On his way home the previous night he had reconnoitred the Middle Street premises and felt uneasy, but he had postponed any investigation until the following day. Too late. His reason had been sound, he needed firmer evidence of the dead girl's connection with the premises; but it was possible that his caution had cost a man his life and it was certain that evidence which might have been obtained from the flat had now been destroyed.

A casual tap on the door and Jimmy Gill walked in.

'I thought you might like to be brought up to date on Bates, the estate agent.' Gill took his usual seat and lit the inevitable cheroot. 'Bates left home just after eleven this morning and went to his office where he stayed until one o'clock. Young Dixon was parked outside trying to look like a lamp post. About half past twelve Bates was joined by a chap called Ellis, a lawyer of Morley, Prisk and Ellis. I've made some enquiries and it seems that, despite the brass plate, Ellis is the sole member of the firm; he's been doing Bates's conveyancing for years and he's been responsible for the legal side of all the girl's deals which involved Bates. Bates and Ellis went out to lunch at the Plume of Feathers and, after lunch, our intrepid young detective followed them here.'

'Here?'

'Here. They asked to speak to you but settled for me. Bates obviously had the wind up and might have done something silly but Ellis had his head screwed on. "My client has done nothing illegal." He is a little chap, wizened like a monkey.' Gill's hand and features brought the words to startling life. 'He agrees that Bates and the girl operated as a team with the girl providing the brains. Bates has been buying and selling property for years but only since he got together with the girl about two years ago has he been making real money. Ellis admits that the girl had inside information on a number of deals, but he claims that there was no reason to think that it had been obtained illegally and, even if it had been, neither he nor his client had had any part in it.'

Gill sighed. 'A smooth bastard, twisted as a corkscrew, but I've no reason to think he was telling outright lies.'

'Did he tell you where his client spent last night?'

'Believe it or not, Bates has a fancy woman. She lives in a flat in Belle Vue. I found that much out before this pair of clowns arrived and I've seen the lady – all mouth and tit as you might expect; but it isn't every girl who will share her bed with a box of Kleenex.'

'He was with her all night?'

'That's his story and she confirms it.'

Gill had also had a report from the detective who had been given the job of tracing Morris's movements. Morris had left home the previous morning to go to work and had arrived there, as usual, just before nine o'clock. At the offices of Lloyd and Winter the staff had been questioned and Jane Williams, the plump blonde in the reception desk had tried to be helpful.

'He wasn't himself, I could see that the minute he came through that door. Usually he was so polite, not like some of them. Always a pleasant "Good morning, Miss Williams" and a remark about the weather. He's a nice young man – not married and he supports his widowed mother . . .'

'How was he different yesterday morning?'

'Different? Oh, yes, well, he looked like a ghost and he just walked through here and up the stairs without a word. When I took him his coffee round eleven he was just sitting there—' She frowned. 'What's it all about? I mean, he's missing now, isn't he?'

'Do you operate the switchboard?'

'Except in my lunchtime when another girl does it.'

'Can you remember if Mr Morris received any phone calls yesterday?'

A brief silence while she thought. 'I was trying to remember; I know I put through one call but there could have been more. Most of the calls go to one of the senior partners. I know he had one call before lunch because he was a long time answering. Mr Winter was waiting for me to get a call for him and I was a bit flustered. Then,

750

about the middle of the afternoon, he made a call, he asked me for a line. I offered to get the number for him but he said, "No, it's personal".'

'You didn't happen to overhear?'

'I don't listen in!'

Mr Lloyd, one of the senior partners, had not seen Morris all that day but Mr Winter had talked to him about a certain specification and thought that he was sickening for something. 'It seemed to me that he was coming down with 'flu. There's a lot of it about and I wasn't a bit surprised when he didn't turn up this morning.'

Morris had left the office at about six and vanished.

'At least we should be able to trace his car,' Wycliffe said. 'Keep them at it, Jimmy.'

When Gill had gone Wycliffe was about to settle down to read the accumulated reports when the telephone rang. 'Wycliffe.'

'Switchboard, sir. We have a woman on the line who insists on speaking to you personally. She says she has information about Christine Powell.'

'Put her through.' Some kink probably. All detectives should be anonymous, once your name appears in the press you become a sitting duck.

'Wycliffe.'

A girlish voice, creamy with the local brogue. She was matter-of-fact. 'I want to speak to you, I think I should have done it before but it's best not to know much when your chaps ask questions. All the same, I don't want him to get away with it.'

'Who?'

'The man who killed her, of course.'

'Who are you?'

Hesitation. 'I'm not coming down to the nick.'

That explained it. Somebody who had had more than one brush with the law – and a girl at that. 'Do you live in Stanley Street?'

Another pause. 'Make up your mind.'

'Yes.'

'Number fifteen?'

'How did you know?'

'Upper or lower flat?'

'Lower.'

One of the girls from the other house in Stanley Street which had belonged to Christine Powell. 'I'll come over.'

'Now?'

'I'll be there in twenty minutes.'

In Prince's Street he was held up behind a convoy of lorries making for the docks but Stanley Street was deserted. Number fifteen, like number nine, had had a face lift. The orange front door was opened before he could ring the bell.

'Are you Lesley Birch?' He had looked her up in the reports before leaving the office.

'That's me, you'd best come in.'

She was plump, running to fat but still pretty. Fair hair, blue eyes and a pink and white complexion. She wore a loose fitting blue frock cut low so that it showed her heavy, sagging breasts. She gave the impression of slovenly opulence. The sort of girl men tell their troubles to. Mammary psychology. Her room too, was frayed and tatty with lots of grubby chintz. Wycliffe was not immune to the seductive appeal of controlled sluttishness. An invitation to unbutton, morally as well as physically.

He sat opposite her in one of the chintz covered armchairs. She was entirely relaxed, flopped in her chair. 'I knew her, you see, she was a friend . . .' She said it defensively as though he might doubt her word. 'She used to drop in two or three times a week when she wanted to talk to somebody.'

'You knew her real name?'

'Oh, yes. Not at first but she told me a long time ago.'

'And did you know that she owned this house?'

She nodded. 'She wanted to cut my rent but I wouldn't have that. I've never sponged on my friends.' She shifted in her chair to reach a packet of cigarettes from a side table. 'Smoke?'

Wycliffe took his pipe from his pocket and felt for matches. She lit a cigarette and inhaled deeply, trickling the smoke out through nostrils and lips. She must be allowed to tell her story in her own way.

'She had a very unhappy childhood.' The baby-blue eyes were serious and confiding. 'Money isn't everything. It was her father, he was very rich. When she told me first I didn't believe her but afterwards I could tell she was speaking the truth. In any case you could see she was different—'

'Different?'

'Well, educated for one thing.

'It started with her asking me about my family, what they were like and all that . . . Her father was a right bastard, he had a taste for under-age girls and once or twice they all got into a hell of a twist to hush it up.

'The boy, her brother, was everything and she was just an after-thought. Her father tried to bring her up very strict and when it didn't work he'd take a stick to her and tell her he was doing it for her own good. I've seen some of that sort. Her mother couldn't do anything with him and she used to console herself with quiet nips from the gin bottle.' She smiled. 'A happy home.'

Wycliffe was puffing away at his pipe, the light from the single electric bulb was yellow and filtered through a plastic shade with a pink fringe.

'I think she felt that she was getting her own back on men, the way she went on. But I used to tell her she was just biting her nose to spite her face—'

'She told you something which you think might have to do with her death?'

She looked at him, her eyes disarmingly frank. 'Well, I don't know, do I?' She tapped ash from her cigarette. 'First going off I persuaded myself it couldn't be anything to do with her being killed but when I thought it over I couldn't be sure and I wouldn't like to think the bastard got away with it because of me.'

'What did she tell you?'

She looked at him with sudden curiosity. 'Are you really a chief super?'

'Yes, why?'

She shrugged. 'I dunno. Anyway, to get back to Chris, she had a boy friend, a regular.'

'She told you?' Wycliffe felt bound to offer encouragement.

She wriggled in her chair to settle her body more comfortably. 'She told me one day when she was feeling a bit down. I said, "A girl like you ought to have a man of your own, get married and have kids." She said, "I've got a man" and I said, "Won't he marry you?" She didn't say anything for a bit then she said, "I think he'd marry me all right but I'm not sure that's what I want."' She looked at Wycliffe in a confiding way, sure that she wouldn't have to explain everything. 'Of course you can imagine what I thought – some old man with one foot in the grave looking for a last kick. But it wasn't like that, this chap was young.'

'She told you about him?'

'Not at first. It was funny really, she was shy about him – her! Then one day she said, "I've never really wanted it before, not until I met him. He's got under my skin, the bastard." A bit later she said, "The funny thing is, he's vicious with it. I never thought I would take that again from any man." She kept coming back to it at different times when she came in. You know what it's like when a girl really falls for a man, she's just got to talk. Once she showed me bruises and I said, "You want to be careful of that sort, my girl." But I mean, she ought to know if anybody did.'

'You've never seen this man?'

'Never.'

'And she never mentioned his name?'

'No, I'd have remembered.'

'Did she tell you about Paul Morris?'

'The Monk?' She laughed. 'That's what she used to call him. She said he was still wet behind the ears. You're not thinking that he—?'

'It's not impossible.'

She looked at him as though he had disappointed her. 'You must be joking!' She reached over and crushed out her cigarette. 'She told me about him and you can take it from me, that boy hardly knows what he's got it for.'

'Did she ever mention going to the Old Custom House with Morris?'

She chuckled, a rich sound of pure enjoyment. 'The bookshop. That was always good for a laugh. Old Jarvis who runs it is a queer and she used to imitate him. She could be a real comic when she felt like it.'

'Apart from that did she tell you anything else about her visits there?'

She stared, frowning, trying to remember. 'No, I don't think so. I know she said she never knew there was so much money in second-hand books.'

Wycliffe produced a photostat of the note he had found in the pocket of Morris's painting coat.

'YOUR GIRL FRIEND IS A WHORE . . .'

'Did you write that?'

'You don't think that I—'

'No, I don't think so. Have you any idea who might?'

She shook her head.

'Brenda?'

'Brenda wouldn't hurt a fly!'

They sat without speaking for a while. A goods train rattled past at the end of the road, not twenty yards away, and the house vibrated. It seemed to go on interminably. When the sound finally died away the ticking of the alarm clock on the mantelpiece was suddenly intrusive.

'Can you remember anything more about the man?'

Another silence. 'I've been trying to think. He had a car,' she added, abruptly. 'I forget how it came up but she said he had a car.'

Wycliffe was content to sit in the chintz-covered armchair which had a fusty smell, just smoking and waiting.

'She said several times "He treats me like dirt and I don't know why I stick it." But then she would say, "Of course we're two of a kind". Once she said, "He likes to live dangerously and I suppose I do too".'

'What did she mean by that? How did she live dangerously?'

It was a silly question and she was contemptuous. 'If you know anything about the game you've no need to ask that.'

'She seems to have confided in you more than in anyone else.'

She nodded. 'I'd have rung up before but I didn't want to do the dirt on anybody – not if I was wrong. I mean, after all, he was the only man who ever gave her what she wanted.' She glanced up at the clock. 'I suppose you wouldn't like a cup of something?'

'I must get back. You can't think of anything else?'

'Nothing you don't know already.'

'I suppose he never came to her flat down the road?'

'What do you think?'

'You'll be asked a lot more questions and you may have to make a statement.'

'I'm not coming to the nick.'

'You won't have to, I'll send a WPC.'

'Shall I be in trouble for not having spoken up before?'

'Why should you be? You don't actually *know* anything.'

She came to the door with him and stood on the step, hugging herself against the cold. A woman passing by gave him an odd look as he closed the gate behind him.

He decided to look in on Franks, the pathologist. The pathology laboratories comprised a couple of communicating huts in the grounds of the city's general hospital, a great white wedding-cake of a building with hundreds of square windows. It was visiting time and people were crossing the car park carrying little parcels and bags and bunches of flowers. Wycliffe had difficulty in finding a place for his car but managed to slot it in where a notice said 'Medical Staff Only'.

Franks was in his office dictating notes on the case to his secretary. Franks and his secretaries were notorious – this one was blonde with shoulder length hair and the serene expression of a nun but, by all accounts, she was following the same path as her predecessors. What it was that appealed to these young women about the roly-poly doctor had escaped Wycliffe's notice. Unless it was the romance of the macabre.

Franks went on dictating, waving Wycliffe to a chair. He was full of more or less harmless affectations and his white office was one of them, even the desk, the chairs and the filing cabinets were white. His rows of books, which happened to include many with red or blue bindings, provided a startling splash of colour. The astringent odour of formalin penetrated through from the laboratory adding to the unreal atmosphere of the place. Why did it suggest to Wycliffe the absurd notion of an administrative office in Heaven?

Franks finished his dictation, dismissed his secretary and turned to Wycliffe almost in the same breath. 'Subject male, probably between twenty-five and thirty years old. Height about one hundred and eighty-five centimetres – you see, we've gone metric – but it means that he was tall.

'As to the cause of death, he was shot.' He took a small specimen tube from his desk drawer and placed it on the top. In the tube a bullet rested on a pad of cotton wool. 'Don't ask me, I've never seen one like it before.'

'Shot!' Wycliffe had been taken by surprise.

'As I removed the bullet from his skull that seems a reasonable deduction. The bullet penetrated the palatine process of the right superior maxillary bone, ricocheted in the skull vault and ended by splintering but not penetrating the left parietal near the coronal suture.'

'In other words he was shot through the roof of the mouth, that usually means suicide in my book.'

'Perhaps you read the wrong book. The fact that the bullet failed to penetrate the roof of the skull made me look further and I found definite signs that it had grazed the inside of the mandible on the right side which would be consistent with the gun having been held under the chin, an uncommon method for suicide, you'll agree.'

'Or for murder.'

Franks nodded. 'As you say.'

'So?'

Franks rearranged his crystal pen tray and his white pig-skin blotter. 'I wouldn't care to have to back this in court but I *think* the bullet was fired from lower down, about the level of the chap's navel. The ribs are in a very bad state but I'm of the opinion that the bullet scored two or three of them.'

Wycliffe was impressed. He lit his pipe and waited until it was drawing before speaking. 'A struggle, in the course of which a shot was fired.'

'A fatal shot,' Franks added. 'I would go along with that. If the bullet was fired low down and followed a path which penetrated clothing and scored several ribs before entering under the chin it might account for the fact that the residual momentum was insufficient for a final penetration of the skull table.'

'The question now is, whose gun?'

Franks smiled smugly. 'Outside my province. Have you any idea who the chap is?'

'Your description fits with a young chap called Morris, an architect, who's been missing since the evening of the fire. We shall have to try to get some sort of identification so anything from you will be welcome – dentition, old fractures, skeletal abnormalities – anything.'

Franks shook his head. 'Nothing, except that he seems to have had a perfect set of teeth which is rare these days. I say, seems, because there is one odd feature, the top four incisors and the left canine are missing—'

'That hardly sounds like a perfect set of teeth.'

'No, but to the best of my belief, he lost those five teeth with

757

considerable damage to the maxillary bones at about the time he died, perhaps a little before, perhaps after.'

'Not due to the bullet?'

'No, the path of the bullet is clearly defined and did not traverse the actual tooth row at any point.'

'Damage caused by the fall when the floors collapsed?'

Franks shrugged. 'It's possible, but it seems odd; the lower jaw, for example, is undamaged save by the fire.'

'A blow before death, perhaps in the struggle?'

Franks looked pompous. 'I would favour that possibility though I would not be prepared to testify to it in court. The blow would have needed to be particularly vicious. Obviously there would have been no point in administering such a blow after death.'

'So you think it was a blow?'

'Entirely between ourselves, I do.'

Wycliffe was thoughtful. 'Nothing else you can tell me?'

Franks was fiddling with the tube containing the bullet, rolling it between his finger and thumb. He loved to dramatize his rôle. 'There could be. I have not yet completed the autopsy. I was able to retrieve small amounts of undamaged tissue and I may be able to give you a grouping – not necessarily based on the blood, but equally valid.'

Wycliffe stood up. 'Good. I'll leave you to it.'

When he left the hospital visitors were leaving too and he was caught up in a long line of slow-moving traffic. A Salvation Army band playing carols near the hospital gate reminded him again that tomorrow would be Christmas Eve. One more year when he had given Helen no help with the preparations. When he got home tonight the twins would be there, they had been staying with friends since the end of the university term. He felt depressed, deprived was a better word, a little resentful that his job seemed to cut him off. It wasn't only the long hours, he was emotionally cut off. For days or even weeks together when he was on a big case he seemed to be living other people's lives, to be immersed in their problems, prying into their secrets. Helen had said that a doctor must feel the same, but a doctor is involved in many cases at the same time and detachment is easier.

The traffic sorted itself out at the roundabout where six roads met.

Two killings and arson for good measure.

Somebody had to warn Mrs Morris that it was probably her son's body which lay on Dr Franks's dissecting table. He pulled into a parking space to consult a map of the city. Spencer Gardens where the Morrises lived was regarded as a respectable neighbourhood, the people who lived there got monthly pay cheques instead of weekly pay packets and their kids did not commonly smash up telephone boxes or nick cigarettes. The houses were semi-detached and between each pair there were two garages set back from the road. People who lived in Spencer Gardens read the *Daily Mail* or even the *Telegraph*. Most of the sitting-room windows had the curtains drawn back and displayed Christmas trees elaborately decorated and lit.

Wycliffe drove slowly along the street trying to make out the numbers. Number forty-two, when he came to it, seemed tatty compared with the rest. By the light of the street lamp he could see that the brickwork had not been pointed and that paint was flaking off the gate and the front door. He had to ring three times before a light went on in the hall, he heard movement then the door was opened by a tall, gaunt woman wearing a woollen two-piece which hung on her as if on a hanger.

He showed his warrant card. 'Detective Chief Superintendent Wycliffe.'

She made no response and continued to block the doorway.

'May I come in?'

She stood aside and switched on the light in a room to the left of the front door. It was a sitting-room and it looked as though it had been neither used nor cleaned in years. A copper pot containing dried grasses and the dusty, faded feathers of some exotic bird stood in the centre of a large round table made of a yellow wood. A low-powered bulb covered by a pink satin shade hung low over the table so that the rest of the room was barely visible. She did not invite him to sit down.

'I've come about your son, Paul Morris.'

'He's not here.'

'I know.'

'His home is not good enough for him, he just uses it like an hotel.' They were stock phrases that she used whenever the occasion arose.

'Perhaps we could sit down?'

'If you like.' But she remained standing as though waiting for him to go.

'It is quite possible that your son has been involved in a serious accident.'

She seemed not to have heard him, she was arranging the ornamental grasses.

'It's a question of identification . . . I'm very much afraid that it may be your son.'

'An accident, you say?'

'It's possible that your son has been killed.'

'No.' She spoke without emphasis but with certainty while she smoothed the table runner with the edge of her palm to remove creases.

'You don't know where your son is?'

'I never know where he is. If you ask me, he's just gone off like his father. Like father like son, that's what I always say. He'll come back if it suits him.' She gave a dry, sarcastic little laugh. 'His father went when Paul was fourteen. You didn't know that, did you?'

'I know that you are a widow, Mrs Morris.'

'Nothing of the kind. I'm no widow, not as far as I know. His father just walked out – vanished. One morning after breakfast – through that door. He went out and never came back.' She massaged her threadbare sleeves with bony hands. The room was bitterly cold.

'I didn't let it interfere with Paul's chances, he's an architect – qualified.' She threw out the statement like a challenge. 'I gave him every chance in spite of his father. It was a struggle and you'd think he'd be grateful, but I never see him, off every morning after he's bolted down his breakfast, evenings, week-ends.'

Wycliffe felt that he must keep running to stay where he was. 'In case it is your son I'd like to ask you one or two questions.'

She smiled in a way that made him feel uncomfortable. 'It isn't him, I tell you.' At last she sat down, on the edge of one of the upright chairs. 'His father was an accountant, he worked with a firm called Martin, Spender and Jukes. After he'd gone I found he'd given them a month's notice. He wouldn't let the firm down.'

'Did your son ever break a limb?'

The question focused her attention for a moment. 'Paul? No, never.'

'Did he ever have any sort of operation?'

760

'No, nothing like that. He was a perfect child; perfect, physically, the doctor said when he was born. Perfect.'

'Had he lost any teeth? Did he ever go to the dentist?'

'Paul has never been to the dentist in his life. No need, he has perfect teeth. He has a little gap between two of his front teeth and I used to tell him when he was little that it meant he would die rich.'

Wycliffe was beaten. 'Could I see his room?'

'If you want to.' Her composure was unnerving. 'It's on the left at the top of the stairs.'

The carpet on the stairs was threadbare and the wallpaper had faded to an indeterminate shade. The room was a back room, it was bare, a single bed, a tiny wardrobe and a chest of drawers. A cheap bookcase contained mainly works on architecture but there were several physical culture books including three or four on judo. Chest expanders hung on a hook behind the door and there was a species of rowing machine on the floor. These things surprised Wycliffe who had thought of Morris as a weedy youth.

She had followed him upstairs and she now stood in the doorway, watching, as though some invisible barrier stopped her from crossing the threshold.

'Is your son keen on sport?'

'Not on sport. Only on judo, it was the one thing apart from his work which interested him at school.'

Wycliffe lacked the courage to make any sort of search but it would have to be done some time. 'Where does he do his painting?'

She looked at him as though he had taken leave of his senses. 'Painting? He's never done any painting since he was at the junior school.'

'You say that he is not at home much, does he sleep away from home?'

'Never.'

'What about holidays?'

'Just the same – off all day, I never see him except when he's getting up or going to bed.'

'Does he never ask you to go out with him?'

She made a curious sound, half between a laugh and a sneer. 'He used to, but where would I want to go?'

She saw him to the door and stood on the doorstep until he had closed the gate. 'Thank you, Mrs Morris. I will keep in touch.'

She did not bother to reply.

The air was sharp with frost, clear and still. The sky overhead was almost saxe blue. In a house opposite a family was watching television with the curtains undrawn and the room lit only by the light of the flickering screen and the coloured lamps on the Christmas tree.

Wycliffe decided to go home. The city seemed empty, the Christmas lights shone over empty streets. The only sign of revelry came from the pubs in snatches of song as he passed. He stopped at a newsvendor's pitch, the man had gone home but he had left a few papers and a box for money. He bought a paper and glanced at the headlines in the light of a street lamp. BODY IN BLAZE – LINK WITH STANLEY STREET MURDER? After an account of the fire and the finding of the body the report went on:

'The police are investigating the possibility of a link between this tragedy and the murder of Christine Powell on Wednesday evening. The body found in the débris of the fire had not been identified at the time of going to press but there is informed speculation that it may turn out to be that of a young professional man employed by a local firm.'

As he neared home a half-moon rode high in the sky above the estuary and the Watch House stood out white in the landscape. The old banger which belonged to the twins was parked across the entrance to the garage so that he had to leave his car on the gravel. But his wife and his daughter kissed him under the mistletoe and his son handed him a glass of sherry.

8

Lesley Birch, the prostitute, quoting the dead girl, had said, 'The funny thing is he's vicious with it. I never thought I would take that again from any man . . .'

And Andrew Jarvis had told him, 'Derek isn't above taking advantage of a situation like that; in fact, I sometimes think he has a cruel streak in his nature.'

The words sounded inside his head as though they were being spoken, he could recall the tone and the manner of their delivery so exactly. Yet it was only now that he linked the two statements together.

It was half past five on Christmas Eve morning and he had been lying awake for more than an hour. In the stillness he had heard a clock, somewhere across the water, strike four then, after an infinity of time, five. The night-light by the telephone at his bedside played tricks on his eyes. Sometimes its pale radiance seemed to fill the whole room then it would shrink to a point of light so intense that it hurt his eyes and confused his sense of direction.

Derek Robson.

But why should he kill the girl? Killing is, presumably, the logical end of the sadist's progress but the crime had not been notably sadistic. And why would Robson set fire to the flat in Middle Street?

Paul Morris. The Monk.

Morris is missing and there is a dead man of his approximate age and height in the mortuary.

Robson is missing too. Missing? Well, nobody seems to know where he is but his car is still at the Old Custom House. Morris and Robson are both 'between twenty-five and thirty' and both are tall.

Coincidence. Imagination has been the downfall of more than one good jack.

A struggle and a shot, a fatal shot. Was the fire a vain attempt to cover the killing? Or was the incendiary disturbed in his work?

If he lay very still and listened intently he could just hear the clang of a bell-buoy out to sea, and, with the eye of his mind, he could watch the slow undulant surge of black water, gleaming in the darkness.

There was a gap, he must have dozed.

'I never knew there was so much money in secondhand books.' So much money—

'We sell books of antiquarian interest and importance . . . We specialize in foreign books, mainly French. Three or four times a year Derek takes the van across the ferry . . . Our last consignment, we haven't had a chance to sort them yet.'

He wished that he had taken a closer look at those books. But why?

Helen whispered tensely in her sleep and he put his hand on her thigh.

Christine Powell had been uniquely eligible as a victim. She qualified as a tart, as a blackmailer playing off substantial business interests, as a woman who seemed to delight in putting men through the hoop. Added to that she had taken up with a man who seemed to have specialized sexual needs.

For the twentieth time he decided to clear his mind, to 'go blank' and so fall asleep.

Any one of the dubious crowd she mixed with might have killed her and any one of them might have decided to protect himself by setting alight to the Middle Street flat. Why should Morris go there? Or Robson?

Powell . . . Salt . . . Bates . . . His thoughts were wandering, he was getting further away, losing the thread instead of following it.

'He has perfect teeth . . .'

'The top four incisors and the left canine are missing . . . considerable damage to the maxillary bones at or about the time he died, perhaps a little before, perhaps after.'

'So you think it was a blow?'

'Obviously there would have been no point in administering such a blow after death.'

Powell . . . Salt . . . Bates . . . Harkness . . . Purvis . . . Powell . . . The names were sounding in his head in time with the swinging bell. Once more he could see the black water rising and falling, rising and falling. This time he slept.

The alarm clock blared insanely and Helen switched it off. Then she switched on the bedside lamp and, as always, turned to kiss him on the forehead. As always, her lips were cool.

'Slept well, dear?'

'Bloody! And you?'

'Like a log.'

Their new surroundings certainly agreed with Helen. He got up, pulled on his dressing-gown and went over to the window. Standing with the curtains behind him he could feel the cold coming off the glass. The stars were still out, not a cloud anywhere. Fine and frosty. He went back and switched on the radio.

'The Bank of England says that it will be a record spending Christmas with an increase in the note circulation of eight per cent . . . The weather is set fair, not, perhaps a traditional Christmas for, say the Met Office, snow is unlikely anywhere in the British Isles; but it will be cold and the old Yule log will come in handy if you can find one and you have somewhere to burn it. Now for the News Headlines at seven-thirty precisely . . .

A Union spokesman for the car strikers said last night that officials will be available all over Christmas, ready to enter into meaningful discussions with the management . . .

'In the Powell murder case police say that the man whose charred remains were found after a fire in the murdered girl's flat had been shot at close range—'

'Shall I go first?' The same question on every working morning of his married life. As though Helen would take possession of the bathroom before him. Fortunately now, they had two, one on the ground floor.

He remembered that he had thought a good deal about the case during the night. As he bathed and shaved he tried to recall those thoughts without much success. He had the disturbing feeling amounting almost to conviction that he had made a discovery or reached a conclusion but he could not focus his recollection.

By the time he set out on his drive to the city the sun was above the horizon and the sky was turquoise blue. People were going to work with a cheerful air. A queue of lorries lined the street to the pannier market. WPC Saxton was waiting for him with his post and the chrysanthemums had been rearranged. Instead of attending to the post he went to the duty room. DC Dixon was there.

'I've found him, sir.' The satisfaction in his voice was unmistakable.

'Who?'

'The lame man who was with the prostitute in the top flat on the night of the murder.'

It had been a question of tying up a loose end, or so they had thought.

'I brought him in this morning, sir, he's in number four interview room. I think you might like to hear what he's got to say.'

Dixon's little lame man was sitting at a bare deal table, dejected and resigned. He had on the mackintosh he had been wearing when Brenda picked him up.

'Mr Watkins, sir. Mr Watkins is an unemployed bricklayer.'

'Mr Watkins?'

'That's me, sir.'

'I think you have something to tell me.'

He was probably no older than Wycliffe but his face was lined and seemed to have been cast in a mould of permanent sadness. He looked at Dixon, standing near the door, 'I told the lad, sir.'

Wycliffe saw the flush on Dixon's cheeks. 'Now tell me.'

The man lifted his shoulders in a gesture of helplessness. 'It's just that I met him, when I was going in to that house he was coming out.'

'You were going into 9 Stanley Street, is that right?'

'It was the first time. I swear to God! And it will be the last.' He wiped his lips with a grubby handkerchief. 'As I was going to open the door, he opened it first—'

'Who are you talking about, Mr Watkins?'

'The young man.'

'What young man?'

Watkins' brow furrowed with the effort required of him. 'Well, he was in a grey overcoat, a tall young fellow, thin—'

'You recognized him?'

'Not then, sir, but now I know who he was. Mr . . . this young man showed me a photograph and then I knew him.'

'Mr Dixon showed you a photograph of a young man and you

recognized him as being the same man you had seen leaving the flat?'

'I think so, sir, and I saw then that it was this architect chap. I mean, I remembered that I'd seen him before on building sites when I was a brickie.'

'Mr Dixon has your address?'

'Oh yes, sir.'

'Then we can ask you to come in and make a statement later. Thank you, Mr Watkins.'

The lame man, not quite sure what had happened to him, got up and after looking at the two policemen doubtfully, made off down the passage. The expression on Dixon's face made Wycliffe want to laugh. 'It's not the end of the world, Dixon.'

Dixon shook his head. 'I don't get it, sir.'

'Think what would happen if we let Watkins go into court. He says he saw a young man in a grey overcoat leaving the house in Stanley Street. He told me a moment ago that he didn't recognize him at the time but when you showed him a photograph of Morris he recognized it as the architect chap he had seen on building sites and he *thought* it was the same man he had seen coming out of the house. The Defence would accuse us of having led the witness and they would make mincemeat out of poor old Watkins in the box.'

'So we need an identity parade, sir.'

'If we find Morris it would be an idea but even if Watkins picked him out of a parade it could be argued that he was identifying the man he saw in your photograph rather than the one he saw in Stanley Street.'

Dixon looked crestfallen. 'I've balled up a good witness.'

Wycliffe grinned. 'I wouldn't have called Watkins a good witness but next time don't be in such a hurry to show a witness photographs.'

'I'm very sorry, sir.'

'I expect you are but don't dwell on it, I've got more important things for you to think about. You'd better come with me.' They walked along the corridor to the lift together.

'By the way, how did you pick him up?'

'Tim Parnell, landlord of The Joiners in Prince's Street recognized his description. It seems he's a harmless old boy, his wife left him a few years back and he's lived on his own ever since. Last year he had an accident and injured his leg, since then he hasn't been able to climb ladders.'

Back in his office Wycliffe picked up the telephone and asked to be put through to Mr Winter of Lloyd and Winter. Mr Winter was distressed.

'Disappeared? But where could he have gone and why? . . . Yes, a first class young man, a very promising architect . . . Yes, we have tried to keep him by the offer of a junior partnership . . . Well worth it . . . Yes, he seems to have a thing about his mother, almost a morbid sense of responsibility . . . Between you and me I think the old girl imposes on the lad . . . No, I know nothing about his private life, he is not at all communicative, quite the reverse . . . If he wasn't such a good architect it would have held him back – none of the social graces . . . As you and I know only too well a good many professional men owe their success to the nineteenth hole . . . No trouble, a pleasure . . . And to you.'

Wycliffe dropped the receiver with a grimace. He had never had nor wished to have any part in the freemasonry of successful professional men. If he had done he would probably have made chief constable but he had no regrets about that either.

'Do you play golf, Dixon?'

'Golf? No, sir.'

'Perhaps you should take it up.'

'I'll bear it in mind, sir.' The boy was learning fast.

'I want you to go to Morris's home. Be nice to his mother and listen to what she tells you. If you go the right way about it you won't have any difficulty in searching through his stuff without upsetting her. Report directly to me.'

Dixon flushed with pleasure.

When Dixon had gone Wycliffe went down to the yard behind the headquarters buildings where there were garages, stores and a workshop. All the material brought back from the fire was stored in two garages. Larger items had been placed on the floor against the walls while smaller things were laid out on trestle tables with some attempt at classification. Sergeant Scales was there with a constable and a young man from Forensic, an expert on fires.

Wycliffe prowled about looking at the exhibits with a glazed expression. He paused before half-a-dozen metal drawers, scorched

768

and distorted by the fire, which had clearly come from a filing cabinet.

'These drawers, why did you take them out of the cabinet?'

'We didn't sir, they were all over the place, all we did was to collect them together.'

The man from Forensic, who had not previously worked with Wycliffe, volunteered, 'The chap who started the fire must have emptied out the contents of the drawers to make sure that everything in them got burnt. You can see that the paint has been burnt from the parts of the drawers which would normally have been protected by the cabinet.'

All he got for his pains was a cold hard stare which made him feel uncomfortable.

On the tables there were heaps of pottery scraps, twisted and discoloured cutlery, bits of electrical wizardry which must have come from a record player or a television set or both. There were all manner of tortured bits of metal which had once been parts of chairs and other furniture and the workings of a clock. All the débris had been sifted and the 'finds' brought to these sheds. It was like an archaeological dig.

'No sign of a gun?'

Scales came over. 'Not yet, sir, and they're almost through on the site. We did find this though.' He pointed to a specimen tube containing a bullet which could have been the twin of the one Wycliffe had seen in Dr Franks's laboratory.

'So there must have been two shots.'

'Looks like it, sir. I'm sending this over to Waddington for comparison and report.' The area force had no ballistics expert on the staff but they made use of a local gunsmith who had a national reputation and had testified in several cases for the Crown.

In the middle of one of the tables, apparently perfect, scarcely tarnished, were two bronze elephants, exquisitely modelled and standing eighteen inches or more at the shoulders.

'Nice elephants.'

'Sir?' It was the man from Forensic.

'I said, these are nice elephants.'

'Very nice, sir.'

It was from such exchanges that the Wycliffe legend grew and some said that the *non sequitur* was a deliberate and cultivated eccentricity. In fact, it usually followed, as now, an occasion when he had snubbed somebody and wanted to say something mildly placatory but could think of nothing.

He tried again. 'When can I expect your report on the fire?'

'I think it's on the way to you, sir, but I can give you the gist of it.' The young man took a deep breath as though about to recite. 'From our study of the incendiary device recovered—'

'You mean the candle and the bucket?'

'Yes, sir. Well, as I was saying, from our study we came to the conclusion that it would have taken about five-and-a-half hours for the device to become effective—'

'For the candle to burn down to the paraffin?'

'That is correct, sir. The fire, as I understand it, was discovered at 0340 hours, not long alter it started, so, if the other devices were similar they must have been activated around 2200 hours.'

In other words the fire-raiser had lit his candles and cleared off before Wycliffe arrived but the one in the bedroom had blown out. When Wycliffe was peering in through the glass door of the kitchen the dead man was already lying in the front room and Forensic's 'incendiary devices' had already been 'activated'.

'How much paraffin was there in the bucket?'

'About one point five litres, sir.'

'In translation?'

'About a third of a gallon.'

'So a gallon of paraffin could have done the lot?'

'That is so, sir.'

Wycliffe continued to browse around like a bargain hunter in a jumble sale. There seemed to be a lot of fragments of porcelain figurines and Scales, who knew about such things, confirmed that the girl must have been a collector. 'I think this will interest you, sir. I've just come across it in the lot which has just arrived.'

It was a steel identity disc on a chain, one of the links of the chain had been broken near the clasp. On one side of the disc an inscription read: Derek Robson 4. XI. 44

Robson! If the disc had come from the body—

'I suppose the chain could have snapped as the body fell,' Scales suggested, uninhibited by preconceived notions.

Wycliffe changed the subject. 'I suppose a lot of this stuff comes from the tobacconist's?'

'We've done our best and he's been quite helpful considering everything but we can't be sure.'

'It doesn't matter.'

'There are sacks of carbonized paper and card, it would take months to go through it all.'

'Don't waste time over it. Forget it.' Wycliffe seemed to have lost interest. He walked over to the scorched and twisted remains of an oil heater. 'Was this the tobacconist's?'

'He says not, it must have belonged to the flat. She had night-storage heaters and electric fires but she probably kept this in case of a power failure.'

Wycliffe walked slowly back to his office. He used the stairs and not the lift and he seemed unaware of the people who passed him. Sergeant Bourne, the young man who seemed destined to be chief constable, was waiting for him in WPC Saxton's office. Wycliffe thought, not entirely without malice, what a splendid pair they would make.

'I've made some progress, sir, and I thought you might wish to hear.'

With a gesture Wycliffe swept him into his office. Bourne had been busy. The city librarian had put him on to a real bibliophile, an elderly gentleman who lived in a large house about thirty miles up the coast. Bourne had been to see him the previous evening.

'He knew Jarvis?'

'Very well, sir. Jarvis is, apparently, quite a figure in the book world.'

'As a dealer?'

Bourne frowned. 'He is certainly known as a dealer but Mr Baldwin – that's the gentleman's name – knew him best as a collector of illustrated books and prints. Apparently he has been collecting for years and he has contributed numerous papers to the journals. Until recently, the last two or three years, he built up his collection from items he happened to come across in the course of business, usually for much less than their market value; now he attends major sales and he has purchased three or four items at considerable cost.'

'How considerable?'

'Mr Baldwin estimates that his purchases in the past three years must have cost him many thousands of pounds.'

'I never knew there was so much money in secondhand books.'

'I beg your pardon, sir?'

'Never mind.' He congratulated Bourne and told him to return to his normal duties.

Whatever else the finding of Robson's identity disc might mean it left little doubt that he had visited the Middle Street flat. Could it, after all, be his body in the mortuary? If so, what had happened to Morris?

He picked up the telephone and put through a call to Andrew Jarvis. 'I wondered if you have had any news of your assistant?'

There was a brief silence then Jarvis spoke, tense and anxious. 'No, I have not. As a matter of fact I was about to ring you. I'm afraid that I was not entirely frank when you were here yesterday . . .' He waited for some comment from Wycliffe and when none was forthcoming, went on, 'I wonder if I might come over to explain?'

'There is no need, Mr Jarvis, I shall be coming to see you during the day . . . Sometime today, I can't say exactly when. As it is Christmas Eve I suppose you are likely to be there all day?'

Jarvis agreed.

'There is one question, does Robson wear dentures?'

'Dentures?' Jarvis sounded surprised by the question, as well he might. 'Yes, he has a small plate, four of his top front teeth were knocked out when he was a lad. He is quite sensitive about it.'

'What about his other teeth?'

'As far as I know he has excellent teeth but I really can't see—'

Wycliffe rang off. The 'dear boy' interpolations were notably absent. Jarvis was a worried man. So much the better. He was on the point of putting out a general call but changed his mind. Instead he arranged for the Old Custom House to be watched.

He worked at his reorganization plan for a while but his thoughts were elsewhere. From time to time he walked to the window and stood watching the seemingly endless flow of traffic into the city. Twice WPC Saxton came in with queries about sections of the report she was typing and she had the surprising impression that he was glad to be interrupted. Her third intrusion was to tell him that DC Dixon was waiting to report.

But Dixon had little to tell. He had met with no difficulty in dealing with Mrs Morris. 'She couldn't have cared less what I did. Have you ever seen her, sir? It was incredible. If I'd been missing for twenty-four hours my mother would have been calling out the marines.' All he had found of possible interest were three photo-graphs in a yellow, paper wallet. 'I thought I ought to bring them though they probably don't mean anything.'

Wycliffe spread them on his desk, three colour snaps. The first had been taken on a beach and showed Robson, in swimming trunks, with his arms round two girls in bikinis. One of the girls, petite and smiling, was Christine Powell; the other, sturdy and grinning dutifully into the camera, seemed familiar but Wycliffe could not immediately place her. Then he remembered, it was almost certainly the freckled Irish girl from the café in Bear Street where Jarvis and Robson got their meals. The second snap was a clever or lucky one of Christine Powell standing under the cedar in dappled sunlight. She was looking up into the branches, apparently unaware of the camera.

'I found them in one of the drawers in his chest-of-drawers. I showed them to his mother and she said she had never seen the girls or the man in her life. "How would you expect me to know who he spends his time with?"' Dixon could not resist imitating her tone and manner.

Wycliffe was looking at the third snap. Again the girl from the café, this time sitting in the driving seat of a red Mini. She had her head through the open window, laughing. She appealed to Wycliffe, there was something practical, even earthy about her, the sort of girl who might have done Morris a lot of good, giving him the kicks and the ha'pence he so badly needed.

Just as he was leaving for lunch a telex came through from Criminal Records. Nothing known of Andrew Jarvis but Robson had a record. Two convictions for violence against women. He had served two years and he had not troubled to change his name.

Wycliffe went to lunch with Gill at Teague's and they had to wait for a table. The set meal was roast turkey and Christmas pudding, there was a sprig of holly on each table and paper chains were sus-pended from the ceiling. Already Wycliffe resented the invasion of the place by 'casuals'.

Gill had been spending time on the dead girl's clients and as-sociates, in particular, Harkness, Purvis, Salt and Bates. He was morose. 'Reluctantly, I think we've got to count Salt out of this one, he had a lot to gain from continued association with the girl. Purvis and Harkness were being blackmailed, in a mild sort of way, for inside information, not for money.' Gill sipped his beer in a pre-occupied way, 'It was all fairly low-key, no high drama as far as I can see and no reason for it.'

'What did she have on them?'

'She threatened Harkness that she would send naughty pictures to his wife, the pictures probably didn't exist but the threat was enough. With Purvis she said she had evidence, and he believed her, of a bit of dirty work he was involved in six or seven years back.' Gill became the burly rock-faced contractor. ' "Of course I've never taken advantage of my position on the council to further my own interests but a few years back I allowed myself to oppose a development (a foolish one) which would have been inconvenient to a friend of mine."

' "And your friend rewarded you. How much?"

'Purvis wasn't anxious to talk figures but in the end he did. "Five thousand. It was several years ago and we were going through a sticky patch at the time, the money came in handy." The bastard was less ashamed of the fact than of the amount. He thought his integrity rated a higher bid.'

'How did you get all this?'

Gill gave one of his horrific grins. 'I put the fear of God into the bastard and I enjoyed every minute of it.' He emptied his glass and signalled the waitress for another. He rarely had to ask for anything twice where a woman was concerned and the beer came with grati-fying promptitude.

'So none of them killed the girl?'

'In my opinion, no.'

'To tidy the thing up we need alibis for Middle Street. We can't be certain that it was the same operator.'

Gill nodded. 'I've attended to that and as far as I can see they are all in the clear. Bates and his girl friend were at the *Nite Spot* in Fuller Road. At least that's what they say and so does Alec Bose, the owner. Purvis was at a council meeting and Harkness was attending a bun-fight organized by the chartered surveyors. Salt's alibi is thinner, he was home with his wife but, for once, I believe him.' He took a deep draught of his beer. 'No report on the gun?'

'Nothing useful. Sure to be unregistered. Waddington says that, judging from the condition of the first bullet – he hadn't seen the second when he made his report – it was almost certainly from an old

774

service revolver from the First World War. He thinks it was a Belgian gun, it's an odd calibre. He also said that the gun couldn't have been cleaned or fired in years.'

'That's what I like about experts.' Gill said. 'Helpful.'

9

Before going to see Jarvis Wycliffe called on the girl in the Bear Street café. Her last lunchtime customer was paying his bill. 'Thank *you*, sir. Shall we see you tomorrow?' The open smile and easy manner must be good for trade. She followed her customer to the door and shot the bolts behind him then she turned to Wycliffe. 'Well?'

Wycliffe laid his three snapshots on one of the café tables and she looked at them cursorily. 'Where did you get those?'

Wycliffe pointed to the one of Robson with the two girls. 'You didn't tell me that you were on such good terms.'

'You didn't ask me.'

'Are you fond of him?'

'I suppose you could say that.'

'I understand that he has gone away for Christmas.'

'Really?'

'Didn't you know?'

'I haven't seen him around.'

He realized that he would get more by frontal attack than by subterfuge. 'How well do you know Robson?'

'I know him.'

'Do you sleep with him?'

'Sometimes.'

'I suppose Morris took this snap?'

She nodded. 'As far as I can remember.'

'Did the four of you go round much together?'

'Not a lot. Now and then Derek would take us all somewhere in his car, usually on a Sunday afternoon.'

'Two couples, you and Robson, Christine and Morris.'

She was clearing the tables as they talked, stacking dishes on a tray. 'You know it wasn't like that.'

'How was it?'

'Christine didn't give a damn for Paul Morris, she collected men like kids collect stamps and Paul was an odd specimen she happened to pick up.'

'And Robson?'

'That was different. No woman will ever collect Derek.'

'So you and Christine Powell were after the same man?'

She turned to him, her snub nose wrinkled with distaste. 'If you want to put it that way, but if you're trying to say that I was jealous then you're wrong. I knew Derek wasn't the sort to settle for one woman, if it hadn't been Christine Powell it would have been somebody else.' She lifted the heavy tray on to the counter. 'I'm not daft, I knew there was no future in it for me.'

Wycliffe pointed to the snap of her sitting in the driving seat of a red Mini. 'Your car?'

'Mine, my dad's, I drive it anyway.' She was standing beside him, waiting for him to go. 'If you've got no more questions . . .'

Wycliffe felt sure that she was under stress, her anxiety to be rid of him arose from more than a desire to get on with her work. She had not asked him any questions. Surely, in the circumstances, this was unnatural?

'You've read about the fire in Middle Street?'

'I heard about it on the News.'

'You know that we found a body?'

'Yes.'

'In the débris we also found an identity disc with Derek Robson's name on it.'

'I see.' Her face and voice were both expressionless.

'When did you last see Robson?'

She hesitated as though trying to recall. 'It must have been Thursday evening when I took in their meal.' He said nothing and she went on, 'You can't tell for sure who it is?'

'Not yet, no.' He was reluctant to leave, sensing that there was something which she was holding back but unable to guess what it might be. 'If you decide that you have something to tell me you can telephone police headquarters at any time.'

She looked blank. 'I don't know what you mean.'

When Wycliffe arrived at the bookshop Jarvis had a customer who was trying to decide whether or not to spend his money on a set of

Fabre's *Souvenirs Entomologiques*. Jarvis had clearly lost interest in the transaction before Wycliffe arrived, now he almost drove the poor man out of his shop. He shut the door behind him and reversed the card from OPEN to CLOSED.

'I'm glad you've come. Please come into my office.' He was agitated and his movements were quick and jerky. 'I'm very worried.'

'About your assistant?'

'About Derek, yes. I ought to have been more frank with you but I didn't want to stir up a lot of fuss about nothing.'

In his little office he lifted a pile of books off the seat of a cane-bottomed chair for Wycliffe and sat, himself, in the swivel chair by his desk. 'As I told you, Derek goes off for a day or two now and then but he always tells me well in advance to make sure that it will be convenient and he always lets me know when to expect him back.'

'Not this time?'

'No. I had no idea that he was going and I don't know when to expect him back.' He clasped his hands together, studied his paired thumbs then unclasped them again. 'I'd better tell you.' He turned in his chair to face Wycliffe with an expression of great candour. 'The night before last – Thursday night – we had a difference of opinion about the business – you might call it a row, I suppose – and after our evening meal Derek went out without a word. That was the last I saw of him.' Jarvis paused then added. 'But I heard him. I'd gone to bed and I heard him come in around midnight. I sleep in a room on this floor, along the passage. To be honest, I thought he was drunk, he made such a noise. He seemed to blunder about in the little hall for a time then, finally, I heard him going up the stairs.'

'And then?'

'I must have fallen asleep.' He looked apologetic. 'I suppose I must have woken from time to time during the night but I certainly heard nothing more of Derek. It was not until after ten o'clock next morning when he had failed to put in an appearance that I went up to his room and found that his bed had not been slept in.'

'He has never done such a thing before?'

'Never!'

Wycliffe felt sure that Jarvis had still not told him all there was to tell. 'Yesterday you went to some trouble to conceal all this, Mr Jarvis, today you seem anxious to tell me – why the change?'

Jarvis swung round to face his desk. 'Well, dear boy, twenty-four hours have gone by with no news.'

'The truth, Mr Jarvis.'

Jarvis looked intensely miserable. 'You are right, of course, dear boy, but I don't want to make trouble for Derek.'

'By being reticent in a murder case you are making trouble for yourself.'

'He took some books of mine with him and that convinces me that he has no intention of coming back.'

'Valuable books?'

'That is beside the point, I am not primarily concerned about the books.'

'All the same, were the books valuable?'

Jarvis still could not bring himself to give a straight answer. 'You can't price old books like groceries, dear boy.'

'How much were the books worth?' Wycliffe was becoming aggressive, impatient with Jarvis's evasions and pretensions which made it difficult to decide whether his story as a whole should be believed.

The bookseller sighed. 'We are talking of many hundreds.'

'Negotiable?'

Jarvis pursed his thin lips. 'In the right market; the books were obviously chosen with this in mind. None of them was sufficiently rare to draw attention and might have been bought over the counter by any good dealer.'

Wycliffe was watching him closely, half convinced that the tale was just another fabrication. 'I shall want a list of the missing books.'

'But I'm making no complaint—'

Wycliffe snapped: 'That's up to you. If you tell me that Robson has gone off with these books they may help us to trace him and that is my concern.'

The little office had only a tiny, rather murky, window high up over the desk. It was like being at the bottom of a well and Wycliffe got up to switch on the light without asking leave. The action was not lost on Jarvis.

'Robson didn't take his car with him which must be worth more than the books, how do you explain that?'

'I can't explain it, dear boy, it is very puzzling.'

'When Robson came in at midnight you heard him but you didn't
see him, is that right?'

'Quite right, I told you I was in bed—'

'So that it might not have been him?'

Jarvis stiffened as though struck by an entirely new possibility.
'But who else could it have been? I mean, whoever it was had a key.'

'An identity disc with Robson's name on it was found in the débris
of the Middle Street fire.'

'Good God! Does that mean—?'

'I don't know what it means but there is a possibility that it is
Robson's body which lies in the mortuary.'

Jarvis shook his head hopelessly. 'I don't know what to think.'
He stared at his desk in silence for a while before turning again to
Wycliffe. 'But if it wasn't Derek I heard, who could it have been?'

'Paul Morris?'

'Paul? But why should Paul—?'

'If he had shot Robson and wanted to get away.'

Jarvis stared at him without speaking for a while then, with
apparent reluctance, he said, 'What you are saying begins to make a
horrible kind of sense.

'The books, the car – Paul knew enough about my books to
choose those which he could sell and, of course, he would never
have driven Derek's car. He always said that his Mini was as much as
he could manage.' He patted his toupée with the flat of his hand. 'It
would also account for the noise he made, I mean, the place was in
darkness and he probably couldn't find the switches. But if he killed
Derek, I suppose that he must also have killed the girl?' He broke off.
'I know that is what you were trying to tell me yesterday but, frankly,
I couldn't really believe it.'

Wycliffe got out his pipe and lit it. Jarvis stared at his desk as
though his thoughts were completely absorbed with the new and
frightening ideas which had been presented to him.

'Did you know that Derek Robson has a criminal record?'

'No, I certainly did not! I can't believe that—'

'Two convictions for assaults on women. How did you meet him,
Mr Jarvis?'

Jarvis considered. 'It must have been at least three years ago. He
just walked in here one morning and spent some time looking at the
books like any other customer. We got talking and it soon became

obvious that he knew what he was talking about, he had a very good knowledge of French literature and he spoke the language like a native.'

'And you employed him on the strength of that?'

'Not at once. He came back several times and we grew friendly. He told me that he had spent a good deal of his youth in France – at Bordeaux where his father was a wine buyer for a firm of importers in London. He went to the lycée and obtained his baccalauréat. To cut a long story short I ended up by offering him employment.'

'You did not take up references?'

'There seemed no point.'

They sat in silence for a while then Wycliffe said that he would like to take another look at the studio. They went up the two flights of stairs, past the bindery and the book-store and into the studio. Everything seemed to be as he had seen it before. Morris's picture was still on the easel and the stove filled the room with enervating warmth. He stood by the stove looking round him, he was trying to imagine the room at night with the lights on and the blue curtains drawn over the dormer windows.

At half past seven on Wednesday evening Jarvis had left Morris alone in this room.

'What was Morris doing when you left? Had he started to paint?'

Jarvis looked up from a folder of prints. 'He was working up his palette.'

Wycliffe moved over to the picture. 'The painting seems to be finished now but it was not so then?'

'Almost but not quite, he had some work to do on it down in the bottom right, that squat building had only been blocked in.'

'And at the time you left he had not found the anonymous note?'

'If he had, he gave no sign of it.'

Presumably, at some time after Jarvis left, he had found the note in its straw coloured envelope.

'YOUR GIRL FRIEND IS A WHORE . . .'

What had been his reaction? Surprise? Shock? Disbelief? Finally, perhaps, contempt for the writer. Anyway he had stuffed the note into the pocket of his painting jacket and gone on painting.

'How long would it have taken Morris to finish his picture?'

Jarvis was wary. 'You can never tell with Paul. He could have done what he had to do in half-an-hour, equally it might have taken him the whole evening.'

YOUR GIRL FRIEND . . . FIND OUT FOR YOURSELF
. . . 9 STANLEY STREET. BOTTOM FLAT.

While he painted the note would never be out of his mind. Useless to try to dismiss it. Had he finished his painting, changed his jacket, put on his overcoat and driven to Stanley Street?

It was possible – just. Perhaps he had parked in Waterloo Place and walked the rest of the way. He would have been torn between the fear of making a fool of himself and something worse. By chance he would have found Christine alone for she had cancelled her regular appointment with Harkness, the surveyor. (Why?) How would she have received him? Probably with anger, perhaps with disdainful indifference. Unforgettable and unforgivable words might have led him to—'

It was possible.

And now she was lying on the floor, crumpled and limp. He would be horrified, horrified at what he had done and not less at the consequences to himself. He had read of sex crimes, the victim is always nude so he decides to strip the body. It is not easy to undress a dead girl—

'No! I don't believe it.' Wycliffe had spoken the words aloud. Everything he had heard about Morris led him to believe that, intolerably provoked, he might have killed Christine Powell but not that he could have stripped her body, lifted her on to the bed and, finally, arranged her limbs in a suggestive pose.

Jarvis was looking at him with curiosity. 'What don't you believe?'

Wycliffe ignored him. 'Did Robson own a gun?'

'A gun? Only a sort of memento of the first war. His uncle gave it to him or maybe it was his great uncle. Whoever it was had done some cloak and dagger work in Belgium and this was a Belgian officer's revolver.'

'Did he have ammunition?'

'I don't know, dear boy, but I shouldn't think so. It was only a souvenir.'

On the way down Wycliffe stopped at the book-store. 'Have you sorted your new consignment yet?'

'No, dear boy, I haven't had a chance to touch them. What with one thing and another . . .' He started to move off along the passage but Wycliffe went into the little room where books were stored on the shelves in batches of a dozen or so.

He looked them over. Most of the great names of 19th-century French literature were represented: Hugo, Dumas, Flaubert, Maupassant, Zola – Wycliffe recognized many old favourites in the unfamiliar guise of their mother tongue but he was surprised to see that most of them seemed to be in pre-war library editions and in poor condition. No first editions here. With Jarvis watching and looking increasingly concerned, Wycliffe removed books from two or three of the bundles and flicked through their pages. He even shook them by their bindings before replacing them on the shelves. As far as he could judge they were exactly what they seemed to be, second-hand books, moderately priced, popular editions of the French classics published in the years immediately before the first war. Their English counterparts would now sell on market stalls at a few pence each.

'I really don't understand what you are looking for, Mr Wycliffe.' Jarvis's tone was plaintive.

'Are these worth importing?'

'Along with more valuable works, dear boy. It would be foolish to come back with the van more than half empty.'

'But you have a sale for these?'

'Oh, yes, there is quite a demand for them from sixth formers doing modern languages for their "A" levels.'

Wycliffe allowed himself to be piloted down the stairs and through the shop. By the time they reached the shop door Jarvis had recovered a good deal of his poise.

'You will keep me informed of any developments, dear boy? You can imagine how I feel, both those boys were like sons to me.'

Wycliffe had walked away a couple of paces when he turned back. 'Do you know if there is a ferry due in this afternoon?'

'A ferry?'

'Cross-channel.'

All Jarvis's newly won composure deserted him. For a moment he seemed scarcely able to speak then he mumbled, 'I really have no idea.'

'Never mind, I can ring the docks.'

As he turned up the cobbled alley to where he had parked his car he found DC Fowler waiting for him. Fowler was a master at keeping obo, he could stand in a busy street or loiter in a deserted square without drawing attention to himself, he had the knack of looking as much part of the scene as a lamp-post.

'I saw you go in, sir, I wondered if you had any fresh instructions for me?'

Wycliffe hesitated, he was still very unsure of his ground. 'You've got transport?'

'Parked just round the corner.'

'Car radio?'

'Yes, sir.'

'Good! It's just possible that Jarvis may come out driving the van or, perhaps, the Jag. If he does, follow him and report.'

Wycliffe continued up the slope to his car and joined the unending stream of traffic into the city. It took him twenty minutes to cover the three miles to his headquarters.

He was convinced that Robson and Jarvis had been engaged in some profitable swindle but unless it was linked with the murder of Christine Powell he did not feel immediately concerned. Privately, though with no admissible evidence, he had acquitted Paul Morris of killing the girl; but it could still have been Morris who survived the presumed struggle in the Middle Street flat and, later, went to the Old Custom House to steal a few carefully selected books which would enable him to obtain enough money to have some chance of getting away.

He climbed the stairs to his office in a mood of depression. Already he was establishing fixed patterns of behaviour in his new surroundings. When his mood was buoyant he used the lift, when he was gloomy or frustrated he laboured up the stairs. He feared that his case was 'closing down for Christmas'. Police work largely depends on information received from the public and the flow of information is stimulated by press, radio and TV. But for two days there would be no newspapers and murder does not make good Christmas broadcasting.

But there was news for him – two items.

Paul Morris's car, the blue Mini, had been found, abandoned, near Taunton. A farmer had reported the car because it was blocking the entrance to one of his fields. The farm was not far out of the town and close to the main road. The farmer was quite sure that the car had not been there the previous evening at nine o'clock.

Wycliffe consulted a map. Taunton was eighty miles away. Where had the car been since Thursday? Forty-eight hours to travel eighty miles. He put through a call to Taunton CID. They had found a suitcase in the boot containing five large illustrated books, the ignition key was in place on a ring with four other keys. The car had been brought in and was being subjected to rigorous examination. Wycliffe asked for the keys to be sent on at once.

He was led to his second piece of news through a message asking him to telephone Dr Bell, head of Forensic, an old friend.

'You're in luck, my lad! The brooch the girl was wearing – your chap couldn't find any print on it and neither could we, but one of our youngsters decided to try a new test for latents. It's supposed to be better than the old ninhydrin test on some surfaces and it depends on a reaction with urea in the sweat. Frankly, I thought he was wasting his time, the brooch is a cameo-type thing with a surface which looks like glazed porcelain. In fact it came up rather well with two quite good partial thumb prints. I've had them photographed and blown up for you.'

Wycliffe thanked him and rang off. He gave instructions for prints to be obtained from articles handled by Morris and by Robson so that they would have a basis for comparison. Soon he would have a strong pointer to the killer. But what of the car? Presumably one of the two missing men, the one whose body was not now in the mortuary, had driven it to Taunton, abandoned it and gone on from there? But why leave it down a country lane? It would have been far less conspicuous and might have passed unnoticed for days on a public car park in Taunton or anywhere else. And why leave the valuable books which were, supposedly, to be turned into money?

The Taunton police would be questioning railway officials and circulars were going out for drivers who might have picked up a hitch-hiker on the Taunton road, but Wycliffe was by no means satisfied. Could the car be a deliberate plant? If so, with what purpose? In any event somebody must have driven it to where it was found. Sheer panic might explain the whole thing if the runaway was Morris.

A tap at the door and Bellings, the assistant chief, came in. The two men fenced more or less amicably for a quarter of an hour then

Beltings said, with an air of discovery, 'It's Christmas, Charles.' Which was followed a little later by what Wycliffe feared most, 'Do you know, Charles, although we have worked together for years, we have never met socially? Never! Our wives have not met. Do you realize that?'

Wycliffe said that he did but that the case would make it impossible for him to arrange anything over Christmas. His manner of saying it was none too gracious but Belling was not offended.

'You carry too much on your own shoulders, Charles. Delegate. Gill is a good officer, isn't he?'

'First rate.'

'Well, then.'

How could he explain that he enjoyed being on the ground, that the job would not be worth doing unless he was doing the job of a real 'jack'? Bellings was an administrator, born to sit at a desk, and he would never understand. Wycliffe mumbled something about 'getting together in the New Year' and Bellings said that he would hold him to it. 'Relax, Charles.'

As Bellings was leaving the telephone rang. It was DC Fowler who had been keeping an eye on the Old Custom House. 'I'm at the rubbish disposal plant, sir. Three quarters of an hour ago Jarvis drove out in his van as you said he might and I followed him here. He had a word with the foreman then he unloaded a number of parcels from his van and drove off. Instead of following him again I went into the works and asked the foreman not to dispose of the parcels until I had contacted you.'

'I'll be with you as soon as I can.'

He was not yet familiar with the city and he was anxious to become so. Until he knew it at least as well as any taxi-driver he would not be content. He consulted a street map and worked out a route which, at first, took him over familiar ground, down Prince's Street to the docks. Dusk was closing over the city, the street lamps were on and cars were driving with sidelights. Parents, with children trailing behind, were coming away from the market with Christmas trees that they had bought at knock-down prices. Soon Brenda, Lesley Birch and all their colleagues would be walking their beats or sitting, hopefully, in some smoky bar. 'Hullo, darling!'

He entered a maze of streets on the perimeter of the docks, rows of little brick houses. For the most part the fronts of the houses were blind and dark but occasionally there would be a rectangle of yellow light from a sitting-room that was, for once, being used. Then he was out of the maze and driving past warehouses with occasional glimpses of the water between them. The new waste disposal unit, pride of the city, had been built on a promontory of reclaimed ground, a squat complex of buildings and a chimney stack silhouetted against an angry sunset sky.

He drove into the yard and got out of his car. He was surprised at the bitter wind blowing across the estuary from the east. Fowler came out of a little brick box of an office situated at some distance from the plant. He was accompanied by the foreman, both men had their collars up and shoulders hunched against the wind.

The foreman was defensively truculent. 'I don't know what all this is about. Mr Jarvis often brings us parcels of books to burn, books which are of no use to him.'

'How often?'

The man stared out over the darkening water, he was slow moving and slow thinking. 'Three, maybe four times a year.'

'Since when?'

'Since the plant started two-and-a-half years ago.'

'Did it never occur to you to ask him why he wanted to get rid of all these books?'

The man turned his gaze on Wycliffe. 'It's no business of mine what ratepayers do, what they choose to throw away—'

'Did you ever ask him?'

'As a matter of fact, I did, just out of curiosity. He said that in order to buy a particular second-hand book he wanted he often had to buy a lot of rubbish with it.'

'I'm going to take these parcels away with me but I'll give you a receipt.'

The man shrugged. 'I suppose it's all right if you say so.'

They loaded the parcels into the two cars and Fowler and Wycliffe drove back to headquarters. There the parcels were unloaded into one of the interview rooms on the ground floor.

Wycliffe lifted one of the parcels on to the table and opened it: seven books of the kind he had seen in the attic at the Old Custom House. Fowler watched him with phlegmatic calm. He took the first book – Flaubert's *Madame Bovary*, flicked through the pages, shook it, peered down the spine then he looked at the edges of the cover boards.

'Have you got a sharp knife?'

Fowler produced a little knife with a razor-sharp blade and Wycliffe slit the cover boards through their thickness. Nothing. He repeated the same operations on three other books but it was only when he slit the covers of the fifth, a strongly bound edition of Dumas' *The Count of Monte Cristo* that he found what he was looking for: a cavity in each of the covers, rectangular in shape and in depth about half the thickness of the covers.

Fowler said merely, 'Drugs?'

'I suppose so but empty now, of course.'

In the next four books they found another cache.

'There are about two hundred books in this batch; if one in five of them has been treated like this it could mean a kilo of heroin or whatever the stuff is . . . You'd better see if Inspector Webb is in the building.'

Inspector Webb was head of the drugs squad.

Fowler went across the passage to a room with a telephone and a few minutes later Webb arrived. His work was a crusade. Given any lead he was unremitting in his efforts to follow it to a conclusion and he spared neither himself nor his men. He hated drugs as though their very chemical substance had been endowed with a terrible malignancy. Perhaps he had seen too much of the misery caused by their misuse to remain objective. He was several years younger than Wycliffe and, of course, junior in rank, but his attitude was brusque, almost rude, as though by his very discovery Wycliffe had incurred a moral responsibility.

Back in his office Wycliffe sent for Jimmy Gill and put him in charge of the operation that would have to be mounted at the Old Custom House. 'I'll leave it to you, Jimmy, to work with Webb.'

Was this what the case was all about? Perhaps. But his interest still centred on the fact that a girl and a man had died violent deaths. Not for the first time he reflected that people have a choice whether or not they take the first steps towards drug addiction, but very few people elect to be maimed or murdered. Society, almost morbid in its anxiety to protect us against ourselves, is less concerned in pro-tecting us against the predations of others.

Wycliffe had decided to spend as much of Christmas day as

possible at home but the mass of paper work on his desk weighed on his conscience. He rang for WPC Saxton and she came in, as always, with her notebook at the ready. 'I'm working on for a while to clear up some of this, perhaps you would ask them to send up a tray from the canteen?'

His tray arrived, tea with two hot mince-pies all runny with fresh cream. He offered one to WPC Saxton and watched her eat it without once having to lick her fingers. How was it done?

He worked steadily while the lights in the offices throughout the building went out, one by one, and the traffic along the highroad dwindled to an occasional car. At half past eight Gill came in, looking tired.

'Well, sir, your friend Jarvis coughed.'

Wycliffe did not deny the soft impeachment. He had to admit that he felt sorry for Jarvis now though he had had little but contempt for him before. It had not taken Gill long to get his story, Jarvis had seemed anxious to unburden himself once confronted. He had refused a lawyer. For years Jarvis had made his trips to France conducting an honest business then, along came Robson with a sound knowledge of books, fluent in French and eminently plausible. An opportunist, he had wormed his way into Jarvis's life and business so that, before long, it was he who made the routine trips across the channel and soon book buying was little more than a cover for drug trafficking. Jarvis said that he did not know the details but Robson had told him that the drug was heroin, prepared from opium brought into Marseilles. Makeshift laboratories, set up in any disused building, flitted ahead of police raids always, apparently, forewarned.

'He doesn't seem a bad little man,' Gill said, 'just weak, but it will go hard with him now.'

The dear boy approach was unlikely to do him much good with prosecuting counsel or with the judge. Judges don't like queers and they have a strong prejudice against drug pedlars.

Despite the most thorough search Webb had failed to find any heroin and Jarvis claimed that he had no idea where Robson had taken it after removing it from the books.

Wycliffe said, 'I wish I knew why Jarvis tried to dispose of the books. He would have been in a much stronger position if he had left them in his store.'

'But you expected him to, you told Fowler—'

'I didn't *expect* him to, I merely gave him the opportunity and he took it.'

'Well?'

'He's not stupid.' Wycliffe looked up at the clock. 'It's Christmas Eve, Jimmy, you should be home with your youngsters.'

Gill yawned and stood up. 'Perhaps you're right. Merry Christmas.'

Wycliffe returned to the papers on his desk but found it impossible to concentrate. At half past nine he gave up. As he left the building through the duty room a single officer wished him 'Good night.'

He drove home once more through empty streets under the neon and tinsel stars. Few of the shops had left their lights on. For them it was over, shelves and stockrooms had been stripped, night-safes were bulging and managers were deciding whether they were 'up' or 'down' on last year and calculating their commissions. Now the cash registers in the pubs were making their own kind of music and soon it would be the turn of the angels.

10

Eleven o'clock on Christmas morning. Wycliffe was standing at the living-room window, looking out over the narrows. Cold and brittle sunshine but brilliant. Helen's embryo trees and shrubs looked forlorn. For once the narrows were deserted, not a craft in sight, only gulls wheeling and swooping, presumably over a school of fish. Presents had been exchanged. Wycliffe was wearing his new finely knitted, lambswool cardigan and his fleece-lined slippers. David was in the bathroom trying out his new electric shaver, Helen was in the kitchen preparing the meal. Ruth's new transistor sounded faintly from her bedroom upstairs. She came into the living-room, still in her dressing-gown, her blonde hair held back by a slide, like a little girl's. She smiled at him, an enigmatic smile, a young woman's smile; he hadn't a clue what she was thinking or what she ever thought. She glided round the house wrapped in herself and sometimes she irritated him, but Helen seemed not to mind. 'It's her age, she'll get over it.'

The day stretched ahead like an expanse of featureless desert. A surfeit of food, emasculated TV, lame efforts at conviviality. The feast of the family. They would end by reading in their separate corners. He left the window and walked through to the kitchen.

The turkey was in the oven, the pudding simmering on the hotplate.

'Bored?'

'I wondered if I could help.'

'You can wash up, if you like, but put your apron on.'

He had a butcher's apron, blue with horizontal, white stripes of which he was secretly proud.

He did not wash up, instead he prowled about the house. He was waiting, but for what? He had no idea himself.

Morris did not kill Christine Powell. He had convinced himself of that. In any case there had been a flaw in his imaginative reconstruction which told in Morris's favour. Robson had gone into the studio at twenty minutes to eight and found Morris there, painting. '. . . working on that city centre thing.' Well, the painting was now finished and Morris's brushes and palette had been cleaned and put away. If Christine Powell had been killed between half past eight and nine, as Franks said, then Morris had to find the note, finish his picture, clean his brushes and palette and get to Stanley Street all in under the hour. Unlikely from any point of view.

His perambulations brought him back to the kitchen. 'What about a sherry?'

'Too early.'

'It's Christmas.'

'All right, but only a small one for me.'

He poured a small one for his wife, a larger one for himself and took his drink into the living-room. He stood, once more, staring out of the window, sipping his drink from time to time. Ruth was sitting in an armchair turning the pages of the *Radio Times*.

If not Morris then Robson . . .

'I'd never realized there was so much money in second-hand books.' Christine Powell speaking. If she had discovered where the money really came from the smallest indiscretion might have cost her her life. Perhaps it had.

Back to Wednesday evening at the Old Custom House. Jarvis had gone out, Morris was in the studio working on his painting. Robson was in his room, probably listening to records. He went to the studio, ostensibly to collect a pen he had left there, actually to satisfy himself that Morris had settled down to work. Robson could have put on Morris's overcoat. Wycliffe had noticed an old-fashioned hall-stand at the bottom of the stairs. Morris probably hung his coat there as he came in. And he probably left his car keys in the pocket of his overcoat. Christine Powell had cancelled Harkness's appointment – because she knew that Robson was coming? In which case the thing had been planned in advance. But there was a snag, the note which he had found in the pocket of Morris's painting jacket. Unless the note was a coincidence but Wycliffe did not like coincidences. If Robson was setting Morris up it would have been easy and prudent to plant such a note *after* the crime.

'Telephone! It's for you.'

He had scarcely heard the telephone ringing and Ruth had answered it. He took the receiver from her.

'Wycliffe.'

It was Scales. 'You left word that you were to be kept informed, sir. I've compared the blow-ups of the prints on the dead girl's brooch with those of Robson and Morris. There's no doubt at all that they match Robson's. I've found fourteen points of correspondence without difficulty.'

'So all we've got to do now is find him.'

'Unless we've already got him, sir.'

That, of course, was the problem, they still did not know whether it was Robson or Morris whose body lay in the mortuary. Dr Franks had succeeded in getting a blood grouping – A, Rhesus positive – but they had been quite unable to find out the groups to which either man belonged.

The finding of Morris's car worried Wycliffe, the evidence of flight was unconvincing. Who, in his right mind, would abandon a road-worthy car and leave in it a large part of his capital, in the middle of the night, in the middle of nowhere? Yet the car had been driven down the farm lane and abandoned by somebody.

And Jarvis had virtually given himself up – why? It could have been panic but Wycliffe did not think so. Once he had seen that the police were suspicious he had almost deliberately laid himself open to arrest.

Wycliffe went to the telephone again and dialled his headquarters. He was put through to the duty officer. 'Has Mr Jarvis gone back to his shop?'

'No, sir, he's still in the cells. He refused bail.'

'On what grounds?'

'He wouldn't give a reason, sir; he just said that he preferred to remain in custody.'

There must be a very good reason why a man as set in his habits as Jarvis would elect to stay in a police cell rather than return to his own home. Wycliffe thought that he could guess that reason.

'I'm coming in to talk to him, have him brought up to my office in half an hour. Is Sergeant Scales still in CID?'

'I don't think so, sir but DC Dixon was there a few minutes ago.'

'If he's still there tell him to join me in my office.'

Wycliffe dropped the receiver and went into the kitchen. His wife was basting the turkey and Ruth was staring out of the window though there was nothing to be seen but the backyard. 'I'm sorry, dear, but I have to go out.'

'For long?'

'Very likely.'

Helen looked ruefully at the turkey. 'I could hold the meal back until this evening.'

'Just save me a bit.' He kissed her on the ear. Ruth had turned away from the window and was looking at him with mild incredulity.

'You should join a union!'

He drove through the city, there were few people about and those few looked out of place, walking aimlessly. He felt guilty because he had escaped. On the CID floor he found Jarvis seated in the waiting room with Dixon. Jarvis looked older, his cavalry twill hung loosely from his shoulders as though he had shrunk.

'Mr Jarvis . . .' Wycliffe ushered him into his office and signalled to Dixon to remain outside. He waved Jarvis to a chair and the bookseller sat blinking in the strong light from the big window.

Jarvis said, vaguely, 'It's Christmas, isn't it?'

'So you refused bail?'

Jarvis blinked and nodded. 'I don't want bail.'

'Any particular reason?'

Jarvis shook his head but did not reply.

'You don't have to answer my questions but there seems no reason for you to make things more unpleasant for yourself than they need to be. Tomorrow you will be remanded and your trial may be weeks ahead. If there was an application for bail the police would not object.'

'No.' Emphatic.

'Why not?'

Again a shake of the head.

'Perhaps you feel safer in custody?'

Jarvis looked at him sharply, 'I don't know what you mean.' His hands rested in his lap, the fingers twitching nervously.

'I think you do.' Wycliffe was watching him with an unwavering stare that was neither antagonistic, nor compassionate. He was beginning to sense the relationship which had grown up between Jarvis and his assistant, it had the smell of fear. To begin with Robson could have been the model employee, intelligent, informed, anxious to please. Jarvis was gently encouraged to loose the reins, to hand over. He was getting old and increasingly aware of his loneliness. Robson took over the buying, the trips to France, and soon there was more money about, more for him to spend on his precious books. At first he did not enquire too closely and by the time he did things had gone too far. Step by step he had been enticed like a pigeon following a trail of scattered grain.

'You have lived with this man on your back for long enough. When did you last have any say in the running of your business or, for that matter, in the running of your life?'

Jarvis shook his head.

'Where is he now?'

'I don't know.'

'But he did come back on Thursday night after the fire?'

'Yes.' In a small voice.

Wycliffe spread his hands in a gesture which invited more.

'He came back after I had gone to bed, that much of what I told you was true. He came into my room . . .'

'And?'

'He just stood inside the door and said, "You're talking to a dead man, you don't get the chance very often so make the most of it." '

'Did he tell you what had happened?'

'Not a word. He just told me what I was to say to the police if they started asking questions.'

'And what was that?'

Jarvis flushed. 'Exactly what I told you. I was to lead you to believe without actually saying so that it was Morris who came back after the fire. Then he said, "You'll be missing a few of your books in the morning, Morris will need some fluid assets and I'm sure you won't begrudge him." He stood there so . . . so arrogant, so pleased with himself, *knowing* that I would do what he wanted . . . If I could have killed him at that moment.'

'Did you see him in the morning?'

'I haven't seen him since.'

'But you don't think he's far away?'

It was pathetic. Jarvis's lips trembled and he shook his head but no words came. In the end he said, 'Is that all?'

'Unless there is something I can do for you?'

'No, nothing.'

'Something to read?'

A very faint smile. 'The sergeant has lent me some thrillers.'

Wycliffe called Dixon in. As Jarvis reached the door he looked back, as though seeing the room for the first time. 'It's odd isn't it?'

'What is?'

'I don't know, you and me . . .'

When he was alone Wycliffe spoke to the officer in charge of crime cars. He gave instructions for two cars to be stationed near the Old Custom House, one in the square and the other in Bear Street but they were not to take up their positions for forty-five minutes.

Dixon came back looking puzzled. 'Is he all right in the head, sir?'

'Why do you ask?'

'He told me to remind you about the gun.'

Wycliffe collected Jarvis's keys from the duty desk and they drove to his customary parking place at the top of the alley leading to the harbour. There was no unending stream of traffic today, not a car in sight, even the parking meters were hooded.'

'Do you know this district, Dixon?'

'Not well, sir, I've been out fishing from the harbour once or twice.'

They reached the harbour; only the gulls mincing along the edge of the wharf, eyeing the water for any scrap of food. The shops had their blinds down. Despite the sunshine it was cold, a cutting wind off the water, and they were glad of their overcoats.

Dixon was mystified and fascinated. He had had his part in the case but he knew little or nothing of its ramifications. He had heard of the drugs raid on the Old Custom House but he had only the haziest notion of how it was linked with the fire in Middle Street and the murder of Christine Powell.

Wycliffe unlocked the shop door and they entered its musty atmosphere. Already the place seemed cold and untenanted. Dixon followed him through the rows of books, through the passage where Jarvis exhibited his pictures, to the back door. Wycliffe fumbled for the right key, found it, and they were out in the sunshine once more, the dappled sunshine which filtered through the great spreading canopy of the cedar.

Wycliffe had not been in the courtyard before and young Dixon did not know of its existence. The weedy cobbles and the cedar backed by weathered stonework gave the place a sense of timelessness, of unreality, but reality intruded from a radio in one of the Bear Street houses.

Robson's Jaguar was still parked beyond the cedar but the black van was in one of several open sheds which occupied the far side of the courtyard. At the Bear Street end there were double doors and next to them a house with a yard railed off from the courtyard by a rotting fence.

Wycliffe said, 'This is where the girl in the snaps you found lives, the freckled girl. It's a café round the front.'

As they reached the fence the girl herself opened the back door and came out into the yard with a bowl of vegetable peelings. She saw them and recognized Wycliffe.

'You! What do you want?'

'Is your father in?'

'He's over to the pub and you'll not see him till closing time.'

There was a crude gate in the fence and Wycliffe passed through followed by Dixon. She eyed them with evident misgiving.

'I suppose you'd better come in.'

The kitchen was not large considering that it must cater for the restaurant trade: a gas range, a hot closet, a freezer, double sinks and draining boards round the walls and a large, deal table in the middle. There was an appetizing smell of stew coming from a pot on the cooker.

'No turkey?'

She grinned. 'We get tired of all that; when the café is closed we go for a good stew.'

'You get on well with your father?'

She looked surprised. 'He's all right when he can keep off the drink.'

'Do you tell him everything?'

'I don't know what you're talking about.'

'Do you enjoy night-driving?'

She had her back to him so that he could not see her expression but her manner was derisive. 'What is this, some sort of game?'

'What did you do on Friday night, the night before last?'

She was putting cloves of garlic in a press and she did not answer.

'What time did you leave? Midnight? About then, I think. Say, two and a half hours driving and you would arrive at about half past two in the morning. You left the car in a lane which you thought was rarely used then you had to walk to the station. There was a train at three-thirty-five which got you here at five-thirty. All you had to do was walk home; in bed by six and father none the wiser. A good night's work.'

She had moved over to the range and was scraping crushed garlic into the stew. 'I can't stop you from talking, can I?'

'How many people were there taking tickets at Taunton Station when you took yours? Not many. The clerk will remember you. You must have travelled down in a compartment with other people, a girl, travelling alone, is noticed. If we put your picture on TV we should soon be hearing from them.'

There was silence broken only by the ticking of the kitchen clock and the gentle, irregular bubbling of the stew. Dixon was mesmerized, unable to guess where it was all leading. In the end she said, 'All right! I helped him to get away, make what you can of it.'

So far Wycliffe's manner had been friendly, relaxed and affable. Suddenly he became peremptory. 'Look at me! You should be quite clear about one thing in your own interest; I know that Paul Morris is dead and it is Robson you are shielding.'

His sudden change of tactics had startled her for a moment, she looked at him with frightened eyes but soon recovered her poise. 'All right, it was Derek I helped to get away.'

Wycliffe relaxed again. 'But you helped nobody to get away, you made the trip alone. Robson is still—'

She was too quick for him, he had fully expected that she would begin by a denial but instead she flew out of the kitchen and almost before he realized what was happening he could hear her racing up the stairs.

'You stay here!' To Dixon.

The stairs led off a small, dark hall between the kitchen and the restaurant. They led to a landing and passage with three or four doors off but the girl had continued up a second flight, narrower and steeper, presumably to an attic or attics. By the time Wycliffe had reached the first landing the girl was at the top of the second flight. He heard a door open then slam and not another sound.

He was angry with himself, what had happened he had foreseen as a possibility yet he had allowed it to happen. In all probability Robson would use the girl as a hostage and there would be a Christmas circus with a police siege of the house with people bleating through loud hailers, a gala day for the press and TV. Unless he could be talked out of it. Wycliffe thought it worth trying. He climbed the remaining stairs at a more leisurely pace.

At the top there was a short passage lit by a skylight with two doors off. The first was open into an empty room with light coming from a dusty, cob-webbed dormer window. The second door was shut.

Wycliffe knew that he was taking a silly risk with a man who delighted in violence but he felt surprisingly calm. It was afterwards, perhaps days later, that he would feel the cold shivers down his spine. He opened the second door and stood in the doorway; there was no immediate threat to him. The girl and Robson were sitting side by side on a camp bed. The man had his hand over her mouth and nostrils, crumpling her cheeks in a cruel grip; in his other hand he held the gun.

Wycliffe showed neither surprise or concern. 'There's no point in stifling her, what possible difference can it make if she screams?'

Robson hesitated for a moment then, with a shrug, released his hold.

Wycliffe said, 'I've come to take you in for questioning.'

'You're a cool bastard, I'll say that for you.'

The girl was feeling her jaw but she showed no disposition to scream.

Wycliffe was trying to judge the temper of the man; his manner was self-confident, cocky. As long as he stayed that way there was little risk of him resorting to violence. 'If you use that gun you will be putting yourself away for a long time.'

'I'm not counting on using it if you and your lot behave. 'I've got it all worked out. All you have to do is to have my car brought round the front with a full tank. Babs and I will go down and drive off together. No trouble to anybody.' He looked at Wycliffe with a crooked grin.

'That sounds reasonable.'

'I'm glad you think so. Just one other thing – no tail. At the first sign of a copper—' He jerked the gun. 'I want sixteen hours, after that you can unleash your bloodhounds.'

'You are taking this young lady as a hostage?'

'If you like to call it that.'

'What do you think about it?' Wycliffe addressed the girl.

'I'll go with him, it will be all right if you do as he says.'

Robson nodded. 'She's a sensible girl.'

Wycliffe looked at him with a quizzical expression. 'Do you read thrillers?'

'What's that got to do with it?'

'You seem anxious to dramatize your situation – to make it sound more desperate than it appears.'

Robson was not smiling now, he was wary, obviously puzzled. 'What are you after, copper?' What exactly do you want me for?'

'For questioning in connection with the deaths of Christine Powell and Paul Morris.'

'There you are, then! That's desperate enough for my money.'

'Did you murder either of these people?'

'No, but with my record—'

Wycliffe cut in: 'I think you should know that the pathologist is satisfied that Morris died in a struggle.'

'Is that on the level?'

'It is, and there's something else: a man has come forward who says he saw Paul Morris leaving the house in Stanley Street shortly after the time at which we believe Christine Powell was murdered.'

Wycliffe salved his conscience with the thought that he was telling the truth, if not the whole truth.

The girl became animated: 'I told you, Derek! . . .'

Robson snapped: 'You shut up!' He turned back to Wycliffe. 'So why do you want me?'

'Because, for whatever reason and in whatever circumstances, it was you who killed Morris. You may still face a lesser charge than murder on that account.'

So far there had been no mention of drugs and Wycliffe counted on the likelihood that Robson did not know that his racket had been discovered. Robson's next question confirmed this: 'What's happened to Jarvis? Babs, here, says he isn't at the shop.'

Wycliffe was casually matter-of-fact: 'He was detained and questioned on suspicion of aiding your escape.'

Robson laughed. 'That's damned funny! Don't you think that's funny, Babs?'

The girl nodded without conviction. Robson sobered, 'I need time to think about this.'

Wycliffe relaxed. For the first time he had a chance to look round the little room. Apart from the camp-bed there was a chair and a card-table with a green baize top. An old fashioned oil-heater with a fretted iron top stood near the bed and gave the room a moist, stuffy warmth. There were newspapers on the floor by the bed and an empty mug. Robson wore the black slacks and sweater he had worn when Wycliffe first met him, but now they were covered with fluff from the bedding and he had two or three days' growth of beard. The girl, apparently passive, was sitting with her hands in her lap.

'Does your father know about your guest?'

She shook her head. 'He's not a man who takes a big interest in what goes on around him unless it's somebody opening a bottle.'

Robson said: 'I'd be ready to make a deal if—'

'No deals!'

Wycliffe saw his jaw muscles tighten along with his grip on the gun. 'You're not in a position to argue, copper.'

Wycliffe spoke quietly. 'Get this into your head: you can drive off with your girl friend, you can have your sixteen hours and much good will it do you. You'll be caught and there'll be an additional crop of charges.' He sounded indifferent, almost bored.

The girl looked from him to her companion and back again; she seemed about to speak but changed her mind.

Robson said: 'You're bloody sure of yourself.'

'Because these hostage tricks are for cocky teenagers and half-wits. They never work.'

There was a minor commotion in the street below. A man's voice, thick with drink, and somebody banging on the door of the café.

'That will be father.'

Wycliffe said, 'You'd better go down and let him in.'

She looked at Robson and after a moment of hesitation he nodded. Wycliffe stepped aside to let her pass and when he heard her footsteps on the stairs he heaved a great sigh of relief. 'If you shoot me they'll give you thirty years straight off so you'd better give me that before it goes off.'

11

'I suppose that, in a way, I was responsible for Christine's death.' Robson was relaxed, almost genial, pleased with himself.

Wycliffe sat at his desk. A stenographer with his pad was placed behind Robson; Jimmy Gill stood by the window. Gill and the stenographer had had their Christmas dinners but Wycliffe and Robson had made do with stale sandwiches and coffee from an understaffed canteen.

Outside, contrary to the forecast, the sky was leaden with snow clouds and at any moment the first fall of the winter would begin.

'You wish to make a statement?'

'That was the idea.'

Wycliffe was subdued, slow and deliberate. 'Very well; you have been cautioned but not yet charged with any offence.' He glanced up at the clock set in the wooden panelling of his office. 'This interview begins at three-twenty.'

Robson spoke without pause or interruption for several minutes. He began confidently and only faltered when he searched for the word which best expressed his meaning. He had written the anonymous note to Paul Morris as a joke but the joke had gone sour. He had never supposed for a moment that it would result in more than an amusing confrontation which he would hear about from Christine later.

'I swear that was how it was.'

He said that he had left the note on Morris's painting table and that he had looked in later to see what had happened. The note had gone. Morris made no reference to it but a few minutes later, after returning to his room, Robson heard him drive off in his Mini.

'You can imagine how I felt next morning when I heard about Christine . . .'

He adopted a tragic expression and turned to Wycliffe for some sign of understanding but Wycliffe was staring at him, his features a blank. Gill was looking out of the window where the scene was like a steel engraving.

'There was nothing I could do. Nothing!'

Robson said that he had spent Thursday in the shop and that towards evening there had been a telephone call from Morris.

'He was like a madman. He insisted on meeting me at the Middle Street flat . . . All right! I'd been there a few times with Chris. The appointment, if that's what you could call it, was for nine o'clock. I walked there because I didn't want my car to be seen around if there was trouble.'

He looked at Wycliffe. 'You can see I'm putting my cards on the table. Anyway, Morris's Mini was parked in a loading bay behind one of the stores and I went up the steps to the flat.

'The place was in darkness and when I rang the bell there was no answer but I tried the door and it was unlocked.'

Wycliffe reflected that it was an hour later that he had stood at the top of the iron steps, ringing the doorbell. He had not had the temerity or the initiative to try the door.

Robson went on: 'I went into the kitchen, using my pocket torch as I didn't want to draw attention by switching on lights.' He looked at Wycliffe and spoke with greater deliberation: 'I had with me an old service revolver which belonged to an uncle of mine. Of course I had no intention of using it but if you'd heard Morris on the phone . . .'

Wycliffe's expression did not change.

'I called out but nobody answered. I must admit that I was more than a bit scared and by the time I reached the passage I had the torch in one hand and the gun in the other. In the passage there was a little light coming from the big front-room, the door of which was partly open. The light was dim and flickering as though some-body was in there with a candle. I called out but there was still no response. I pushed open the door and went in.'

Robson paused to run his hand through his thick, black hair. 'I could scarcely believe my eyes. At each end of the room there was a bucket with a lighted candle somehow floating in it and, over the bucket, somebody had constructed a crazy pyramid of furniture, paper and linen. It went through my mind that it must be part of some sort of ceremony like witchcraft or something, then it dawned on me.

'I went towards one of the things, actually the one on my right. There is an alcove at that end of the room – or there was – and as I drew level with it something made me duck. I'll never know what made me do it but if I hadn't it really would have been me you found in the ashes.' He looked up with the faintest trace of a smile. 'Morris had been standing in the alcove, waiting for me with a heavy brass thing like a pestle which Christine used as a door-stop.

'Of course, he missed me and I was in with a chance. The gun went off almost immediately when I wasn't even thinking of using it but the shot couldn't have touched him for he fought like a madman. I'd never have believed he had it in him. He was trying to get at the gun, forcing my arm down, then it happened, another shot and he went limp and just slid to the ground.' He paused. 'I was petrified!'

Robson shifted his chair so that the casters screeched, glanced behind him, perhaps to see if the stenographer was still there, then he ran his finger round inside the collar of his sweater. 'God! It's hot in here.' No one else moved or spoke and after a brief interval he continued with his story.

For a while, he said, he had just stood there, then, as he recovered from the shock, he realized that he would almost certainly be at the receiving end of a murder charge. 'With my record!' He seemed anxious to make sure that his record was not overlooked.

'I decided to let the candles burn. I knew it was wrong but I thought it would give me a better chance and it couldn't hurt him. Then I remembered something which Christine had once pointed out, Morris and I were exactly the same height, I carried a bit more weight but . . .'

He looked at the carpet as though he had come to a part of his story which he found difficult. 'To cut it short, I took off my identity disc and, after making sure he didn't wear one, I put mine round his neck.' He shrugged. 'I did it on the spur of the moment.'

Robson stopped speaking and there was complete silence. The stenographer cleared his throat as though he found the silence embarrassing. From his place by the window Gill could see myriads of snow flakes scurrying down to settle on the grass and the rockeries below but the high-road was still black and shining under the street lamps.

'Is that your statement, Mr Robson?'

Robson looked mildly surprised. 'Yes.'

'Are you willing to answer one or two questions?'

A smile. 'That's what I'm here for.'

The internal telephone on Wycliffe's desk bleeped and he answered it. 'Wycliffe . . . Yes . . . No, I'll come out.' He replaced the receiver and stood up. 'Excuse me.'

He was gone for two or three minutes but the three men remaining in the room scarcely moved. Every half-minute the big hand of the wall-clock jerked forward with a little click dictated by a 'master' somewhere in the building. Another of Wycliffe's pet hates, he liked a clock he could wind and keep three minutes fast.

When he came back he resumed his former place and took up where he had left off.

'You seem to have left something out of your statement, Mr Robson. You say that you exchanged identities with the dead man, or hoped to do so, by putting your identity disc round his neck, what else did you do?'

Robson's gaze returned to the carpet. 'I'm not proud of that.'

Gill spoke for the first time. 'You took the brass pestle and delivered a smashing blow to Morris' upper jaw. Why did you do that?'

'It occurred to me that his teeth would have . . . well, given me away. He had all his teeth while I have a small plate in front where I lost four teeth in a rough house.'

'And then – after you delivered the blow, did you do anything else? Did you, for example, look round the rest of the flat?'

It was some time before he answered then he said, 'I looked round briefly, I don't know why.'

Wycliffe's gaze was unwavering. 'Did you find any more candles in buckets?'

'There was another in the bedroom.'

'Lit?'

'Like the others.'

'Now, Mr Robson, perhaps you will tell me what you did after you left the flat. If you want to make a full statement it will have to cover the time until your arrest this morning.'

Robson nodded. He spent some time in thought then he went on with his story. He had driven back to the Old Custom House in Morris's car having taken the keys from the body.

'You locked the flat?'

Hesitation. 'Yes, I did, I don't know why.'

'The key?'

'It was on Morris's bunch.'

'Go on.'

He had put Morris's car in a shed in Bear Street where the freckled girl kept her own Mini and, with the girl's help he had established himself in the attic. He worked on the principle that the best place to hide was under the very noses of the searchers. If he had been content to leave it at that for the time being his chances might have been better but he had tried to be too clever. Morris's car had to be found at some safe distance and he had sent the freckled girl to ditch it in some place where it would be found but, preferably, not at once.

All through his statement which had taken almost an hour Robson had spoken in a subdued voice and a controlled manner, striving to appear not only co-operative but remorseful for his admitted part in the events he described. Now that the ordeal seemed to be over his cockiness and self-complacency returned. Almost one could hear him say, 'Make something of that, copper'.

Wycliffe got out his pipe, filled it and lit it. Only when it was drawing nicely did he speak and the interval was long enough for Robson to begin to fidget. 'As far as I can judge, you seem to have told very few unnecessary lies. That is an achievement; most criminals cannot resist the temptation to embroider.'

Robson's expression became wooden. 'I don't understand . . .'

'There are two facts which your statement does not explain. When you were brought here your fingerprints were taken as a matter of routine. An expert from Forensic has compared them with a photograph of latent prints developed from the brooch Christine Powell was wearing when she died. I understand that there are more than enough points of similarity to connect you with the killing.' Wycliffe held up his hand. 'The witness who at first said that he had seen Morris leaving the Stanley Street flat turned out to be unreliable. He could, of course, be called for the defence but I doubt if they will use him.'

Robson exercised great self-control. He said, merely, 'There must be some mistake.'

Wycliffe ignored him. 'I said that there were two facts. After you were arrested this morning I arranged for officers of the drugs squad to search the premises where you were hiding. I heard just now that they have recovered approximately a kilogramme of a substance which appears to be heroin. I have evidence that heroin has been smuggled into this country by you in consignments of books.'

Robson's lips moved but he did not trust himself to speak.

'These facts will involve you in fresh charges so it is my duty to caution you afresh.' Wychffe's voice and manner were calm, indifferent, almost disdainful.

By seven o'clock on Christmas evening Robson had completed a second statement and the CID floor was a blaze of light with someone in occupation of almost every room. Repercussions were beginning to be felt in London and several provincial towns which were regularly visited by Robson. Messages had gone out to Marseilles, Toulon, Béziers and Lyons which would rouse a good many policemen from their Christmas lethargy. A kilo of heroin is a substantial haul but it was the implication that similar amounts had travelled by a regular route which put officials on their mettle.

For Wycliffe it was the least important aspect of his case, a side-issue. What mattered to him was that a violent man would be restrained from further violence for a long time to come.

In making his second statement Robson's whole attitude seemed to have changed, he was like a different person, bombastic, truculent. Now that he realized that nothing could save him from a life sentence, that the very word mitigation was a sour joke in the context of his case, he seemed determined to get what satisfaction he could from his situation by making a parade of his guilt. Even his voice and his manner of speech had changed. So far he had been articulate, even cultured, now his words came in bursts, disjointed phrases often difficult to link together, interspersed with invective against almost anyone he happened to mention.

His real motive for killing Christine Powell remained uncertain. He said that she had started to ask awkward questions about the second-hand rubbish he took the trouble to import; then, one evening, by an unlucky chance, she had caught him in the act of removing heroin from the covers of a book.

'So you killed her to keep her quiet?'

A complacent smile. 'Wrong again, copper. I killed her because she tried to screw me like she screwed the stupid bastards in Stanley Street.'

'Blackmail?'

He nodded. 'Of a sort. The chick had really fallen for me and she wanted me to marry her to shut her mouth.'

For some reason which he could not quite analyse, Wycliffe hoped that this was a lie.

Whatever his motive Robson had told the girl to expect him at a time when he knew that Paul Morris would be alone in the studio at the Old Custom House. He had worn Morris's overcoat and he had driven the blue Mini.

The note – 'YOUR GIRL FRIEND IS A WHORE . . .' had been part of his scheme to incriminate Morris and he had placed it in the painting jacket after the crime. Morris had never set eyes on it.

Real trouble began for Robson late on Thursday afternoon when Morris telephoned in a highly excited state. He accused Robson outright and demanded to talk to him under threat of going to the police.

'Christ! he scared me, I couldn't make out his angle then. I mean, if he had the dirt on me, why didn't he sing straight? But I couldn't risk calling his bluff, he always was an unpredictable sod.'

He stuck to his story that it was Morris who had insisted on meeting in the Middle Street flat and that it was Morris who had rigged the fire. 'You think that I would have put a foot in there with the cops likely to bust in at any minute? But I had no option.' He paused. 'It was like I said, he'd fixed to burn the place down and me with it. He was a bloody madman, not fit to be loose. And all for a bloody tart!'

It was as far as they got but it was far enough. To Wycliffe it made a kind of sense, it completed a pattern. Paul Morris had decided there was nothing left for him to live for; he had tried Robson, found him guilty, and decided that they should go together. But like most of the really important things in his life it had gone wrong.

At a little after nine o'clock Wycliffe drove home over roads that were crisp with newly fallen snow. The moon had risen and the sky was clear. The navigation lights in the estuary twinkled like stars. Helen and the twins were playing Canasta but they stopped to feed him with cold turkey and salad washed down with his favourite hock.

As he ate he was thinking; not of Robson or Jarvis; not of the dead girl, nor of the ill-starred Morris; he had in his mind an image of the little upstair flat at 9 Stanley Street, and of Brenda, the prostitute, with her feet up, watching the television.